# The Best of
# Archie
# AMERICANA
## *Bronze Age*
### 1980s-1990s

# The Best of

# Archie

# AMERICANA

## Bronze Age

**FEATURING THE TALENTS OF:**

Howard Bender, Ed Berdej, Bob Bolling, Nate Butler, Doug Crane,
Jon D'Agostino, Dan DeCarlo, Dan DeCarlo Jr., Jim DeCarlo, Angelo DeCesare,
Frank Doyle, Joe Edwards, Hy Eisman, Mike Esposito, Alison Flood, George Gladir,
Stan Goldberg, Bill Golliher, Barry Grossman, Rich Koslowski, Rudy Lapick,
Eric Lee, Hal Lifson, Rex Lindsey, Sean Murphey, Rod Ollerenshaw, Dan Parent,
Mike Pellowski, Fernando Ruiz, Henry Scarpelli, Jeff Shultz, Bob Smith, Hal Smith,
Sal Trapani, Kathleen Webb and Bill Yoshida

**FOREWORD BY:** Dan Parent

**INTRODUCTIONS BY:** Steve Geppi and Paul Castiglia

Published by Archie Comic Publications, Inc. 629 Fifth Avenue, Suite 100, Pelham, NY 10803-1242

Printed in Canada. First Printing. ISBN: 978-1-68255-855-3

# ArchieComics.com

**Jon Goldwater** Publisher / Co-CEO

**Victor Gorelick** Co-President / Editor-In-Chief

**Mike Pellerito** Co-President

**Alex Segura** Co-President

**Roberto Aguirre-Sacasa** Chief Creative Officer

**William Mooar** Chief Operating Officer

**Robert Wintle** Chief Financial Officer

**Jonathan Betancourt** Director of Book Sales & Operations

**Stephen Oswald** Production Manager

**Kari McLachlan** Lead Designer

**Carlos Antunes** Associate Editor

**Jamie Lee Rotante** Assistant Editor / Proofreader

**Nancy Silberkleit** Co-CEO

# TABLE OF CONTENTS

**14  FOREWORD**
by Dan Parent

**16  THE 1980s**

**18  ARCHIE IN THE 1980s**
Introduction by Steve Geppi

**21  BOOGIE BUGGY**
Disco started to subside in the late 1970s, but not before a brief resurgence in
the early1980s — on roller skates!
Originally presented in ARCHIE #289, February 1980

**27  1980s ARCHIE COMICS COVER GALLERY**
Originally printed between 1980 and 1981

**31  HEALTH NUTS**
The health club craze really took off in the '80s... and it took a few pounds of
Veronica's pride with it!
Originally presented in BETTY & VERONICA #302, February, 1981

**36  IN THE SWING**
Veronica has always been on the cutting edge of fashion and was the first to
bring the popular "Preppy" look to Riverdale!.
Originally presented in BETTY & VERONICA #302, February, 1981

**41  BO WOE**
Popular movie star Bo Derek's beaded hairstyle inspired women everywhere
to try something new with their hair.
Originally presented in BETTY & VERONICA SPECTACULAR #506, June, 1981

**46  A ZEST FOR THE WEST**
The hit '80s movie *Urban Cowboy* turned western wear into standard
wear as people across the nation put on their boots and ten gallon hats!
Originally presented in PEP #374, June, 1981

**51  FLEETING MEETING**
Throughout the 1980s, John Travolta's star continued to shine, making him the
heartthrob of teenage girls everywhere— including Betty and Veronica!
Originally printed in BETTY & VERONICA #310, October, 1981

**57  TEST ZEST**
Video arcades are zapping all of Archie's date money... until Mr. Lodge pays
him to test out his company's new space game!
Originally printed in BETTY & VERONICA #312, December, 1981

**62  1980s ARCHIE COMICS COVER GALLERY**
Originally printed between 1982 and 1983

**66  GAME ACCLAIM**
Jughead is no expert at arcade games but if a high score means free burgers
he'll find a way to win!
Originally presented in ARCHIE'S PALS 'N' GALS #162, January, 1983

**71  BUCKEROO FEVER**
The success of the movie *Urban Cowboy* brought cowboy style back in
fashion — and made mechanical bulls a national pastime!
First appearance in LAUGH #376, January, 1983

**76  THE PUNK**
Jughead has always been an outsider, but what happens when he aligns
himself with the revolutionary punk rock movement?! A pivotal 1980s tale.
Originally presented in JUGHEAD #327, February, 1983

**84  E.T. TRAVESTY**
*E.T.* was the movie event of the decade, so it was only a matter of time
before Archie had an alien encounter of his own!
Originally presented in ARCHIE #322, March, 1983

**90  INPUT AND OUTLAY**
Weatherbee gets a computer, but how will it work with Archie programming it?
Originally presented in ARCHIE & ME #140, August, 1983

**96    SCHEME SCAMP**
In the 1980s musical acts like the Go-Go's and the Bangles brought all-girl groups back into vogue!
Originally presented in ARCHIE #327, January, 1984

**101  UNTITLED "FLASHDANCE" STORY**
The phenomenal success of the movie *Flashdance* resulted in an increased interest in dancing, and it spawned its own unique fashions.
Originally presented in BETTY & ME #137, January, 1984

**107  VIDIOCY**
Arcade games came into their own in the 1980s.
Originally presented in PEP #393, March, 1984

**108  THE BREAKDANCING BREAK**
This athletic form of dance combined acrobatics with the latest urban fashions, all set to a thumping rap music beat!
Originally presented in EVERYTHING'S ARCHIE #112, July, 1984

**114  CABLE CABOODLE**
Cable TV exploded in the '80s with multiple channels to choose from... and multiple fights for the remote!
Originally presented in ARCHIE'S PALS 'N' GALS #171, September, 1984.

**119  1980s ARCHIE COMICS COVER GALLERY**
Originally printed between 1984 and 1985

**121  THE FAME GAME**
Everyone knows that Michael Jackson ruled as "The King of Pop" in the 1980s. But did you know he had an inestimable influence on The Archies?
Originally presented in EVERYTHING'S ARCHIE #115, January, 1985

**127  A FLAIR FOR WEAR**
In the 1980s, it wasn't enough to sound cool... you had to look cool, too!
Originally presented in EVERYTHING'S ARCHIE #116, March, 1985

**133  THE BOOK**
When The Archies become the opening band for the "King of Pop," they find themselves neck deep in mystery!
Originally presented in ARCHIE'S TV LAUGH-OUT #100, April, 1985

**143  TRIVIA TRAVESTY**
As fascination with nostalgia increased with every passing decade, it was
inevitable that the board game Trivial Pursuit would capture the nation's fancy.
Originally presented in EVERYTHING'S ARCHIE #117, May, 1985

**148  LOOKALIKE LOONY**
The advent and success of MTV forced musicians to be more visual, often
resulting in outrageous costumes,makeup and hairstyles!
Originally presented in ARCHIE #336, July, 1985

**154  FASHION FROLIC**
The faculty's music video chic leads to high school teen shock!
Originally presented in ARCHIE'S PALS 'N' GALS #176, July, 1985.

**159  DELIGHTFUL DILEMMA**
Veronica thinks about who she should date: the latest flashy pop star or
wannabe rocker Archie!
Originally presented in ARCHIE GIANT SERIES #550, August, 1985.

**164  DIMRIDER**
Archie's jalopy gets an upgrade in this parody of 1982's *Knight Rider*.
Originally presented in ARCHIE'S TV LAUGH-OUT #102, August, 1985.

**170  ROCK 'N RASSLE**
The Archies land a ringside gig at a pro wrestling match!
Originally presented in EVERYTHING'S ARCHIE #120, November, 1985.

**175  THE CELEBRITY**
Rocker Bruce Springsteen was a hero to blue collar workers everywhere and
scored his greatest success in the 1980s.
Originally presented in BETTY'S DIARY #1, April, 1986

**181  WHEEL OF LOOT**
Television game shows became big business in the 1980s due to the
phenomenal success of programs like *Wheel of Fortune*.
Originally presented in BETTY & ME #160, August, 1987

**186  1980s ARCHIE COMICS COVER GALLERY**
Originally printed between 1987 and 1988

**190   OUT OF THE ORDINARY**
Arch and Reg get Mohawk makeovers to impress a pretty punkette!
Originally presented in ARCHIE #354, January, 1988

**195   WE, THE JURY**
Every decade has its share of "love triangle" stories and in this classic tale, Betty
and Veronica go to court to settle the matter of Archie's heart once and for all!
Originally presented in BETTY & VERONICA VOL. 2 #9, April, 1988

**200   A PASSION FOR FASHION**
From preppy to punk, from new wave to *Flashdance*, from break dancing to
MTV— the fashions of the '80s meshed together by decade's end on TV shows
like *Miami Vice!*
Originally presented in EVERYTHING'S ARCHIE #137, August, 1988

**201   ROBO-TEEN**
Archie suits up for mecha-fun in this parody of 1987's *RoboCop*.
Originally presented in LAUGH #13, April, 1989.

**207   SHLOCK ROCK**
The Archies plan to take the music video world by storm!
Originally presented in EVERYTHING'S ARCHIE #143, June, 1989.

**214   THE 1990s**

**216   LIVIN' IN THE '90s WITH MY COMIC BOOK FRIENDS**
Introduction by Paul Castiglia

**221   RATMAN**
The biggest hit movie of the summer of '89 featured a certain caped crime-
fighter, and the buzz continued well into the '90s.
Originally presented in LAUGH #19, February, 1990

**227   MESSAGE MESS-UP**
Fearing technology has passed them by, Archie's parents finally get the message
– literally – when they purchase an answering machine!
Originally presented in EVERYTHING'S ARCHIE #152, November, 1990

**232   1990s ARCHIE COMICS COVER GALLERY**
Originally printed between 1990 and 1991

**236 ON THE WRONG WAVELENGTH**
Veronica has a remote control for everything, but when it comes to
controlling Archie, she doesn't need a "clicker"!
Originally presented in ARCHIE #385, March, 1991

**241 THE FUNNIEST VIDEO**
The teens see stars when a TV show offers big cash prizes for hilarious
animal videos, but do their pets share their vision?
Originally presented in EVERYTHING'S ARCHIE #154, March, 1991

**246 DUGGY WUGGY, M.D.**
Medical shows have been a staple of prime-time fare, but the '90s brought
a new twist to the medical show genre with TV's first teenage doctor.
Originally presented in LAUGH #27, April, 1991

**252 DISH MOUNTING**
Archie's dad gets "mixed signals" when he tries to install a satellite dish.
Originally presented in ARCHIE #389, July, 1991

**257 PEACE PIPES**
What starts as an effort to honor Betty's serviceman uncle soon develops
into a full-fledged salute to the varied heritages of Riverdale High's teens.
This story makes special mention of Operation Desert Storm.
Originally presented in BETTY & VERONICA #47, January, 1992

**262 I RATINGS – FEATURING HAL & ROBERTA**
The '90s was the era of the morning radio shock jock, but these trash talkers
may have met their match when they take on testy Veronica!
Originally presented in VERONICA #20, April, 1992

**267 SKATE DATE**
Rollerblading was the coolest way to get around...
Originally presented in ARCHIE #404, October, 1992

**272 1990s ARCHIE COMICS COVER GALLERY**
Originally printed between 1992 and 1993

**275 THE STAR**
While the '70s and '80s had a few eccentric basketball stars, the 1990s
was the first decade dominated by showmanship and flashy personalities.
Has Archie "got game" on Riverdale High's court?
Originally presented in ARCHIE #411, May, 1993

281  **THE ALTERNATIVE WHIRL**
Betty enjoys the alternative music scene, but a music industry pro hits a sour note by asking her to change her pro-Archie song to an anti-Archie rant!
Originally presented in BETTY #6, June, 1993

286  **GENERATION GASP**
B&V show off their "teen spirit" when they model the latest in "grunge" fashions!
Originally presented in BETTY & VERONICA #69, November, 1993

291  **THE UNKINDEST CUT**
It's a tale of hair shorn and grown... and that's the long and the short of it, in this examination of popular '90s hairdos!
Originally presented in BETTY & VERONICA #70, December, 1993

296  **JERSEY CITY 07303**
One of the most popular TV shows of the 1990s traced the life of teens with a west coast zip code, but it never saw more melodrama than this tantalizing Betty & Veronica tale!
Originally presented in BETTY & VERONICA SPECTACULAR #7, April, 1994

301  **THE TRENDSETTERS**
Betty and Veronica have always been at the forefront of fashion, and the 1990s were no exception!
Originally presented in BETTY & VERONICA #76, June, 1994

306  **BLARNEY BLUES**
Many a '90s baby grew up in the glow of a televised purple dinosaur... and Jughead's baby sister Jellybean was no exception! Will Jughead ever be able to regain her attention?
Originally presented in JUGHEAD #57, June, 1994

312  **SIMULATION STIMULATION**
Virtual reality is a dream come true for hamburger-loving Jughead... as well as for Jughead-loving Ethel!
Originally presented in JUGHEAD #58, July, 1994

317  **FAT FREE FERVOR**
The '90s fat free food craze is put to the test – literally – by Riverdale's resident culinary connoisseur, Jughead.
Originally presented in JUGHEAD #61, October, 1994

**323 LOVE AND LEARN**
Long before Oprah and Dr. Phil, Donohue featured guests that offered advice for the lovelorn!
Originally presented in WORLD OF ARCHIE #22, March, 1996

**329 P.C. PAL**
Originally presented in ARCHIE #454, December, 1996

**330 1990s ARCHIE COMICS COVER GALLERY**
Originally printed between 1996 and 1997

**333 INTERACTIVE COMICS**
Archie decides to give interactive entertainment a whirl... by letting the readers of his comic decide his fate!
Originally presented in ARCHIE #457, March, 1997

**338 CRIME DAZE**
*America's Most Wanted* inspired a generation of amateur detectives to phone in tips on wanted fugitives... just wait until you see who Betty and Veronica turn in!
Originally presented in BETTY & VERONICA SPECTACULAR #24, July, 1997

**343 WISH UPON A STAR**
Superstar Brad Pitt has been making hearts throb since the early '90s... perhaps none more so than Ethel's!
Originally presented in ARCHIE & FRIENDS #24, August, 1997

**348 E-MAIL CALL**
The world wide web leads to world wide panic when Veronica's computer goes down and her e-mail pals across the globe wonder where she's been!
Originally presented in VERONICA #68, October, 1997

**353 NOVEL JOB**
When shock DJ Howie Severe has a book signing, it's up to Betty to stem the tide of fans that have shown up.
Originally presented in BETTY #56, December, 1997

**359 THE NEW GIRL IN TOWN**
One of the most popular supporting characters in Archie Comics, Brigitte Reilly, made her first appearance in this poignant tale.
Originally presented in BETTY & VERONICA #119, January, 1998

**364  CHANGING HIS TOON**
It's a brush stroke of genius when Mr. Weatherbee asks Chuck to take
a break from cartooning and draw a portrait of him instead.
Originally presented in ARCHIE #470, April, 1998

**370  THAT CERTAIN RING**
Betty is on the cutting edge when she gets a nose ring!
Originally presented in BETTY #62, June, 1998

**376  GROUP THERAPY**
When Betty and Veronica meet their favorite '90s teen heartthrobs, the
behavior of the all-brother rock group has the girls screaming, "Oh, brother!"
Originally presented in BETTY & VERONICA #126, July, 1998

**382  LAPTOP LAMENT**
The popularity of laptop computers and wireless connections
made it easier than ever to have information at your fingertips!
Originally presented in ARCHIE #475, September, 1998

**388  THE BIG OBSESSION**
In the late '90s, one celebrity had a "titanic" rise to fame,
but can he handle the starstruck teens of Riverdale?
*Originally presented in BETTY & VERONICA #129, November, 1998*

**394  VIRTUAL VIRTUOSO**
Originally presented in JUGHEAD #110, November, 1998

**395  1990s ARCHIE COMICS COVER GALLERY**
Originally printed between 1998 and 1999

**399  WHATEVER-!**
Every decade has its catchphrases, but none can top "Whatever"!
Originally presented in VERONICA #85, March, 1999

**404  WHAT A TANGLED WEB THEY WEAVE**
Fed up with an internet advice columnist, Veronica starts an advice website
of her own... let the web wars begin!
Originally presented in VERONICA #89, July, 1999

**410  THE BIG RIDE**
The '90s was the greatest decade for amusement park rides.
Originally presented in ARCHIE & FRIENDS #38, December, 1999

# FOREWORD BY DAN PARENT

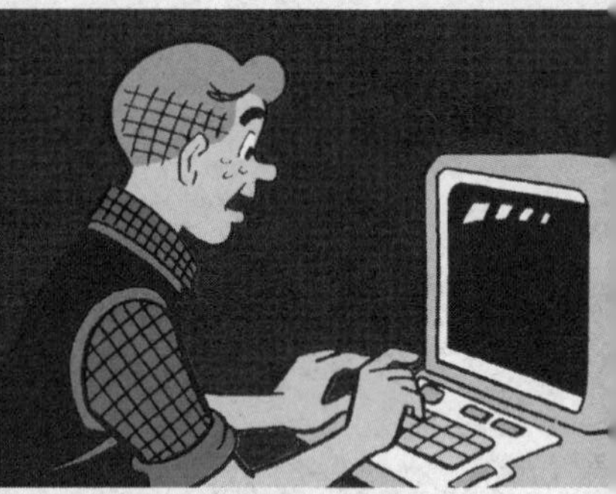

I started at Archie in the late '80s, so the '90s was my first full decade there. I worked on lots of titles like *Veronica* and some classics of the decade ones, like *Jughead's Diner* and *Archie 3000*.

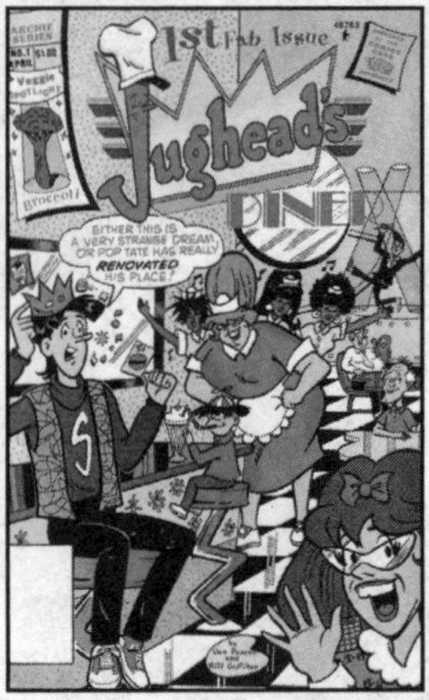
1st Fab Issue
Jughead's
DINER
EITHER THIS IS A VERY STRANGE DREAM OR POP TATE HAS REALLY RENOVATED HIS PLACE!

**JUGHEAD'S DINER #1, April, 1990**

When "the powers that be" wanted a storyline to shake things up a bit, Bill Golliher and I came up with the greatest received story of the decade from Archie Comics: "Love Showdown."

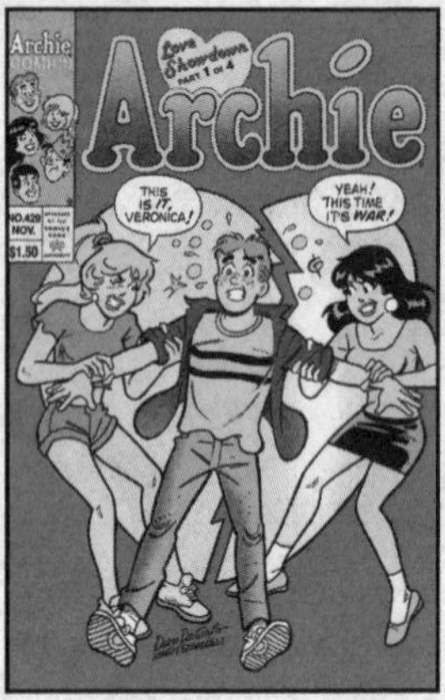
Archie
Love Showdown PART 1 of 4
Archie
THIS IS IT, VERONICA!
YEAH! THIS TIME IT'S WAR!
NO.429 NOV.
$1.50

**ARCHIE #429, November, 1994**

Or as I call it, "any excuse to get Cheryl Blossom back in the comics!"

We came up with the idea of Archie choosing someone other than Betty and Veronica. Archie going for Cheryl over the other two girls made worldwide headlines!

All this lead to my favorite part of the nineties, the resurgence of Cheryl, who was so popular from "Love Showdown" that she received a mini-series then her own title! We had no idea the impact the story would have. It was EVERYWHERE! There are tapes of Bill and me on national morning shows with '90s mullets to prove it!

Other additions came to the World of Archie in the '90s. We brought Jellybean, Jughead's baby sister, into the mix, Brigitte Reilly came on board and so many more. There was also the big Sabrina the Teenage Witch resurgence thanks to the TV show and I wrote some of those issues.

SABRINA THE TEENAGE WITCH, 1999

Archie entered the digital age with ArchieComics.com! It was very cutting edge at the time, even with a 48k modem! Shortly after the Archie Internet fan sites started, and there are now countless sites and blogs devoted to Archie. The Archie stories started to change too, with the kids having PCs

and cell phones. When the decade ended the digital revolution was fully upon us, from the way we printed our books to Archie's ever-growing presence online. We were on that road that lead to Facebook, Twitter and our new Archie App (which has been downloaded 12 million times as I write this!). The new decade of the new millennium brought even more changes; Archie got Married... twice!

He has new friends like Kevin Keller plus a whole school full of new faces. Archie Comics is now more than ever the most vibrant publisher in comics. The modern World of Archie has never seemed more energized or vibrant. But some things shouldn't change. What I mean is that Archie Comics has remained Archie Comics; times may change, but our characters don't –they get better with age! As time marches on, we still need our friends to be there and you can always count on Archie and the Gang being there!

Caricature of Dan Parent circa 1990

The Best of

# Archie
# AMERICANA

*Bronze Age*

## The 1980s

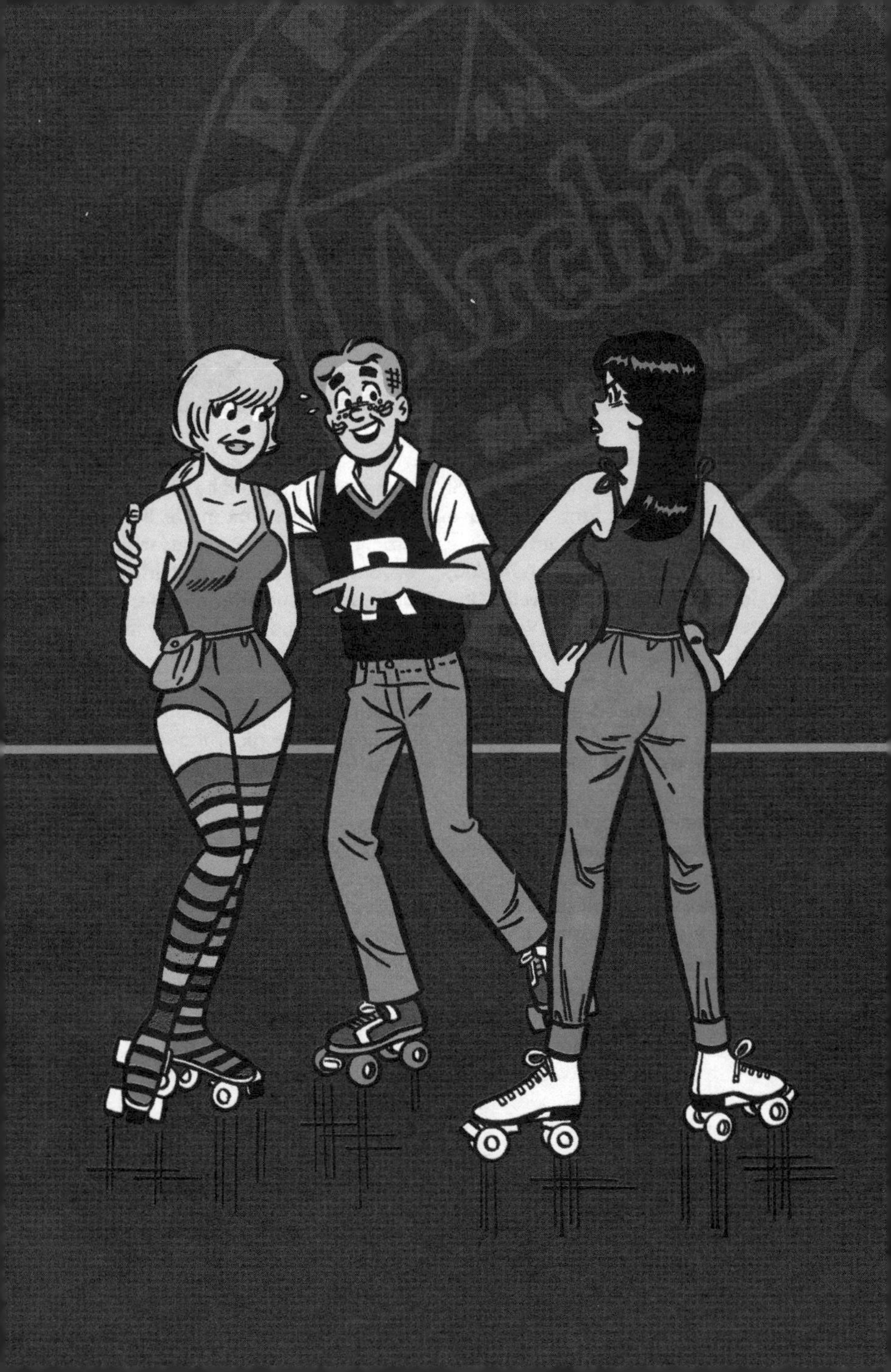

# ARCHIE IN THE 1980s
## INTRODUCTION BY STEVE GEPPI

## -THE 1980s-

Archie and I go way back. In that sense at least, I'm not much different than the millions of fans who have spent at least some amount of time with the gang in Riverdale. As a kid, I anxiously read and re-read the adventures of Archie, Betty, Veronica, Jughead, Reggie, their friends, family and teachers. My mother would prepare a big, Jughead-esque plate of hamburgers, and I would dig into them and a huge stack of Archie Comics at the same time. It was a wonderful world that simultaneously offered an escape from reality and sparked my imagination of the perfect teenaged life, particularly the malt shop and the impossible task of choosing between Betty and Veronica.

Escapism and enjoyment weren't the only things I got from those fantastic comics, though. There were things there to be learned, as well. Like many other children, my vocabulary was expanded because the stories often contained words I hadn't seen previously. "Spelunking," an example I like to use, was one I found in a *Life*

*With Archie* story. While it's not as common as it should be in other media, Archie Comics has made it standard practice to offer amusement that broadens the minds of children, while at the same time offering entertainment that parents can feel safe with. This is no small thing.

As hard as it is for people who know me now to imagine, though, I drifted away from comics while I was growing up and beginning a career. The separation didn't last long. When I got back into the field, it was full speed ahead. It was no time at all before I opened my first comic book store, Geppi's Comic World, in the basement of a TV repair shop.

Every day people would come into my shop to buy and sell comics. Superheroes, westerns, science fiction, monsters, horror, humor...You name it, I saw it. I've always said there's at least one comic book for everyone, but I was particularly fortunate that there were so many that appealed to me.

As my business expanded, I found out very quickly that I'd never lost my love of Archie and his friends. They remained—and remain—very dear to me. Many people have written eloquently about their timelessness or the different reasons for their continued appeal. It would be difficult to sing their praises in a way you haven't heard before, but surely the consistent combination of lively art, entertaining stories, solid values and adaptability have enabled their appeal to transcend the trends and fads of each successive era.

In the preceding volumes of the *Archie Americana* Series, we've seen selections of the best Archie stories from the '40s, '50s, '60s and '70s. That, not surprisingly, brings us to the edition, *Best of Archie Americana: Bronze Age*. Despite the fact that my introduction to the group came many years earlier, for me it's just simply impossible to think of Archie Comics in the '80s and not think of them fondly.

When I founded Diamond Comic Distributors in 1982, Archie Comics was one of the first big publishers to sign on with us. The perfect counterpart to my love of the comics was that the folks who produced them turned out to be such good people.

This, of course, did nothing to dampen my enthusiasm for collecting Archie. In fact, Archie has always enjoyed a prized position in my collection. Over the years I've had the opportunity to acquire perhaps the finest known copies of *Pep Comics* #22 (Archie's first appearance) and *Archie Comics* #1 (his first title, the same one that continues to this day), and even the first six Archie newspaper daily comic strips drawn by Bob Montana. I can never resist the urge to show my Archie treasures to my fellow collectors, so several pieces from my collection are always on display in our gallery.

Now it's many years later, Diamond has become the largest distributor of English language comics in the world, and Archie is still a very important part of our family. You can take a look at this book and the others in the series to see the fashions or crazes of a particular era, but you'll also see that the things that made Archie and his friends who they are have not changed. They're still people any kid would love to know.

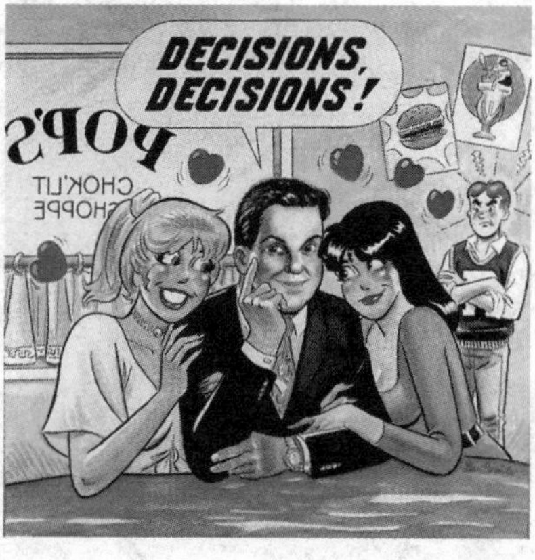
DECISIONS, DECISIONS!

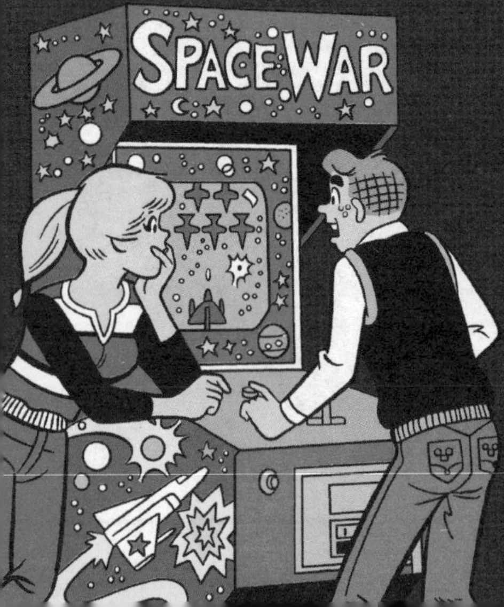
SPACE WAR

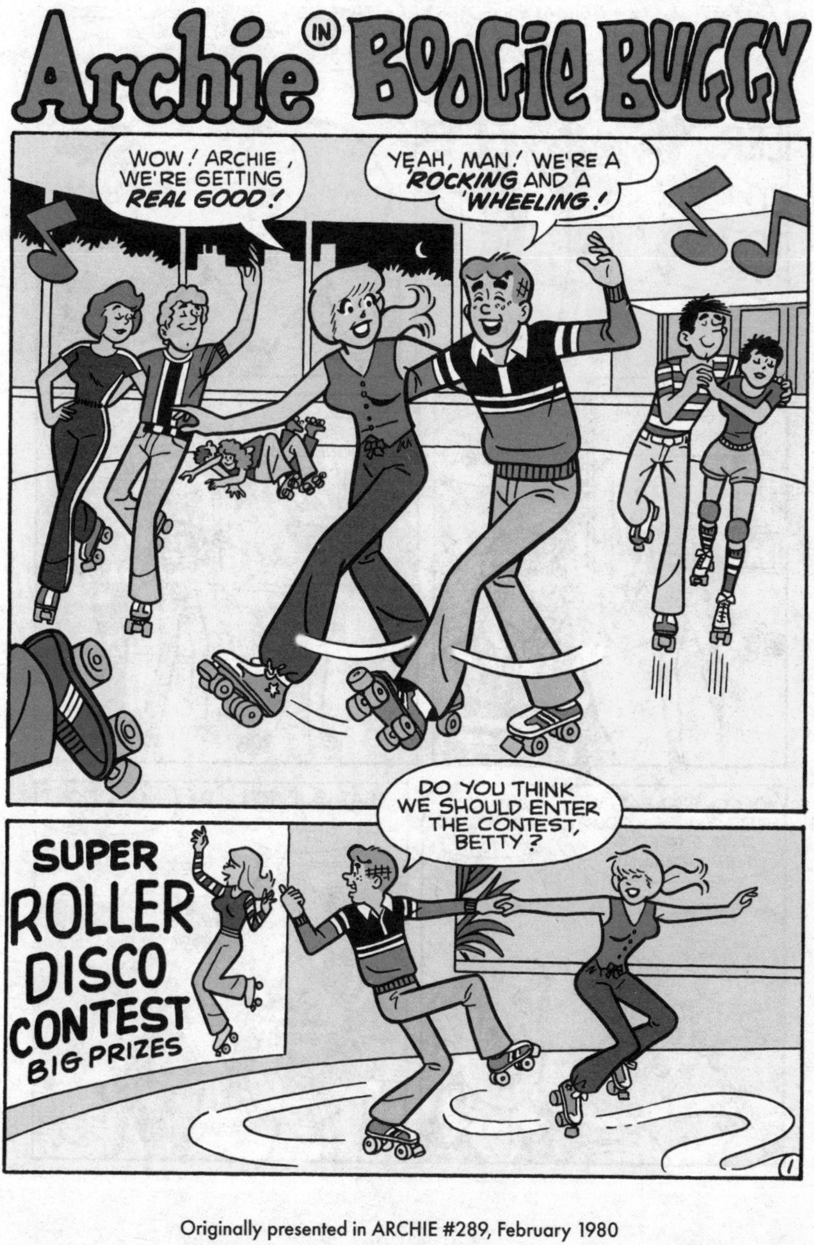
Archie IN Boogie Buggy
WOW! ARCHIE, WE'RE GETTING REAL GOOD!
YEAH, MAN! WE'RE A 'ROCKING AND A 'WHEELING!
SUPER ROLLER DISCO CONTEST BIG PRIZES
DO YOU THINK WE SHOULD ENTER THE CONTEST, BETTY?
1

Originally presented in ARCHIE #289, February 1980

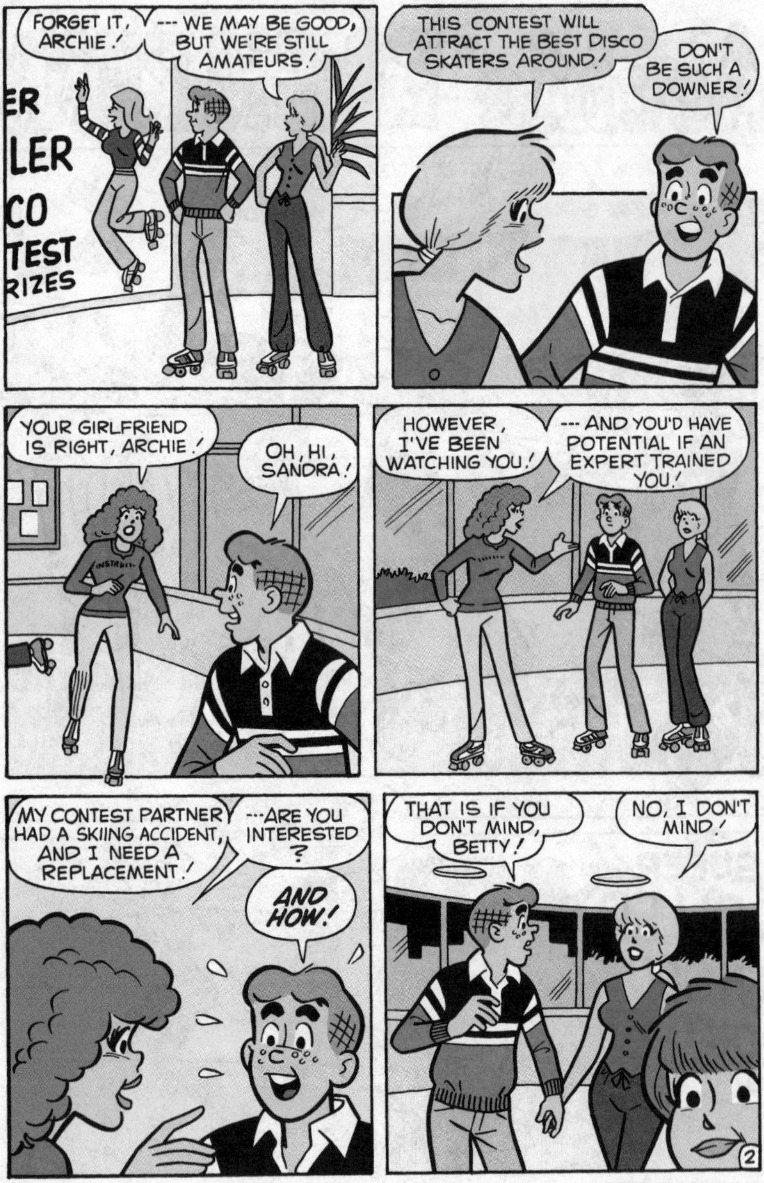
FORGET IT, ARCHIE!
--- WE MAY BE GOOD, BUT WE'RE STILL AMATEURS!
ER
LER
CO
TEST
RIZES
THIS CONTEST WILL ATTRACT THE BEST DISCO SKATERS AROUND!
DON'T BE SUCH A DOWNER!
YOUR GIRLFRIEND IS RIGHT, ARCHIE!
OH, HI, SANDRA!
HOWEVER, I'VE BEEN WATCHING YOU!
--- AND YOU'D HAVE POTENTIAL IF AN EXPERT TRAINED YOU!
MY CONTEST PARTNER HAD A SKIING ACCIDENT, AND I NEED A REPLACEMENT!
---ARE YOU INTERESTED?
AND HOW!
THAT IS IF YOU DON'T MIND, BETTY!
NO, I DON'T MIND!
2

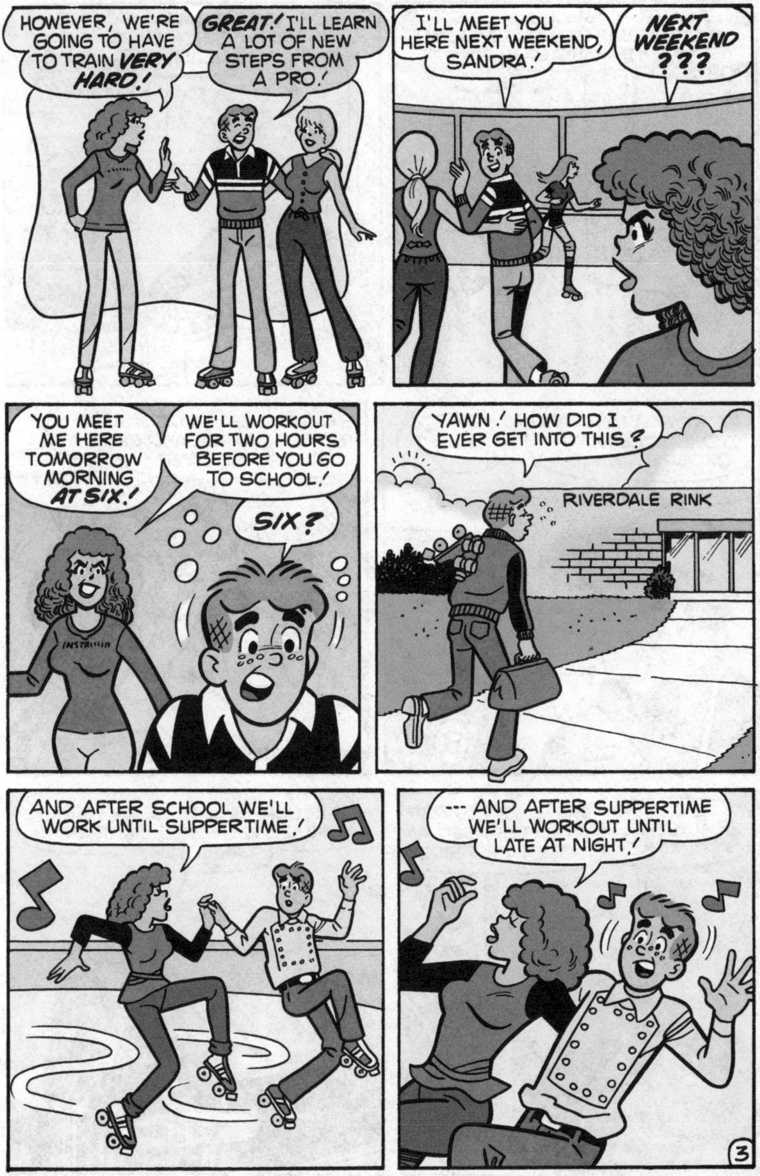
HOWEVER, WE'RE GOING TO HAVE TO TRAIN VERY HARD!
GREAT! I'LL LEARN A LOT OF NEW STEPS FROM A PRO!
I'LL MEET YOU HERE NEXT WEEKEND, SANDRA!
NEXT WEEKEND???
YOU MEET ME HERE TOMORROW MORNING AT SIX!
WE'LL WORKOUT FOR TWO HOURS BEFORE YOU GO TO SCHOOL!
SIX?
YAWN! HOW DID I EVER GET INTO THIS?
RIVERDALE RINK
AND AFTER SCHOOL WE'LL WORK UNTIL SUPPERTIME!
--- AND AFTER SUPPERTIME WE'LL WORKOUT UNTIL LATE AT NIGHT!
3

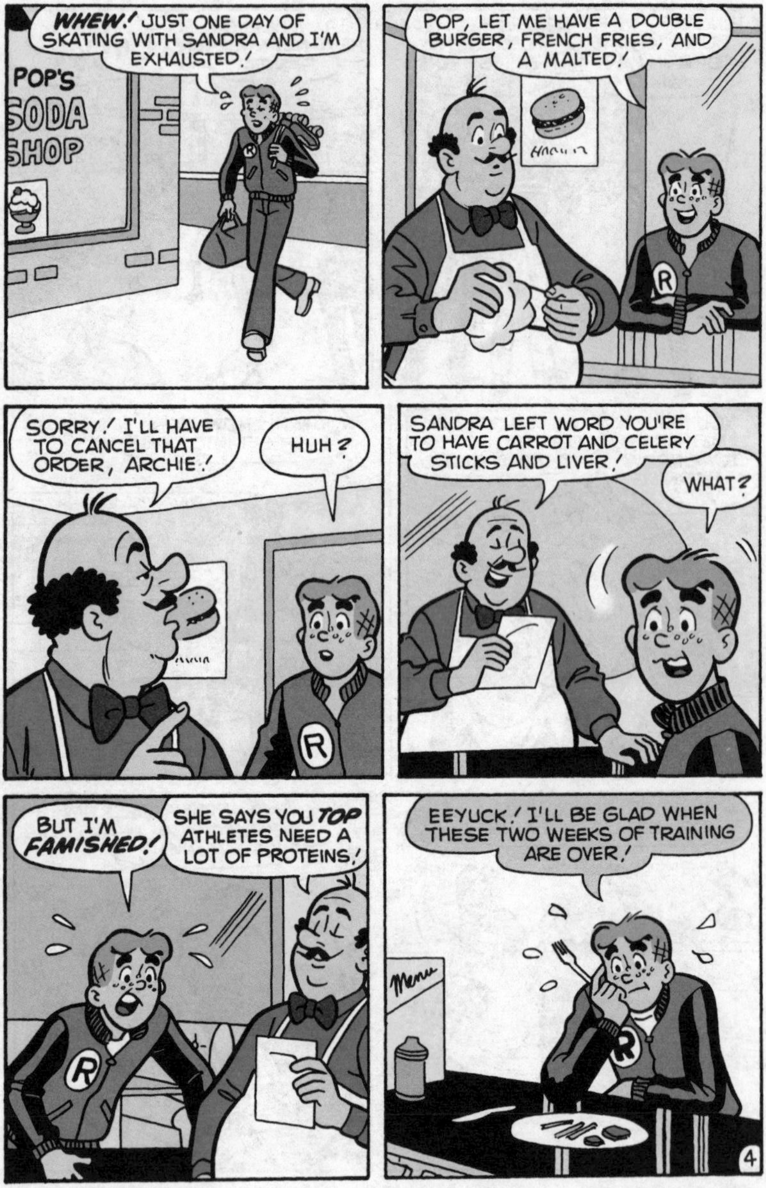
WHEW! JUST ONE DAY OF SKATING WITH SANDRA AND I'M EXHAUSTED!
POP'S SODA SHOP
POP, LET ME HAVE A DOUBLE BURGER, FRENCH FRIES, AND A MALTED!
SORRY! I'LL HAVE TO CANCEL THAT ORDER, ARCHIE!
HUH?
SANDRA LEFT WORD YOU'RE TO HAVE CARROT AND CELERY STICKS AND LIVER!
WHAT?
BUT I'M FAMISHED!
SHE SAYS YOU TOP ATHLETES NEED A LOT OF PROTEINS!
EEYUCK! I'LL BE GLAD WHEN THESE TWO WEEKS OF TRAINING ARE OVER!
Menu
4

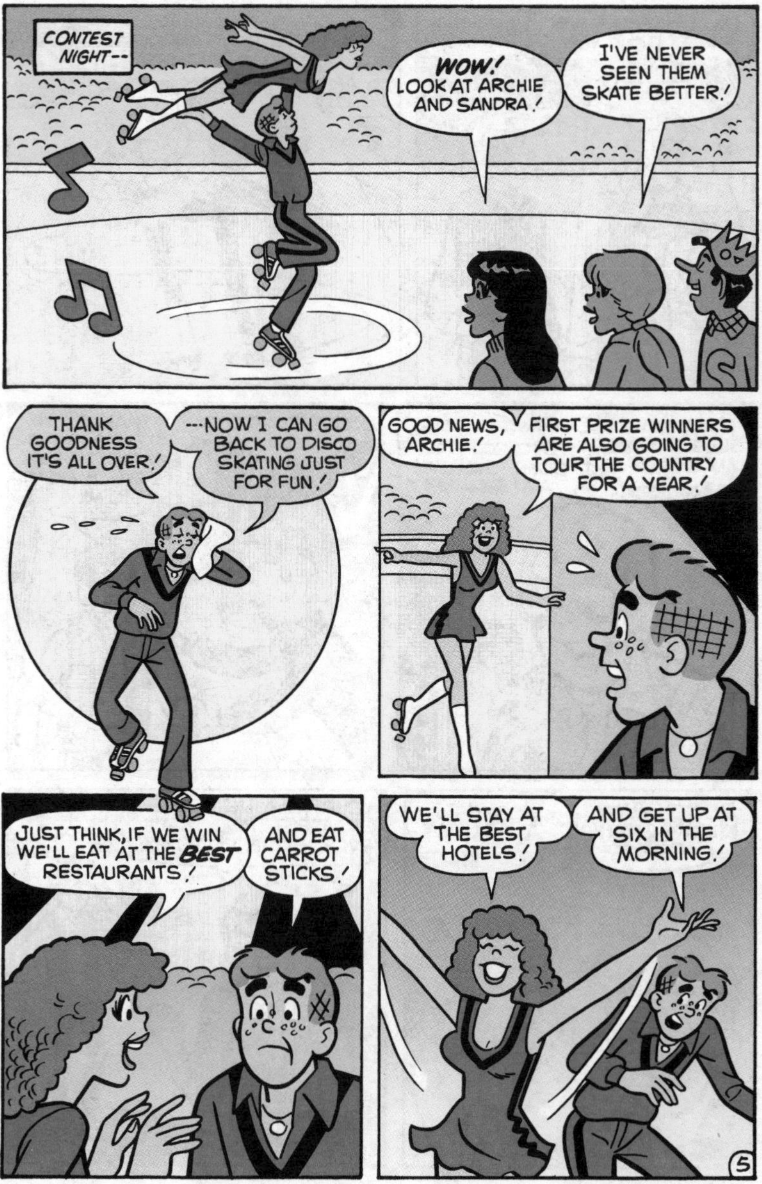
CONTEST NIGHT--
WOW! LOOK AT ARCHIE AND SANDRA!
I'VE NEVER SEEN THEM SKATE BETTER!
THANK GOODNESS IT'S ALL OVER!
---NOW I CAN GO BACK TO DISCO SKATING JUST FOR FUN!
GOOD NEWS, ARCHIE!
FIRST PRIZE WINNERS ARE ALSO GOING TO TOUR THE COUNTRY FOR A YEAR!
JUST THINK, IF WE WIN WE'LL EAT AT THE BEST RESTAURANTS!
AND EAT CARROT STICKS!
WE'LL STAY AT THE BEST HOTELS!
AND GET UP AT SIX IN THE MORNING!
5

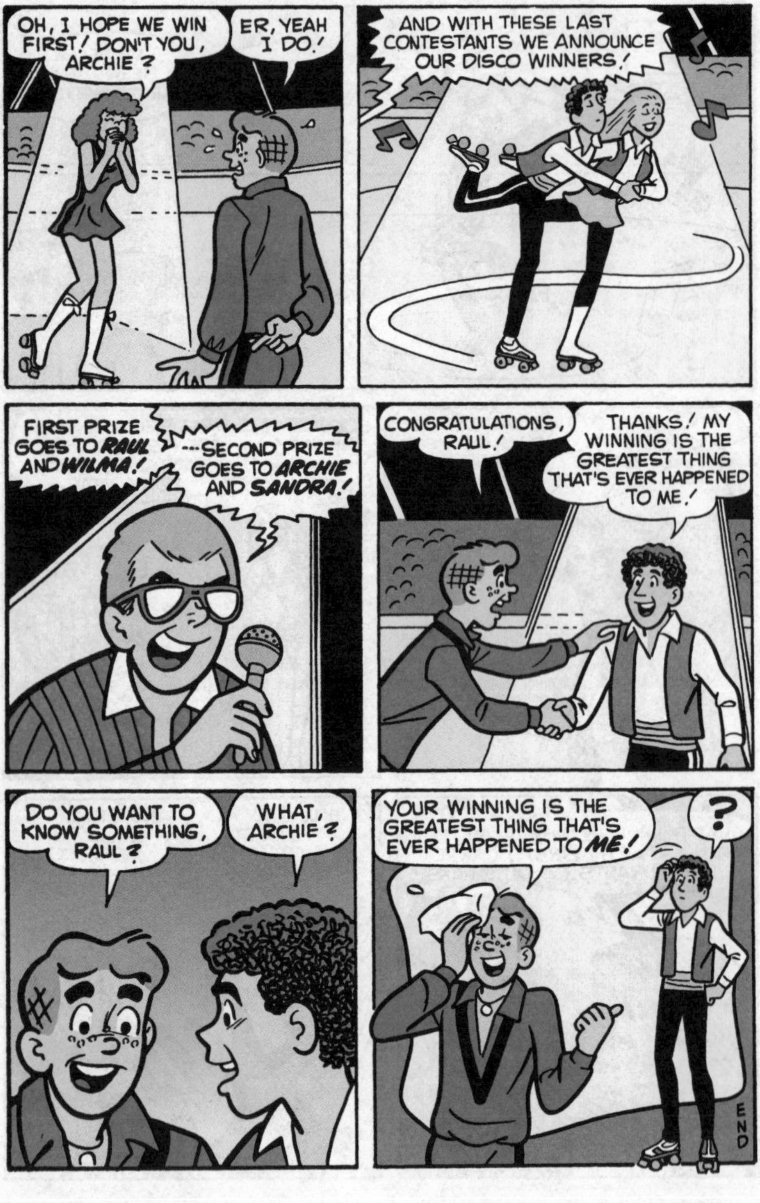
OH, I HOPE WE WIN FIRST! DON'T YOU, ARCHIE?
ER, YEAH I DO!
AND WITH THESE LAST CONTESTANTS WE ANNOUNCE OUR DISCO WINNERS!
FIRST PRIZE GOES TO RAUL AND WILMA!
---SECOND PRIZE GOES TO ARCHIE AND SANDRA!
CONGRATULATIONS, RAUL!
THANKS! MY WINNING IS THE GREATEST THING THAT'S EVER HAPPENED TO ME!
DO YOU WANT TO KNOW SOMETHING, RAUL?
WHAT, ARCHIE?
YOUR WINNING IS THE GREATEST THING THAT'S EVER HAPPENED TO ME!
?
END

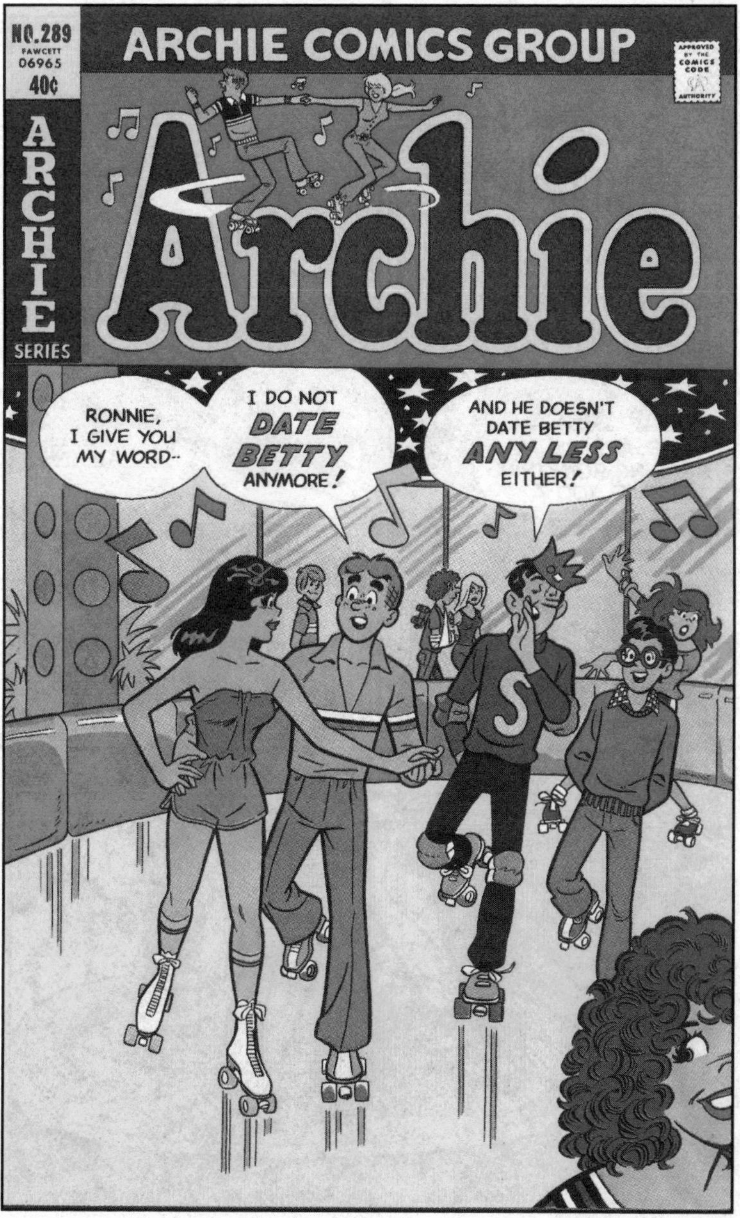
NO.289
FAWCETT
06965
40¢
ARCHIE COMICS GROUP
APPROVED BY THE COMICS CODE AUTHORITY
ARCHIE
SERIES
Archie
RONNIE, I GIVE YOU MY WORD--
I DO NOT DATE BETTY ANYMORE!
AND HE DOESN'T DATE BETTY ANY LESS EITHER!

Originally printed in 1980

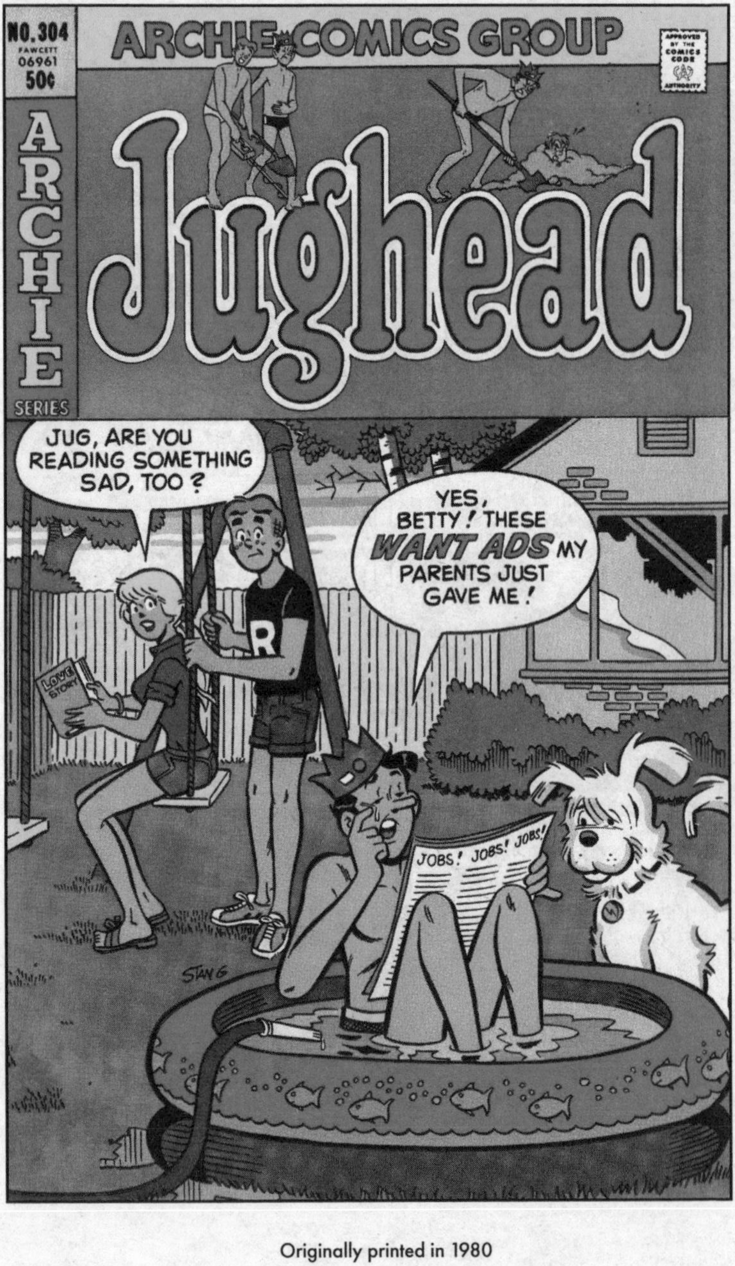
NO. 304
FAWCETT
06961
50¢
ARCHIE COMICS GROUP
APPROVED BY THE COMICS CODE AUTHORITY
ARCHIE SERIES
Jughead
JUG, ARE YOU READING SOMETHING SAD, TOO ?
YES, BETTY ! THESE WANT ADS MY PARENTS JUST GAVE ME !
LOVE STORY
R
JOBS! JOBS! JOBS!
STAN G

Originally printed in 1980

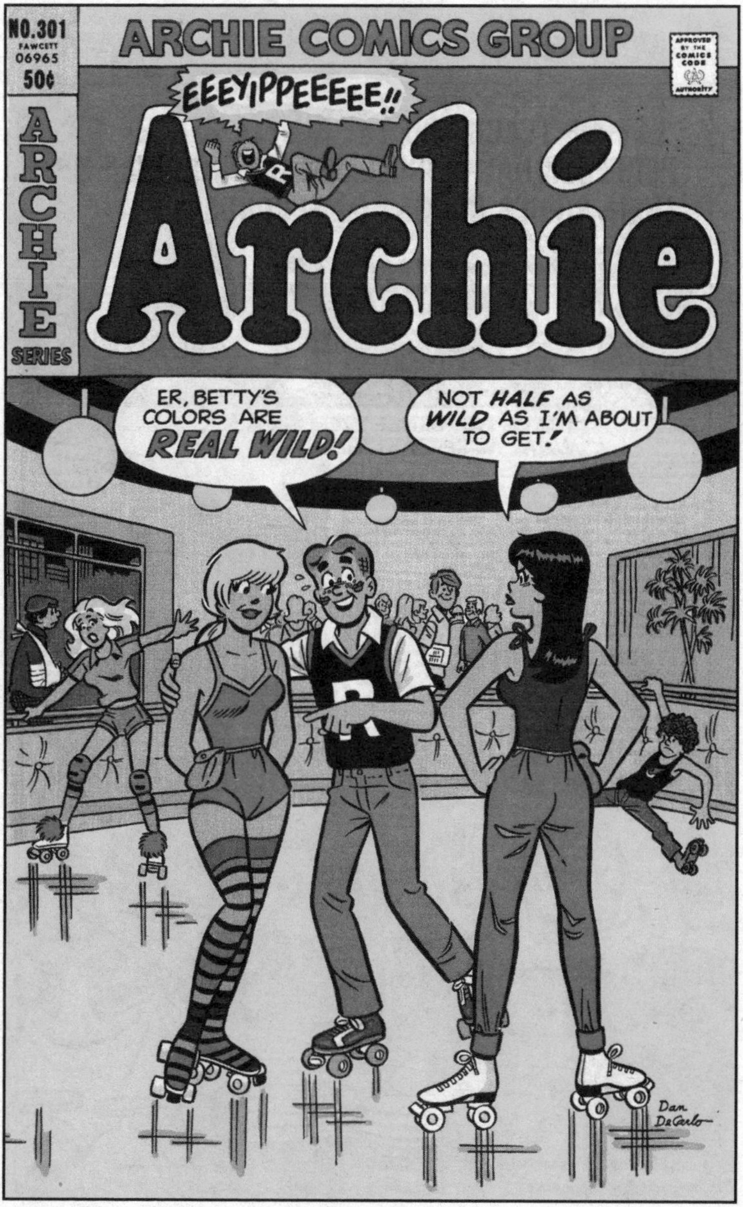
NO.301
FAWCETT
06965
50¢
ARCHIE COMICS GROUP
APPROVED BY THE COMICS CODE AUTHORITY
ARCHIE
ARCHIE SERIES
EEEYIPPEEEEE!!
Archie
ER, BETTY'S COLORS ARE REAL WILD!
NOT HALF AS WILD AS I'M ABOUT TO GET!
Dan DeCarlo

Originally printed in 1981

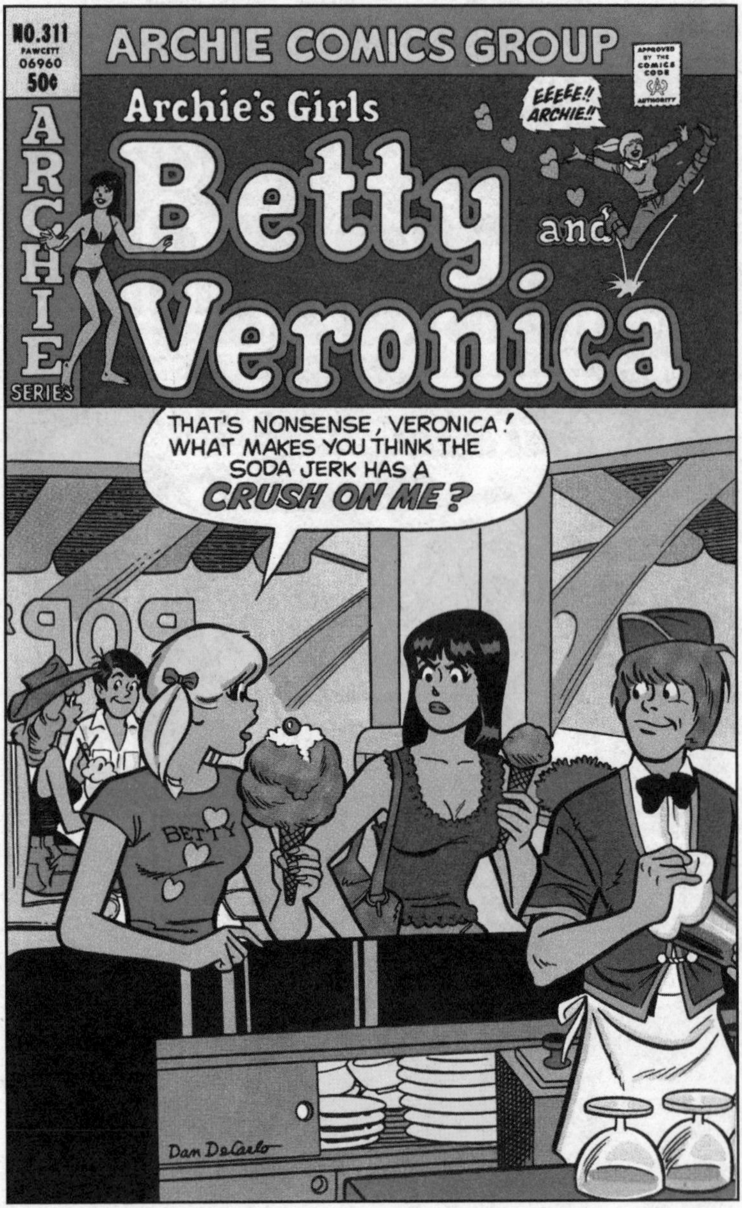
NO.311
FAWCETT
06960
50¢
ARCHIE COMICS GROUP
APPROVED BY THE COMICS CODE AUTHORITY
Archie's Girls
Betty and Veronica
ARCHIE SERIES
EEEEE!! ARCHIE!!
THAT'S NONSENSE, VERONICA! WHAT MAKES YOU THINK THE SODA JERK HAS A CRUSH ON ME?
BETTY
Dan DeCarlo

Originally printed in 1981

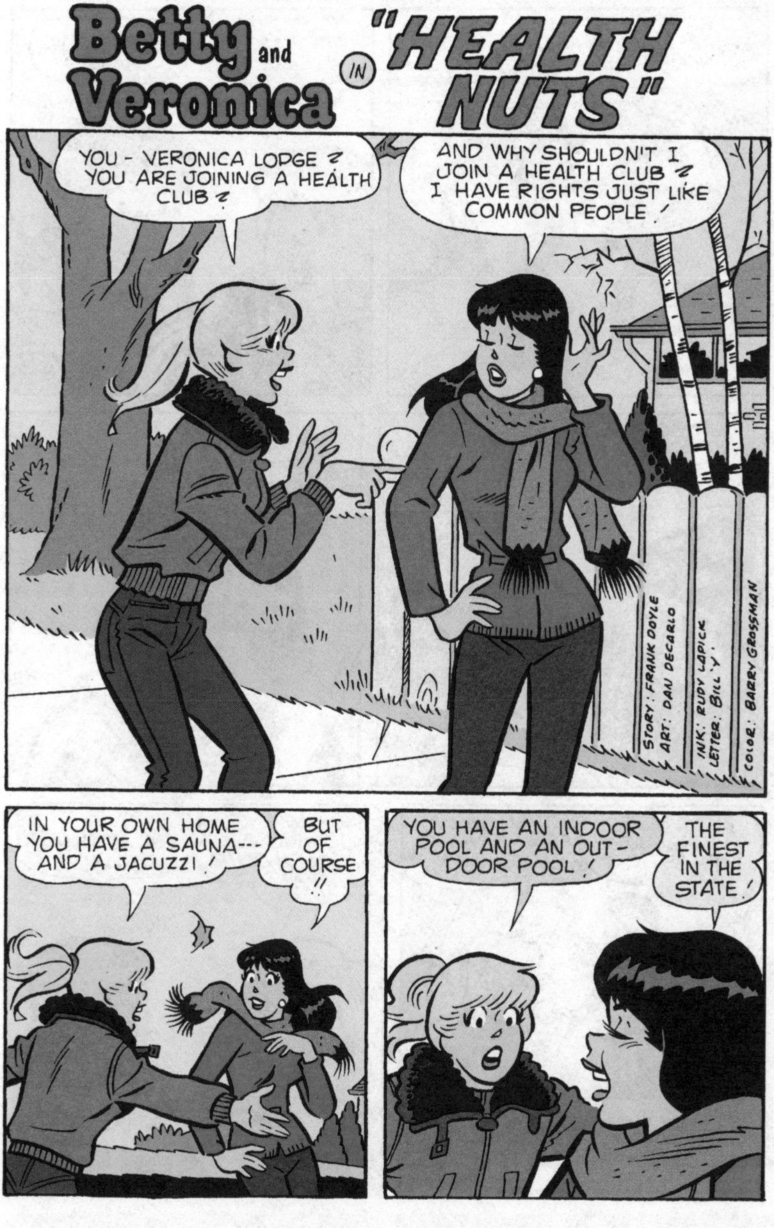
Betty and Veronica
IN
"HEALTH NUTS"
YOU - VERONICA LODGE? YOU ARE JOINING A HEALTH CLUB?
AND WHY SHOULDN'T I JOIN A HEALTH CLUB? I HAVE RIGHTS JUST LIKE COMMON PEOPLE!
STORY: FRANK DOYLE
ART: DAN DECARLO
INK: RUDY LAPICK
LETTER: BILL 'Y'
COLOR: BARRY GROSSMAN
IN YOUR OWN HOME YOU HAVE A SAUNA--- AND A JACUZZI!
BUT OF COURSE!!
YOU HAVE AN INDOOR POOL AND AN OUT-DOOR POOL!
THE FINEST IN THE STATE!

Originally presented in BETTY & VERONICA #302, February, 1981

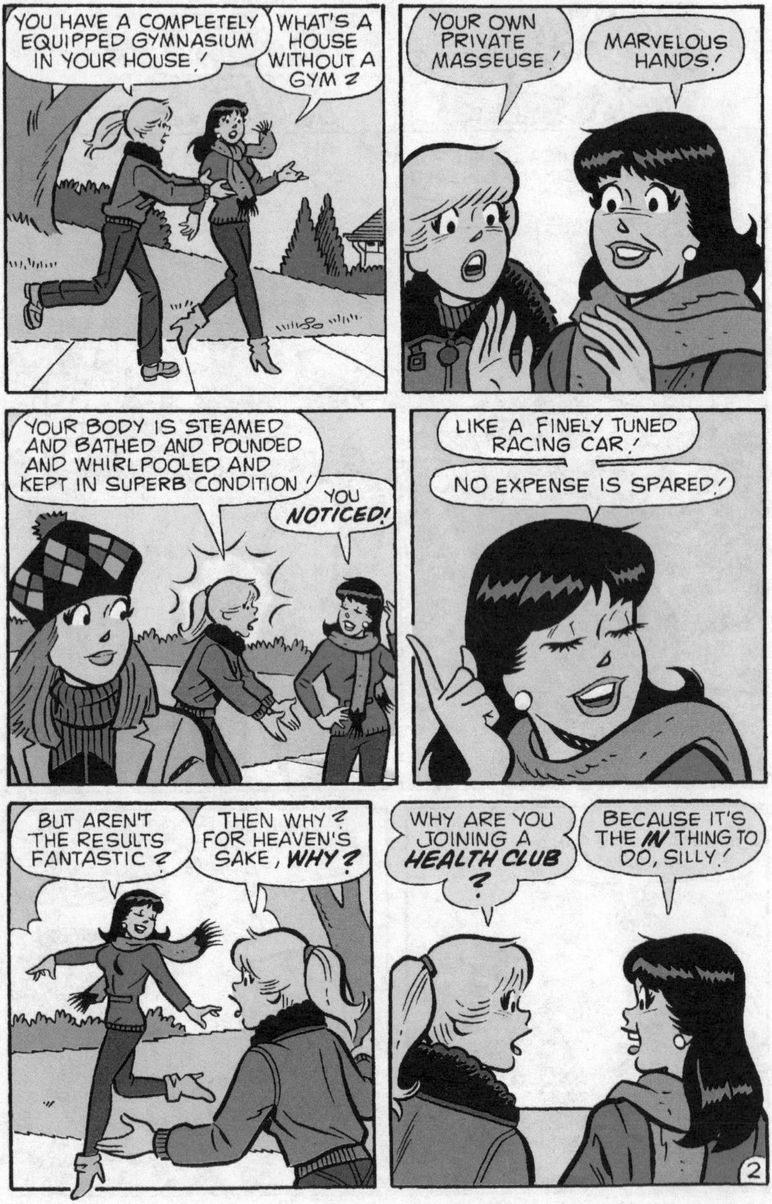
YOU HAVE A COMPLETELY EQUIPPED GYMNASIUM IN YOUR HOUSE!
WHAT'S A HOUSE WITHOUT A GYM?
YOUR OWN PRIVATE MASSEUSE!
MARVELOUS HANDS!
YOUR BODY IS STEAMED AND BATHED AND POUNDED AND WHIRLPOOLED AND KEPT IN SUPERB CONDITION!
YOU NOTICED!
LIKE A FINELY TUNED RACING CAR!
NO EXPENSE IS SPARED!
BUT AREN'T THE RESULTS FANTASTIC?
THEN WHY? FOR HEAVEN'S SAKE, WHY?
WHY ARE YOU JOINING A HEALTH CLUB?
BECAUSE IT'S THE IN THING TO DO, SILLY!
2

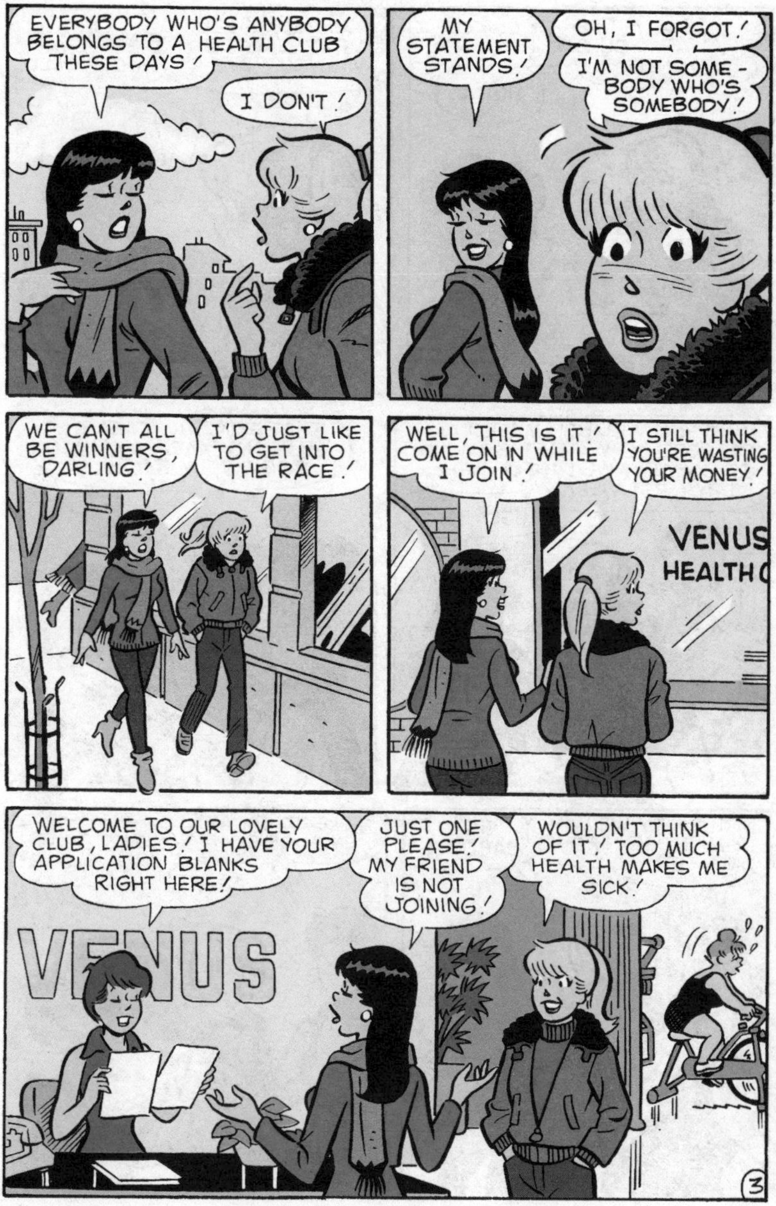
EVERYBODY WHO'S ANYBODY BELONGS TO A HEALTH CLUB THESE DAYS!
I DON'T!
MY STATEMENT STANDS!
OH, I FORGOT!
I'M NOT SOME-BODY WHO'S SOMEBODY!
WE CAN'T ALL BE WINNERS, DARLING!
I'D JUST LIKE TO GET INTO THE RACE!
WELL, THIS IS IT! COME ON IN WHILE I JOIN!
I STILL THINK YOU'RE WASTING YOUR MONEY!
VENUS
HEALTH
WELCOME TO OUR LOVELY CLUB, LADIES! I HAVE YOUR APPLICATION BLANKS RIGHT HERE!
JUST ONE PLEASE! MY FRIEND IS NOT JOINING!
WOULDN'T THINK OF IT! TOO MUCH HEALTH MAKES ME SICK!
VENUS
3

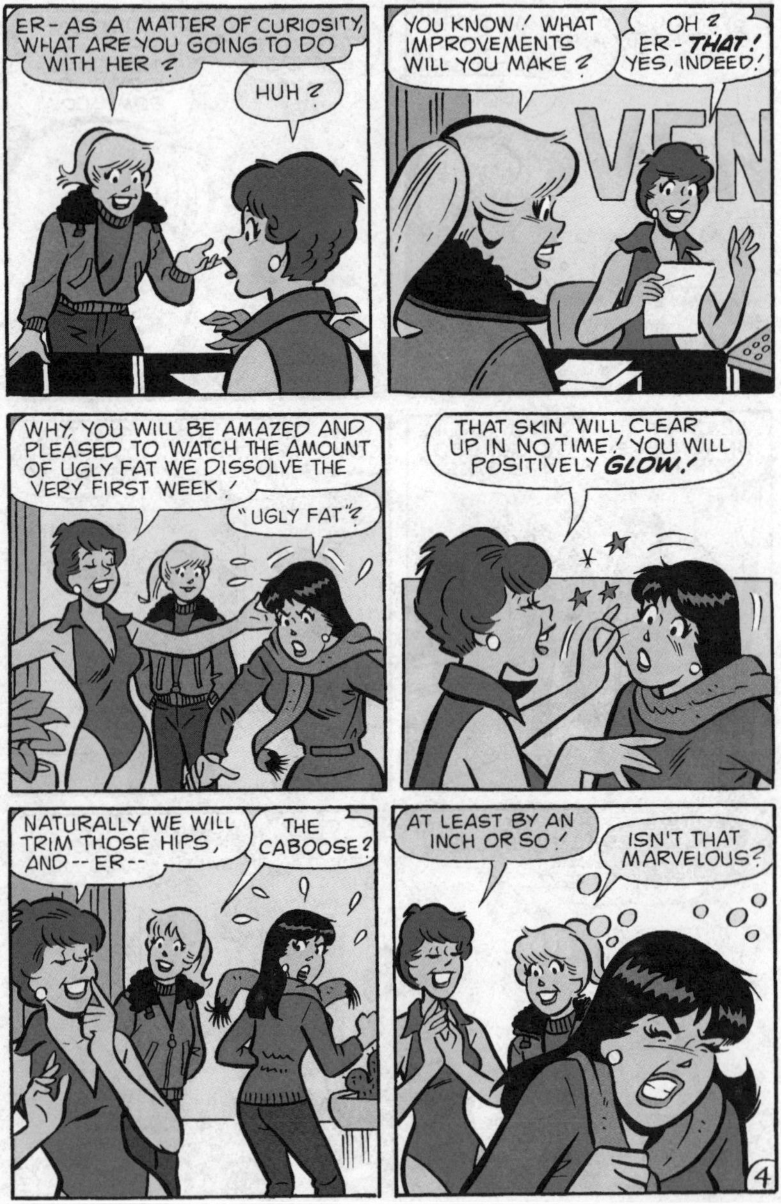
ER- AS A MATTER OF CURIOSITY, WHAT ARE YOU GOING TO DO WITH HER ?
HUH ?
YOU KNOW ! WHAT IMPROVEMENTS WILL YOU MAKE ?
OH ? ER- THAT ! YES, INDEED !
VEN
WHY, YOU WILL BE AMAZED AND PLEASED TO WATCH THE AMOUNT OF UGLY FAT WE DISSOLVE THE VERY FIRST WEEK !
"UGLY FAT"?
THAT SKIN WILL CLEAR UP IN NO TIME ! YOU WILL POSITIVELY GLOW !
NATURALLY WE WILL TRIM THOSE HIPS, AND -- ER --
THE CABOOSE ?
AT LEAST BY AN INCH OR SO !
ISN'T THAT MARVELOUS?
4

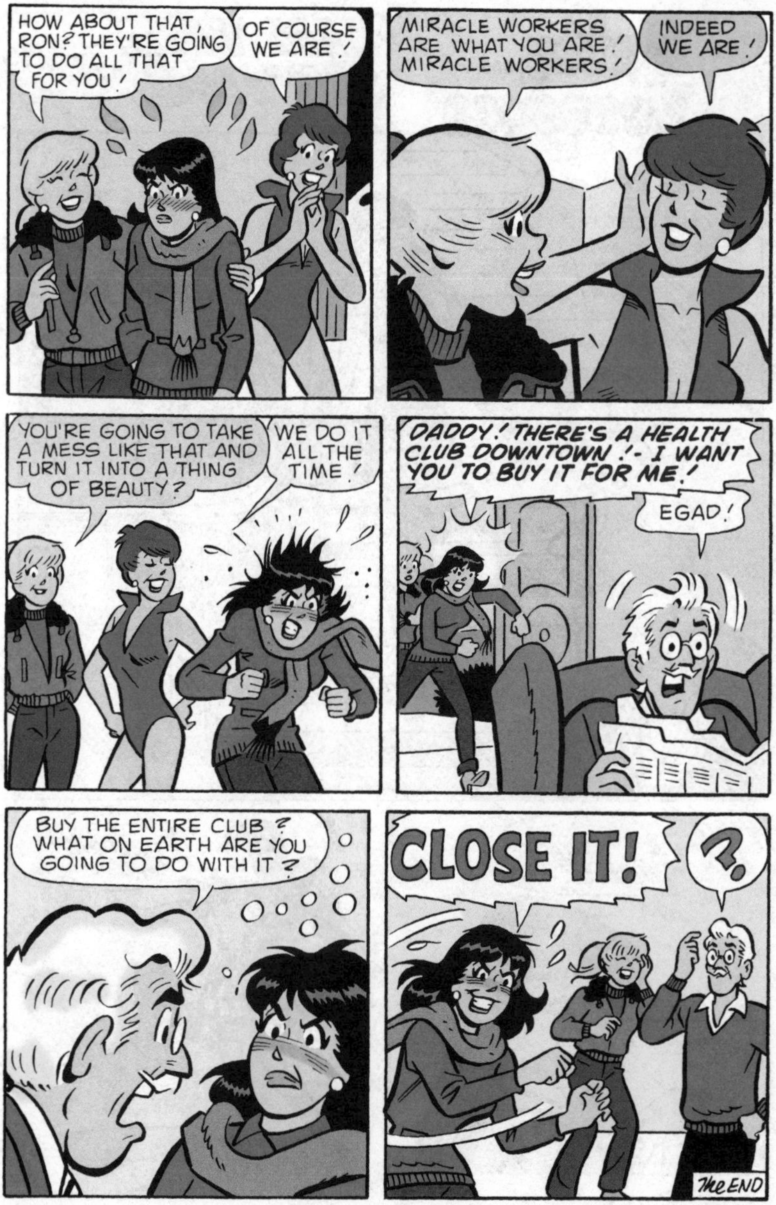
HOW ABOUT THAT, RON? THEY'RE GOING TO DO ALL THAT FOR YOU!
OF COURSE WE ARE!
MIRACLE WORKERS ARE WHAT YOU ARE! MIRACLE WORKERS!
INDEED WE ARE!
YOU'RE GOING TO TAKE A MESS LIKE THAT AND TURN IT INTO A THING OF BEAUTY?
WE DO IT ALL THE TIME!
DADDY! THERE'S A HEALTH CLUB DOWNTOWN! - I WANT YOU TO BUY IT FOR ME!
EGAD!
BUY THE ENTIRE CLUB? WHAT ON EARTH ARE YOU GOING TO DO WITH IT?
CLOSE IT!
?
THE END

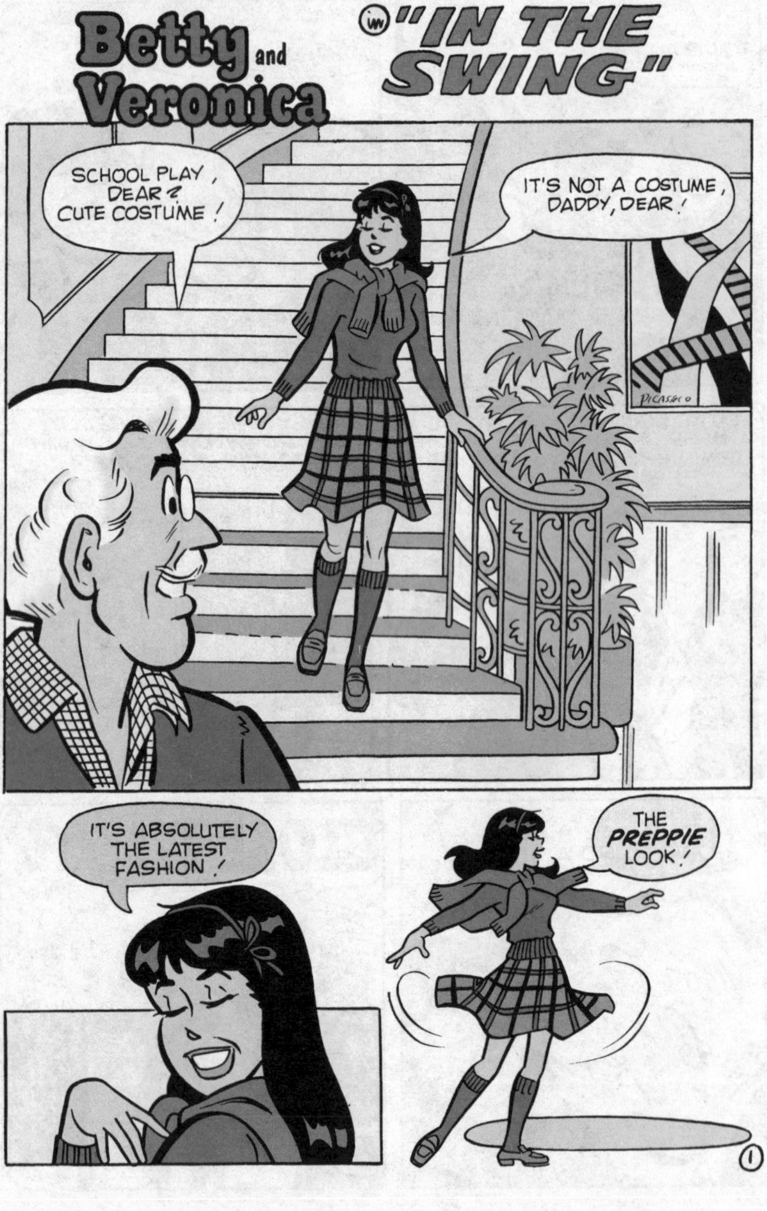
Betty and Veronica
in "IN THE SWING"
SCHOOL PLAY, DEAR? CUTE COSTUME!
IT'S NOT A COSTUME, DADDY, DEAR!
PICASSCO
IT'S ABSOLUTELY THE LATEST FASHION!
THE PREPPIE LOOK!
1

Originally presented in BETTY & VERONICA #302, February, 1981

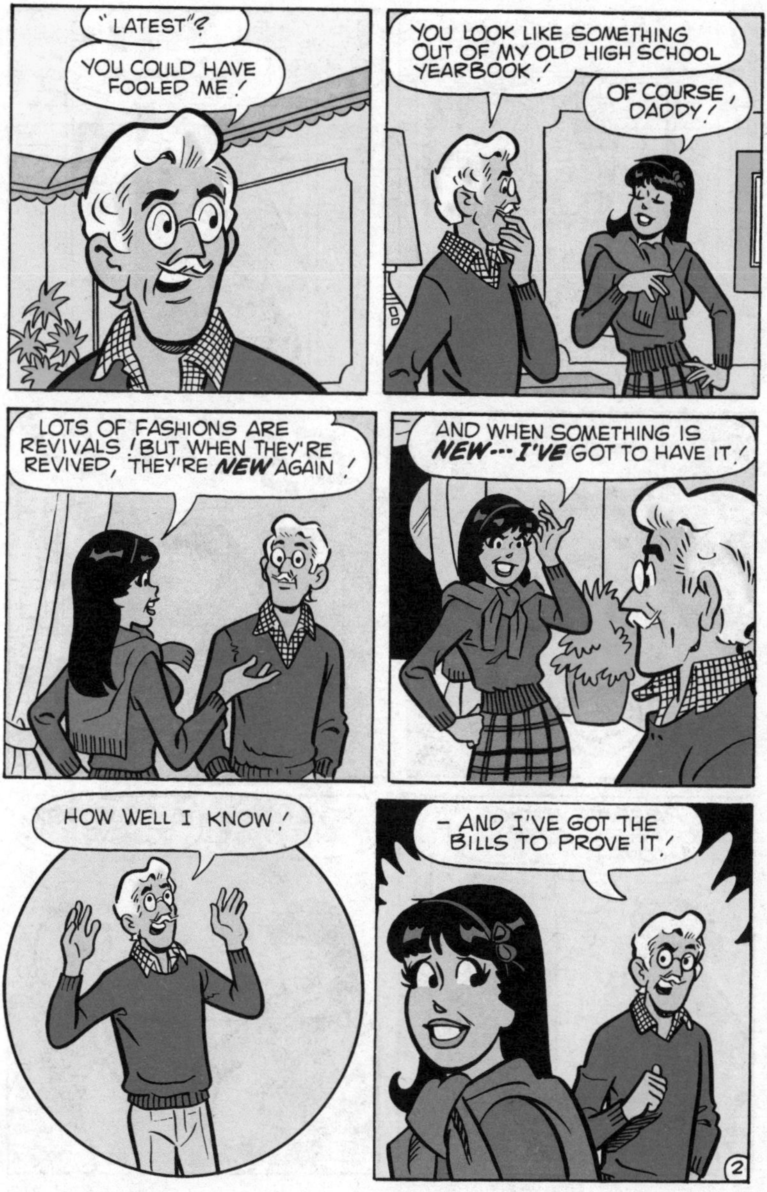
"LATEST"?
YOU COULD HAVE FOOLED ME!
YOU LOOK LIKE SOMETHING OUT OF MY OLD HIGH SCHOOL YEARBOOK!
OF COURSE, DADDY!
LOTS OF FASHIONS ARE REVIVALS! BUT WHEN THEY'RE REVIVED, THEY'RE **NEW** AGAIN!
AND WHEN SOMETHING IS **NEW**--- **I'VE** GOT TO HAVE IT!
HOW WELL I KNOW!
- AND I'VE GOT THE BILLS TO PROVE IT!
2

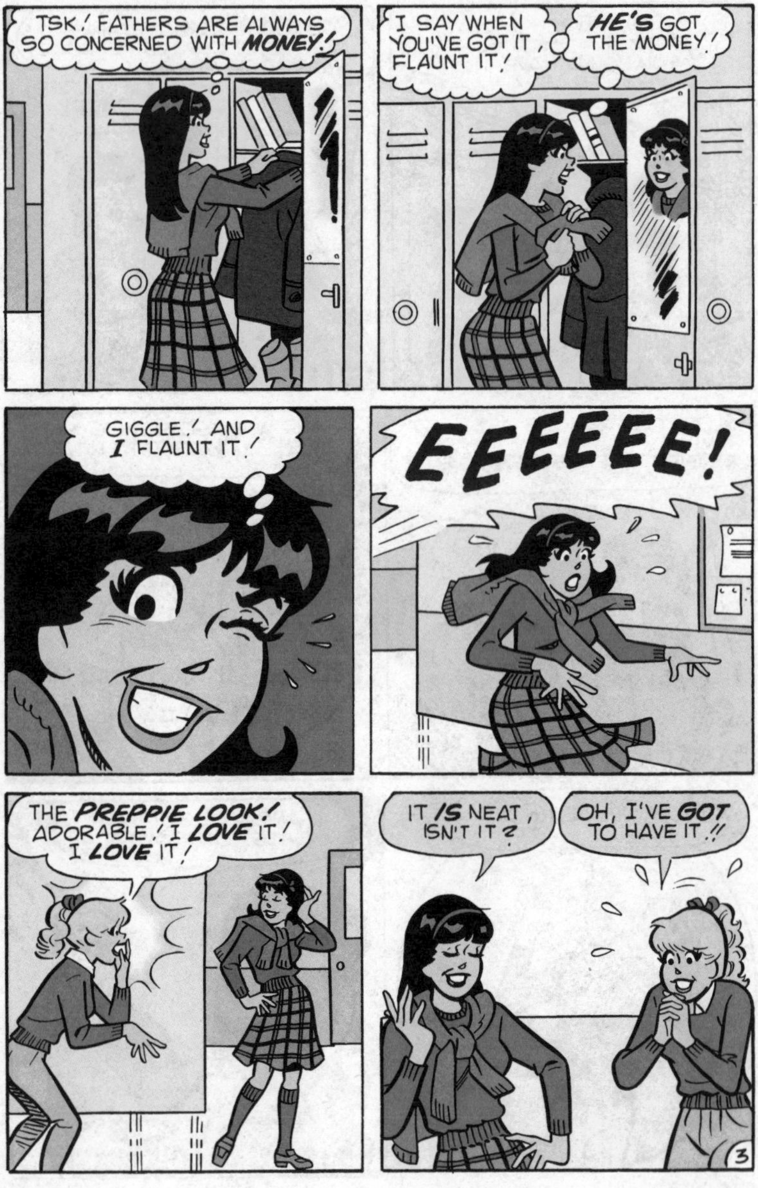
TSK! FATHERS ARE ALWAYS SO CONCERNED WITH MONEY!
I SAY WHEN YOU'VE GOT IT, FLAUNT IT!
HE'S GOT THE MONEY!
GIGGLE! AND I FLAUNT IT!
EEEEEE!
THE PREPPIE LOOK! ADORABLE! I LOVE IT! I LOVE IT!
IT IS NEAT, ISN'T IT?
OH, I'VE GOT TO HAVE IT!!
3

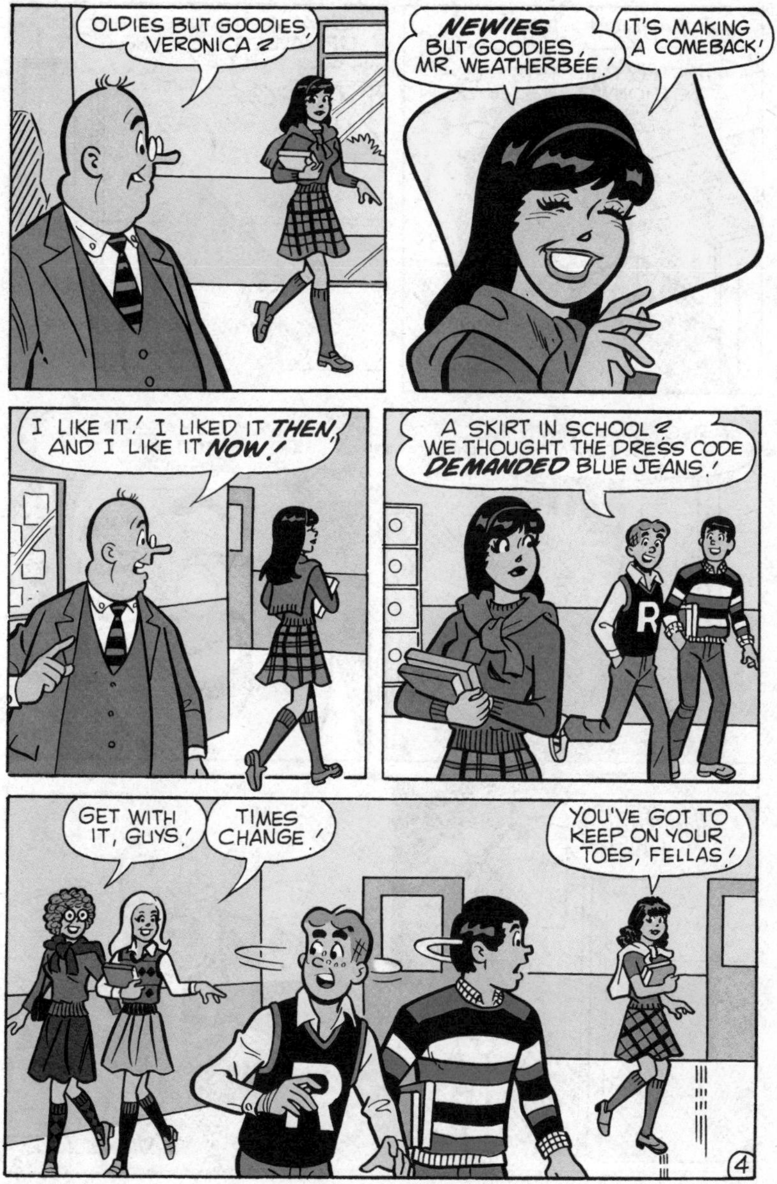
OLDIES BUT GOODIES, VERONICA ?
NEWIES BUT GOODIES, MR. WEATHERBEE!
IT'S MAKING A COMEBACK!
I LIKE IT! I LIKED IT THEN, AND I LIKE IT NOW!
A SKIRT IN SCHOOL? WE THOUGHT THE DRESS CODE DEMANDED BLUE JEANS!
GET WITH IT, GUYS!
TIMES CHANGE!
YOU'VE GOT TO KEEP ON YOUR TOES, FELLAS!
4

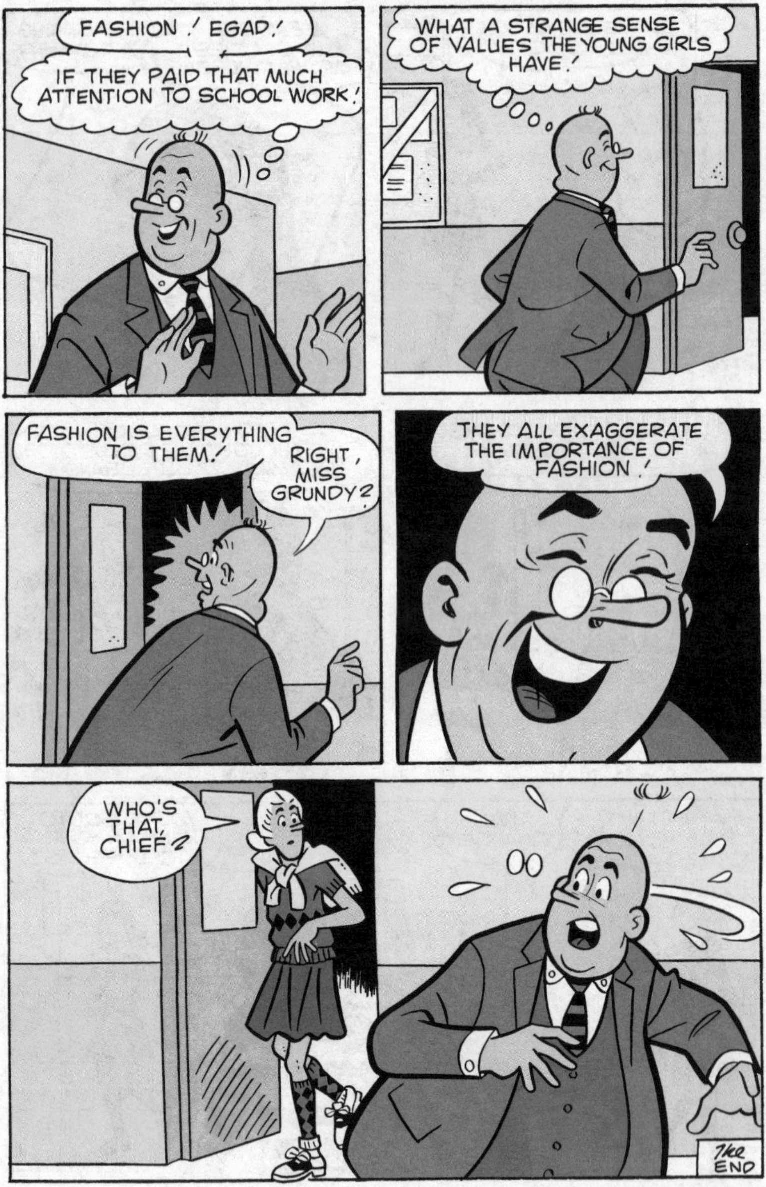
FASHION! EGAD!
IF THEY PAID THAT MUCH ATTENTION TO SCHOOL WORK!
WHAT A STRANGE SENSE OF VALUES THE YOUNG GIRLS HAVE!
FASHION IS EVERYTHING TO THEM!
RIGHT, MISS GRUNDY?
THEY ALL EXAGGERATE THE IMPORTANCE OF FASHION!
WHO'S THAT, CHIEF?
END

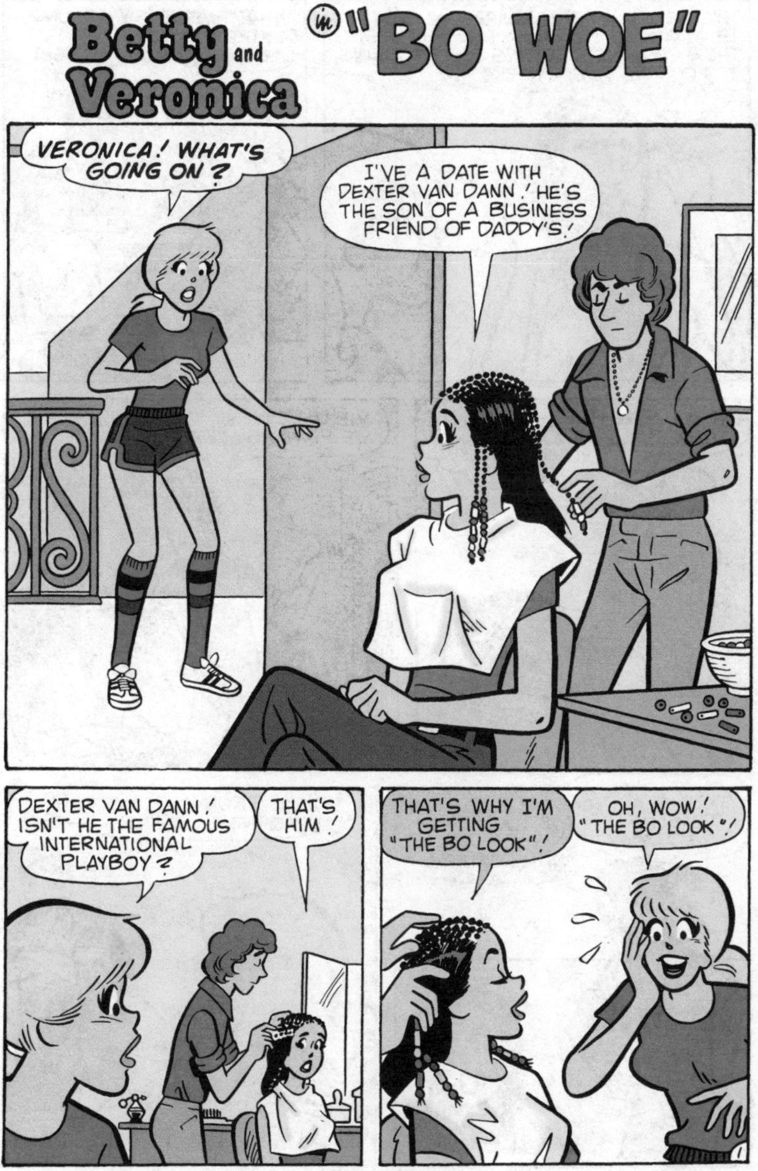
Betty and Veronica
in "BO WOE"
VERONICA! WHAT'S GOING ON?
I'VE A DATE WITH DEXTER VAN DANN! HE'S THE SON OF A BUSINESS FRIEND OF DADDY'S!
DEXTER VAN DANN! ISN'T HE THE FAMOUS INTERNATIONAL PLAYBOY?
THAT'S HIM!
THAT'S WHY I'M GETTING "THE BO LOOK"!
OH, WOW! "THE BO LOOK"!

Originally presented in BETTY & VERONICA SPECTACULAR #506, June, 1981

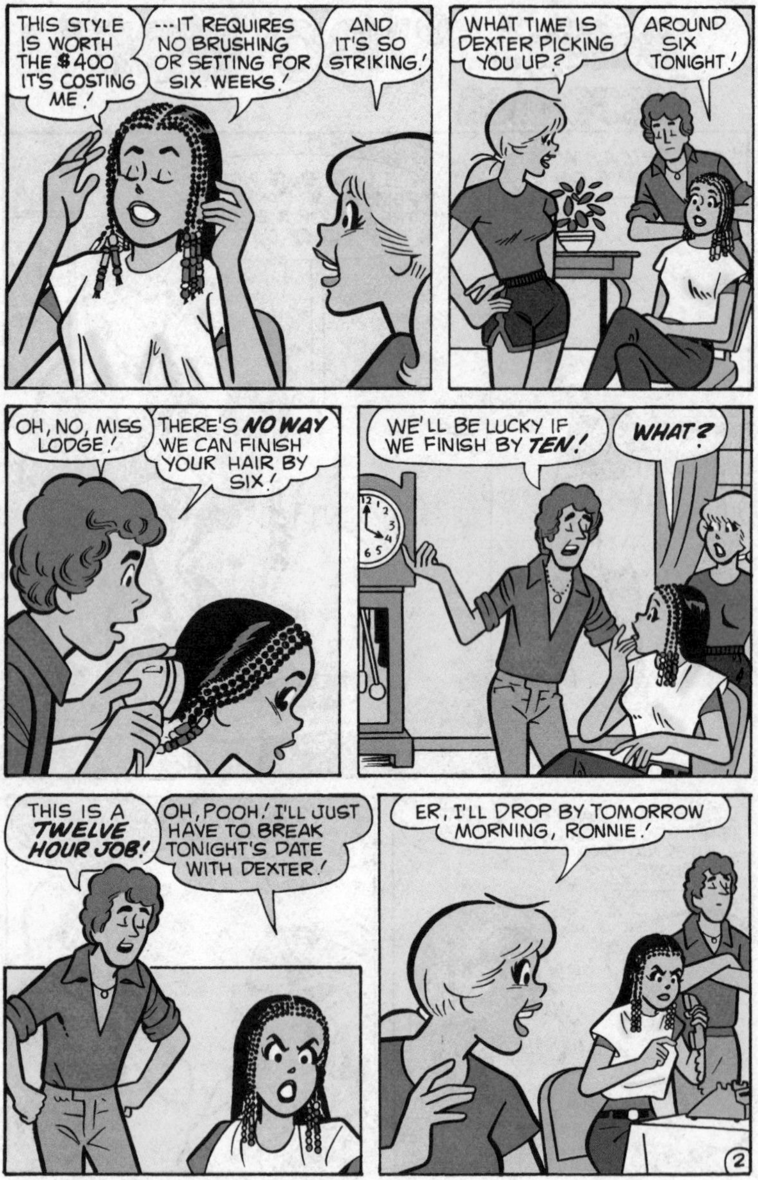
THIS STYLE IS WORTH THE $400 IT'S COSTING ME!
---IT REQUIRES NO BRUSHING OR SETTING FOR SIX WEEKS!
AND IT'S SO STRIKING!
WHAT TIME IS DEXTER PICKING YOU UP?
AROUND SIX TONIGHT!
OH, NO, MISS LODGE!
THERE'S NO WAY WE CAN FINISH YOUR HAIR BY SIX!
WE'LL BE LUCKY IF WE FINISH BY TEN!
WHAT?
THIS IS A TWELVE HOUR JOB!
OH, POOH! I'LL JUST HAVE TO BREAK TONIGHT'S DATE WITH DEXTER!
ER, I'LL DROP BY TOMORROW MORNING, RONNIE!
2

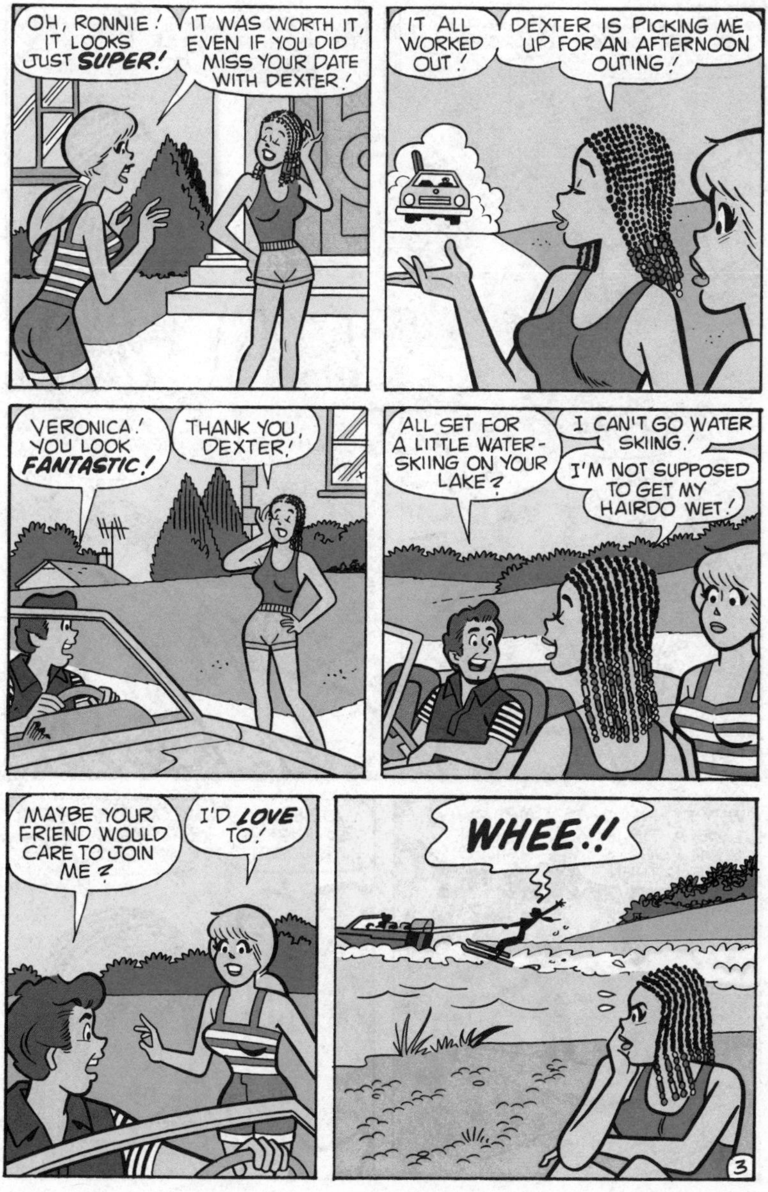
OH, RONNIE! IT LOOKS JUST SUPER!
IT WAS WORTH IT, EVEN IF YOU DID MISS YOUR DATE WITH DEXTER!
IT ALL WORKED OUT!
DEXTER IS PICKING ME UP FOR AN AFTERNOON OUTING!
VERONICA! YOU LOOK FANTASTIC!
THANK YOU, DEXTER!
ALL SET FOR A LITTLE WATER-SKIING ON YOUR LAKE?
I CAN'T GO WATER SKIING!
I'M NOT SUPPOSED TO GET MY HAIRDO WET!
MAYBE YOUR FRIEND WOULD CARE TO JOIN ME?
I'D LOVE TO!
WHEE!!
3

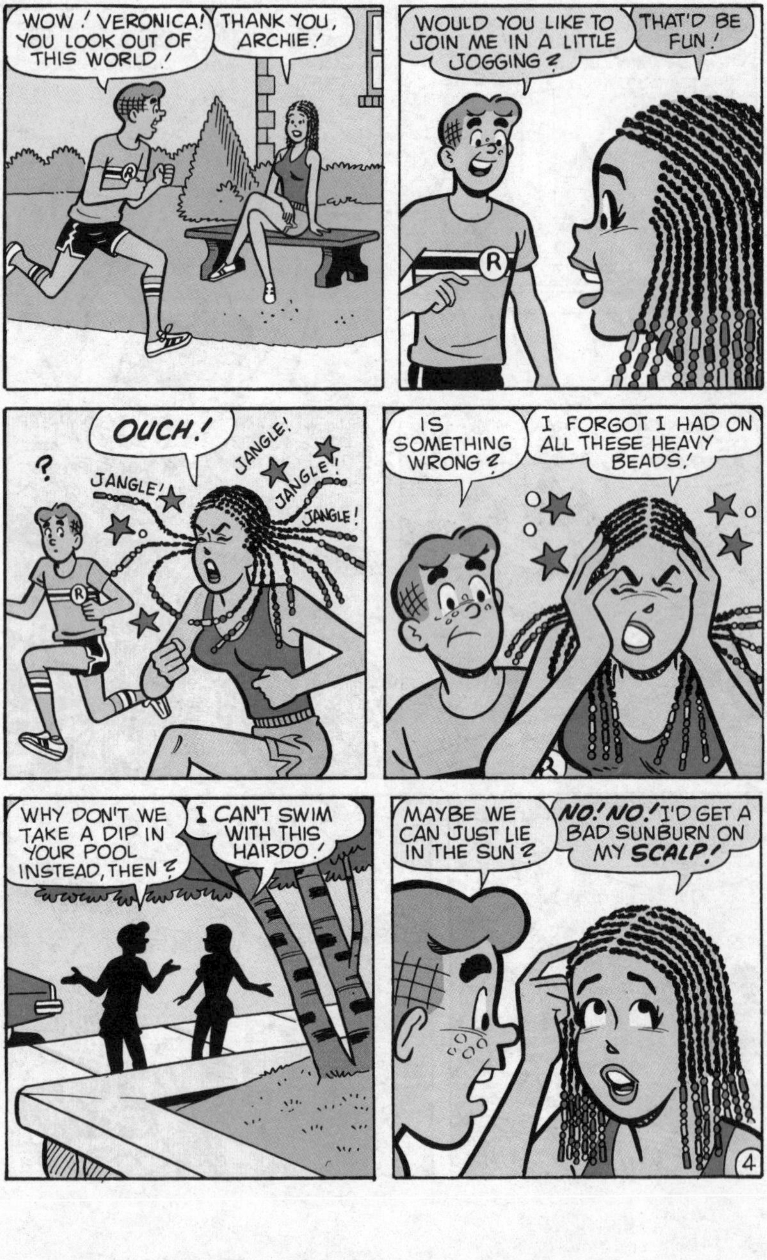
WOW! VERONICA! YOU LOOK OUT OF THIS WORLD!
THANK YOU, ARCHIE!
WOULD YOU LIKE TO JOIN ME IN A LITTLE JOGGING?
THAT'D BE FUN!
?
OUCH!
JANGLE!
JANGLE!
JANGLE!
JANGLE!
IS SOMETHING WRONG?
I FORGOT I HAD ON ALL THESE HEAVY BEADS!
WHY DON'T WE TAKE A DIP IN YOUR POOL INSTEAD, THEN?
I CAN'T SWIM WITH THIS HAIRDO!
MAYBE WE CAN JUST LIE IN THE SUN?
NO! NO! I'D GET A BAD SUNBURN ON MY SCALP!
4

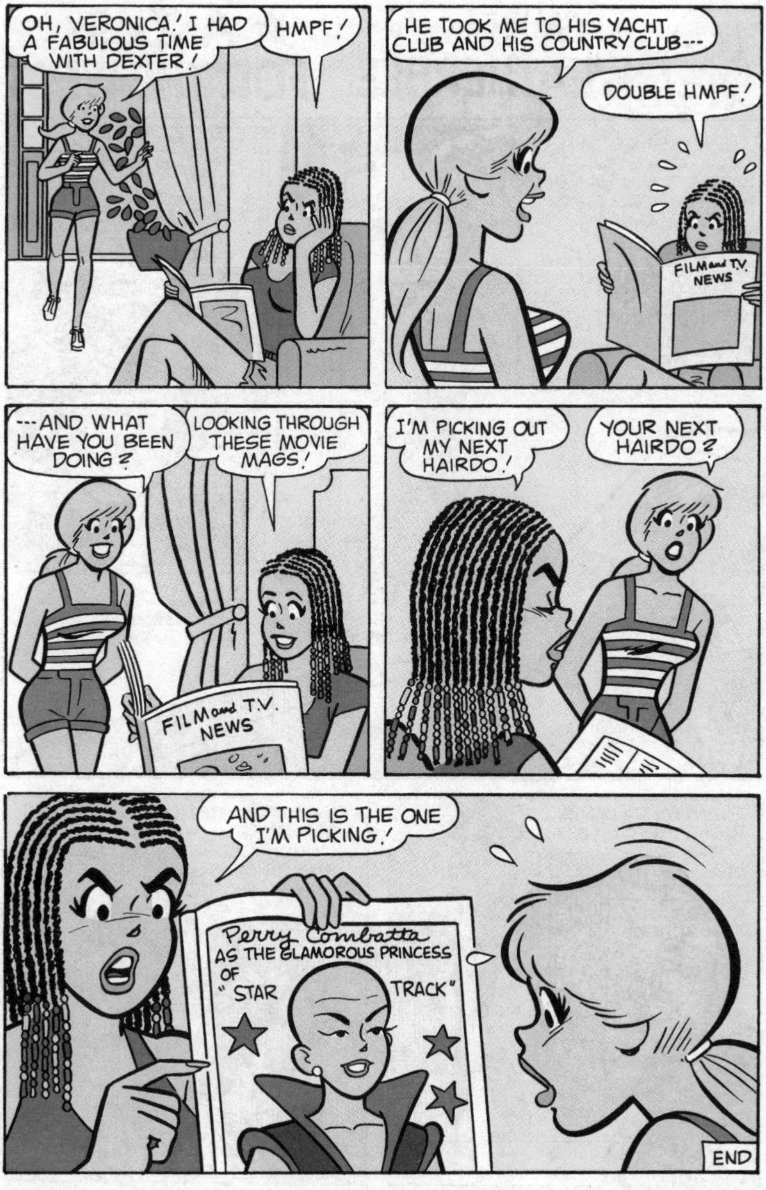
OH, VERONICA! I HAD A FABULOUS TIME WITH DEXTER!
HMPF!
HE TOOK ME TO HIS YACHT CLUB AND HIS COUNTRY CLUB---
DOUBLE HMPF!
FILM and T.V. NEWS
---AND WHAT HAVE YOU BEEN DOING?
LOOKING THROUGH THESE MOVIE MAGS!
FILM and T.V. NEWS
I'M PICKING OUT MY NEXT HAIRDO!
YOUR NEXT HAIRDO?
AND THIS IS THE ONE I'M PICKING!
Perry Combatta
AS THE GLAMOROUS PRINCESS OF "STAR TRACK"
END

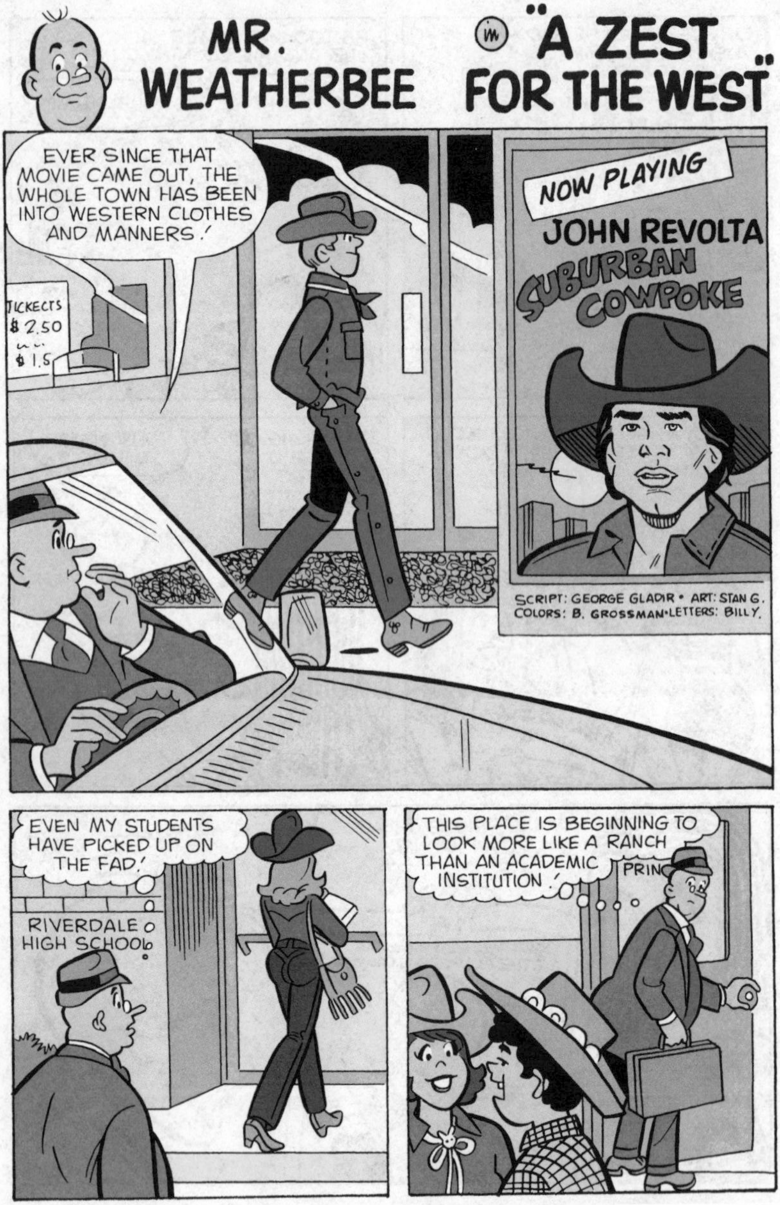
MR. WEATHERBEE in "A ZEST FOR THE WEST"
EVER SINCE THAT MOVIE CAME OUT, THE WHOLE TOWN HAS BEEN INTO WESTERN CLOTHES AND MANNERS!
TICKECTS $2.50
NOW PLAYING
JOHN REVOLTA
SUBURBAN COWPOKE
SCRIPT: GEORGE GLADIR • ART: STAN G.
COLORS: B. GROSSMAN • LETTERS: BILLY.
EVEN MY STUDENTS HAVE PICKED UP ON THE FAD!
RIVERDALE HIGH SCHOOL
THIS PLACE IS BEGINNING TO LOOK MORE LIKE A RANCH THAN AN ACADEMIC INSTITUTION!
PRIN

Originally presented in PEP #374, June, 1981

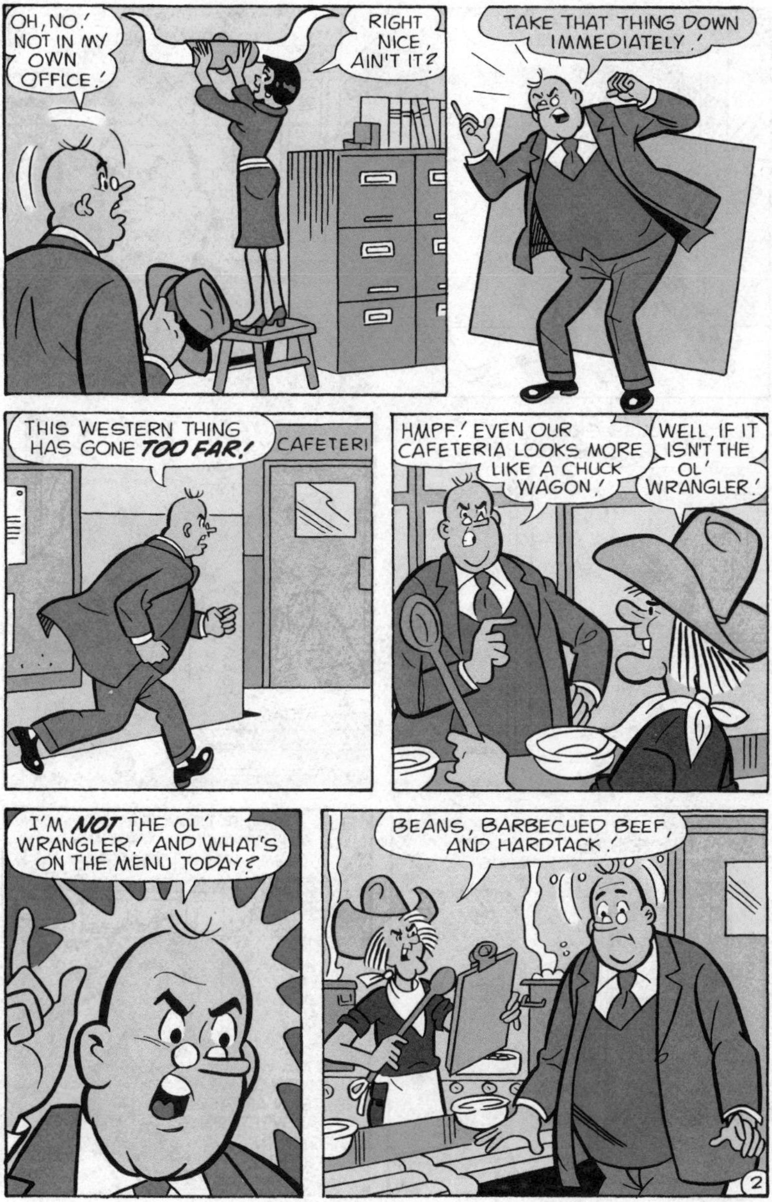
OH, NO! NOT IN MY OWN OFFICE!
RIGHT NICE, AIN'T IT?
TAKE THAT THING DOWN IMMEDIATELY!
THIS WESTERN THING HAS GONE TOO FAR!
CAFETERI
HMPF! EVEN OUR CAFETERIA LOOKS MORE LIKE A CHUCK WAGON!
WELL, IF IT ISN'T THE OL' WRANGLER!
I'M NOT THE OL' WRANGLER! AND WHAT'S ON THE MENU TODAY?
BEANS, BARBECUED BEEF, AND HARDTACK!
2

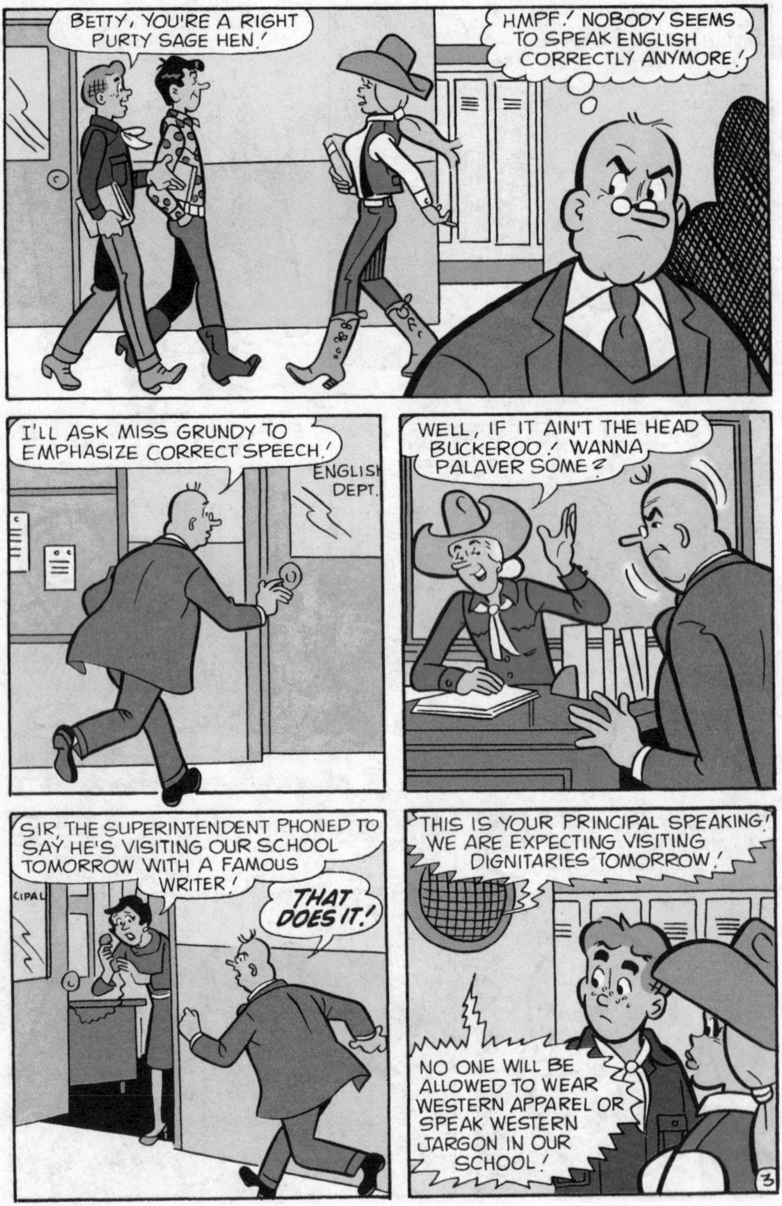
BETTY, YOU'RE A RIGHT PURTY SAGE HEN!
HMPF! NOBODY SEEMS TO SPEAK ENGLISH CORRECTLY ANYMORE!
I'LL ASK MISS GRUNDY TO EMPHASIZE CORRECT SPEECH!
ENGLISH DEPT.
WELL, IF IT AIN'T THE HEAD BUCKEROO! WANNA PALAVER SOME?
SIR, THE SUPERINTENDENT PHONED TO SAY HE'S VISITING OUR SCHOOL TOMORROW WITH A FAMOUS WRITER!
THAT DOES IT!
THIS IS YOUR PRINCIPAL SPEAKING! WE ARE EXPECTING VISITING DIGNITARIES TOMORROW!
NO ONE WILL BE ALLOWED TO WEAR WESTERN APPAREL OR SPEAK WESTERN JARGON IN OUR SCHOOL!
3

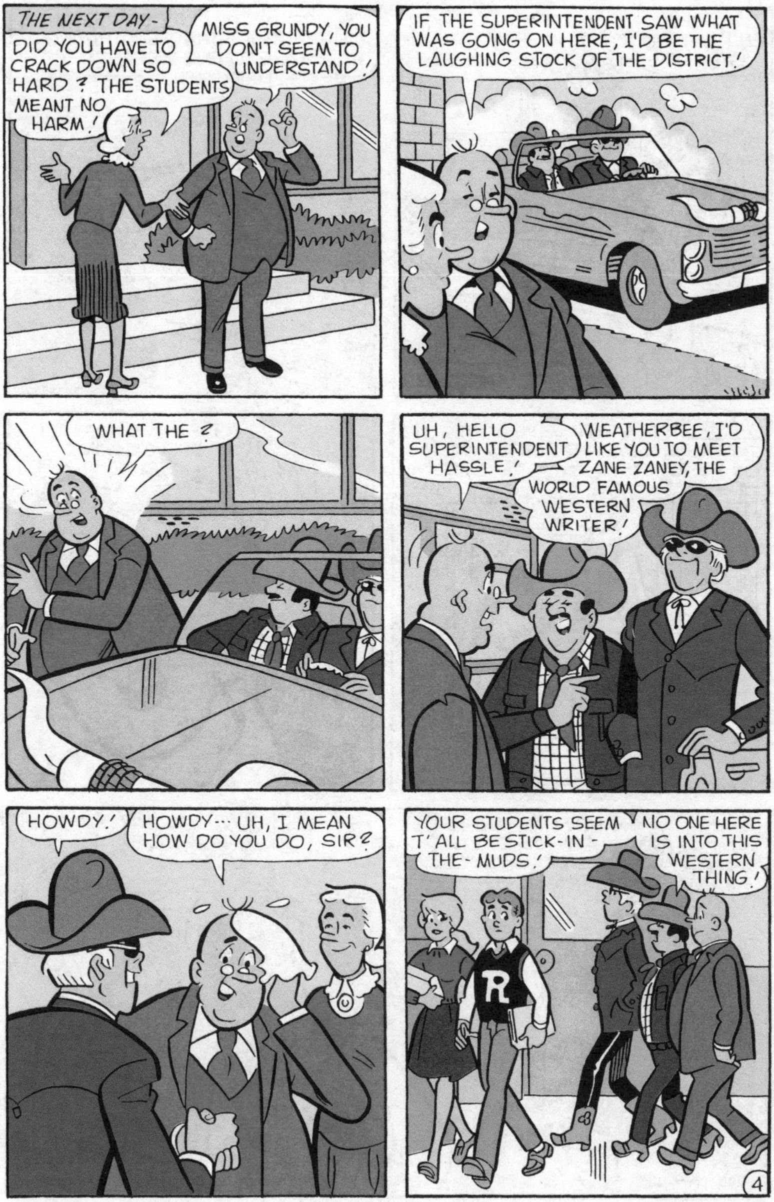
THE NEXT DAY-
DID YOU HAVE TO CRACK DOWN SO HARD? THE STUDENTS MEANT NO HARM!
MISS GRUNDY, YOU DON'T SEEM TO UNDERSTAND!
IF THE SUPERINTENDENT SAW WHAT WAS GOING ON HERE, I'D BE THE LAUGHING STOCK OF THE DISTRICT!
WHAT THE ?
UH, HELLO SUPERINTENDENT HASSLE!
WEATHERBEE, I'D LIKE YOU TO MEET ZANE ZANEY, THE WORLD FAMOUS WESTERN WRITER!
HOWDY!
HOWDY... UH, I MEAN HOW DO YOU DO, SIR?
YOUR STUDENTS SEEM T' ALL BE STICK-IN-THE-MUDS!
NO ONE HERE IS INTO THIS WESTERN THING!
4

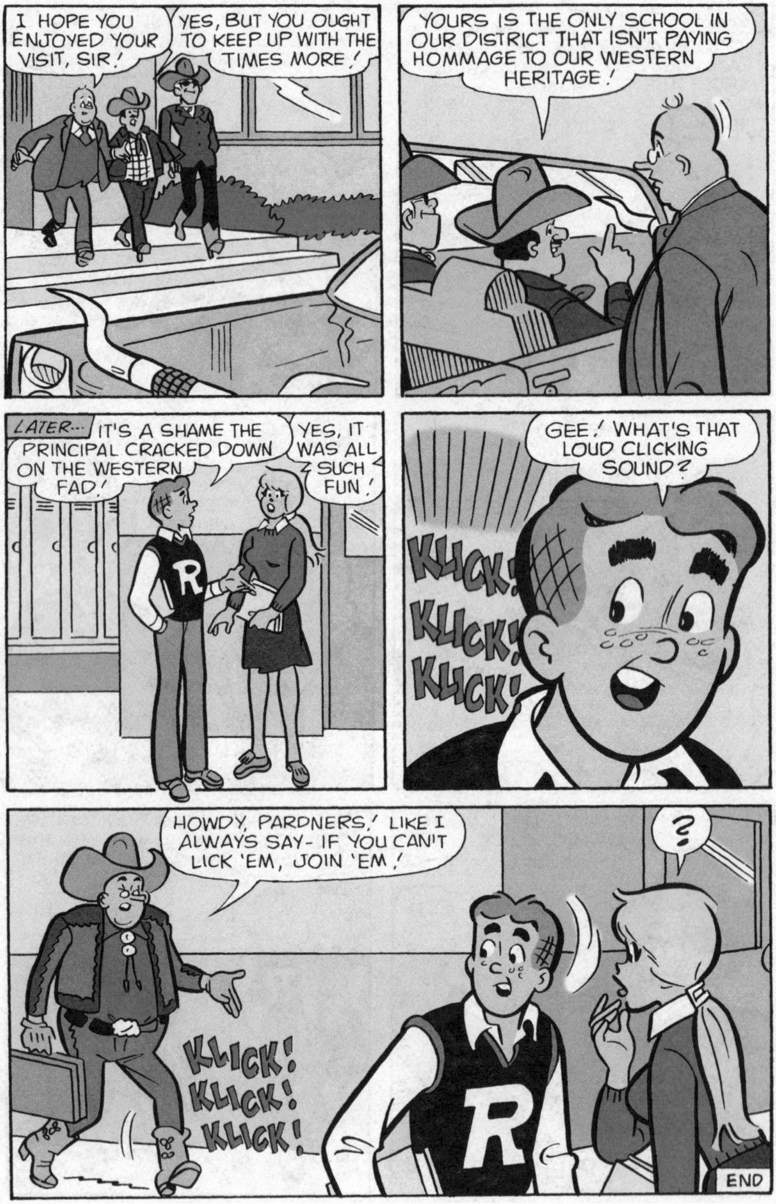
I HOPE YOU ENJOYED YOUR VISIT, SIR!
YES, BUT YOU OUGHT TO KEEP UP WITH THE TIMES MORE!
YOURS IS THE ONLY SCHOOL IN OUR DISTRICT THAT ISN'T PAYING HOMMAGE TO OUR WESTERN HERITAGE!
LATER...
IT'S A SHAME THE PRINCIPAL CRACKED DOWN ON THE WESTERN FAD!
YES, IT WAS ALL SUCH FUN!
GEE! WHAT'S THAT LOUD CLICKING SOUND?
KLICK! KLICK! KLICK!
HOWDY, PARDNERS! LIKE I ALWAYS SAY- IF YOU CAN'T LICK 'EM, JOIN 'EM!
?
KLICK! KLICK! KLICK!
END

# Betty and Veronica in FLEETING MEETING

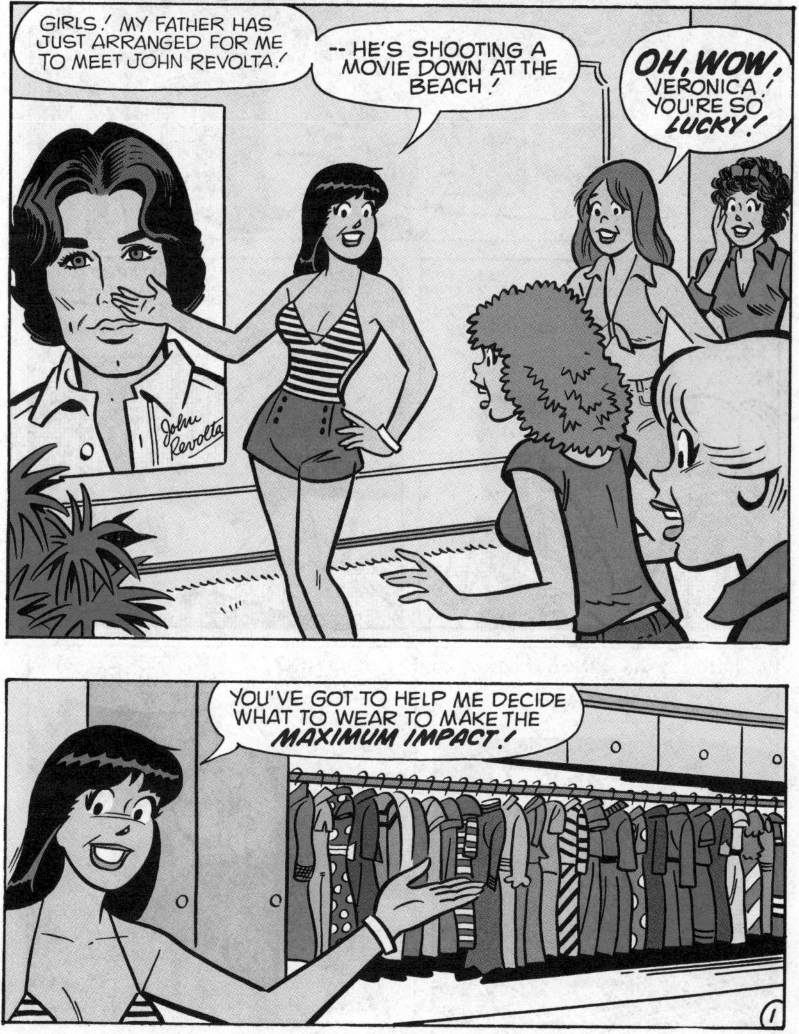
GIRLS! MY FATHER HAS JUST ARRANGED FOR ME TO MEET JOHN REVOLTA!
-- HE'S SHOOTING A MOVIE DOWN AT THE BEACH!
OH, WOW, VERONICA! YOU'RE SO LUCKY!
John Revolta
YOU'VE GOT TO HELP ME DECIDE WHAT TO WEAR TO MAKE THE MAXIMUM IMPACT!
1

Originally printed in BETTY & VERONICA #310, October, 1981

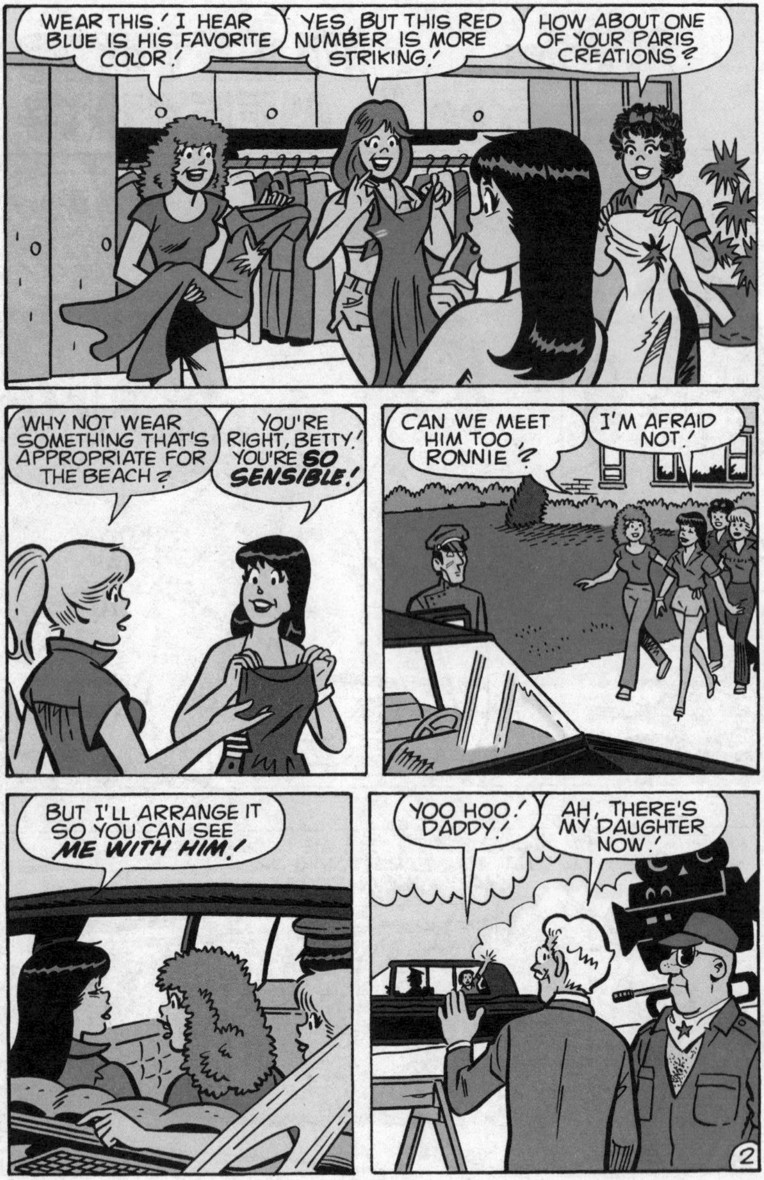
WEAR THIS! I HEAR BLUE IS HIS FAVORITE COLOR!
YES, BUT THIS RED NUMBER IS MORE STRIKING!
HOW ABOUT ONE OF YOUR PARIS CREATIONS?
WHY NOT WEAR SOMETHING THAT'S APPROPRIATE FOR THE BEACH?
YOU'RE RIGHT, BETTY! YOU'RE SO SENSIBLE!
CAN WE MEET HIM TOO, RONNIE?
I'M AFRAID NOT!
BUT I'LL ARRANGE IT SO YOU CAN SEE ME WITH HIM!
YOO HOO! DADDY!
AH, THERE'S MY DAUGHTER NOW!
2

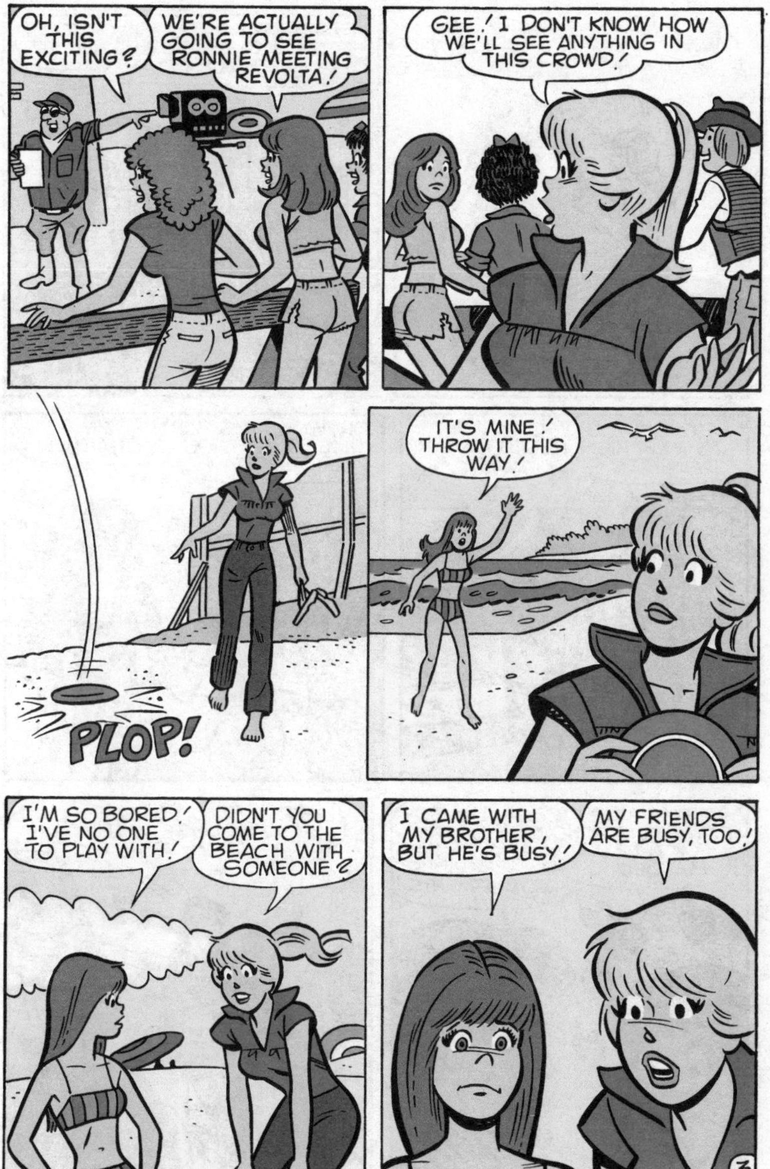
OH, ISN'T THIS EXCITING?
WE'RE ACTUALLY GOING TO SEE RONNIE MEETING REVOLTA!
GEE! I DON'T KNOW HOW WE'LL SEE ANYTHING IN THIS CROWD!
PLOP!
IT'S MINE! THROW IT THIS WAY!
I'M SO BORED! I'VE NO ONE TO PLAY WITH!
DIDN'T YOU COME TO THE BEACH WITH SOMEONE?
I CAME WITH MY BROTHER, BUT HE'S BUSY!
MY FRIENDS ARE BUSY, TOO!
3

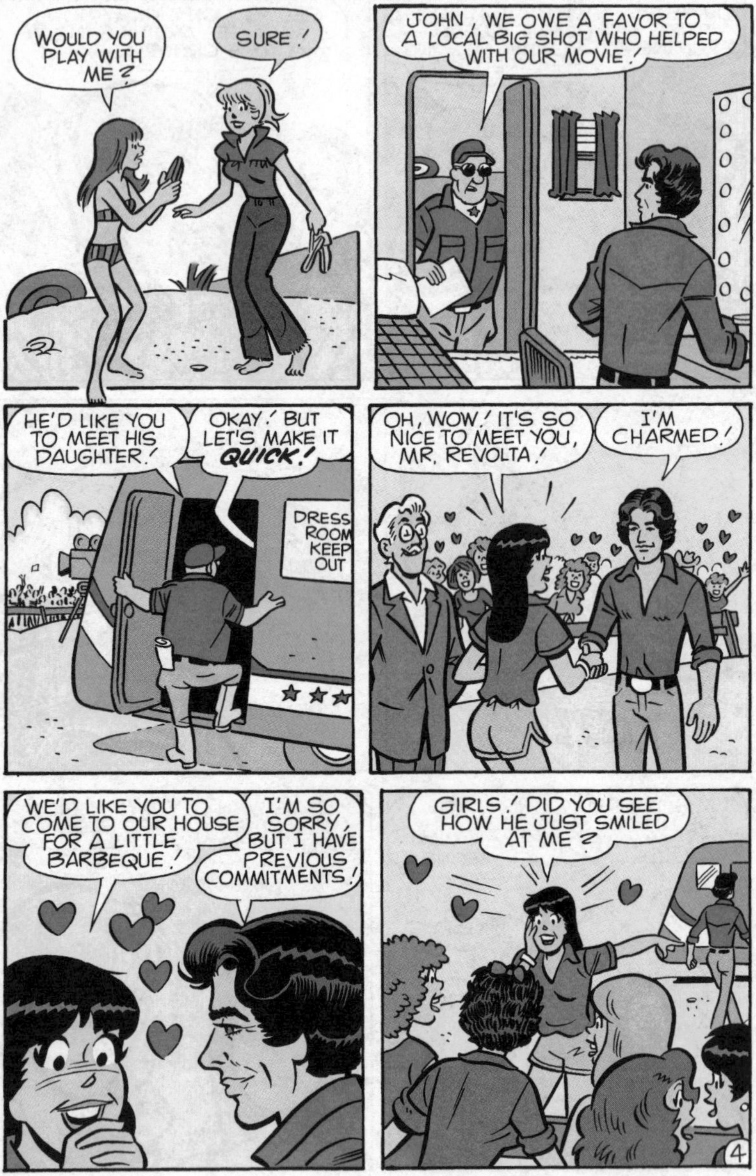
WOULD YOU PLAY WITH ME?
SURE!
JOHN, WE OWE A FAVOR TO A LOCAL BIG SHOT WHO HELPED WITH OUR MOVIE!
HE'D LIKE YOU TO MEET HIS DAUGHTER!
OKAY! BUT LET'S MAKE IT QUICK!
DRESS ROOM KEEP OUT
OH, WOW! IT'S SO NICE TO MEET YOU, MR. REVOLTA!
I'M CHARMED!
WE'D LIKE YOU TO COME TO OUR HOUSE FOR A LITTLE BARBEQUE!
I'M SO SORRY, BUT I HAVE PREVIOUS COMMITMENTS!
GIRLS! DID YOU SEE HOW HE JUST SMILED AT ME?
4

WHERE'S BETTY? DIDN'T SHE SEE ME TALKING TO REVOLTA?
SHE WANDERED OFF SOMEWHERE!
HMPF! THAT JEALOUS CAT COULDN'T STAND TO SEE ME IN MY MOMENT OF GLORY!
LINDA!
WHERE'S MY KID SISTER?
SHE'S RIGHT OVER THERE, MR. REVOLTA!
SCRIPT GIRL
I'M SORRY I WAS TIED UP, LINDA!
I DIDN'T KNOW HE WAS YOUR BROTHER!
I'LL MAKE IT UP TO YOU!
I'M GIVING A PARTY FOR YOU RIGHT NOW!
CAN MY FRIEND BETTY COME?
SURE!
OH, WOW!
5

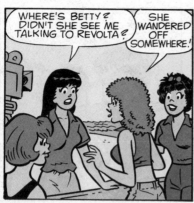

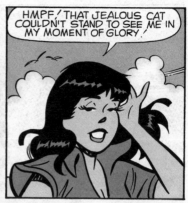

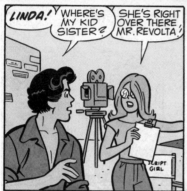

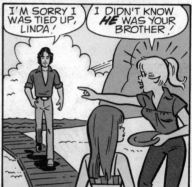

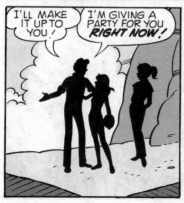

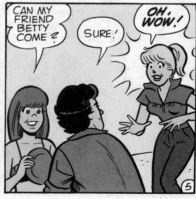

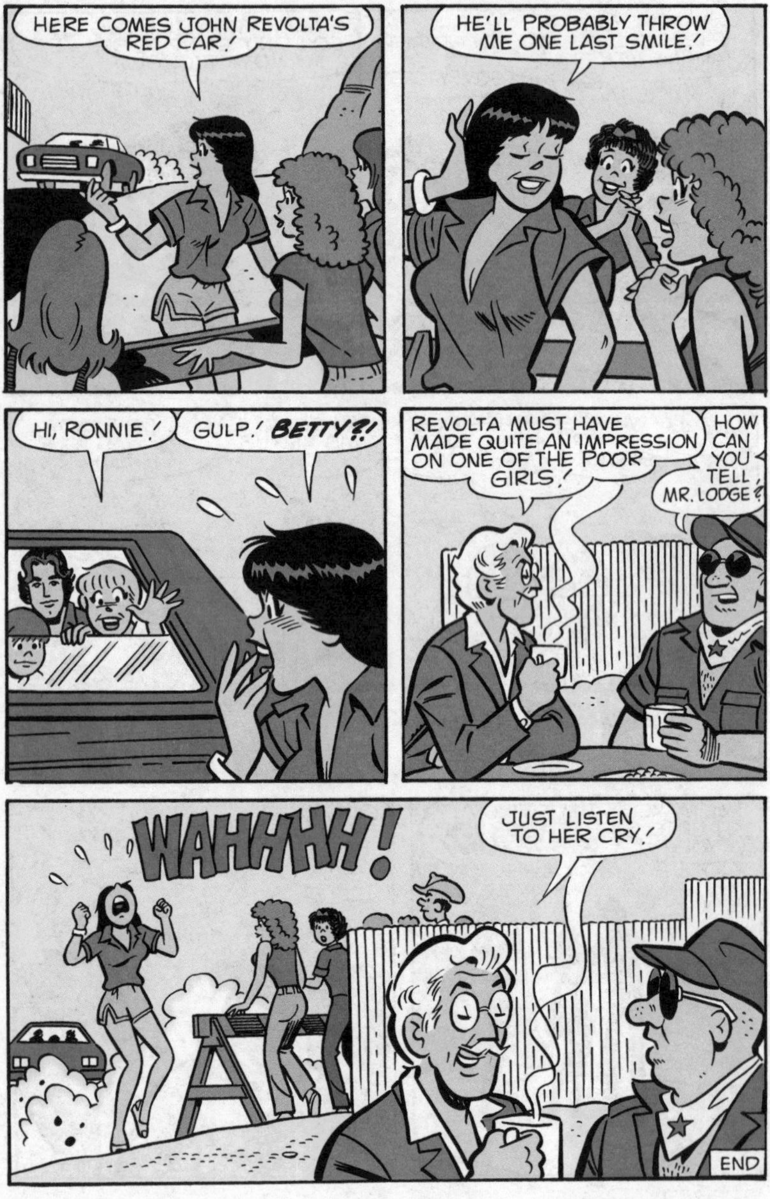
HERE COMES JOHN REVOLTA'S RED CAR!
HE'LL PROBABLY THROW ME ONE LAST SMILE!
HI, RONNIE!
GULP! BETTY?!
REVOLTA MUST HAVE MADE QUITE AN IMPRESSION ON ONE OF THE POOR GIRLS!
HOW CAN YOU TELL, MR. LODGE?
WAHHHH!
JUST LISTEN TO HER CRY!
END

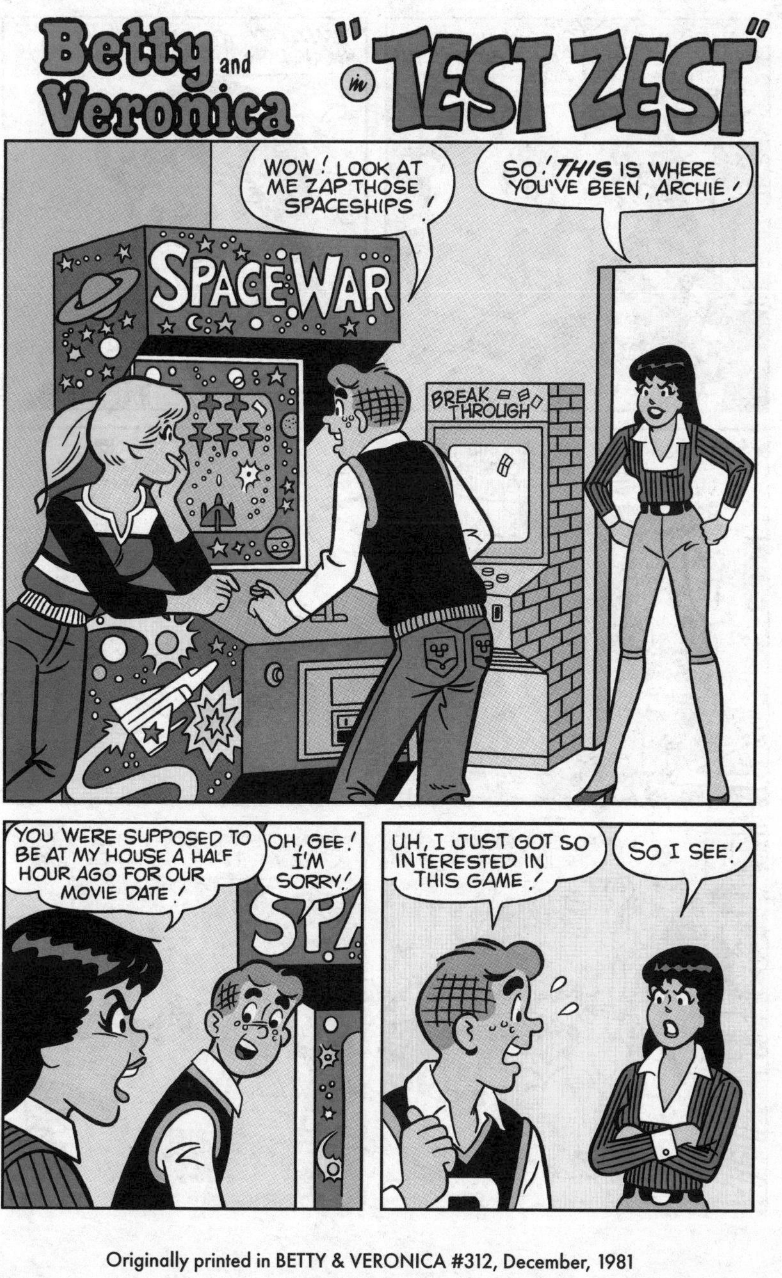
Betty and Veronica
in
"TEST ZEST"
WOW! LOOK AT ME ZAP THOSE SPACESHIPS!
SO! THIS IS WHERE YOU'VE BEEN, ARCHIE!
SPACE WAR
BREAK THROUGH
YOU WERE SUPPOSED TO BE AT MY HOUSE A HALF HOUR AGO FOR OUR MOVIE DATE!
OH, GEE! I'M SORRY!
UH, I JUST GOT SO INTERESTED IN THIS GAME!
SO I SEE!

Originally printed in BETTY & VERONICA #312, December, 1981

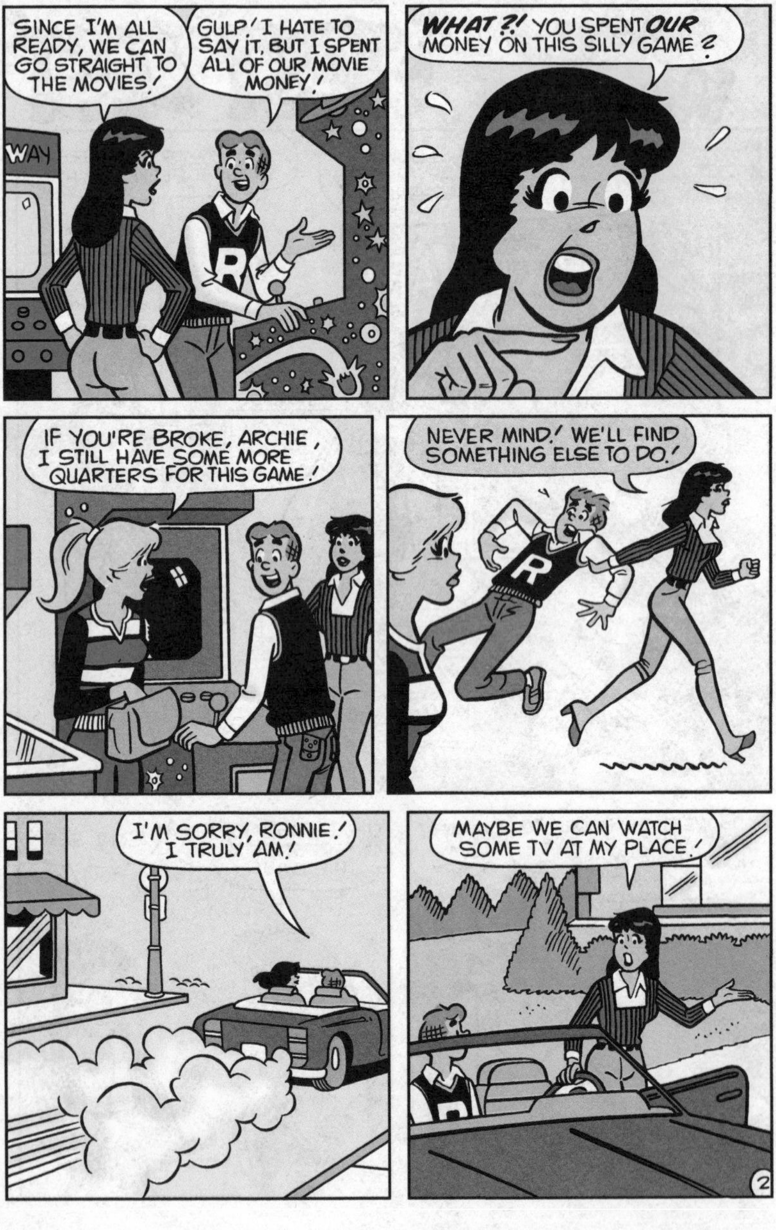
SINCE I'M ALL READY, WE CAN GO STRAIGHT TO THE MOVIES!
GULP! I HATE TO SAY IT, BUT I SPENT ALL OF OUR MOVIE MONEY!
WAY
WHAT?! YOU SPENT OUR MONEY ON THIS SILLY GAME?
IF YOU'RE BROKE, ARCHIE, I STILL HAVE SOME MORE QUARTERS FOR THIS GAME!
NEVER MIND! WE'LL FIND SOMETHING ELSE TO DO!
I'M SORRY, RONNIE! I TRULY AM!
MAYBE WE CAN WATCH SOME TV AT MY PLACE!
2

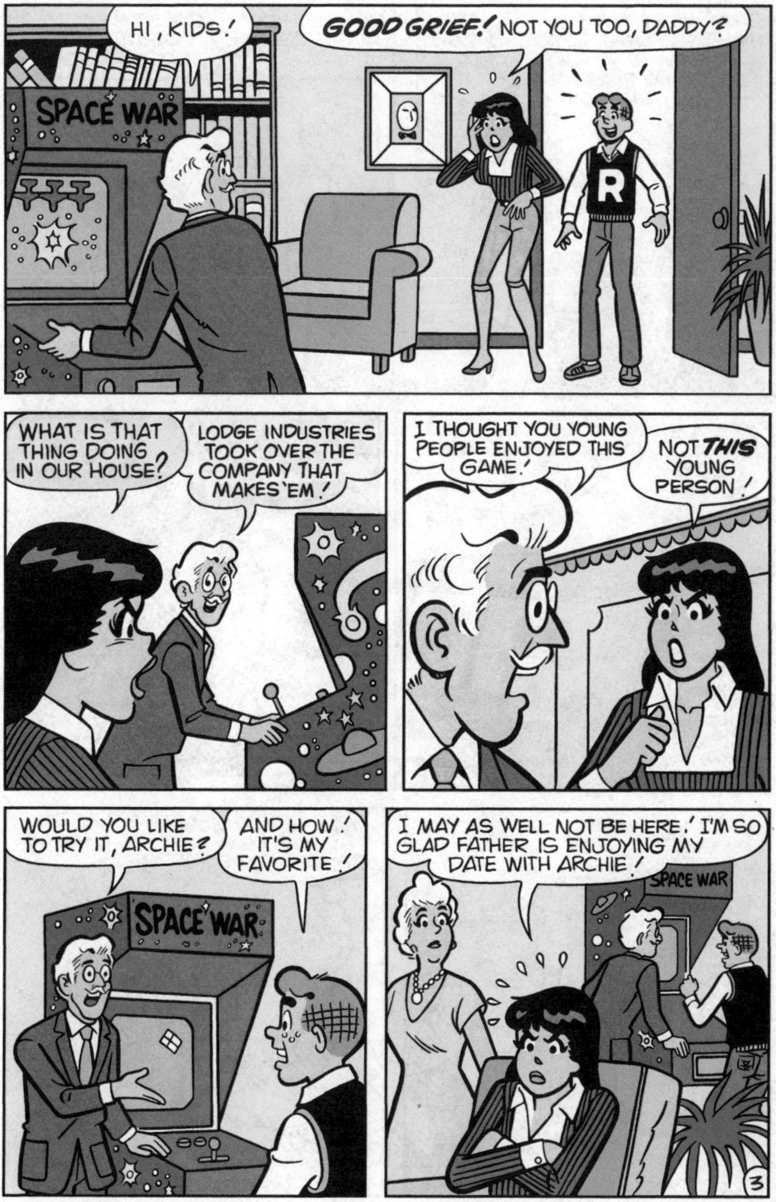
HI, KIDS!
SPACE WAR
GOOD GRIEF! NOT YOU TOO, DADDY?
R
WHAT IS THAT THING DOING IN OUR HOUSE?
LODGE INDUSTRIES TOOK OVER THE COMPANY THAT MAKES 'EM!
I THOUGHT YOU YOUNG PEOPLE ENJOYED THIS GAME!
NOT THIS YOUNG PERSON!
WOULD YOU LIKE TO TRY IT, ARCHIE?
AND HOW! IT'S MY FAVORITE!
SPACE WAR
I MAY AS WELL NOT BE HERE! I'M SO GLAD FATHER IS ENJOYING MY DATE WITH ARCHIE!
SPACE WAR
3

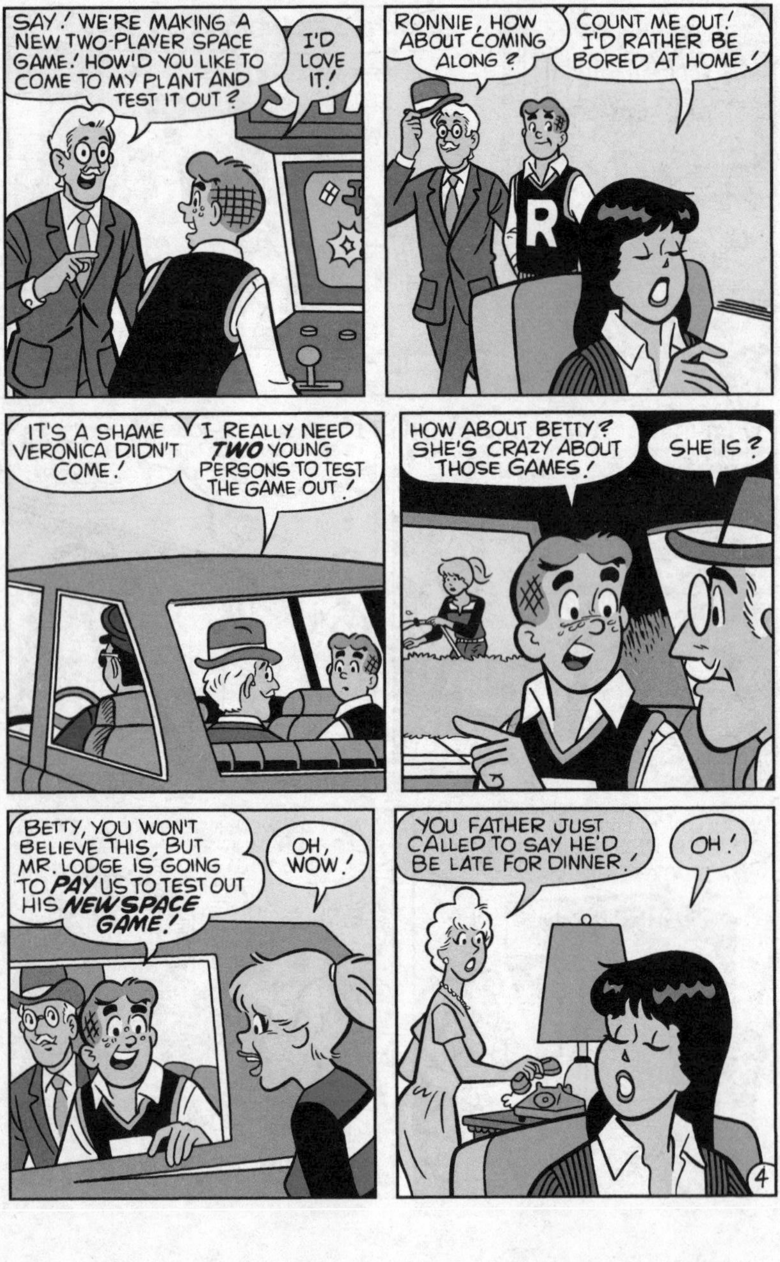
SAY! WE'RE MAKING A NEW TWO-PLAYER SPACE GAME! HOW'D YOU LIKE TO COME TO MY PLANT AND TEST IT OUT?
I'D LOVE IT!
RONNIE, HOW ABOUT COMING ALONG?
COUNT ME OUT! I'D RATHER BE BORED AT HOME!
IT'S A SHAME VERONICA DIDN'T COME!
I REALLY NEED TWO YOUNG PERSONS TO TEST THE GAME OUT!
HOW ABOUT BETTY? SHE'S CRAZY ABOUT THOSE GAMES!
SHE IS?
BETTY, YOU WON'T BELIEVE THIS, BUT MR. LODGE IS GOING TO PAY US TO TEST OUT HIS NEW SPACE GAME!
OH, WOW!
YOU FATHER JUST CALLED TO SAY HE'D BE LATE FOR DINNER!
OH!
4

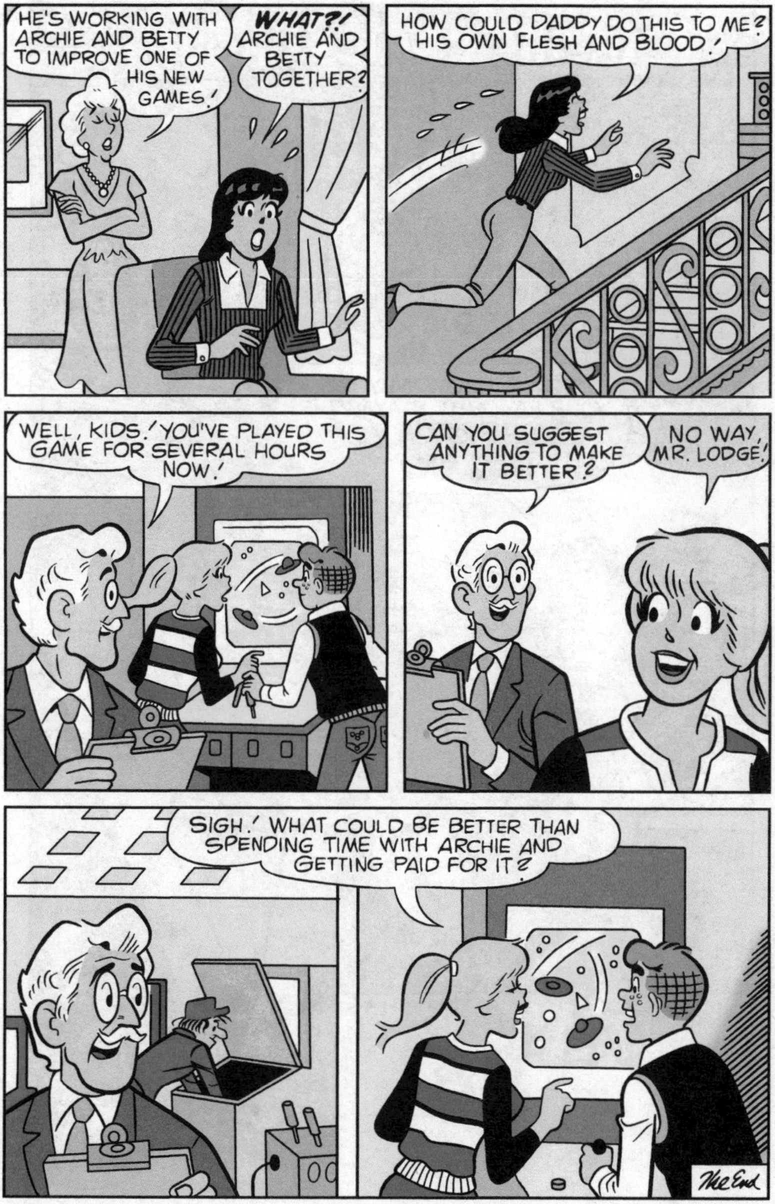
HE'S WORKING WITH ARCHIE AND BETTY TO IMPROVE ONE OF HIS NEW GAMES!
WHAT?! ARCHIE AND BETTY TOGETHER?
HOW COULD DADDY DO THIS TO ME? HIS OWN FLESH AND BLOOD!
WELL, KIDS! YOU'VE PLAYED THIS GAME FOR SEVERAL HOURS NOW!
CAN YOU SUGGEST ANYTHING TO MAKE IT BETTER?
NO WAY, MR. LODGE!
SIGH! WHAT COULD BE BETTER THAN SPENDING TIME WITH ARCHIE AND GETTING PAID FOR IT?
The End

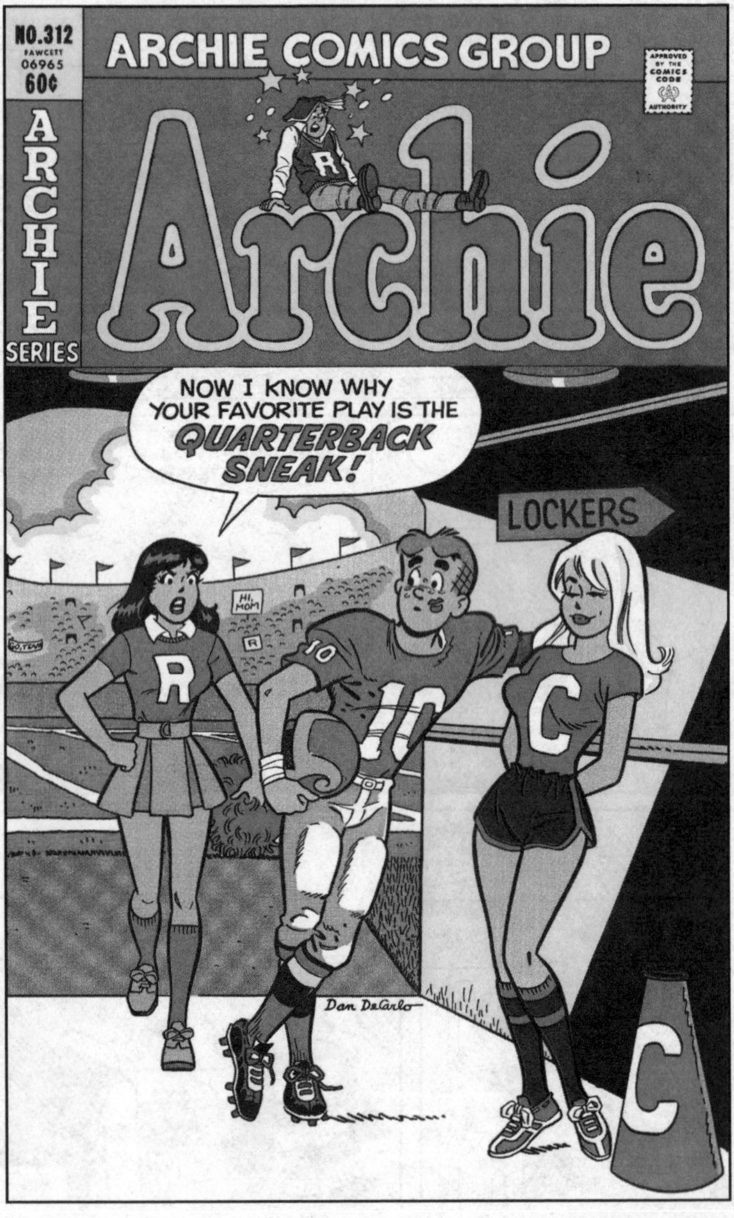
NO.312
FAWCETT
06965
60¢
ARCHIE COMICS GROUP
APPROVED BY THE COMICS CODE AUTHORITY
ARCHIE
SERIES
Archie
NOW I KNOW WHY YOUR FAVORITE PLAY IS THE QUARTERBACK SNEAK!
LOCKERS
HI, MOM
Dan DeCarlo

Originally printed in 1982

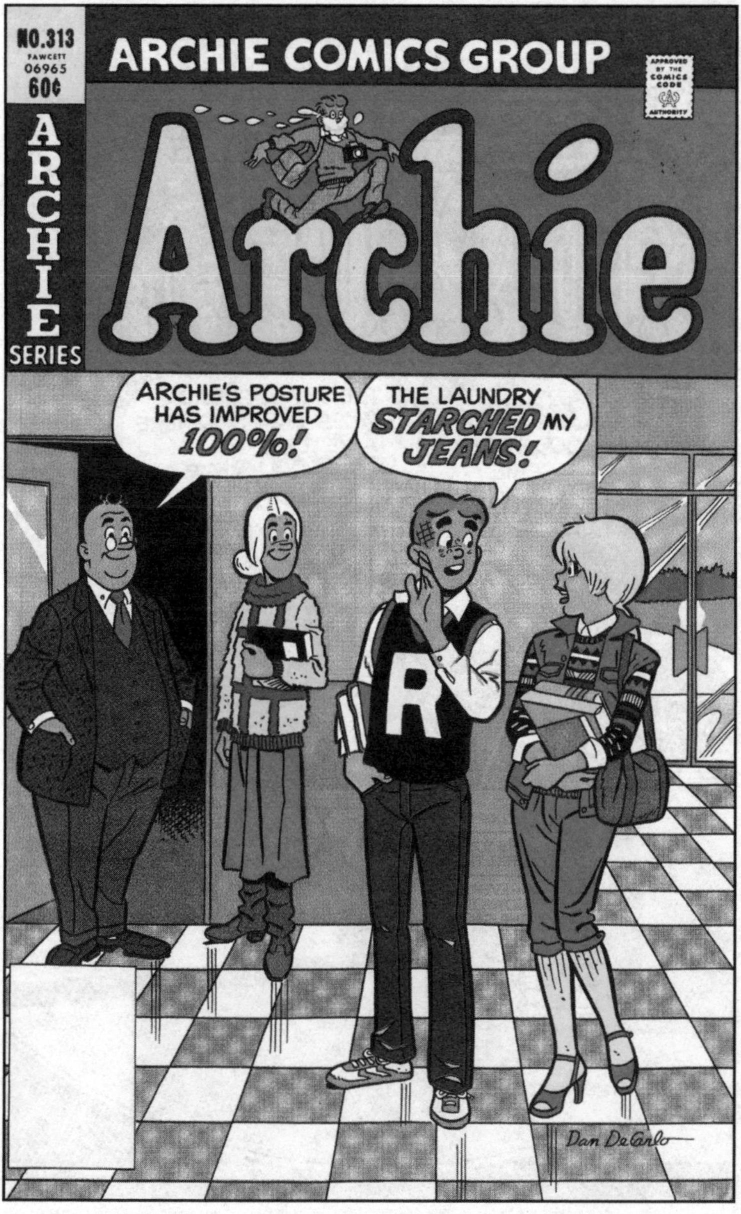
NO.313
FAWCETT
06965
60¢
ARCHIE COMICS GROUP
APPROVED BY THE COMICS CODE AUTHORITY
ARCHIE
SERIES
Archie
ARCHIE'S POSTURE HAS IMPROVED 100%!
THE LAUNDRY STARCHED MY JEANS!
Dan DeCarlo

Originally printed in 1982

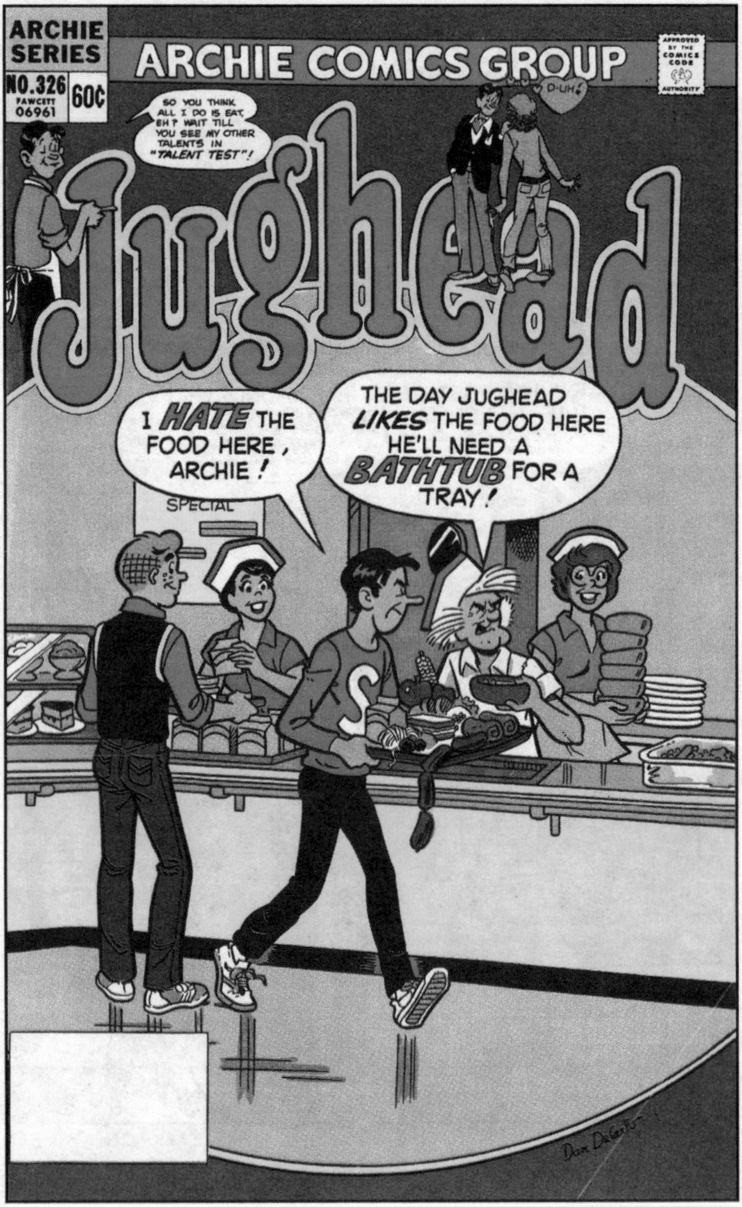
ARCHIE SERIES
NO.326 FAWCETT 06961
60¢
ARCHIE COMICS GROUP
APPROVED BY THE COMICS CODE AUTHORITY
SO YOU THINK ALL I DO IS EAT, EH? WAIT TILL YOU SEE MY OTHER TALENTS IN "TALENT TEST"!
D-UH!
Jughead
I HATE THE FOOD HERE, ARCHIE!
THE DAY JUGHEAD LIKES THE FOOD HERE HE'LL NEED A BATHTUB FOR A TRAY!
SPECIAL

Originally printed in 1982

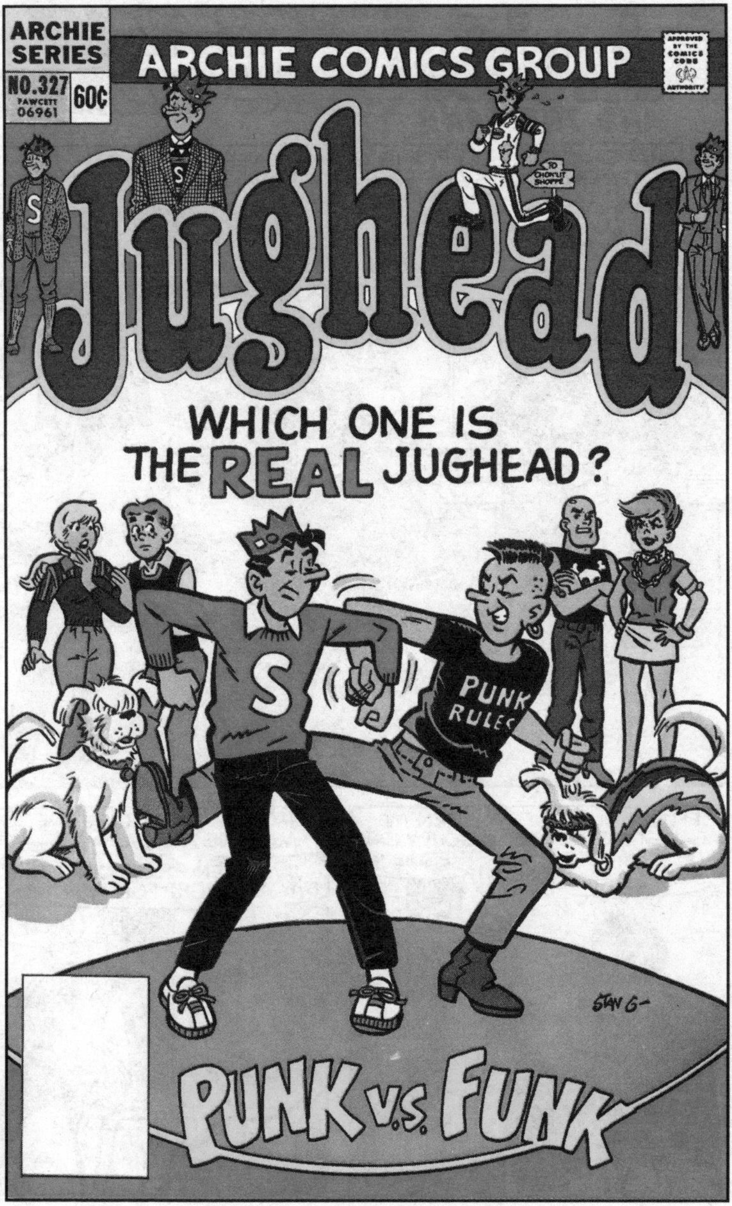
ARCHIE SERIES
NO.327 FAWCETT 06961
60¢
ARCHIE COMICS GROUP
APPROVED BY THE COMICS CODE AUTHORITY
Jughead
TO CHOK'LIT SHOPPE
WHICH ONE IS THE REAL JUGHEAD?
S
PUNK RULES
STAN G-
PUNK v.s. FUNK

Originally printed in 1983

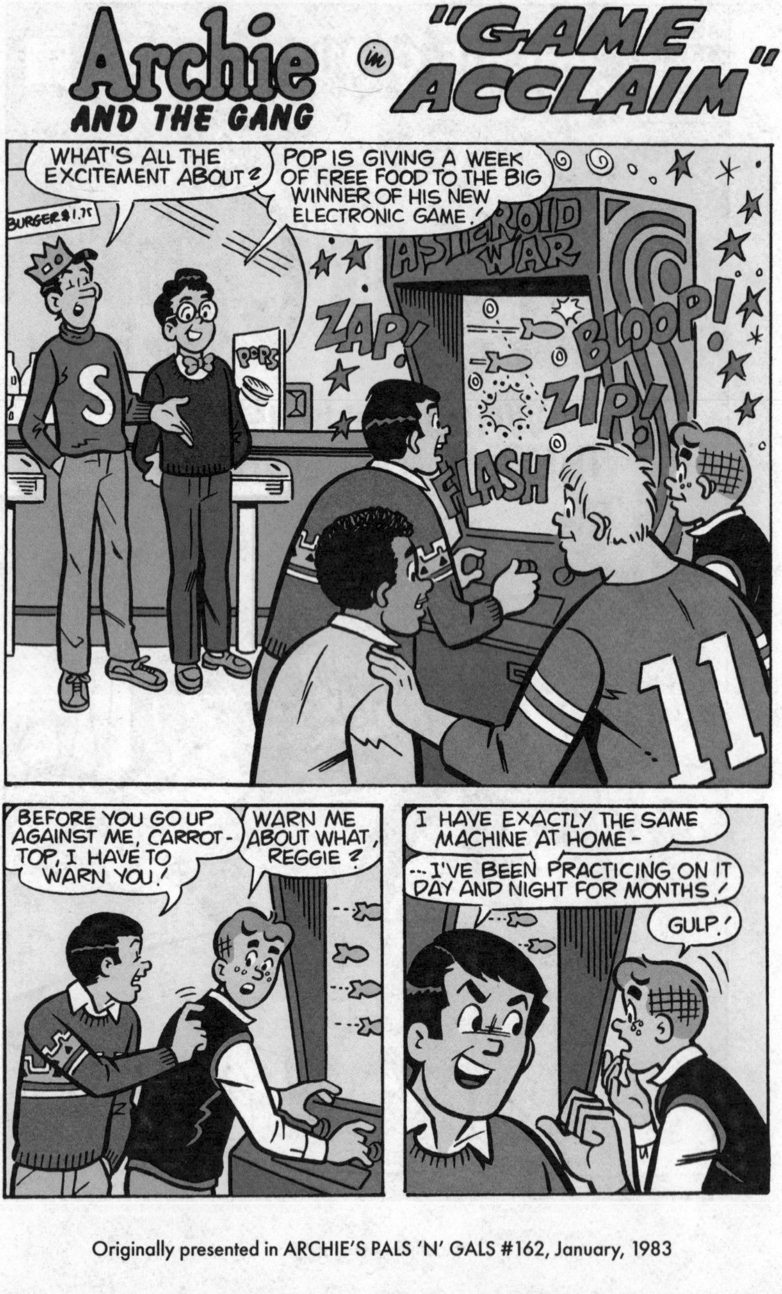
Archie AND THE GANG in "GAME ACCLAIM"
WHAT'S ALL THE EXCITEMENT ABOUT?
POP IS GIVING A WEEK OF FREE FOOD TO THE BIG WINNER OF HIS NEW ELECTRONIC GAME!
BURGER $1.75
ASTEROID WAR
ZAP!
BLOOP!
ZIP!
FLASH
BEFORE YOU GO UP AGAINST ME, CARROT-TOP, I HAVE TO WARN YOU!
WARN ME ABOUT WHAT, REGGIE?
I HAVE EXACTLY THE SAME MACHINE AT HOME--
...I'VE BEEN PRACTICING ON IT DAY AND NIGHT FOR MONTHS!
GULP!

Originally presented in ARCHIE'S PALS 'N' GALS #162, January, 1983

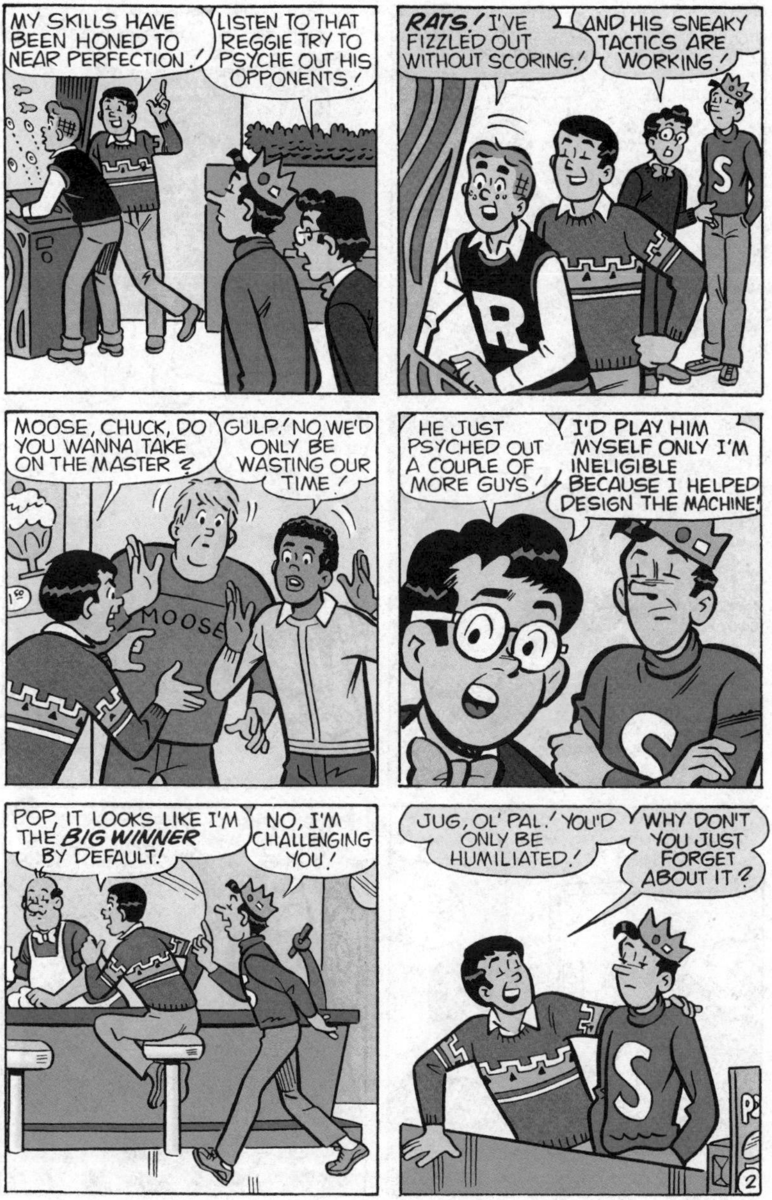
MY SKILLS HAVE BEEN HONED TO NEAR PERFECTION!
LISTEN TO THAT REGGIE TRY TO PSYCHE OUT HIS OPPONENTS!
RATS! I'VE FIZZLED OUT WITHOUT SCORING!
AND HIS SNEAKY TACTICS ARE WORKING!
R
S
MOOSE, CHUCK, DO YOU WANNA TAKE ON THE MASTER?
GULP! NO, WE'D ONLY BE WASTING OUR TIME!
MOOSE
HE JUST PSYCHED OUT A COUPLE OF MORE GUYS!
I'D PLAY HIM MYSELF ONLY I'M INELIGIBLE BECAUSE I HELPED DESIGN THE MACHINE!
POP, IT LOOKS LIKE I'M THE BIG WINNER BY DEFAULT!
NO, I'M CHALLENGING YOU!
JUG, OL' PAL! YOU'D ONLY BE HUMILIATED!
WHY DON'T YOU JUST FORGET ABOUT IT?
2

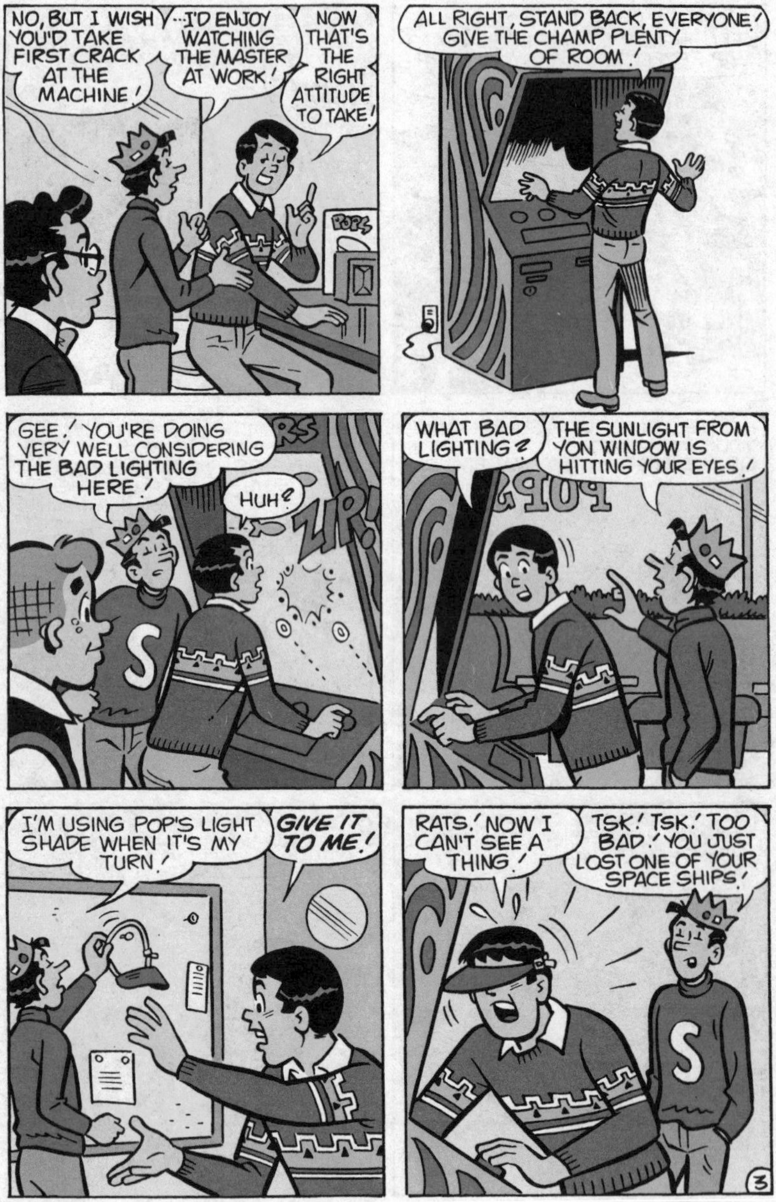
NO, BUT I WISH YOU'D TAKE FIRST CRACK AT THE MACHINE!
...I'D ENJOY WATCHING THE MASTER AT WORK!
NOW THAT'S THE RIGHT ATTITUDE TO TAKE!
POPS
ALL RIGHT, STAND BACK, EVERYONE! GIVE THE CHAMP PLENTY OF ROOM!
GEE! YOU'RE DOING VERY WELL CONSIDERING THE BAD LIGHTING HERE!
HUH?
ZIP!
WHAT BAD LIGHTING?
THE SUNLIGHT FROM YON WINDOW IS HITTING YOUR EYES!
I'M USING POP'S LIGHT SHADE WHEN IT'S MY TURN!
GIVE IT TO ME!
RATS! NOW I CAN'T SEE A THING!
TSK! TSK! TOO BAD! YOU JUST LOST ONE OF YOUR SPACE SHIPS!
3

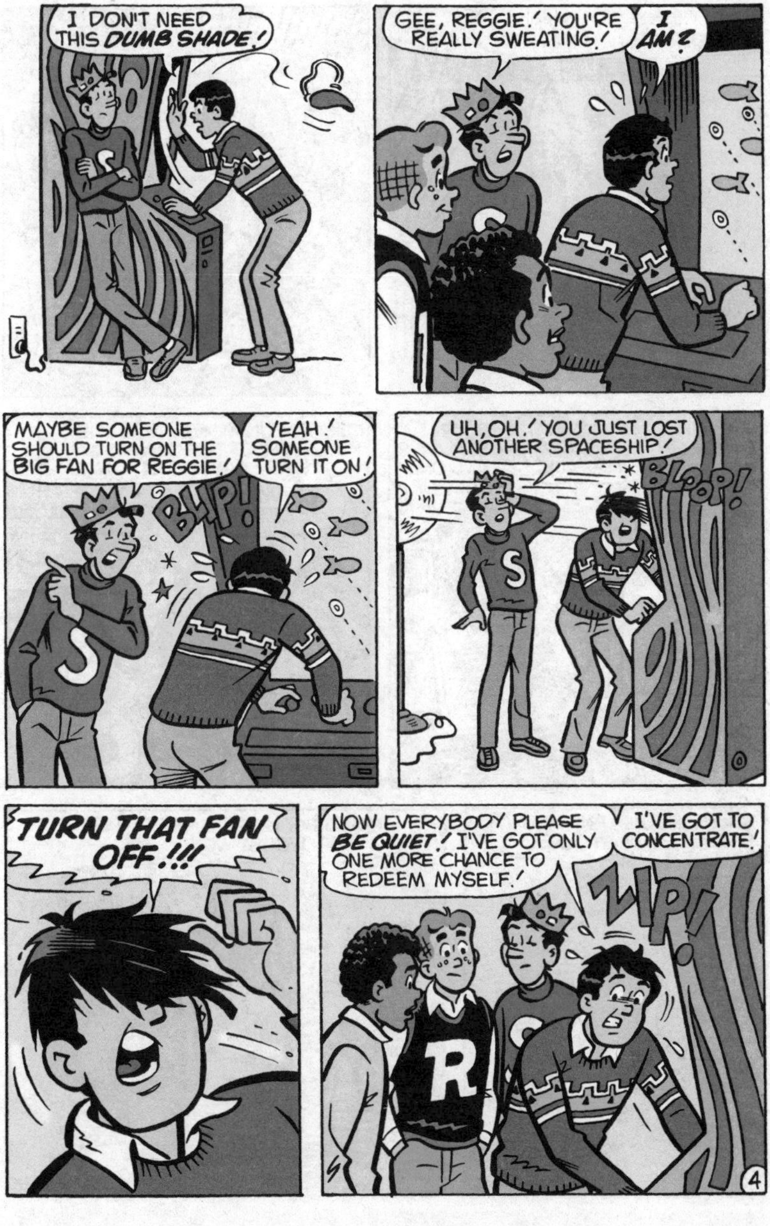
I DON'T NEED THIS DUMB SHADE!
GEE, REGGIE! YOU'RE REALLY SWEATING!
I AM?
MAYBE SOMEONE SHOULD TURN ON THE BIG FAN FOR REGGIE!
YEAH! SOMEONE TURN IT ON!
BLIP!
UH, OH! YOU JUST LOST ANOTHER SPACESHIP!
BLOOP!
TURN THAT FAN OFF!!!
NOW EVERYBODY PLEASE BE QUIET! I'VE GOT ONLY ONE MORE CHANCE TO REDEEM MYSELF!
I'VE GOT TO CONCENTRATE!
ZIP!
4

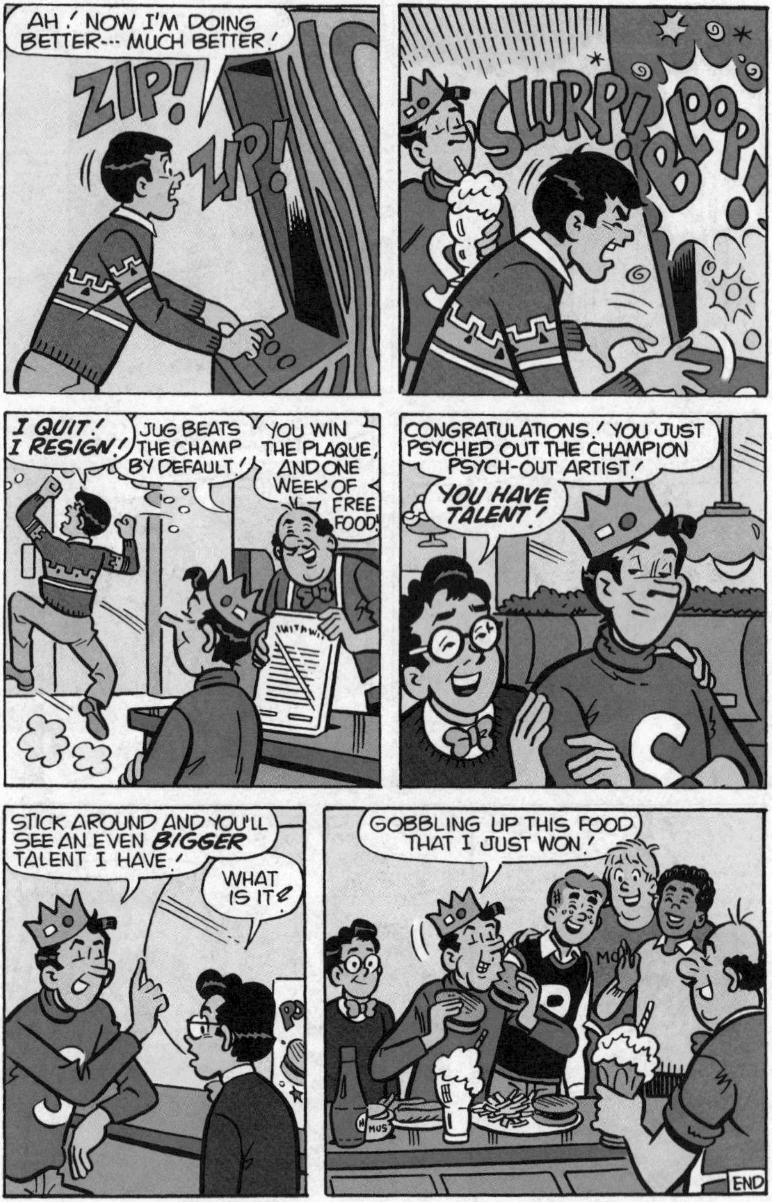
AH! NOW I'M DOING BETTER--- MUCH BETTER!
ZIP!
ZIP!
SLURP!
BLOOP!
I QUIT! I RESIGN!
JUG BEATS THE CHAMP BY DEFAULT!
YOU WIN THE PLAQUE, AND ONE WEEK OF FREE FOOD!
CONGRATULATIONS! YOU JUST PSYCHED OUT THE CHAMPION PSYCH-OUT ARTIST!
YOU HAVE TALENT!
STICK AROUND AND YOU'LL SEE AN EVEN BIGGER TALENT I HAVE!
WHAT IS IT?
GOBBLING UP THIS FOOD THAT I JUST WON!
END

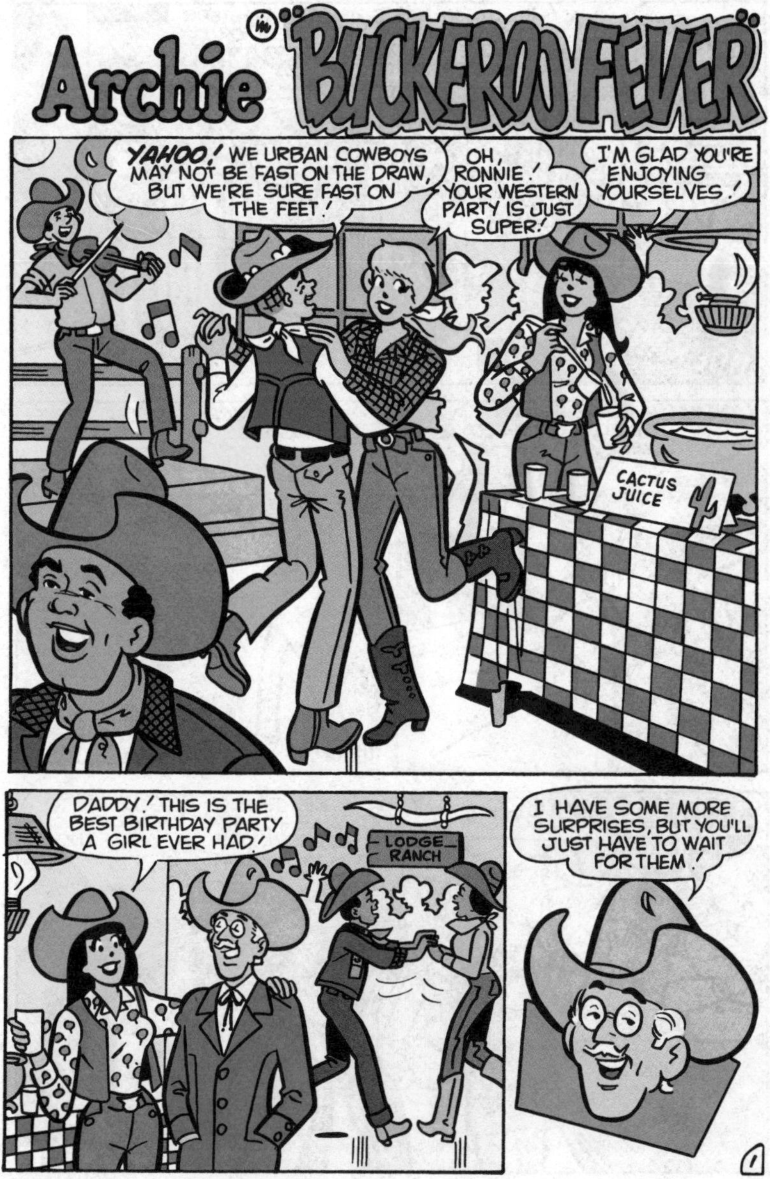
Archie in "BUCKEROO FEVER"
YAHOO! WE URBAN COWBOYS MAY NOT BE FAST ON THE DRAW, BUT WE'RE SURE FAST ON THE FEET!
OH, RONNIE! YOUR WESTERN PARTY IS JUST SUPER!
I'M GLAD YOU'RE ENJOYING YOURSELVES!
CACTUS JUICE
DADDY! THIS IS THE BEST BIRTHDAY PARTY A GIRL EVER HAD!
LODGE RANCH
I HAVE SOME MORE SURPRISES, BUT YOU'LL JUST HAVE TO WAIT FOR THEM!
1

First appearance in LAUGH #376, January, 1983

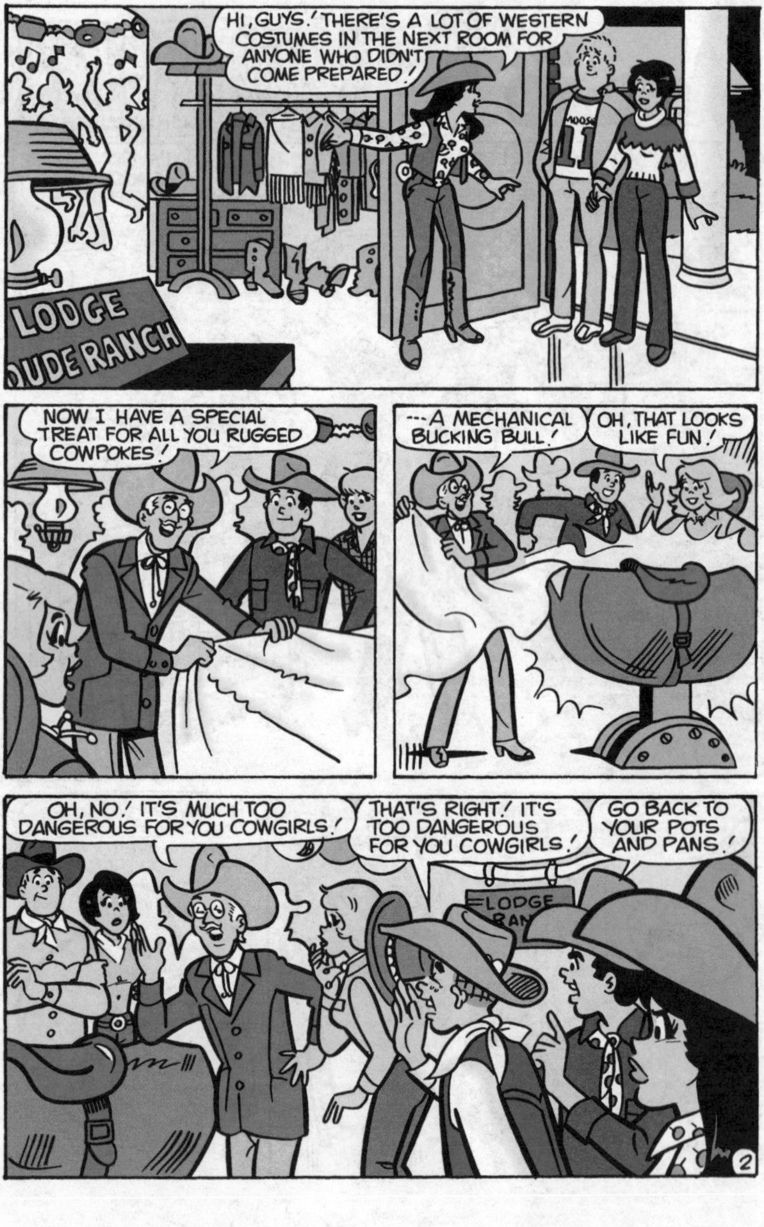
HI, GUYS! THERE'S A LOT OF WESTERN COSTUMES IN THE NEXT ROOM FOR ANYONE WHO DIDN'T COME PREPARED!
LODGE DUDE RANCH
NOW I HAVE A SPECIAL TREAT FOR ALL YOU RUGGED COWPOKES!
---A MECHANICAL BUCKING BULL!
OH, THAT LOOKS LIKE FUN!
OH, NO! IT'S MUCH TOO DANGEROUS FOR YOU COWGIRLS!
THAT'S RIGHT! IT'S TOO DANGEROUS FOR YOU COWGIRLS!
GO BACK TO YOUR POTS AND PANS!
2

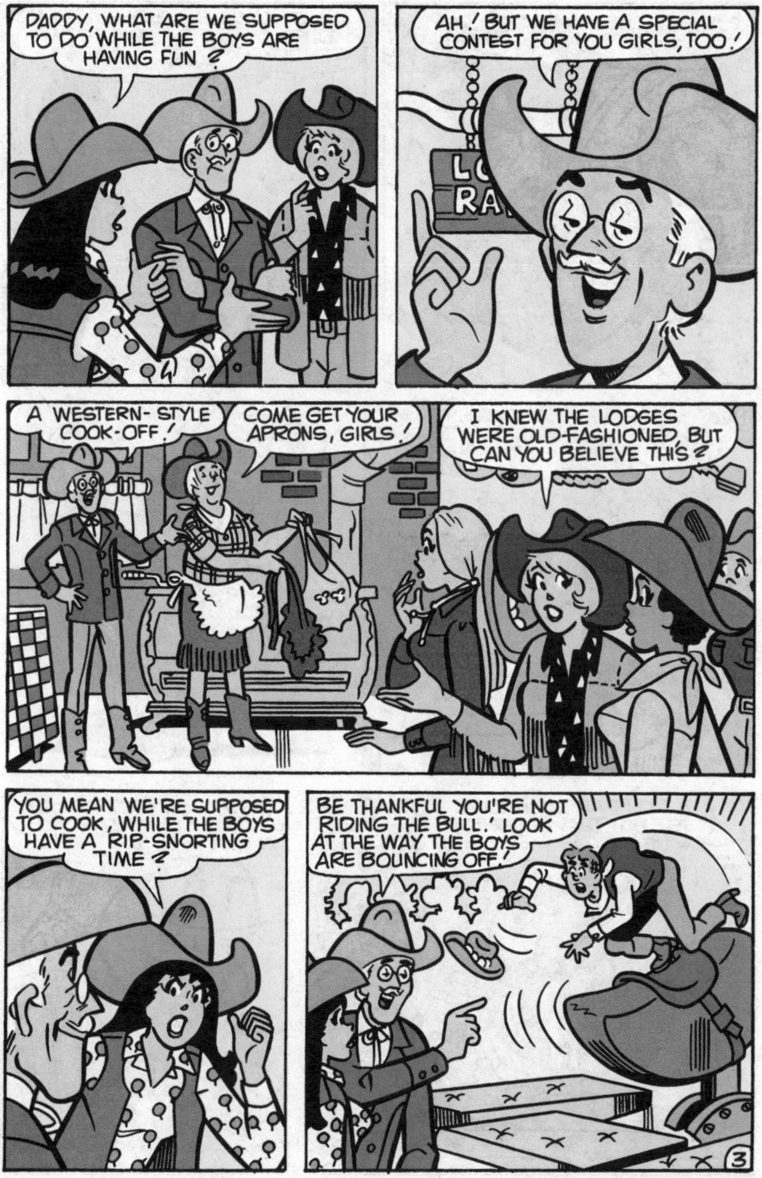
DADDY, WHAT ARE WE SUPPOSED TO DO WHILE THE BOYS ARE HAVING FUN ?
AH! BUT WE HAVE A SPECIAL CONTEST FOR YOU GIRLS, TOO!
A WESTERN-STYLE COOK-OFF!
COME GET YOUR APRONS, GIRLS!
I KNEW THE LODGES WERE OLD-FASHIONED, BUT CAN YOU BELIEVE THIS ?
YOU MEAN WE'RE SUPPOSED TO COOK, WHILE THE BOYS HAVE A RIP-SNORTING TIME ?
BE THANKFUL YOU'RE NOT RIDING THE BULL! LOOK AT THE WAY THE BOYS ARE BOUNCING OFF!
3

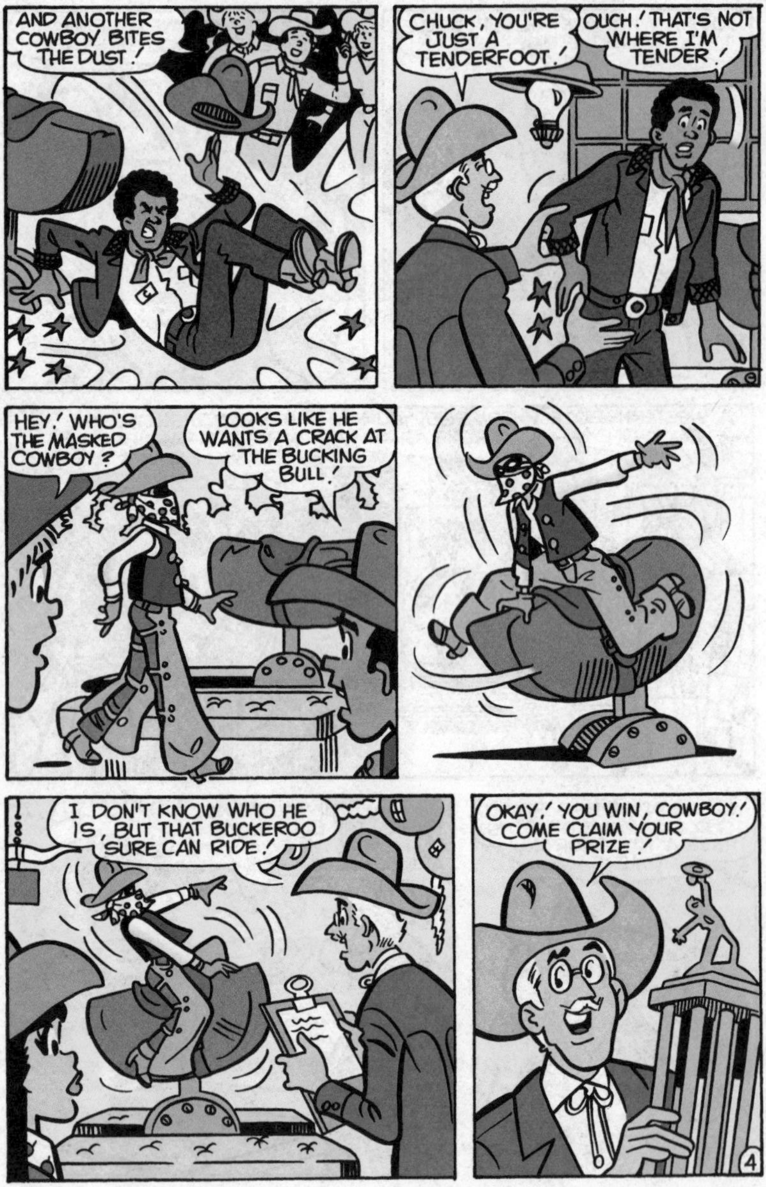
AND ANOTHER COWBOY BITES THE DUST!
CHUCK, YOU'RE JUST A TENDERFOOT!
OUCH! THAT'S NOT WHERE I'M TENDER!
HEY! WHO'S THE MASKED COWBOY?
LOOKS LIKE HE WANTS A CRACK AT THE BUCKING BULL!
I DON'T KNOW WHO HE IS, BUT THAT BUCKEROO SURE CAN RIDE!
OKAY! YOU WIN, COWBOY! COME CLAIM YOUR PRIZE!
4

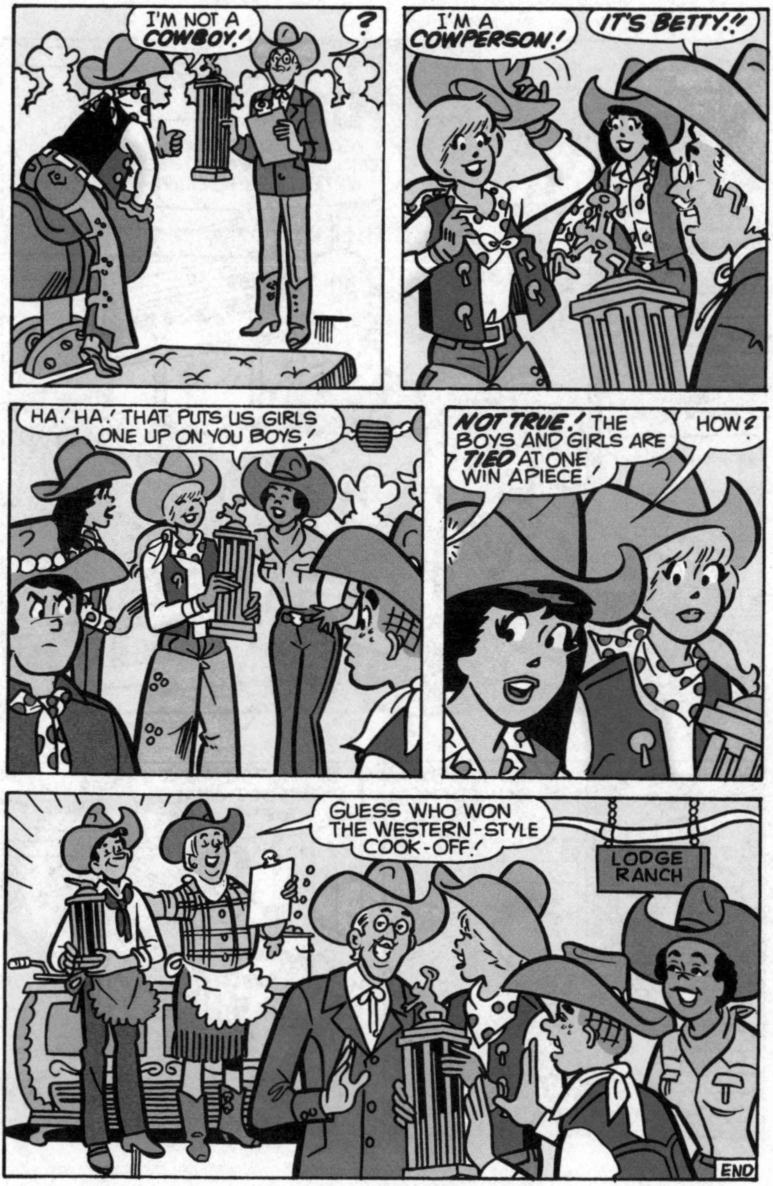
I'M NOT A COWBOY!
?
I'M A COWPERSON!
IT'S BETTY!!
HA! HA! THAT PUTS US GIRLS ONE UP ON YOU BOYS!
NOT TRUE! THE BOYS AND GIRLS ARE TIED AT ONE WIN APIECE!
HOW?
GUESS WHO WON THE WESTERN-STYLE COOK-OFF!
LODGE RANCH
END

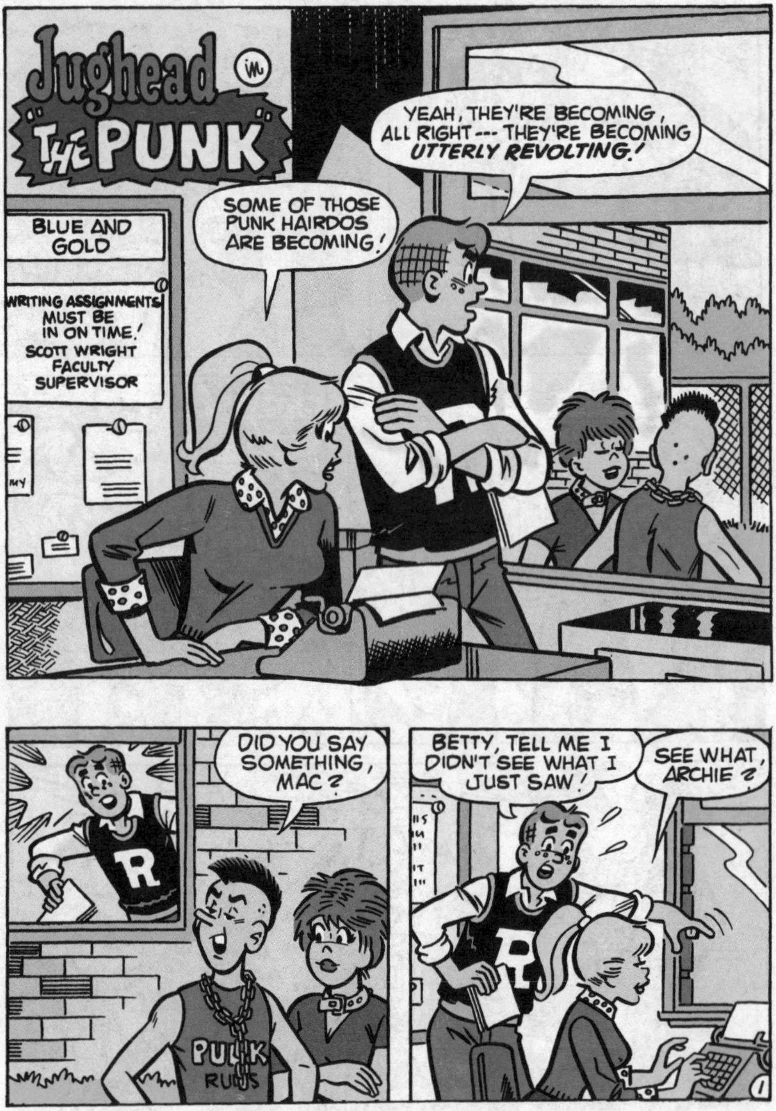
Jughead in "The PUNK"
BLUE AND GOLD
WRITING ASSIGNMENTS MUST BE IN ON TIME! SCOTT WRIGHT FACULTY SUPERVISOR
SOME OF THOSE PUNK HAIRDOS ARE BECOMING!
YEAH, THEY'RE BECOMING, ALL RIGHT --- THEY'RE BECOMING UTTERLY REVOLTING!
DID YOU SAY SOMETHING, MAC?
BETTY, TELL ME I DIDN'T SEE WHAT I JUST SAW!
SEE WHAT, ARCHIE?

Originally presented in JUGHEAD #327, February, 1983

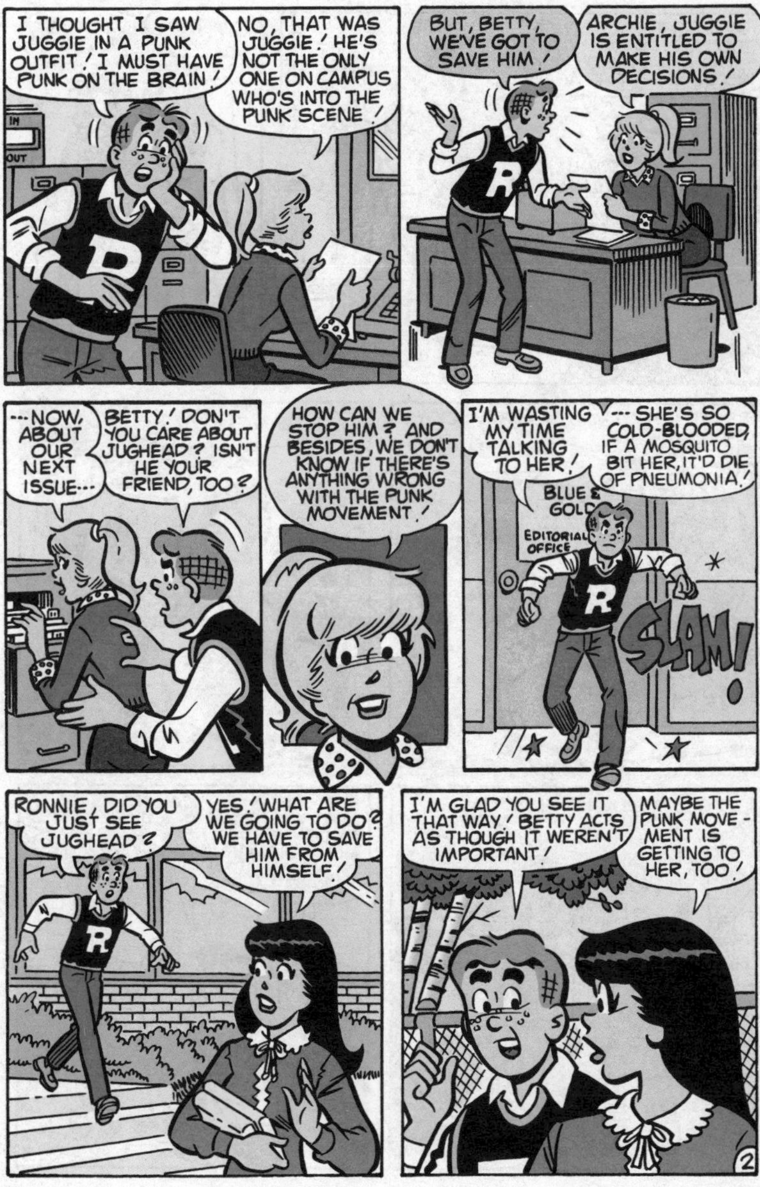
I THOUGHT I SAW JUGGIE IN A PUNK OUTFIT! I MUST HAVE PUNK ON THE BRAIN!
NO, THAT WAS JUGGIE! HE'S NOT THE ONLY ONE ON CAMPUS WHO'S INTO THE PUNK SCENE!
IN
OUT
BUT, BETTY, WE'VE GOT TO SAVE HIM!
ARCHIE, JUGGIE IS ENTITLED TO MAKE HIS OWN DECISIONS!
---NOW, ABOUT OUR NEXT ISSUE---
BETTY! DON'T YOU CARE ABOUT JUGHEAD? ISN'T HE YOUR FRIEND, TOO?
HOW CAN WE STOP HIM? AND BESIDES, WE DON'T KNOW IF THERE'S ANYTHING WRONG WITH THE PUNK MOVEMENT!
I'M WASTING MY TIME TALKING TO HER!
--- SHE'S SO COLD-BLOODED, IF A MOSQUITO BIT HER, IT'D DIE OF PNEUMONIA!
BLUE & GOLD
EDITORIAL OFFICE
SLAM!
RONNIE, DID YOU JUST SEE JUGHEAD?
YES! WHAT ARE WE GOING TO DO? WE HAVE TO SAVE HIM FROM HIMSELF!
I'M GLAD YOU SEE IT THAT WAY! BETTY ACTS AS THOUGH IT WEREN'T IMPORTANT!
MAYBE THE PUNK MOVEMENT IS GETTING TO HER, TOO!
2

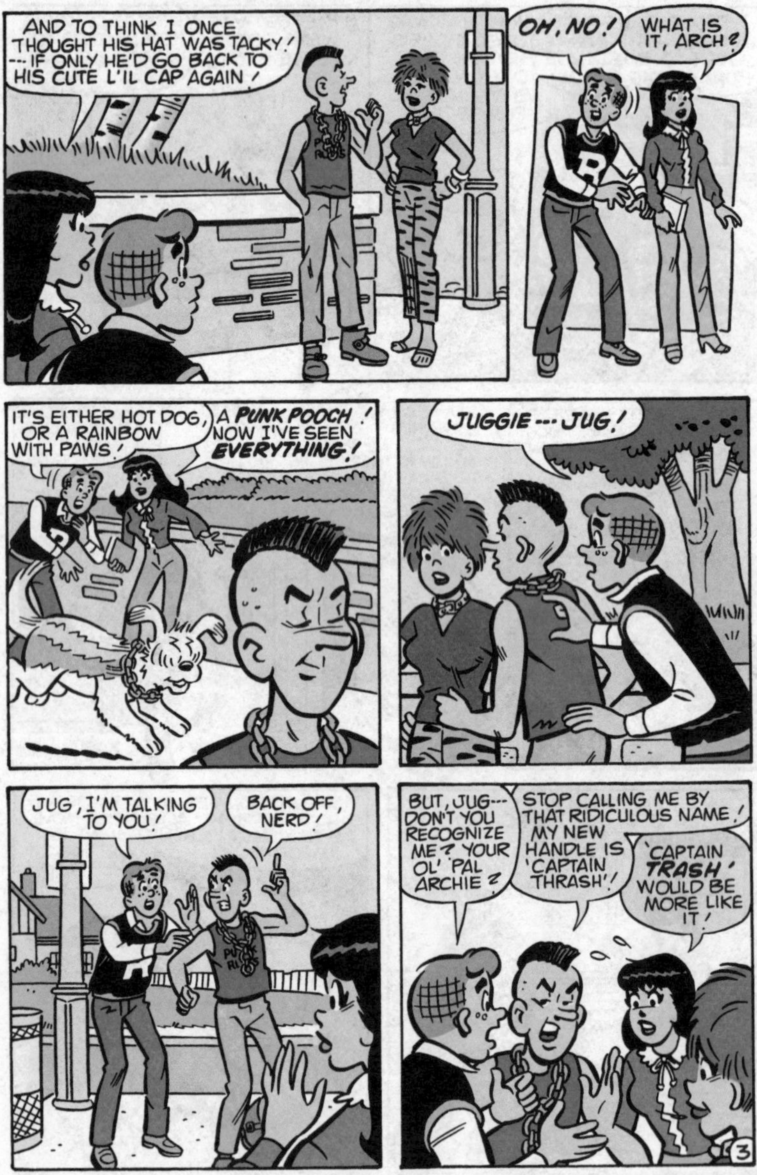
AND TO THINK I ONCE THOUGHT HIS HAT WAS TACKY! --- IF ONLY HE'D GO BACK TO HIS CUTE L'IL CAP AGAIN!
OH, NO!
WHAT IS IT, ARCH?
IT'S EITHER HOT DOG, OR A RAINBOW WITH PAWS!
A PUNK POOCH! NOW I'VE SEEN EVERYTHING!
JUGGIE --- JUG!
JUG, I'M TALKING TO YOU!
BACK OFF, NERD!
BUT, JUG--- DON'T YOU RECOGNIZE ME? YOUR OL' PAL ARCHIE?
STOP CALLING ME BY THAT RIDICULOUS NAME! MY NEW HANDLE IS 'CAPTAIN THRASH'!
'CAPTAIN TRASH' WOULD BE MORE LIKE IT!
3

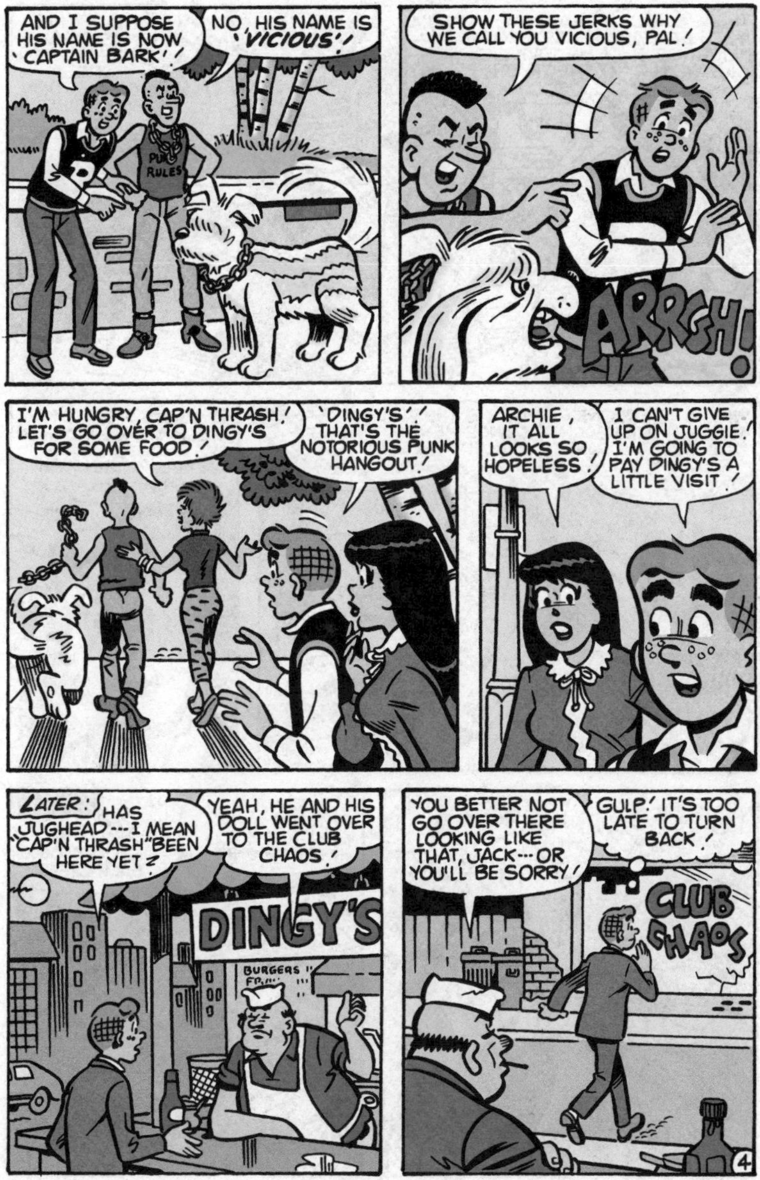
AND I SUPPOSE HIS NAME IS NOW 'CAPTAIN BARK'!
NO, HIS NAME IS 'VICIOUS'!
PUNK RULES
SHOW THESE JERKS WHY WE CALL YOU VICIOUS, PAL!
ARRGH!
I'M HUNGRY, CAP'N THRASH! LET'S GO OVER TO DINGY'S FOR SOME FOOD!
'DINGY'S'! THAT'S THE NOTORIOUS PUNK HANGOUT!
ARCHIE, IT ALL LOOKS SO HOPELESS!
I CAN'T GIVE UP ON JUGGIE! I'M GOING TO PAY DINGY'S A LITTLE VISIT!
LATER:
HAS JUGHEAD --- I MEAN "CAP'N THRASH" BEEN HERE YET?
YEAH, HE AND HIS DOLL WENT OVER TO THE CLUB CHAOS!
DINGY'S
BURGERS
YOU BETTER NOT GO OVER THERE LOOKING LIKE THAT, JACK--- OR YOU'LL BE SORRY!
GULP! IT'S TOO LATE TO TURN BACK!
CLUB CHAOS
4

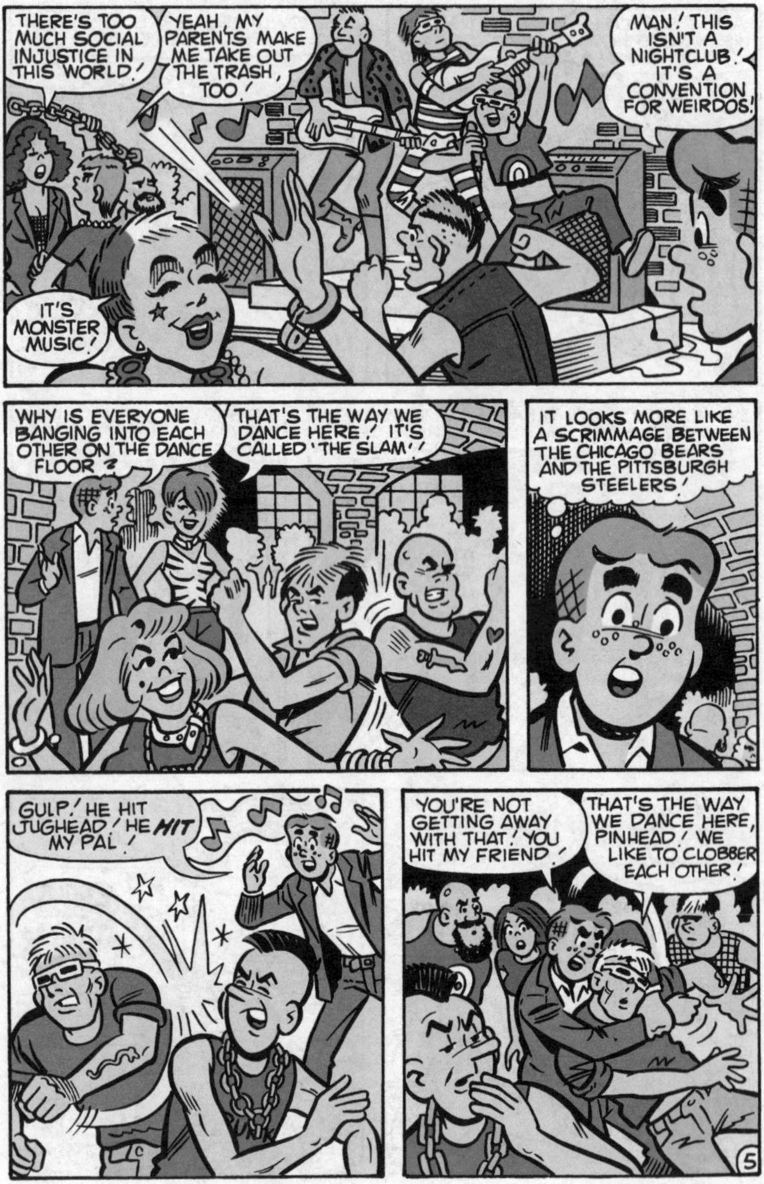
THERE'S TOO MUCH SOCIAL INJUSTICE IN THIS WORLD!
YEAH, MY PARENTS MAKE ME TAKE OUT THE TRASH, TOO!
MAN! THIS ISN'T A NIGHTCLUB! IT'S A CONVENTION FOR WEIRDOS!
IT'S MONSTER MUSIC!
WHY IS EVERYONE BANGING INTO EACH OTHER ON THE DANCE FLOOR?
THAT'S THE WAY WE DANCE HERE! IT'S CALLED 'THE SLAM'!
IT LOOKS MORE LIKE A SCRIMMAGE BETWEEN THE CHICAGO BEARS AND THE PITTSBURGH STEELERS!
GULP! HE HIT JUGHEAD! HE *HIT* MY PAL!
YOU'RE NOT GETTING AWAY WITH THAT! YOU HIT MY FRIEND!
THAT'S THE WAY WE DANCE HERE, PINHEAD! WE LIKE TO CLOBBER EACH OTHER!
5

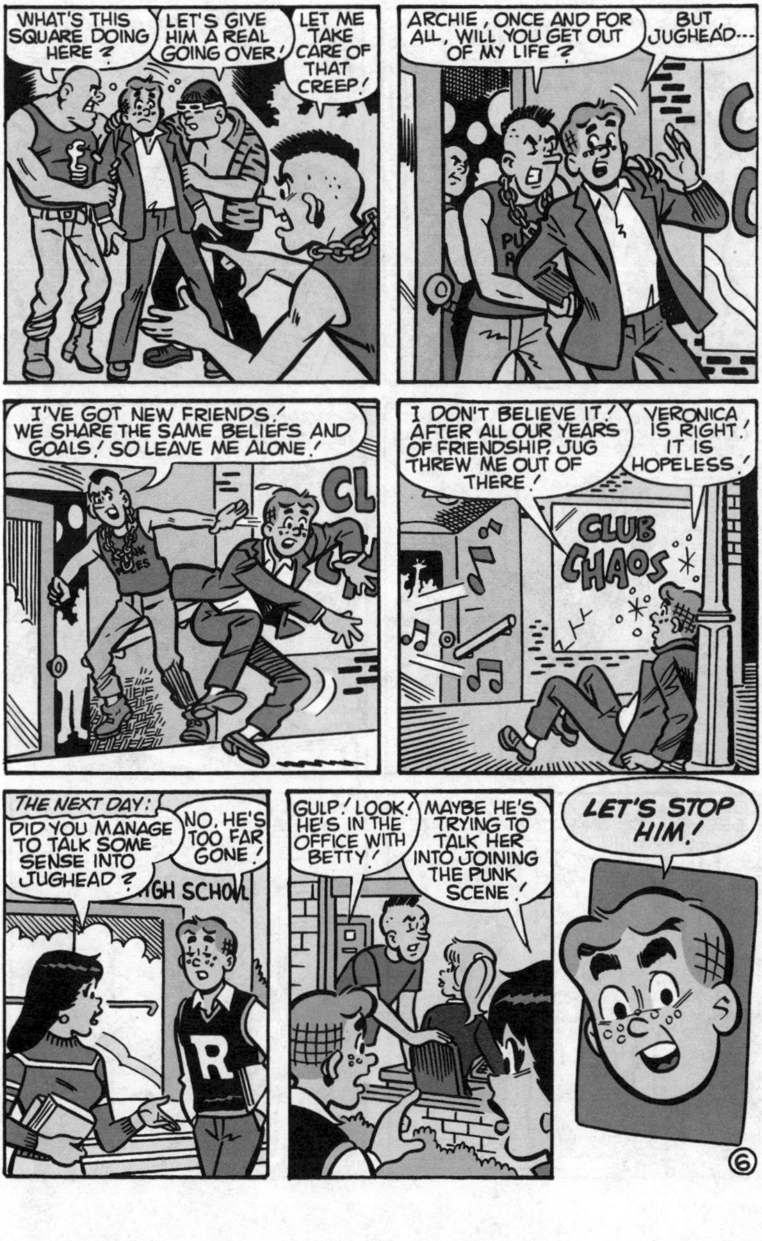
WHAT'S THIS SQUARE DOING HERE ?
LET'S GIVE HIM A REAL GOING OVER!
LET ME TAKE CARE OF THAT CREEP!
ARCHIE, ONCE AND FOR ALL, WILL YOU GET OUT OF MY LIFE ?
BUT JUGHEAD...
I'VE GOT NEW FRIENDS! WE SHARE THE SAME BELIEFS AND GOALS! SO LEAVE ME ALONE!
I DON'T BELIEVE IT! AFTER ALL OUR YEARS OF FRIENDSHIP, JUG THREW ME OUT OF THERE!
VERONICA IS RIGHT! IT IS HOPELESS!
CLUB CHAOS
THE NEXT DAY:
DID YOU MANAGE TO TALK SOME SENSE INTO JUGHEAD ?
NO, HE'S TOO FAR GONE!
GULP! LOOK! HE'S IN THE OFFICE WITH BETTY!
MAYBE HE'S TRYING TO TALK HER INTO JOINING THE PUNK SCENE!
LET'S STOP HIM!
6

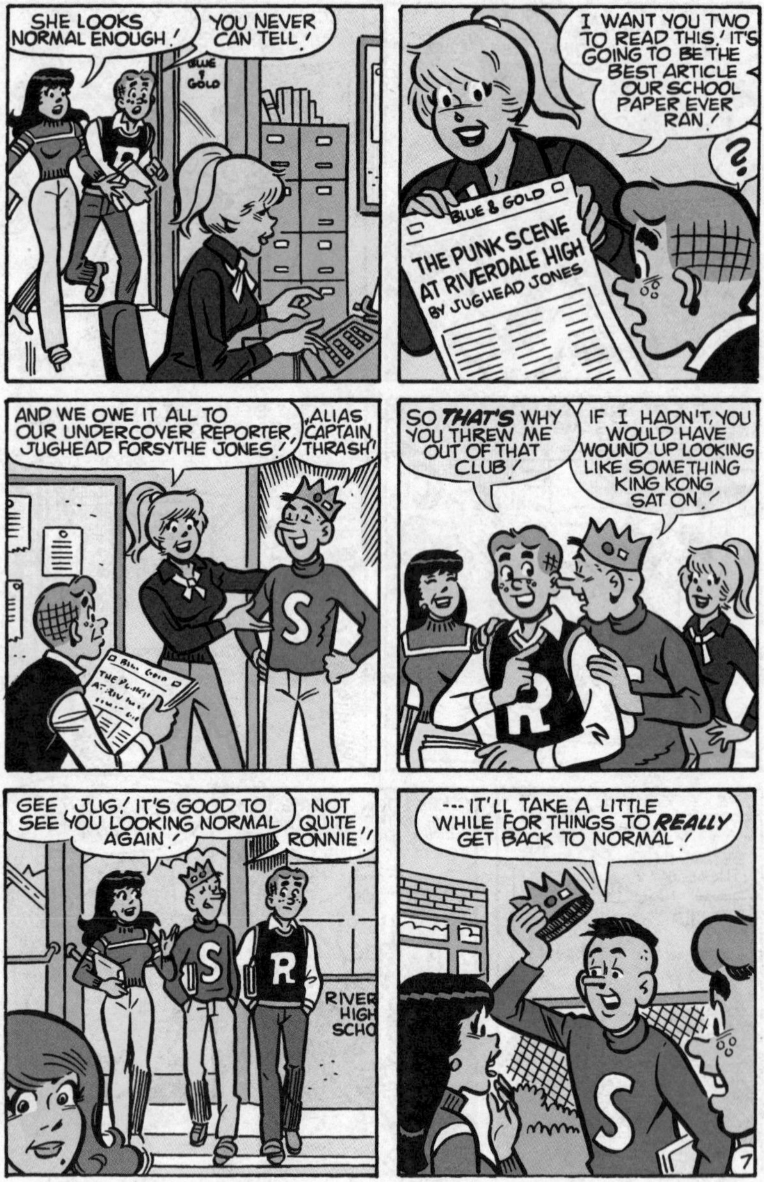
SHE LOOKS NORMAL ENOUGH!
YOU NEVER CAN TELL!
I WANT YOU TWO TO READ THIS! IT'S GOING TO BE THE BEST ARTICLE OUR SCHOOL PAPER EVER RAN!
?
BLUE & GOLD
THE PUNK SCENE AT RIVERDALE HIGH
BY JUGHEAD JONES
AND WE OWE IT ALL TO OUR UNDERCOVER REPORTER, JUGHEAD FORSYTHE JONES!
ALIAS "CAPTAIN THRASH"!
SO THAT'S WHY YOU THREW ME OUT OF THAT CLUB!
IF I HADN'T, YOU WOULD HAVE WOUND UP LOOKING LIKE SOMETHING KING KONG SAT ON!
GEE JUG! IT'S GOOD TO SEE YOU LOOKING NORMAL AGAIN!
NOT QUITE, RONNIE!
RIVER HIGH SCHO
--- IT'LL TAKE A LITTLE WHILE FOR THINGS TO REALLY GET BACK TO NORMAL!
7

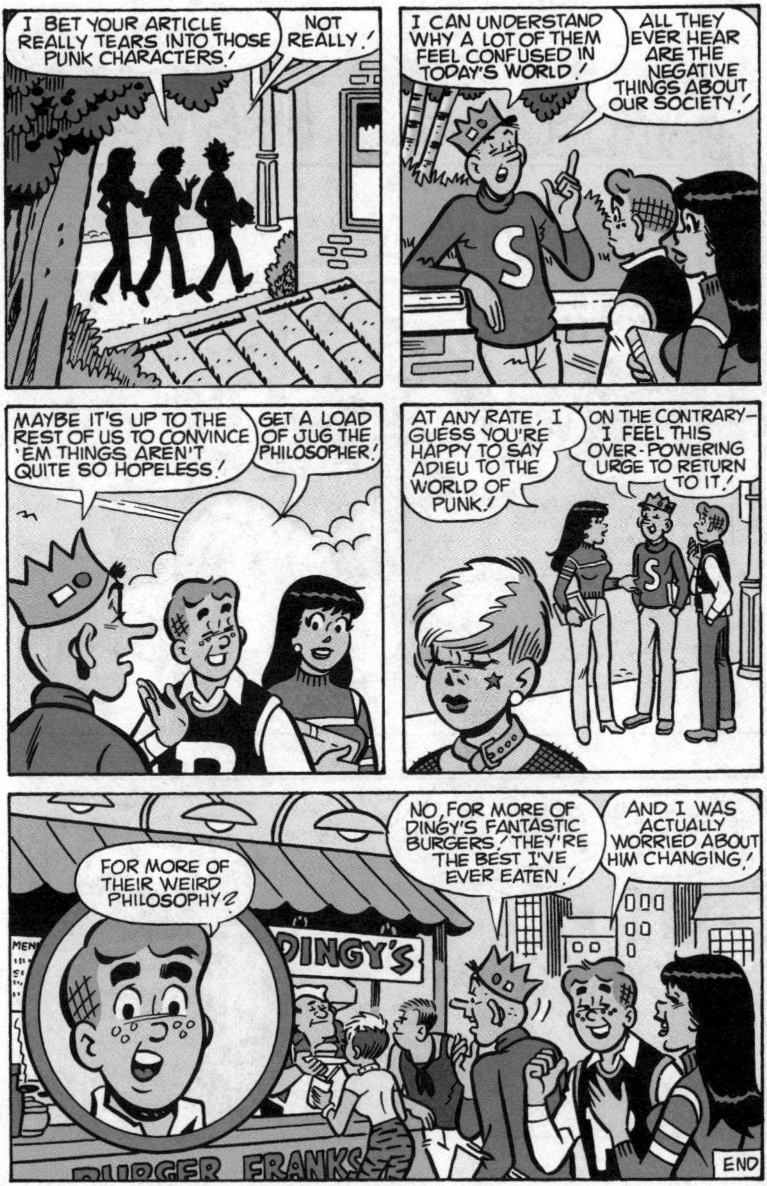
I BET YOUR ARTICLE REALLY TEARS INTO THOSE PUNK CHARACTERS!
NOT REALLY!
I CAN UNDERSTAND WHY A LOT OF THEM FEEL CONFUSED IN TODAY'S WORLD!
ALL THEY EVER HEAR ARE THE NEGATIVE THINGS ABOUT OUR SOCIETY!
MAYBE IT'S UP TO THE REST OF US TO CONVINCE 'EM THINGS AREN'T QUITE SO HOPELESS!
GET A LOAD OF JUG THE PHILOSOPHER!
AT ANY RATE, I GUESS YOU'RE HAPPY TO SAY ADIEU TO THE WORLD OF PUNK!
ON THE CONTRARY—I FEEL THIS OVER-POWERING URGE TO RETURN TO IT!
FOR MORE OF THEIR WEIRD PHILOSOPHY?
NO, FOR MORE OF DINGY'S FANTASTIC BURGERS! THEY'RE THE BEST I'VE EVER EATEN!
AND I WAS ACTUALLY WORRIED ABOUT HIM CHANGING!
DINGY'S
BURGER FRANKS
END

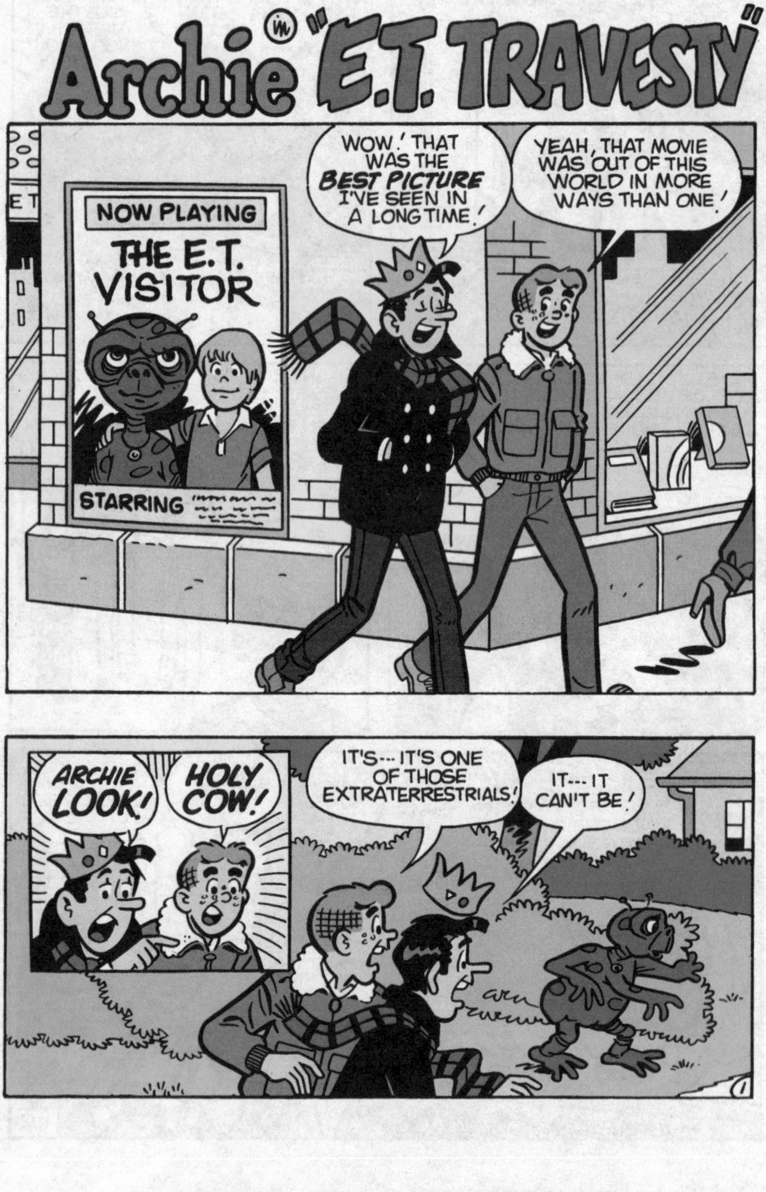
Archie in "E.T. TRAVESTY"
NOW PLAYING
THE E.T. VISITOR
STARRING
WOW! THAT WAS THE BEST PICTURE I'VE SEEN IN A LONG TIME!
YEAH, THAT MOVIE WAS OUT OF THIS WORLD IN MORE WAYS THAN ONE!
ARCHIE LOOK!
HOLY COW!
IT'S--- IT'S ONE OF THOSE EXTRATERRESTRIALS!
IT--- IT CAN'T BE!

Originally presented in ARCHIE #322, March, 1983

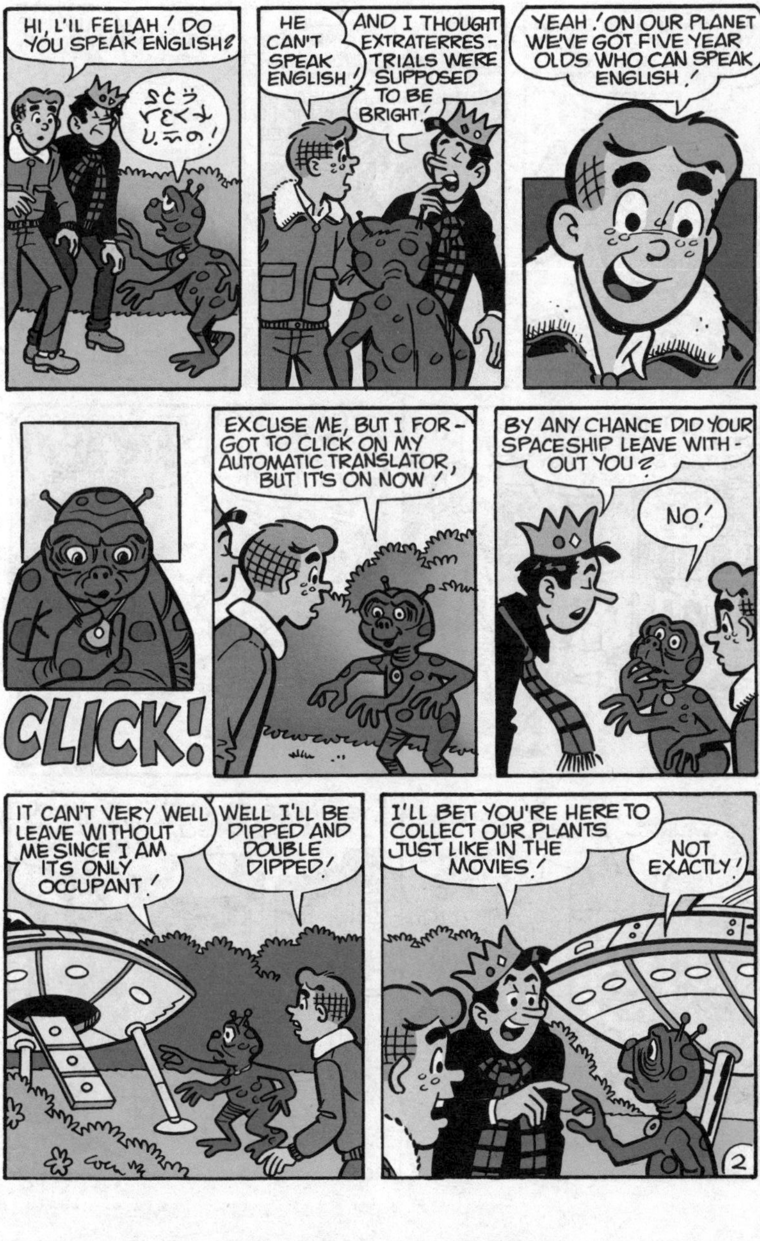
HI, L'IL FELLAH! DO YOU SPEAK ENGLISH?
HE CAN'T SPEAK ENGLISH!
AND I THOUGHT EXTRATERRES-TRIALS WERE SUPPOSED TO BE BRIGHT!
YEAH! ON OUR PLANET WE'VE GOT FIVE YEAR OLDS WHO CAN SPEAK ENGLISH!
CLICK!
EXCUSE ME, BUT I FOR-GOT TO CLICK ON MY AUTOMATIC TRANSLATOR, BUT IT'S ON NOW!
BY ANY CHANCE DID YOUR SPACESHIP LEAVE WITH-OUT YOU?
NO!
IT CAN'T VERY WELL LEAVE WITHOUT ME SINCE I AM ITS ONLY OCCUPANT!
WELL I'LL BE DIPPED AND DOUBLE DIPPED!
I'LL BET YOU'RE HERE TO COLLECT OUR PLANTS JUST LIKE IN THE MOVIES!
NOT EXACTLY!
2

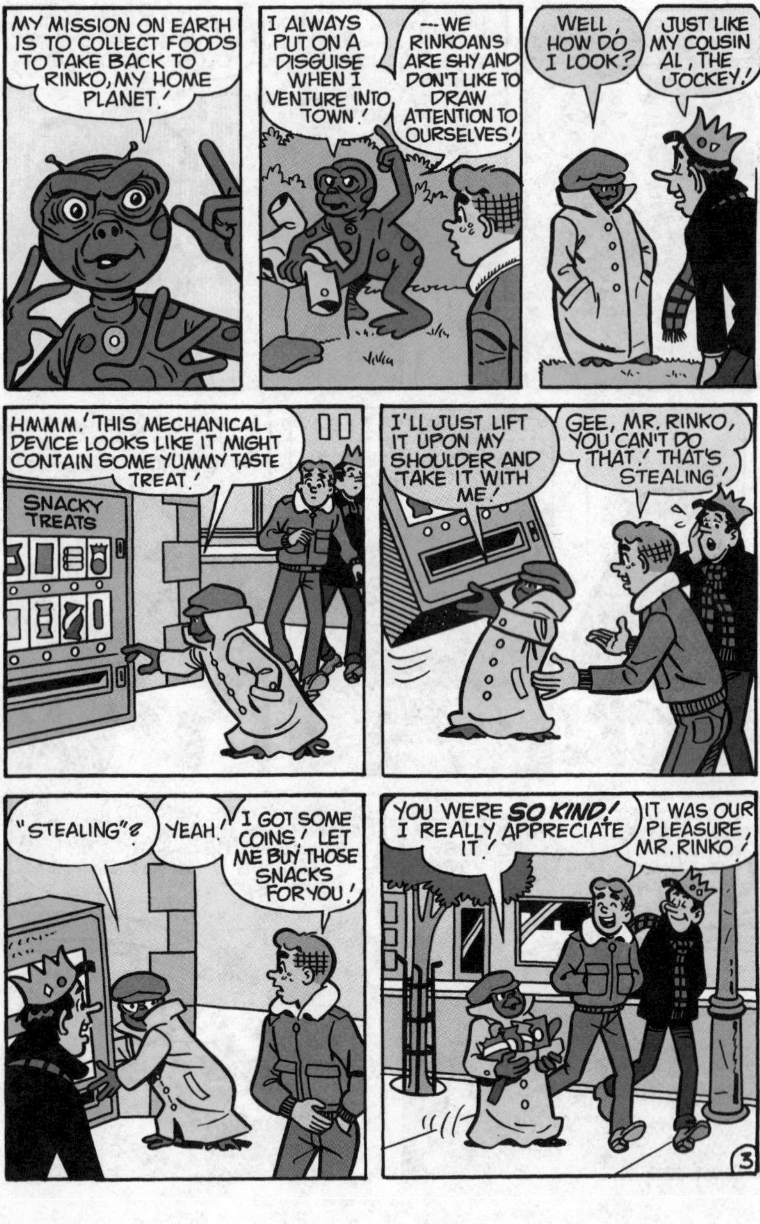
MY MISSION ON EARTH IS TO COLLECT FOODS TO TAKE BACK TO RINKO, MY HOME PLANET!
I ALWAYS PUT ON A DISGUISE WHEN I VENTURE INTO TOWN!
---WE RINKOANS ARE SHY AND DON'T LIKE TO DRAW ATTENTION TO OURSELVES!
WELL, HOW DO I LOOK?
JUST LIKE MY COUSIN AL, THE JOCKEY!
HMMM! THIS MECHANICAL DEVICE LOOKS LIKE IT MIGHT CONTAIN SOME YUMMY TASTE TREAT!
SNACKY TREATS
I'LL JUST LIFT IT UPON MY SHOULDER AND TAKE IT WITH ME!
GEE, MR. RINKO, YOU CAN'T DO THAT! THAT'S STEALING!
"STEALING"?
YEAH!
I GOT SOME COINS! LET ME BUY THOSE SNACKS FOR YOU!
YOU WERE SO KIND! I REALLY APPRECIATE IT!
IT WAS OUR PLEASURE, MR. RINKO!
3

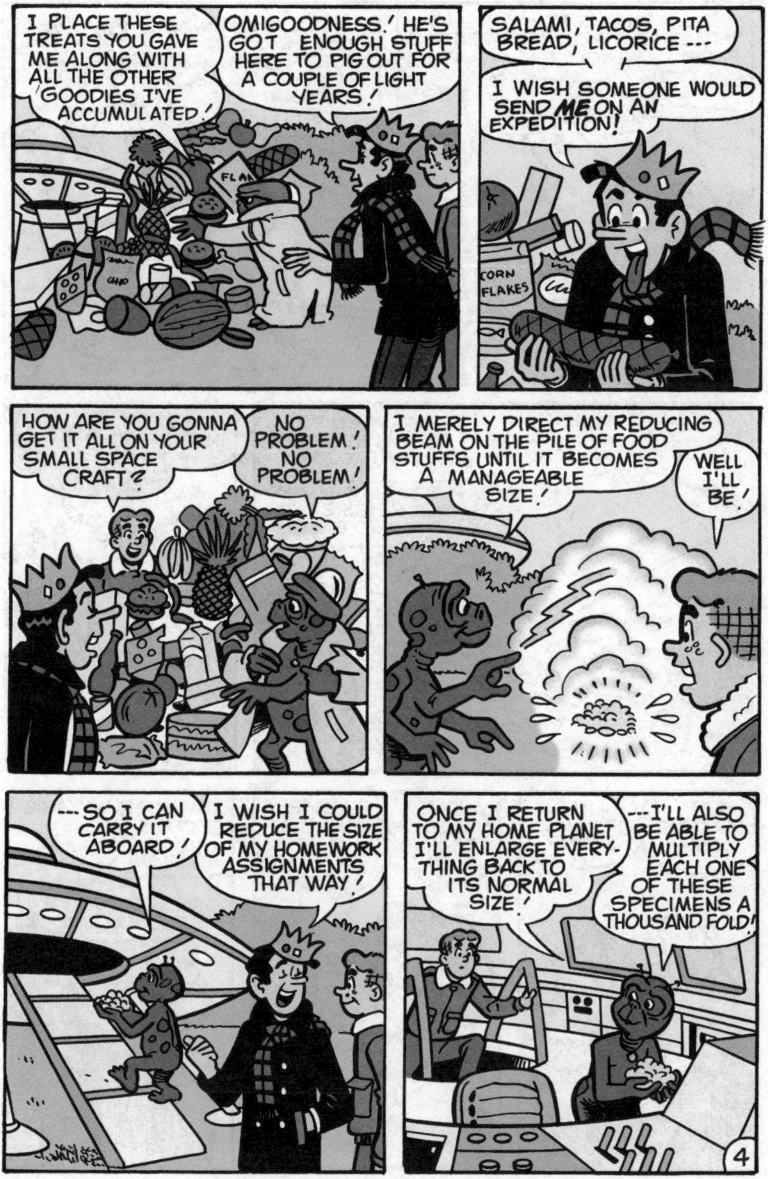
I PLACE THESE TREATS YOU GAVE ME ALONG WITH ALL THE OTHER GOODIES I'VE ACCUMULATED!
OMIGOODNESS! HE'S GOT ENOUGH STUFF HERE TO PIG OUT FOR A COUPLE OF LIGHT YEARS!
SALAMI, TACOS, PITA BREAD, LICORICE ---
I WISH SOMEONE WOULD SEND ME ON AN EXPEDITION!
CORN FLAKES
HOW ARE YOU GONNA GET IT ALL ON YOUR SMALL SPACE CRAFT?
NO PROBLEM! NO PROBLEM!
I MERELY DIRECT MY REDUCING BEAM ON THE PILE OF FOOD STUFFS UNTIL IT BECOMES A MANAGEABLE SIZE!
WELL I'LL BE!
--- SO I CAN CARRY IT ABOARD!
I WISH I COULD REDUCE THE SIZE OF MY HOMEWORK ASSIGNMENTS THAT WAY!
ONCE I RETURN TO MY HOME PLANET I'LL ENLARGE EVERYTHING BACK TO ITS NORMAL SIZE!
--- I'LL ALSO BE ABLE TO MULTIPLY EACH ONE OF THESE SPECIMENS A THOUSAND FOLD!
4

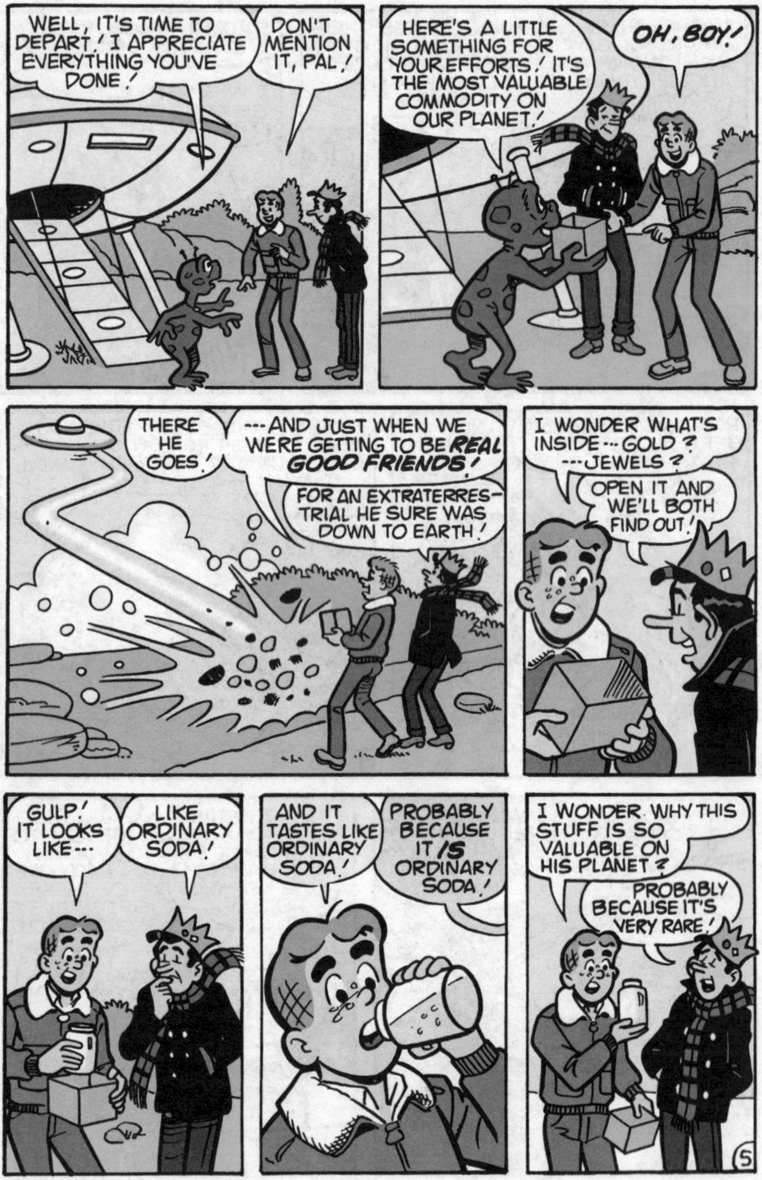
WELL, IT'S TIME TO DEPART! I APPRECIATE EVERYTHING YOU'VE DONE!
DON'T MENTION IT, PAL!
HERE'S A LITTLE SOMETHING FOR YOUR EFFORTS! IT'S THE MOST VALUABLE COMMODITY ON OUR PLANET!
OH, BOY!
THERE HE GOES!
---AND JUST WHEN WE WERE GETTING TO BE REAL GOOD FRIENDS!
FOR AN EXTRATERRES-TRIAL HE SURE WAS DOWN TO EARTH!
I WONDER WHAT'S INSIDE---GOLD? ---JEWELS?
OPEN IT AND WE'LL BOTH FIND OUT!
GULP! IT LOOKS LIKE---
LIKE ORDINARY SODA!
AND IT TASTES LIKE ORDINARY SODA!
PROBABLY BECAUSE IT IS ORDINARY SODA!
I WONDER WHY THIS STUFF IS SO VALUABLE ON HIS PLANET?
PROBABLY BECAUSE IT'S VERY RARE!
5

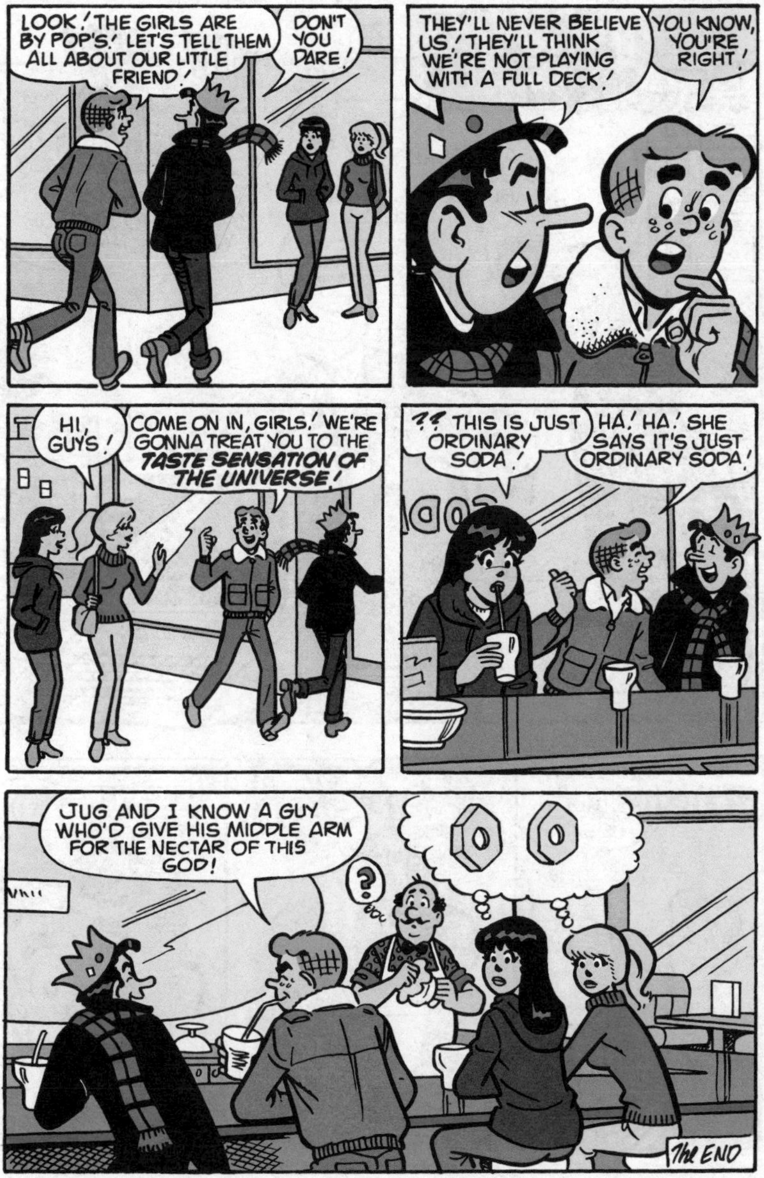
LOOK! THE GIRLS ARE BY POP'S! LET'S TELL THEM ALL ABOUT OUR LITTLE FRIEND!
DON'T YOU DARE!
THEY'LL NEVER BELIEVE US! THEY'LL THINK WE'RE NOT PLAYING WITH A FULL DECK!
YOU KNOW, YOU'RE RIGHT!
HI, GUYS!
COME ON IN, GIRLS! WE'RE GONNA TREAT YOU TO THE TASTE SENSATION OF THE UNIVERSE!
?? THIS IS JUST ORDINARY SODA!
HA! HA! SHE SAYS IT'S JUST ORDINARY SODA!
JUG AND I KNOW A GUY WHO'D GIVE HIS MIDDLE ARM FOR THE NECTAR OF THIS GOD!
?
The END

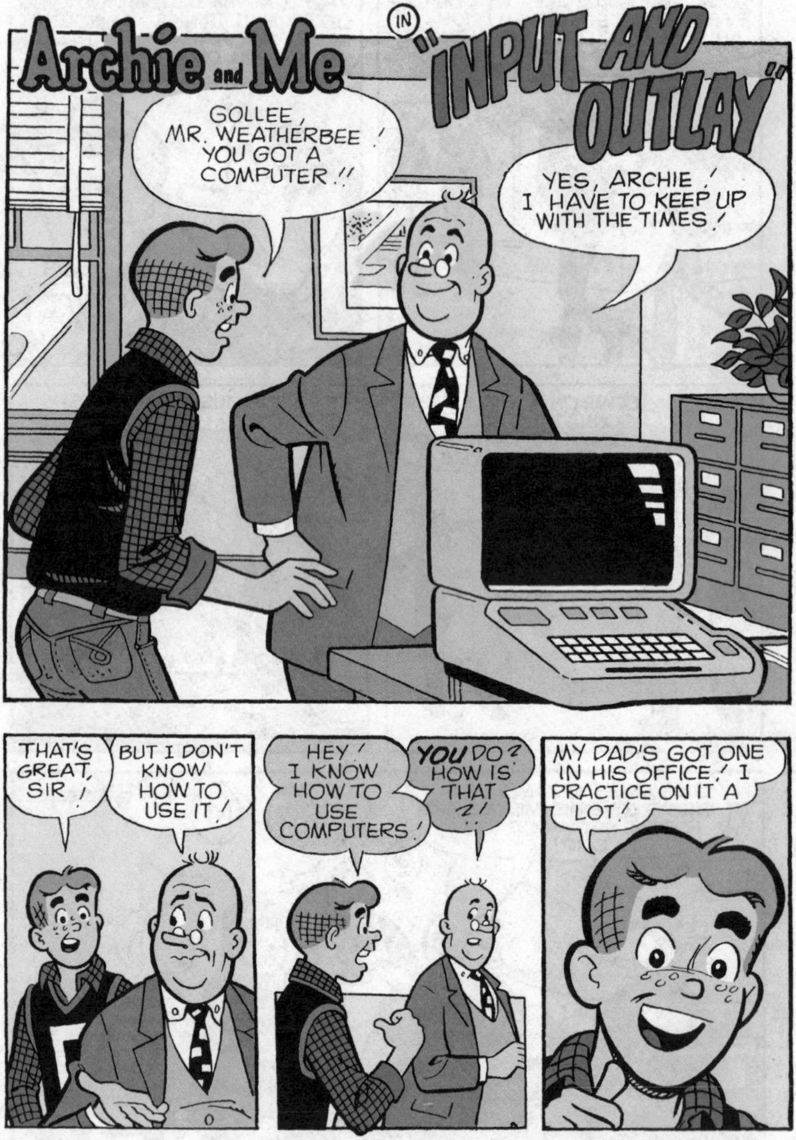
Archie and Me
IN
"INPUT AND OUTLAY"
GOLLEE, MR. WEATHERBEE! YOU GOT A COMPUTER!!
YES, ARCHIE! I HAVE TO KEEP UP WITH THE TIMES!
THAT'S GREAT, SIR!
BUT I DON'T KNOW HOW TO USE IT!
HEY! I KNOW HOW TO USE COMPUTERS!
YOU DO? HOW IS THAT?!
MY DAD'S GOT ONE IN HIS OFFICE! I PRACTICE ON IT A LOT!

Originally presented in ARCHIE & ME #140, August, 1983

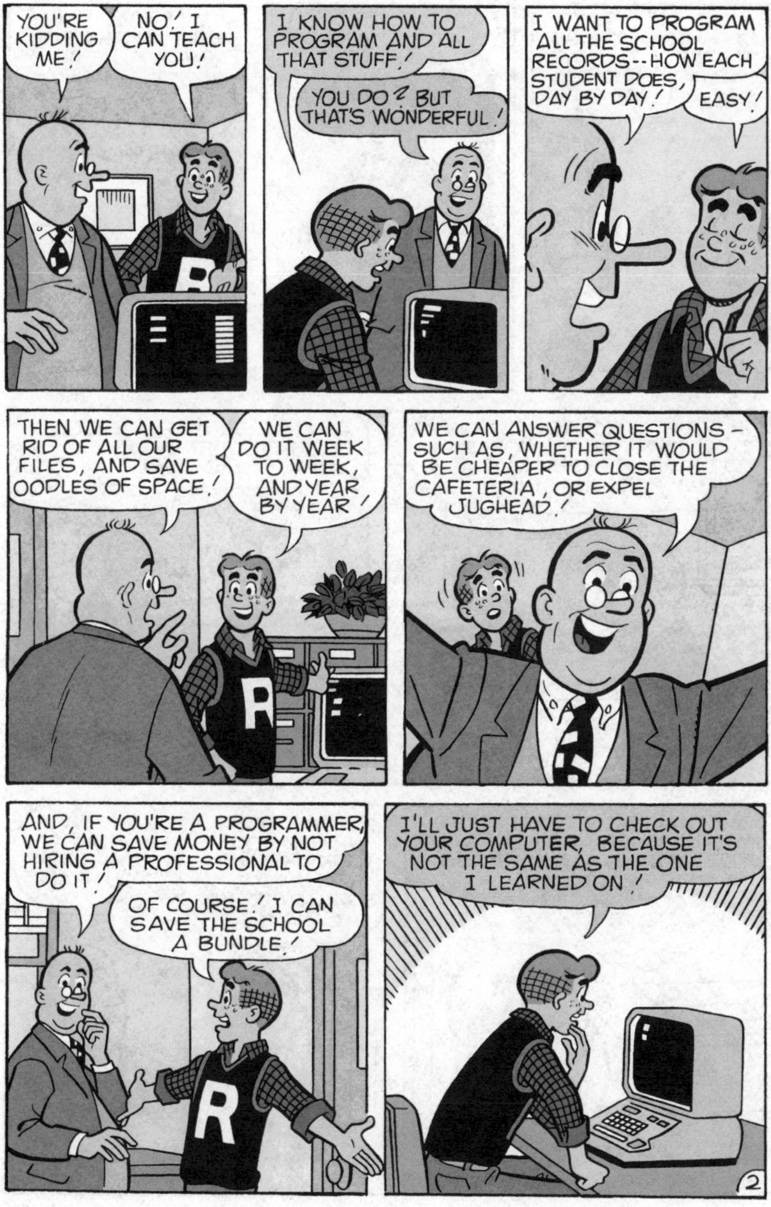
YOU'RE KIDDING ME!
NO! I CAN TEACH YOU!
I KNOW HOW TO PROGRAM AND ALL THAT STUFF!
YOU DO? BUT THAT'S WONDERFUL!
I WANT TO PROGRAM ALL THE SCHOOL RECORDS--HOW EACH STUDENT DOES, DAY BY DAY!
EASY!
THEN WE CAN GET RID OF ALL OUR FILES, AND SAVE OODLES OF SPACE!
WE CAN DO IT WEEK TO WEEK, AND YEAR BY YEAR!
WE CAN ANSWER QUESTIONS - SUCH AS, WHETHER IT WOULD BE CHEAPER TO CLOSE THE CAFETERIA, OR EXPEL JUGHEAD!
AND, IF YOU'RE A PROGRAMMER, WE CAN SAVE MONEY BY NOT HIRING A PROFESSIONAL TO DO IT!
OF COURSE! I CAN SAVE THE SCHOOL A BUNDLE!
I'LL JUST HAVE TO CHECK OUT YOUR COMPUTER, BECAUSE IT'S NOT THE SAME AS THE ONE I LEARNED ON!
2

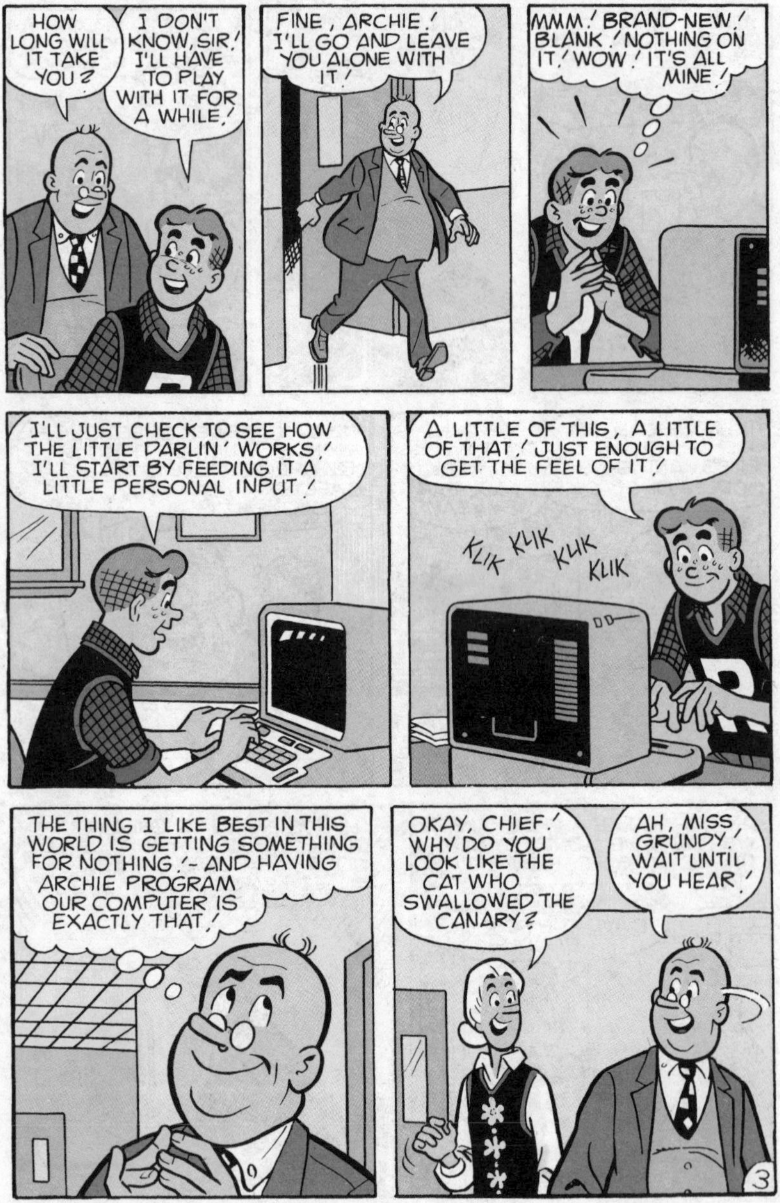
HOW LONG WILL IT TAKE YOU?
I DON'T KNOW, SIR! I'LL HAVE TO PLAY WITH IT FOR A WHILE!
FINE, ARCHIE! I'LL GO AND LEAVE YOU ALONE WITH IT!
MMM! BRAND-NEW! BLANK! NOTHING ON IT! WOW! IT'S ALL MINE!
I'LL JUST CHECK TO SEE HOW THE LITTLE DARLIN' WORKS! I'LL START BY FEEDING IT A LITTLE PERSONAL INPUT!
A LITTLE OF THIS, A LITTLE OF THAT! JUST ENOUGH TO GET THE FEEL OF IT!
KLIK KLIK KLIK KLIK
THE THING I LIKE BEST IN THIS WORLD IS GETTING SOMETHING FOR NOTHING!- AND HAVING ARCHIE PROGRAM OUR COMPUTER IS EXACTLY THAT!
OKAY, CHIEF! WHY DO YOU LOOK LIKE THE CAT WHO SWALLOWED THE CANARY?
AH, MISS GRUNDY! WAIT UNTIL YOU HEAR!
3

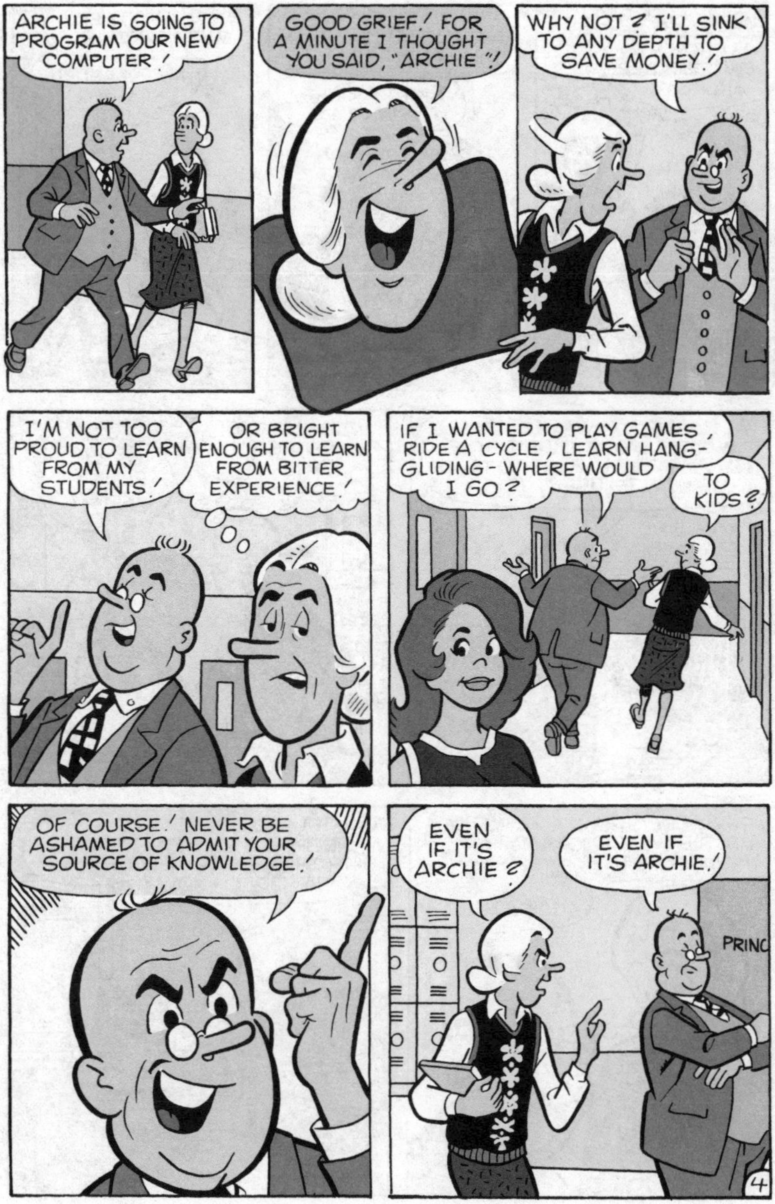
ARCHIE IS GOING TO PROGRAM OUR NEW COMPUTER!
GOOD GRIEF! FOR A MINUTE I THOUGHT YOU SAID, "ARCHIE"!
WHY NOT? I'LL SINK TO ANY DEPTH TO SAVE MONEY!
I'M NOT TOO PROUD TO LEARN FROM MY STUDENTS!
OR BRIGHT ENOUGH TO LEARN FROM BITTER EXPERIENCE!
IF I WANTED TO PLAY GAMES, RIDE A CYCLE, LEARN HANG-GLIDING - WHERE WOULD I GO?
TO KIDS?
OF COURSE! NEVER BE ASHAMED TO ADMIT YOUR SOURCE OF KNOWLEDGE!
EVEN IF IT'S ARCHIE?
EVEN IF IT'S ARCHIE!
PRINC
4

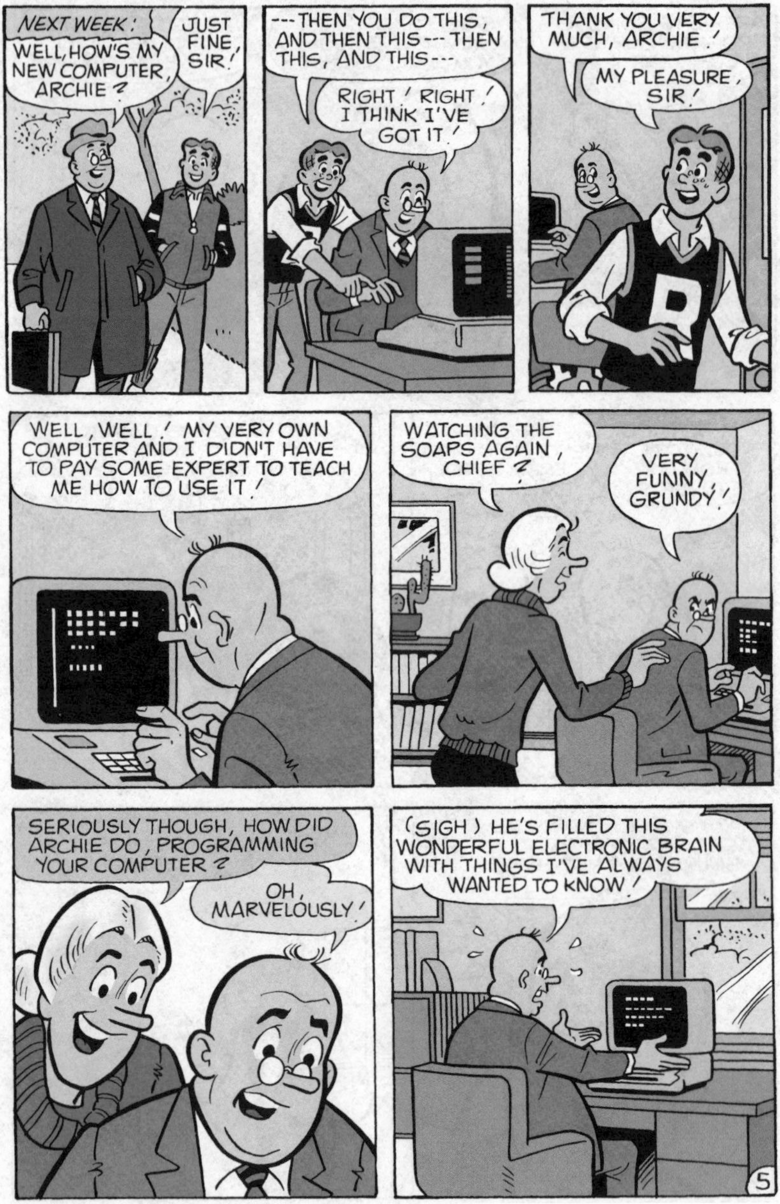
NEXT WEEK:
WELL, HOW'S MY NEW COMPUTER, ARCHIE?
JUST FINE, SIR!
---THEN YOU DO THIS, AND THEN THIS--- THEN THIS, AND THIS---
RIGHT! RIGHT! I THINK I'VE GOT IT!
THANK YOU VERY MUCH, ARCHIE!
MY PLEASURE, SIR!
WELL, WELL! MY VERY OWN COMPUTER AND I DIDN'T HAVE TO PAY SOME EXPERT TO TEACH ME HOW TO USE IT!
WATCHING THE SOAPS AGAIN, CHIEF?
VERY FUNNY, GRUNDY!
SERIOUSLY THOUGH, HOW DID ARCHIE DO, PROGRAMMING YOUR COMPUTER?
OH, MARVELOUSLY!
(SIGH) HE'S FILLED THIS WONDERFUL ELECTRONIC BRAIN WITH THINGS I'VE ALWAYS WANTED TO KNOW!
5

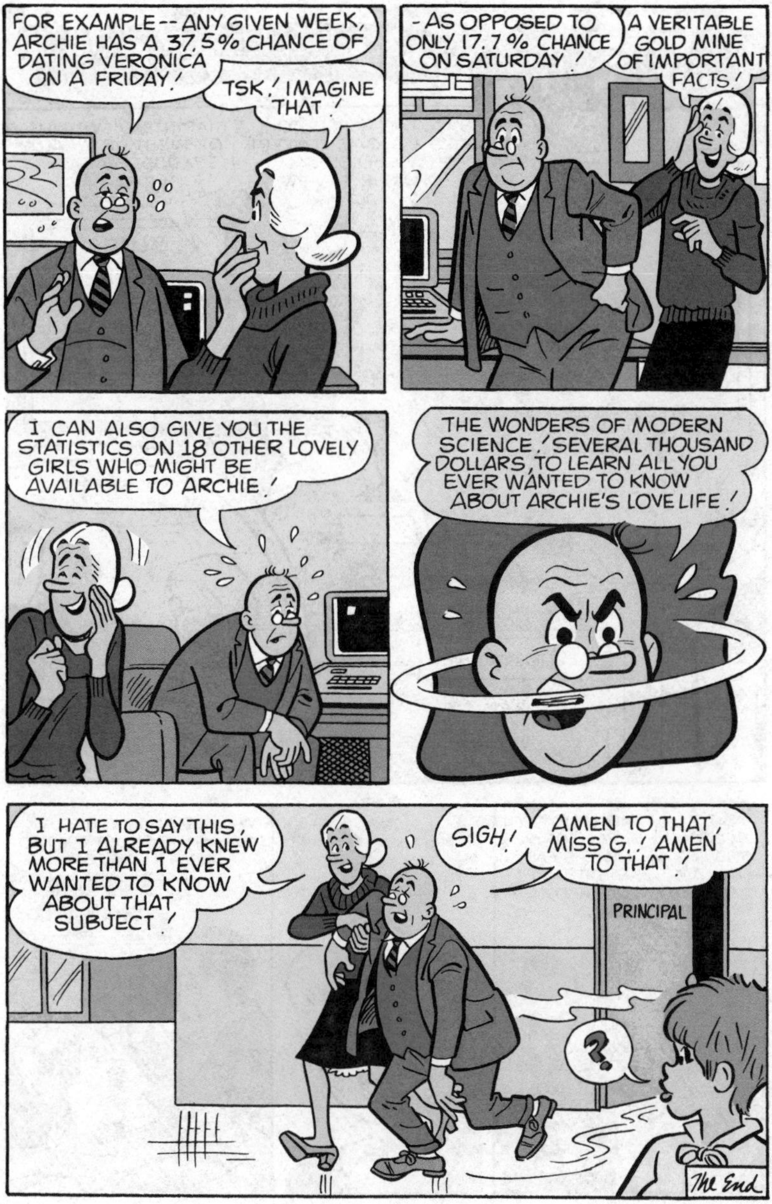
FOR EXAMPLE -- ANY GIVEN WEEK, ARCHIE HAS A 37.5% CHANCE OF DATING VERONICA ON A FRIDAY!
TSK! IMAGINE THAT!
- AS OPPOSED TO ONLY 17.7% CHANCE ON SATURDAY!
A VERITABLE GOLD MINE OF IMPORTANT FACTS!
I CAN ALSO GIVE YOU THE STATISTICS ON 18 OTHER LOVELY GIRLS WHO MIGHT BE AVAILABLE TO ARCHIE!
THE WONDERS OF MODERN SCIENCE! SEVERAL THOUSAND DOLLARS, TO LEARN ALL YOU EVER WANTED TO KNOW ABOUT ARCHIE'S LOVE LIFE!
I HATE TO SAY THIS, BUT I ALREADY KNEW MORE THAN I EVER WANTED TO KNOW ABOUT THAT SUBJECT!
SIGH!
AMEN TO THAT, MISS G.! AMEN TO THAT!
PRINCIPAL
?
The End

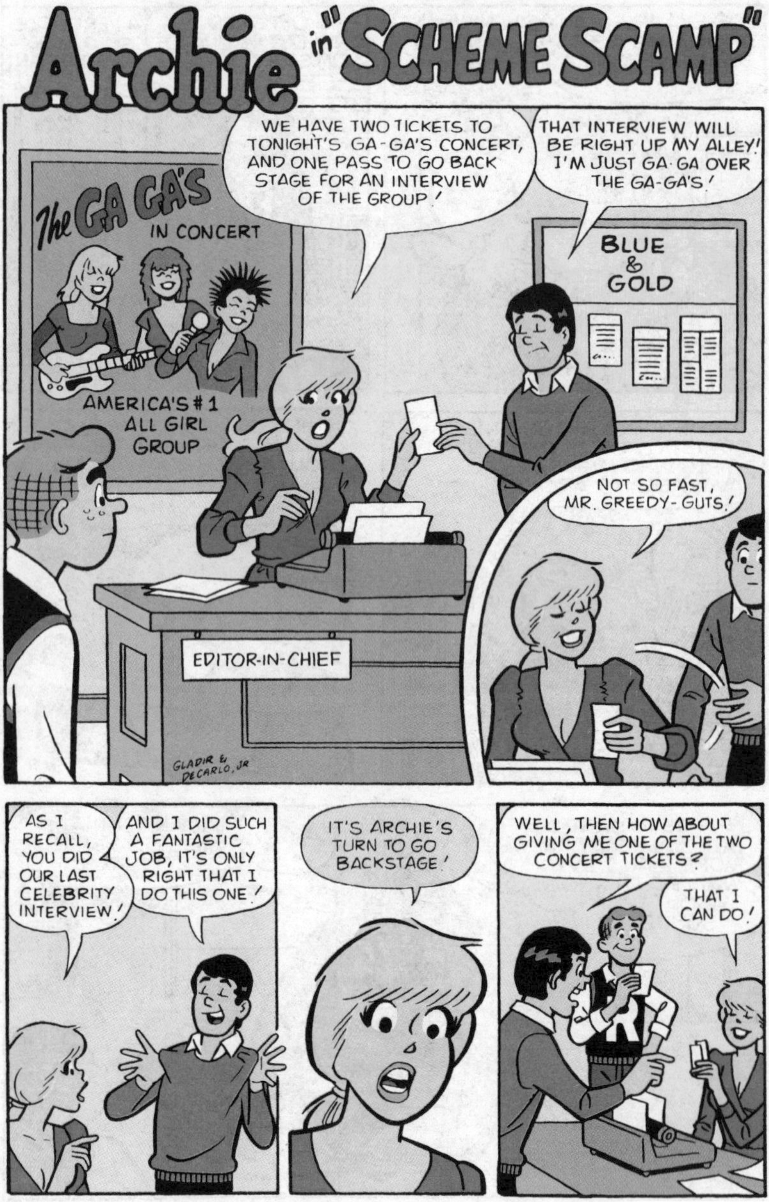
Archie in "SCHEME SCAMP"
WE HAVE TWO TICKETS TO TONIGHT'S GA-GA'S CONCERT, AND ONE PASS TO GO BACK STAGE FOR AN INTERVIEW OF THE GROUP!
THAT INTERVIEW WILL BE RIGHT UP MY ALLEY! I'M JUST GA-GA OVER THE GA-GA'S!
The GA GA'S IN CONCERT
AMERICA'S #1 ALL GIRL GROUP
BLUE & GOLD
EDITOR-IN-CHIEF
GLADIR & DECARLO, JR
NOT SO FAST, MR. GREEDY-GUTS!
AS I RECALL, YOU DID OUR LAST CELEBRITY INTERVIEW!
AND I DID SUCH A FANTASTIC JOB, IT'S ONLY RIGHT THAT I DO THIS ONE!
IT'S ARCHIE'S TURN TO GO BACKSTAGE!
WELL, THEN HOW ABOUT GIVING ME ONE OF THE TWO CONCERT TICKETS?
THAT I CAN DO!

Originally presented in ARCHIE #327, January, 1984

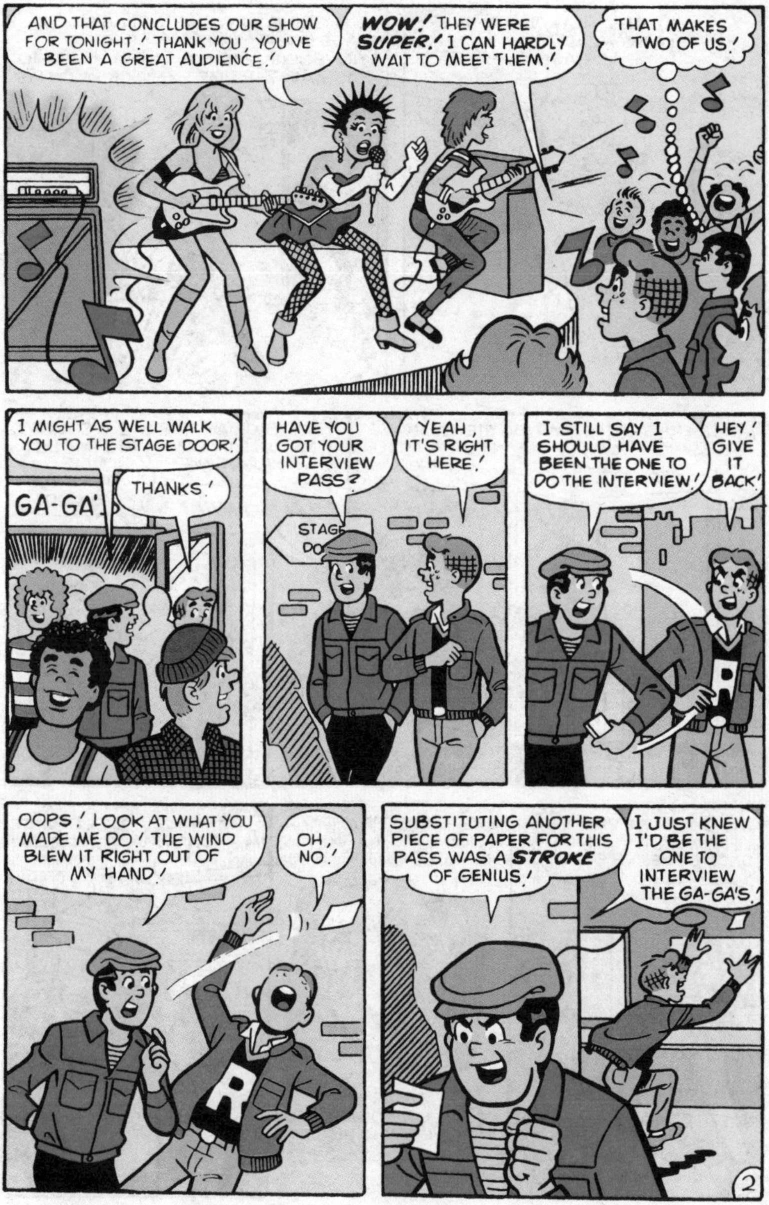
AND THAT CONCLUDES OUR SHOW FOR TONIGHT! THANK YOU, YOU'VE BEEN A GREAT AUDIENCE!
WOW! THEY WERE SUPER! I CAN HARDLY WAIT TO MEET THEM!
THAT MAKES TWO OF US!
I MIGHT AS WELL WALK YOU TO THE STAGE DOOR!
THANKS!
GA-GA'S
HAVE YOU GOT YOUR INTERVIEW PASS?
YEAH, IT'S RIGHT HERE!
I STILL SAY I SHOULD HAVE BEEN THE ONE TO DO THE INTERVIEW!
HEY! GIVE IT BACK!
OOPS! LOOK AT WHAT YOU MADE ME DO! THE WIND BLEW IT RIGHT OUT OF MY HAND!
OH, NO!
SUBSTITUTING ANOTHER PIECE OF PAPER FOR THIS PASS WAS A STROKE OF GENIUS!
I JUST KNEW I'D BE THE ONE TO INTERVIEW THE GA-GA'S!
2

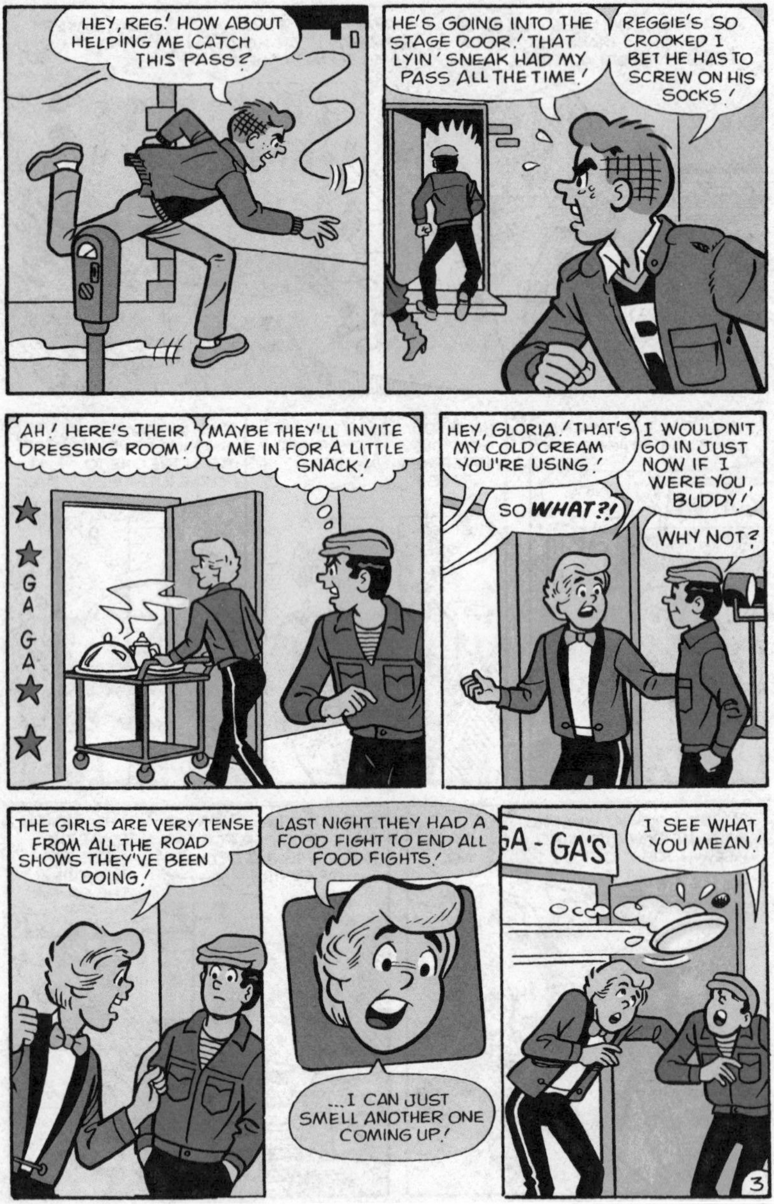
HEY, REG! HOW ABOUT HELPING ME CATCH THIS PASS?
HE'S GOING INTO THE STAGE DOOR! THAT LYIN' SNEAK HAD MY PASS ALL THE TIME!
REGGIE'S SO CROOKED I BET HE HAS TO SCREW ON HIS SOCKS!
AH! HERE'S THEIR DRESSING ROOM!
MAYBE THEY'LL INVITE ME IN FOR A LITTLE SNACK!
GA GA
HEY, GLORIA! THAT'S MY COLD CREAM YOU'RE USING!
SO WHAT?!
I WOULDN'T GO IN JUST NOW IF I WERE YOU, BUDDY!
WHY NOT?
THE GIRLS ARE VERY TENSE FROM ALL THE ROAD SHOWS THEY'VE BEEN DOING!
LAST NIGHT THEY HAD A FOOD FIGHT TO END ALL FOOD FIGHTS!
...I CAN JUST SMELL ANOTHER ONE COMING UP!
GA - GA'S
I SEE WHAT YOU MEAN!
3

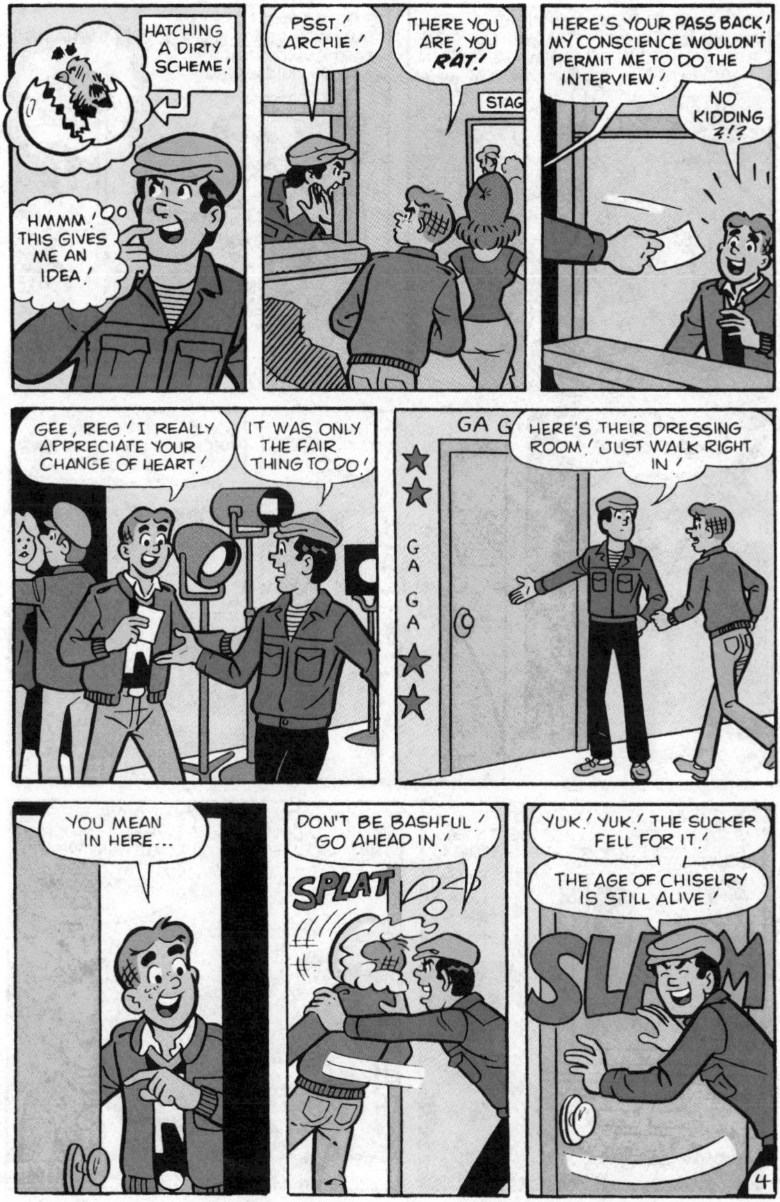
HATCHING A DIRTY SCHEME!
HMMM! THIS GIVES ME AN IDEA!
PSST! ARCHIE!
THERE YOU ARE, YOU RAT!
STAG
HERE'S YOUR PASS BACK! MY CONSCIENCE WOULDN'T PERMIT ME TO DO THE INTERVIEW!
NO KIDDING ?!?
GEE, REG! I REALLY APPRECIATE YOUR CHANGE OF HEART!
IT WAS ONLY THE FAIR THING TO DO!
GA G
HERE'S THEIR DRESSING ROOM! JUST WALK RIGHT IN!
GA GA
YOU MEAN IN HERE...
DON'T BE BASHFUL! GO AHEAD IN!
SPLAT
YUK! YUK! THE SUCKER FELL FOR IT!
THE AGE OF CHISELRY IS STILL ALIVE!
SLAM
4

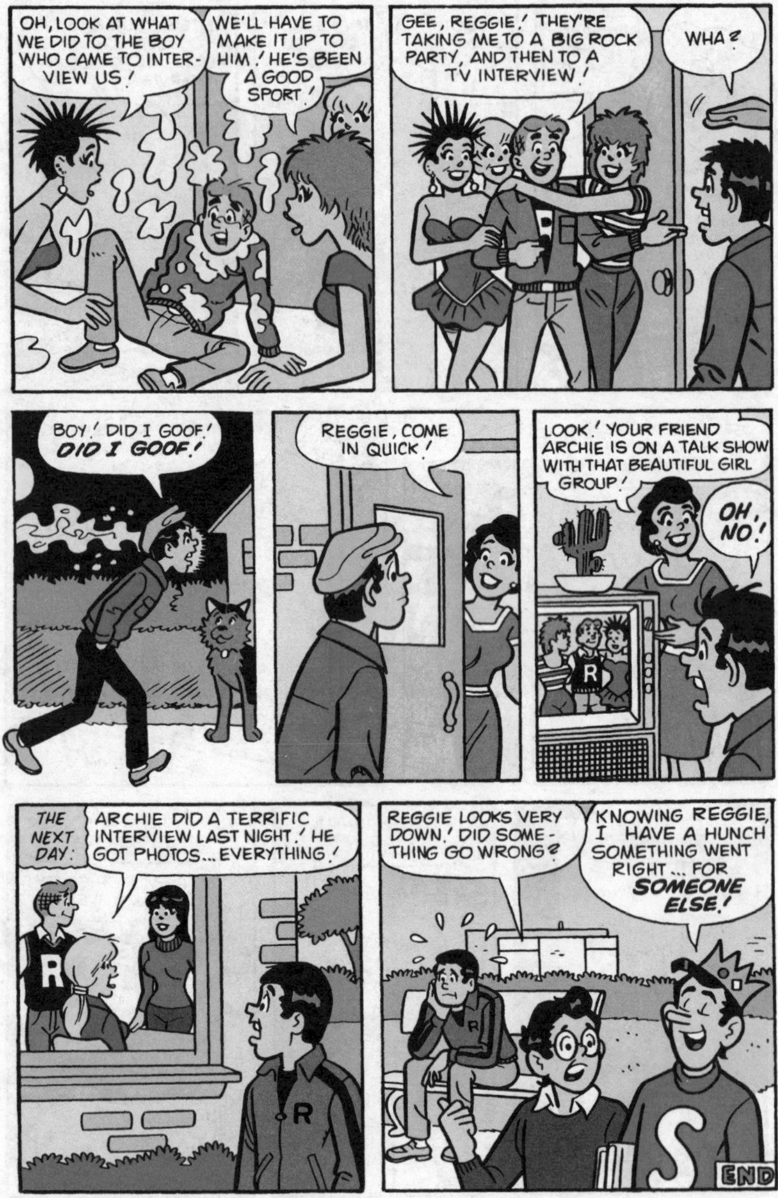
OH, LOOK AT WHAT WE DID TO THE BOY WHO CAME TO INTERVIEW US!
WE'LL HAVE TO MAKE IT UP TO HIM! HE'S BEEN A GOOD SPORT!
GEE, REGGIE! THEY'RE TAKING ME TO A BIG ROCK PARTY, AND THEN TO A TV INTERVIEW!
WHA?
BOY! DID I GOOF! DID I GOOF!
REGGIE, COME IN QUICK!
LOOK! YOUR FRIEND ARCHIE IS ON A TALK SHOW WITH THAT BEAUTIFUL GIRL GROUP!
OH, NO!
THE NEXT DAY:
ARCHIE DID A TERRIFIC INTERVIEW LAST NIGHT! HE GOT PHOTOS... EVERYTHING!
REGGIE LOOKS VERY DOWN! DID SOMETHING GO WRONG?
KNOWING REGGIE, I HAVE A HUNCH SOMETHING WENT RIGHT ... FOR SOMEONE ELSE!
END

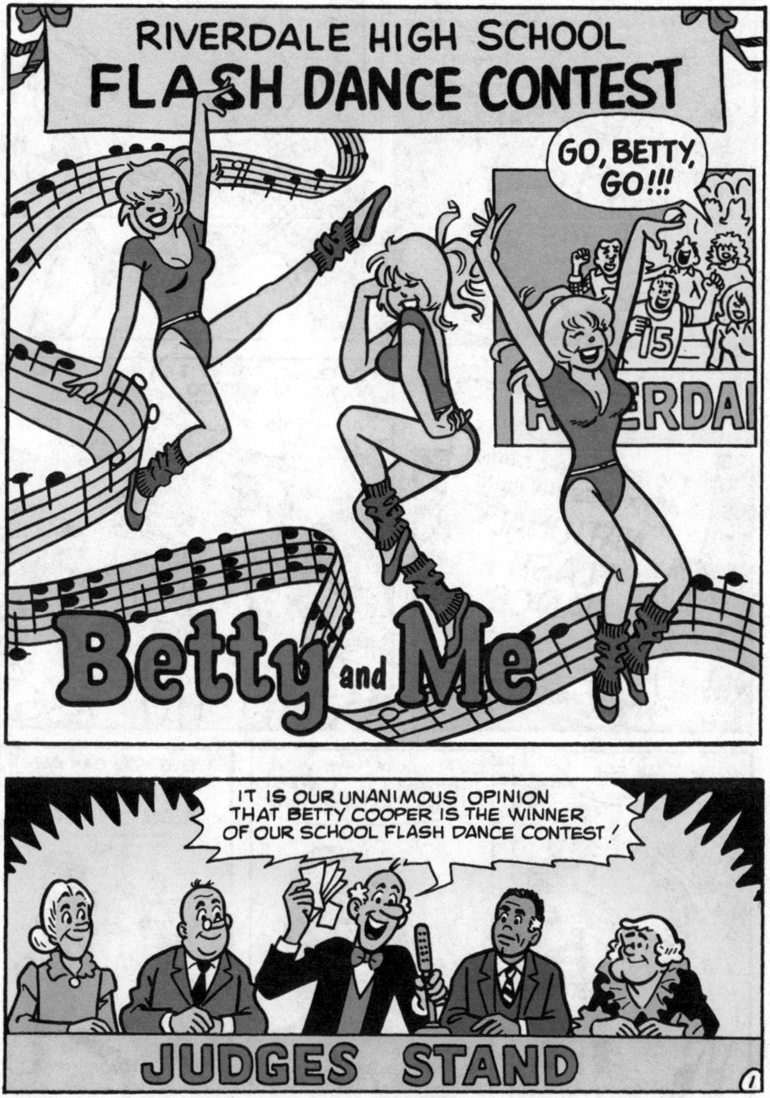
RIVERDALE HIGH SCHOOL
FLASH DANCE CONTEST
GO, BETTY, GO!!!
RIVERDAL
15
Betty and Me
IT IS OUR UNANIMOUS OPINION THAT BETTY COOPER IS THE WINNER OF OUR SCHOOL FLASH DANCE CONTEST!
JUDGES STAND
1

Originally presented in BETTY & ME #137, January, 1984

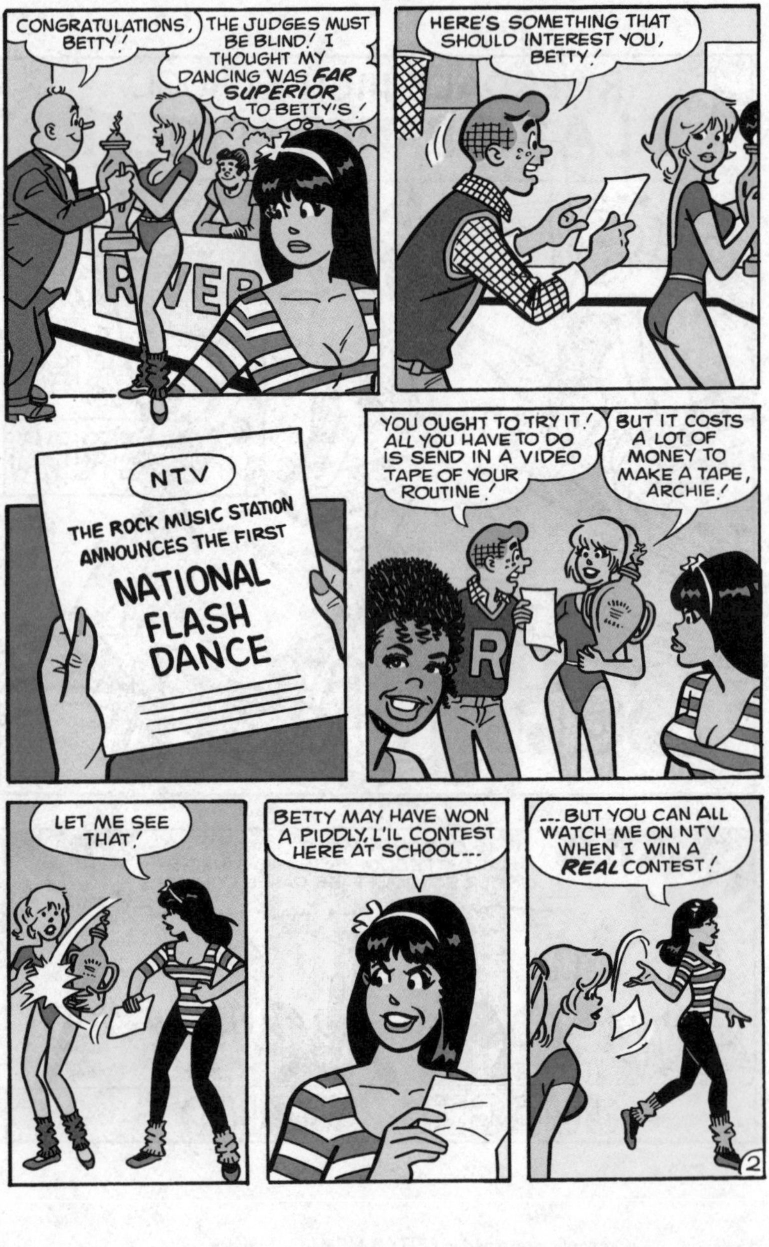
CONGRATULATIONS, BETTY!
THE JUDGES MUST BE BLIND! I THOUGHT MY DANCING WAS FAR SUPERIOR TO BETTY'S!
HERE'S SOMETHING THAT SHOULD INTEREST YOU, BETTY!
NTV
THE ROCK MUSIC STATION ANNOUNCES THE FIRST
NATIONAL FLASH DANCE
YOU OUGHT TO TRY IT! ALL YOU HAVE TO DO IS SEND IN A VIDEO TAPE OF YOUR ROUTINE!
BUT IT COSTS A LOT OF MONEY TO MAKE A TAPE, ARCHIE!
LET ME SEE THAT!
BETTY MAY HAVE WON A PIDDLY, L'IL CONTEST HERE AT SCHOOL...
...BUT YOU CAN ALL WATCH ME ON NTV WHEN I WIN A REAL CONTEST!
2

HEY, GUYS! HAVE YOU HEARD, RONNIE IS FLYING IN A HOLLYWOOD DIRECTOR TO TAPE HER FLASH DANCE ROUTINE FOR THE CONTEST!

NO KIDDING!

"...AND I ALSO HEAR SHE EVEN HIRED THE GREAT "RAP FLASH" HIMSELF, TO CHOREOGRAPH HER STEPS --

"SHE'S ALSO HAVING HER OUTFIT MADE BY MOVIE COSTUME DESIGNERS!"

TOO BAD BETTY ISN'T ENTERING! SHE'S THE BETTER DANCER!

BY FAR!

LET'S GO TO THE GYM AND SHOOT A FEW BASKETS!

GOOD IDEA, CHUCK!

SOUNDS LIKE SOMEONE ELSE HAS THE SAME IDEA!!

GYM

THUMP!

THUMP!

IT'S BETTY!!

③

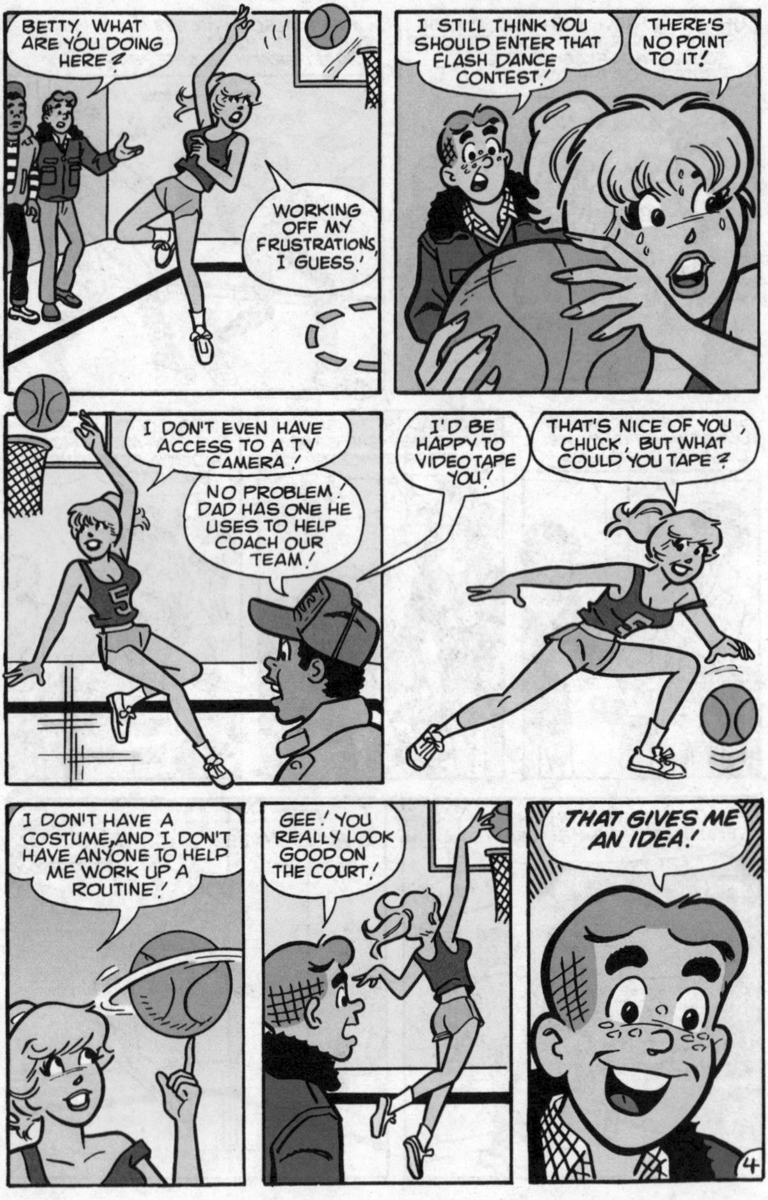
BETTY, WHAT ARE YOU DOING HERE?
WORKING OFF MY FRUSTRATIONS, I GUESS!
I STILL THINK YOU SHOULD ENTER THAT FLASH DANCE CONTEST!
THERE'S NO POINT TO IT!
I DON'T EVEN HAVE ACCESS TO A TV CAMERA!
NO PROBLEM! DAD HAS ONE HE USES TO HELP COACH OUR TEAM!
I'D BE HAPPY TO VIDEOTAPE YOU!
THAT'S NICE OF YOU, CHUCK, BUT WHAT COULD YOU TAPE?
I DON'T HAVE A COSTUME, AND I DON'T HAVE ANYONE TO HELP ME WORK UP A ROUTINE!
GEE! YOU REALLY LOOK GOOD ON THE COURT!
THAT GIVES ME AN IDEA!
4

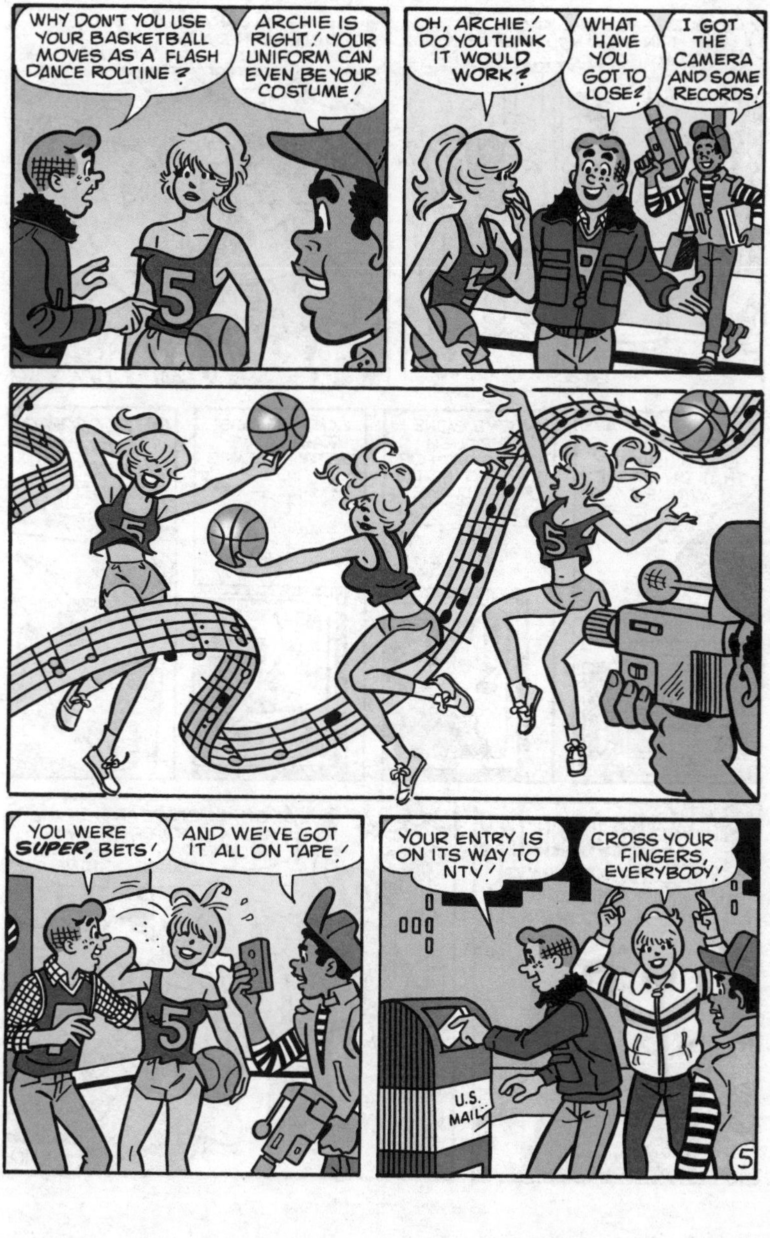
WHY DON'T YOU USE YOUR BASKETBALL MOVES AS A FLASH DANCE ROUTINE?
ARCHIE IS RIGHT! YOUR UNIFORM CAN EVEN BE YOUR COSTUME!
OH, ARCHIE! DO YOU THINK IT WOULD WORK?
WHAT HAVE YOU GOT TO LOSE?
I GOT THE CAMERA AND SOME RECORDS!
YOU WERE SUPER, BETS!
AND WE'VE GOT IT ALL ON TAPE!
YOUR ENTRY IS ON ITS WAY TO NTV!
CROSS YOUR FINGERS, EVERYBODY!
U.S. MAIL
5

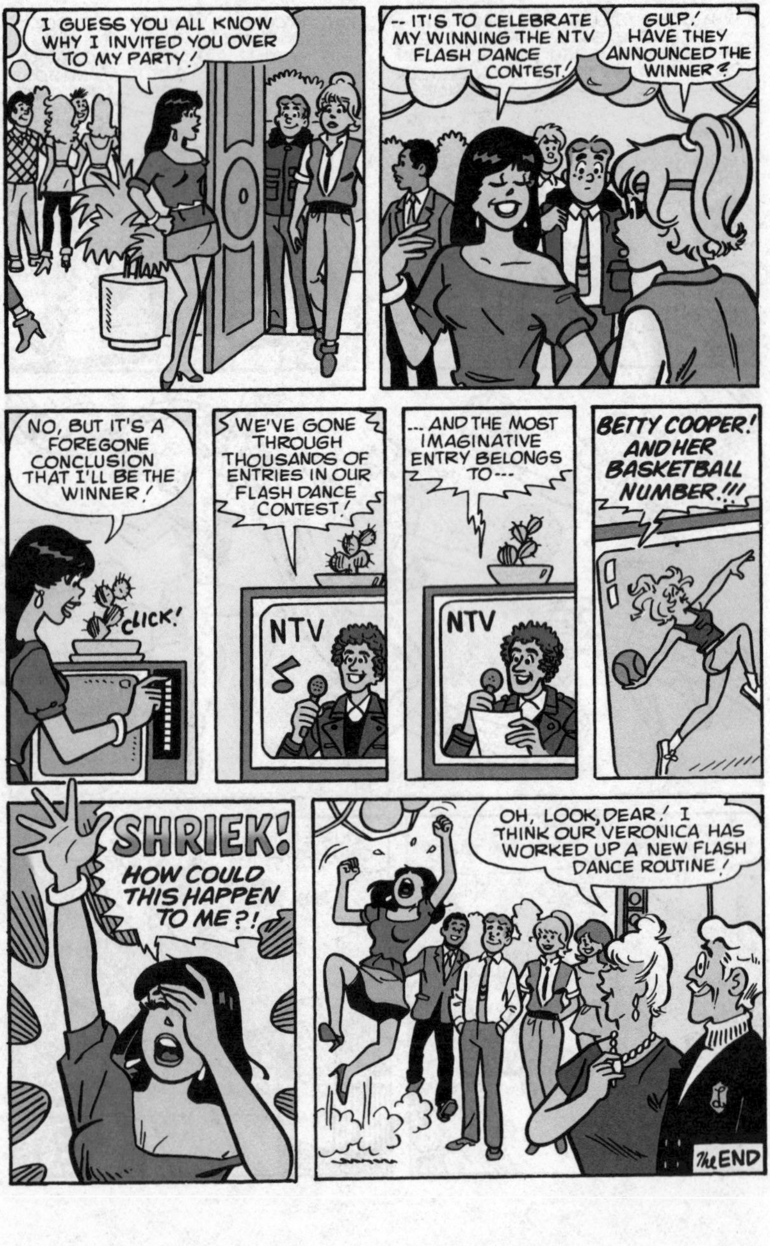
I GUESS YOU ALL KNOW WHY I INVITED YOU OVER TO MY PARTY!
-- IT'S TO CELEBRATE MY WINNING THE NTV FLASH DANCE CONTEST!
GULP! HAVE THEY ANNOUNCED THE WINNER?
NO, BUT IT'S A FOREGONE CONCLUSION THAT I'LL BE THE WINNER!
CLICK!
WE'VE GONE THROUGH THOUSANDS OF ENTRIES IN OUR FLASH DANCE CONTEST!
NTV
... AND THE MOST IMAGINATIVE ENTRY BELONGS TO---
NTV
BETTY COOPER! AND HER BASKETBALL NUMBER!!!
SHRIEK!
HOW COULD THIS HAPPEN TO ME?!
OH, LOOK, DEAR! I THINK OUR VERONICA HAS WORKED UP A NEW FLASH DANCE ROUTINE!
The END

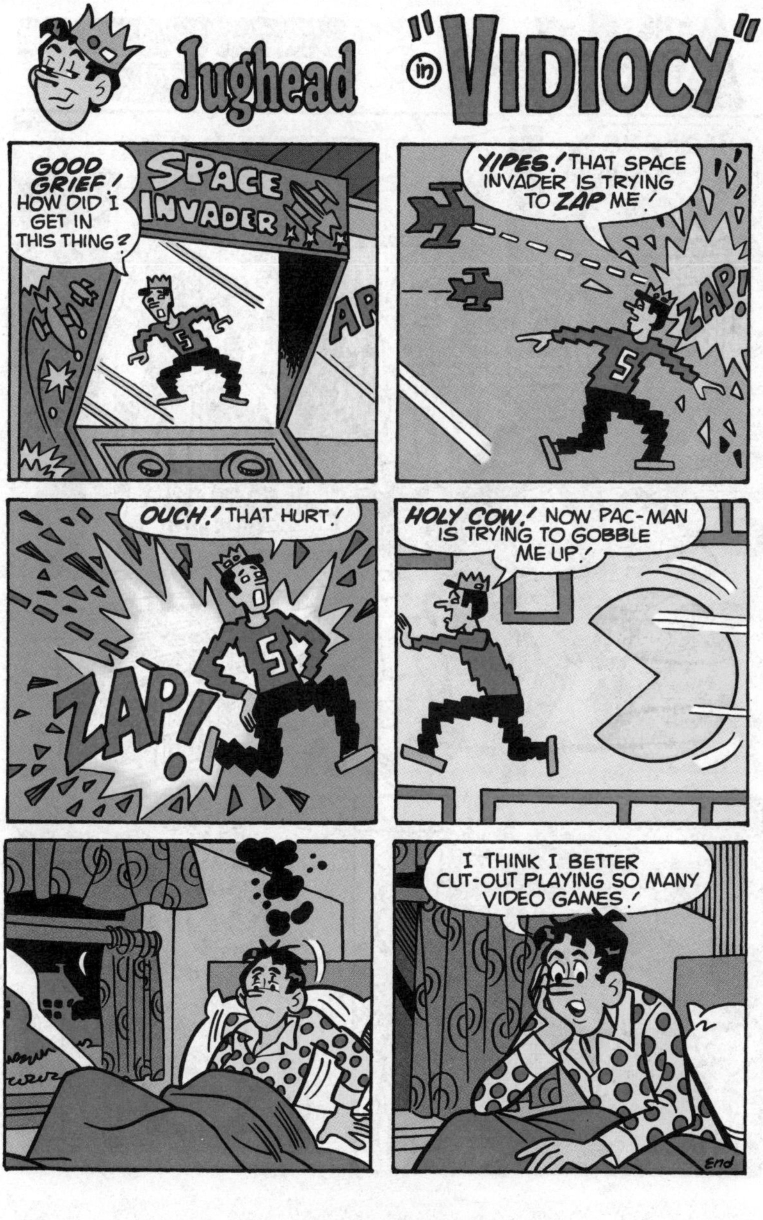
Jughead
in
"VIDIOCY"
GOOD GRIEF! HOW DID I GET IN THIS THING?
SPACE INVADER
YIPES! THAT SPACE INVADER IS TRYING TO ZAP ME!
ZAP!
OUCH! THAT HURT!
ZAP!
HOLY COW! NOW PAC-MAN IS TRYING TO GOBBLE ME UP!
I THINK I BETTER CUT-OUT PLAYING SO MANY VIDEO GAMES!
End

Originally presented in PEP #393, March, 1984

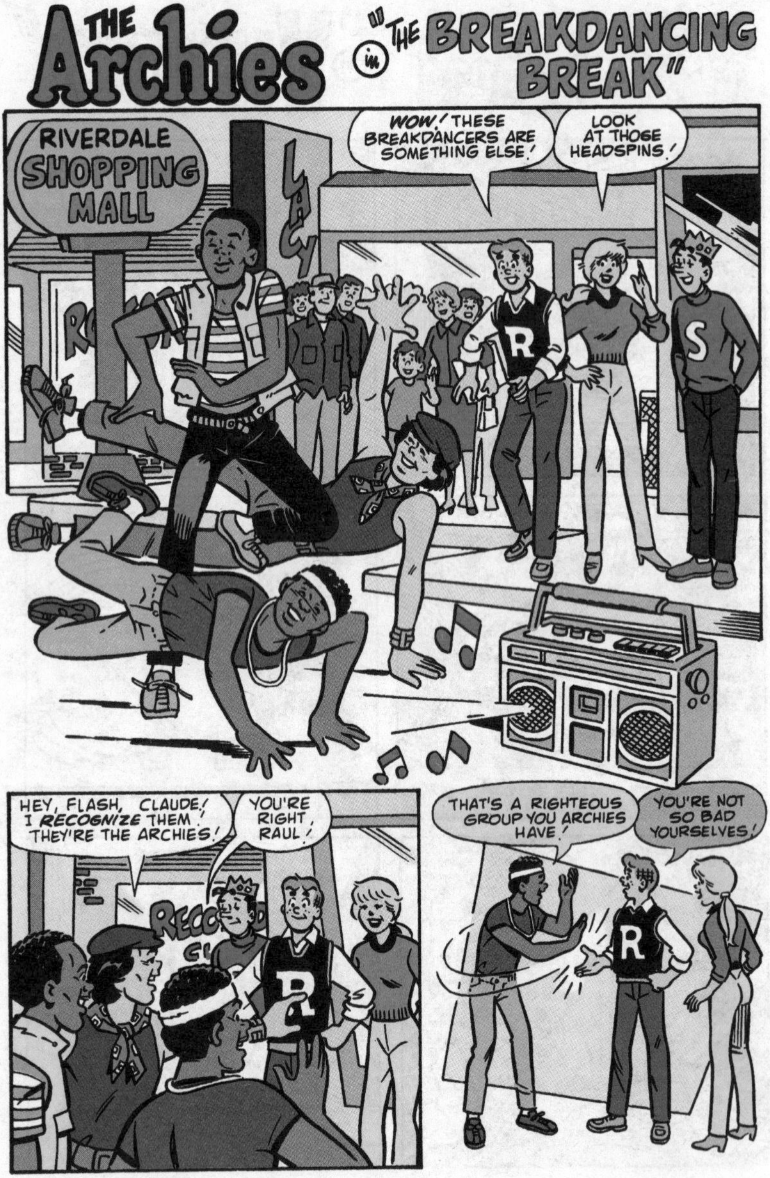
THE Archies in "THE BREAKDANCING BREAK"
RIVERDALE SHOPPING MALL
WOW! THESE BREAKDANCERS ARE SOMETHING ELSE!
LOOK AT THOSE HEADSPINS!
HEY, FLASH, CLAUDE! I RECOGNIZE THEM! THEY'RE THE ARCHIES!
YOU'RE RIGHT, RAUL!
THAT'S A RIGHTEOUS GROUP YOU ARCHIES HAVE!
YOU'RE NOT SO BAD YOURSELVES!

Originally presented in EVERYTHING'S ARCHIE #112, July, 1984

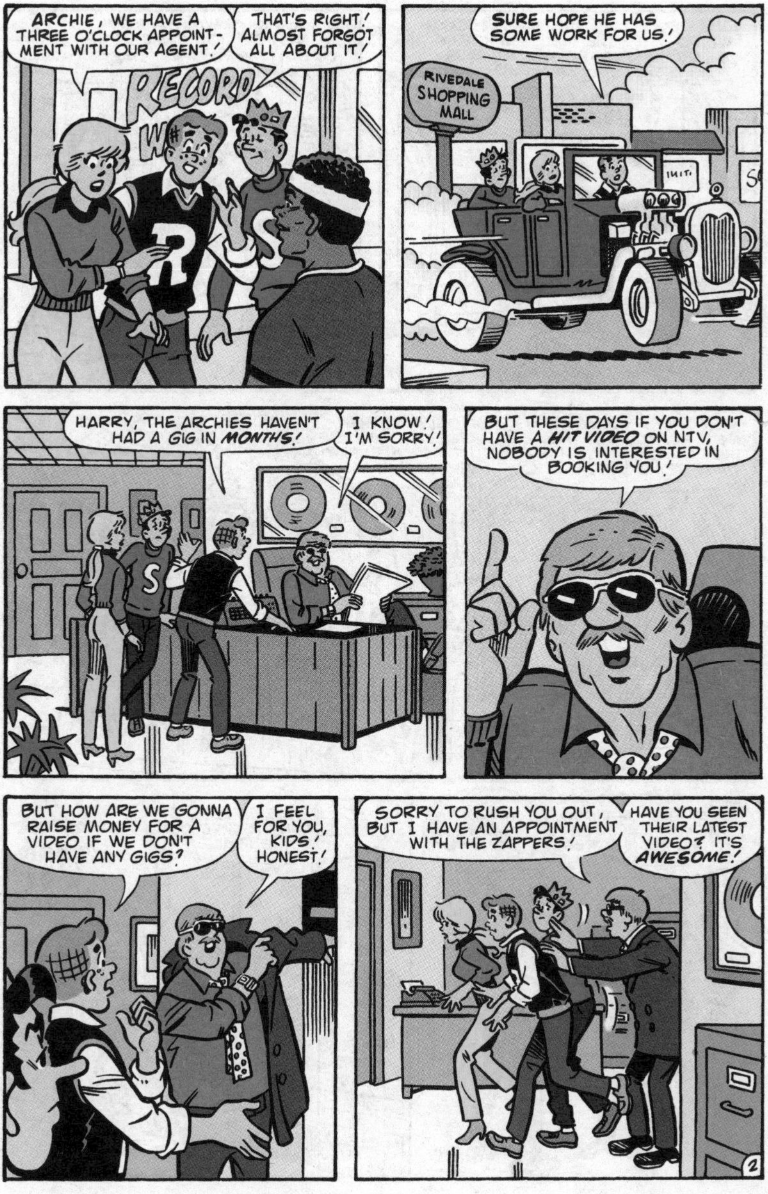
ARCHIE, WE HAVE A THREE O'CLOCK APPOINT-MENT WITH OUR AGENT!
THAT'S RIGHT! ALMOST FORGOT ALL ABOUT IT!
RECORD
SURE HOPE HE HAS SOME WORK FOR US!
RIVEDALE SHOPPING MALL
HARRY, THE ARCHIES HAVEN'T HAD A GIG IN MONTHS!
I KNOW! I'M SORRY!
BUT THESE DAYS IF YOU DON'T HAVE A HIT VIDEO ON NTV, NOBODY IS INTERESTED IN BOOKING YOU!
BUT HOW ARE WE GONNA RAISE MONEY FOR A VIDEO IF WE DON'T HAVE ANY GIGS?
I FEEL FOR YOU, KIDS! HONEST!
SORRY TO RUSH YOU OUT, BUT I HAVE AN APPOINTMENT WITH THE ZAPPERS!
HAVE YOU SEEN THEIR LATEST VIDEO? IT'S AWESOME!
2

WHAT DO WE DO NOW, ARCHIE?
WE STILL HAVE $500 IN THE TILL! I'M HOPING THIS OUTFIT WILL MAKE US A VIDEO!
VIDEO PRODUCTIONS
VP
YOU KIDS WANT A ROCK VIDEO? YOU CAME TO THE RIGHT PLACE!
FOR ONLY A MILLION, WE'LL FLY YOU DOWN TO THE CARIBBEAN WITH A CAST OF HUNDREDS!
...FOR ONLY ANOTHER QUARTER OF A MILLION WE'LL THROW IN SUPER FIREWORKS!
WHAT KIND OF VIDEO CAN YOU MAKE FOR ...UH, FIVE HUNDRED DOLLARS?
FIVE HUNDRED DOLLARS?
FOR $500 WE'LL TAPE YOU GETTING KICKED OUT OF THIS PLACE!
3

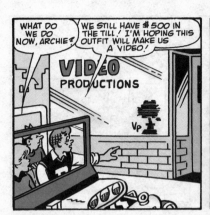

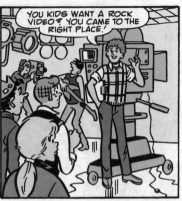

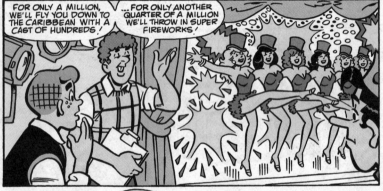

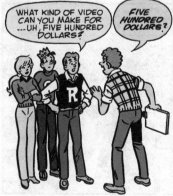

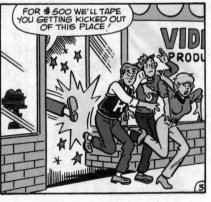

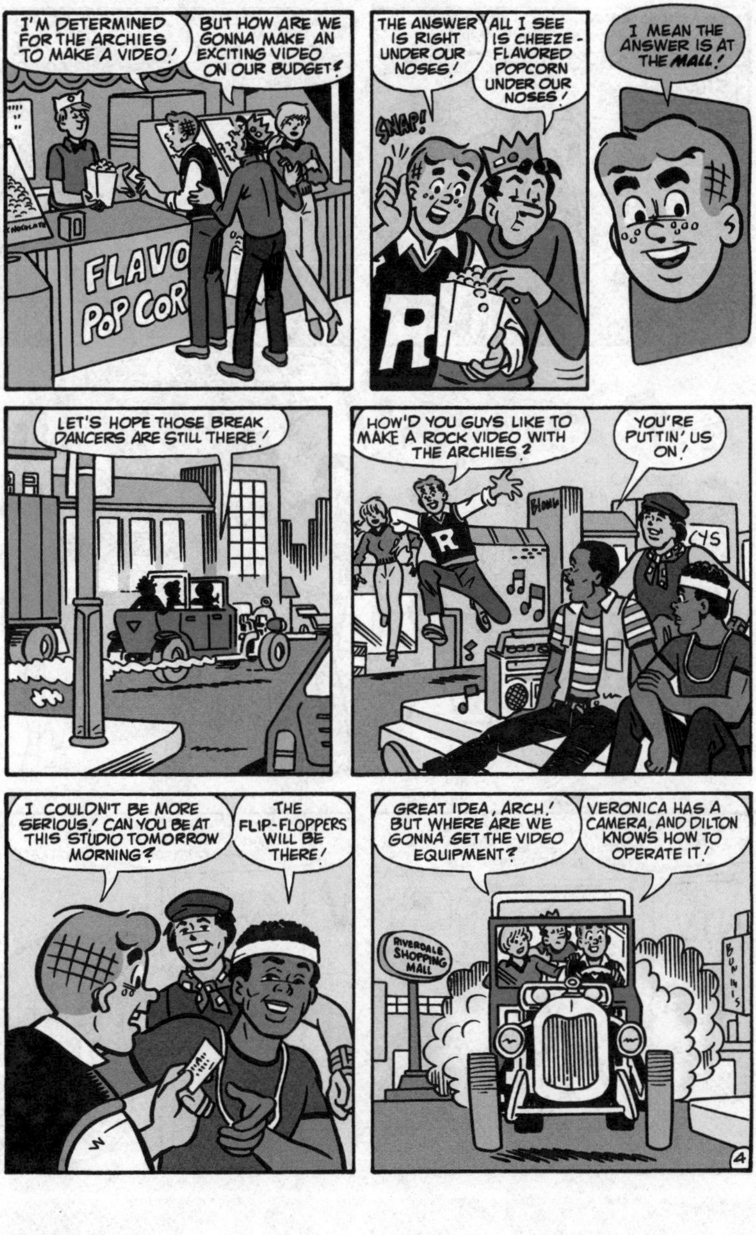
I'M DETERMINED FOR THE ARCHIES TO MAKE A VIDEO!
BUT HOW ARE WE GONNA MAKE AN EXCITING VIDEO ON OUR BUDGET?!
FLAVO POP COR
THE ANSWER IS RIGHT UNDER OUR NOSES!
ALL I SEE IS CHEEZE-FLAVORED POPCORN UNDER OUR NOSES!
SNAP!
I MEAN THE ANSWER IS AT THE MALL!
LET'S HOPE THOSE BREAK DANCERS ARE STILL THERE!
HOW'D YOU GUYS LIKE TO MAKE A ROCK VIDEO WITH THE ARCHIES?
YOU'RE PUTTIN' US ON!
I COULDN'T BE MORE SERIOUS! CAN YOU BE AT THIS STUDIO TOMORROW MORNING?
THE FLIP-FLOPPERS WILL BE THERE!
GREAT IDEA, ARCH! BUT WHERE ARE WE GONNA GET THE VIDEO EQUIPMENT?
VERONICA HAS A CAMERA, AND DILTON KNOWS HOW TO OPERATE IT!
RIVERDALE SHOPPING MALL
4

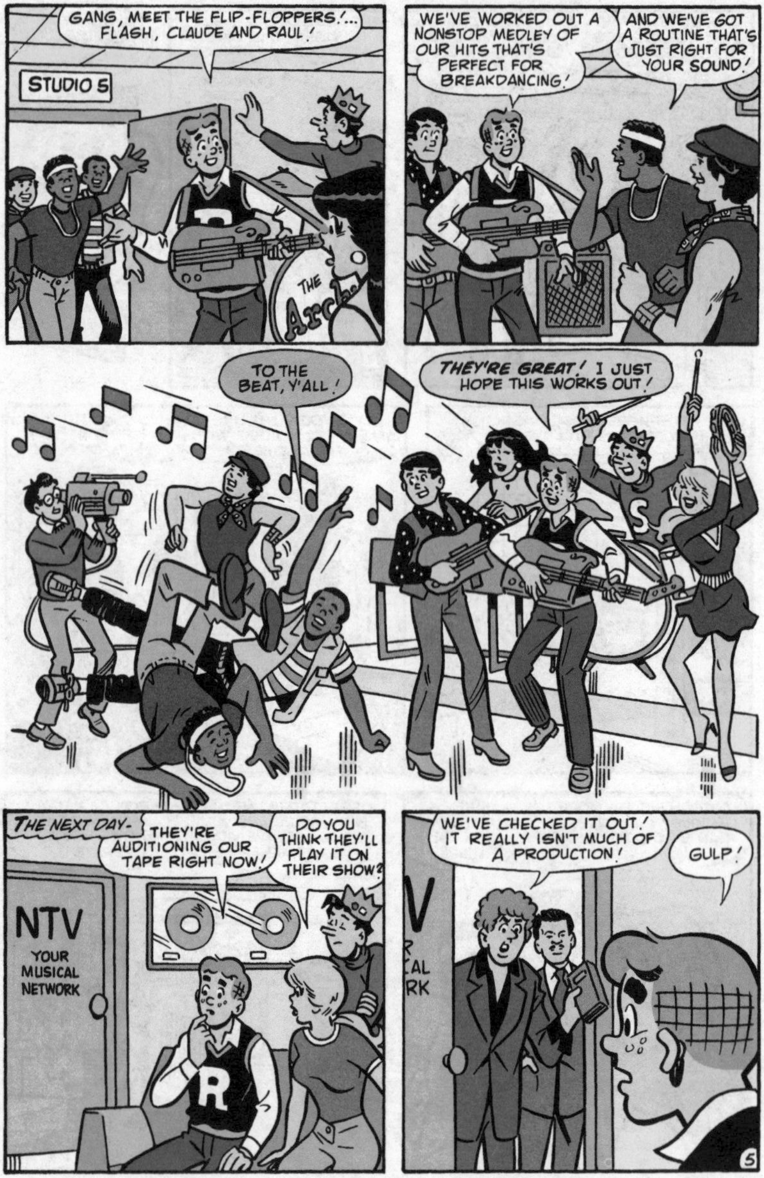
GANG, MEET THE FLIP-FLOPPERS!... FLASH, CLAUDE AND RAUL!
STUDIO 5
WE'VE WORKED OUT A NONSTOP MEDLEY OF OUR HITS THAT'S PERFECT FOR BREAKDANCING!
AND WE'VE GOT A ROUTINE THAT'S JUST RIGHT FOR YOUR SOUND!
TO THE BEAT, Y'ALL!
THEY'RE GREAT! I JUST HOPE THIS WORKS OUT!
THE NEXT DAY-
THEY'RE AUDITIONING OUR TAPE RIGHT NOW!
DO YOU THINK THEY'LL PLAY IT ON THEIR SHOW?
NTV
YOUR MUSICAL NETWORK
WE'VE CHECKED IT OUT! IT REALLY ISN'T MUCH OF A PRODUCTION!
GULP!
5

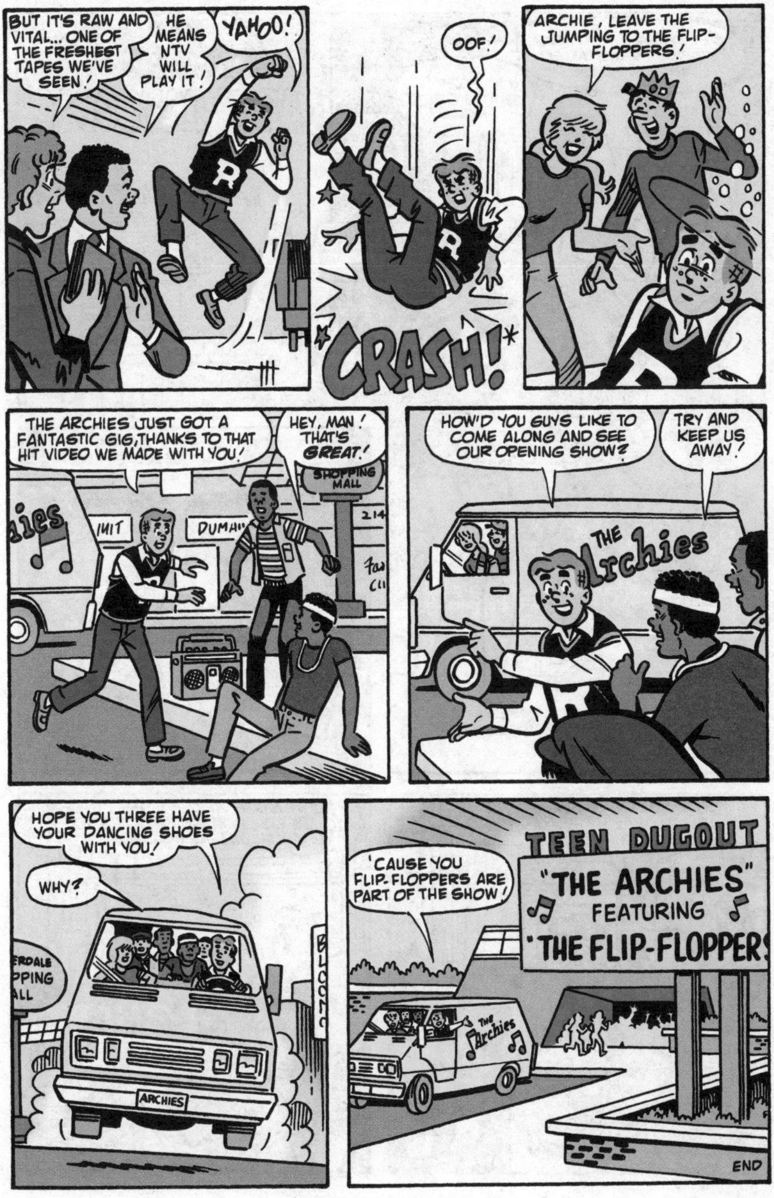
BUT IT'S RAW AND VITAL... ONE OF THE FRESHEST TAPES WE'VE SEEN!
HE MEANS NTV WILL PLAY IT!
YAHOO!
OOF!
CRASH!
ARCHIE, LEAVE THE JUMPING TO THE FLIP-FLOPPERS!
THE ARCHIES JUST GOT A FANTASTIC GIG, THANKS TO THAT HIT VIDEO WE MADE WITH YOU!
HEY, MAN! THAT'S GREAT!
SHOPPING MALL
HOW'D YOU GUYS LIKE TO COME ALONG AND SEE OUR OPENING SHOW?
TRY AND KEEP US AWAY!
THE Archies
HOPE YOU THREE HAVE YOUR DANCING SHOES WITH YOU!
WHY?
ARCHIES
TEEN DUGOUT
"THE ARCHIES" FEATURING "THE FLIP-FLOPPERS
'CAUSE YOU FLIP-FLOPPERS ARE PART OF THE SHOW!
END

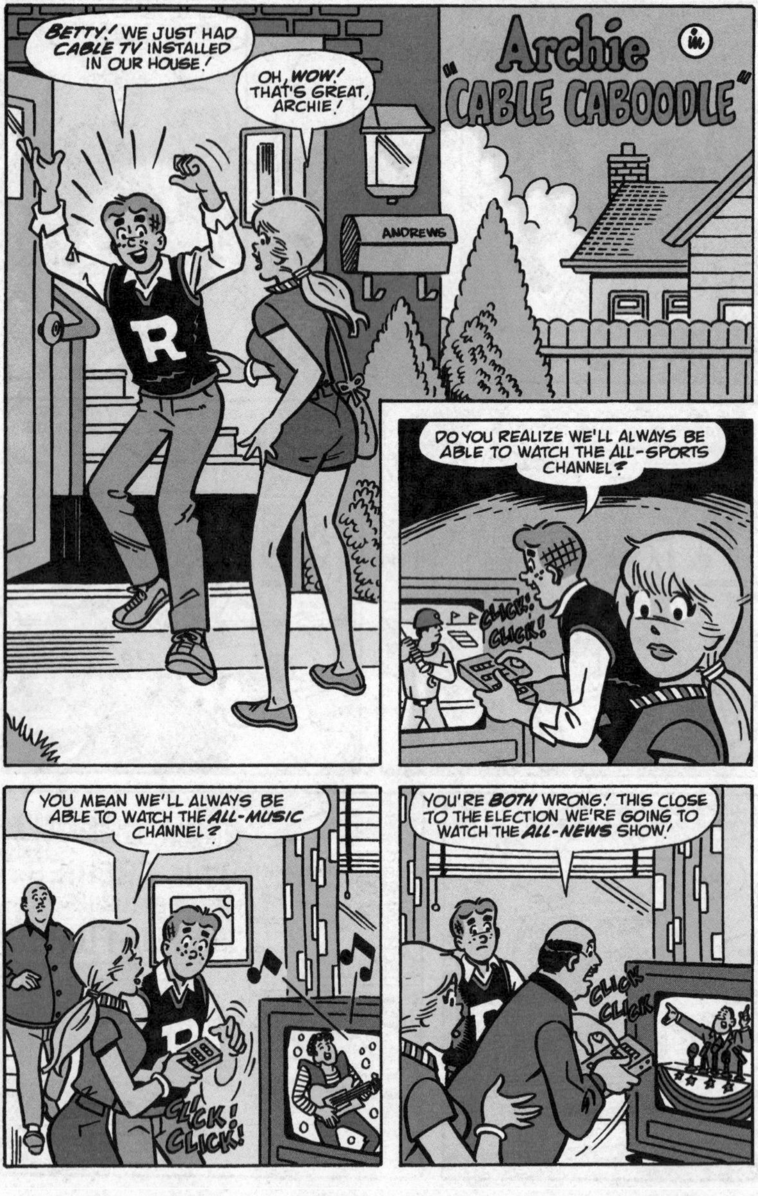
BETTY! WE JUST HAD CABLE TV INSTALLED IN OUR HOUSE!
OH, WOW! THAT'S GREAT, ARCHIE!
ANDREWS
Archie in "CABLE CABOODLE"
DO YOU REALIZE WE'LL ALWAYS BE ABLE TO WATCH THE ALL-SPORTS CHANNEL?
CLICK! CLICK!
YOU MEAN WE'LL ALWAYS BE ABLE TO WATCH THE ALL-MUSIC CHANNEL?
CLICK! CLICK!
YOU'RE BOTH WRONG! THIS CLOSE TO THE ELECTION WE'RE GOING TO WATCH THE ALL-NEWS SHOW!
CLICK CLICK

Originally presented in ARCHIE'S PALS 'N' GALS #171, September, 1984

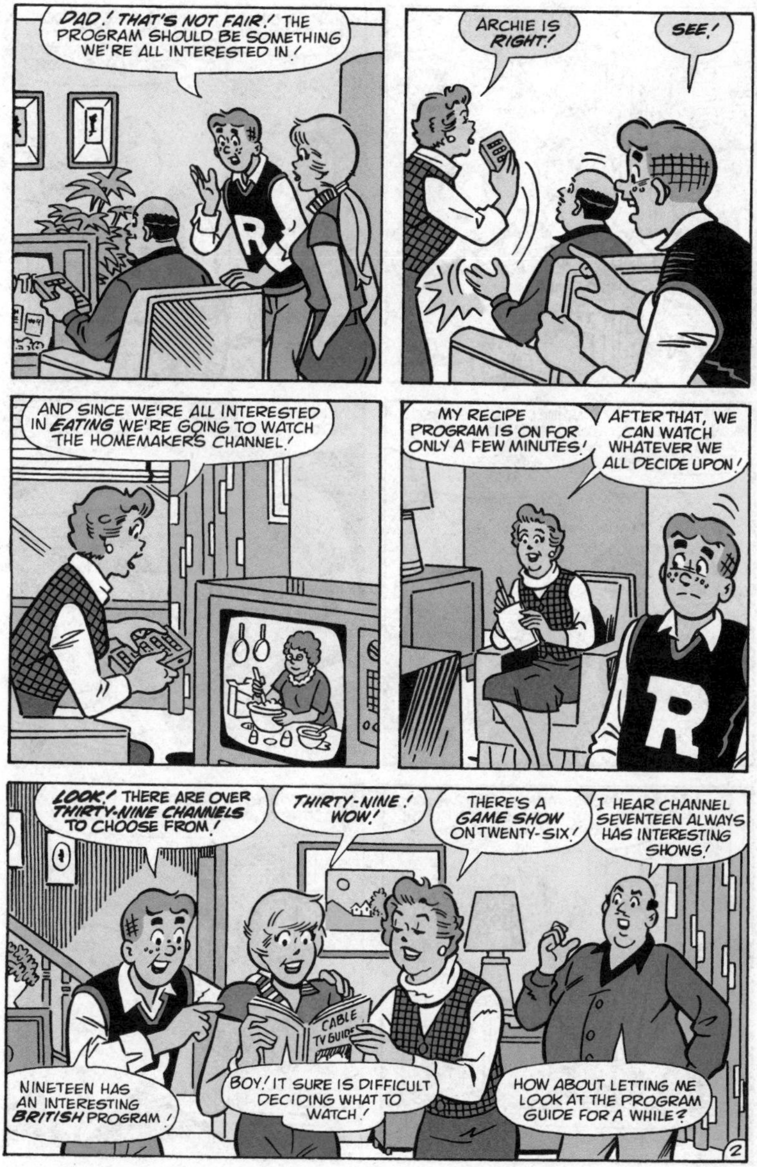
DAD! THAT'S NOT FAIR! THE PROGRAM SHOULD BE SOMETHING WE'RE ALL INTERESTED IN!
ARCHIE IS RIGHT!
SEE!
AND SINCE WE'RE ALL INTERESTED IN EATING WE'RE GOING TO WATCH THE HOMEMAKERS CHANNEL!
MY RECIPE PROGRAM IS ON FOR ONLY A FEW MINUTES!
AFTER THAT, WE CAN WATCH WHATEVER WE ALL DECIDE UPON!
LOOK! THERE ARE OVER THIRTY-NINE CHANNELS TO CHOOSE FROM!
THIRTY-NINE! WOW!
THERE'S A GAME SHOW ON TWENTY-SIX!
I HEAR CHANNEL SEVENTEEN ALWAYS HAS INTERESTING SHOWS!
CABLE TV GUIDE
NINETEEN HAS AN INTERESTING BRITISH PROGRAM!
BOY! IT SURE IS DIFFICULT DECIDING WHAT TO WATCH!
HOW ABOUT LETTING ME LOOK AT THE PROGRAM GUIDE FOR A WHILE?
2

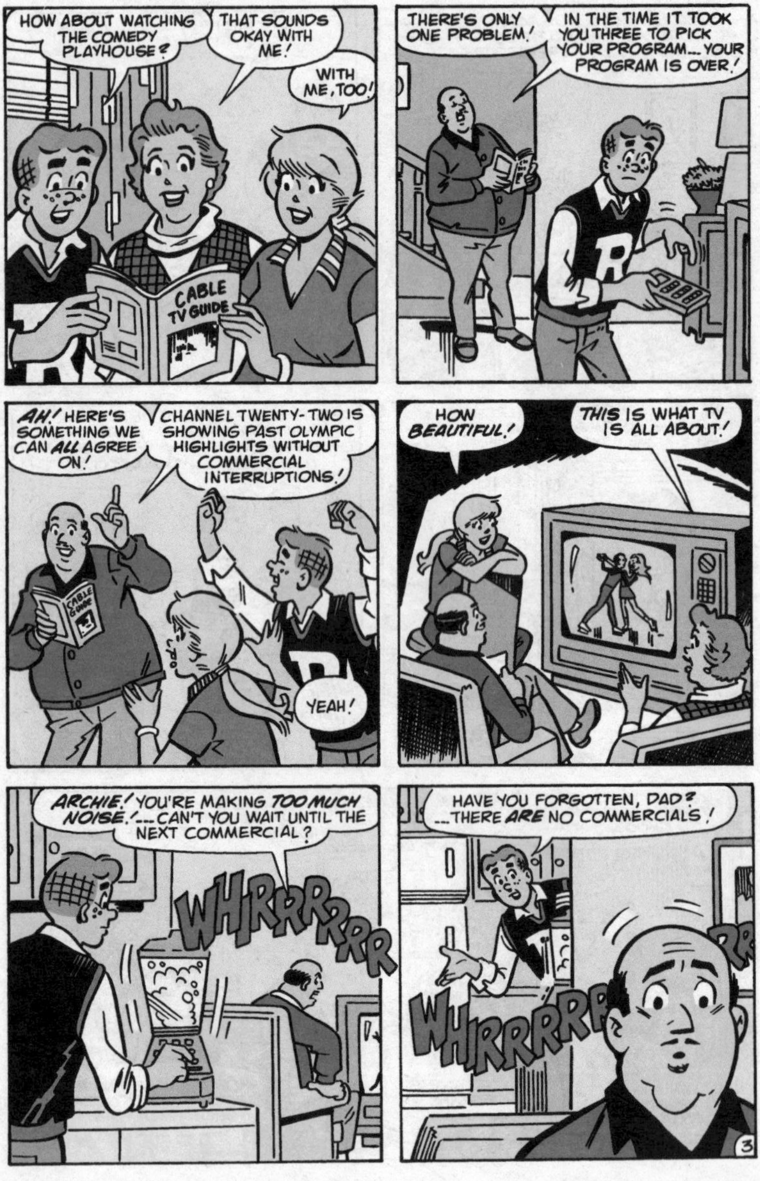
HOW ABOUT WATCHING THE COMEDY PLAYHOUSE?
THAT SOUNDS OKAY WITH ME!
WITH ME, TOO!
CABLE TV GUIDE
THERE'S ONLY ONE PROBLEM!
IN THE TIME IT TOOK YOU THREE TO PICK YOUR PROGRAM... YOUR PROGRAM IS OVER!
AH! HERE'S SOMETHING WE CAN ALL AGREE ON!
CHANNEL TWENTY-TWO IS SHOWING PAST OLYMPIC HIGHLIGHTS WITHOUT COMMERCIAL INTERRUPTIONS!
CABLE GUIDE
YEAH!
HOW BEAUTIFUL!
THIS IS WHAT TV IS ALL ABOUT!
ARCHIE! YOU'RE MAKING TOO MUCH NOISE!... CAN'T YOU WAIT UNTIL THE NEXT COMMERCIAL?
WHIRRRRRRR
HAVE YOU FORGOTTEN, DAD? ...THERE ARE NO COMMERCIALS!
WHIRRRRRR
3

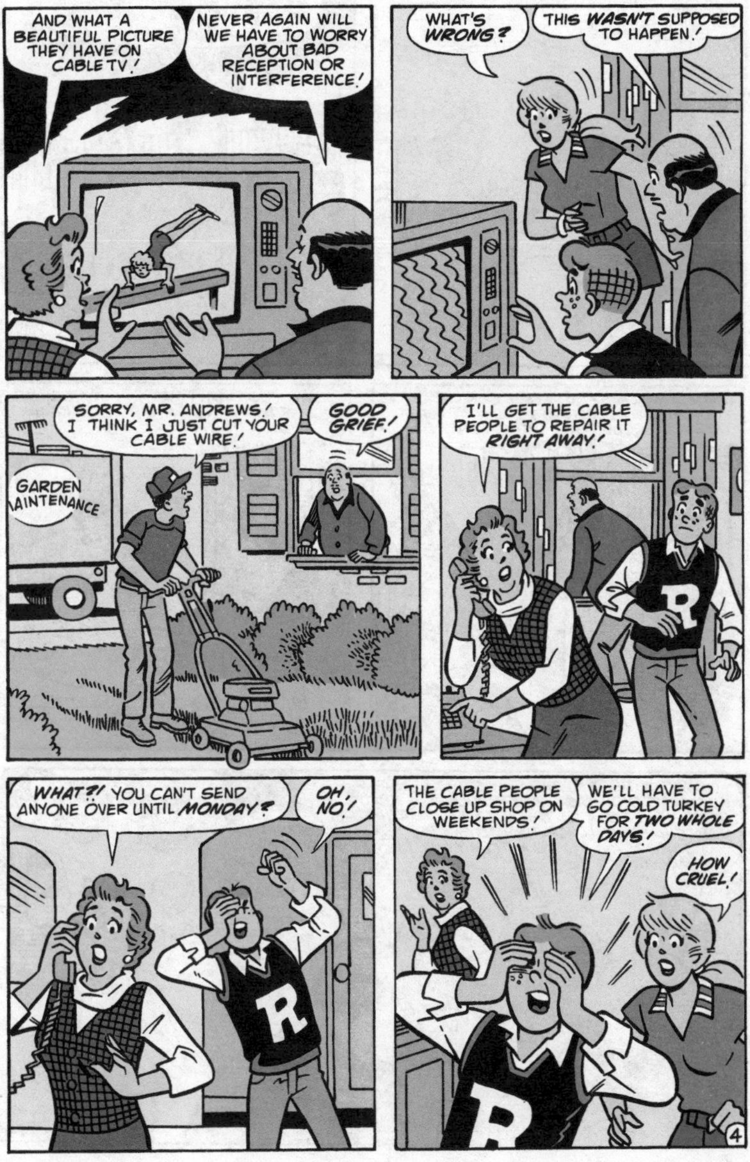
AND WHAT A BEAUTIFUL PICTURE THEY HAVE ON CABLE TV!
NEVER AGAIN WILL WE HAVE TO WORRY ABOUT BAD RECEPTION OR INTERFERENCE!
WHAT'S WRONG?
THIS WASN'T SUPPOSED TO HAPPEN!
SORRY, MR. ANDREWS! I THINK I JUST CUT YOUR CABLE WIRE!
GOOD GRIEF!
GARDEN MAINTENANCE
I'LL GET THE CABLE PEOPLE TO REPAIR IT RIGHT AWAY!
WHAT?! YOU CAN'T SEND ANYONE OVER UNTIL MONDAY?
OH, NO!
THE CABLE PEOPLE CLOSE UP SHOP ON WEEKENDS!
WE'LL HAVE TO GO COLD TURKEY FOR TWO WHOLE DAYS!
HOW CRUEL!
4

JUG, I HEAR ARCHIE'S FAMILY JUST SIGNED UP FOR CABLE TV!

I WISH OUR HOUSE HAD IT!

WELL, AT LEAST MY PAL ARCHIE WILL LET ME COME OVER AND WATCH WITH HIM!

WHAT'S WRONG? YOUR PLACE LOOKS LIKE A MORGUE!

IT *IS!* OUR CABLE TV IS DEAD... AT LEAST UNTIL MONDAY!

SAY, JUG! ISN'T THAT ONE OF THOSE NEW MINI TV'S YOU HAVE THERE?

YES, MR. ANDREWS!

GOSH! WITH REGULAR TV YOU DON'T HAVE SO MANY CHANNELS TO WORRY ABOUT!

AND IT HAS *COMMERCIALS* ... WHICH GIVE YOU TIME TO GO TO THE *KITCHEN!*

... *AND* TO THE *BATHROOM!*

AND WITH REGULAR TV YOU DON'T HAVE TO WORRY ABOUT CABLE REPAIRS!

The End

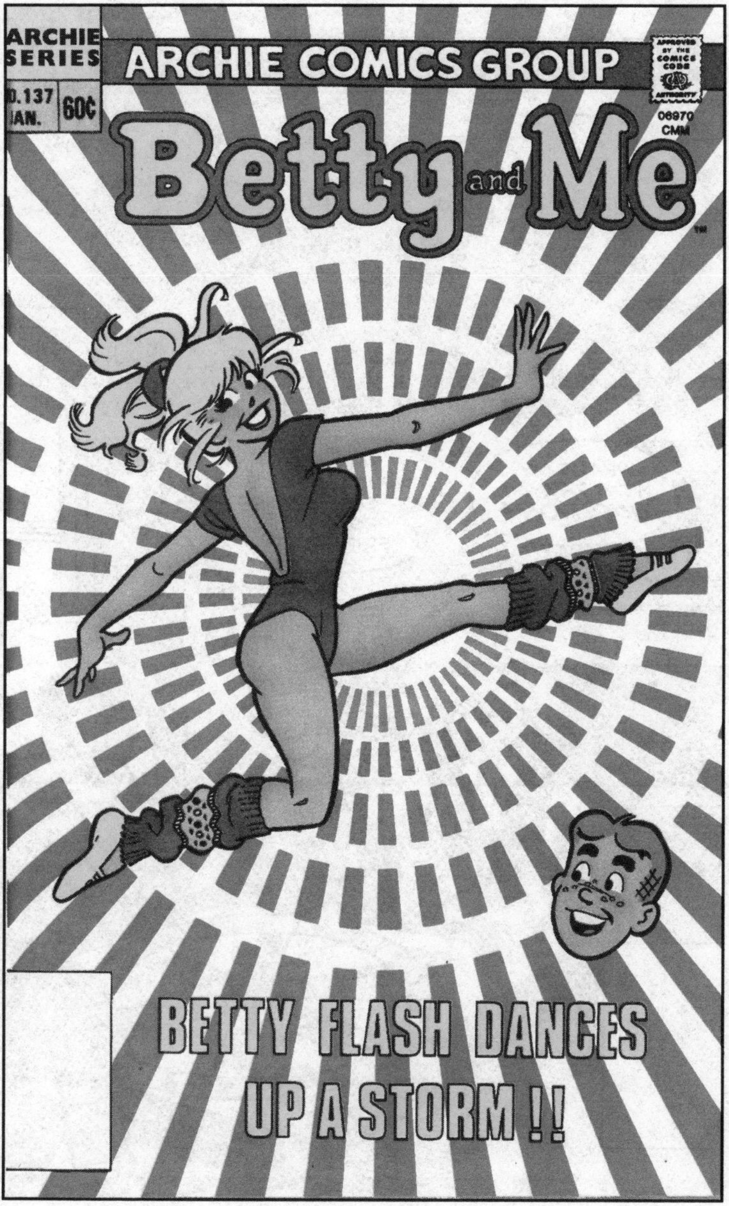
ARCHIE SERIES
ARCHIE COMICS GROUP
APPROVED BY THE COMICS CODE AUTHORITY
0.137 JAN.
60¢
06970 CMM
Betty and Me
BETTY FLASH DANCES UP A STORM !!

Originally printed in 1984

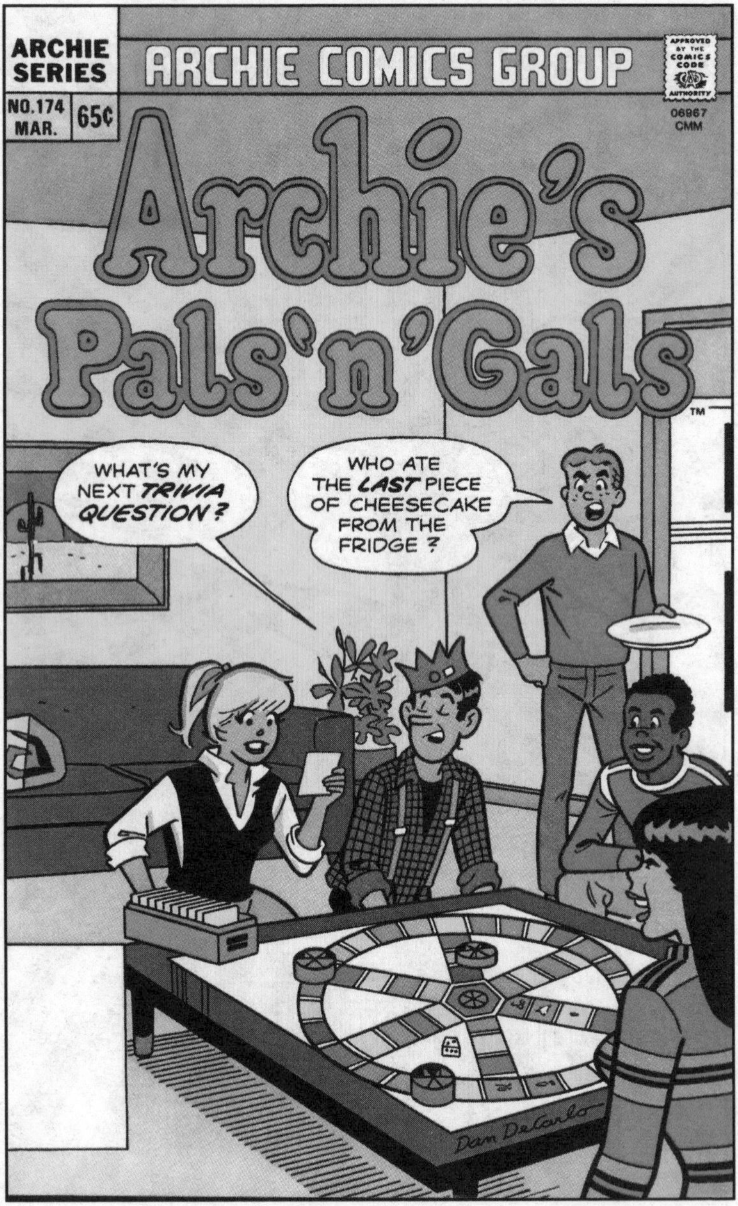
ARCHIE SERIES
ARCHIE COMICS GROUP
APPROVED BY THE COMICS CODE AUTHORITY
NO.174 MAR.
65¢
06967 CMM
Archie's Pals 'n' Gals
TM
WHAT'S MY NEXT TRIVIA QUESTION?
WHO ATE THE LAST PIECE OF CHEESECAKE FROM THE FRIDGE?
Dan DeCarlo

Originally printed in 1985

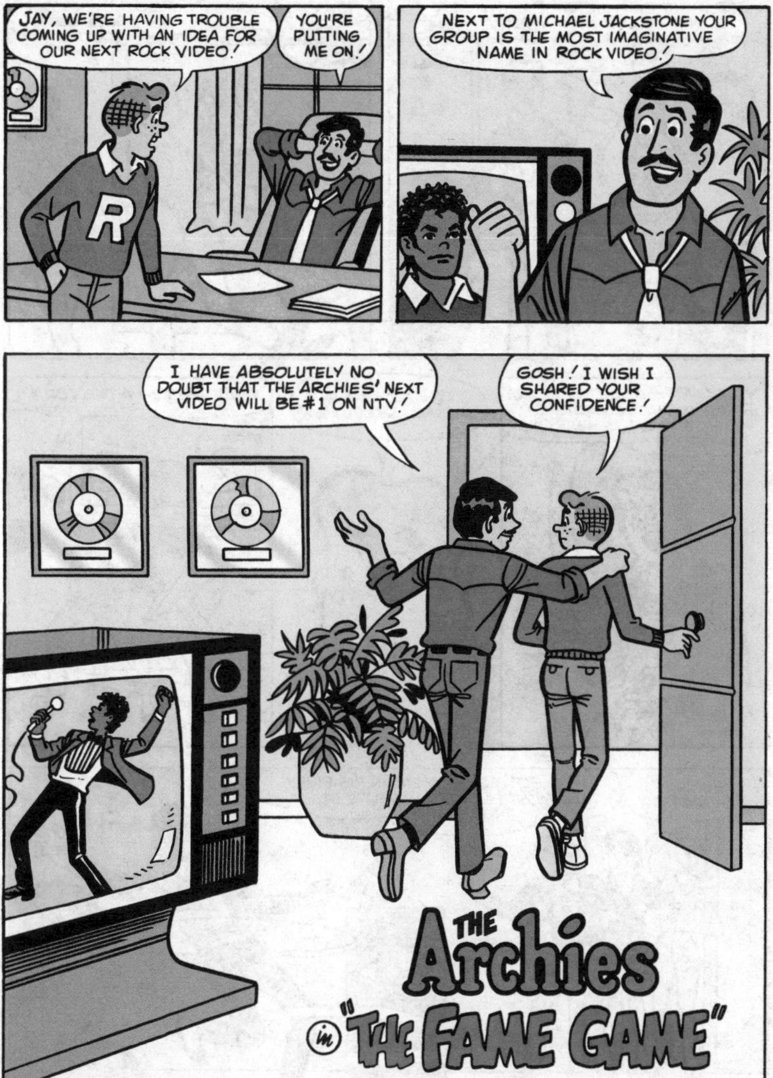
JAY, WE'RE HAVING TROUBLE COMING UP WITH AN IDEA FOR OUR NEXT ROCK VIDEO!
YOU'RE PUTTING ME ON!
NEXT TO MICHAEL JACKSTONE YOUR GROUP IS THE MOST IMAGINATIVE NAME IN ROCK VIDEO!
I HAVE ABSOLUTELY NO DOUBT THAT THE ARCHIES' NEXT VIDEO WILL BE #1 ON NTV!
GOSH! I WISH I SHARED YOUR CONFIDENCE!
THE Archies
in "THE FAME GAME"

Originally presented in EVERYTHING'S ARCHIE #115, January, 1985

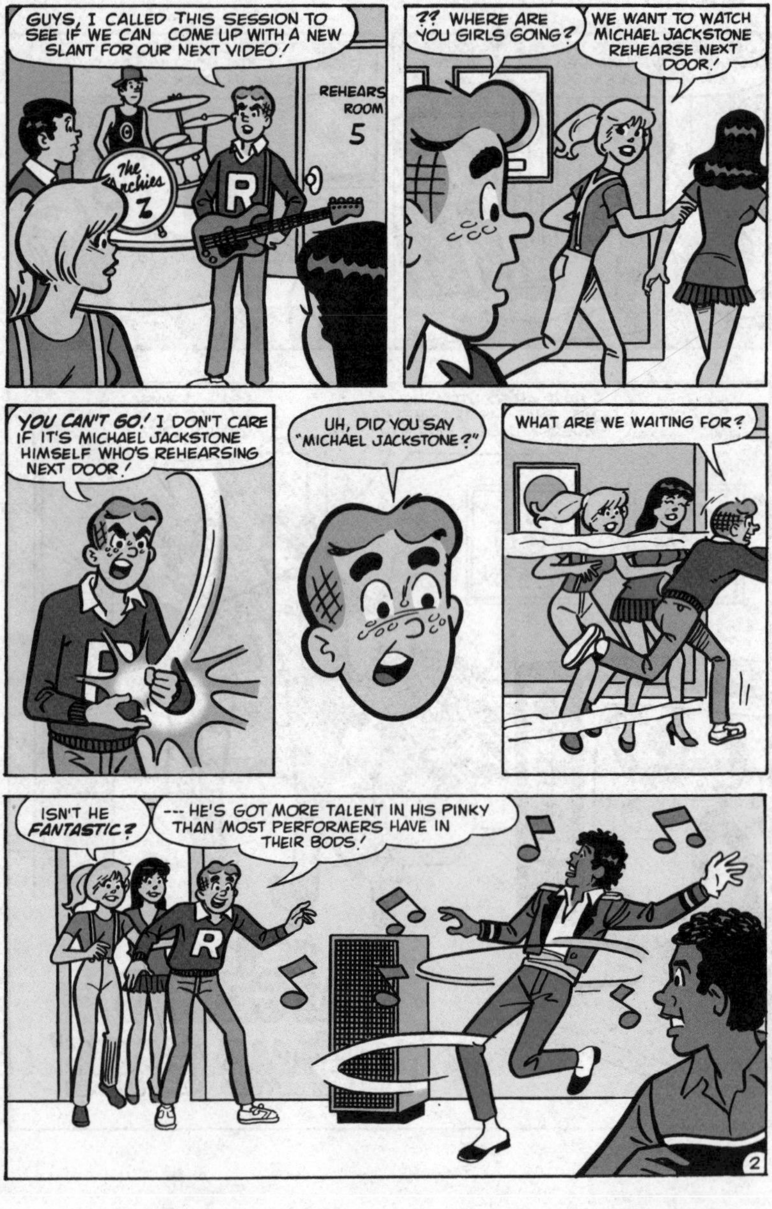
GUYS, I CALLED THIS SESSION TO SEE IF WE CAN COME UP WITH A NEW SLANT FOR OUR NEXT VIDEO!
REHEARS ROOM 5
The Archies
?? WHERE ARE YOU GIRLS GOING?
WE WANT TO WATCH MICHAEL JACKSTONE REHEARSE NEXT DOOR!
YOU CAN'T GO! I DON'T CARE IF IT'S MICHAEL JACKSTONE HIMSELF WHO'S REHEARSING NEXT DOOR!
UH, DID YOU SAY "MICHAEL JACKSTONE?"
WHAT ARE WE WAITING FOR?
ISN'T HE FANTASTIC?
--- HE'S GOT MORE TALENT IN HIS PINKY THAN MOST PERFORMERS HAVE IN THEIR BODS!
2

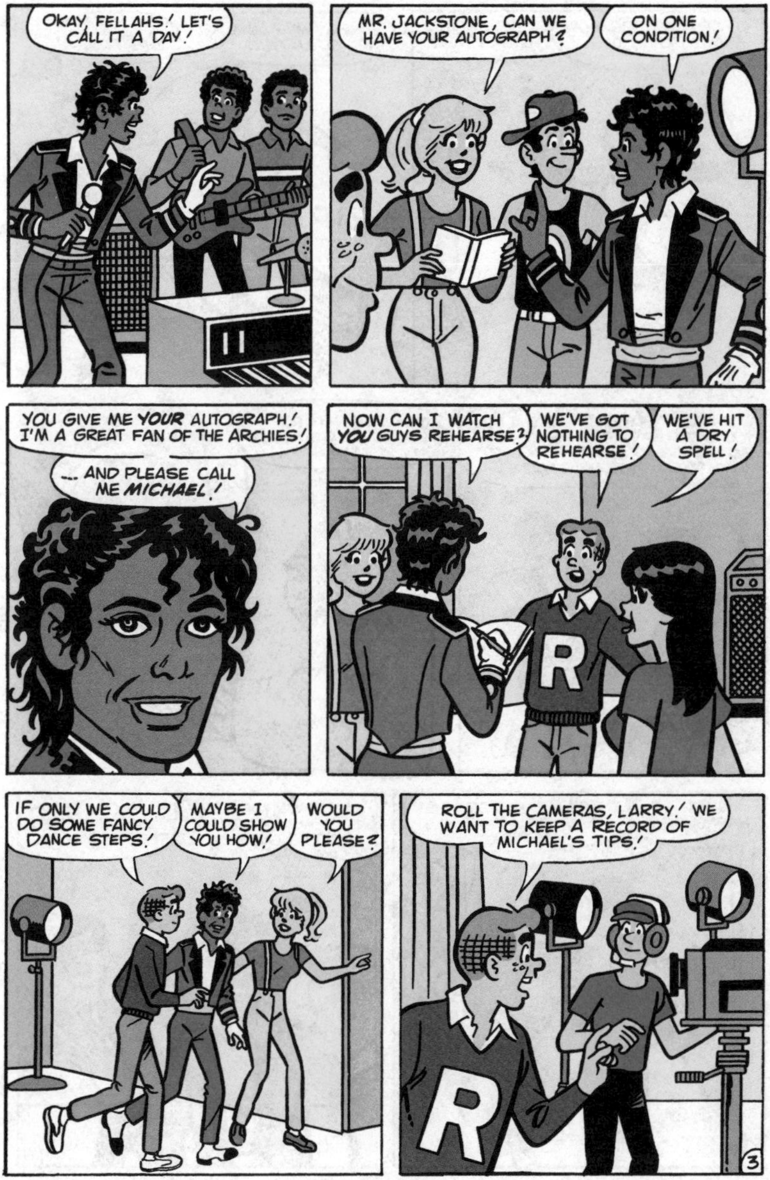
OKAY, FELLAHS! LET'S CALL IT A DAY!
MR. JACKSTONE, CAN WE HAVE YOUR AUTOGRAPH?
ON ONE CONDITION!
YOU GIVE ME YOUR AUTOGRAPH! I'M A GREAT FAN OF THE ARCHIES!
... AND PLEASE CALL ME MICHAEL!
NOW CAN I WATCH YOU GUYS REHEARSE?
WE'VE GOT NOTHING TO REHEARSE!
WE'VE HIT A DRY SPELL!
IF ONLY WE COULD DO SOME FANCY DANCE STEPS!
MAYBE I COULD SHOW YOU HOW!
WOULD YOU PLEASE?
ROLL THE CAMERAS, LARRY! WE WANT TO KEEP A RECORD OF MICHAEL'S TIPS!
3

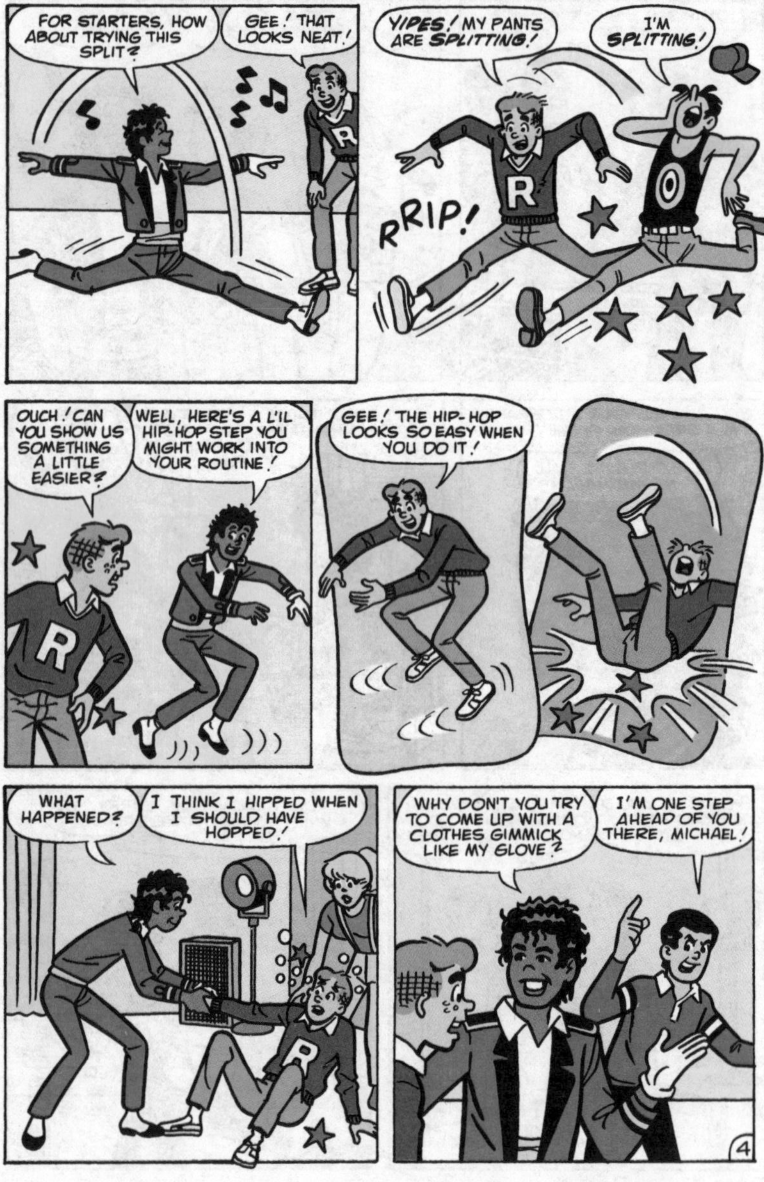
FOR STARTERS, HOW ABOUT TRYING THIS SPLIT?
GEE! THAT LOOKS NEAT!
YIPES! MY PANTS ARE SPLITTING!
I'M SPLITTING!
RRIP!
OUCH! CAN YOU SHOW US SOMETHING A LITTLE EASIER?
WELL, HERE'S A L'IL HIP-HOP STEP YOU MIGHT WORK INTO YOUR ROUTINE!
GEE! THE HIP-HOP LOOKS SO EASY WHEN YOU DO IT!
WHAT HAPPENED?
I THINK I HIPPED WHEN I SHOULD HAVE HOPPED!
WHY DON'T YOU TRY TO COME UP WITH A CLOTHES GIMMICK LIKE MY GLOVE?
I'M ONE STEP AHEAD OF YOU THERE, MICHAEL!
4

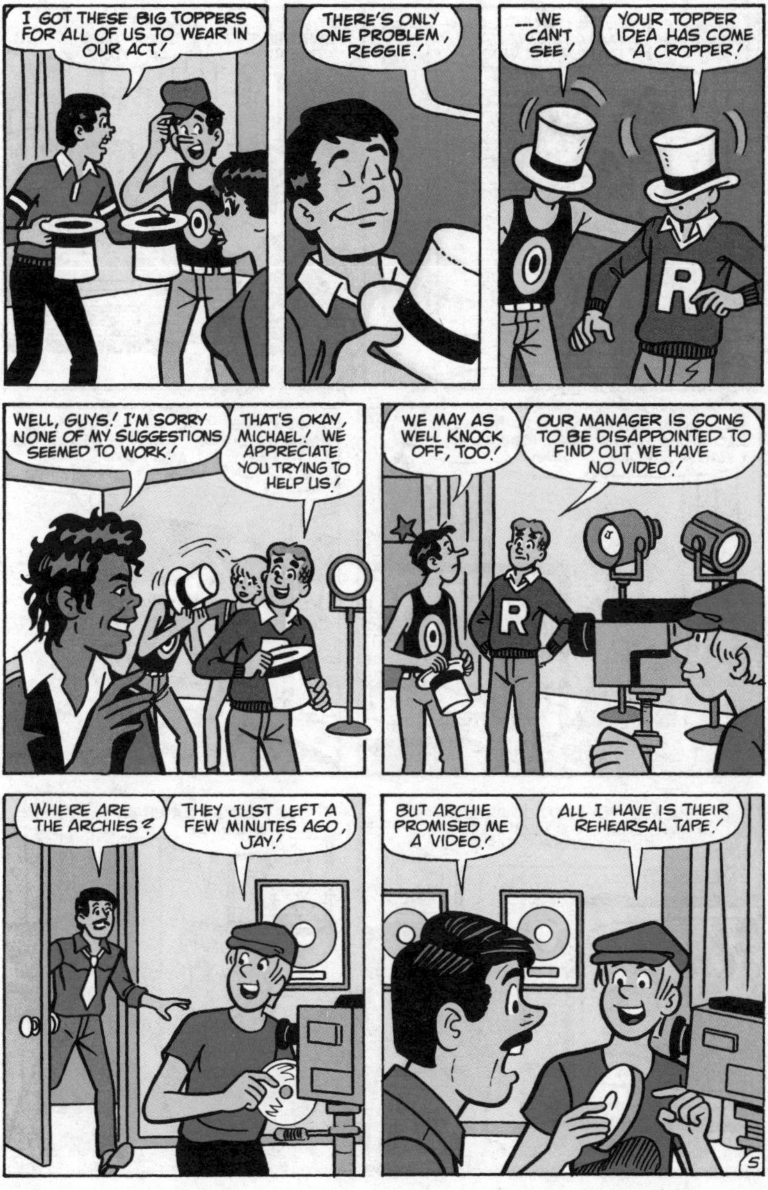
I GOT THESE BIG TOPPERS FOR ALL OF US TO WEAR IN OUR ACT!
THERE'S ONLY ONE PROBLEM, REGGIE!
...WE CAN'T SEE!
YOUR TOPPER IDEA HAS COME A CROPPER!
WELL, GUYS! I'M SORRY NONE OF MY SUGGESTIONS SEEMED TO WORK!
THAT'S OKAY, MICHAEL! WE APPRECIATE YOU TRYING TO HELP US!
WE MAY AS WELL KNOCK OFF, TOO!
OUR MANAGER IS GOING TO BE DISAPPOINTED TO FIND OUT WE HAVE NO VIDEO!
WHERE ARE THE ARCHIES?
THEY JUST LEFT A FEW MINUTES AGO, JAY!
BUT ARCHIE PROMISED ME A VIDEO!
ALL I HAVE IS THEIR REHEARSAL TAPE!
5

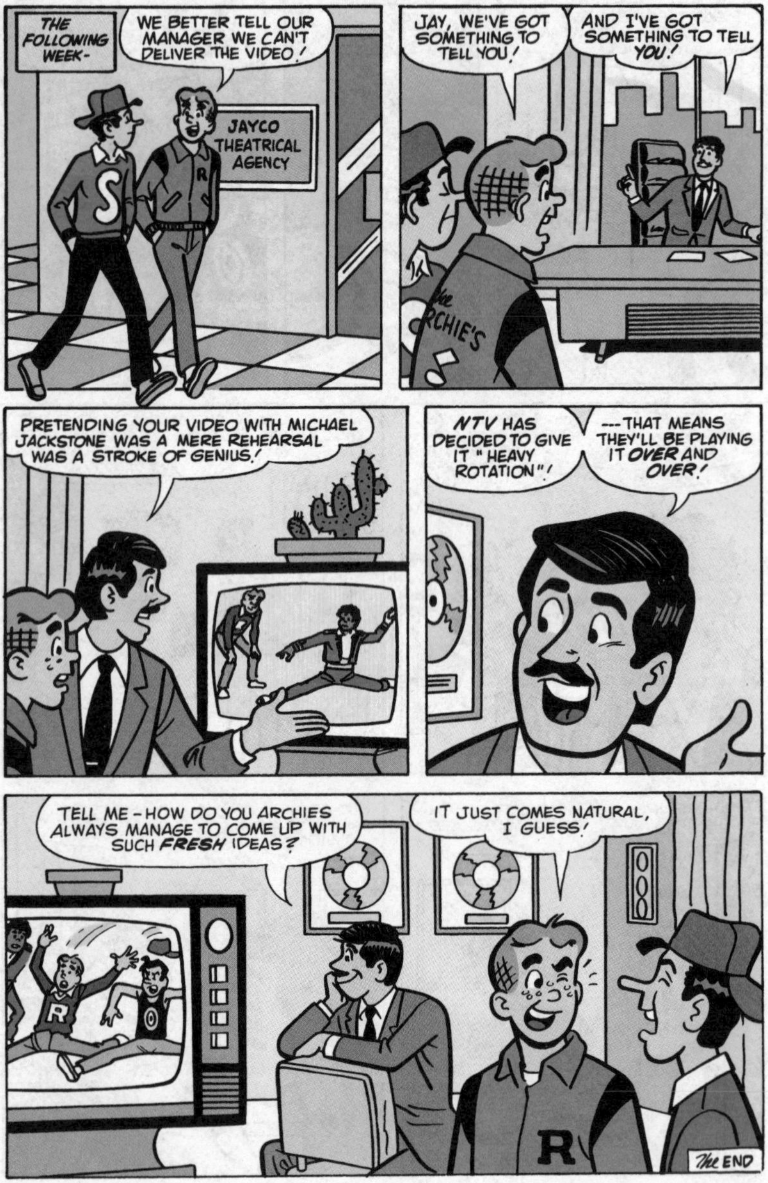
THE FOLLOWING WEEK-
WE BETTER TELL OUR MANAGER WE CAN'T DELIVER THE VIDEO!
JAYCO THEATRICAL AGENCY
JAY, WE'VE GOT SOMETHING TO TELL YOU!
AND I'VE GOT SOMETHING TO TELL YOU!
PRETENDING YOUR VIDEO WITH MICHAEL JACKSTONE WAS A MERE REHEARSAL WAS A STROKE OF GENIUS!
NTV HAS DECIDED TO GIVE IT "HEAVY ROTATION"!
---THAT MEANS THEY'LL BE PLAYING IT OVER AND OVER!
TELL ME - HOW DO YOU ARCHIES ALWAYS MANAGE TO COME UP WITH SUCH FRESH IDEAS?
IT JUST COMES NATURAL, I GUESS!
The END

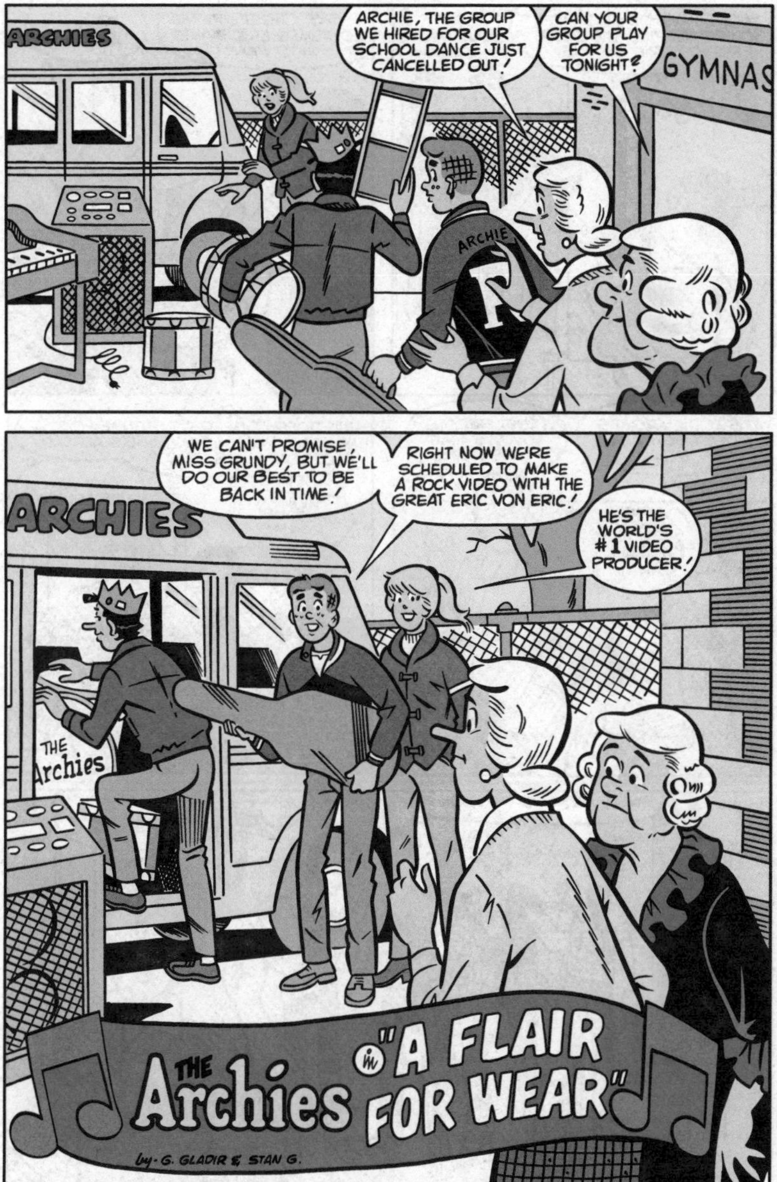
ARCHIES
ARCHIE, THE GROUP WE HIRED FOR OUR SCHOOL DANCE JUST CANCELLED OUT!
CAN YOUR GROUP PLAY FOR US TONIGHT?
GYMNAS
ARCHIE
WE CAN'T PROMISE, MISS GRUNDY, BUT WE'LL DO OUR BEST TO BE BACK IN TIME!
RIGHT NOW WE'RE SCHEDULED TO MAKE A ROCK VIDEO WITH THE GREAT ERIC VON ERIC!
HE'S THE WORLD'S #1 VIDEO PRODUCER!
ARCHIES
THE Archies
THE Archies in "A FLAIR FOR WEAR"
by G. GLADIR & STAN G.

Originally presented in EVERYTHING'S ARCHIE #116, March, 1985

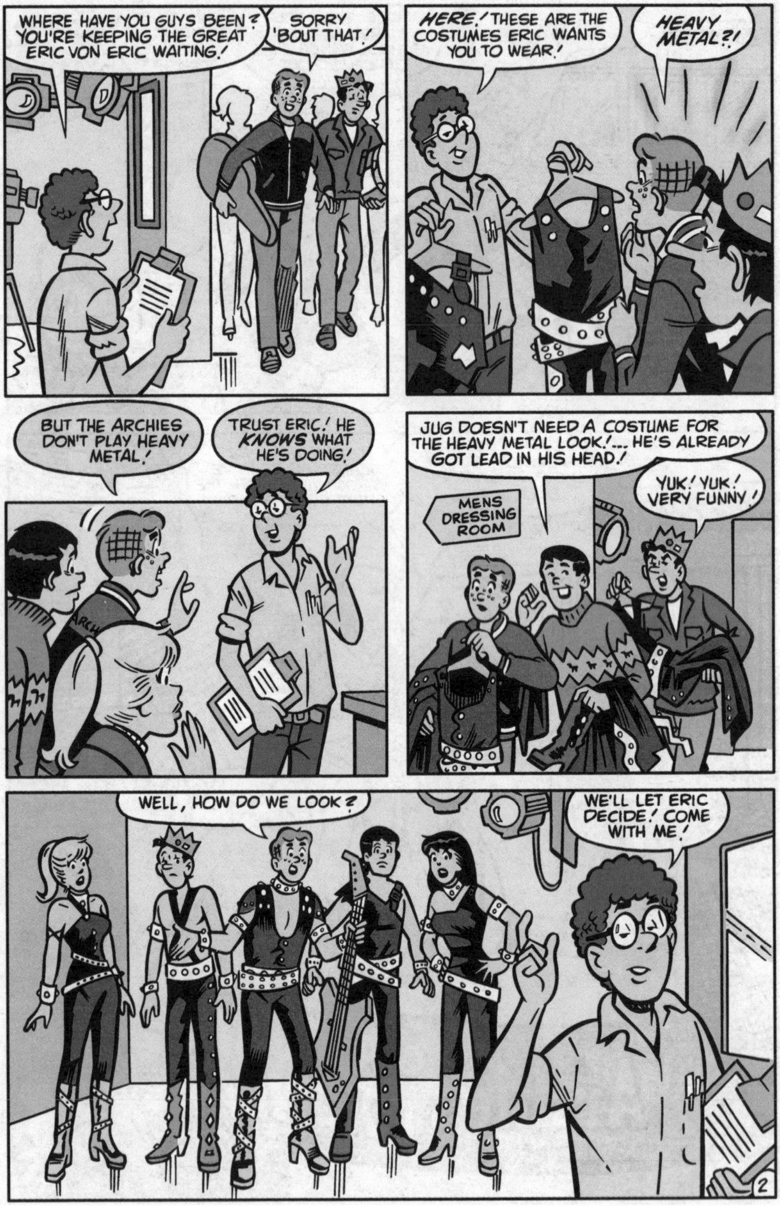

WHERE HAVE YOU GUYS BEEN? YOU'RE KEEPING THE GREAT ERIC VON ERIC WAITING!
SORRY 'BOUT THAT!
HERE! THESE ARE THE COSTUMES ERIC WANTS YOU TO WEAR!
HEAVY METAL?!
BUT THE ARCHIES DON'T PLAY HEAVY METAL!
TRUST ERIC! HE KNOWS WHAT HE'S DOING!
JUG DOESN'T NEED A COSTUME FOR THE HEAVY METAL LOOK!... HE'S ALREADY GOT LEAD IN HIS HEAD!
MENS DRESSING ROOM
YUK! YUK! VERY FUNNY!
WELL, HOW DO WE LOOK?
WE'LL LET ERIC DECIDE! COME WITH ME!
2

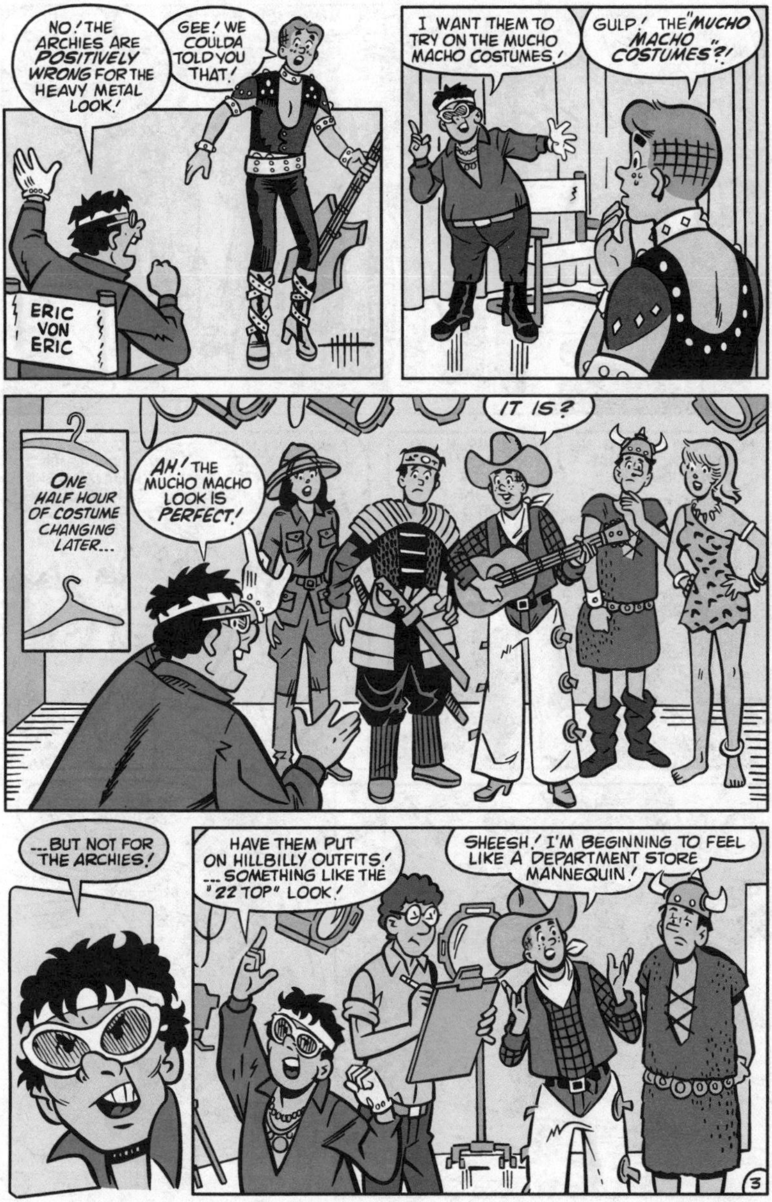
NO! THE ARCHIES ARE POSITIVELY WRONG FOR THE HEAVY METAL LOOK!
GEE! WE COULDA TOLD YOU THAT!
ERIC VON ERIC
I WANT THEM TO TRY ON THE MUCHO MACHO COSTUMES!
GULP! THE "MUCHO MACHO COSTUMES"?!
ONE HALF HOUR OF COSTUME CHANGING LATER...
AH! THE MUCHO MACHO LOOK IS PERFECT!
IT IS?
...BUT NOT FOR THE ARCHIES!
HAVE THEM PUT ON HILLBILLY OUTFITS! ...SOMETHING LIKE THE "22 TOP" LOOK!
SHEESH! I'M BEGINNING TO FEEL LIKE A DEPARTMENT STORE MANNEQUIN!
3

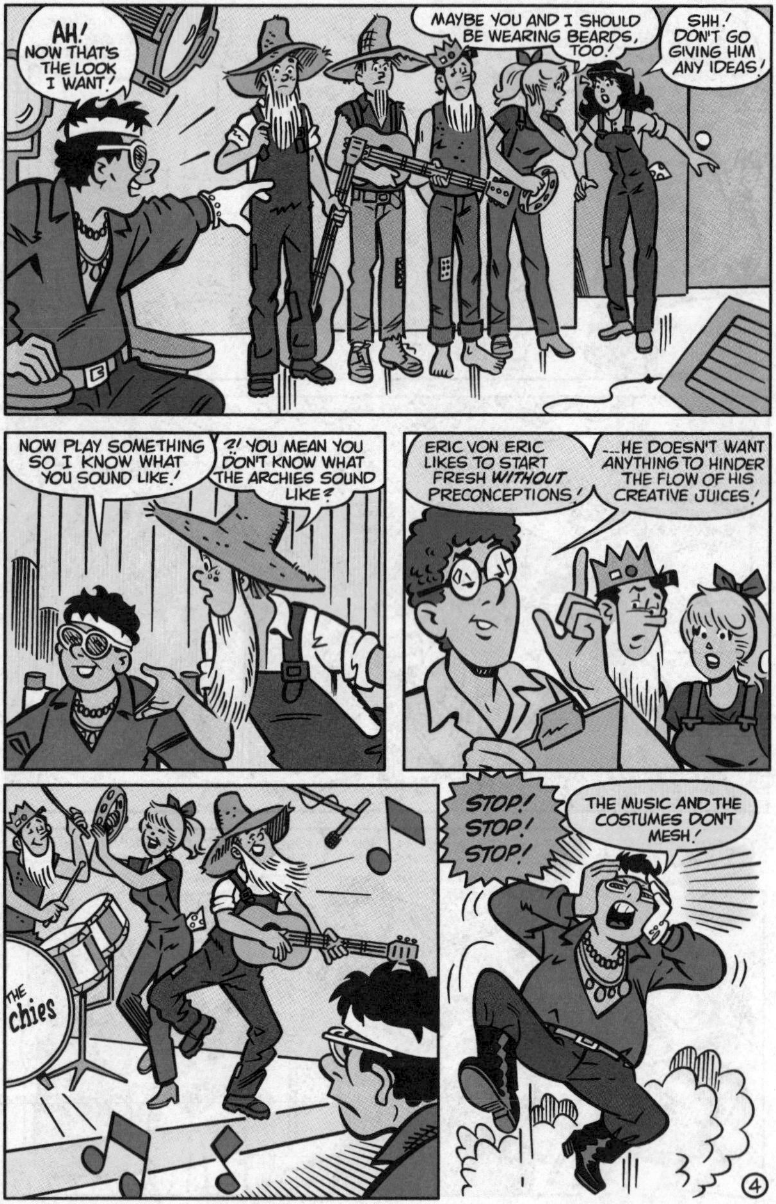
AH! NOW THAT'S THE LOOK I WANT!
MAYBE YOU AND I SHOULD BE WEARING BEARDS, TOO!
SHH! DON'T GO GIVING HIM ANY IDEAS!
NOW PLAY SOMETHING SO I KNOW WHAT YOU SOUND LIKE!
?! YOU MEAN YOU DON'T KNOW WHAT THE ARCHIES SOUND LIKE?
ERIC VON ERIC LIKES TO START FRESH *WITHOUT* PRECONCEPTIONS!
...HE DOESN'T WANT ANYTHING TO HINDER THE FLOW OF HIS CREATIVE JUICES!
THE chies
STOP! STOP! STOP!
THE MUSIC AND THE COSTUMES DON'T MESH!
4

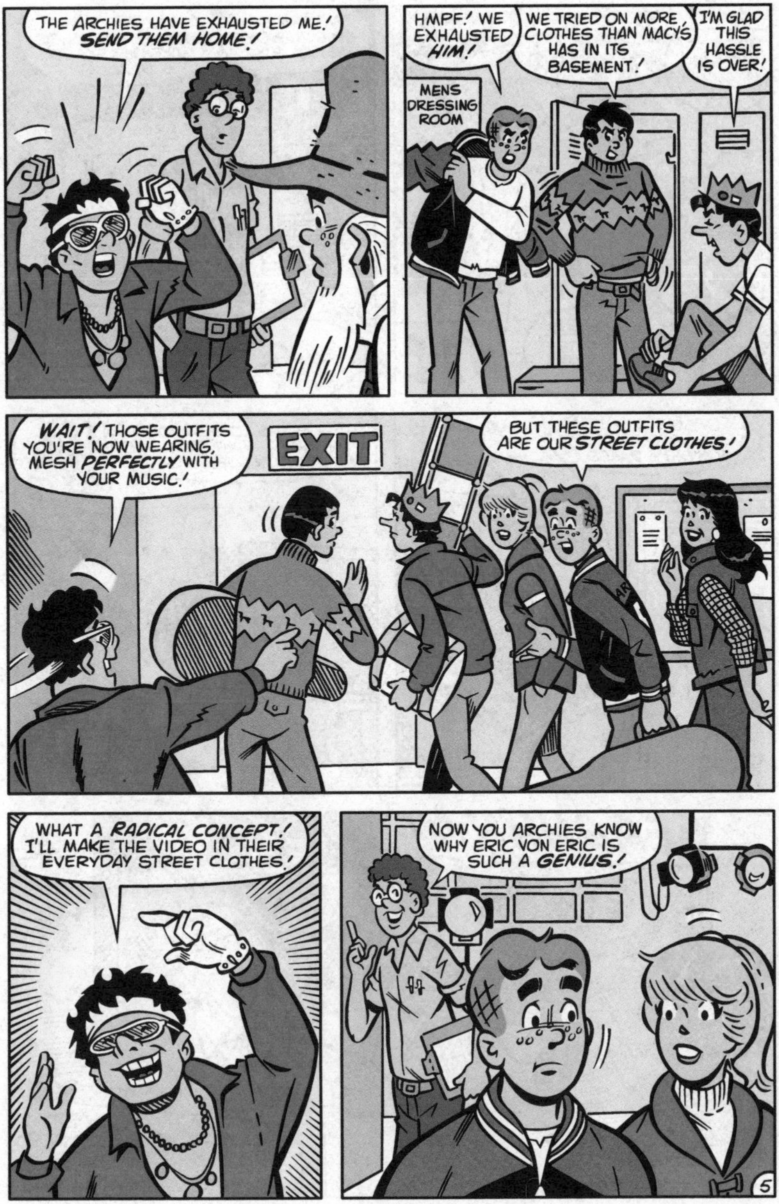
THE ARCHIES HAVE EXHAUSTED ME! SEND THEM HOME!
HMPF! WE EXHAUSTED HIM!
WE TRIED ON MORE CLOTHES THAN MACY'S HAS IN ITS BASEMENT!
I'M GLAD THIS HASSLE IS OVER!
MENS DRESSING ROOM
WAIT! THOSE OUTFITS YOU'RE NOW WEARING, MESH PERFECTLY WITH YOUR MUSIC!
EXIT
BUT THESE OUTFITS ARE OUR STREET CLOTHES!
WHAT A RADICAL CONCEPT! I'LL MAKE THE VIDEO IN THEIR EVERYDAY STREET CLOTHES!
NOW YOU ARCHIES KNOW WHY ERIC VON ERIC IS SUCH A GENIUS!
5

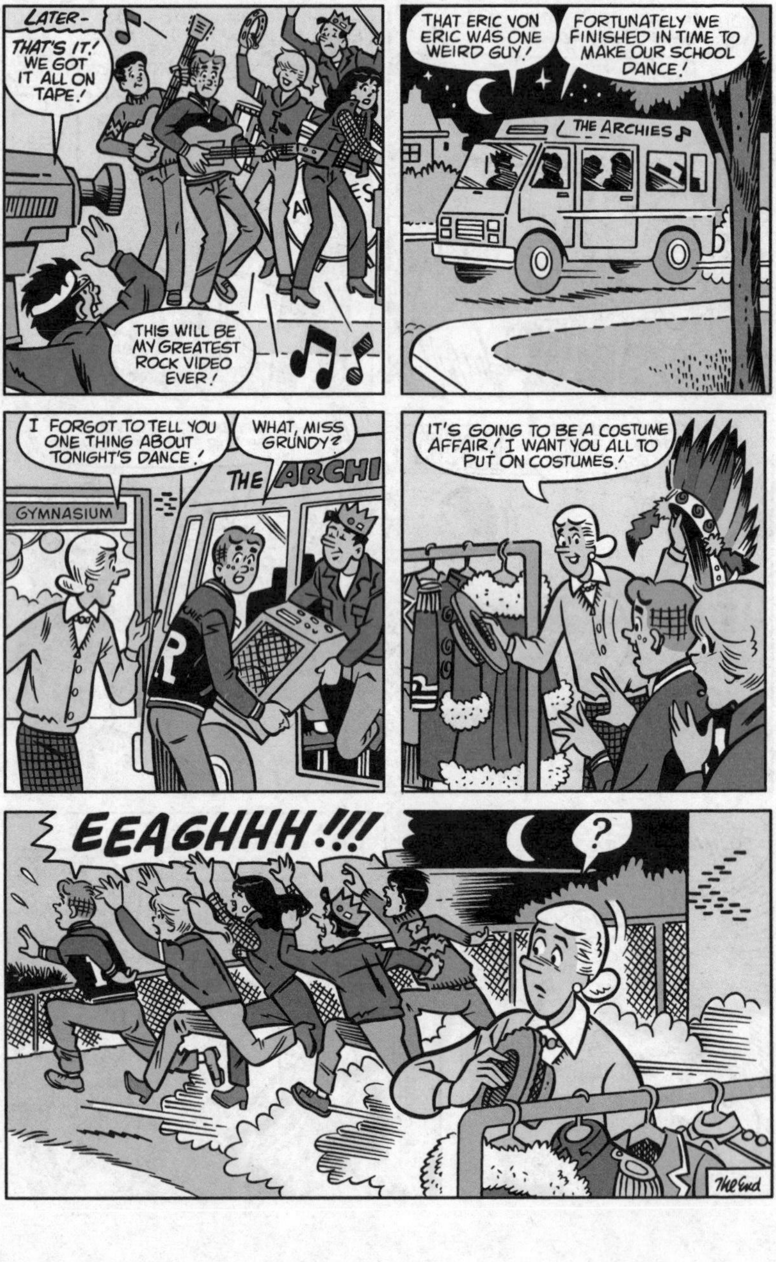
LATER-
THAT'S IT! WE GOT IT ALL ON TAPE!
THIS WILL BE MY GREATEST ROCK VIDEO EVER!
THAT ERIC VON ERIC WAS ONE WEIRD GUY!
FORTUNATELY WE FINISHED IN TIME TO MAKE OUR SCHOOL DANCE!
THE ARCHIES
I FORGOT TO TELL YOU ONE THING ABOUT TONIGHT'S DANCE!
WHAT, MISS GRUNDY?
GYMNASIUM
THE ARCHI
IT'S GOING TO BE A COSTUME AFFAIR! I WANT YOU ALL TO PUT ON COSTUMES!
EEAGHHH!!!
?
The End

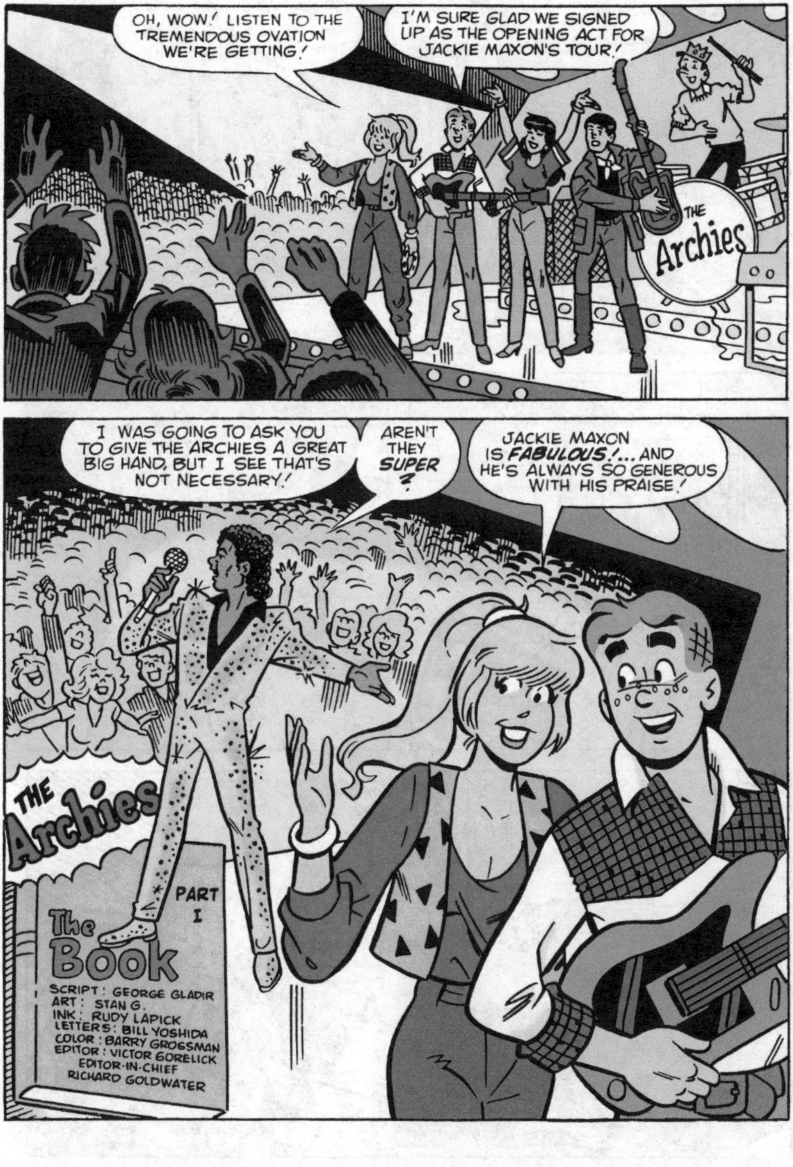
OH, WOW! LISTEN TO THE TREMENDOUS OVATION WE'RE GETTING!
I'M SURE GLAD WE SIGNED UP AS THE OPENING ACT FOR JACKIE MAXON'S TOUR!
THE Archies
I WAS GOING TO ASK YOU TO GIVE THE ARCHIES A GREAT BIG HAND, BUT I SEE THAT'S NOT NECESSARY!
AREN'T THEY SUPER ?
JACKIE MAXON IS FABULOUS!... AND HE'S ALWAYS SO GENEROUS WITH HIS PRAISE!
THE Archies
PART I
The Book
SCRIPT: GEORGE GLADIR
ART: STAN G.
INK: RUDY LAPICK
LETTERS: BILL YOSHIDA
COLOR: BARRY GROSSMAN
EDITOR: VICTOR GORELICK
EDITOR-IN-CHIEF RICHARD GOLDWATER

Originally presented in ARCHIE'S TV LAUGH-OUT #100, April, 1985

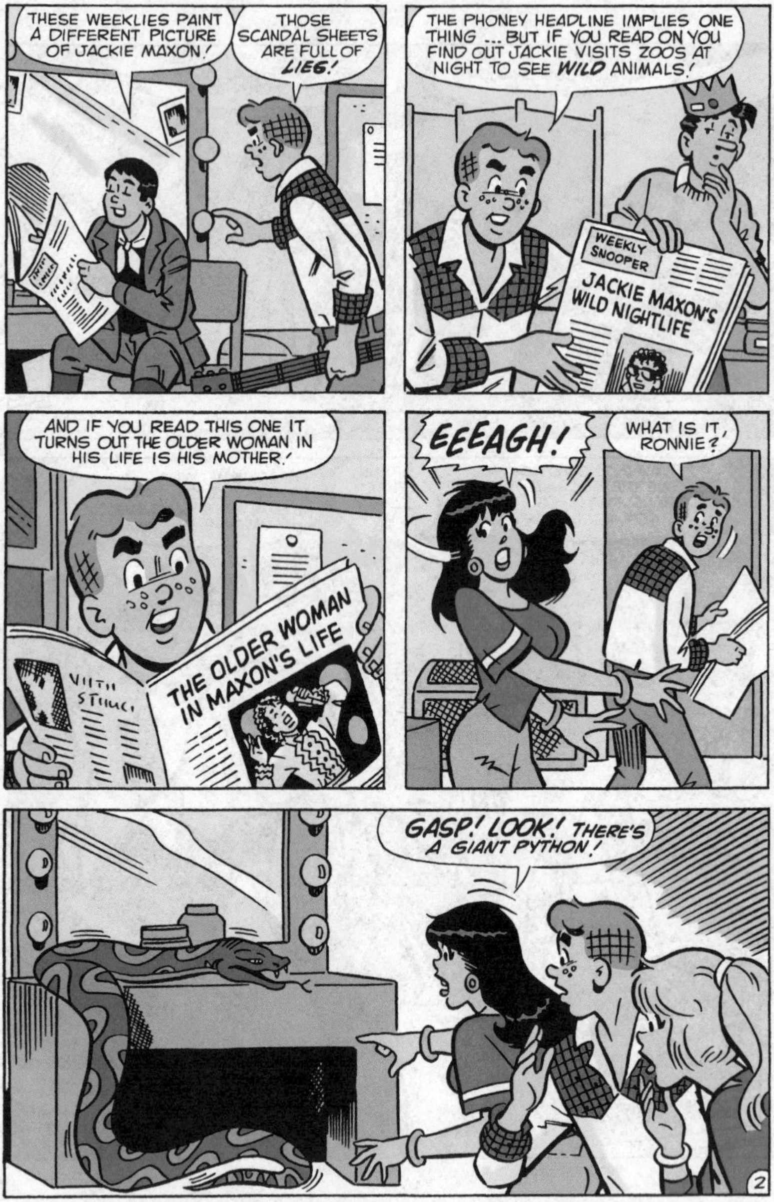
THESE WEEKLIES PAINT A DIFFERENT PICTURE OF JACKIE MAXON!
THOSE SCANDAL SHEETS ARE FULL OF LIES!
THE PHONEY HEADLINE IMPLIES ONE THING ... BUT IF YOU READ ON YOU FIND OUT JACKIE VISITS ZOOS AT NIGHT TO SEE WILD ANIMALS!
WEEKLY SNOOPER
JACKIE MAXON'S WILD NIGHTLIFE
AND IF YOU READ THIS ONE IT TURNS OUT THE OLDER WOMAN IN HIS LIFE IS HIS MOTHER!
THE OLDER WOMAN IN MAXON'S LIFE
EEEAGH!
WHAT IS IT, RONNIE?
GASP! LOOK! THERE'S A GIANT PYTHON!
2

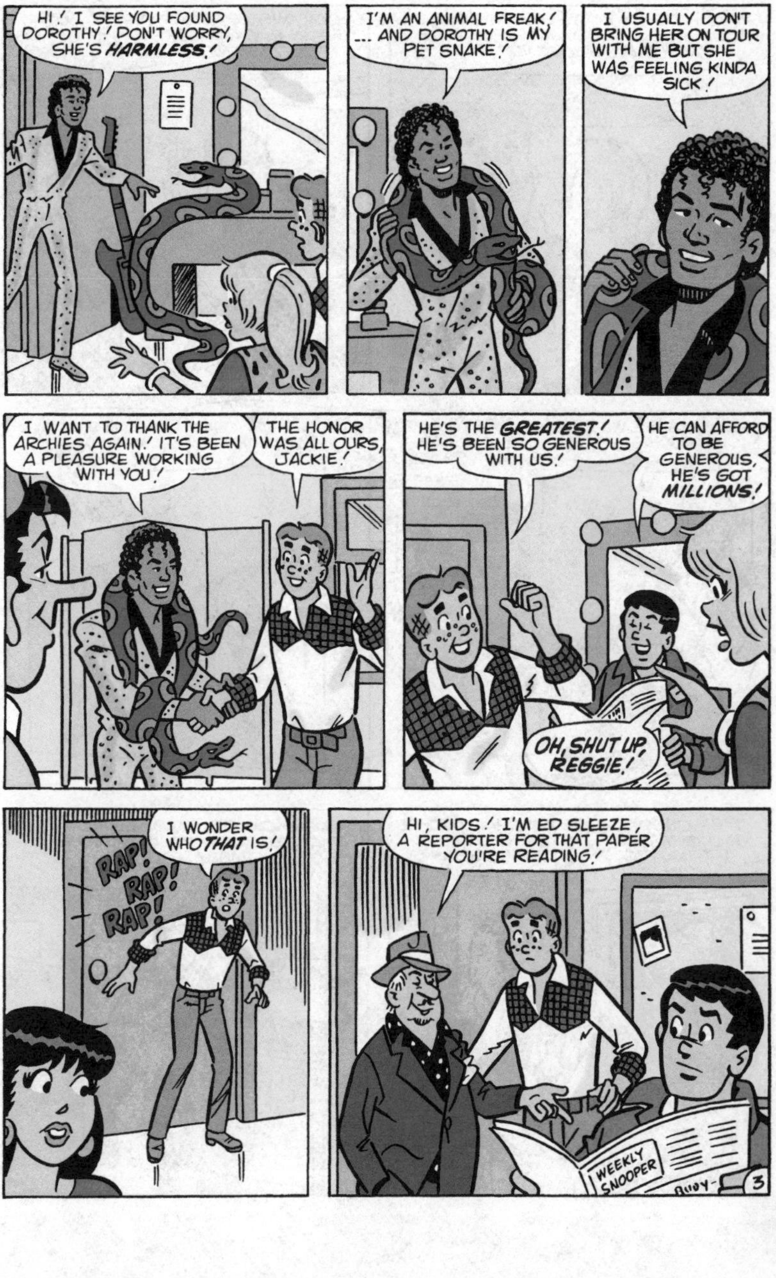
HI! I SEE YOU FOUND DOROTHY! DON'T WORRY, SHE'S HARMLESS!
I'M AN ANIMAL FREAK! ... AND DOROTHY IS MY PET SNAKE!
I USUALLY DON'T BRING HER ON TOUR WITH ME BUT SHE WAS FEELING KINDA SICK!
I WANT TO THANK THE ARCHIES AGAIN! IT'S BEEN A PLEASURE WORKING WITH YOU!
THE HONOR WAS ALL OURS, JACKIE!
HE'S THE GREATEST! HE'S BEEN SO GENEROUS WITH US!
HE CAN AFFORD TO BE GENEROUS, HE'S GOT MILLIONS!
OH, SHUT UP, REGGIE!
I WONDER WHO THAT IS!
RAP! RAP! RAP!
HI, KIDS! I'M ED SLEEZE, A REPORTER FOR THAT PAPER YOU'RE READING!
WEEKLY SNOOPER
3

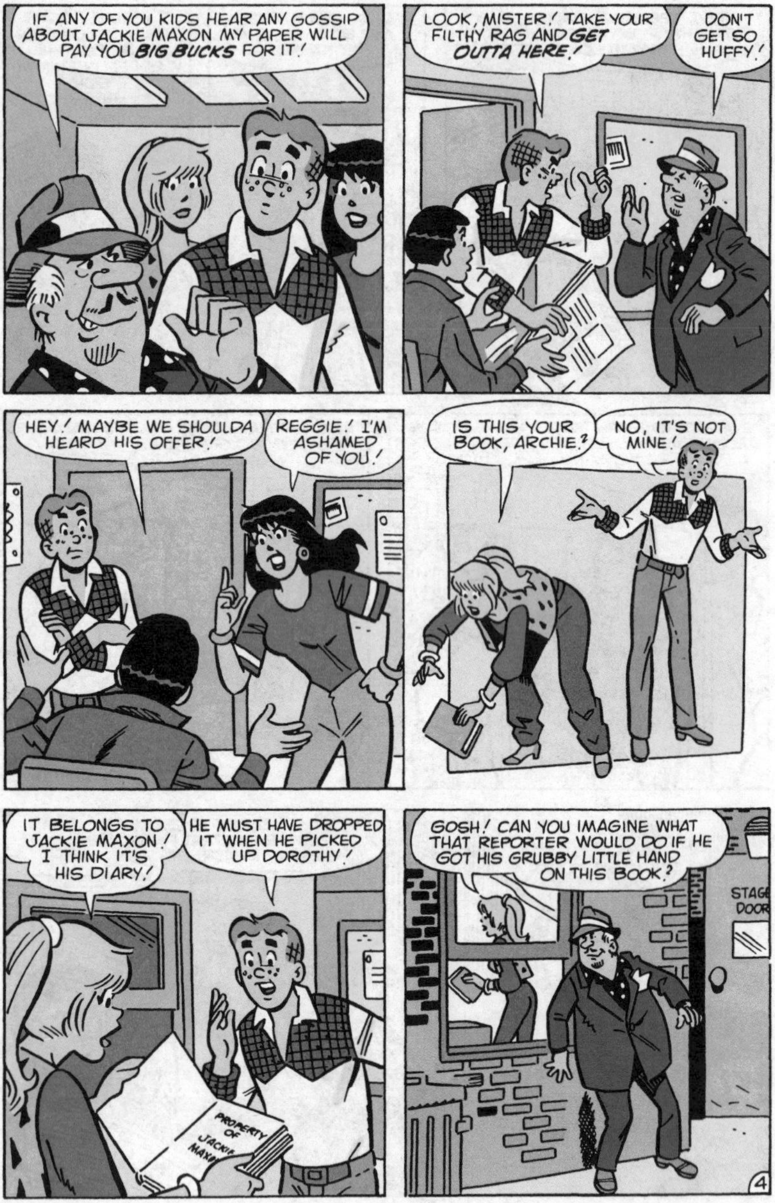
IF ANY OF YOU KIDS HEAR ANY GOSSIP ABOUT JACKIE MAXON MY PAPER WILL PAY YOU BIG BUCKS FOR IT!
LOOK, MISTER! TAKE YOUR FILTHY RAG AND GET OUTTA HERE!
DON'T GET SO HUFFY!
HEY! MAYBE WE SHOULDA HEARD HIS OFFER!
REGGIE! I'M ASHAMED OF YOU!
IS THIS YOUR BOOK, ARCHIE?
NO, IT'S NOT MINE!
IT BELONGS TO JACKIE MAXON! I THINK IT'S HIS DIARY!
HE MUST HAVE DROPPED IT WHEN HE PICKED UP DOROTHY!
PROPERTY OF JACKIE MAXON
GOSH! CAN YOU IMAGINE WHAT THAT REPORTER WOULD DO IF HE GOT HIS GRUBBY LITTLE HAND ON THIS BOOK?
STAGE DOOR
4

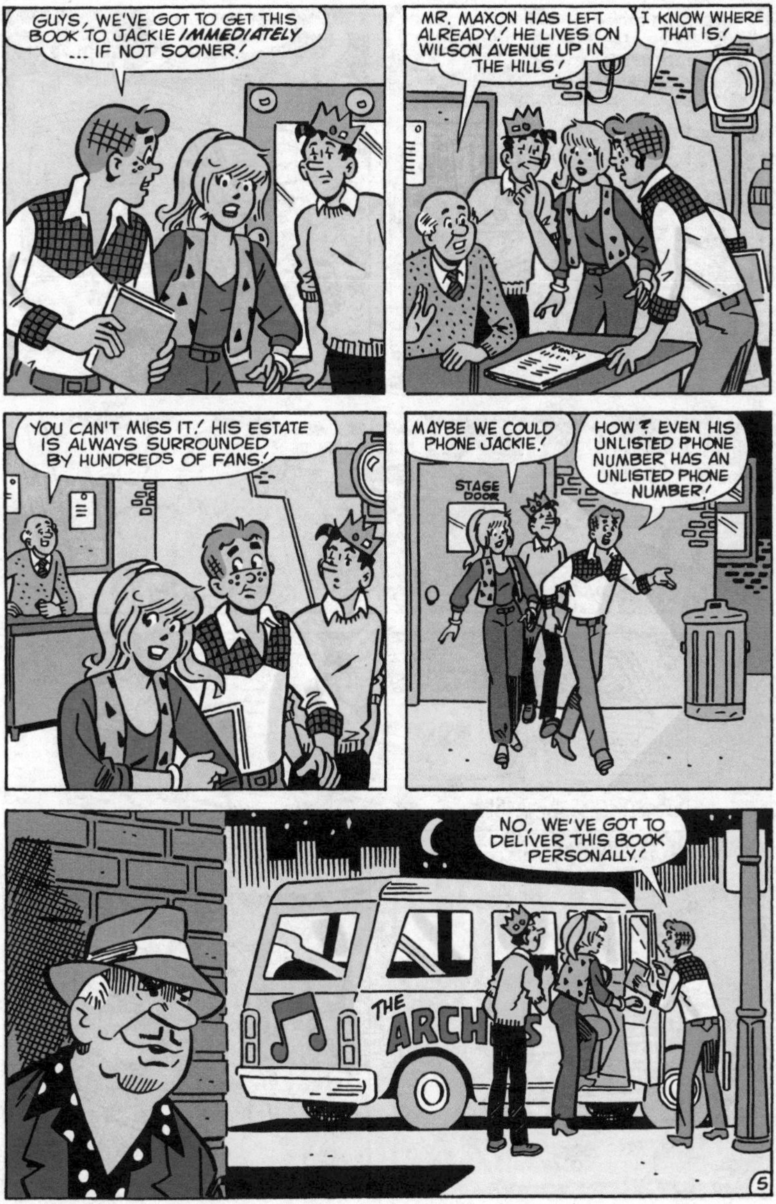
GUYS, WE'VE GOT TO GET THIS BOOK TO JACKIE *IMMEDIATELY* ... IF NOT SOONER!
MR. MAXON HAS LEFT ALREADY! HE LIVES ON WILSON AVENUE UP IN THE HILLS!
I KNOW WHERE THAT IS!
YOU CAN'T MISS IT! HIS ESTATE IS ALWAYS SURROUNDED BY HUNDREDS OF FANS!
MAYBE WE COULD PHONE JACKIE!
STAGE DOOR
HOW? EVEN HIS UNLISTED PHONE NUMBER HAS AN UNLISTED PHONE NUMBER!
NO, WE'VE GOT TO DELIVER THIS BOOK PERSONALLY!
THE ARCH
5

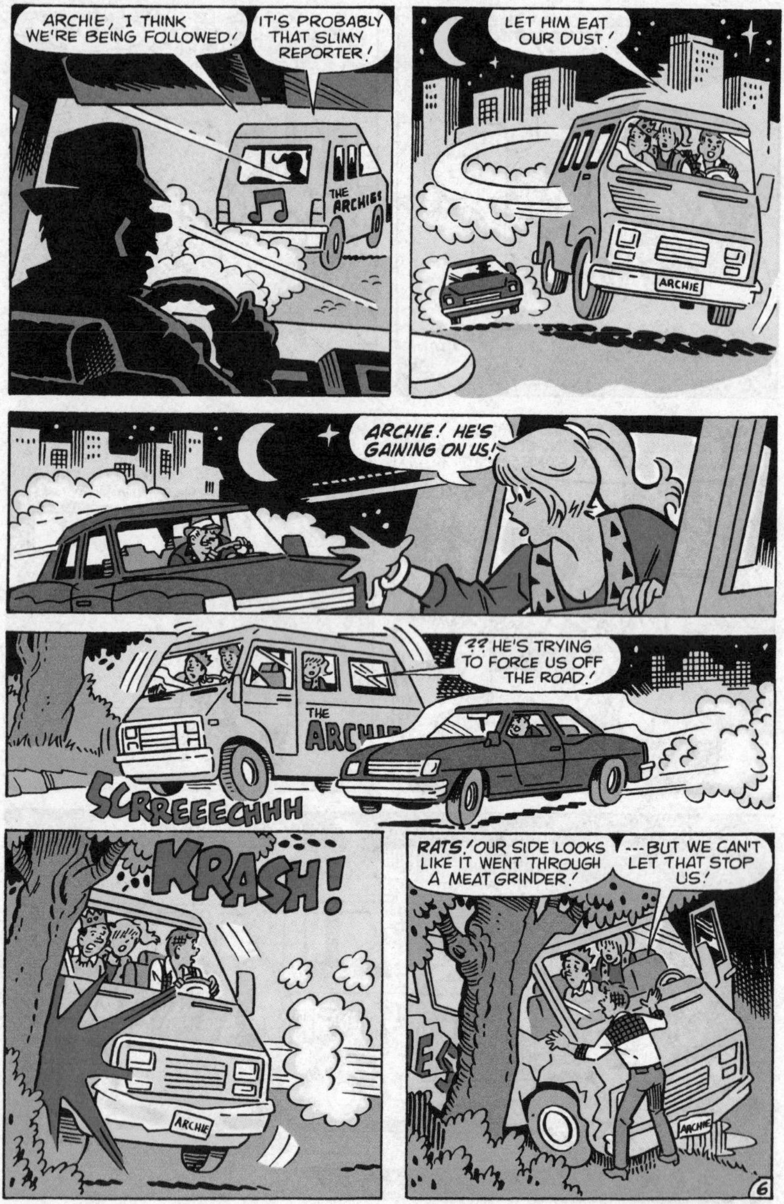
ARCHIE, I THINK WE'RE BEING FOLLOWED!
IT'S PROBABLY THAT SLIMY REPORTER!
THE ARCHIES
LET HIM EAT OUR DUST!
ARCHIE
ARCHIE! HE'S GAINING ON US!
?? HE'S TRYING TO FORCE US OFF THE ROAD!
SCRREEEECHHH
KRASH!
ARCHIE
RATS! OUR SIDE LOOKS LIKE IT WENT THROUGH A MEAT GRINDER!
---BUT WE CAN'T LET THAT STOP US!
ARCHIE
6

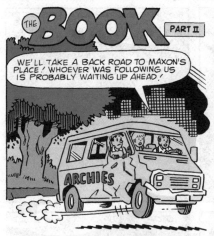

THE BOOK PART II

WE'LL TAKE A BACK ROAD TO MAXON'S PLACE! WHOEVER WAS FOLLOWING US IS PROBABLY WAITING UP AHEAD!

LOOK AT THE MOB IN FRONT OF MAXON'S HOME!

IT FIGURES! HE'S THE WORLD'S MOST POPULAR ENTERTAINER!

WE HAVE TO SEE JACKIE MAXON RIGHT AWAY!

YOU AND ABOUT A THOUSAND OTHER FANS!

WE'RE THE ARCHIES! WE HAVE SOMETHING *VERY IMPORTANT* TO DELIVER TO HIM!

SORRY, HE'S ASLEEP, AND LEFT WORD NOT TO BE DISTURBED!

ARCHIE, I THINK I JUST SPOTTED THE REPORTER'S CAR!

WE'VE GOT TO GET BEHIND THESE WALLS SOMEHOW! GIVE US A BOOST JUG!

HOW WILL WE GET DOWN ON THE OTHER SIDE?

WE'LL FIGURE OUT SOMETHING!

7

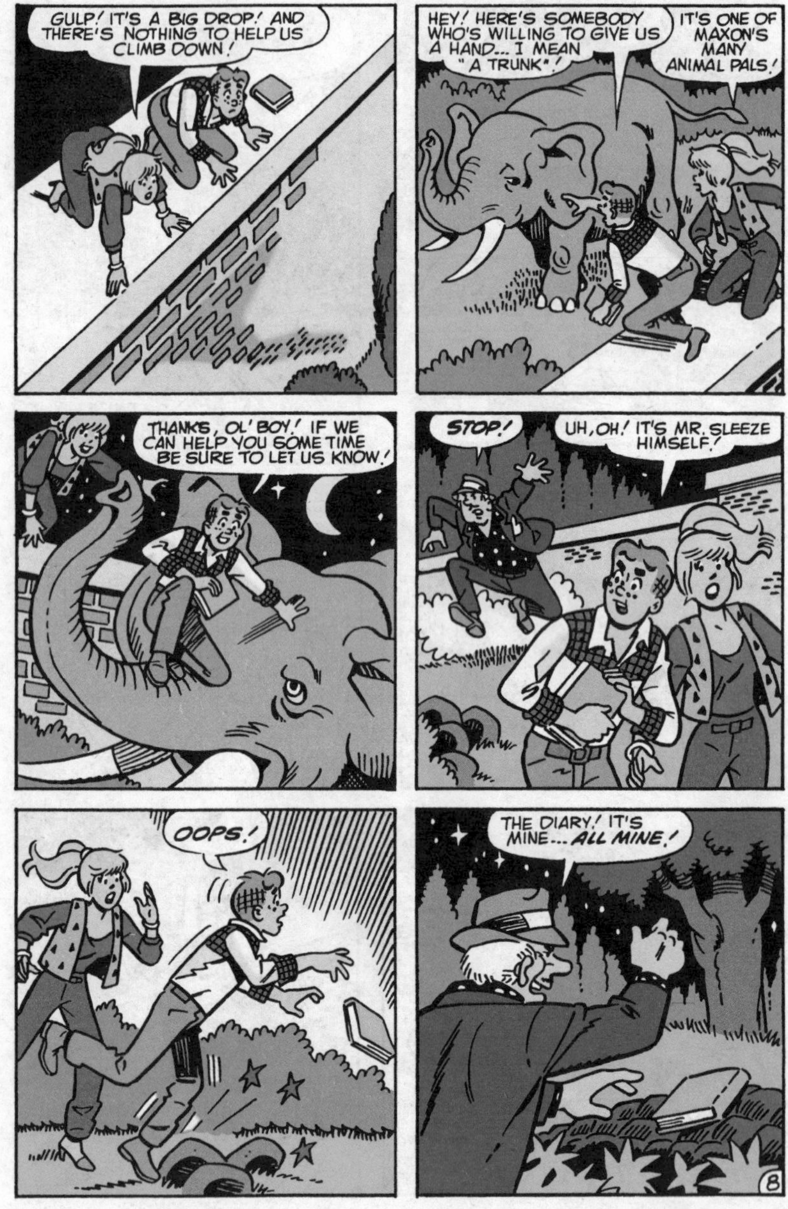
GULP! IT'S A BIG DROP! AND THERE'S NOTHING TO HELP US CLIMB DOWN!
HEY! HERE'S SOMEBODY WHO'S WILLING TO GIVE US A HAND... I MEAN "A TRUNK"!
IT'S ONE OF MAXON'S MANY ANIMAL PALS!
THANKS, OL' BOY! IF WE CAN HELP YOU SOME TIME BE SURE TO LET US KNOW!
STOP!
UH, OH! IT'S MR. SLEEZE HIMSELF!
OOPS!
THE DIARY! IT'S MINE... ALL MINE!
8

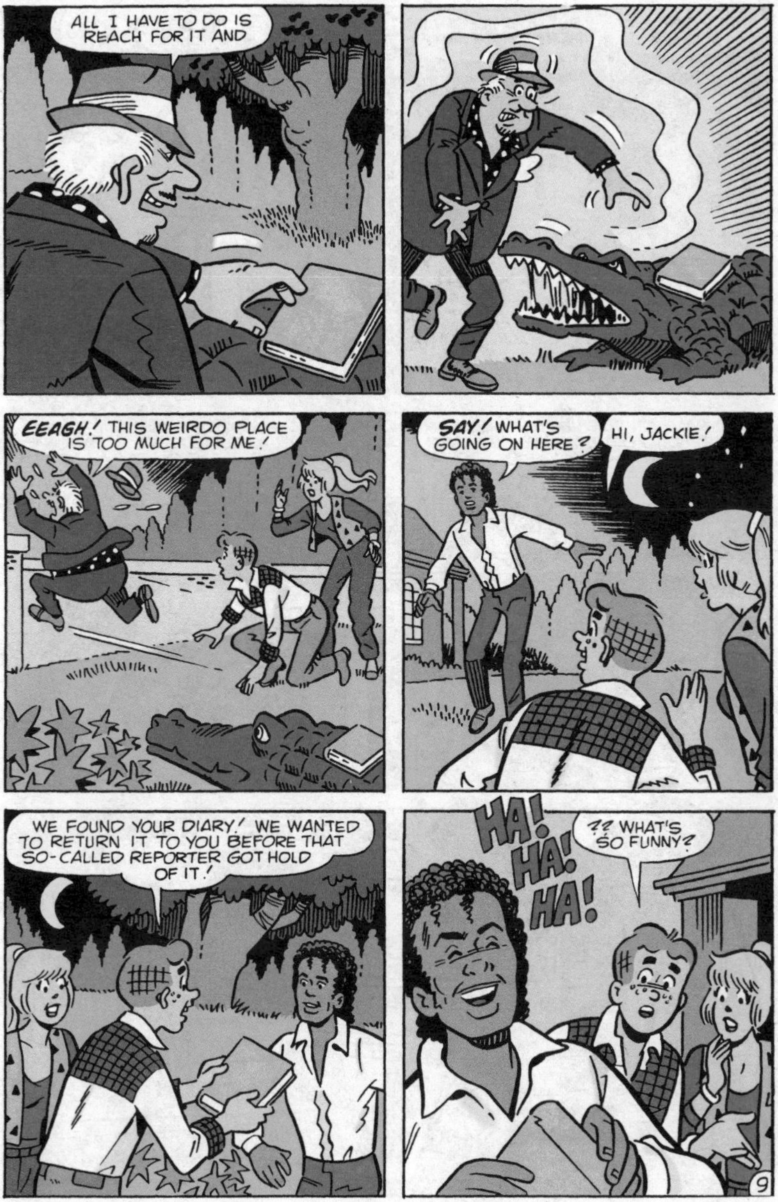
ALL I HAVE TO DO IS REACH FOR IT AND
EEAGH! THIS WEIRDO PLACE IS TOO MUCH FOR ME!
SAY! WHAT'S GOING ON HERE?
HI, JACKIE!
WE FOUND YOUR DIARY! WE WANTED TO RETURN IT TO YOU BEFORE THAT SO-CALLED REPORTER GOT HOLD OF IT!
HA! HA! HA!
?? WHAT'S SO FUNNY?
9

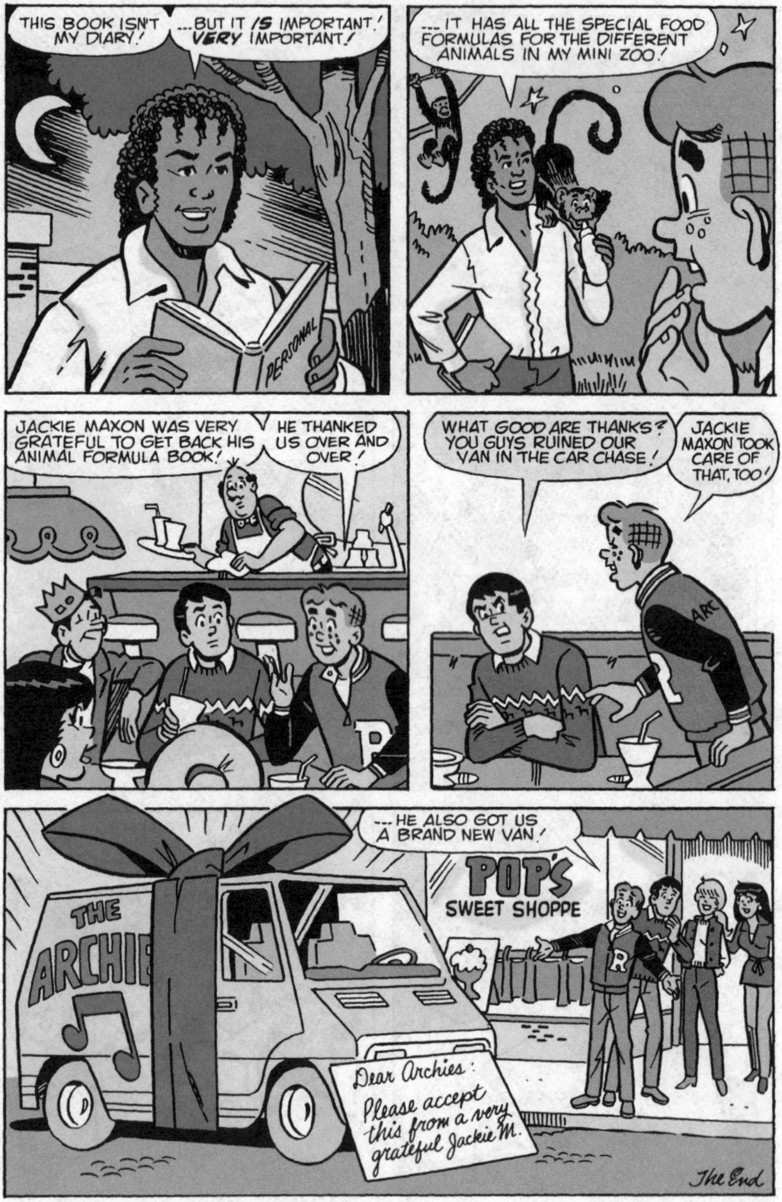
THIS BOOK ISN'T MY DIARY!
...BUT IT IS IMPORTANT! VERY IMPORTANT!
PERSONAL
... IT HAS ALL THE SPECIAL FOOD FORMULAS FOR THE DIFFERENT ANIMALS IN MY MINI ZOO!
JACKIE MAXON WAS VERY GRATEFUL TO GET BACK HIS ANIMAL FORMULA BOOK!
HE THANKED US OVER AND OVER!
WHAT GOOD ARE THANKS? YOU GUYS RUINED OUR VAN IN THE CAR CHASE!
JACKIE MAXON TOOK CARE OF THAT, TOO!
--- HE ALSO GOT US A BRAND NEW VAN!
POP'S SWEET SHOPPE
THE ARCHIES
Dear Archies: Please accept this from a very grateful Jackie M.
The End

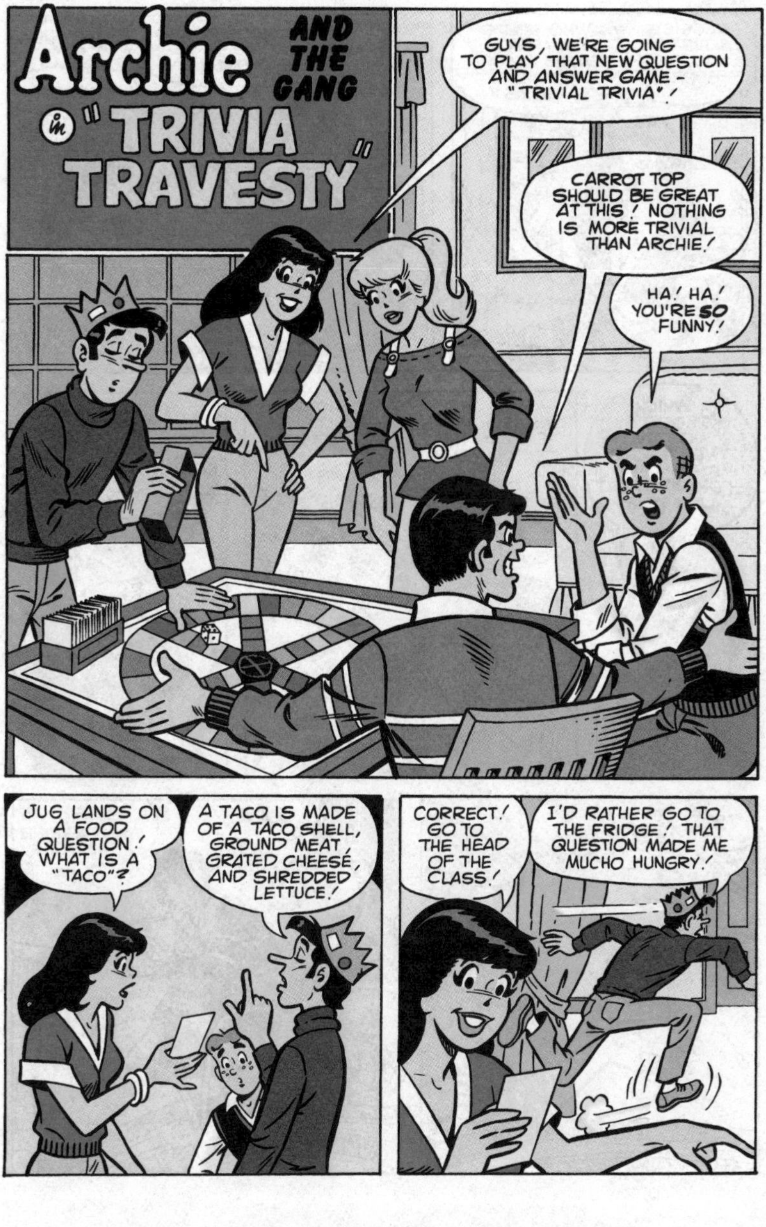
Archie AND THE GANG in "TRIVIA TRAVESTY"
GUYS, WE'RE GOING TO PLAY THAT NEW QUESTION AND ANSWER GAME - "TRIVIAL TRIVIA"!
CARROT TOP SHOULD BE GREAT AT THIS! NOTHING IS MORE TRIVIAL THAN ARCHIE!
HA! HA! YOU'RE SO FUNNY!
JUG LANDS ON A FOOD QUESTION! WHAT IS A "TACO"?
A TACO IS MADE OF A TACO SHELL, GROUND MEAT, GRATED CHEESE, AND SHREDDED LETTUCE!
CORRECT! GO TO THE HEAD OF THE CLASS!
I'D RATHER GO TO THE FRIDGE! THAT QUESTION MADE ME MUCHO HUNGRY!

Originally presented in EVERYTHING'S ARCHIE #117, May, 1985

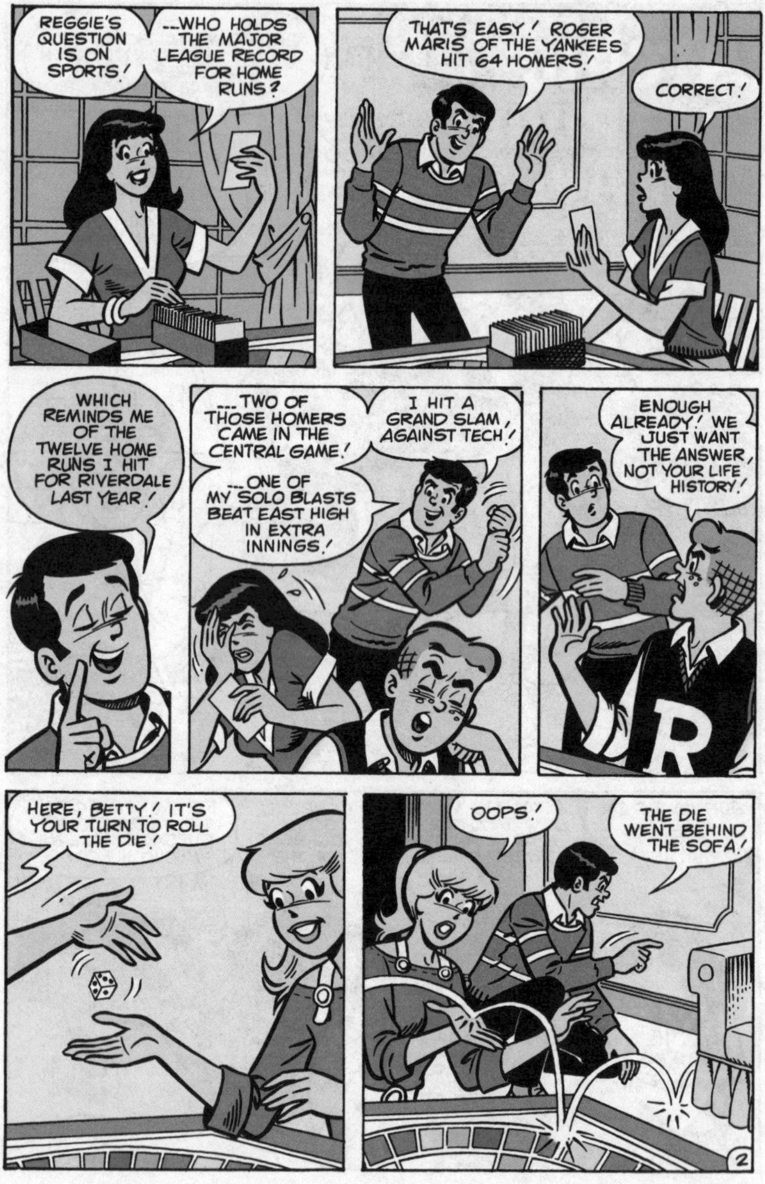
REGGIE'S QUESTION IS ON SPORTS!
--WHO HOLDS THE MAJOR LEAGUE RECORD FOR HOME RUNS?
THAT'S EASY! ROGER MARIS OF THE YANKEES HIT 64 HOMERS!
CORRECT!
WHICH REMINDS ME OF THE TWELVE HOME RUNS I HIT FOR RIVERDALE LAST YEAR!
...TWO OF THOSE HOMERS CAME IN THE CENTRAL GAME!
I HIT A GRAND SLAM AGAINST TECH!
...ONE OF MY SOLO BLASTS BEAT EAST HIGH IN EXTRA INNINGS!
ENOUGH ALREADY! WE JUST WANT THE ANSWER, NOT YOUR LIFE HISTORY!
HERE, BETTY! IT'S YOUR TURN TO ROLL THE DIE!
OOPS!
THE DIE WENT BEHIND THE SOFA!
2

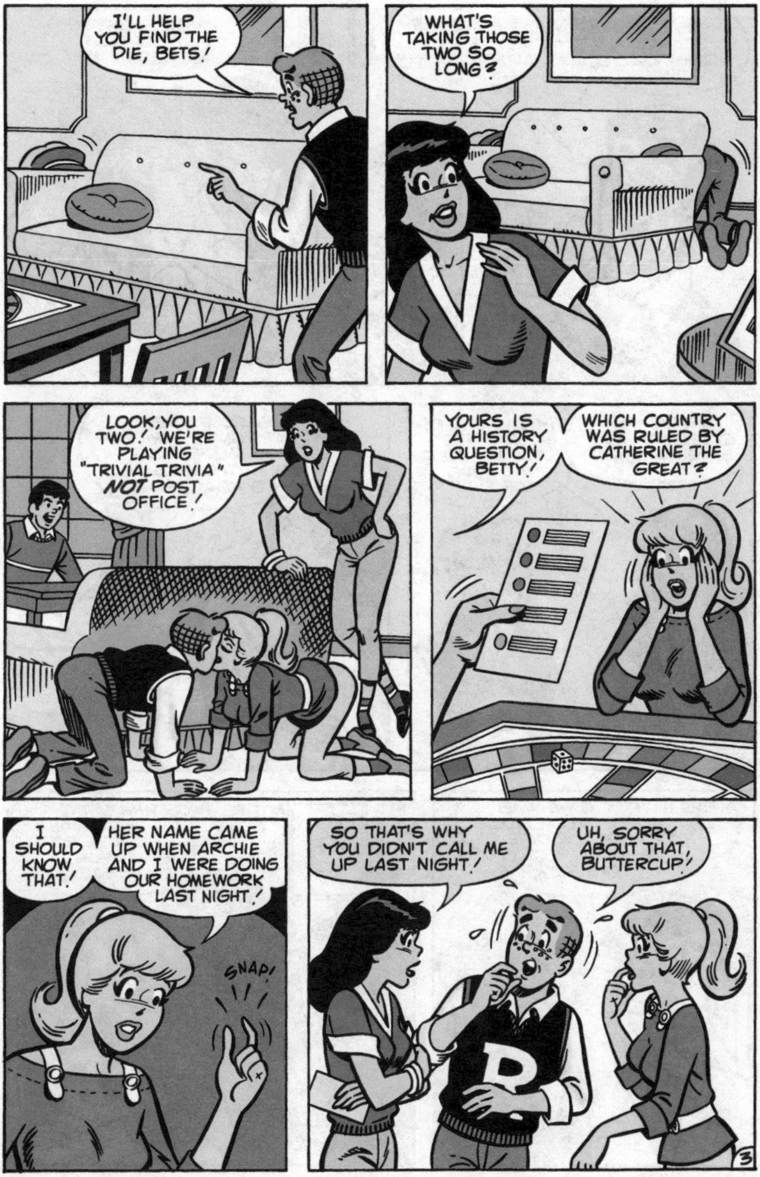
I'LL HELP YOU FIND THE DIE, BETS!
WHAT'S TAKING THOSE TWO SO LONG?
LOOK, YOU TWO! WE'RE PLAYING "TRIVIAL TRIVIA" NOT POST OFFICE!
YOURS IS A HISTORY QUESTION, BETTY!
WHICH COUNTRY WAS RULED BY CATHERINE THE GREAT?
I SHOULD KNOW THAT!
HER NAME CAME UP WHEN ARCHIE AND I WERE DOING OUR HOMEWORK LAST NIGHT!
SNAP!
SO THAT'S WHY YOU DIDN'T CALL ME UP LAST NIGHT!
UH, SORRY ABOUT THAT, BUTTERCUP!
3

HERE'S YOUR SCIENCE QUESTION, RONNIE!
WHAT IS THE WORLD'S BIGGEST WORM?
HE'S SITTING HERE RIGHT BESIDE ME!
ARCHIE'S CATEGORY IS ENTERTAINMENT!
WHICH ACTRESS HAD THE LEADING ROLE IN "GUNS OF FIRE"?
I SHOULD KNOW THAT, RONNIE! WE SAW THAT MOVIE RIGHT AFTER THE HILLSIDE FOOTBALL GAME!
THE HILLSIDE GAME WAS ON THE NIGHT YOU CALLED TO BREAK OUR DATE BECAUSE YOU WERE SICK!
THIS TWO-TIMING RAT GOES OUT WITH SO MANY GIRLS HE CAN'T EVEN REMEMBER THEIR NAMES!
4

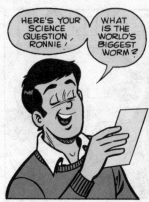

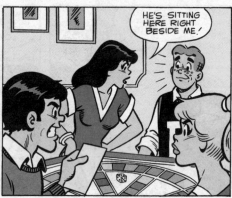

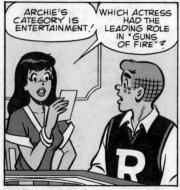

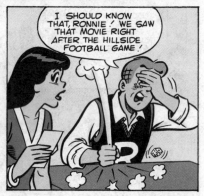

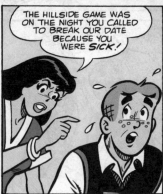

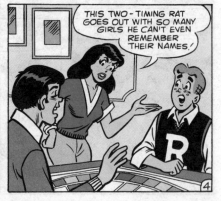

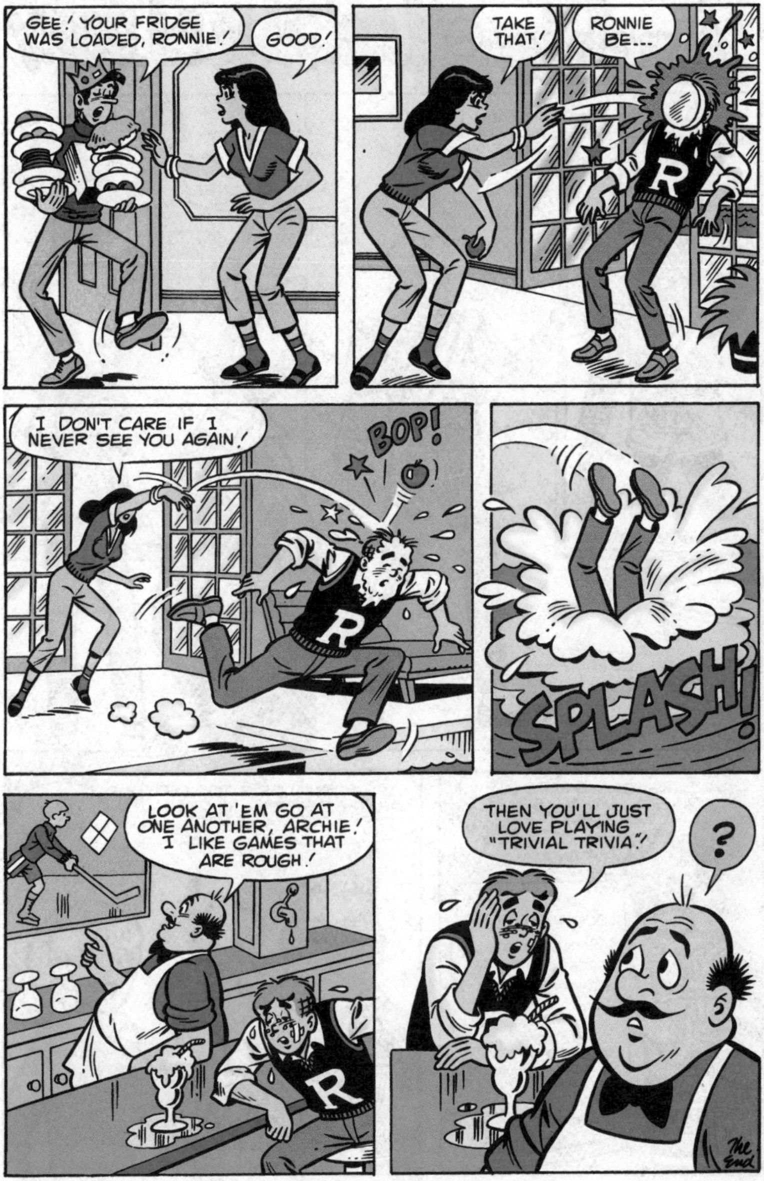
GEE! YOUR FRIDGE WAS LOADED, RONNIE!
GOOD!
TAKE THAT!
RONNIE BE...
I DON'T CARE IF I NEVER SEE YOU AGAIN!
BOP!
SPLASH!
LOOK AT 'EM GO AT ONE ANOTHER, ARCHIE! I LIKE GAMES THAT ARE ROUGH!
THEN YOU'LL JUST LOVE PLAYING "TRIVIAL TRIVIA"!
?
The End

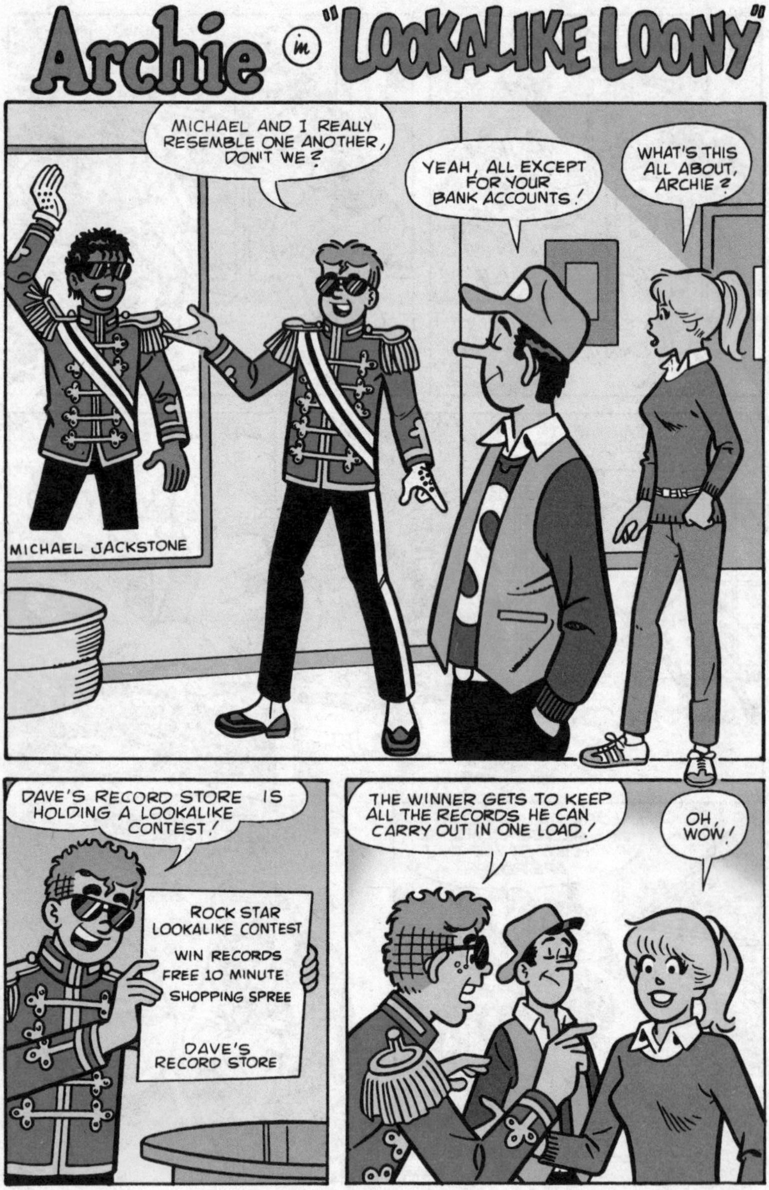
Archie in "LOOKALIKE LOONY"
MICHAEL AND I REALLY RESEMBLE ONE ANOTHER, DON'T WE?
YEAH, ALL EXCEPT FOR YOUR BANK ACCOUNTS!
WHAT'S THIS ALL ABOUT, ARCHIE?
MICHAEL JACKSTONE
DAVE'S RECORD STORE IS HOLDING A LOOKALIKE CONTEST!
ROCK STAR LOOKALIKE CONTEST
WIN RECORDS
FREE 10 MINUTE SHOPPING SPREE
DAVE'S RECORD STORE
THE WINNER GETS TO KEEP ALL THE RECORDS HE CAN CARRY OUT IN ONE LOAD!
OH, WOW!

Originally presented in ARCHIE #336, July, 1985

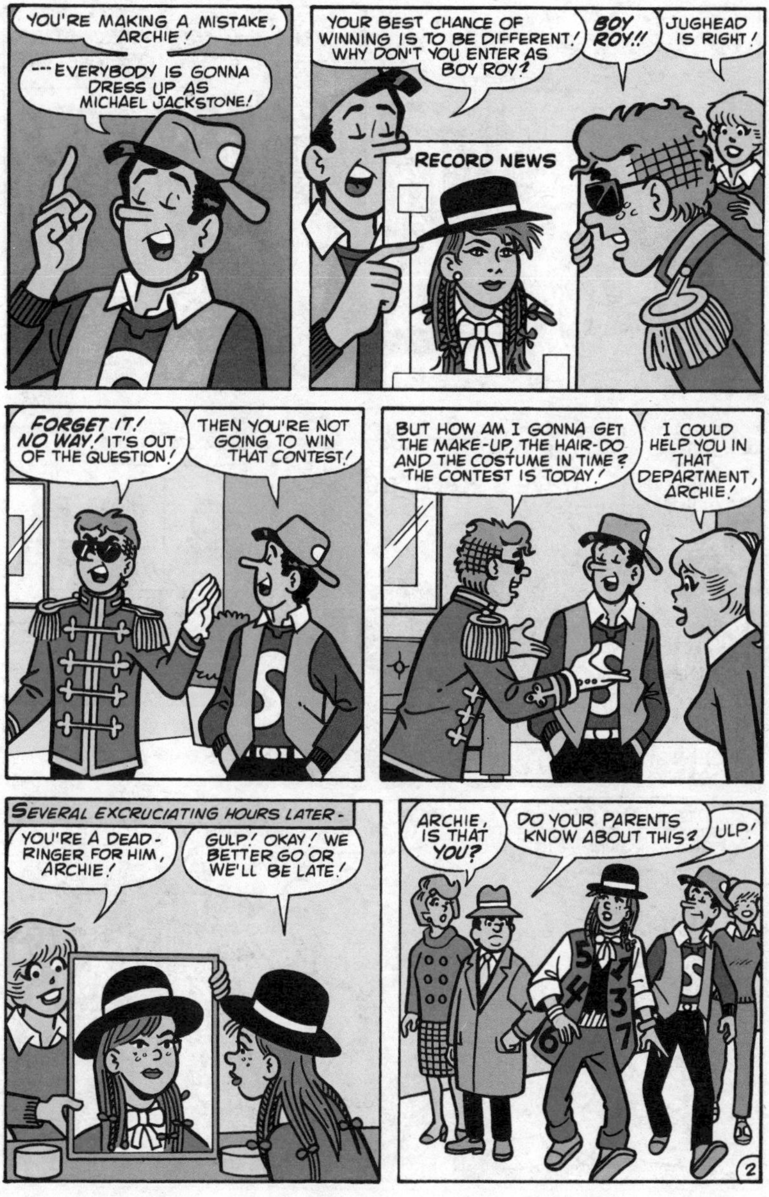
YOU'RE MAKING A MISTAKE, ARCHIE!
---EVERYBODY IS GONNA DRESS UP AS MICHAEL JACKSTONE!
YOUR BEST CHANCE OF WINNING IS TO BE DIFFERENT! WHY DON'T YOU ENTER AS BOY ROY?
RECORD NEWS
BOY ROY!!
JUGHEAD IS RIGHT!
FORGET IT! NO WAY! IT'S OUT OF THE QUESTION!
THEN YOU'RE NOT GOING TO WIN THAT CONTEST!
BUT HOW AM I GONNA GET THE MAKE-UP, THE HAIR-DO AND THE COSTUME IN TIME? THE CONTEST IS TODAY!
I COULD HELP YOU IN THAT DEPARTMENT, ARCHIE!
SEVERAL EXCRUCIATING HOURS LATER-
YOU'RE A DEAD-RINGER FOR HIM, ARCHIE!
GULP! OKAY! WE BETTER GO OR WE'LL BE LATE!
ARCHIE, IS THAT YOU?
DO YOUR PARENTS KNOW ABOUT THIS?
ULP!
2

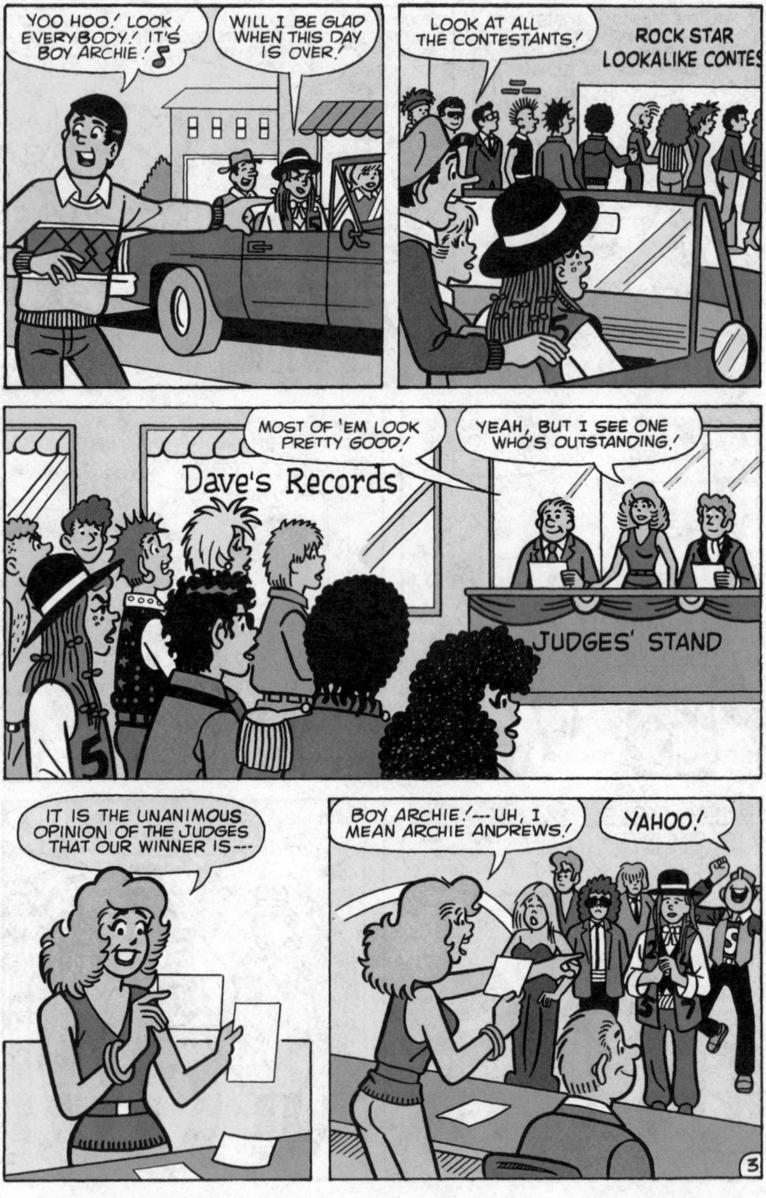
YOO HOO! LOOK, EVERYBODY! IT'S BOY ARCHIE!
WILL I BE GLAD WHEN THIS DAY IS OVER!
LOOK AT ALL THE CONTESTANTS!
ROCK STAR LOOKALIKE CONTES
MOST OF 'EM LOOK PRETTY GOOD!
YEAH, BUT I SEE ONE WHO'S OUTSTANDING!
Dave's Records
JUDGES' STAND
IT IS THE UNANIMOUS OPINION OF THE JUDGES THAT OUR WINNER IS---
BOY ARCHIE!--- UH, I MEAN ARCHIE ANDREWS!
YAHOO!
3

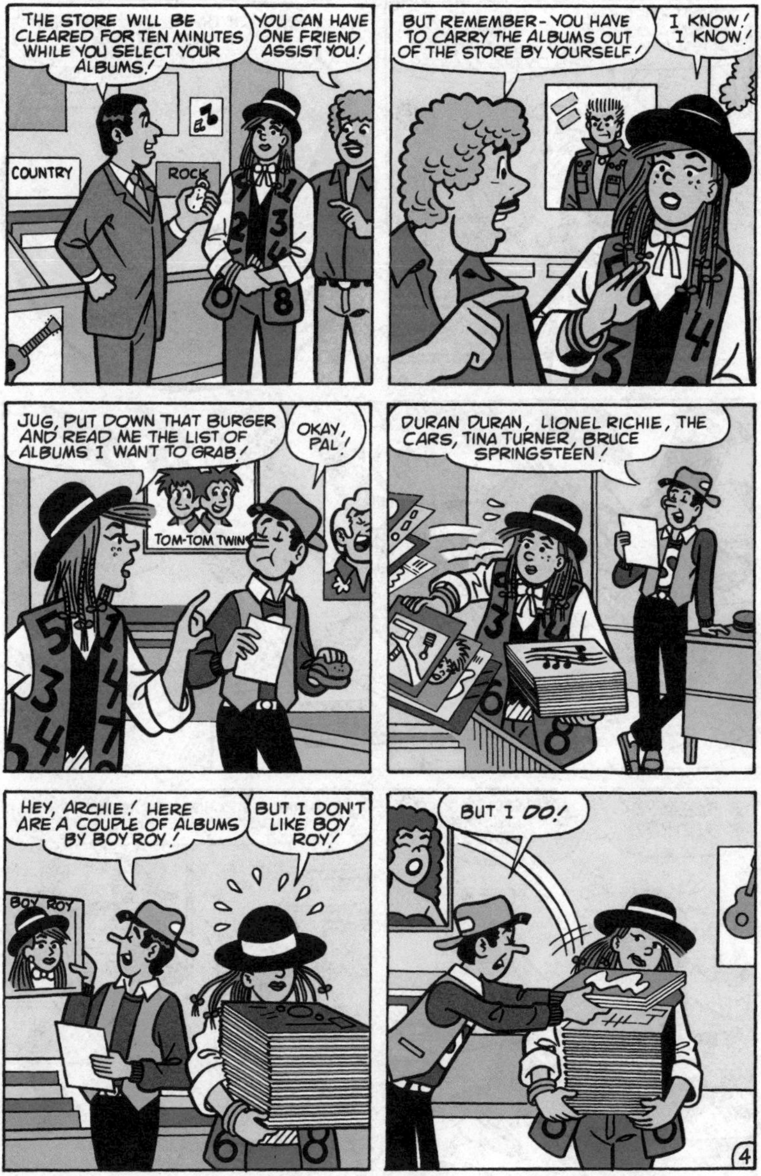
THE STORE WILL BE CLEARED FOR TEN MINUTES WHILE YOU SELECT YOUR ALBUMS!
YOU CAN HAVE ONE FRIEND ASSIST YOU!
COUNTRY
ROCK
BUT REMEMBER- YOU HAVE TO CARRY THE ALBUMS OUT OF THE STORE BY YOURSELF!
I KNOW! I KNOW!
JUG, PUT DOWN THAT BURGER AND READ ME THE LIST OF ALBUMS I WANT TO GRAB!
OKAY, PAL!
TOM-TOM TWIN
DURAN DURAN, LIONEL RICHIE, THE CARS, TINA TURNER, BRUCE SPRINGSTEEN!
HEY, ARCHIE! HERE ARE A COUPLE OF ALBUMS BY BOY ROY!
BUT I DON'T LIKE BOY ROY!
BOY ROY
BUT I DO!
4

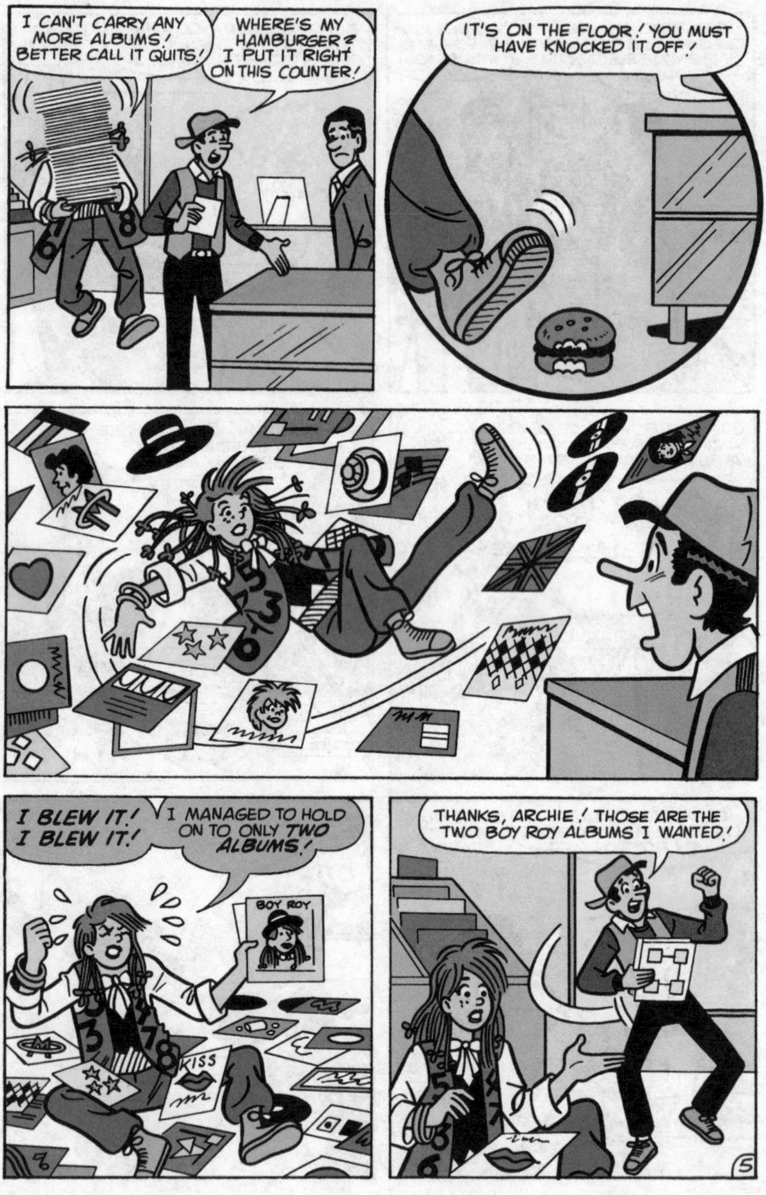
I CAN'T CARRY ANY MORE ALBUMS! BETTER CALL IT QUITS!
WHERE'S MY HAMBURGER? I PUT IT RIGHT ON THIS COUNTER!
IT'S ON THE FLOOR! YOU MUST HAVE KNOCKED IT OFF!
I BLEW IT! I BLEW IT!
I MANAGED TO HOLD ON TO ONLY TWO ALBUMS!
BOY ROY
KISS
THANKS, ARCHIE! THOSE ARE THE TWO BOY ROY ALBUMS I WANTED!
5

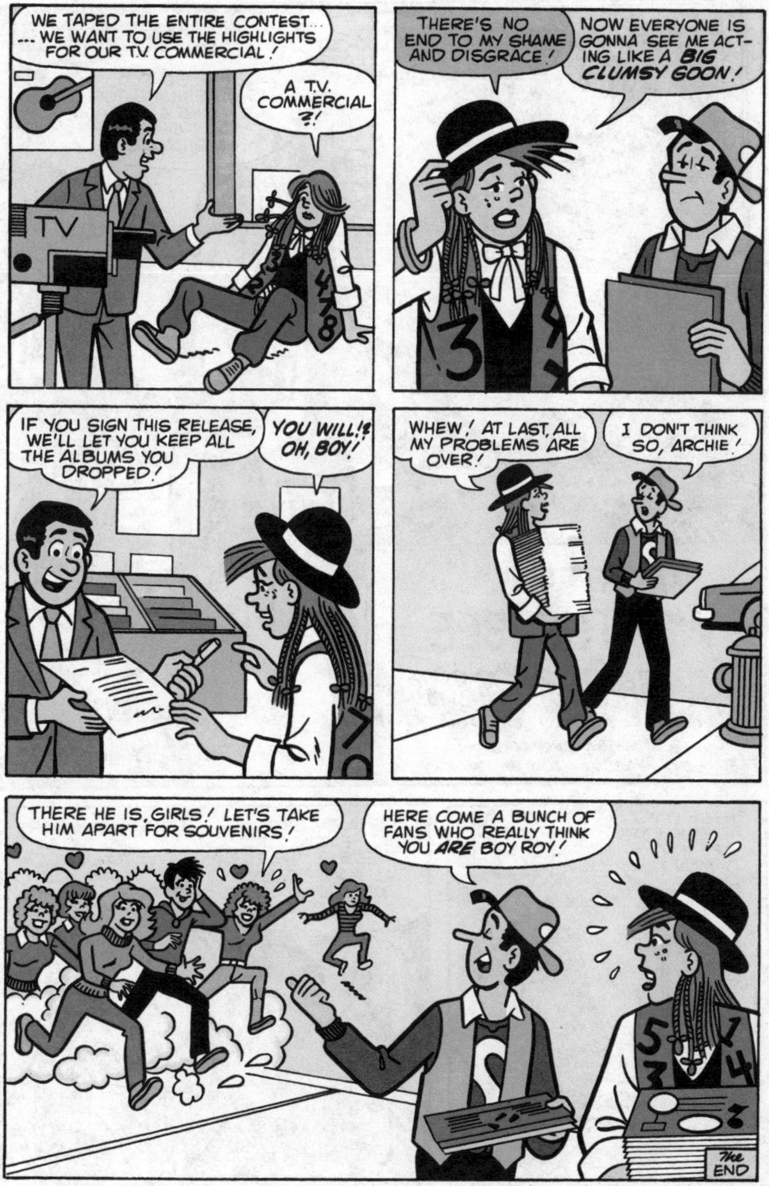
WE TAPED THE ENTIRE CONTEST... ...WE WANT TO USE THE HIGHLIGHTS FOR OUR T.V. COMMERCIAL!
A T.V. COMMERCIAL ?!
THERE'S NO END TO MY SHAME AND DISGRACE!
NOW EVERYONE IS GONNA SEE ME ACTING LIKE A BIG CLUMSY GOON!
IF YOU SIGN THIS RELEASE, WE'LL LET YOU KEEP ALL THE ALBUMS YOU DROPPED!
YOU WILL!? OH, BOY!
WHEW! AT LAST, ALL MY PROBLEMS ARE OVER!
I DON'T THINK SO, ARCHIE!
THERE HE IS, GIRLS! LET'S TAKE HIM APART FOR SOUVENIRS!
HERE COME A BUNCH OF FANS WHO REALLY THINK YOU ARE BOY ROY!
The END

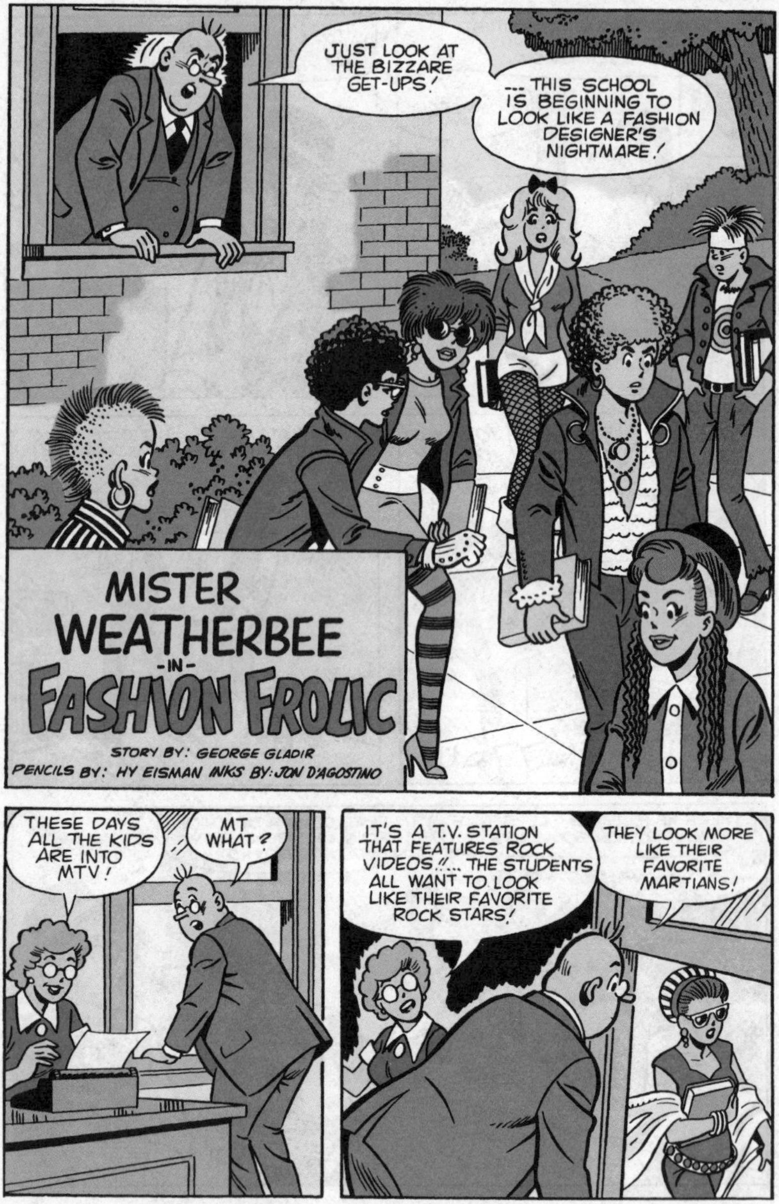
JUST LOOK AT THE BIZZARE GET-UPS!
... THIS SCHOOL IS BEGINNING TO LOOK LIKE A FASHION DESIGNER'S NIGHTMARE!
MISTER WEATHERBEE -IN- FASHION FROLIC
STORY BY: GEORGE GLADIR
PENCILS BY: HY EISMAN INKS BY: JON D'AGOSTINO
THESE DAYS ALL THE KIDS ARE INTO MTV!
MT WHAT?
IT'S A T.V. STATION THAT FEATURES ROCK VIDEOS!!... THE STUDENTS ALL WANT TO LOOK LIKE THEIR FAVORITE ROCK STARS!
THEY LOOK MORE LIKE THEIR FAVORITE MARTIANS!

Originally presented in ARCHIE'S PALS 'N' GALS #176, July, 1985

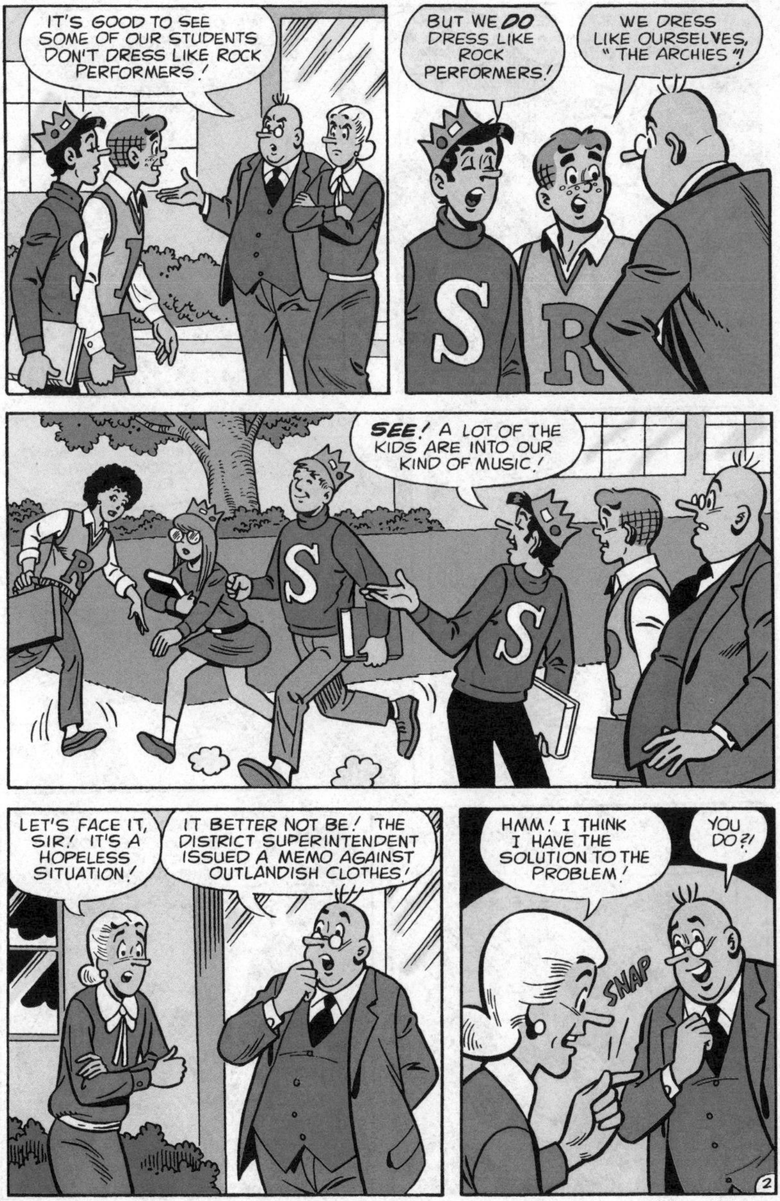
IT'S GOOD TO SEE SOME OF OUR STUDENTS DON'T DRESS LIKE ROCK PERFORMERS!
BUT WE DO DRESS LIKE ROCK PERFORMERS!
WE DRESS LIKE OURSELVES, "THE ARCHIES"!
SEE! A LOT OF THE KIDS ARE INTO OUR KIND OF MUSIC!
LET'S FACE IT, SIR! IT'S A HOPELESS SITUATION!
IT BETTER NOT BE! THE DISTRICT SUPERINTENDENT ISSUED A MEMO AGAINST OUTLANDISH CLOTHES!
HMM! I THINK I HAVE THE SOLUTION TO THE PROBLEM!
YOU DO?!
SNAP
2

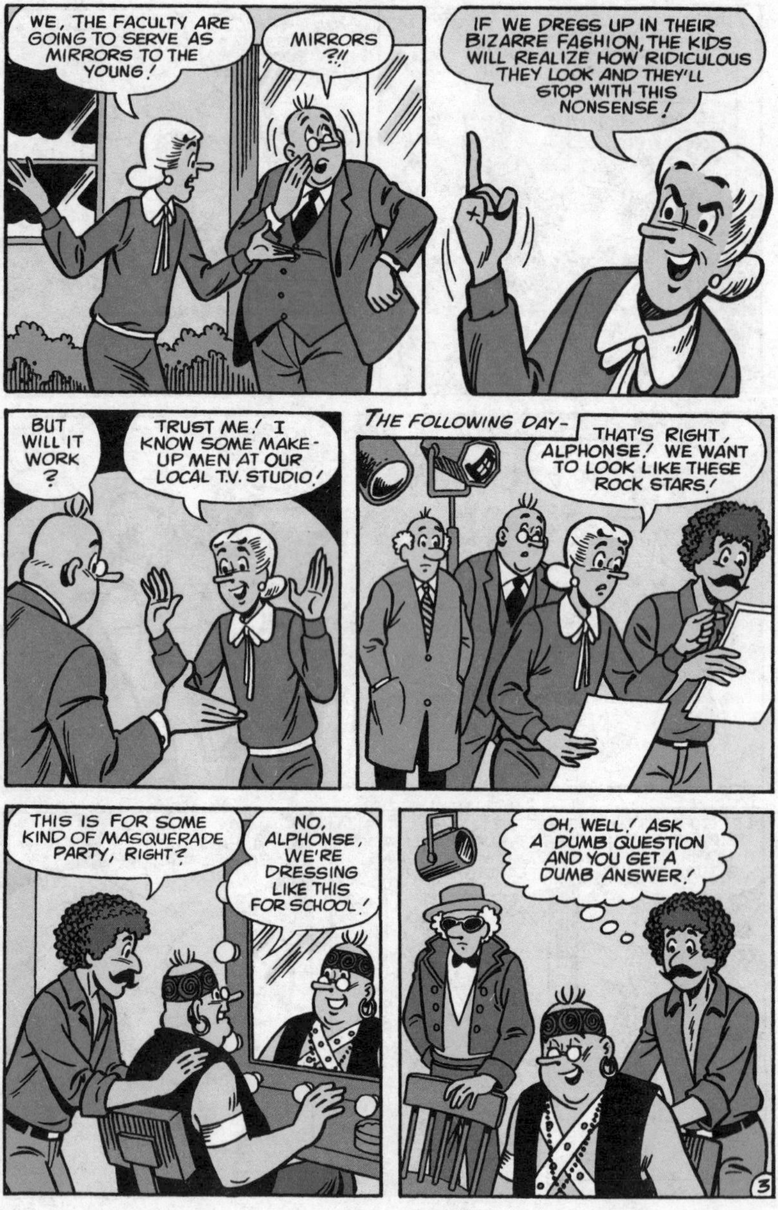
WE, THE FACULTY ARE GOING TO SERVE AS MIRRORS TO THE YOUNG!
MIRRORS ?!!
IF WE DRESS UP IN THEIR BIZARRE FASHION, THE KIDS WILL REALIZE HOW RIDICULOUS THEY LOOK AND THEY'LL STOP WITH THIS NONSENSE!
BUT WILL IT WORK ?
TRUST ME! I KNOW SOME MAKE-UP MEN AT OUR LOCAL T.V. STUDIO!
THE FOLLOWING DAY-
THAT'S RIGHT, ALPHONSE! WE WANT TO LOOK LIKE THESE ROCK STARS!
THIS IS FOR SOME KIND OF MASQUERADE PARTY, RIGHT?
NO, ALPHONSE, WE'RE DRESSING LIKE THIS FOR SCHOOL!
OH, WELL! ASK A DUMB QUESTION AND YOU GET A DUMB ANSWER!
3

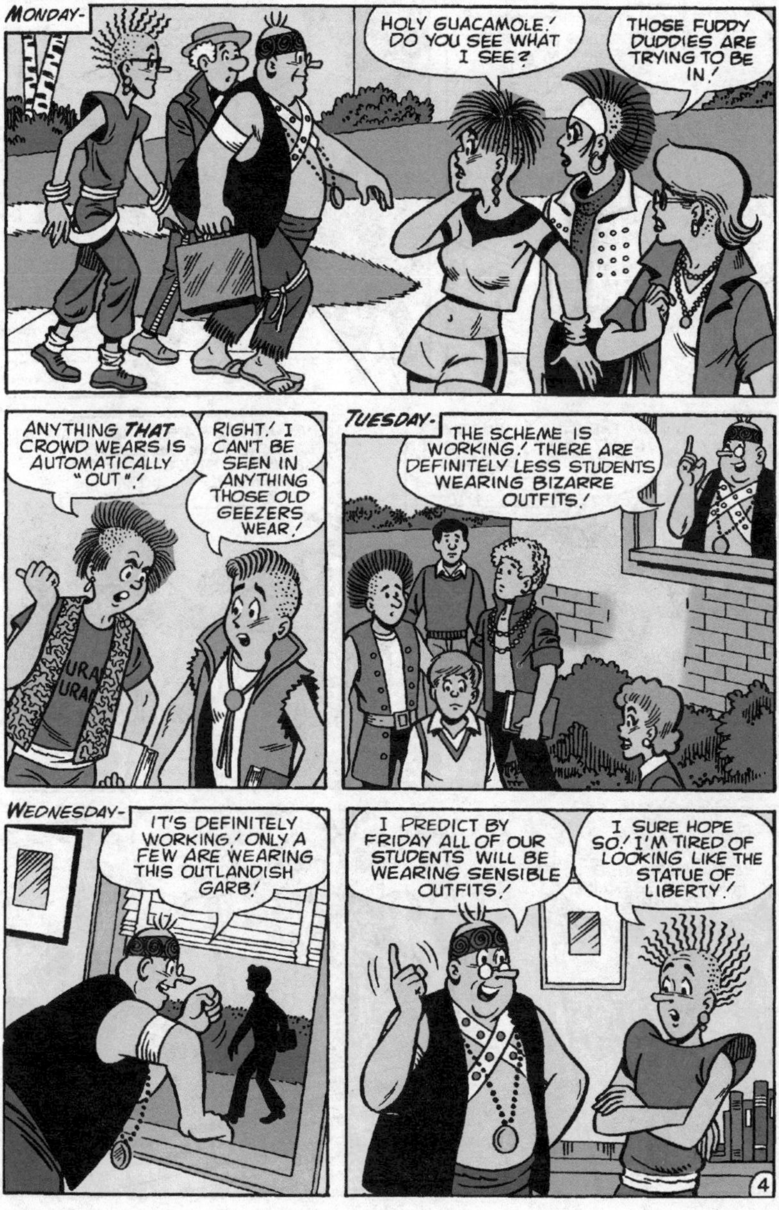
MONDAY-
HOLY GUACAMOLE! DO YOU SEE WHAT I SEE?
THOSE FUDDY DUDDIES ARE TRYING TO BE IN!
ANYTHING THAT CROWD WEARS IS AUTOMATICALLY "OUT"!
RIGHT! I CAN'T BE SEEN IN ANYTHING THOSE OLD GEEZERS WEAR!
TUESDAY-
THE SCHEME IS WORKING! THERE ARE DEFINITELY LESS STUDENTS WEARING BIZARRE OUTFITS!
WEDNESDAY-
IT'S DEFINITELY WORKING! ONLY A FEW ARE WEARING THIS OUTLANDISH GARB!
I PREDICT BY FRIDAY ALL OF OUR STUDENTS WILL BE WEARING SENSIBLE OUTFITS!
I SURE HOPE SO! I'M TIRED OF LOOKING LIKE THE STATUE OF LIBERTY!
4

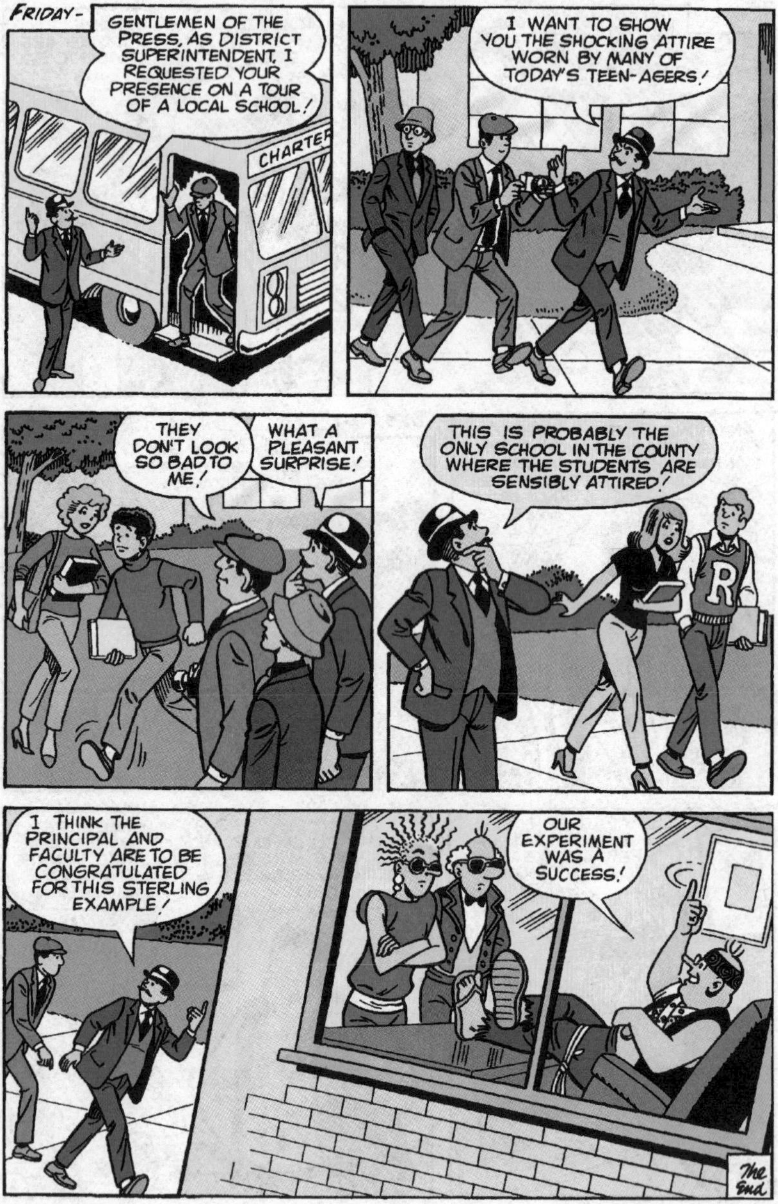
FRIDAY-
GENTLEMEN OF THE PRESS, AS DISTRICT SUPERINTENDENT, I REQUESTED YOUR PRESENCE ON A TOUR OF A LOCAL SCHOOL!
CHARTER
I WANT TO SHOW YOU THE SHOCKING ATTIRE WORN BY MANY OF TODAY'S TEEN-AGERS!
THEY DON'T LOOK SO BAD TO ME!
WHAT A PLEASANT SURPRISE!
THIS IS PROBABLY THE ONLY SCHOOL IN THE COUNTY WHERE THE STUDENTS ARE SENSIBLY ATTIRED!
I THINK THE PRINCIPAL AND FACULTY ARE TO BE CONGRATULATED FOR THIS STERLING EXAMPLE!
OUR EXPERIMENT WAS A SUCCESS!
The End

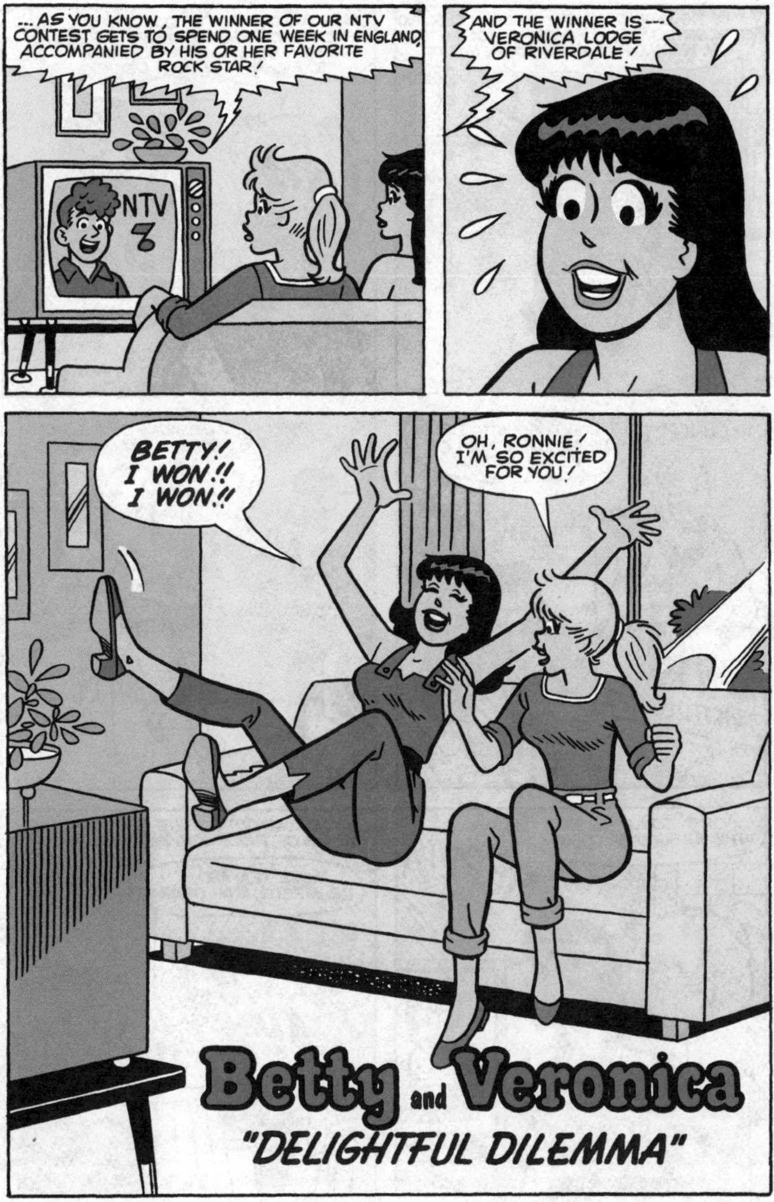
...AS YOU KNOW, THE WINNER OF OUR NTV CONTEST GETS TO SPEND ONE WEEK IN ENGLAND ACCOMPANIED BY HIS OR HER FAVORITE ROCK STAR!
NTV
AND THE WINNER IS --- VERONICA LODGE OF RIVERDALE!
BETTY! I WON!! I WON!!
OH, RONNIE! I'M SO EXCITED FOR YOU!
Betty and Veronica
"DELIGHTFUL DILEMMA"

Originally presented in ARCHIE GIANT SERIES #550, August, 1985

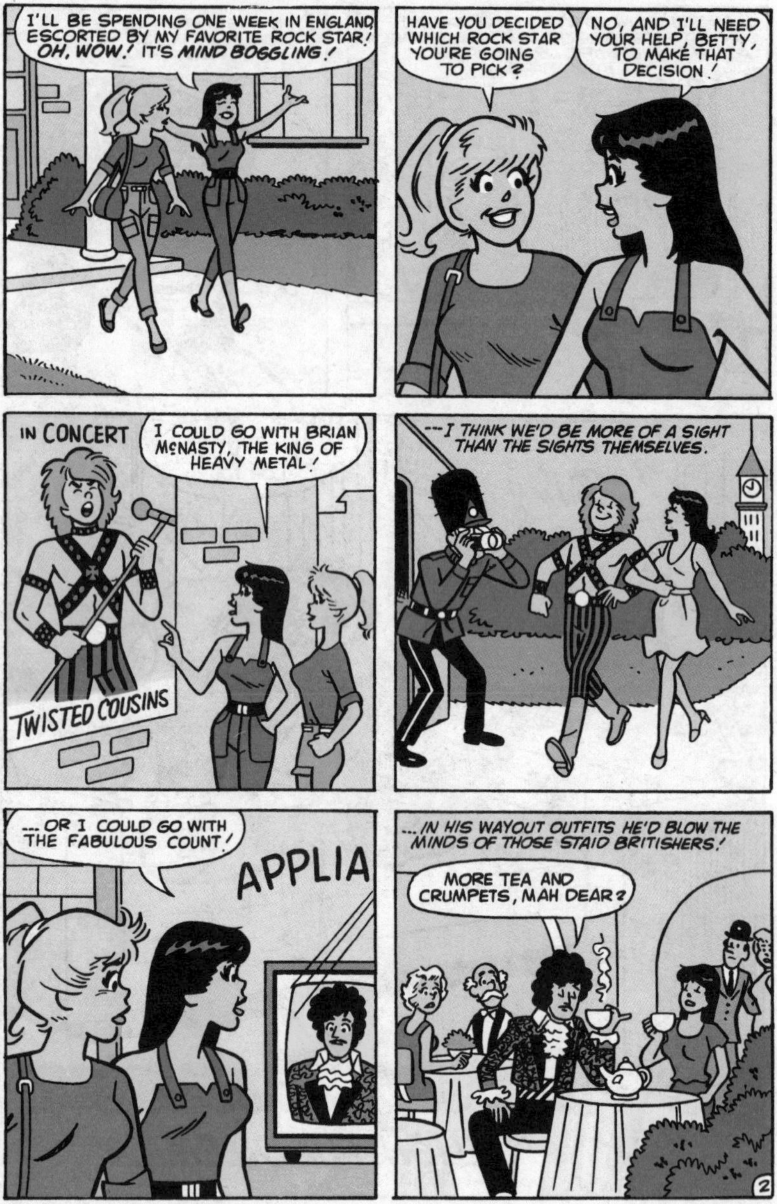
I'LL BE SPENDING ONE WEEK IN ENGLAND ESCORTED BY MY FAVORITE ROCK STAR! OH, WOW! IT'S MIND BOGGLING!
HAVE YOU DECIDED WHICH ROCK STAR YOU'RE GOING TO PICK?
NO, AND I'LL NEED YOUR HELP, BETTY, TO MAKE THAT DECISION!
IN CONCERT
TWISTED COUSINS
I COULD GO WITH BRIAN McNASTY, THE KING OF HEAVY METAL!
---I THINK WE'D BE MORE OF A SIGHT THAN THE SIGHTS THEMSELVES.
--- OR I COULD GO WITH THE FABULOUS COUNT!
APPLIA
...IN HIS WAYOUT OUTFITS HE'D BLOW THE MINDS OF THOSE STAID BRITISHERS!
MORE TEA AND CRUMPETS, MAH DEAR?
2

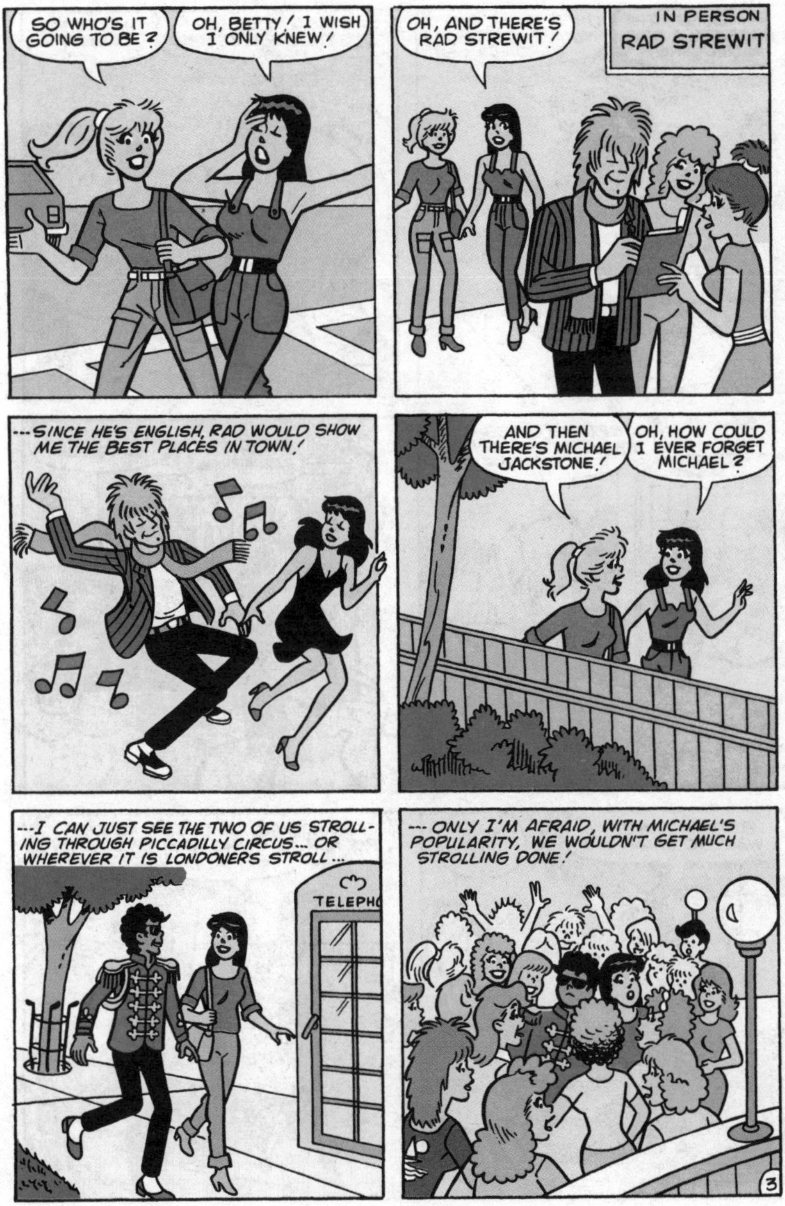
SO WHO'S IT GOING TO BE?
OH, BETTY! I WISH I ONLY KNEW!
OH, AND THERE'S RAD STREWIT!
IN PERSON
RAD STREWIT
---SINCE HE'S ENGLISH, RAD WOULD SHOW ME THE BEST PLACES IN TOWN!
AND THEN THERE'S MICHAEL JACKSTONE!
OH, HOW COULD I EVER FORGET MICHAEL?
---I CAN JUST SEE THE TWO OF US STROLL-ING THROUGH PICCADILLY CIRCUS... OR WHEREVER IT IS LONDONERS STROLL...
TELEPHO
--- ONLY I'M AFRAID, WITH MICHAEL'S POPULARITY, WE WOULDN'T GET MUCH STROLLING DONE!
3

SO YOU SEE THE PROBLEM I HAVE IN DECIDING!
OH, IF ONLY I HAD *YOUR* PROBLEM, VERONICA!
---INSTEAD I'LL HAVE TO SETTLE FOR SECOND BEST!
WHAT DO YOU MEAN?
CAN'T YOU GUESS WITH WHOM I'LL BE COZYING UP WITH?
The Archies
SIGH! OH, ARCHIEKINS!
MY PRECIOUS BUTTERCUP!
BETTY, DEAREST, I WANT TO THANK YOU!
FOR WHAT?
FOR HELPING ME DECIDE WHICH ROCKER IS GOING TO BE MY LONDON ESCORT!
?
4

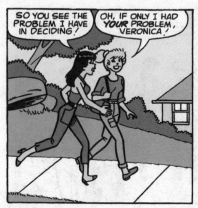

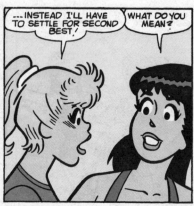

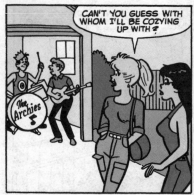

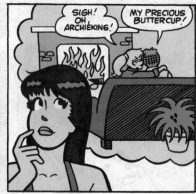

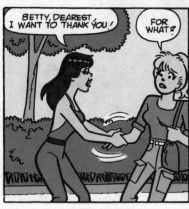

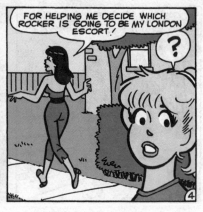

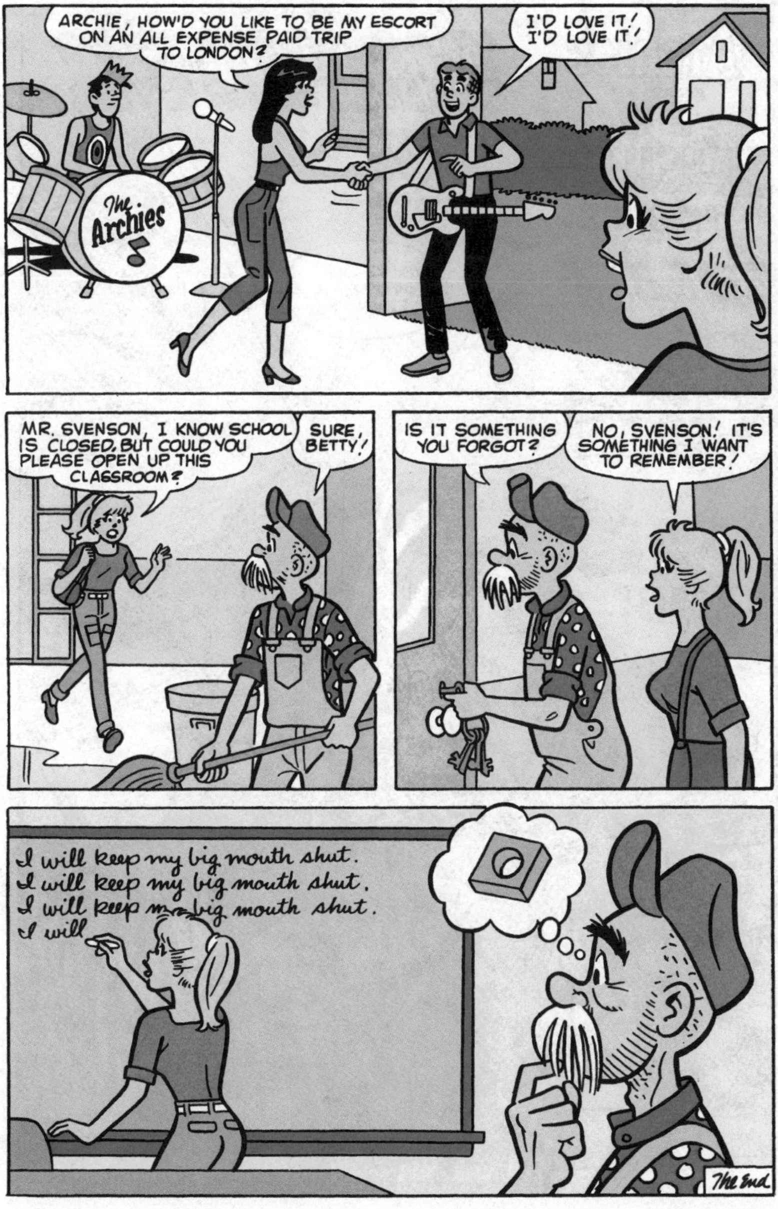
ARCHIE, HOW'D YOU LIKE TO BE MY ESCORT ON AN ALL EXPENSE PAID TRIP TO LONDON?
I'D LOVE IT! I'D LOVE IT!
The Archies
MR. SVENSON, I KNOW SCHOOL IS CLOSED, BUT COULD YOU PLEASE OPEN UP THIS CLASSROOM?
SURE, BETTY!
IS IT SOMETHING YOU FORGOT?
NO, SVENSON! IT'S SOMETHING I WANT TO REMEMBER!
I will keep my big mouth shut.
I will keep my big mouth shut.
I will keep my big mouth shut.
I will
The End

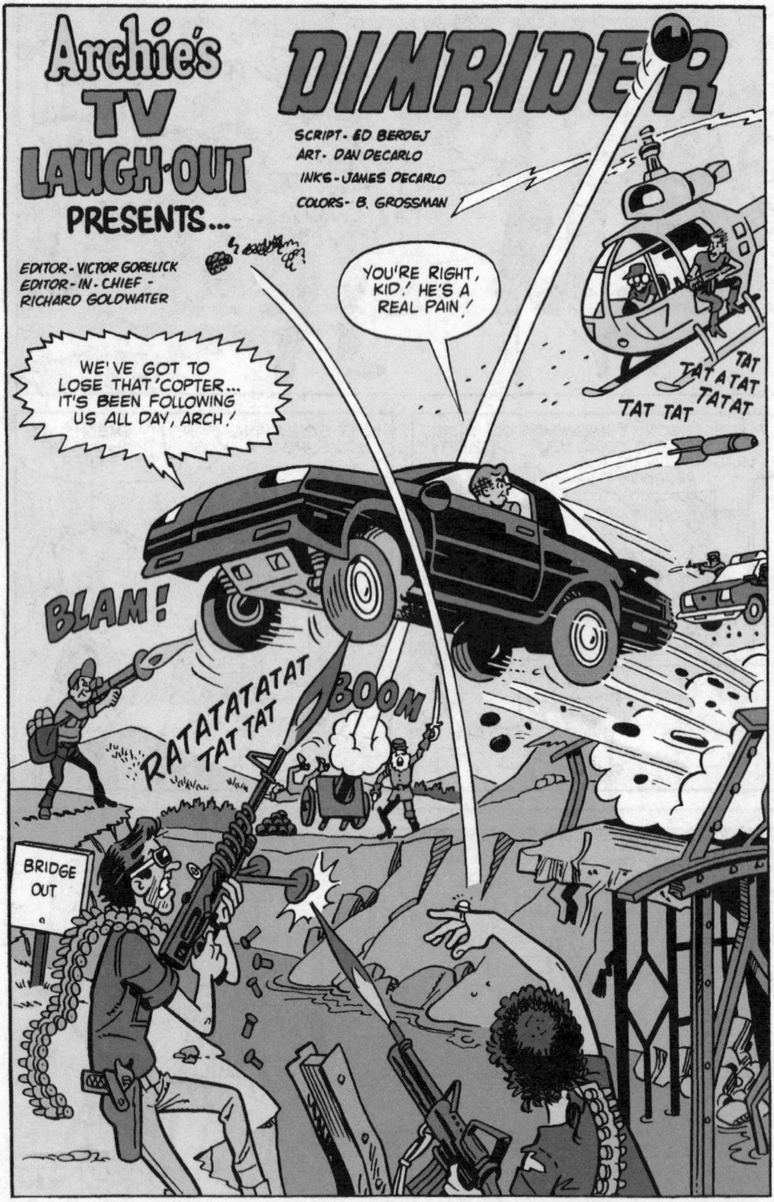

Archie's TV LAUGH-OUT PRESENTS...
DIMRIDER
SCRIPT- ED BERDEJ
ART- DAN DECARLO
INKS- JAMES DECARLO
COLORS- B. GROSSMAN
EDITOR-VICTOR GORELICK
EDITOR-IN-CHIEF - RICHARD GOLDWATER
WE'VE GOT TO LOSE THAT 'COPTER... IT'S BEEN FOLLOWING US ALL DAY, ARCH!
YOU'RE RIGHT, KID! HE'S A REAL PAIN!
TAT TATATAT TATAT TAT TAT
BLAM!
RATATATATAT TAT TAT
BOOM
BRIDGE OUT


Originally presented in ARCHIE'S TV LAUGH-OUT #102, August, 1985

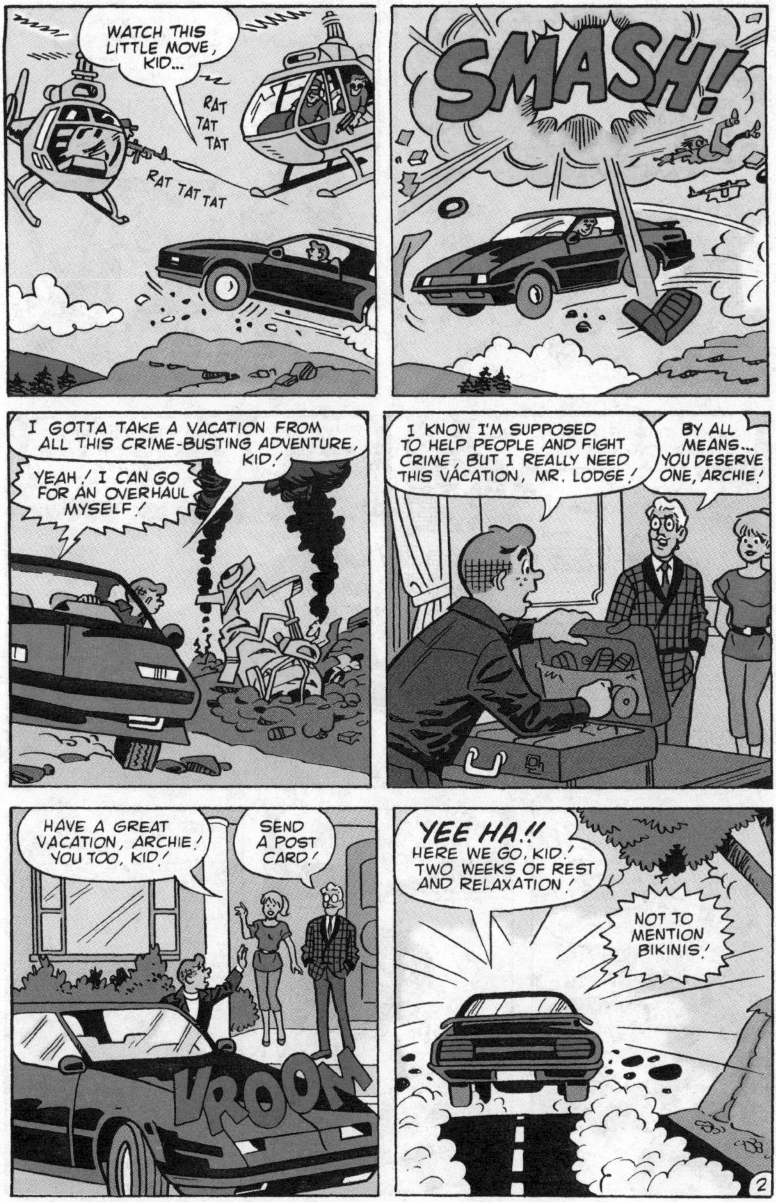
WATCH THIS LITTLE MOVE, KID...
RAT TAT TAT
RAT TAT TAT
SMASH!
I GOTTA TAKE A VACATION FROM ALL THIS CRIME-BUSTING ADVENTURE, KID!
YEAH! I CAN GO FOR AN OVERHAUL MYSELF!
I KNOW I'M SUPPOSED TO HELP PEOPLE AND FIGHT CRIME, BUT I REALLY NEED THIS VACATION, MR. LODGE!
BY ALL MEANS... YOU DESERVE ONE, ARCHIE!
HAVE A GREAT VACATION, ARCHIE! YOU TOO, KID!
SEND A POST CARD!
VROOM
YEE HA!! HERE WE GO, KID! TWO WEEKS OF REST AND RELAXATION!
NOT TO MENTION BIKINIS!
2

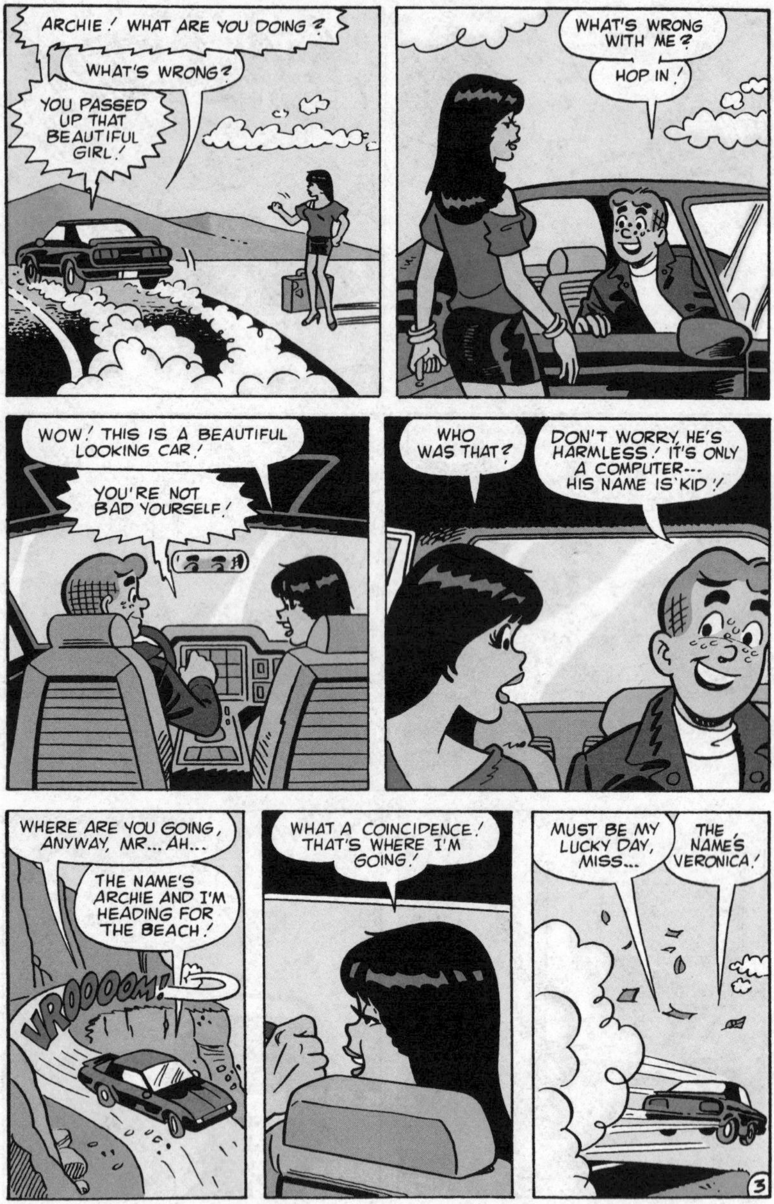
ARCHIE! WHAT ARE YOU DOING?
WHAT'S WRONG?
YOU PASSED UP THAT BEAUTIFUL GIRL!
WHAT'S WRONG WITH ME?
HOP IN!
WOW! THIS IS A BEAUTIFUL LOOKING CAR!
YOU'RE NOT BAD YOURSELF!
WHO WAS THAT?
DON'T WORRY, HE'S HARMLESS! IT'S ONLY A COMPUTER--- HIS NAME IS 'KID'!
WHERE ARE YOU GOING, ANYWAY, MR... AH...
THE NAME'S ARCHIE AND I'M HEADING FOR THE BEACH!
VROOOOM!
WHAT A COINCIDENCE! THAT'S WHERE I'M GOING!
MUST BE MY LUCKY DAY, MISS...
THE NAME'S VERONICA!
3

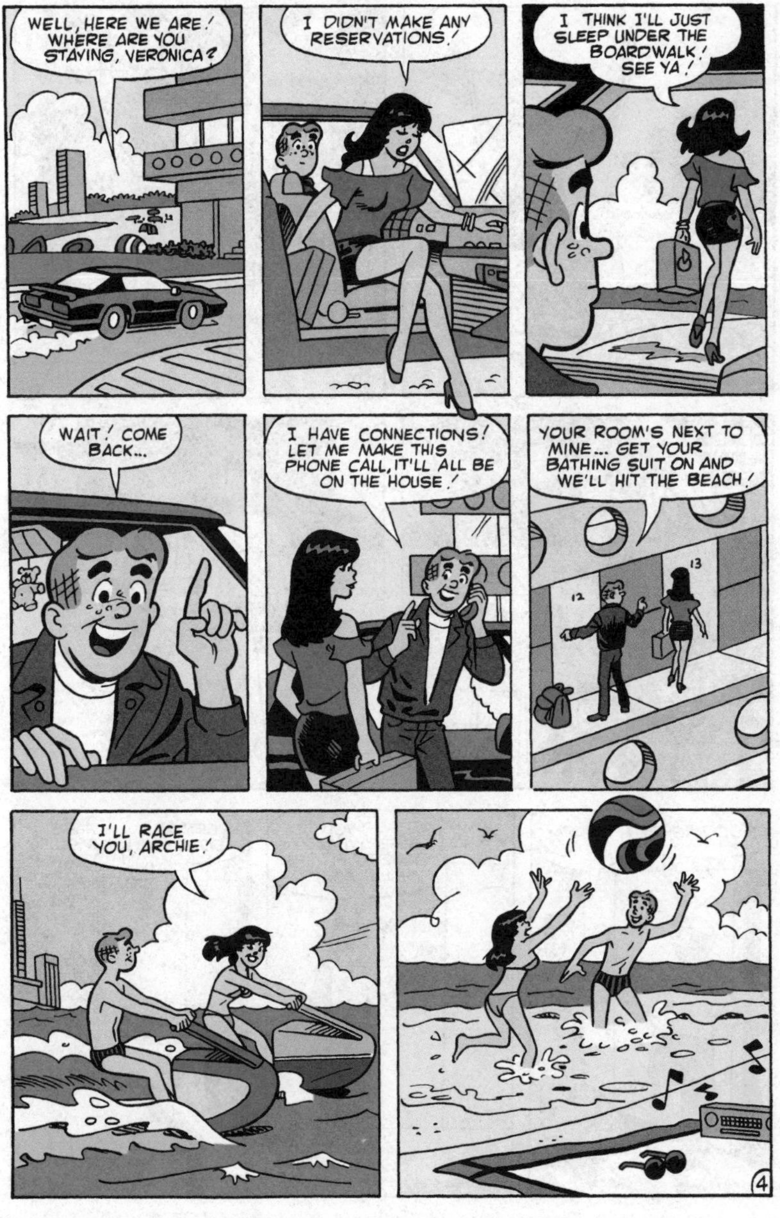
WELL, HERE WE ARE! WHERE ARE YOU STAYING, VERONICA?
I DIDN'T MAKE ANY RESERVATIONS!
I THINK I'LL JUST SLEEP UNDER THE BOARDWALK! SEE YA!
WAIT! COME BACK...
I HAVE CONNECTIONS! LET ME MAKE THIS PHONE CALL, IT'LL ALL BE ON THE HOUSE!
YOUR ROOM'S NEXT TO MINE... GET YOUR BATHING SUIT ON AND WE'LL HIT THE BEACH!
12
13
I'LL RACE YOU, ARCHIE!
4

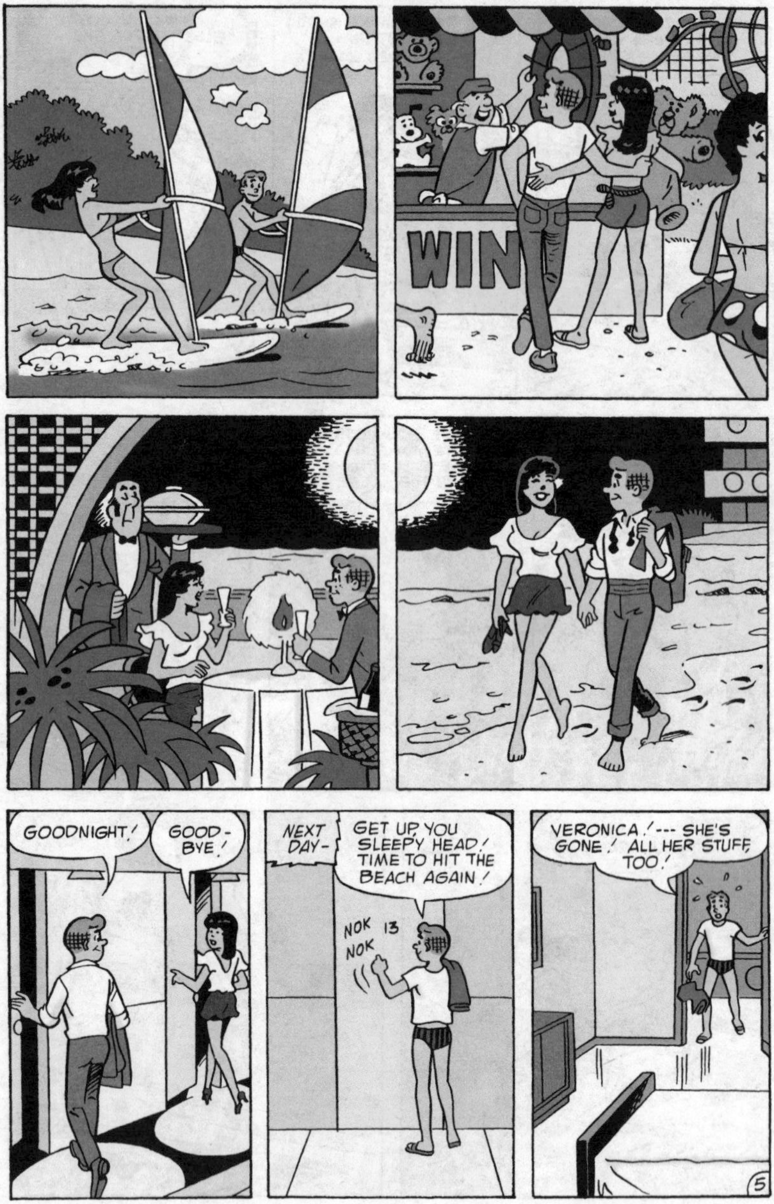
WIN
GOODNIGHT!
GOOD-BYE!
NEXT DAY-
GET UP, YOU SLEEPY HEAD! TIME TO HIT THE BEACH AGAIN!
NOK NOK
13
VERONICA!--- SHE'S GONE! ALL HER STUFF, TOO!
5

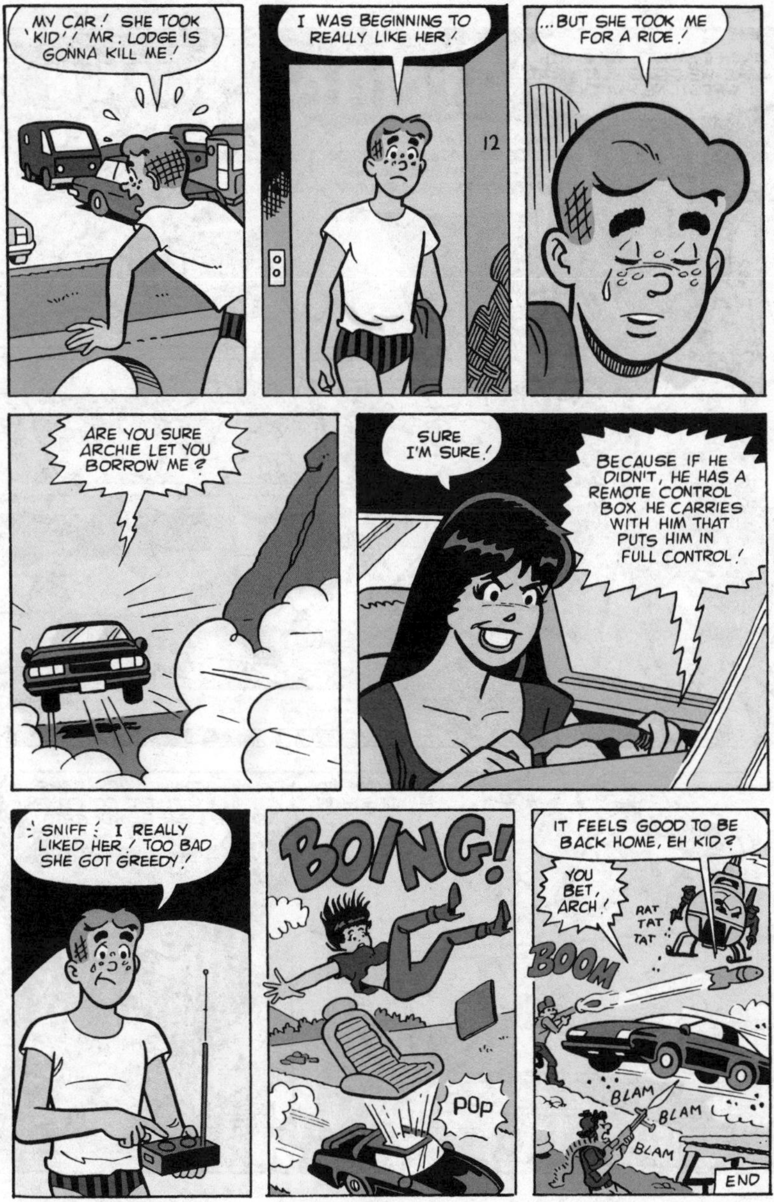
MY CAR! SHE TOOK 'KID'! MR. LODGE IS GONNA KILL ME!
I WAS BEGINNING TO REALLY LIKE HER!
12
...BUT SHE TOOK ME FOR A RIDE!
ARE YOU SURE ARCHIE LET YOU BORROW ME?
SURE I'M SURE!
BECAUSE IF HE DIDN'T, HE HAS A REMOTE CONTROL BOX HE CARRIES WITH HIM THAT PUTS HIM IN FULL CONTROL!
SNIFF! I REALLY LIKED HER! TOO BAD SHE GOT GREEDY!
BOING!
POP
IT FEELS GOOD TO BE BACK HOME, EH KID?
YOU BET, ARCH!
RAT TAT TAT
BOOM
BLAM
BLAM
BLAM
END

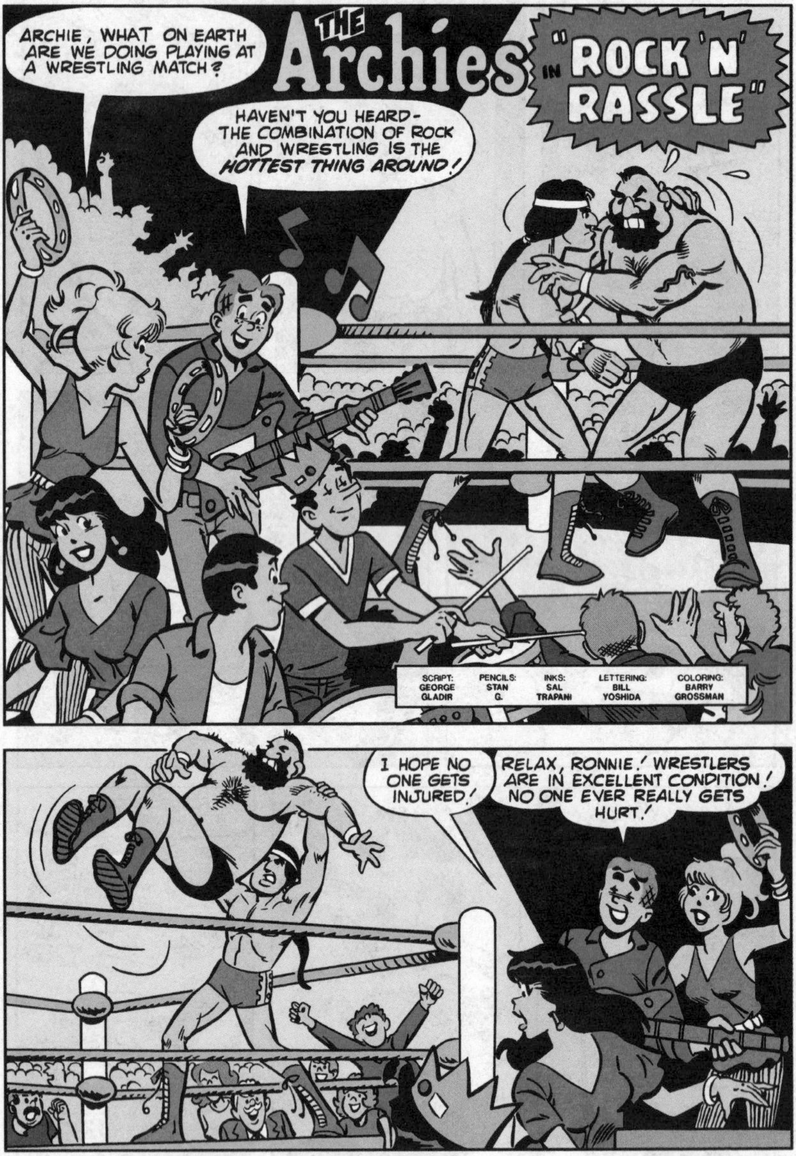
ARCHIE, WHAT ON EARTH ARE WE DOING PLAYING AT A WRESTLING MATCH?
THE Archies IN "ROCK 'N' RASSLE"
HAVEN'T YOU HEARD- THE COMBINATION OF ROCK AND WRESTLING IS THE HOTTEST THING AROUND!
SCRIPT: GEORGE GLADIR
PENCILS: STAN G.
INKS: SAL TRAPANI
LETTERING: BILL YOSHIDA
COLORING: BARRY GROSSMAN
I HOPE NO ONE GETS INJURED!
RELAX, RONNIE! WRESTLERS ARE IN EXCELLENT CONDITION! NO ONE EVER REALLY GETS HURT!

Originally presented in EVERYTHING'S ARCHIE #120, November, 1985

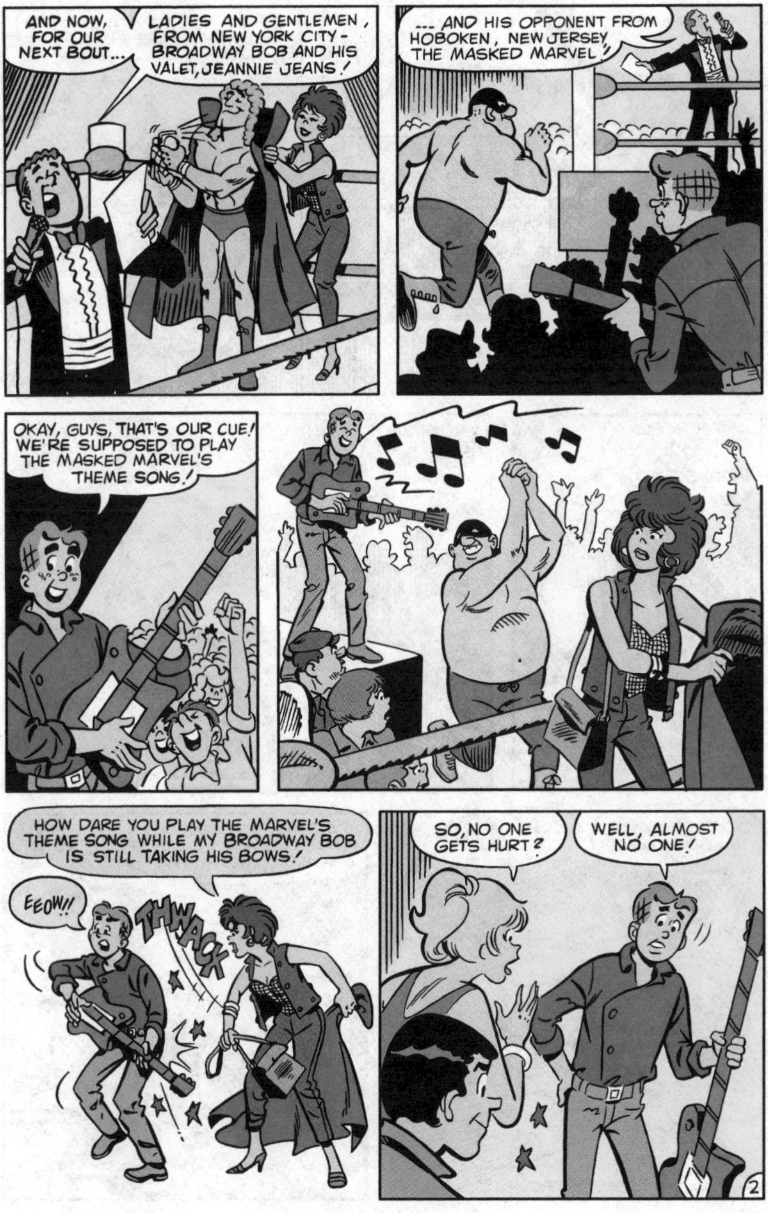
AND NOW, FOR OUR NEXT BOUT...
LADIES AND GENTLEMEN, FROM NEW YORK CITY - BROADWAY BOB AND HIS VALET, JEANNIE JEANS!
... AND HIS OPPONENT FROM HOBOKEN, NEW JERSEY THE MASKED MARVEL!
OKAY, GUYS, THAT'S OUR CUE! WE'RE SUPPOSED TO PLAY THE MASKED MARVEL'S THEME SONG!
HOW DARE YOU PLAY THE MARVEL'S THEME SONG WHILE MY BROADWAY BOB IS STILL TAKING HIS BOWS!
EEOW!!
THWACK
SO, NO ONE GETS HURT?
WELL, ALMOST NO ONE!
2

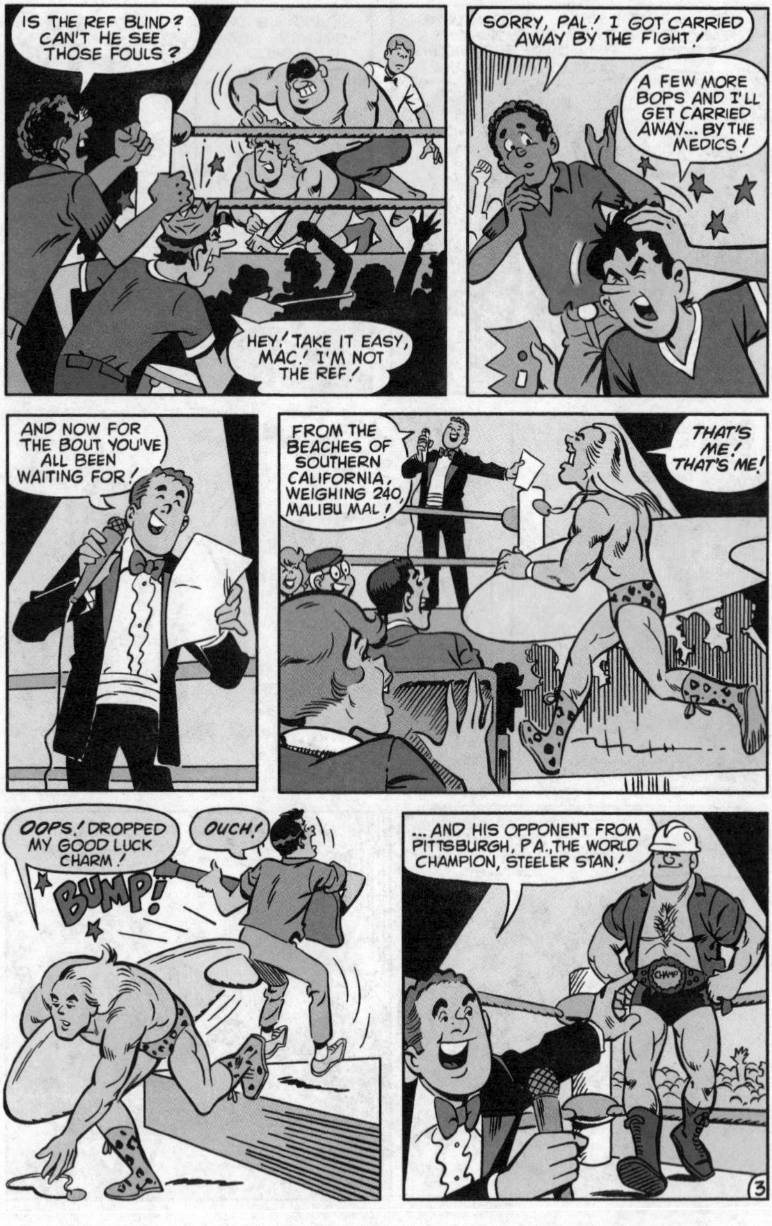
IS THE REF BLIND? CAN'T HE SEE THOSE FOULS?
HEY! TAKE IT EASY, MAC! I'M NOT THE REF!
SORRY, PAL! I GOT CARRIED AWAY BY THE FIGHT!
A FEW MORE BOPS AND I'LL GET CARRIED AWAY... BY THE MEDICS!
AND NOW FOR THE BOUT YOU'VE ALL BEEN WAITING FOR!
FROM THE BEACHES OF SOUTHERN CALIFORNIA, WEIGHING 240, MALIBU MAL!
THAT'S ME! THAT'S ME!
OOPS! DROPPED MY GOOD LUCK CHARM!
OUCH!
BUMP!
...AND HIS OPPONENT FROM PITTSBURGH, PA., THE WORLD CHAMPION, STEELER STAN!
CHAMP
3

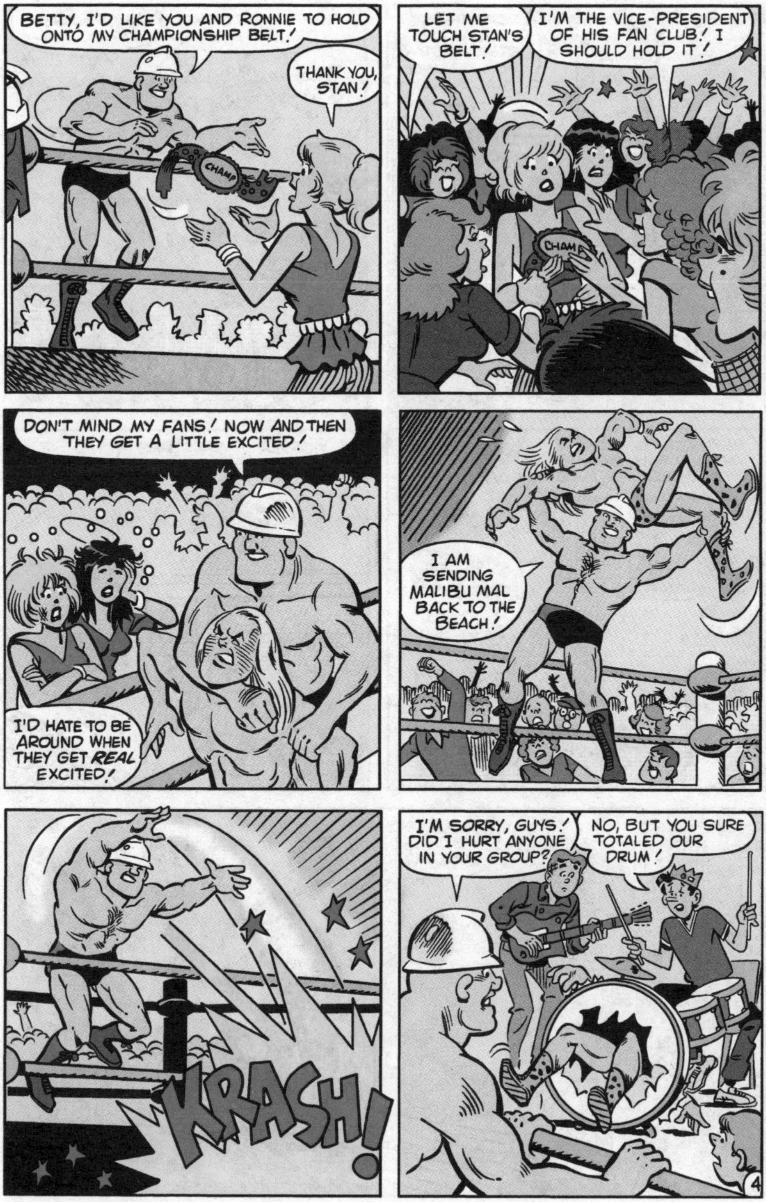
BETTY, I'D LIKE YOU AND RONNIE TO HOLD ONTO MY CHAMPIONSHIP BELT!
THANK YOU, STAN!
CHAMP
LET ME TOUCH STAN'S BELT!
I'M THE VICE-PRESIDENT OF HIS FAN CLUB! I SHOULD HOLD IT!
CHAMP
DON'T MIND MY FANS! NOW AND THEN THEY GET A LITTLE EXCITED!
I'D HATE TO BE AROUND WHEN THEY GET *REAL* EXCITED!
I AM SENDING MALIBU MAL BACK TO THE BEACH!
KRASH!
I'M SORRY, GUYS! DID I HURT ANYONE IN YOUR GROUP?
NO, BUT YOU SURE TOTALED OUR DRUM!
4

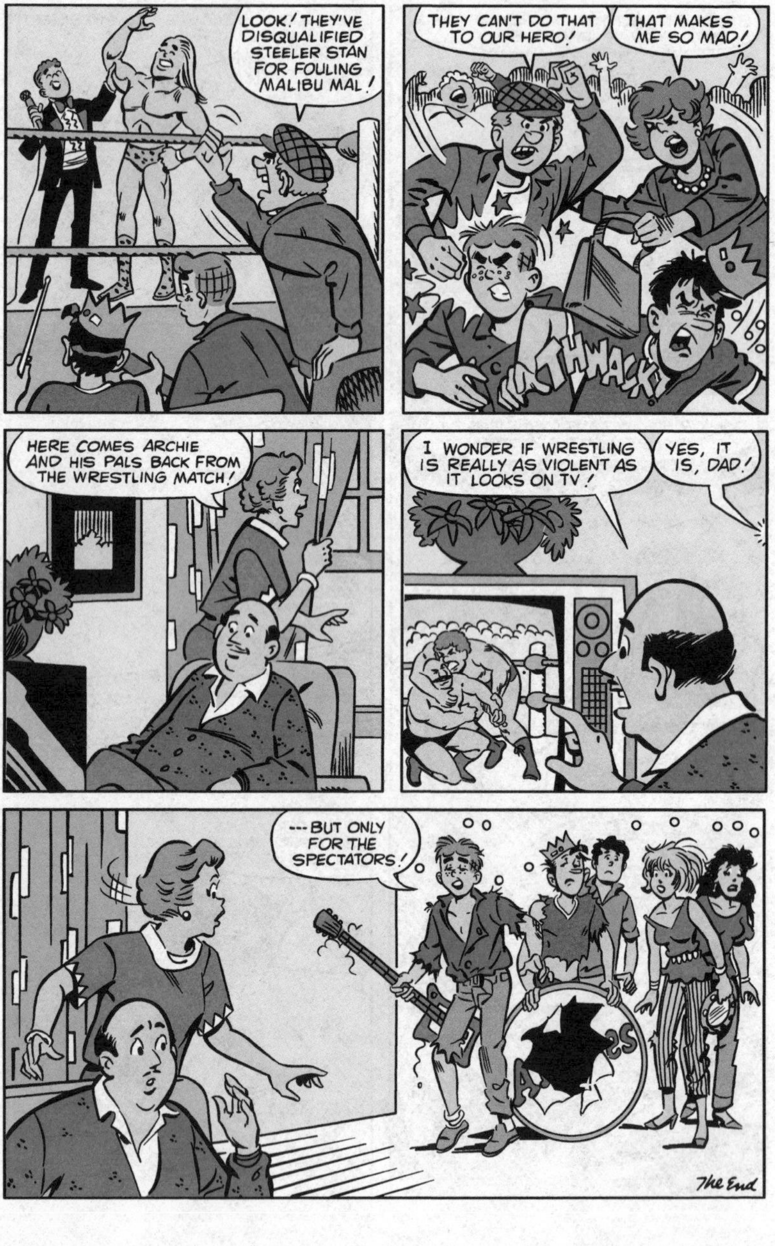
LOOK! THEY'VE DISQUALIFIED STEELER STAN FOR FOULING MALIBU MAL!
THEY CAN'T DO THAT TO OUR HERO!
THAT MAKES ME SO MAD!
THWACK!
HERE COMES ARCHIE AND HIS PALS BACK FROM THE WRESTLING MATCH!
I WONDER IF WRESTLING IS REALLY AS VIOLENT AS IT LOOKS ON TV!
YES, IT IS, DAD!
---BUT ONLY FOR THE SPECTATORS!
The End

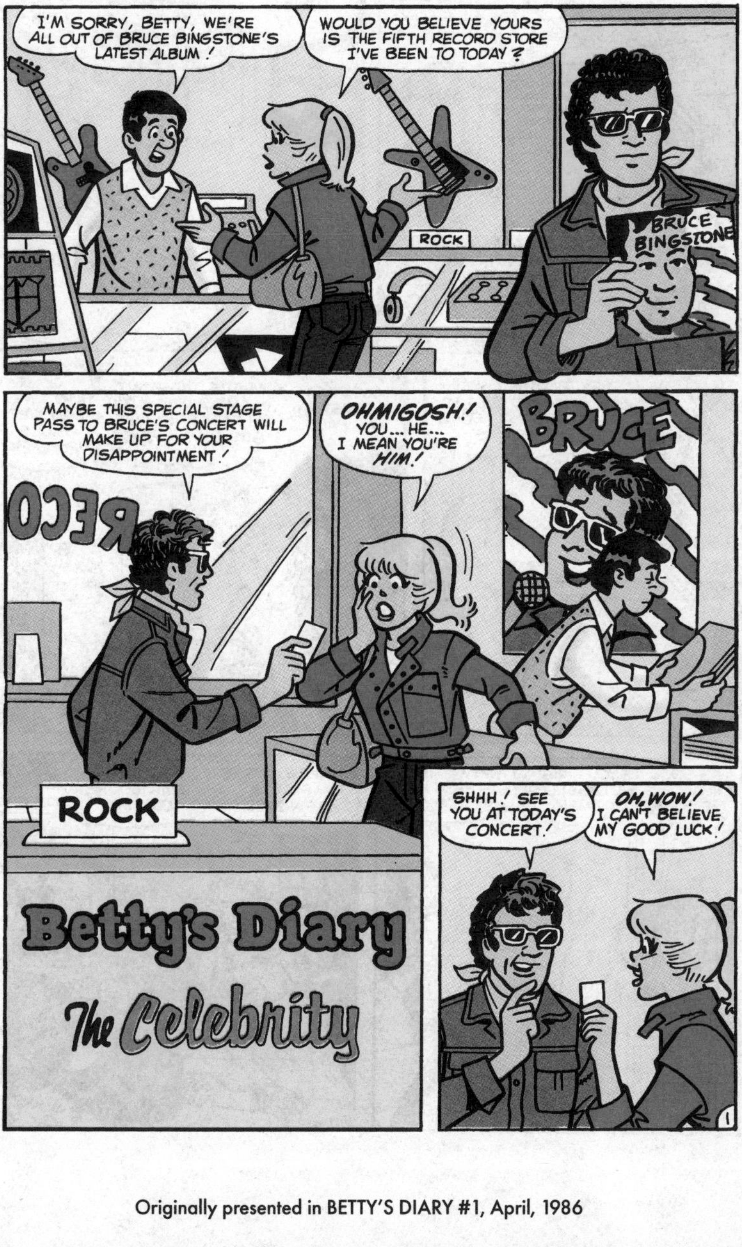
I'M SORRY, BETTY, WE'RE ALL OUT OF BRUCE BINGSTONE'S LATEST ALBUM!
WOULD YOU BELIEVE YOURS IS THE FIFTH RECORD STORE I'VE BEEN TO TODAY?
ROCK
BRUCE BINGSTONE
MAYBE THIS SPECIAL STAGE PASS TO BRUCE'S CONCERT WILL MAKE UP FOR YOUR DISAPPOINTMENT!
OHMIGOSH! YOU... HE... I MEAN YOU'RE HIM!
BRUCE
ROCK
Betty's Diary
The Celebrity
SHHH! SEE YOU AT TODAY'S CONCERT!
OH, WOW! I CAN'T BELIEVE MY GOOD LUCK!
1

Originally presented in BETTY'S DIARY #1, April, 1986

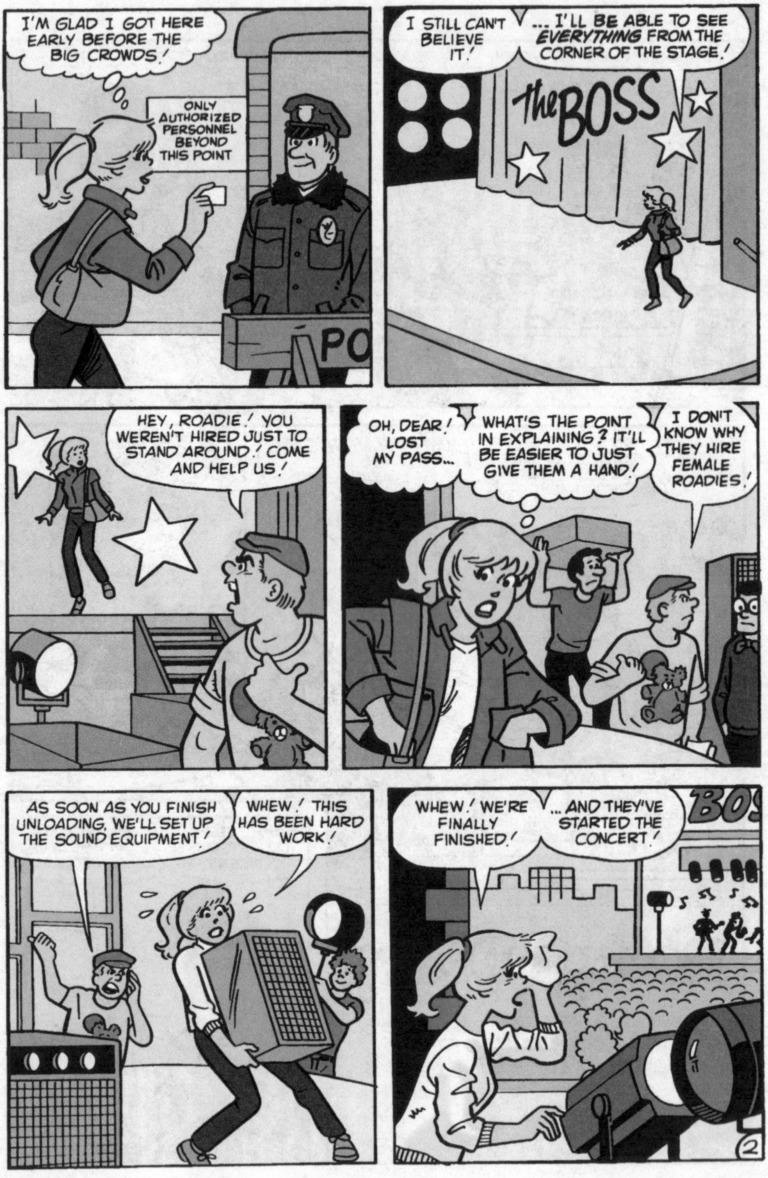
I'M GLAD I GOT HERE EARLY BEFORE THE BIG CROWDS!
ONLY AUTHORIZED PERSONNEL BEYOND THIS POINT
PO
I STILL CAN'T BELIEVE IT!
... I'LL BE ABLE TO SEE *EVERYTHING* FROM THE CORNER OF THE STAGE!
the BOSS
HEY, ROADIE! YOU WEREN'T HIRED JUST TO STAND AROUND! COME AND HELP US!
OH, DEAR! LOST MY PASS...
WHAT'S THE POINT IN EXPLAINING? IT'LL BE EASIER TO JUST GIVE THEM A HAND!
I DON'T KNOW WHY THEY HIRE FEMALE ROADIES!
AS SOON AS YOU FINISH UNLOADING, WE'LL SET UP THE SOUND EQUIPMENT!
WHEW! THIS HAS BEEN HARD WORK!
WHEW! WE'RE FINALLY FINISHED!
... AND THEY'VE STARTED THE CONCERT!
2

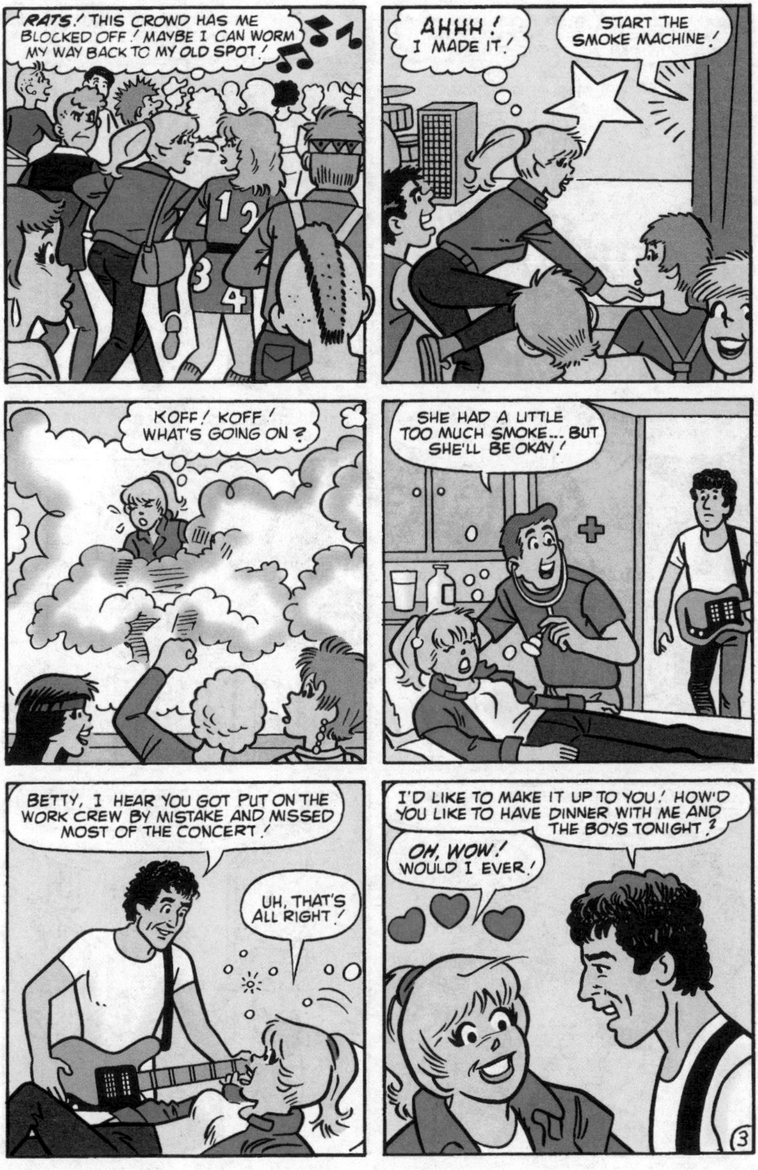
RATS! THIS CROWD HAS ME BLOCKED OFF! MAYBE I CAN WORM MY WAY BACK TO MY OLD SPOT!
AHHH! I MADE IT!
START THE SMOKE MACHINE!
KOFF! KOFF! WHAT'S GOING ON?
SHE HAD A LITTLE TOO MUCH SMOKE... BUT SHE'LL BE OKAY!
BETTY, I HEAR YOU GOT PUT ON THE WORK CREW BY MISTAKE AND MISSED MOST OF THE CONCERT!
UH, THAT'S ALL RIGHT!
I'D LIKE TO MAKE IT UP TO YOU! HOW'D YOU LIKE TO HAVE DINNER WITH ME AND THE BOYS TONIGHT?
OH, WOW! WOULD I EVER!
3

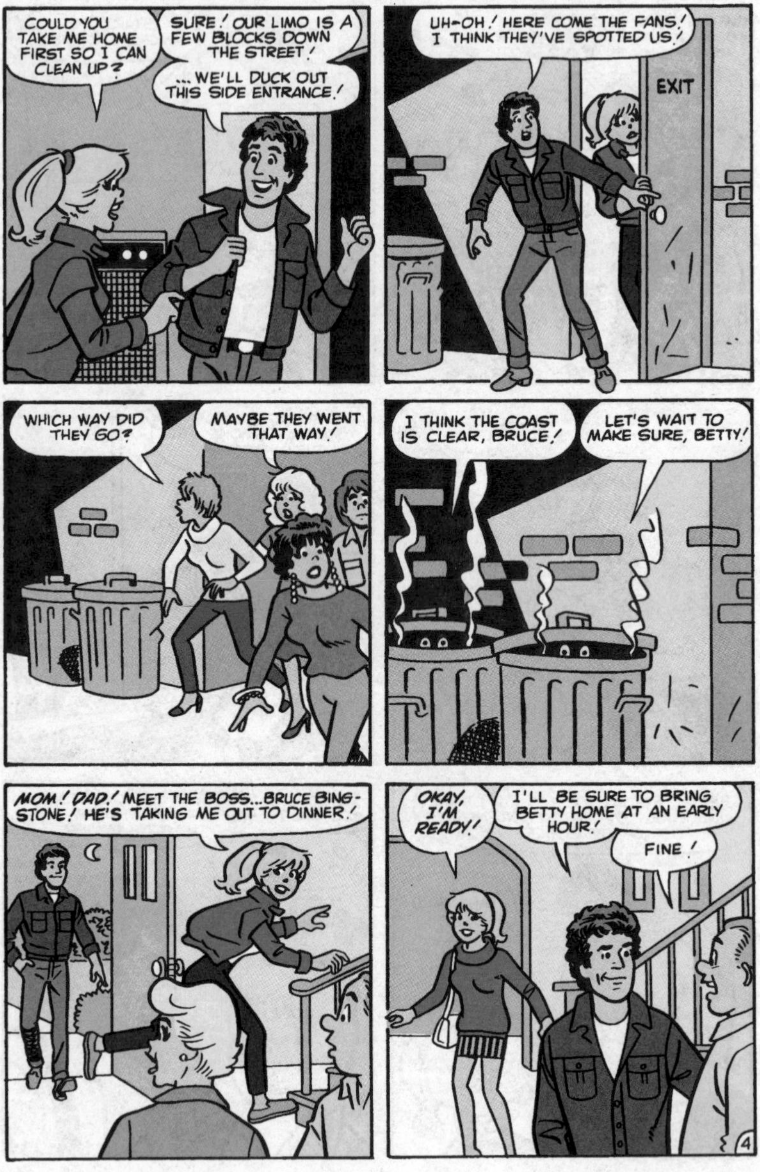
COULD YOU TAKE ME HOME FIRST SO I CAN CLEAN UP?
SURE! OUR LIMO IS A FEW BLOCKS DOWN THE STREET!
... WE'LL DUCK OUT THIS SIDE ENTRANCE!
UH-OH! HERE COME THE FANS! I THINK THEY'VE SPOTTED US!
EXIT
WHICH WAY DID THEY GO?
MAYBE THEY WENT THAT WAY!
I THINK THE COAST IS CLEAR, BRUCE!
LET'S WAIT TO MAKE SURE, BETTY!
MOM! DAD! MEET THE BOSS...BRUCE BINGSTONE! HE'S TAKING ME OUT TO DINNER!
OKAY, I'M READY!
I'LL BE SURE TO BRING BETTY HOME AT AN EARLY HOUR!
FINE!
4

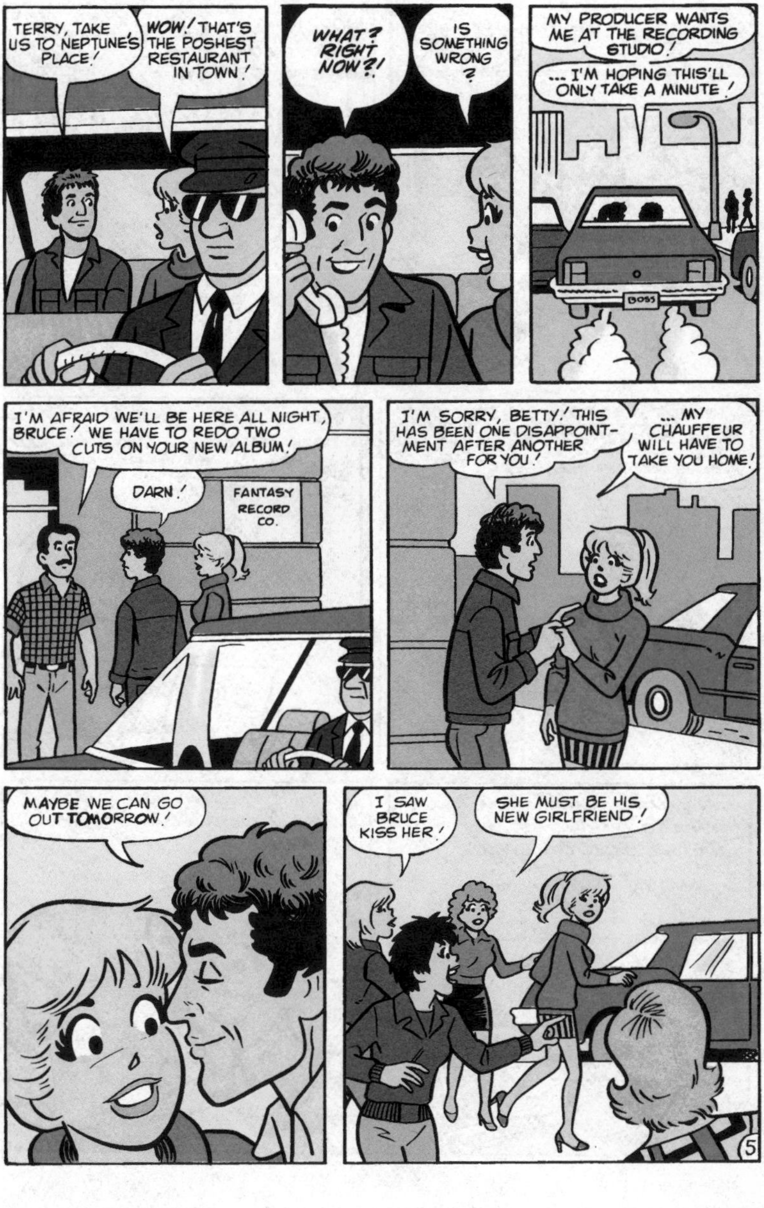
TERRY, TAKE US TO NEPTUNE'S PLACE!
WOW! THAT'S THE POSHEST RESTAURANT IN TOWN!
WHAT? RIGHT NOW?!
IS SOMETHING WRONG?
MY PRODUCER WANTS ME AT THE RECORDING STUDIO!
... I'M HOPING THIS'LL ONLY TAKE A MINUTE!
BOSS
I'M AFRAID WE'LL BE HERE ALL NIGHT, BRUCE! WE HAVE TO REDO TWO CUTS ON YOUR NEW ALBUM!
DARN!
FANTASY RECORD CO.
I'M SORRY, BETTY! THIS HAS BEEN ONE DISAPPOINTMENT AFTER ANOTHER FOR YOU!
... MY CHAUFFEUR WILL HAVE TO TAKE YOU HOME!
MAYBE WE CAN GO OUT TOMORROW!
I SAW BRUCE KISS HER!
SHE MUST BE HIS NEW GIRLFRIEND!
5

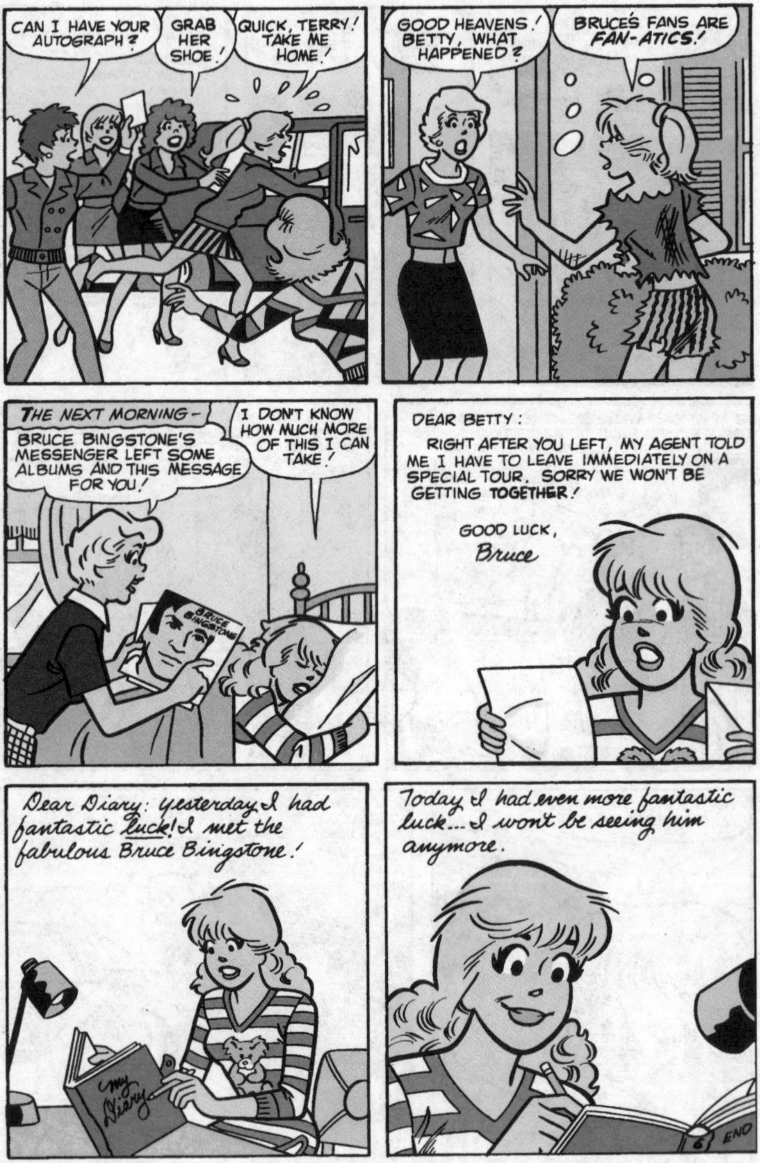
CAN I HAVE YOUR AUTOGRAPH ?
GRAB HER SHOE !
QUICK, TERRY! TAKE ME HOME!
GOOD HEAVENS! BETTY, WHAT HAPPENED ?
BRUCE'S FANS ARE FAN-ATICS!
THE NEXT MORNING-
BRUCE BINGSTONE'S MESSENGER LEFT SOME ALBUMS AND THIS MESSAGE FOR YOU!
I DON'T KNOW HOW MUCH MORE OF THIS I CAN TAKE!
BRUCE BINGSTONE
DEAR BETTY:
RIGHT AFTER YOU LEFT, MY AGENT TOLD ME I HAVE TO LEAVE IMMEDIATELY ON A SPECIAL TOUR. SORRY WE WON'T BE GETTING TOGETHER!
GOOD LUCK,
Bruce
Dear Diary: yesterday I had fantastic luck! I met the fabulous Bruce Bingstone!
My Diary
Today I had even more fantastic luck... I won't be seeing him anymore.
END

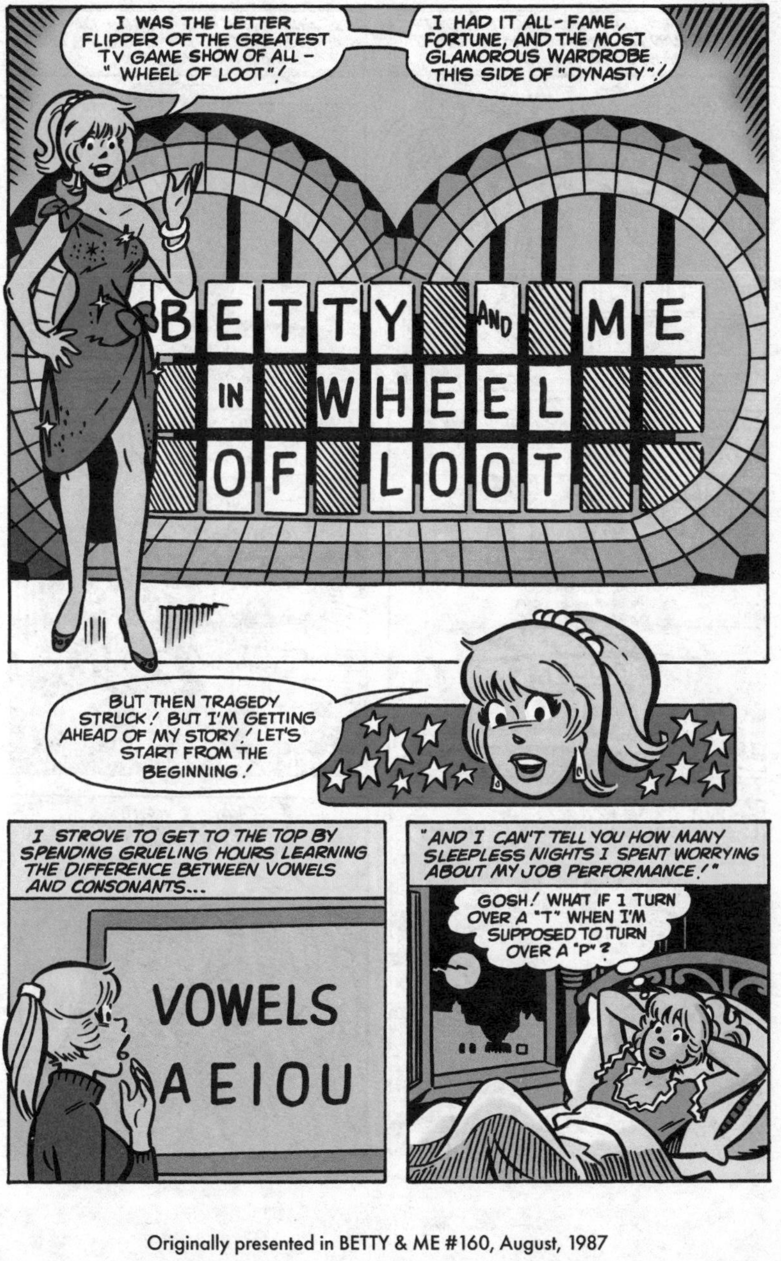
I WAS THE LETTER FLIPPER OF THE GREATEST TV GAME SHOW OF ALL – " WHEEL OF LOOT "!
I HAD IT ALL - FAME, FORTUNE, AND THE MOST GLAMOROUS WARDROBE THIS SIDE OF "DYNASTY"!
BETTY AND ME
IN WHEEL
OF LOOT
BUT THEN TRAGEDY STRUCK! BUT I'M GETTING AHEAD OF MY STORY! LET'S START FROM THE BEGINNING!
I STROVE TO GET TO THE TOP BY SPENDING GRUELING HOURS LEARNING THE DIFFERENCE BETWEEN VOWELS AND CONSONANTS...
VOWELS
A E I O U
"AND I CAN'T TELL YOU HOW MANY SLEEPLESS NIGHTS I SPENT WORRYING ABOUT MY JOB PERFORMANCE!"
GOSH! WHAT IF I TURN OVER A "T" WHEN I'M SUPPOSED TO TURN OVER A "P"?

Originally presented in BETTY & ME #160, August, 1987

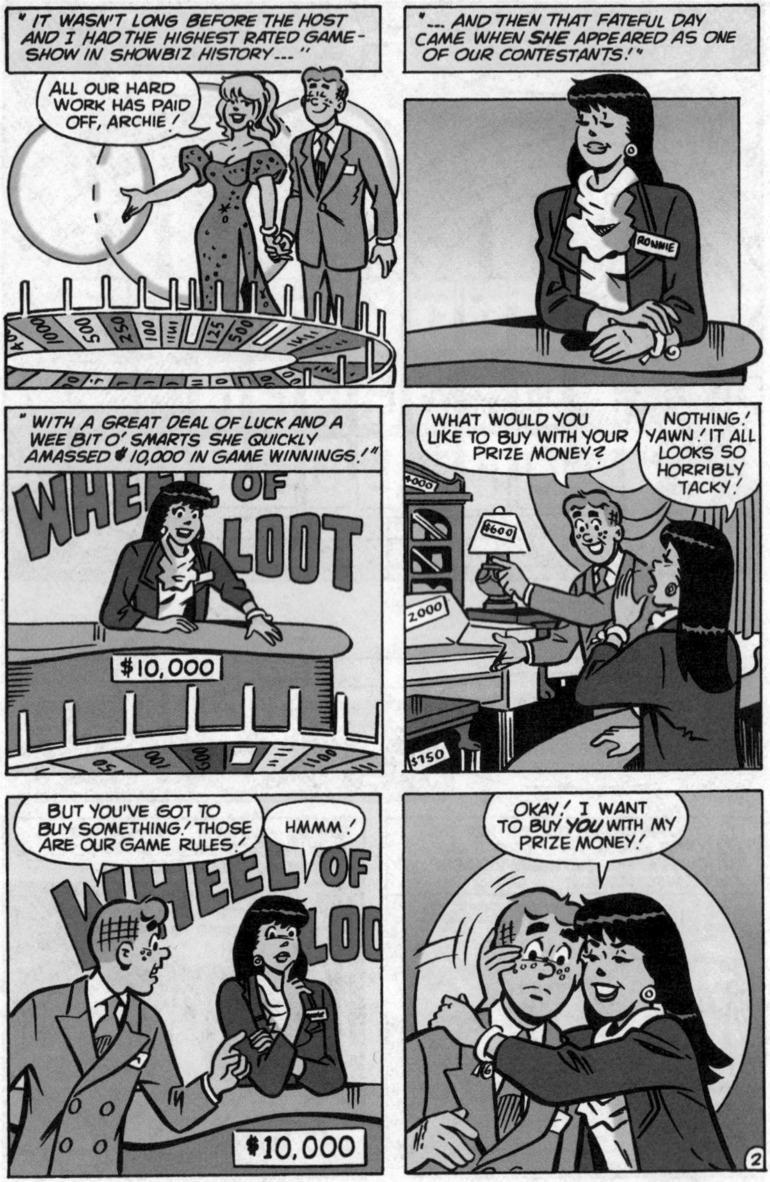

" IT WASN'T LONG BEFORE THE HOST AND I HAD THE HIGHEST RATED GAME-SHOW IN SHOWBIZ HISTORY--- "
ALL OUR HARD WORK HAS PAID OFF, ARCHIE!
"--- AND THEN THAT FATEFUL DAY CAME WHEN SHE APPEARED AS ONE OF OUR CONTESTANTS!"
RONNIE
" WITH A GREAT DEAL OF LUCK AND A WEE BIT O' SMARTS SHE QUICKLY AMASSED $10,000 IN GAME WINNINGS! "
WHEEL OF LOOT
$10,000
WHAT WOULD YOU LIKE TO BUY WITH YOUR PRIZE MONEY?
NOTHING! YAWN! IT ALL LOOKS SO HORRIBLY TACKY!
$600
2000
$750
BUT YOU'VE GOT TO BUY SOMETHING! THOSE ARE OUR GAME RULES!
HMMM!
$10,000
OKAY! I WANT TO BUY YOU WITH MY PRIZE MONEY!
2

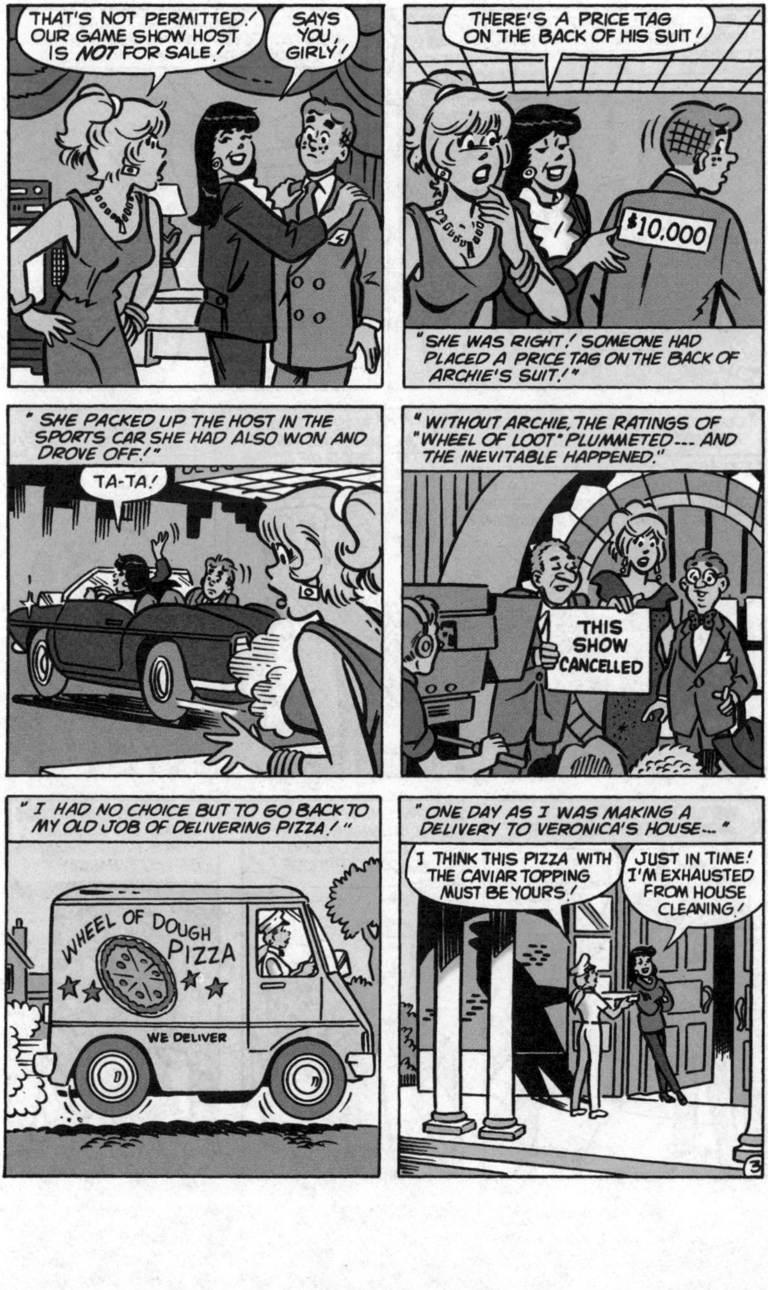
THAT'S NOT PERMITTED! OUR GAME SHOW HOST IS NOT FOR SALE!
SAYS YOU, GIRLY!
THERE'S A PRICE TAG ON THE BACK OF HIS SUIT!
$10,000
"SHE WAS RIGHT! SOMEONE HAD PLACED A PRICE TAG ON THE BACK OF ARCHIE'S SUIT!"
"SHE PACKED UP THE HOST IN THE SPORTS CAR SHE HAD ALSO WON AND DROVE OFF!"
TA-TA!
"WITHOUT ARCHIE, THE RATINGS OF "WHEEL OF LOOT" PLUMMETED--- AND THE INEVITABLE HAPPENED."
THIS SHOW CANCELLED
"I HAD NO CHOICE BUT TO GO BACK TO MY OLD JOB OF DELIVERING PIZZA!"
WHEEL OF DOUGH PIZZA
WE DELIVER
"ONE DAY AS I WAS MAKING A DELIVERY TO VERONICA'S HOUSE..."
I THINK THIS PIZZA WITH THE CAVIAR TOPPING MUST BE YOURS!
JUST IN TIME! I'M EXHAUSTED FROM HOUSE CLEANING!
3

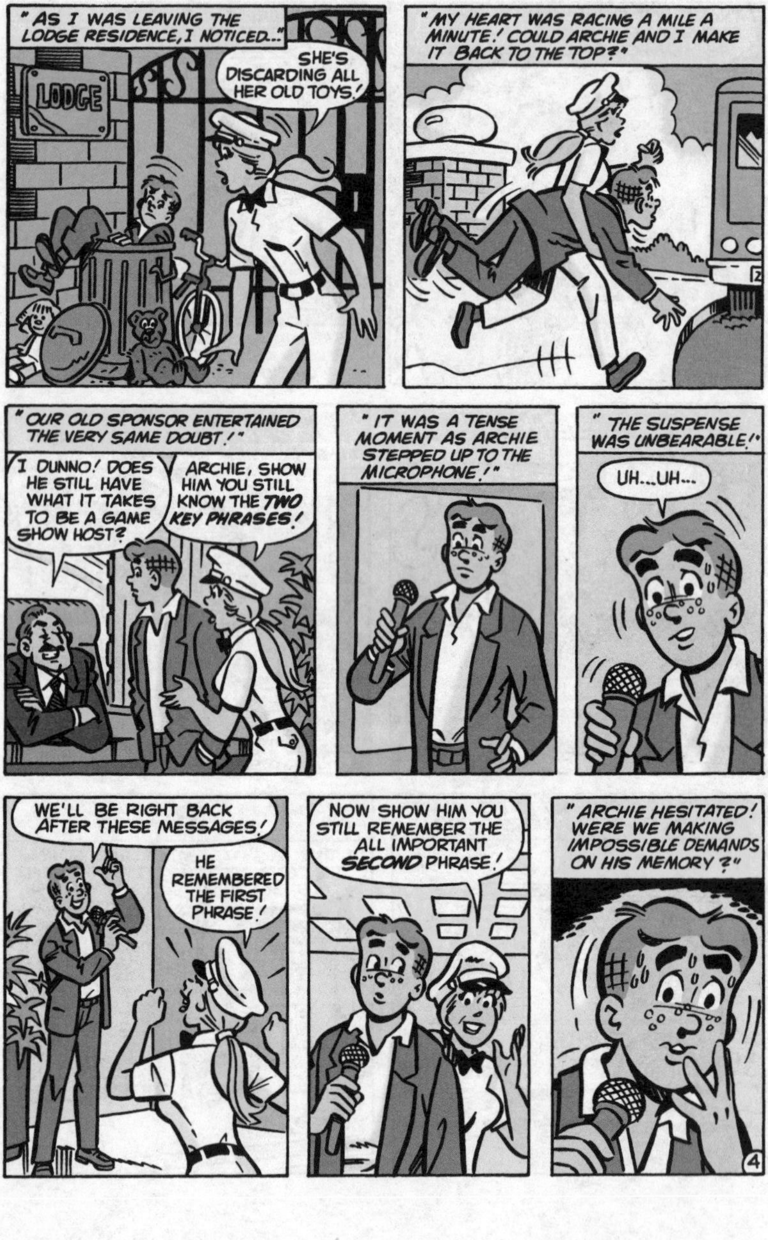
"AS I WAS LEAVING THE LODGE RESIDENCE, I NOTICED..."
LODGE
SHE'S DISCARDING ALL HER OLD TOYS!
"MY HEART WAS RACING A MILE A MINUTE! COULD ARCHIE AND I MAKE IT BACK TO THE TOP?"
"OUR OLD SPONSOR ENTERTAINED THE VERY SAME DOUBT!"
I DUNNO! DOES HE STILL HAVE WHAT IT TAKES TO BE A GAME SHOW HOST?
ARCHIE, SHOW HIM YOU STILL KNOW THE TWO KEY PHRASES!
"IT WAS A TENSE MOMENT AS ARCHIE STEPPED UP TO THE MICROPHONE!"
"THE SUSPENSE WAS UNBEARABLE!"
UH...UH...
WE'LL BE RIGHT BACK AFTER THESE MESSAGES!
HE REMEMBERED THE FIRST PHRASE!
NOW SHOW HIM YOU STILL REMEMBER THE ALL IMPORTANT SECOND PHRASE!
"ARCHIE HESITATED! WERE WE MAKING IMPOSSIBLE DEMANDS ON HIS MEMORY?"
4

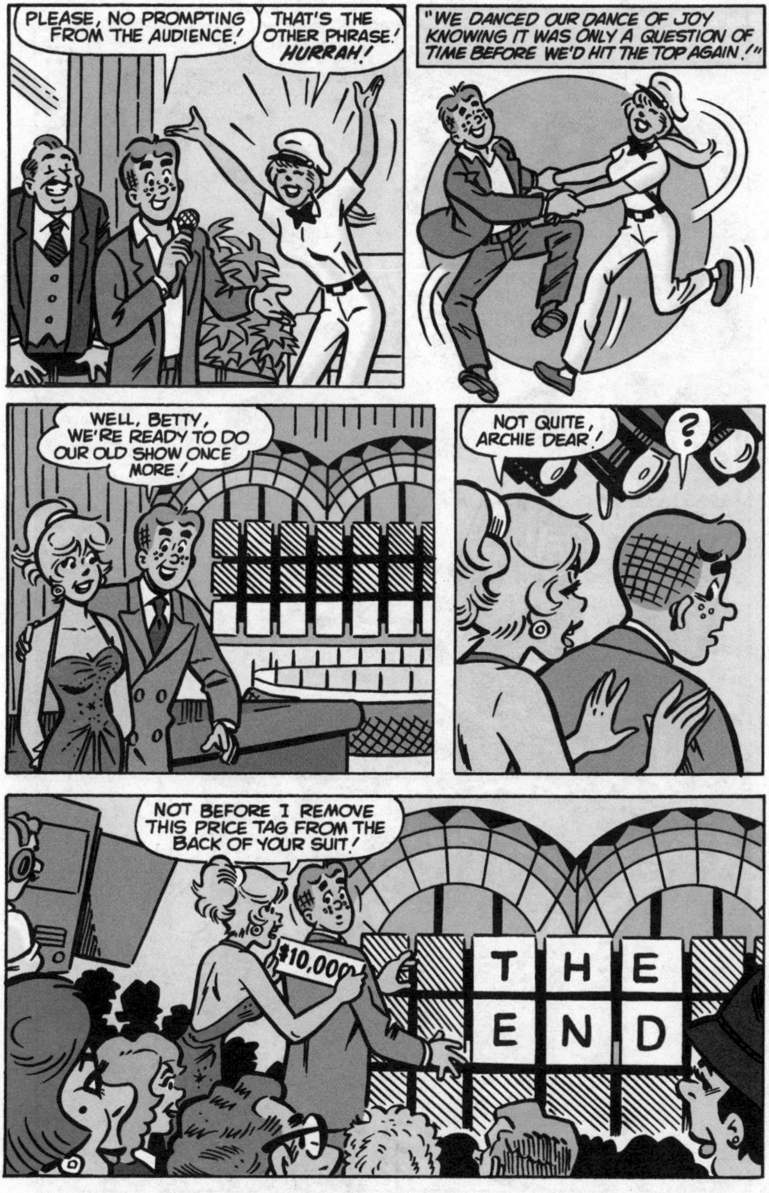
PLEASE, NO PROMPTING FROM THE AUDIENCE!
THAT'S THE OTHER PHRASE! HURRAH!
"WE DANCED OUR DANCE OF JOY KNOWING IT WAS ONLY A QUESTION OF TIME BEFORE WE'D HIT THE TOP AGAIN!"
WELL, BETTY, WE'RE READY TO DO OUR OLD SHOW ONCE MORE!
NOT QUITE, ARCHIE DEAR!
?
NOT BEFORE I REMOVE THIS PRICE TAG FROM THE BACK OF YOUR SUIT!
$10,000
THE END

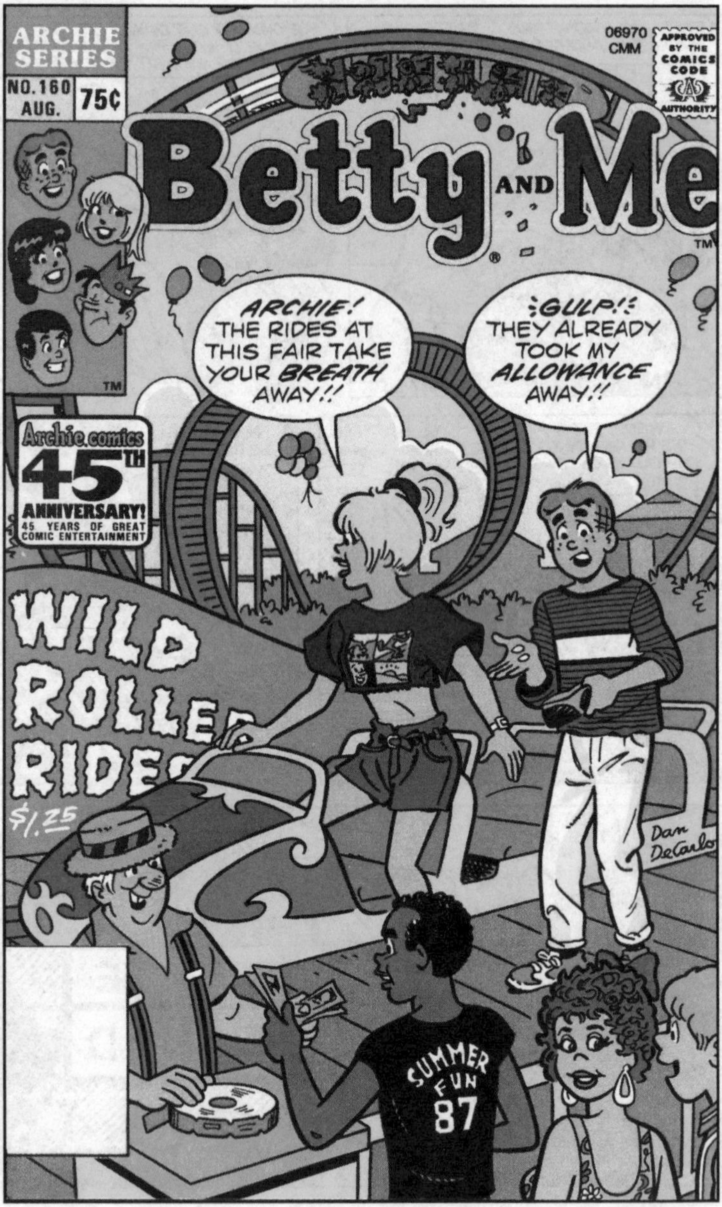
ARCHIE SERIES
NO.160 AUG.
75¢
06970 CMM
APPROVED BY THE COMICS CODE AUTHORITY
Betty and Me
ARCHIE! THE RIDES AT THIS FAIR TAKE YOUR BREATH AWAY!!
GULP! THEY ALREADY TOOK MY ALLOWANCE AWAY!!
Archie comics 45TH ANNIVERSARY! 45 YEARS OF GREAT COMIC ENTERTAINMENT
WILD ROLLER RIDES
$1.25
Dan DeCarlo
SUMMER FUN 87

Originally printed in 1987

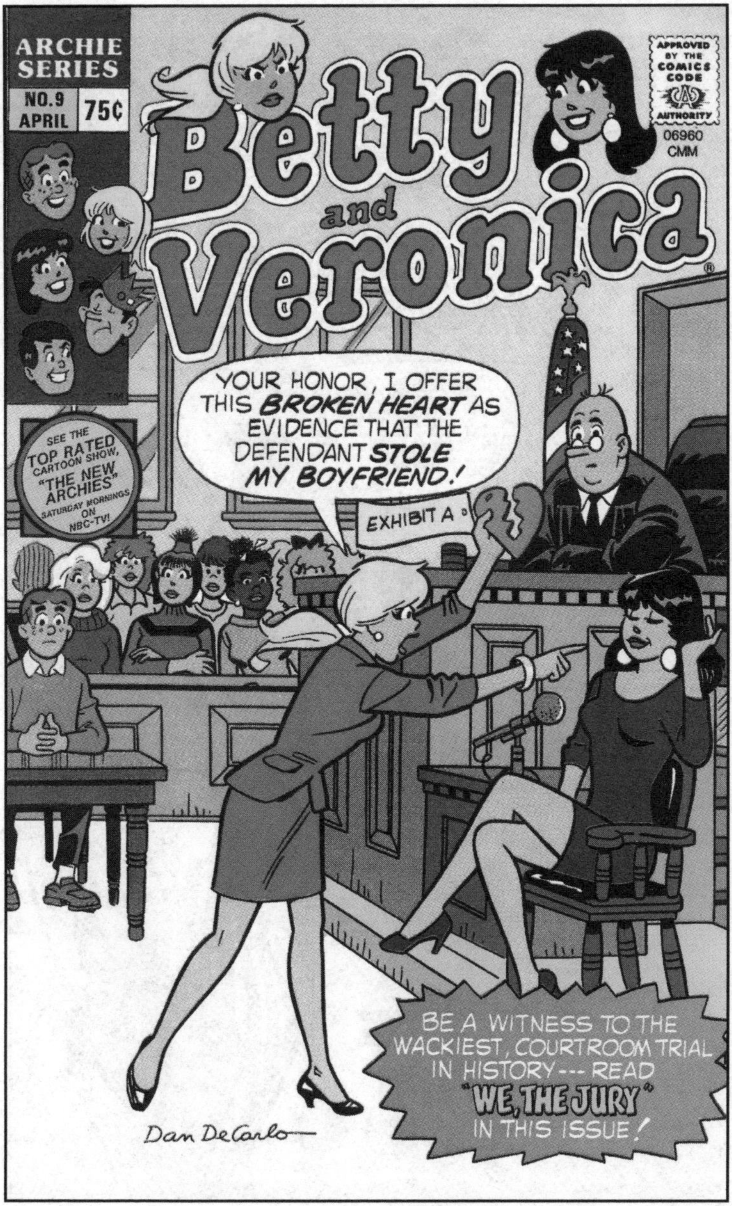
ARCHIE SERIES
NO.9 APRIL
75¢
Betty and Veronica
APPROVED BY THE COMICS CODE AUTHORITY
06960 CMM
SEE THE TOP RATED CARTOON SHOW, "THE NEW ARCHIES" SATURDAY MORNINGS ON NBC-TV!
YOUR HONOR, I OFFER THIS BROKEN HEART AS EVIDENCE THAT THE DEFENDANT STOLE MY BOYFRIEND!
EXHIBIT A
BE A WITNESS TO THE WACKIEST, COURTROOM TRIAL IN HISTORY--- READ "WE, THE JURY" IN THIS ISSUE!
Dan DeCarlo

Originally printed in 1988

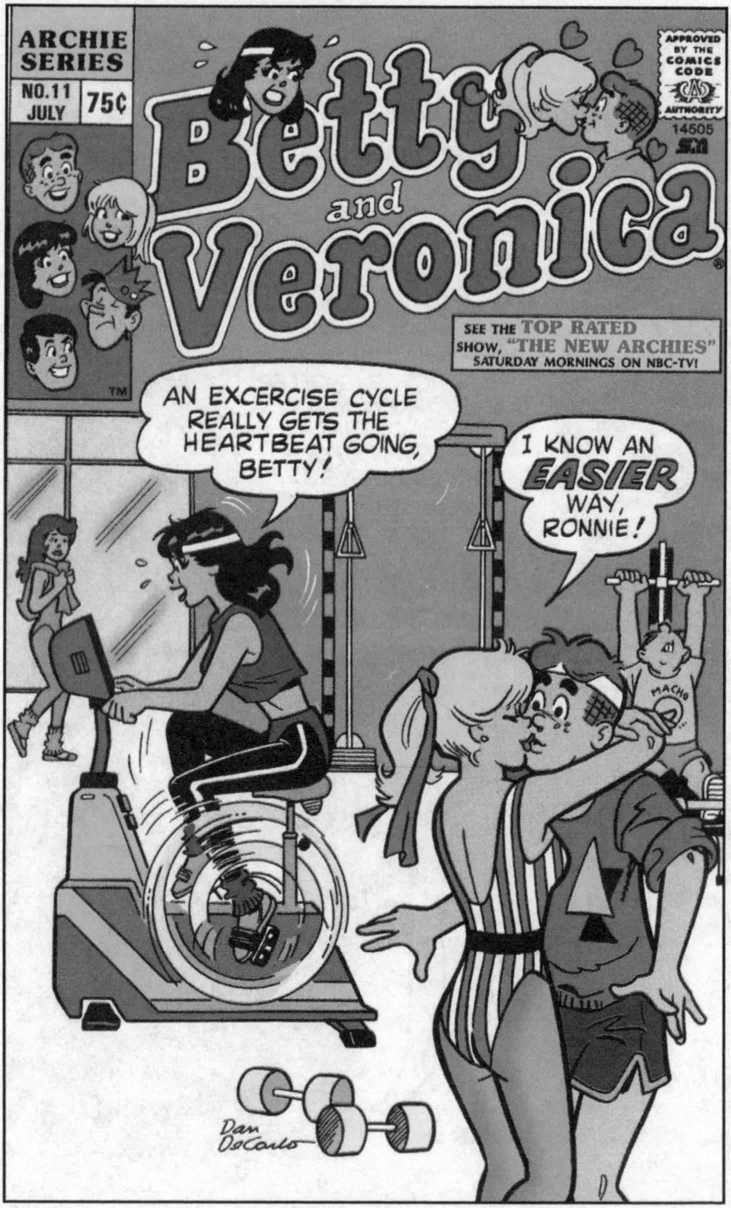
ARCHIE SERIES
NO.11 JULY
75¢
APPROVED BY THE COMICS CODE AUTHORITY
14505
Betty and Veronica
SEE THE TOP RATED SHOW, "THE NEW ARCHIES" SATURDAY MORNINGS ON NBC-TV!
TM
AN EXCERCISE CYCLE REALLY GETS THE HEARTBEAT GOING, BETTY!
I KNOW AN EASIER WAY, RONNIE!
MACHO
Dan DeCarlo

Originally printed in 1988

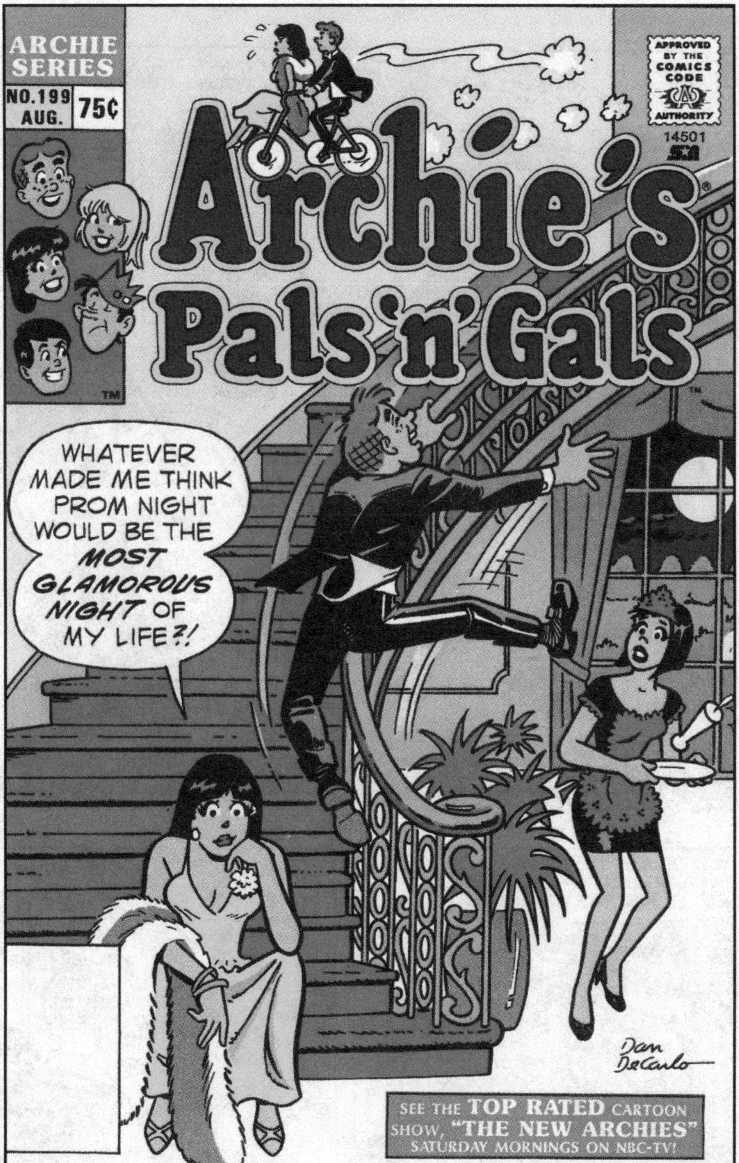
ARCHIE SERIES
NO.199 AUG.
75¢
APPROVED BY THE COMICS CODE AUTHORITY
14501
Archie's Pals 'n' Gals
WHATEVER MADE ME THINK PROM NIGHT WOULD BE THE MOST GLAMOROUS NIGHT OF MY LIFE?!
Dan DeCarlo
SEE THE TOP RATED CARTOON SHOW, "THE NEW ARCHIES" SATURDAY MORNINGS ON NBC-TV!

Originally printed in 1988

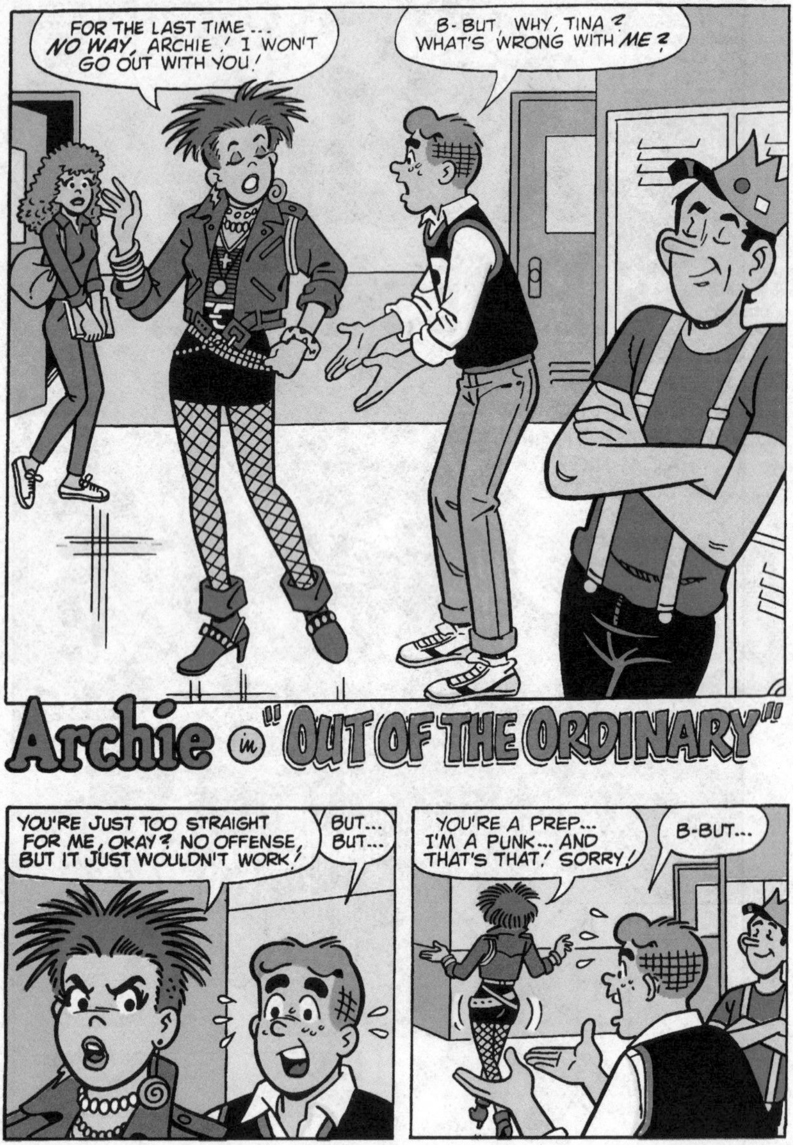
FOR THE LAST TIME... NO WAY, ARCHIE! I WON'T GO OUT WITH YOU!
B-BUT, WHY, TINA? WHAT'S WRONG WITH ME?
Archie in "OUT OF THE ORDINARY"
YOU'RE JUST TOO STRAIGHT FOR ME, OKAY? NO OFFENSE, BUT IT JUST WOULDN'T WORK!
BUT... BUT...
YOU'RE A PREP... I'M A PUNK... AND THAT'S THAT! SORRY!
B-BUT...

Originally presented in ARCHIE #354, January, 1988

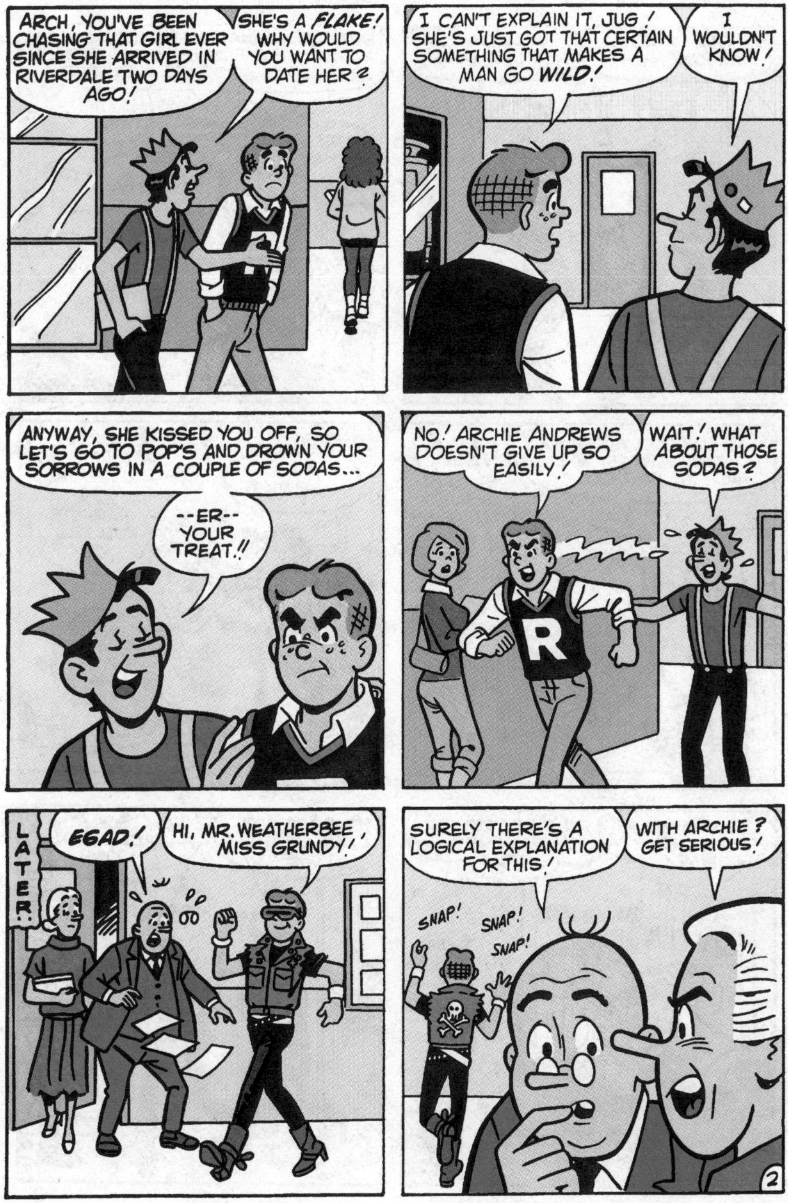
ARCH, YOU'VE BEEN CHASING THAT GIRL EVER SINCE SHE ARRIVED IN RIVERDALE TWO DAYS AGO!
SHE'S A FLAKE! WHY WOULD YOU WANT TO DATE HER?
I CAN'T EXPLAIN IT, JUG! SHE'S JUST GOT THAT CERTAIN SOMETHING THAT MAKES A MAN GO WILD!
I WOULDN'T KNOW!
ANYWAY, SHE KISSED YOU OFF, SO LET'S GO TO POP'S AND DROWN YOUR SORROWS IN A COUPLE OF SODAS...
--ER-- YOUR TREAT.!!
NO! ARCHIE ANDREWS DOESN'T GIVE UP SO EASILY!
WAIT! WHAT ABOUT THOSE SODAS?
LATER.
EGAD!
HI, MR. WEATHERBEE, MISS GRUNDY!
SURELY THERE'S A LOGICAL EXPLANATION FOR THIS!
WITH ARCHIE? GET SERIOUS!
SNAP!
SNAP!
SNAP!
2

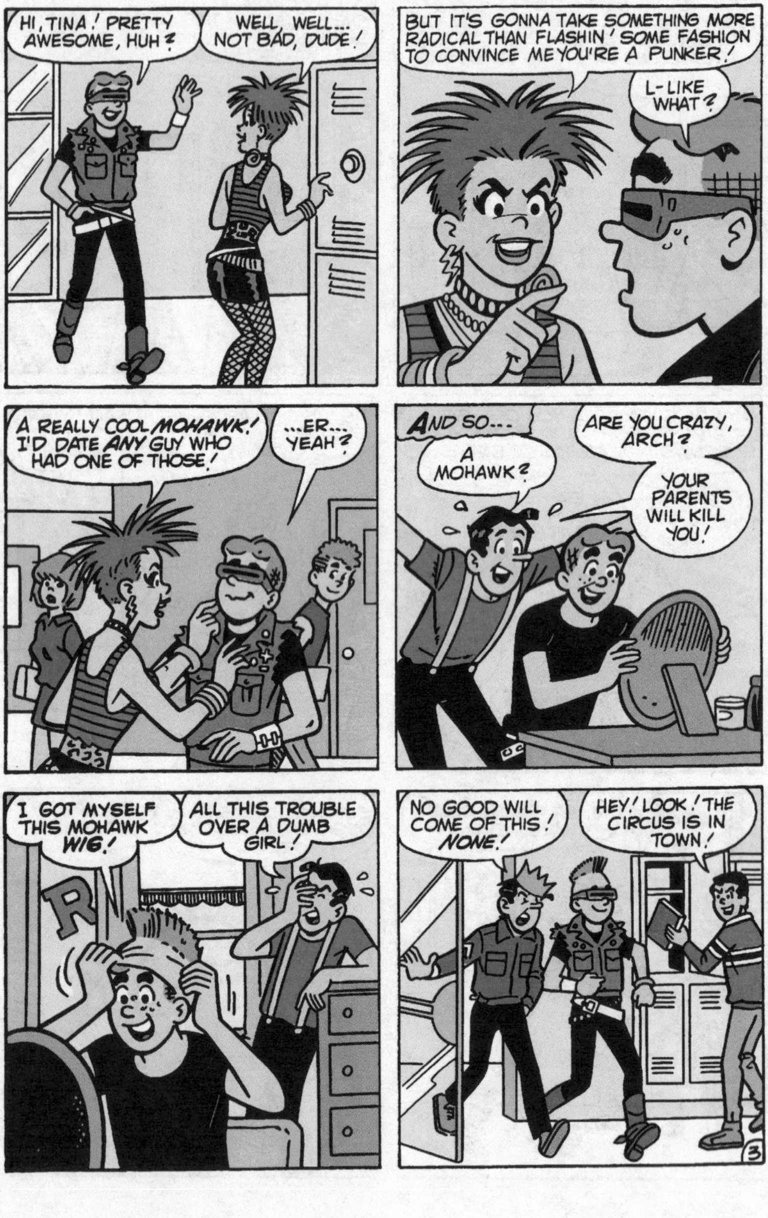
HI, TINA! PRETTY AWESOME, HUH?
WELL, WELL... NOT BAD, DUDE!
BUT IT'S GONNA TAKE SOMETHING MORE RADICAL THAN FLASHIN' SOME FASHION TO CONVINCE ME YOU'RE A PUNKER!
L-LIKE WHAT?
A REALLY COOL MOHAWK! I'D DATE ANY GUY WHO HAD ONE OF THOSE!
...ER... YEAH?
AND SO...
A MOHAWK?
ARE YOU CRAZY, ARCH?
YOUR PARENTS WILL KILL YOU!
I GOT MYSELF THIS MOHAWK WIG!
ALL THIS TROUBLE OVER A DUMB GIRL!
NO GOOD WILL COME OF THIS! NONE!
HEY! LOOK! THE CIRCUS IS IN TOWN!
3

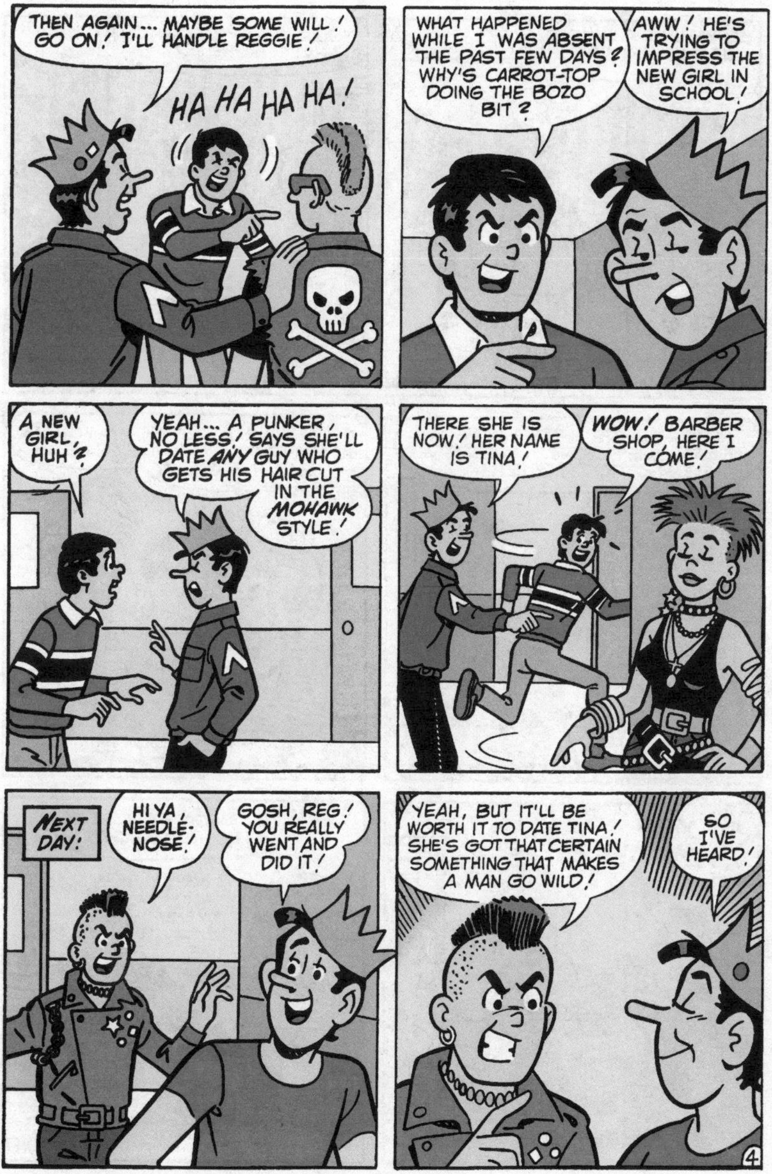
THEN AGAIN... MAYBE SOME WILL! GO ON! I'LL HANDLE REGGIE!
HA HA HA HA!
WHAT HAPPENED WHILE I WAS ABSENT THE PAST FEW DAYS? WHY'S CARROT-TOP DOING THE BOZO BIT?
AWW! HE'S TRYING TO IMPRESS THE NEW GIRL IN SCHOOL!
A NEW GIRL, HUH?
YEAH... A PUNKER, NO LESS! SAYS SHE'LL DATE ANY GUY WHO GETS HIS HAIR CUT IN THE MOHAWK STYLE!
THERE SHE IS NOW! HER NAME IS TINA!
WOW! BARBER SHOP, HERE I COME!
NEXT DAY!
HI YA, NEEDLE-NOSE!
GOSH, REG! YOU REALLY WENT AND DID IT!
YEAH, BUT IT'LL BE WORTH IT TO DATE TINA! SHE'S GOT THAT CERTAIN SOMETHING THAT MAKES A MAN GO WILD!
SO I'VE HEARD!
4

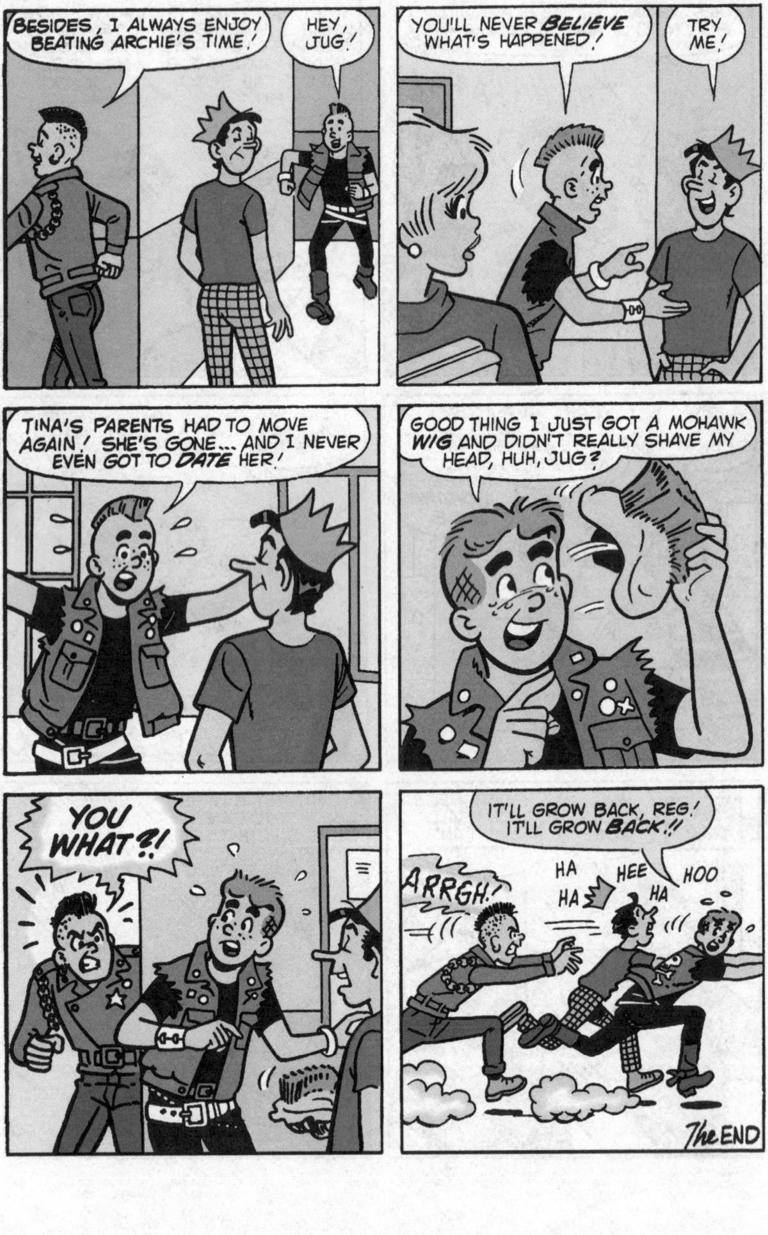
BESIDES, I ALWAYS ENJOY BEATING ARCHIE'S TIME!
HEY, JUG!
YOU'LL NEVER BELIEVE WHAT'S HAPPENED!
TRY ME!
TINA'S PARENTS HAD TO MOVE AGAIN! SHE'S GONE... AND I NEVER EVEN GOT TO DATE HER!
GOOD THING I JUST GOT A MOHAWK WIG AND DIDN'T REALLY SHAVE MY HEAD, HUH, JUG?
YOU WHAT?!
IT'LL GROW BACK, REG! IT'LL GROW BACK!!
ARRGH!
HA HA
HEE
HA
HOO
The END

Betty and Veronica in "WE, THE JURY"
YOUR HONOR, I INTEND TO PROVE BEYOND A SHADOW OF A DOUBT---
--- THAT THE DEFENDANT, VERONICA LODGE, WITH MALICE A FORETHOUGHT, DID ON OCTOBER TENTH ATTEMPT TO STEAL MY BOYFRIEND...
---ONE ARCHIE ANDREWS, WHO SITS BEFORE YOU, MARKED EXHIBIT "A"!
EXHIBIT "A"

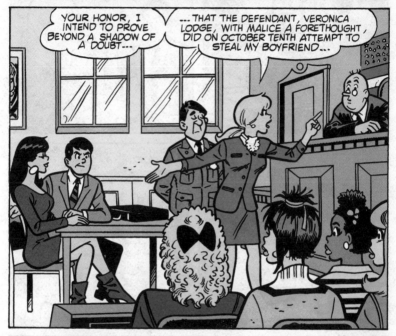

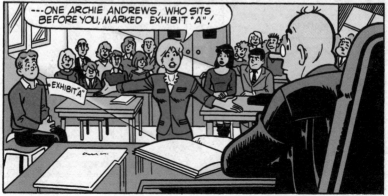

Originally presented in BETTY & VERONICA VOL. 2 #9, April, 1988

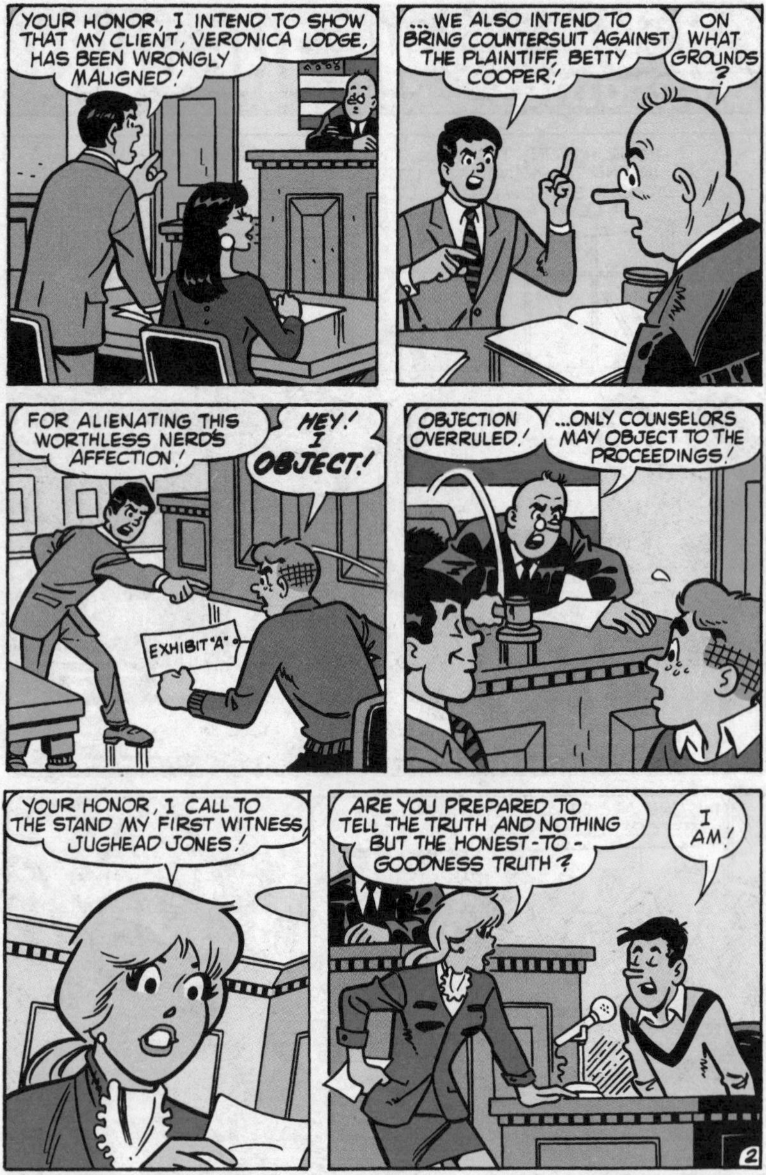
YOUR HONOR, I INTEND TO SHOW THAT MY CLIENT, VERONICA LODGE, HAS BEEN WRONGLY MALIGNED!
...WE ALSO INTEND TO BRING COUNTERSUIT AGAINST THE PLAINTIFF, BETTY COOPER!
ON WHAT GROUNDS?
FOR ALIENATING THIS WORTHLESS NERD'S AFFECTION!
HEY! I OBJECT!
EXHIBIT "A"
OBJECTION OVERRULED!
...ONLY COUNSELORS MAY OBJECT TO THE PROCEEDINGS!
YOUR HONOR, I CALL TO THE STAND MY FIRST WITNESS, JUGHEAD JONES!
ARE YOU PREPARED TO TELL THE TRUTH AND NOTHING BUT THE HONEST-TO-GOODNESS TRUTH?
I AM!
2

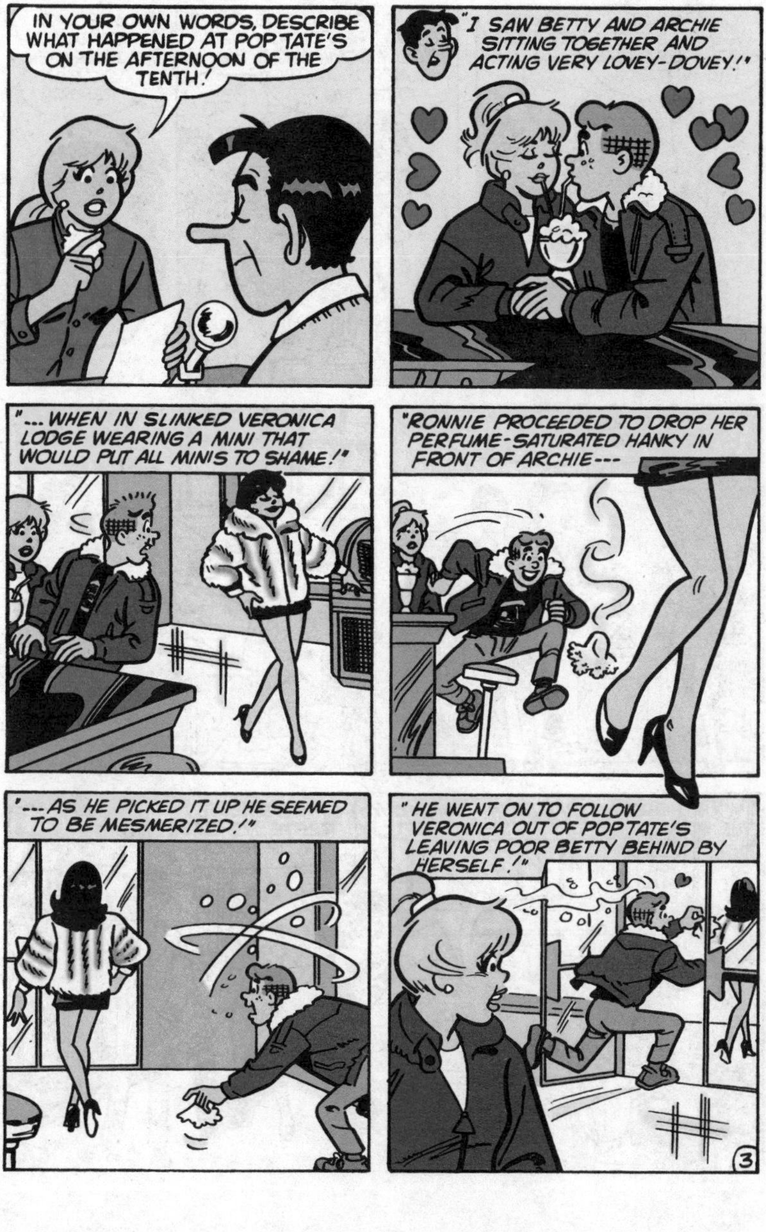
IN YOUR OWN WORDS, DESCRIBE WHAT HAPPENED AT POP TATE'S ON THE AFTERNOON OF THE TENTH!
"I SAW BETTY AND ARCHIE SITTING TOGETHER AND ACTING VERY LOVEY-DOVEY!"
"...WHEN IN SLINKED VERONICA LODGE WEARING A MINI THAT WOULD PUT ALL MINIS TO SHAME!"
"RONNIE PROCEEDED TO DROP HER PERFUME-SATURATED HANKY IN FRONT OF ARCHIE---
"---AS HE PICKED IT UP HE SEEMED TO BE MESMERIZED!"
"HE WENT ON TO FOLLOW VERONICA OUT OF POP TATE'S LEAVING POOR BETTY BEHIND BY HERSELF!"
3

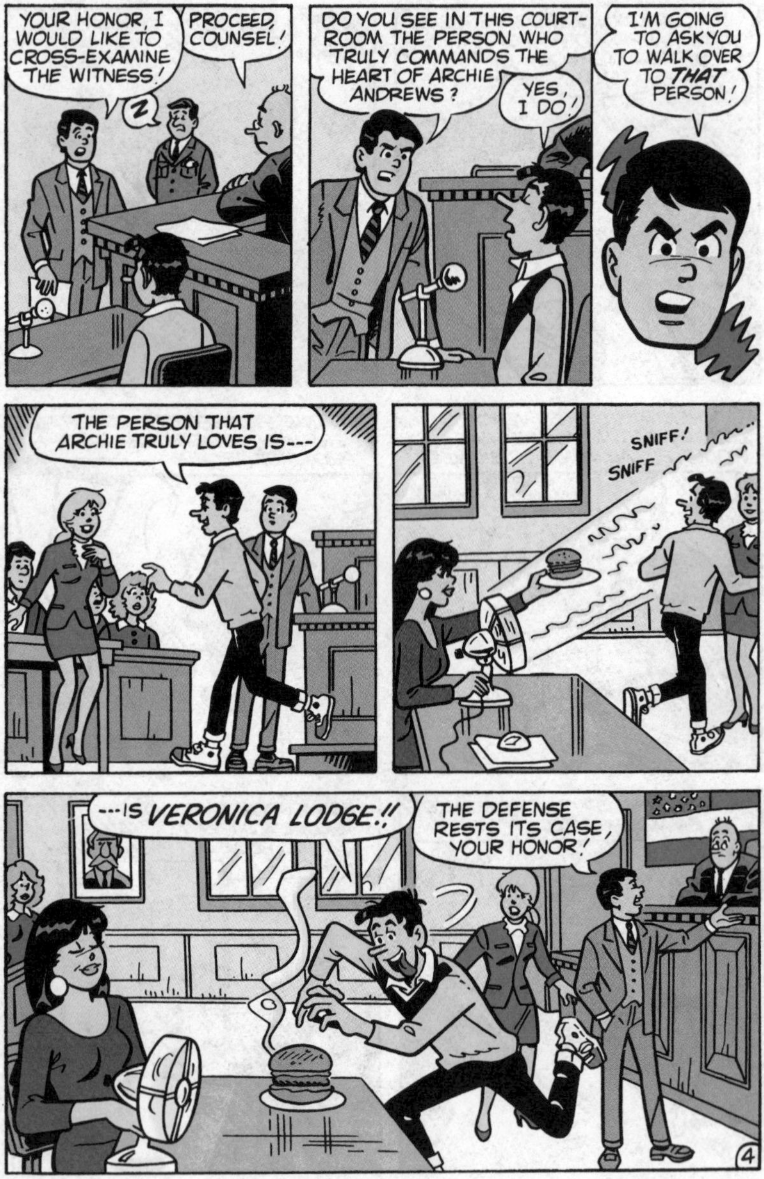
YOUR HONOR, I WOULD LIKE TO CROSS-EXAMINE THE WITNESS!
PROCEED, COUNSEL!
Z
DO YOU SEE IN THIS COURTROOM THE PERSON WHO TRULY COMMANDS THE HEART OF ARCHIE ANDREWS?
YES, I DO!
I'M GOING TO ASK YOU TO WALK OVER TO *THAT* PERSON!
THE PERSON THAT ARCHIE TRULY LOVES IS---
SNIFF!
SNIFF
---IS *VERONICA LODGE!!*
THE DEFENSE RESTS ITS CASE, YOUR HONOR!
4

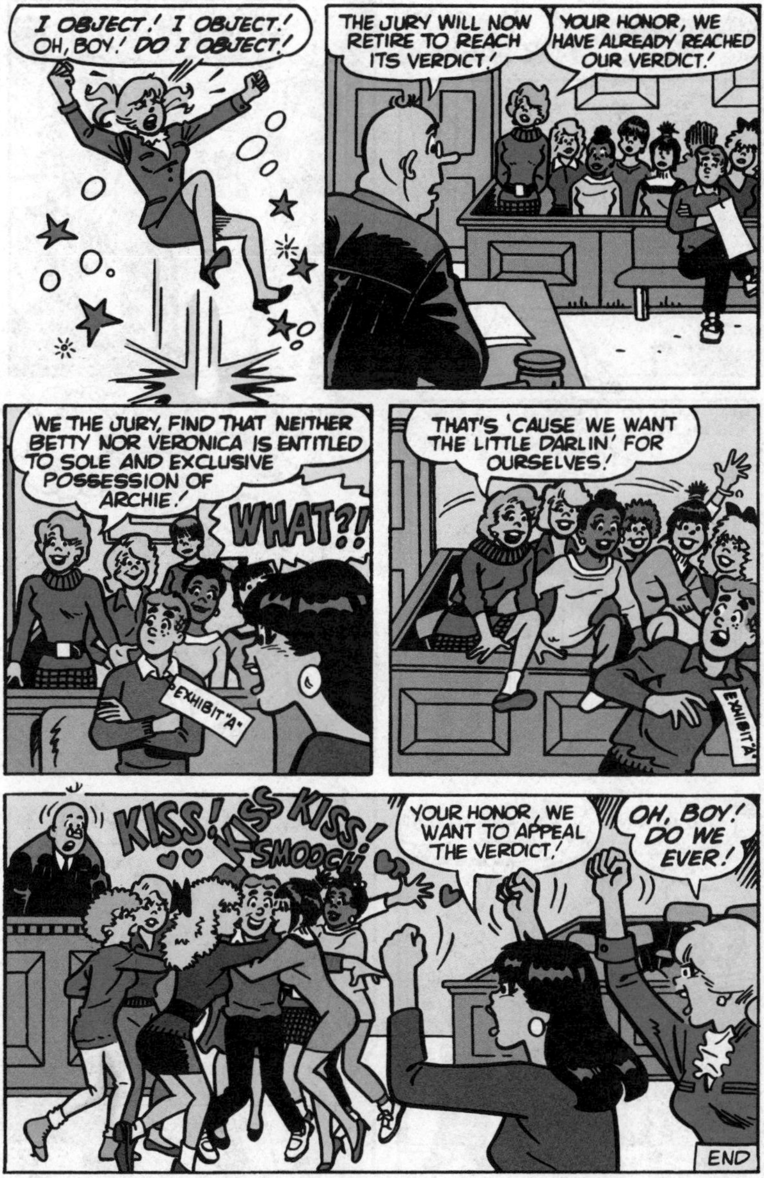
I OBJECT! I OBJECT! OH, BOY! DO I OBJECT!
THE JURY WILL NOW RETIRE TO REACH ITS VERDICT!
YOUR HONOR, WE HAVE ALREADY REACHED OUR VERDICT!
WE THE JURY, FIND THAT NEITHER BETTY NOR VERONICA IS ENTITLED TO SOLE AND EXCLUSIVE POSSESSION OF ARCHIE!
WHAT?!
EXHIBIT "A"
THAT'S 'CAUSE WE WANT THE LITTLE DARLIN' FOR OURSELVES!
EXHIBIT "A"
KISS! KISS KISS!
SMOOCH
YOUR HONOR, WE WANT TO APPEAL THE VERDICT!
OH, BOY! DO WE EVER!
END

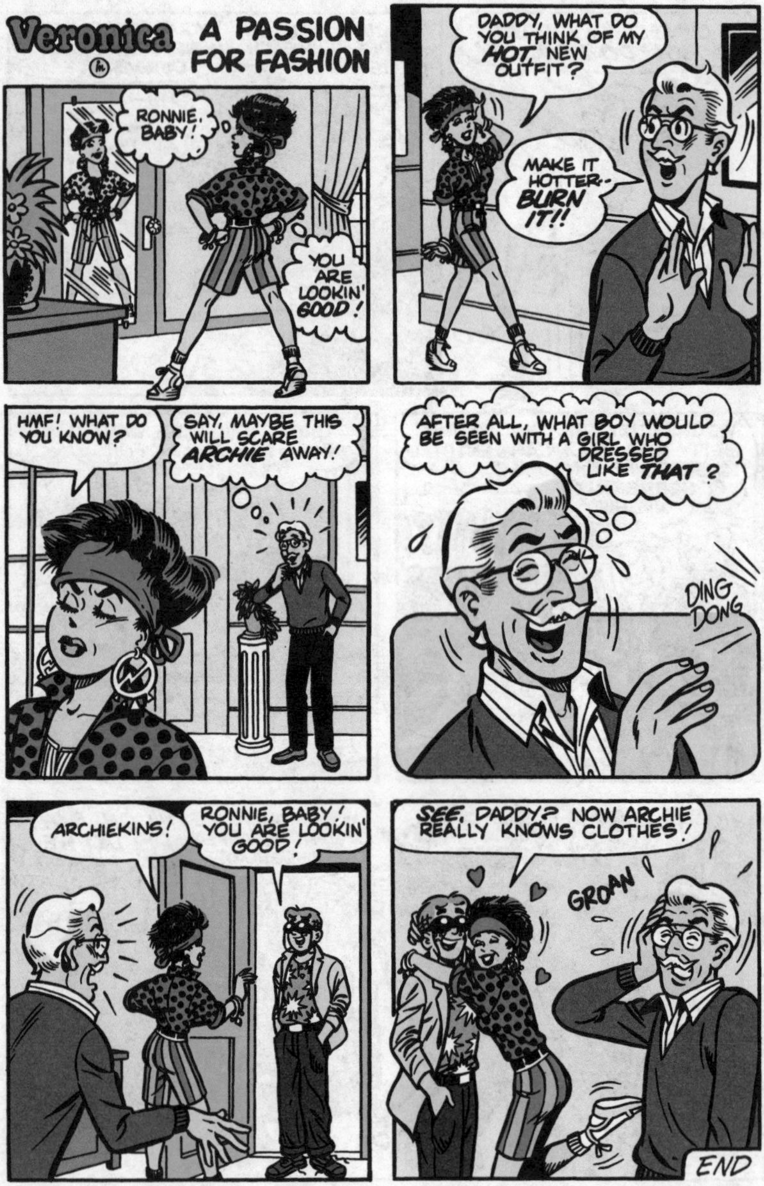
Veronica
A PASSION FOR FASHION
RONNIE, BABY!
YOU ARE LOOKIN' GOOD!
DADDY, WHAT DO YOU THINK OF MY HOT, NEW OUTFIT?
MAKE IT HOTTER... BURN IT!!
HMF! WHAT DO YOU KNOW?
SAY, MAYBE THIS WILL SCARE ARCHIE AWAY!
AFTER ALL, WHAT BOY WOULD BE SEEN WITH A GIRL WHO DRESSED LIKE THAT?
DING DONG
ARCHIEKINS!
RONNIE, BABY! YOU ARE LOOKIN' GOOD!
SEE, DADDY? NOW ARCHIE REALLY KNOWS CLOTHES!
GROAN
END

Originally presented in EVERYTHING'S ARCHIE #137, August, 1988

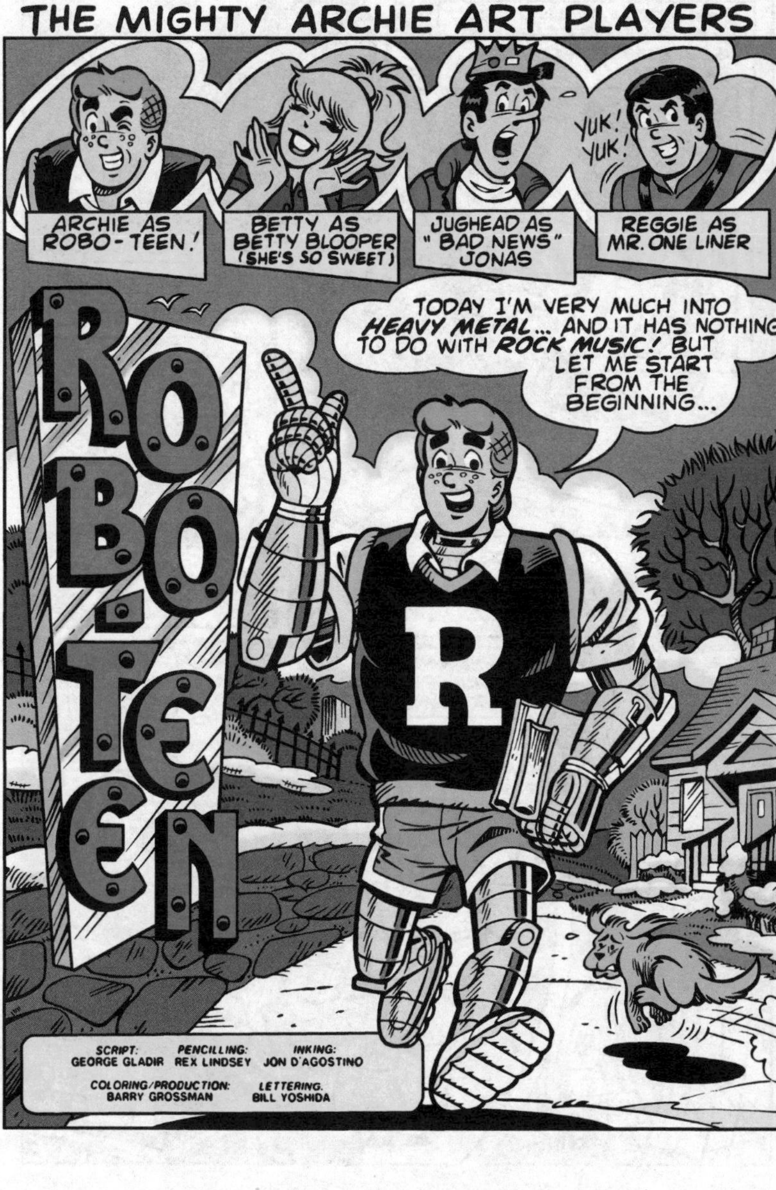
THE MIGHTY ARCHIE ART PLAYERS
YUK! YUK!
ARCHIE AS ROBO-TEEN!
BETTY AS BETTY BLOOPER (SHE'S SO SWEET)
JUGHEAD AS "BAD NEWS" JONAS
REGGIE AS MR. ONE LINER
ROBO-TEEN
TODAY I'M VERY MUCH INTO HEAVY METAL... AND IT HAS NOTHING TO DO WITH ROCK MUSIC! BUT LET ME START FROM THE BEGINNING...
R
SCRIPT: GEORGE GLADIR PENCILLING: REX LINDSEY INKING: JON D'AGOSTINO
COLORING/PRODUCTION: BARRY GROSSMAN LETTERING. BILL YOSHIDA

Originally presented in LAUGH #13, April, 1989

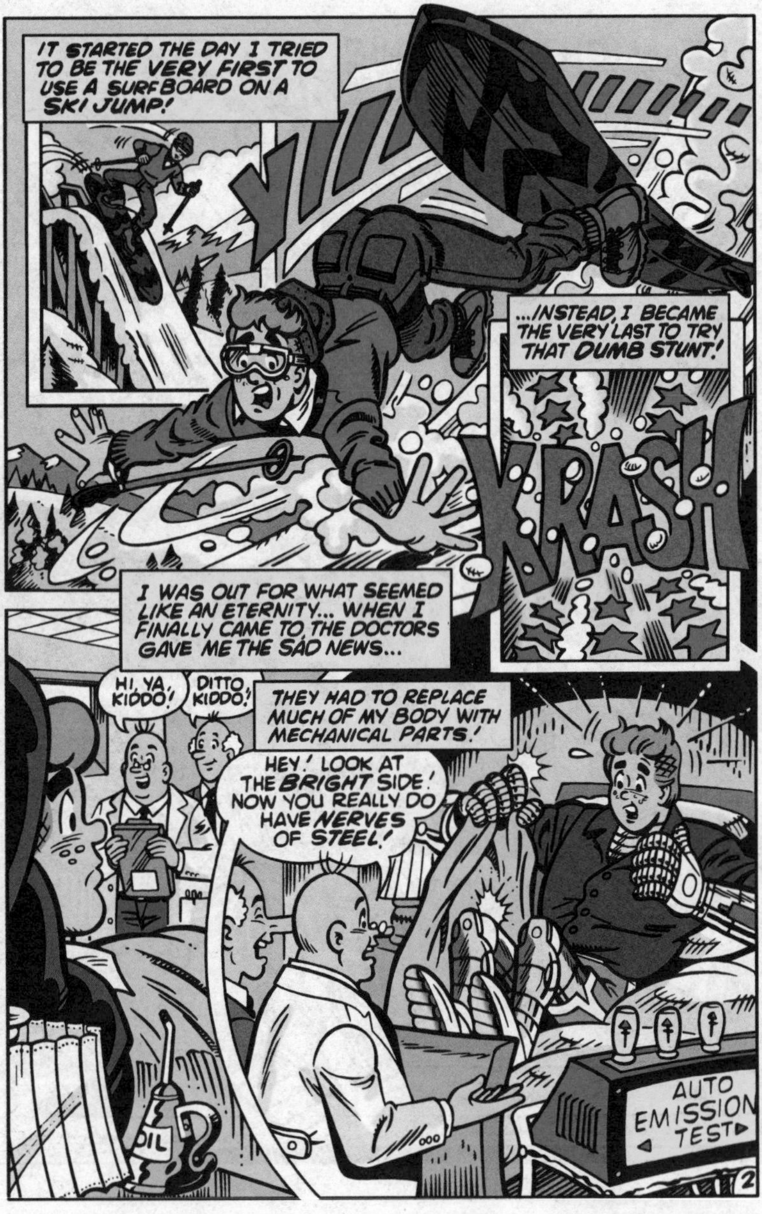
IT STARTED THE DAY I TRIED TO BE THE VERY FIRST TO USE A SURFBOARD ON A SKI JUMP!
...INSTEAD, I BECAME THE VERY LAST TO TRY THAT DUMB STUNT!
KRASH
I WAS OUT FOR WHAT SEEMED LIKE AN ETERNITY... WHEN I FINALLY CAME TO, THE DOCTORS GAVE ME THE SAD NEWS...
HI, YA, KIDDO!
DITTO, KIDDO!
THEY HAD TO REPLACE MUCH OF MY BODY WITH MECHANICAL PARTS!
HEY! LOOK AT THE BRIGHT SIDE! NOW YOU REALLY DO HAVE NERVES OF STEEL!
OIL
AUTO EMISSION TEST
2

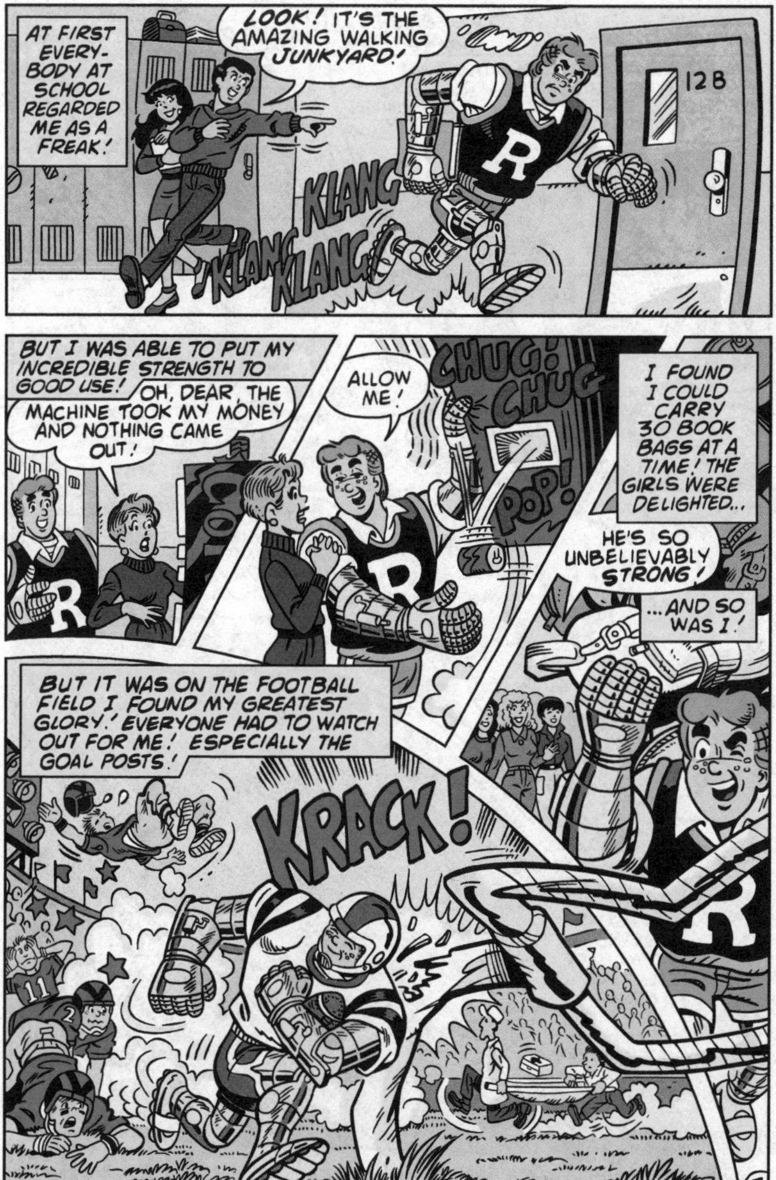
AT FIRST EVERY-BODY AT SCHOOL REGARDED ME AS A FREAK!
LOOK! IT'S THE AMAZING WALKING JUNKYARD!
12B
KLANG KLANG KLANG KLANG
BUT I WAS ABLE TO PUT MY INCREDIBLE STRENGTH TO GOOD USE!
OH, DEAR, THE MACHINE TOOK MY MONEY AND NOTHING CAME OUT!
ALLOW ME!
CHUG! CHUG
POP!
I FOUND I COULD CARRY 30 BOOK BAGS AT A TIME! THE GIRLS WERE DELIGHTED...
HE'S SO UNBELIEVABLY STRONG!
...AND SO WAS I!
BUT IT WAS ON THE FOOTBALL FIELD I FOUND MY GREATEST GLORY! EVERYONE HAD TO WATCH OUT FOR ME! ESPECIALLY THE GOAL POSTS!
KRACK!
11
2
3

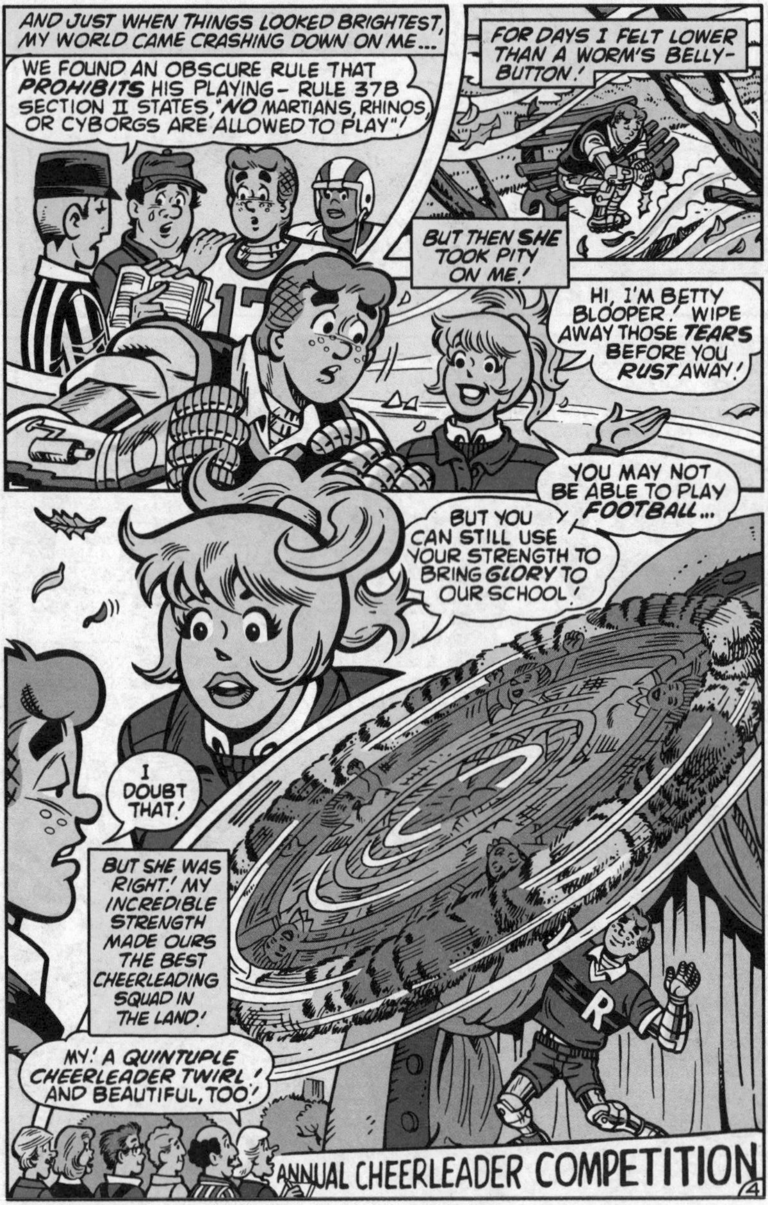
AND JUST WHEN THINGS LOOKED BRIGHTEST, MY WORLD CAME CRASHING DOWN ON ME...
WE FOUND AN OBSCURE RULE THAT PROHIBITS HIS PLAYING - RULE 37B SECTION II STATES, "NO MARTIANS, RHINOS OR CYBORGS ARE ALLOWED TO PLAY"!
FOR DAYS I FELT LOWER THAN A WORM'S BELLY-BUTTON!
BUT THEN SHE TOOK PITY ON ME!
HI, I'M BETTY BLOOPER! WIPE AWAY THOSE TEARS BEFORE YOU RUST AWAY!
YOU MAY NOT BE ABLE TO PLAY FOOTBALL...
BUT YOU CAN STILL USE YOUR STRENGTH TO BRING GLORY TO OUR SCHOOL!
I DOUBT THAT!
BUT SHE WAS RIGHT! MY INCREDIBLE STRENGTH MADE OURS THE BEST CHEERLEADING SQUAD IN THE LAND!
MY! A QUINTUPLE CHEERLEADER TWIRL! AND BEAUTIFUL, TOO!
ANNUAL CHEERLEADER COMPETITION
4

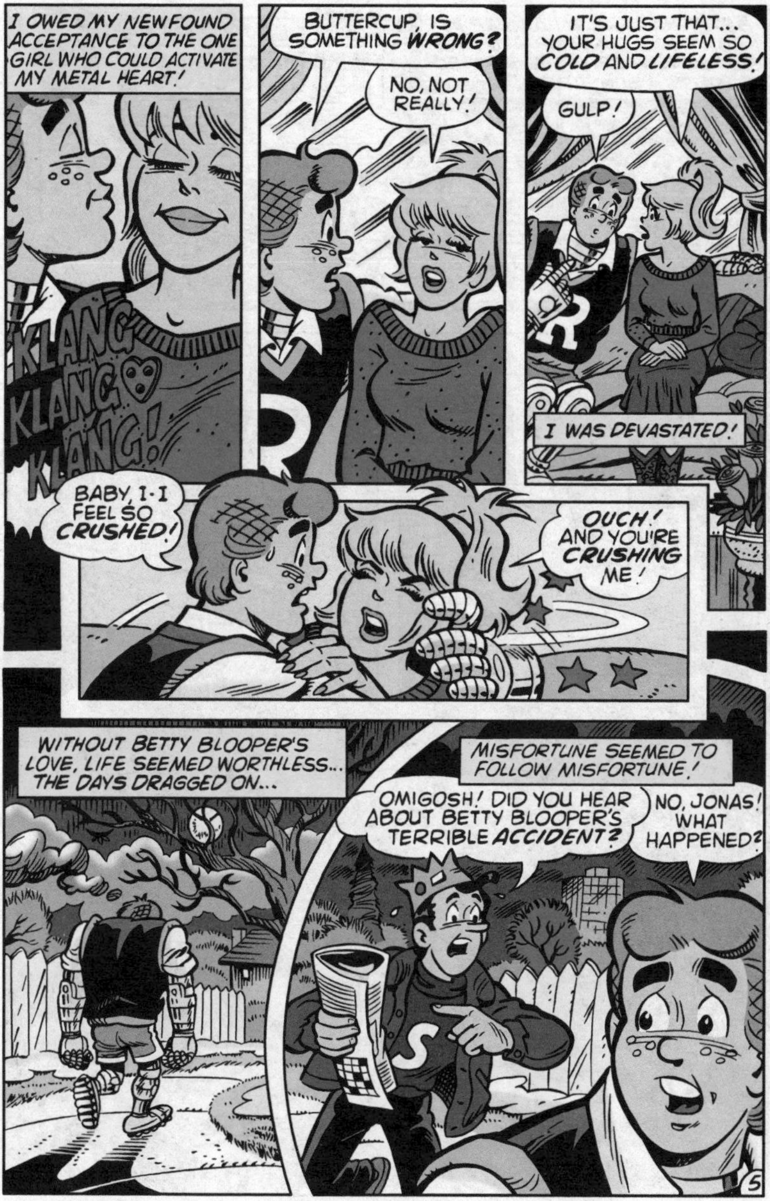
I OWED MY NEWFOUND ACCEPTANCE TO THE ONE GIRL WHO COULD ACTIVATE MY METAL HEART!
KLANG KLANG KLANG KLANG!
BUTTERCUP, IS SOMETHING WRONG?
NO, NOT REALLY!
IT'S JUST THAT... YOUR HUGS SEEM SO COLD AND LIFELESS!
GULP!
I WAS DEVASTATED!
BABY, I-I FEEL SO CRUSHED!
OUCH! AND YOU'RE CRUSHING ME!
WITHOUT BETTY BLOOPER'S LOVE, LIFE SEEMED WORTHLESS... THE DAYS DRAGGED ON...
MISFORTUNE SEEMED TO FOLLOW MISFORTUNE!
OMIGOSH! DID YOU HEAR ABOUT BETTY BLOOPER'S TERRIBLE ACCIDENT?
NO, JONAS! WHAT HAPPENED?
5

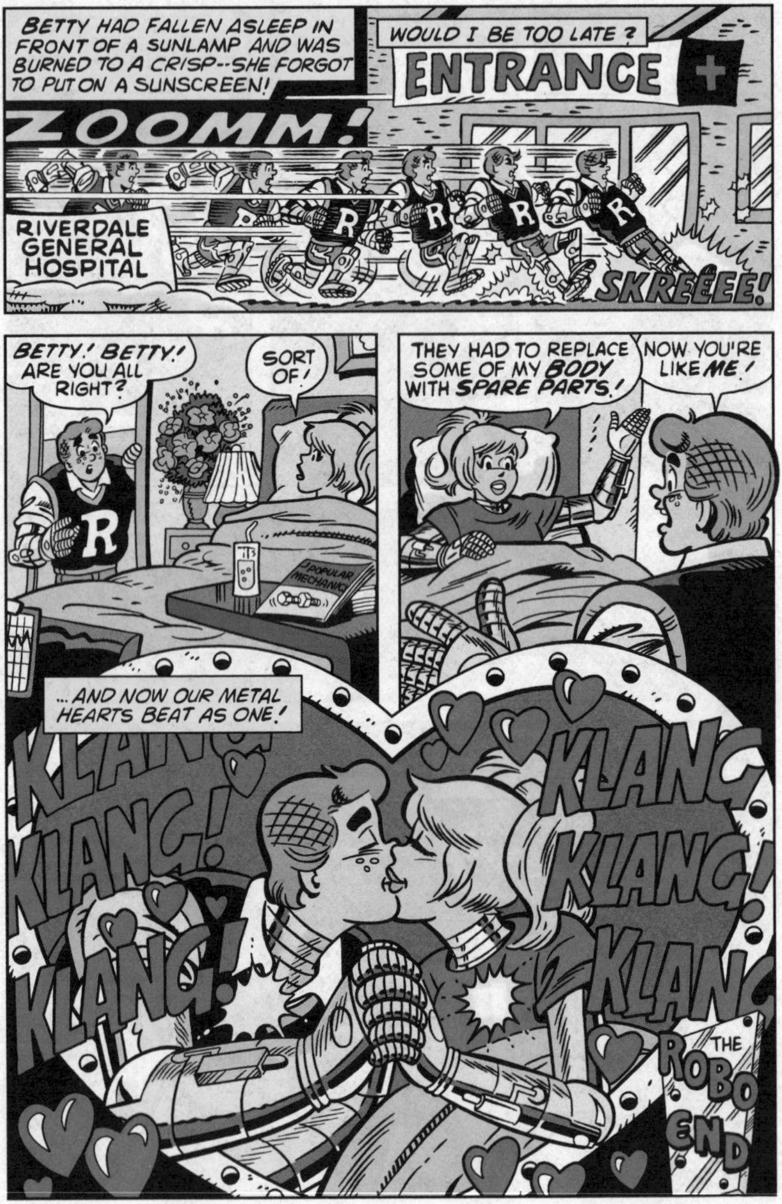
BETTY HAD FALLEN ASLEEP IN FRONT OF A SUNLAMP AND WAS BURNED TO A CRISP--SHE FORGOT TO PUT ON A SUNSCREEN!
WOULD I BE TOO LATE ?
ENTRANCE
ZOOMM!
RIVERDALE GENERAL HOSPITAL
SKREEEEE!
BETTY! BETTY! ARE YOU ALL RIGHT?
SORT OF!
POPULAR MECHANICS
THEY HAD TO REPLACE SOME OF MY BODY WITH SPARE PARTS!
NOW YOU'RE LIKE ME!
...AND NOW OUR METAL HEARTS BEAT AS ONE!
KLANG!
KLANG!
KLANG!
KLANG
KLANG!
KLANG
THE ROBO END

LET'S FACE IT, GUYS, WITHOUT A ROCK VIDEO, THE ARCHIES ARE GOING NOWHERE IN THE MUSIC BUSINESS!
(SIGH!) AND EVERYONE KNOWS A ROCK VIDEO COSTS A FORTUNE TO PRODUCE!
THE Archies
THE Archies IN "SHLOCK ROCK"
AS USUAL, REGGIE MANTLE COMES TO THE RESCUE!
STUDIO B
WE'LL MAKE OUR OWN VIDEO WITH MY DAD'S CAMCORDER!
MY COUSIN IGGY HERE HAS VOLUNTEERED TO SHOOT US!

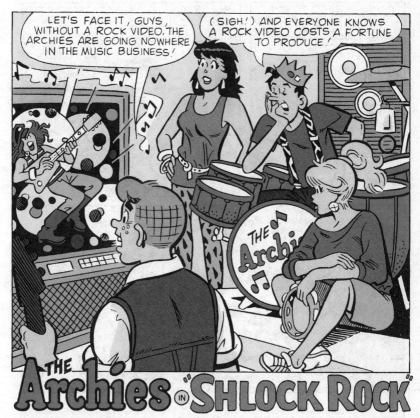

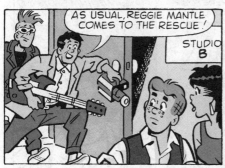

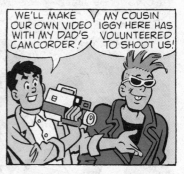

Originally presented in EVERYTHING'S ARCHIE #143, June, 1989

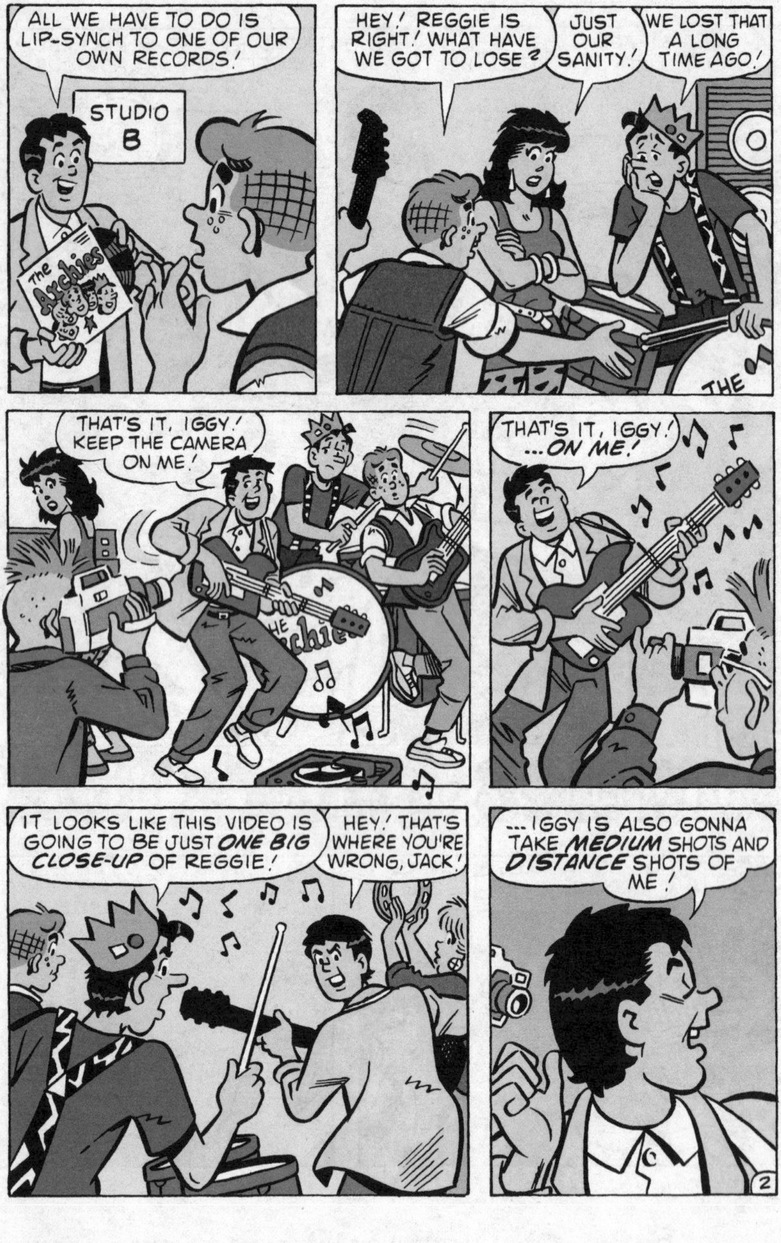
ALL WE HAVE TO DO IS LIP-SYNCH TO ONE OF OUR OWN RECORDS!
STUDIO B
The Archies
HEY! REGGIE IS RIGHT! WHAT HAVE WE GOT TO LOSE?
JUST OUR SANITY!
WE LOST THAT A LONG TIME AGO!
THE
THAT'S IT, IGGY! KEEP THE CAMERA ON ME!
THE Archies
THAT'S IT, IGGY! ...ON ME!
IT LOOKS LIKE THIS VIDEO IS GOING TO BE JUST ONE BIG CLOSE-UP OF REGGIE!
HEY! THAT'S WHERE YOU'RE WRONG, JACK!
...IGGY IS ALSO GONNA TAKE MEDIUM SHOTS AND DISTANCE SHOTS OF ME!
2

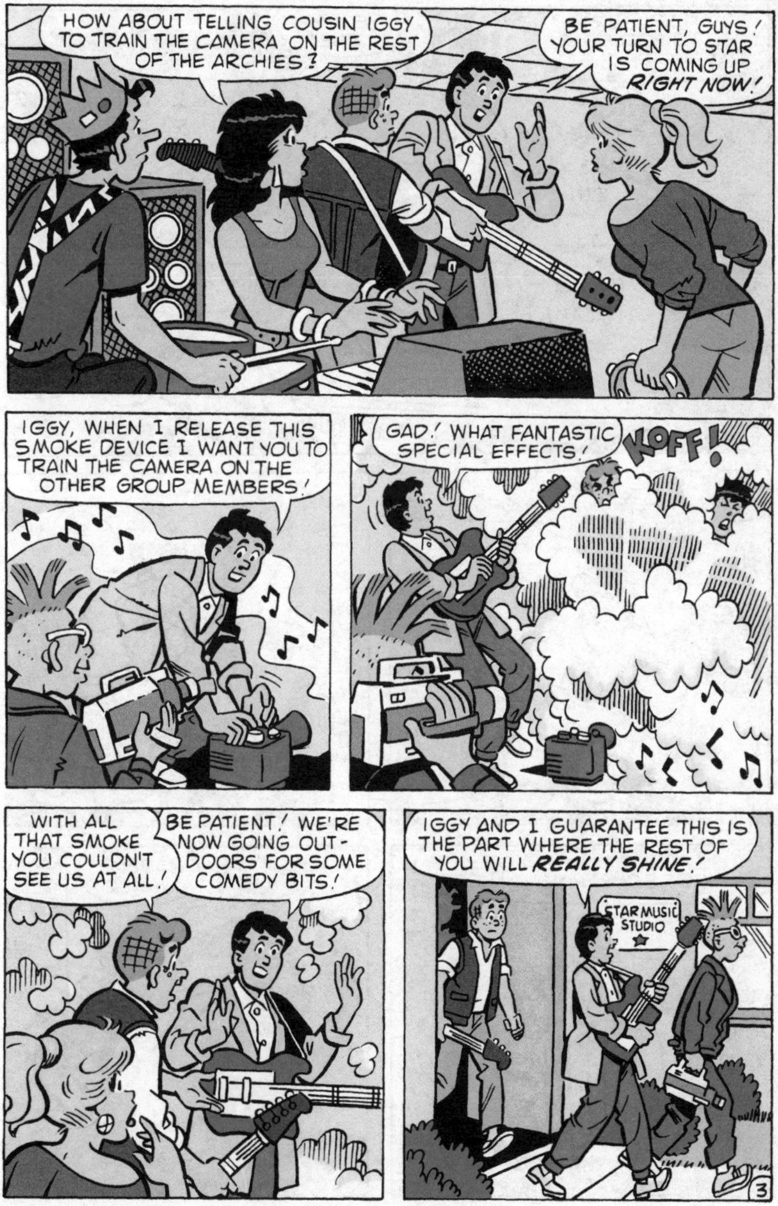
HOW ABOUT TELLING COUSIN IGGY TO TRAIN THE CAMERA ON THE REST OF THE ARCHIES?
BE PATIENT, GUYS! YOUR TURN TO STAR IS COMING UP RIGHT NOW!
IGGY, WHEN I RELEASE THIS SMOKE DEVICE I WANT YOU TO TRAIN THE CAMERA ON THE OTHER GROUP MEMBERS!
GAD! WHAT FANTASTIC SPECIAL EFFECTS!
KOFF!
WITH ALL THAT SMOKE YOU COULDN'T SEE US AT ALL!
BE PATIENT! WE'RE NOW GOING OUT-DOORS FOR SOME COMEDY BITS!
IGGY AND I GUARANTEE THIS IS THE PART WHERE THE REST OF YOU WILL REALLY SHINE!
STAR MUSIC STUDIO
3

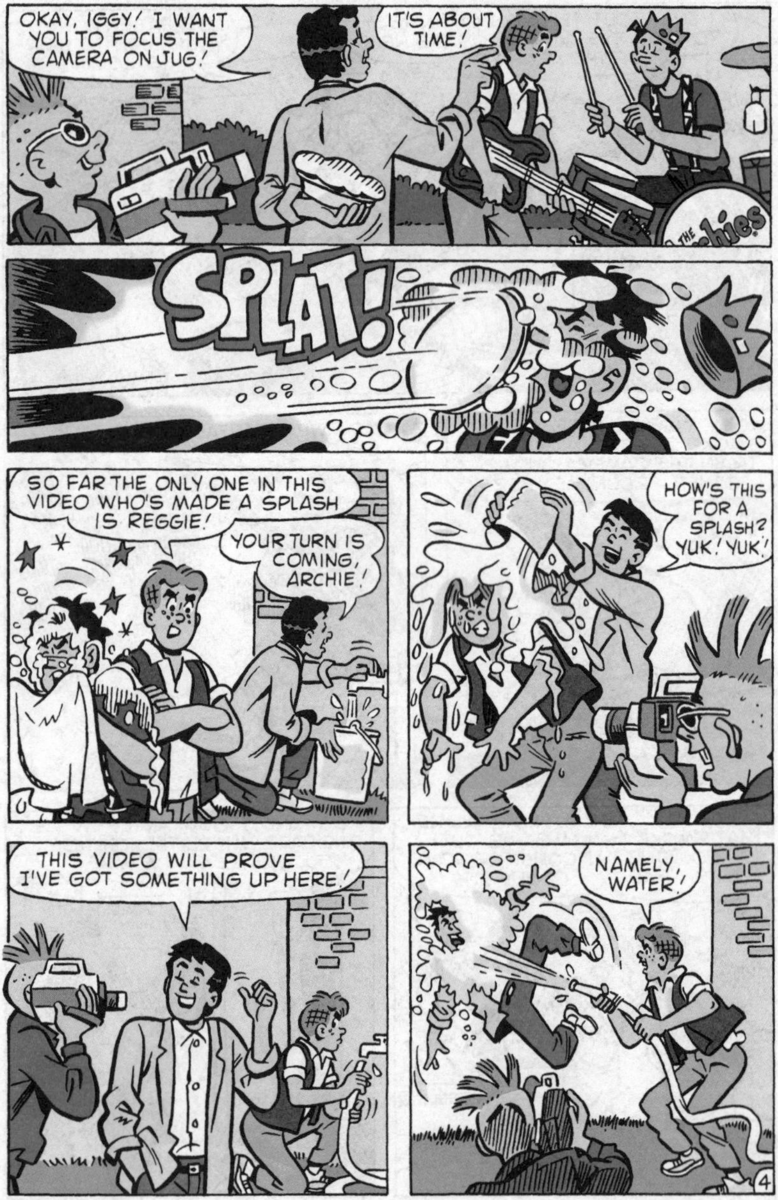
OKAY, IGGY! I WANT YOU TO FOCUS THE CAMERA ON JUG!
IT'S ABOUT TIME!
THE Archies
SPLAT!
SO FAR THE ONLY ONE IN THIS VIDEO WHO'S MADE A SPLASH IS REGGIE!
YOUR TURN IS COMING, ARCHIE!
HOW'S THIS FOR A SPLASH? YUK! YUK!
THIS VIDEO WILL PROVE I'VE GOT SOMETHING UP HERE!
NAMELY, WATER!
4

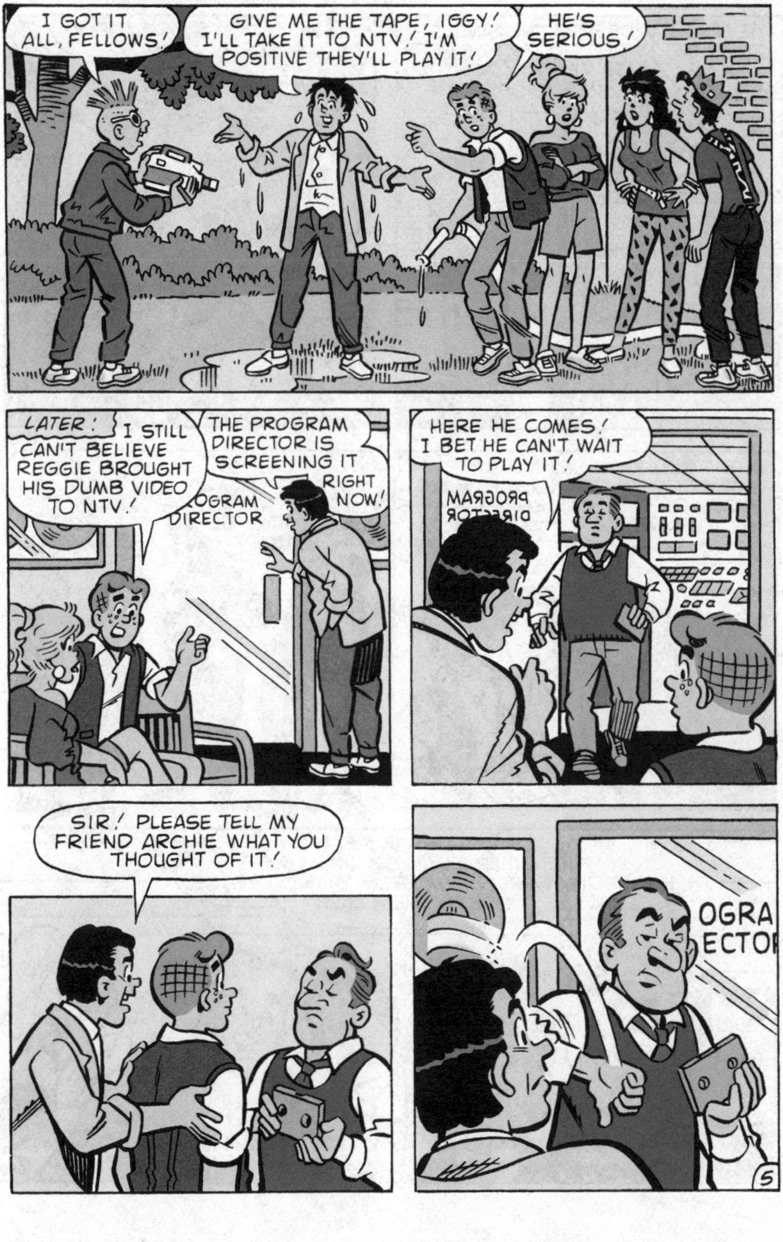
I GOT IT ALL, FELLOWS!
GIVE ME THE TAPE, IGGY! I'LL TAKE IT TO NTV! I'M POSITIVE THEY'LL PLAY IT!
HE'S SERIOUS!
LATER:
I STILL CAN'T BELIEVE REGGIE BROUGHT HIS DUMB VIDEO TO NTV!
THE PROGRAM DIRECTOR IS SCREENING IT RIGHT NOW!
PROGRAM DIRECTOR
HERE HE COMES! I BET HE CAN'T WAIT TO PLAY IT!
SIR! PLEASE TELL MY FRIEND ARCHIE WHAT YOU THOUGHT OF IT!
OGRA ECTOR
5

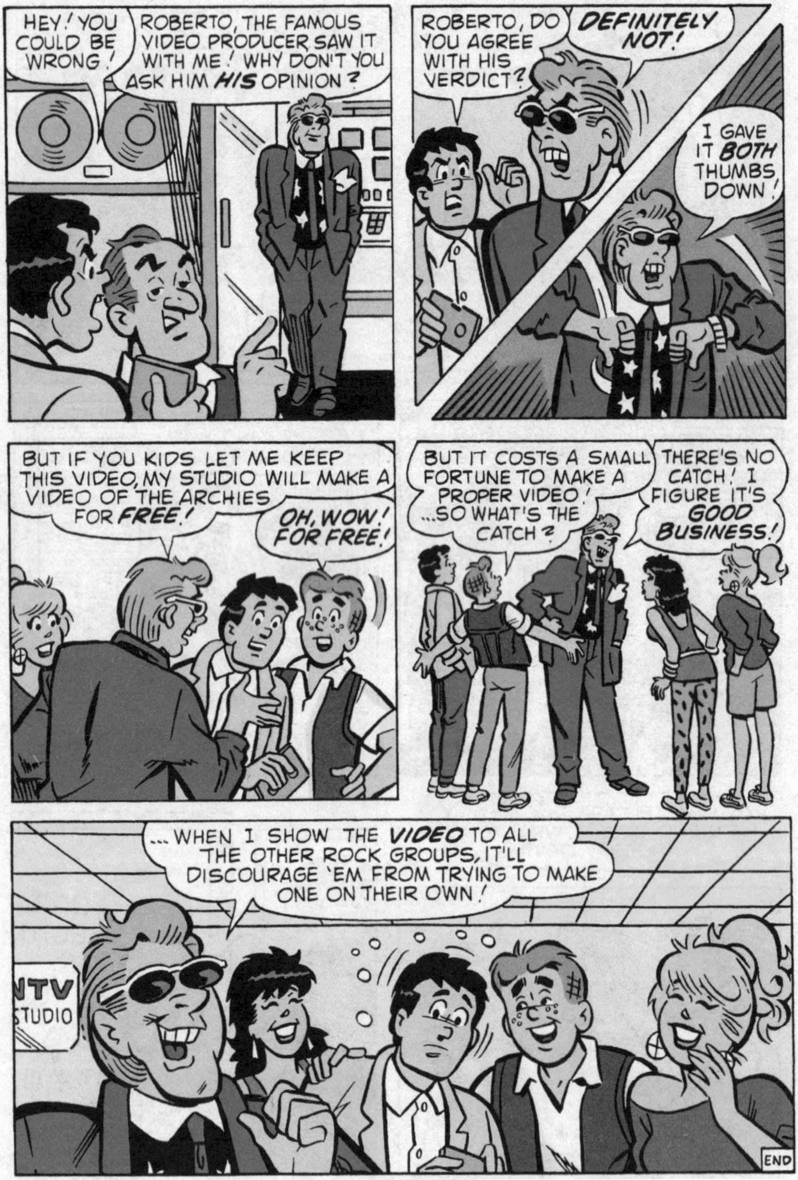
HEY! YOU COULD BE WRONG!
ROBERTO, THE FAMOUS VIDEO PRODUCER SAW IT WITH ME! WHY DON'T YOU ASK HIM HIS OPINION?
ROBERTO, DO YOU AGREE WITH HIS VERDICT?
DEFINITELY NOT!
I GAVE IT BOTH THUMBS DOWN!
BUT IF YOU KIDS LET ME KEEP THIS VIDEO, MY STUDIO WILL MAKE A VIDEO OF THE ARCHIES FOR FREE!
OH, WOW! FOR FREE!
BUT IT COSTS A SMALL FORTUNE TO MAKE A PROPER VIDEO! ...SO WHAT'S THE CATCH?
THERE'S NO CATCH! I FIGURE IT'S GOOD BUSINESS!
...WHEN I SHOW THE VIDEO TO ALL THE OTHER ROCK GROUPS, IT'LL DISCOURAGE 'EM FROM TRYING TO MAKE ONE ON THEIR OWN!
NTV
STUDIO
END

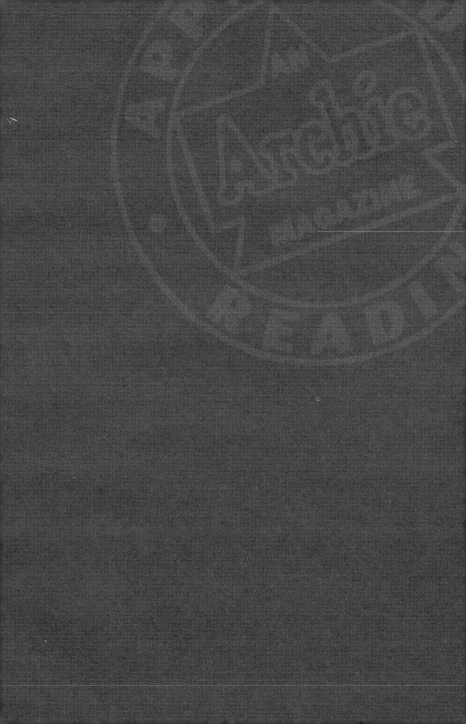

The Best of

# Archie Americana

## Bronze Age

## The 1990s

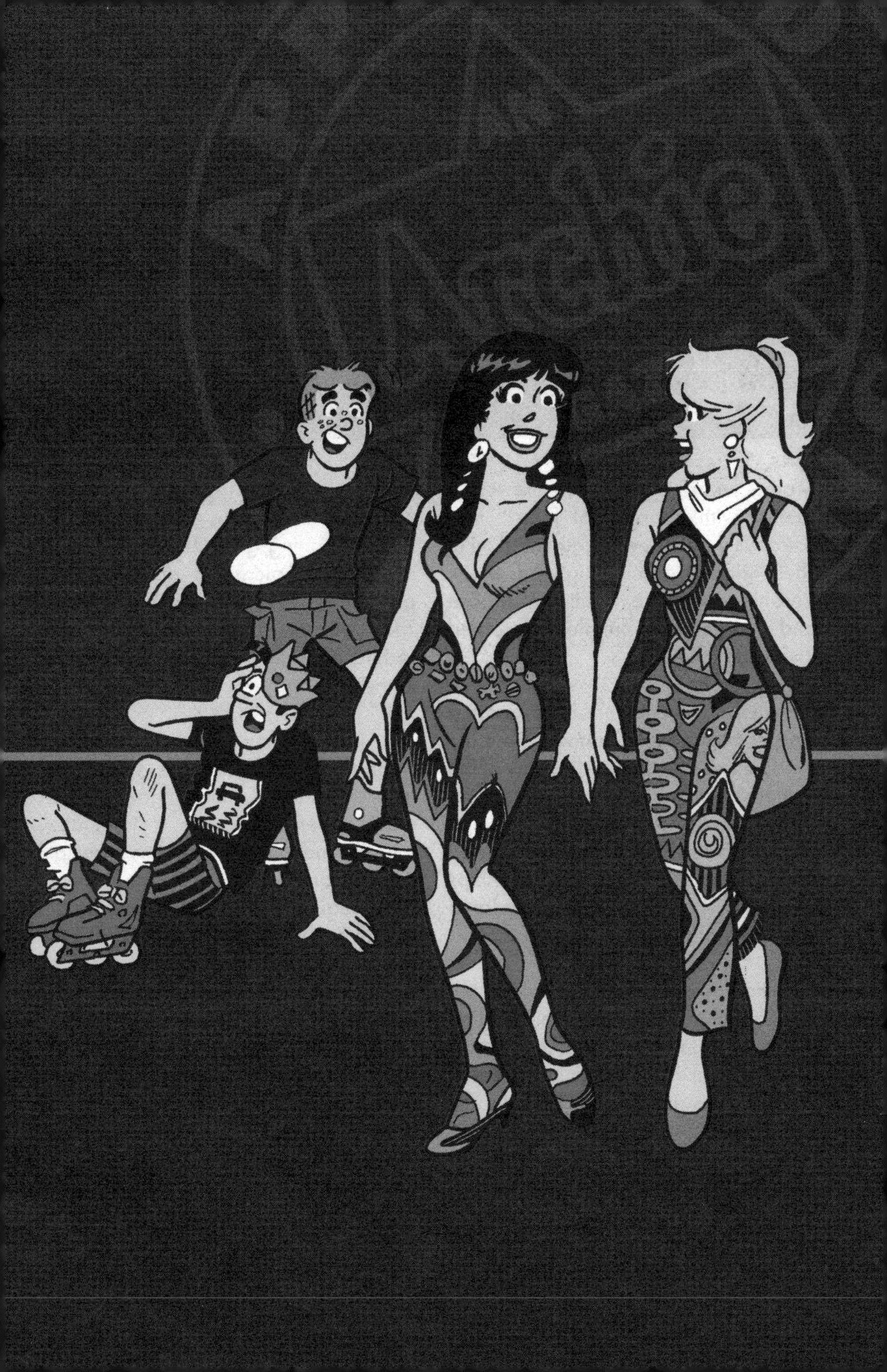

# LIVIN' IN THE '90s WITH MY COMIC BOOK FRIENDS

## INTRODUCTION BY PAUL CASTIGLIA

### -THE 1990s-

Many years ago I became close friends with a group of folks I had previously only been acquainted with. Their names? Archie, Jughead, Betty, Veronica, Reggie, Dilton, Moose and the entire population of fabled Riverdale, USA.

Sure, I had encountered the gang a time or two in my childhood. Be it the random issue of *Jughead*, or any of the numerous Filmation animated cartoon series shown on Saturday morning TV. I liked the characters, their broad archetypes and the relationships between them, and appreciated Archie's world for the fun it was.

Riverdale was a nice diversion, but back then my little boy imagination was more often preoccupied by flights of fantasy. Like most comic book-crazy boys, I was more interested in the super-heroics of Spider-Man, Batman and their ilk. I left the majority of Archie comics reading to the girls.

I should have listened to them. The girls in my life have always been ahead of the curve... especially those Archie-reading girls! They knew that the simplest pleasures are the most profound.... and the most universal. Thankfully, I had a golden opportunity to find out first-hand what those girls knew all along.

The day of my awakening came January 2, 1990. That's when my tenure at Archie Comics began. My life would never be the same. It didn't take long for me to realize just how special Archie Comics were... and are. Where do I begin to chart my memories of Archie in the '90s? There are just too many to list, but I'll try to convey some of the more lasting impressions.

I came into the organization just as they were planning their 50th anniversary. I couldn't have started at a better time, as my first assignment was helping to compile the stories that would make up the first edition of the heralded *Archie Americana Series, the Best of the Forties*. Researching the earliest Archie stories provided me with a unique perspective on where the characters had been, and how their past informed their present. It was those building blocks that formed the firm foundation for the Archie comic book universe throughout the years. The characters and basic situations – the eternal love triangle, Archie being a klutz, Jughead outwitting everyone – remained constant even though the fads and fashions changed. It is a tribute to the universal nature of teenage characters in high school that the series effortlessly reflected these surface changes decade after decade.

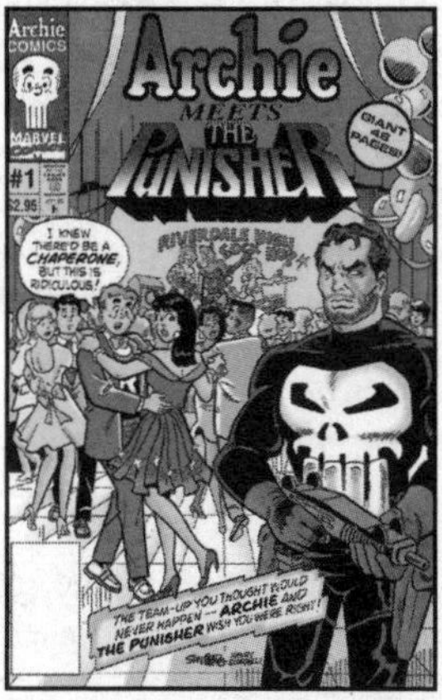
Archie COMICS
Archie
MEETS
THE
PUNISHER
GIANT 48 PAGES!
#1
I KNEW THERE'D BE A CHAPERONE, BUT THIS IS RIDICULOUS!
THE TEAM-UP YOU THOUGHT WOULD NEVER HAPPEN – ARCHIE AND THE PUNISHER WISH YOU WERE RIGHT!

ARCHIE MEETS PUNISHER, 1994

The nineties were no exception. In fact, just as the forties laid the groundwork for all that followed, the nineties likewise foreshadowed the exciting things happening at Archie today. In 1994, the landmark "Love Showdown" storyline received nation-wide coverage. 1994 also saw the famed Archie/Marvel cross-over, "Archie Meets the Punisher," written by Batton Lash, with art by Stan Goldberg and John Buscema. The nineties also saw the launch of the Archie Comics website; today, that site is an integral part of the company and its plans for today and the future.

The nineties were a great time for Archie milestones. Not only did Cheryl return, but several titles celebrated anniversary issues, and new titles including *Archie & Friends, Betty* and *Betty & Veronica Spectacular* were launched. *Sabrina the Teenage Witch* became a sensation on TV, which led to a successful revival of her comic series.

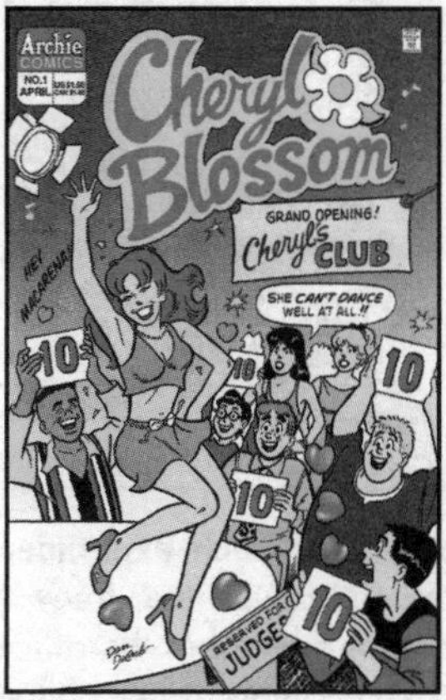
Archie COMICS
Cheryl Blossom
GRAND OPENING! Cheryl's CLUB
HEY MACARENA!
SHE CAN'T DANCE WELL AT ALL!!
RESERVED FOR JUDGES

CHERYL BLOSSOM #1, 1997

The nineties were also one of the great decades for experimentation at Archie Comics. *Archie's Explorers of the Unknown* recast the gang as adventurers while *Archie's R/C Racers* had them competing in a cross-country car race. Veronica's title became a glamorous travelogue as she traveled throughout the world. Jughead toppled through time in *Jughead's Time Police* and served comfort food and kooky comedy in *Jughead's Diner*. But those were just the appetizers for Jughead's main course: a makeover that found the crowned one sporting a Mohawk, and the more lasting addition of his little baby sister, Forsythia "Jellybean" Jones.

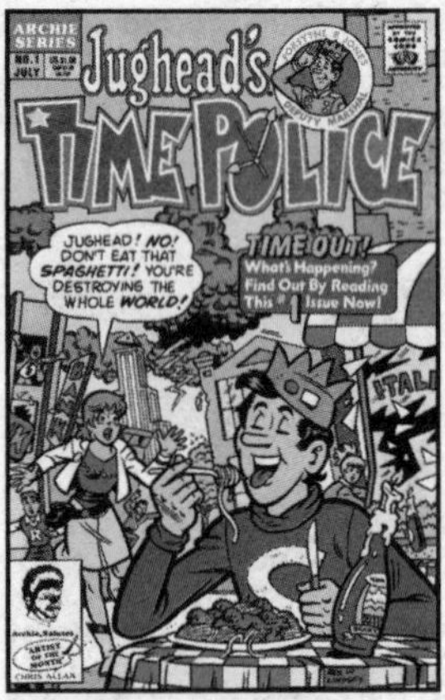
ARCHIE SERIES
NO. 1
JULY
Jughead's
TIME POLICE
FORSYTHE P. JONES
DEPUTY MARSHAL
JUGHEAD! NO! DON'T EAT THAT SPAGHETTI! YOU'RE DESTROYING THE WHOLE WORLD!
TIME OUT!
What's Happening? Find Out By Reading This #1 Issue Now!
ARTIST OF THE MONTH
CHRIS ALLAN

JUGHEAD'S TIME POLICE #1, 1990

It's no surprise such experimentation took place, given the freewheeling times I experienced in the office back then. Archie's internet-less bullpen was a place where people actually spoke to one another on the phone or over cubicle walls or (gasp!) even in person! Good-natured practical jokes were a standard, as were sound bytes over the intercom. A spirit of creativity was fostered, and despite how raucous the room could get at times, all the work was done on time, and was filled with good humor... and good art!

Back in college, I'd heard teachers say working at Archie was an education in the industry. I found out first hand how right they were! At Archie, I learned everything there is to know about comic books—from conception to completion and the promotion that follows, as well as dealing with talent, printers, distributors and retailers. I owe my whole career to that invaluable training. But more importantly, I forged friendships that have lasted a lifetime... not only with my colleagues, but with the world's favorite comic book teens. That's the story of Archie and me in the 1990s... and with this volume, you too can relive just how great a decade the nineties were for Archie and his friends!

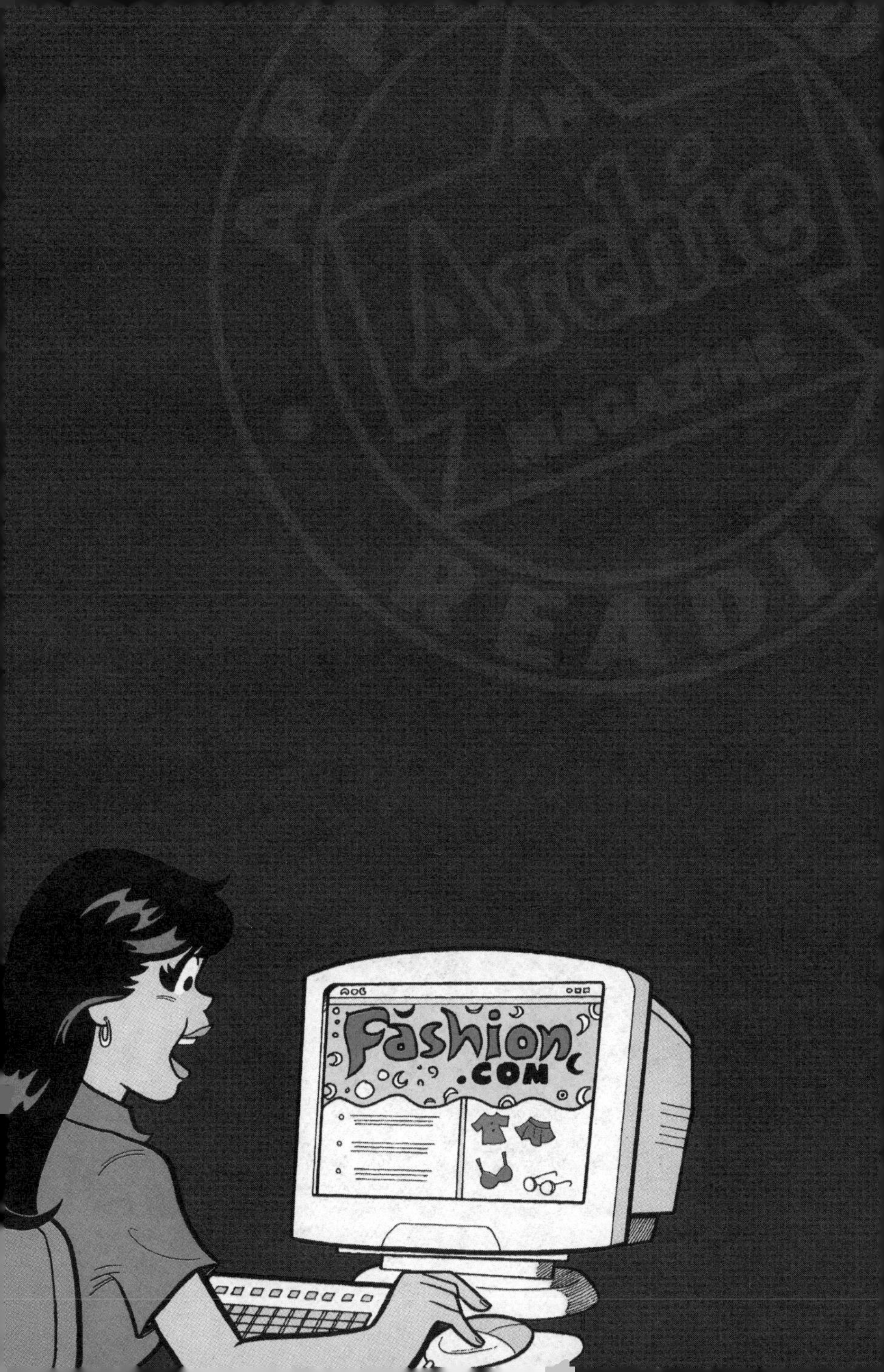
Fashion
.COM

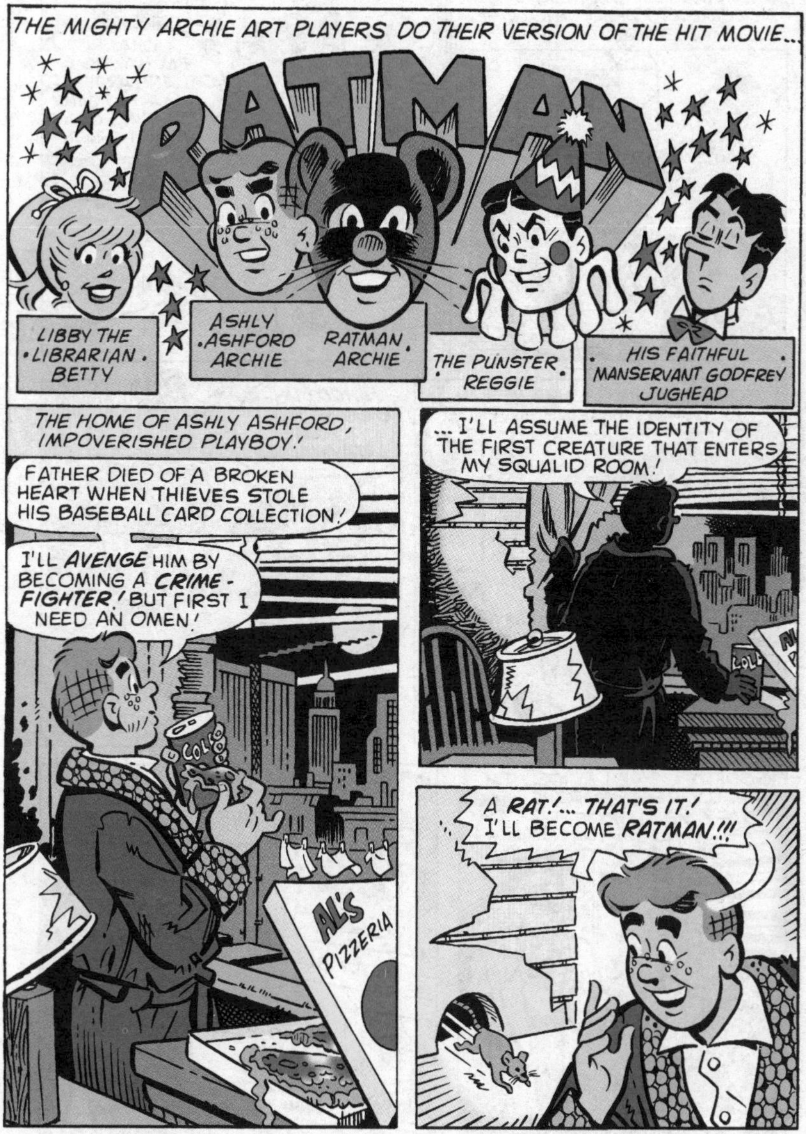
THE MIGHTY ARCHIE ART PLAYERS DO THEIR VERSION OF THE HIT MOVIE...
RATMAN
LIBBY THE LIBRARIAN BETTY
ASHLY ASHFORD ARCHIE
RATMAN ARCHIE
THE PUNSTER REGGIE
HIS FAITHFUL MANSERVANT GODFREY JUGHEAD
THE HOME OF ASHLY ASHFORD, IMPOVERISHED PLAYBOY!
FATHER DIED OF A BROKEN HEART WHEN THIEVES STOLE HIS BASEBALL CARD COLLECTION!
I'LL AVENGE HIM BY BECOMING A CRIME-FIGHTER! BUT FIRST I NEED AN OMEN!
AL'S PIZZERIA
...I'LL ASSUME THE IDENTITY OF THE FIRST CREATURE THAT ENTERS MY SQUALID ROOM!
A RAT!... THAT'S IT! I'LL BECOME RATMAN!!!

Originally presented in LAUGH #19, February, 1990

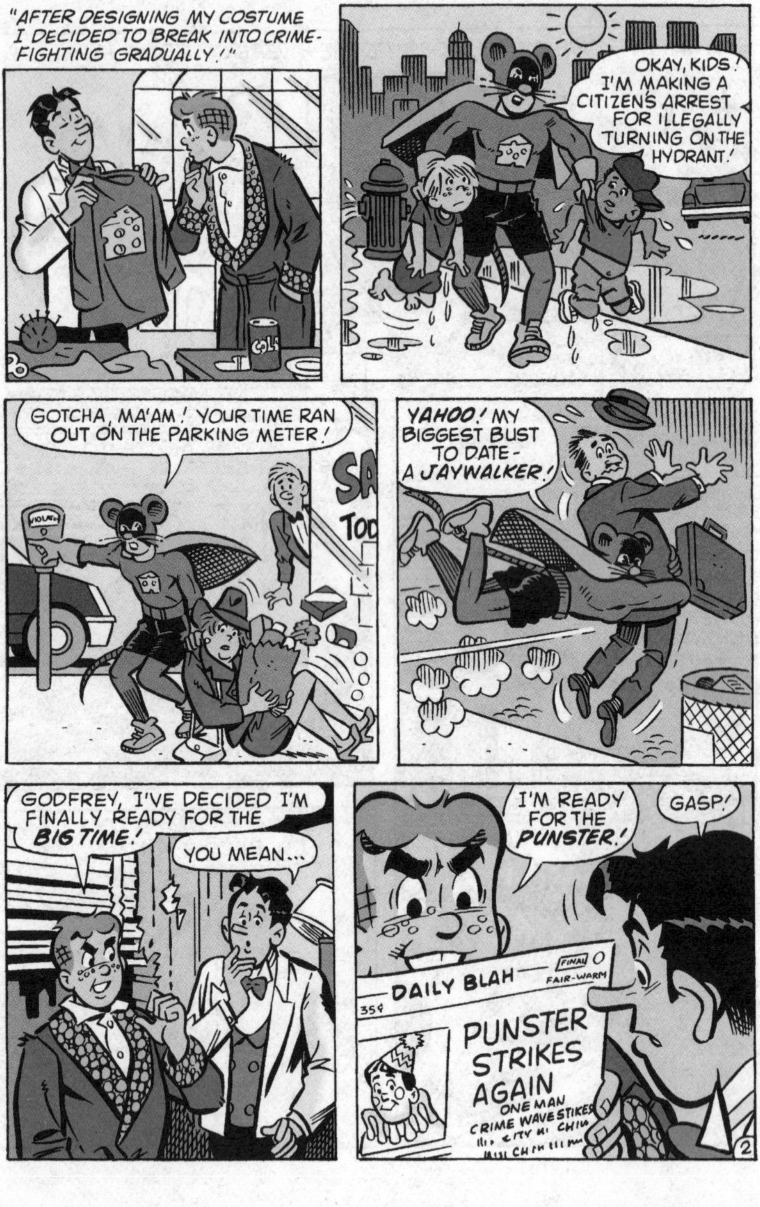
"AFTER DESIGNING MY COSTUME I DECIDED TO BREAK INTO CRIME-FIGHTING GRADUALLY!"
OKAY, KIDS! I'M MAKING A CITIZEN'S ARREST FOR ILLEGALLY TURNING ON THE HYDRANT!
GOTCHA, MA'AM! YOUR TIME RAN OUT ON THE PARKING METER!
YAHOO! MY BIGGEST BUST TO DATE - A JAYWALKER!
GODFREY, I'VE DECIDED I'M FINALLY READY FOR THE BIG TIME!
YOU MEAN...
I'M READY FOR THE PUNSTER!
GASP!
DAILY BLAH
FINAL
FAIR-WARM
35¢
PUNSTER STRIKES AGAIN
ONE MAN CRIME WAVE STIKES
2

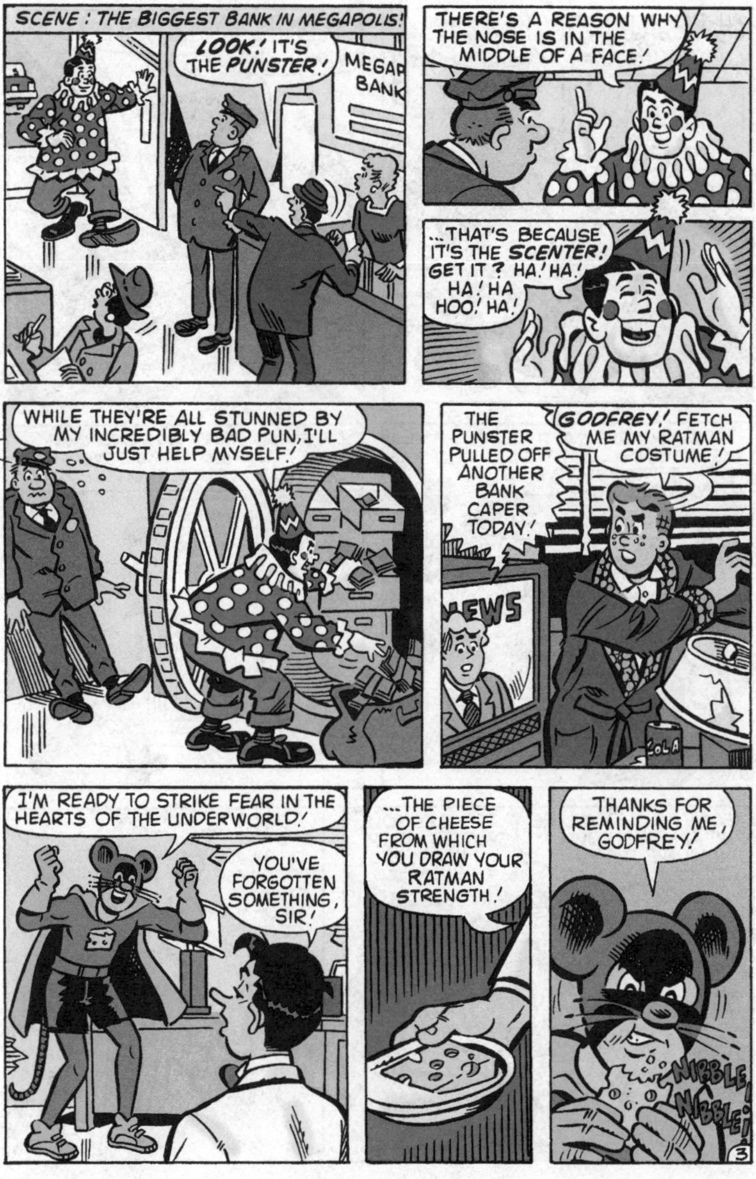
SCENE : THE BIGGEST BANK IN MEGAPOLIS!
LOOK! IT'S THE PUNSTER!
MEGAP BANK
THERE'S A REASON WHY THE NOSE IS IN THE MIDDLE OF A FACE!
...THAT'S BECAUSE IT'S THE SCENTER! GET IT ? HA! HA! HA! HA HOO! HA!
WHILE THEY'RE ALL STUNNED BY MY INCREDIBLY BAD PUN, I'LL JUST HELP MYSELF!
THE PUNSTER PULLED OFF ANOTHER BANK CAPER TODAY!
GODFREY! FETCH ME MY RATMAN COSTUME!
NEWS
COLA
I'M READY TO STRIKE FEAR IN THE HEARTS OF THE UNDERWORLD!
YOU'VE FORGOTTEN SOMETHING, SIR!
...THE PIECE OF CHEESE FROM WHICH YOU DRAW YOUR RATMAN STRENGTH!
THANKS FOR REMINDING ME, GODFREY!
NIBBLE! NIBBLE!
3

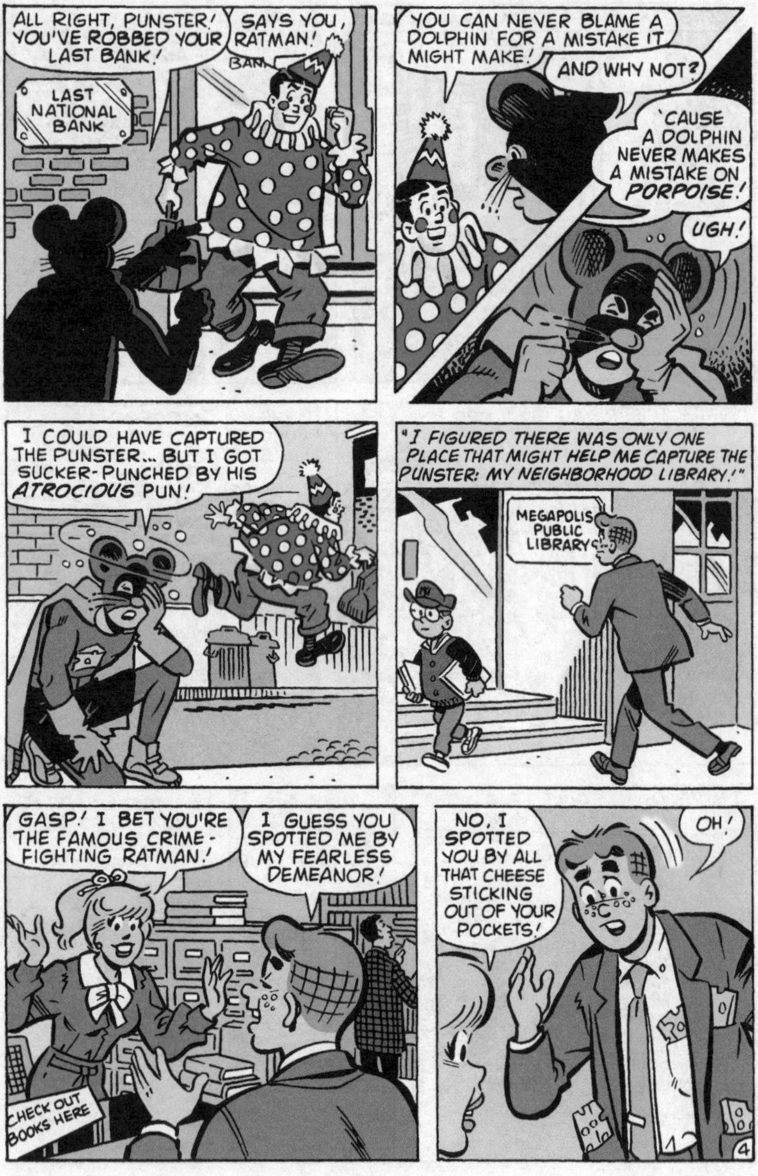
ALL RIGHT, PUNSTER! YOU'VE ROBBED YOUR LAST BANK!
SAYS YOU, RATMAN!
LAST NATIONAL BANK
YOU CAN NEVER BLAME A DOLPHIN FOR A MISTAKE IT MIGHT MAKE!
AND WHY NOT?
'CAUSE A DOLPHIN NEVER MAKES A MISTAKE ON PORPOISE!
UGH!
I COULD HAVE CAPTURED THE PUNSTER... BUT I GOT SUCKER-PUNCHED BY HIS ATROCIOUS PUN!
"I FIGURED THERE WAS ONLY ONE PLACE THAT MIGHT HELP ME CAPTURE THE PUNSTER: MY NEIGHBORHOOD LIBRARY!"
MEGAPOLIS PUBLIC LIBRARY
GASP! I BET YOU'RE THE FAMOUS CRIME-FIGHTING RATMAN!
I GUESS YOU SPOTTED ME BY MY FEARLESS DEMEANOR!
CHECK OUT BOOKS HERE
NO, I SPOTTED YOU BY ALL THAT CHEESE STICKING OUT OF YOUR POCKETS!
OH!
4

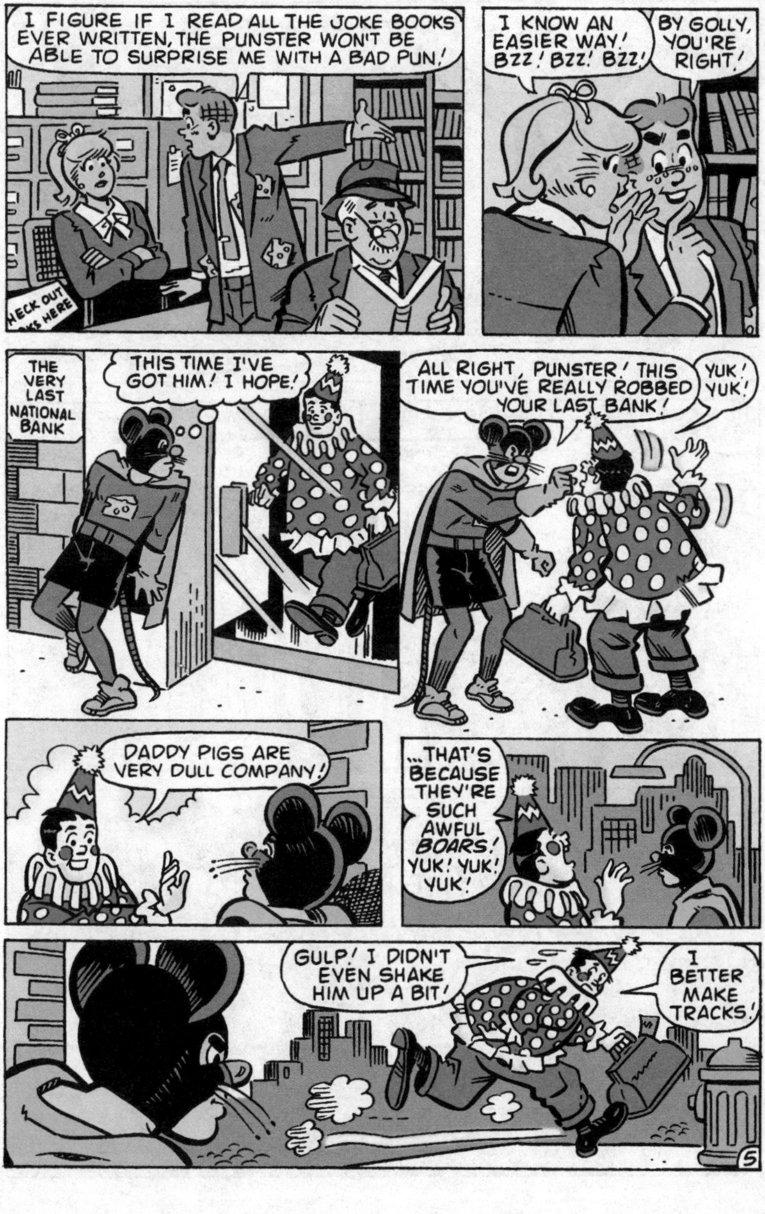
I FIGURE IF I READ ALL THE JOKE BOOKS EVER WRITTEN, THE PUNSTER WON'T BE ABLE TO SURPRISE ME WITH A BAD PUN!
I KNOW AN EASIER WAY! BZZ! BZZ! BZZ!
BY GOLLY, YOU'RE RIGHT!
THE VERY LAST NATIONAL BANK
THIS TIME I'VE GOT HIM! I HOPE!
ALL RIGHT, PUNSTER! THIS TIME YOU'VE REALLY ROBBED YOUR LAST BANK!
YUK! YUK!
DADDY PIGS ARE VERY DULL COMPANY!
...THAT'S BECAUSE THEY'RE SUCH AWFUL BOARS! YUK! YUK! YUK!
GULP! I DIDN'T EVEN SHAKE HIM UP A BIT!
I BETTER MAKE TRACKS!
5

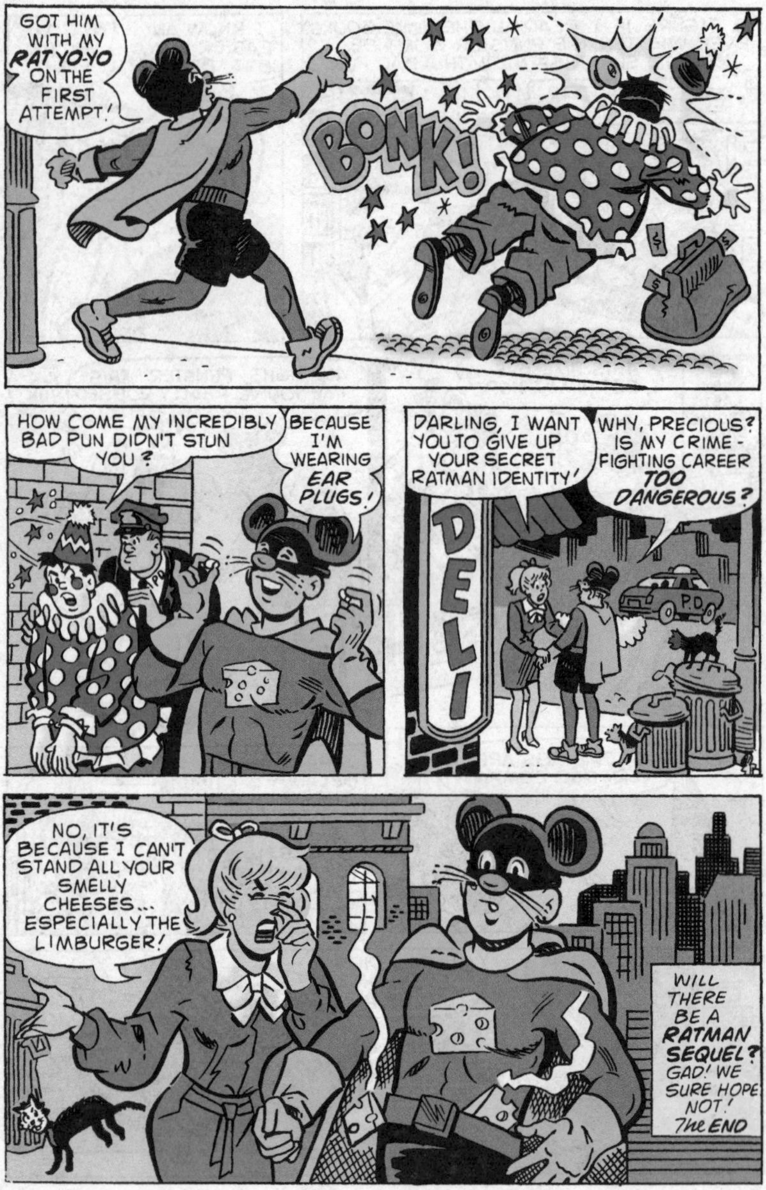
GOT HIM WITH MY RAT YO-YO ON THE FIRST ATTEMPT!
BONK!
HOW COME MY INCREDIBLY BAD PUN DIDN'T STUN YOU?
BECAUSE I'M WEARING EAR PLUGS!
DARLING, I WANT YOU TO GIVE UP YOUR SECRET RATMAN IDENTITY!
WHY, PRECIOUS? IS MY CRIME-FIGHTING CAREER TOO DANGEROUS?
DELI
P.D.
NO, IT'S BECAUSE I CAN'T STAND ALL YOUR SMELLY CHEESES... ESPECIALLY THE LIMBURGER!
WILL THERE BE A RATMAN SEQUEL? GAD! WE SURE HOPE NOT!
The END

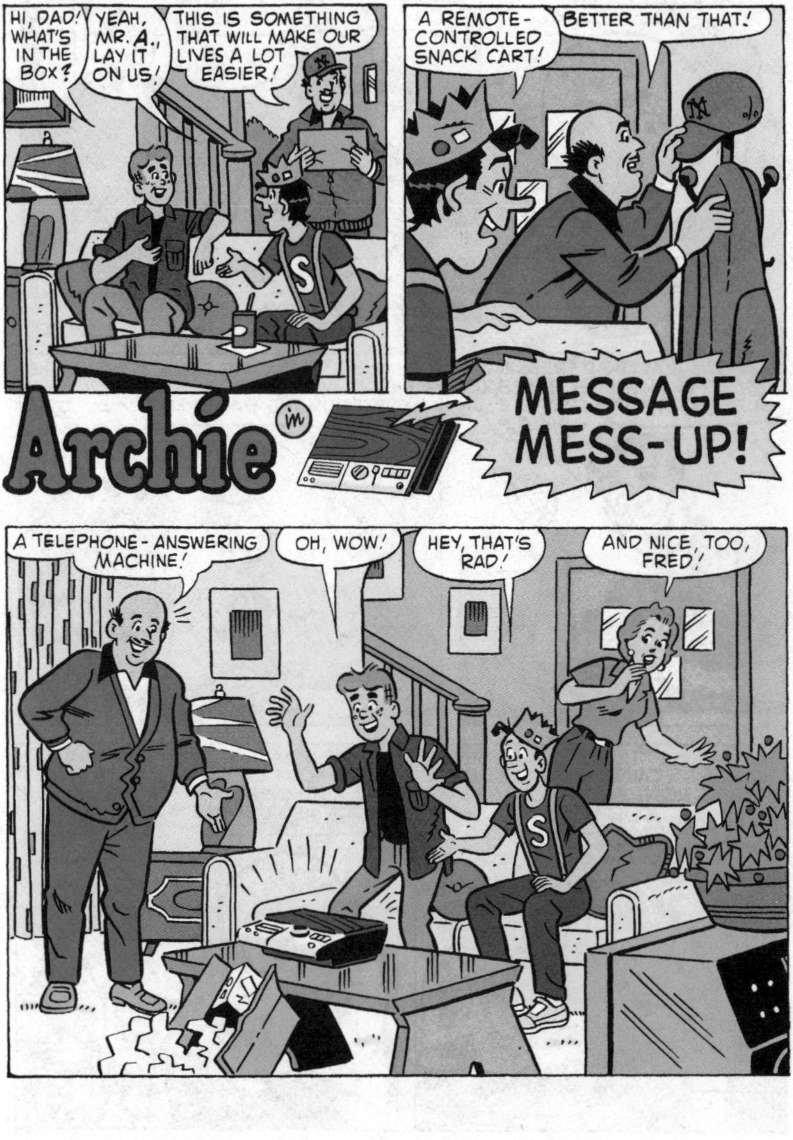
HI, DAD! WHAT'S IN THE BOX?
YEAH, MR. A., LAY IT ON US!
THIS IS SOMETHING THAT WILL MAKE OUR LIVES A LOT EASIER!
A REMOTE-CONTROLLED SNACK CART!
BETTER THAN THAT!
Archie in
MESSAGE MESS-UP!
A TELEPHONE-ANSWERING MACHINE!
OH, WOW!
HEY, THAT'S RAD!
AND NICE, TOO, FRED!

Originally presented in EVERYTHING'S ARCHIE #152, November, 1990

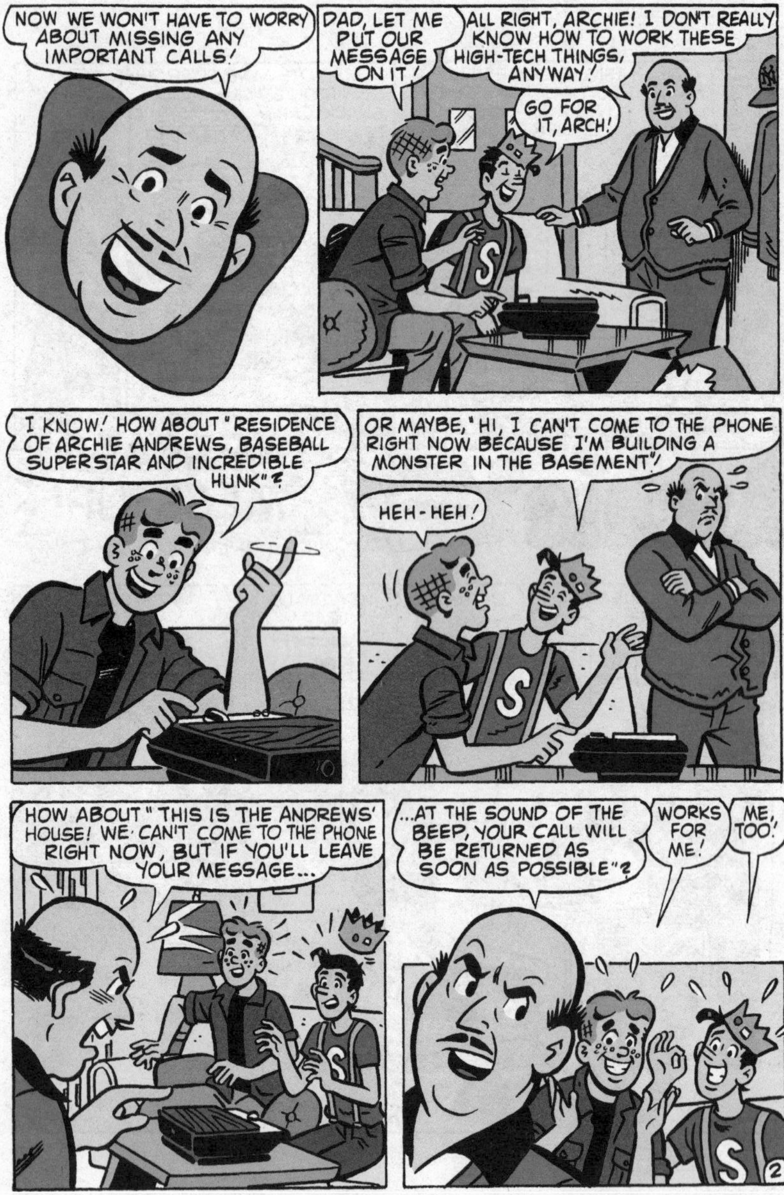
NOW WE WON'T HAVE TO WORRY ABOUT MISSING ANY IMPORTANT CALLS!
DAD, LET ME PUT OUR MESSAGE ON IT!
ALL RIGHT, ARCHIE! I DON'T REALLY KNOW HOW TO WORK THESE HIGH-TECH THINGS, ANYWAY!
GO FOR IT, ARCH!
I KNOW! HOW ABOUT "RESIDENCE OF ARCHIE ANDREWS, BASEBALL SUPERSTAR AND INCREDIBLE HUNK"?
OR MAYBE, "HI, I CAN'T COME TO THE PHONE RIGHT NOW BECAUSE I'M BUILDING A MONSTER IN THE BASEMENT"!
HEH-HEH!
HOW ABOUT "THIS IS THE ANDREWS' HOUSE! WE CAN'T COME TO THE PHONE RIGHT NOW, BUT IF YOU'LL LEAVE YOUR MESSAGE...
...AT THE SOUND OF THE BEEP, YOUR CALL WILL BE RETURNED AS SOON AS POSSIBLE"?
WORKS FOR ME!
ME, TOO!
2

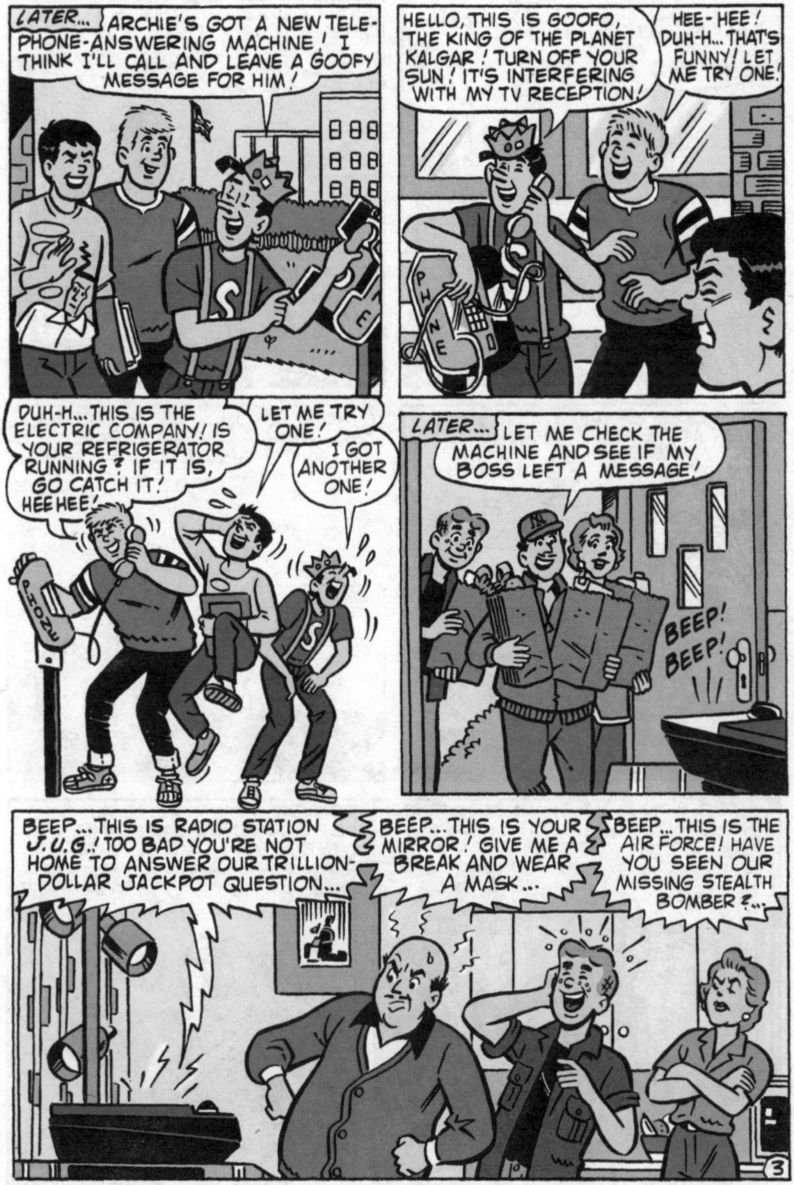
LATER...
ARCHIE'S GOT A NEW TELEPHONE-ANSWERING MACHINE! I THINK I'LL CALL AND LEAVE A GOOFY MESSAGE FOR HIM!
HELLO, THIS IS GOOFO, THE KING OF THE PLANET KALGAR! TURN OFF YOUR SUN! IT'S INTERFERING WITH MY TV RECEPTION!
HEE-HEE! DUH-H... THAT'S FUNNY! LET ME TRY ONE!
DUH-H... THIS IS THE ELECTRIC COMPANY! IS YOUR REFRIGERATOR RUNNING? IF IT IS, GO CATCH IT! HEE HEE!
LET ME TRY ONE!
I GOT ANOTHER ONE!
LATER...
LET ME CHECK THE MACHINE AND SEE IF MY BOSS LEFT A MESSAGE!
BEEP! BEEP!
BEEP... THIS IS RADIO STATION J.U.G.! TOO BAD YOU'RE NOT HOME TO ANSWER OUR TRILLION-DOLLAR JACKPOT QUESTION...
BEEP... THIS IS YOUR MIRROR! GIVE ME A BREAK AND WEAR A MASK...
BEEP... THIS IS THE AIR FORCE! HAVE YOU SEEN OUR MISSING STEALTH BOMBER?...
3

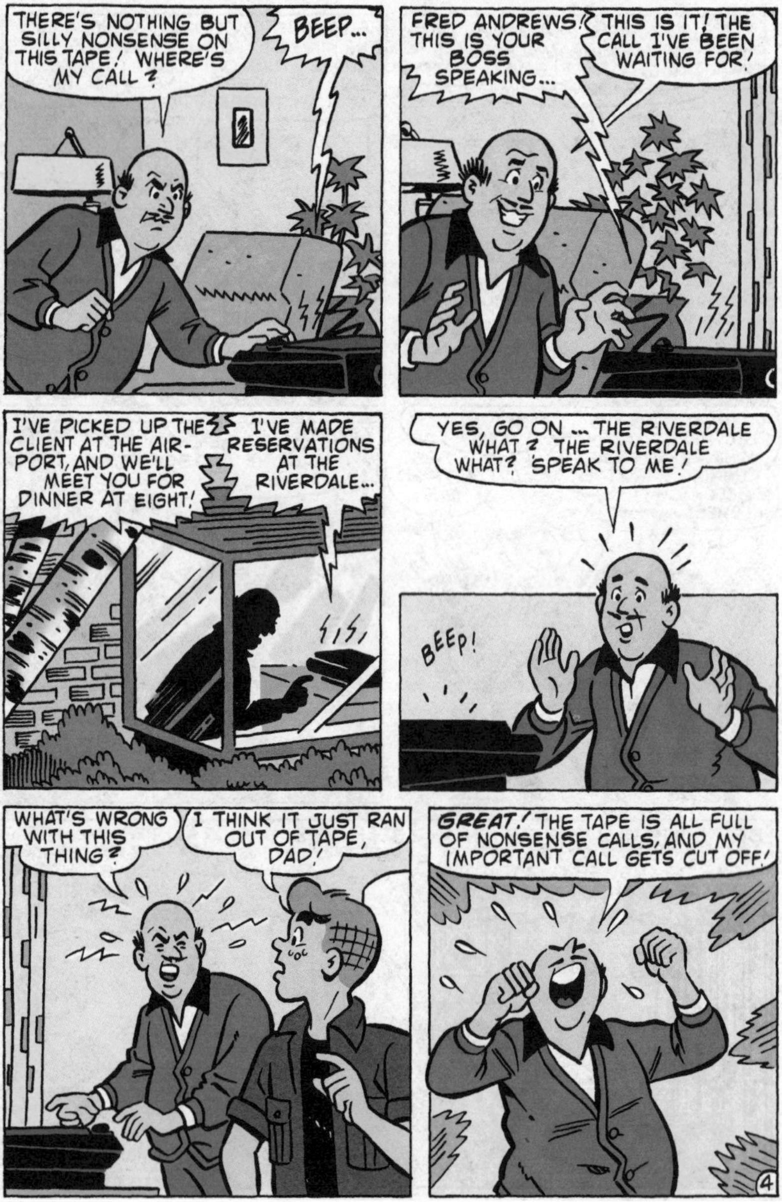
THERE'S NOTHING BUT SILLY NONSENSE ON THIS TAPE! WHERE'S MY CALL?
BEEP...
FRED ANDREWS! THIS IS YOUR BOSS SPEAKING...
THIS IS IT! THE CALL I'VE BEEN WAITING FOR!
I'VE PICKED UP THE CLIENT AT THE AIR-PORT, AND WE'LL MEET YOU FOR DINNER AT EIGHT!
I'VE MADE RESERVATIONS AT THE RIVERDALE...
YES, GO ON ... THE RIVERDALE WHAT? THE RIVERDALE WHAT? SPEAK TO ME!
BEEP!
WHAT'S WRONG WITH THIS THING?
I THINK IT JUST RAN OUT OF TAPE, DAD!
GREAT! THE TAPE IS ALL FULL OF NONSENSE CALLS, AND MY IMPORTANT CALL GETS CUT OFF!
4

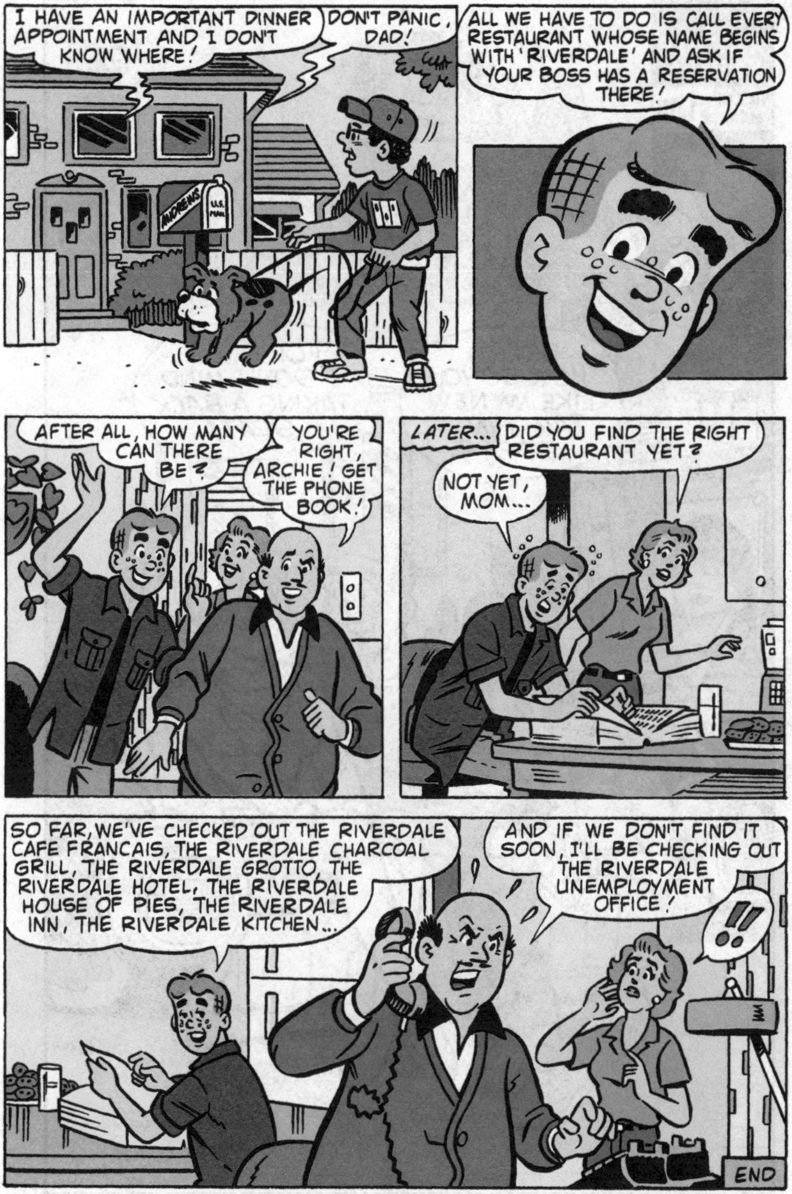
I HAVE AN IMPORTANT DINNER APPOINTMENT AND I DON'T KNOW WHERE!
DON'T PANIC, DAD!
ALL WE HAVE TO DO IS CALL EVERY RESTAURANT WHOSE NAME BEGINS WITH 'RIVERDALE' AND ASK IF YOUR BOSS HAS A RESERVATION THERE!
AFTER ALL, HOW MANY CAN THERE BE?
YOU'RE RIGHT, ARCHIE! GET THE PHONE BOOK!
LATER...
DID YOU FIND THE RIGHT RESTAURANT YET?
NOT YET, MOM...
SO FAR, WE'VE CHECKED OUT THE RIVERDALE CAFE FRANCAIS, THE RIVERDALE CHARCOAL GRILL, THE RIVERDALE GROTTO, THE RIVERDALE HOTEL, THE RIVERDALE HOUSE OF PIES, THE RIVERDALE INN, THE RIVERDALE KITCHEN...
AND IF WE DON'T FIND IT SOON, I'LL BE CHECKING OUT THE RIVERDALE UNEMPLOYMENT OFFICE!
!!
END

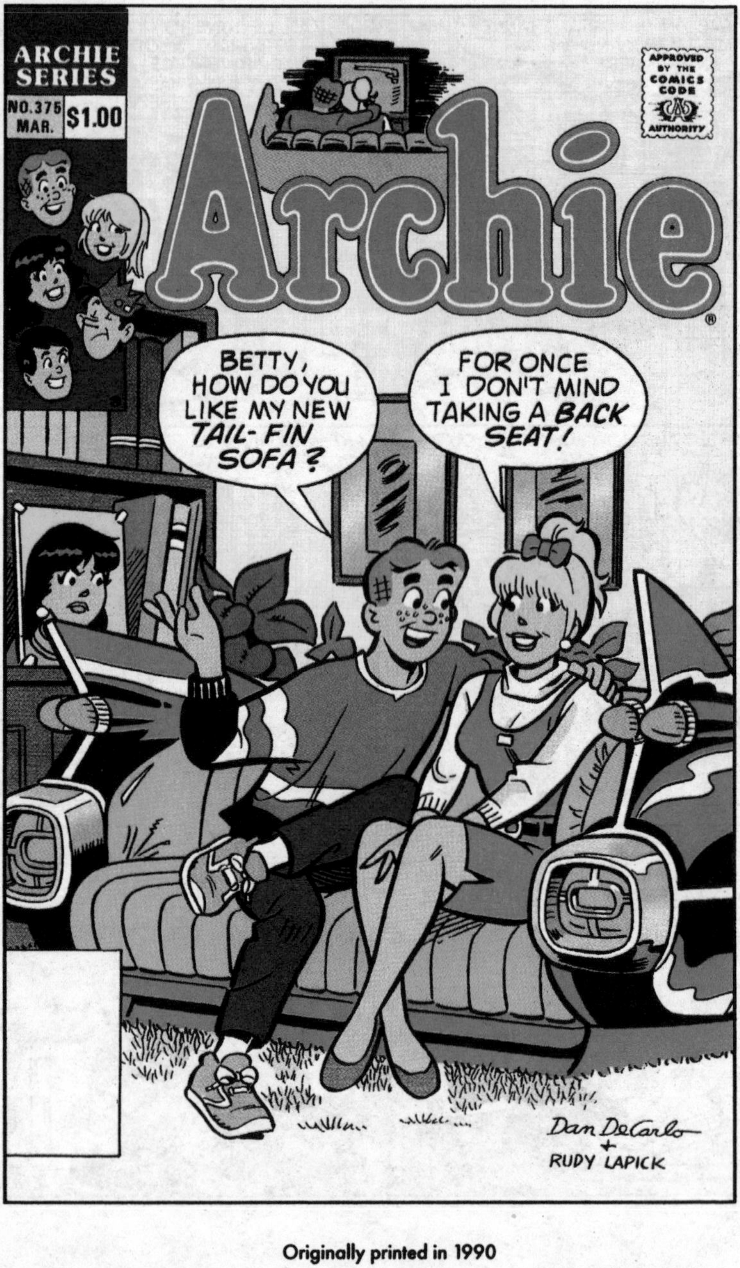
ARCHIE SERIES
NO.375 MAR.
$1.00
APPROVED BY THE COMICS CODE AUTHORITY
Archie
BETTY, HOW DO YOU LIKE MY NEW TAIL-FIN SOFA?
FOR ONCE I DON'T MIND TAKING A BACK SEAT!
Dan DeCarlo + RUDY LAPICK

Originally printed in 1990

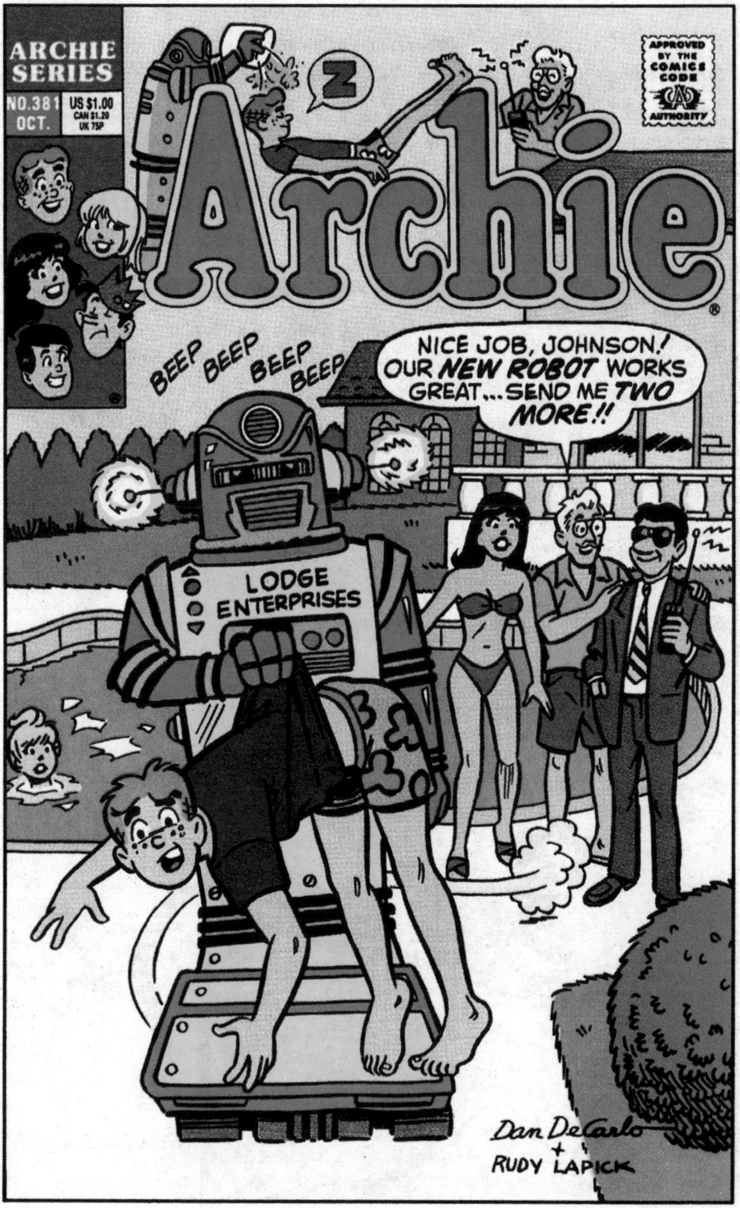
ARCHIE SERIES
NO.381 OCT.
US $1.00 CAN $1.20 UK 75P
APPROVED BY THE COMICS CODE AUTHORITY
Archie
Z
BEEP BEEP BEEP BEEP
NICE JOB, JOHNSON! OUR NEW ROBOT WORKS GREAT... SEND ME TWO MORE!!
LODGE ENTERPRISES
Dan DeCarlo + RUDY LAPICK

Originally printed in 1990

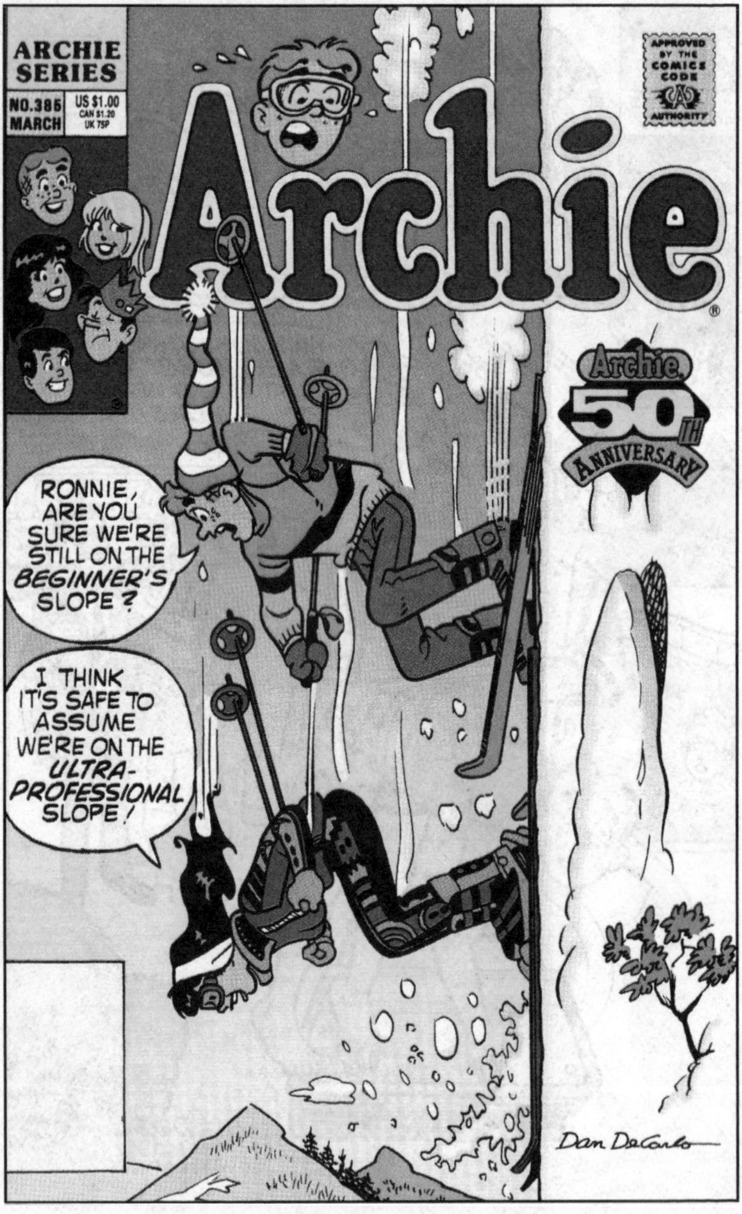
ARCHIE SERIES
NO.385 MARCH
US $1.00 CAN $1.20 UK 75P
APPROVED BY THE COMICS CODE AUTHORITY
Archie
Archie 50TH ANNIVERSARY
RONNIE, ARE YOU SURE WE'RE STILL ON THE BEGINNER'S SLOPE?
I THINK IT'S SAFE TO ASSUME WE'RE ON THE ULTRA-PROFESSIONAL SLOPE!
Dan DeCarlo

Originally printed in 1991

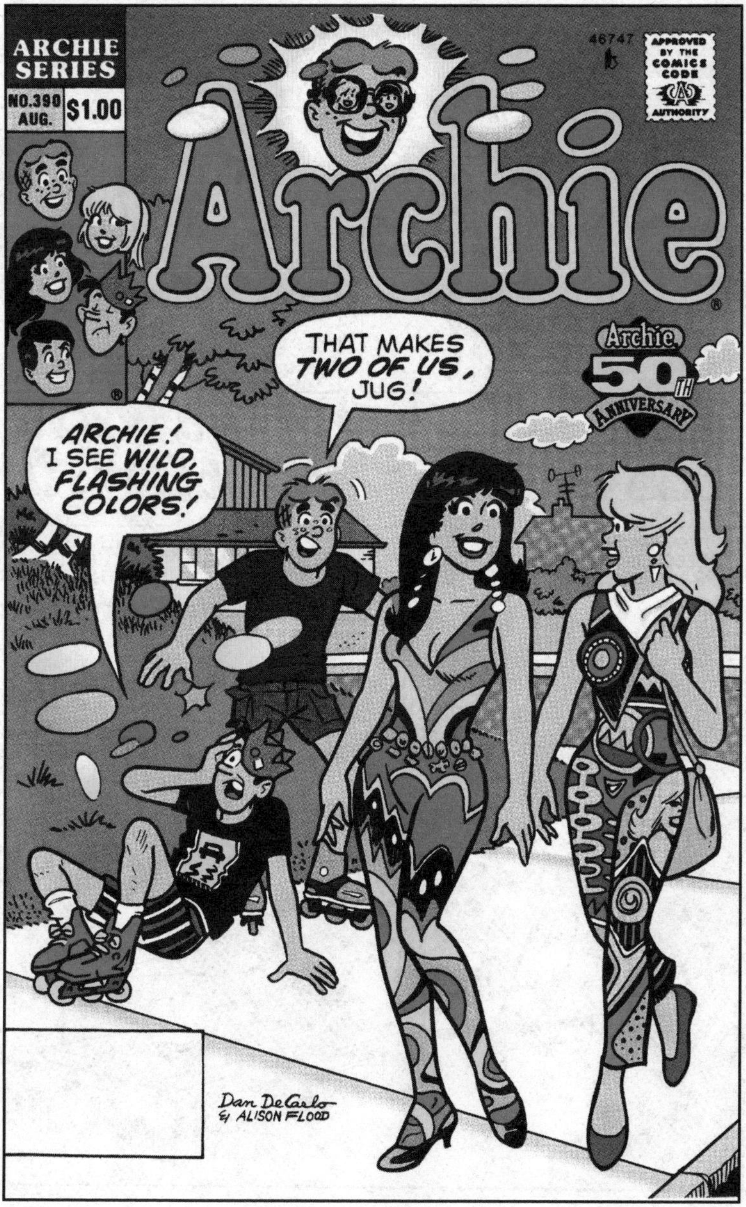
ARCHIE SERIES
NO.390 AUG.
$1.00
46747
APPROVED BY THE COMICS CODE AUTHORITY
Archie
Archie 50TH ANNIVERSARY
THAT MAKES TWO OF US, JUG!
ARCHIE! I SEE WILD, FLASHING COLORS!
Dan DeCarlo & ALISON FLOOD

Originally printed in 1991

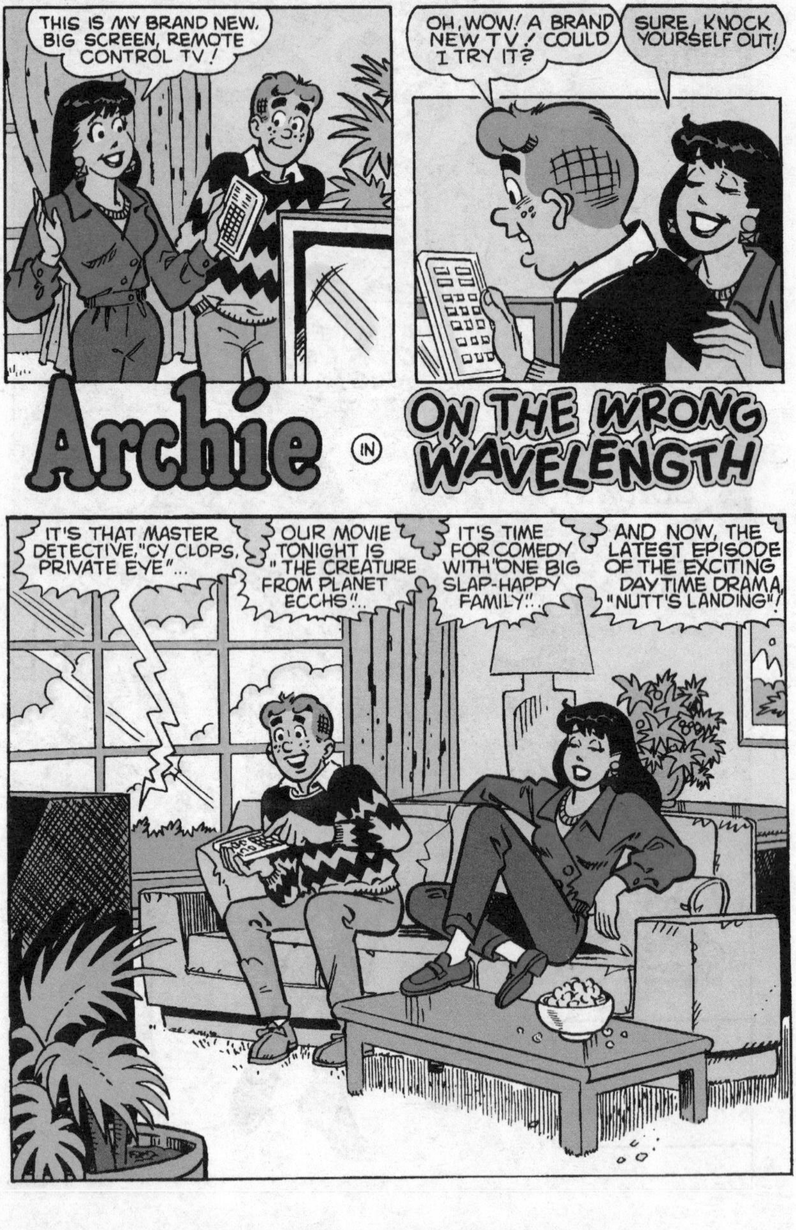
THIS IS MY BRAND NEW, BIG SCREEN, REMOTE CONTROL TV!
OH, WOW! A BRAND NEW TV! COULD I TRY IT?
SURE, KNOCK YOURSELF OUT!
Archie
IN
ON THE WRONG WAVELENGTH
IT'S THAT MASTER DETECTIVE, "CY CLOPS, PRIVATE EYE"...
OUR MOVIE TONIGHT IS "THE CREATURE FROM PLANET ECCHS"...
IT'S TIME FOR COMEDY WITH "ONE BIG SLAP-HAPPY FAMILY"...
AND NOW, THE LATEST EPISODE OF THE EXCITING DAYTIME DRAMA, "NUTT'S LANDING"!

Originally presented in ARCHIE #385, March, 1991

THE DOOR OPENED AND IN WALKED THIS KNOCK-OUT WHO WAS...

...A GRUESOME ALIEN SPACE CREATURE WHO SENT ME AN ESP MESSAGE THAT SAID...

...WE CAN INSTALL THE PLUMBING OURSELVES! IT'LL BE AS EASY AS...

A HOSTILE TAKEOVER OF A MULTI-BILLION-DOLLAR CORPORATION!

WHAT ARE YOU KIDS WATCHING?

IT'S HARD TO TELL THE WAY ARCHIE IS SWITCHING CHANNELS, BUT...

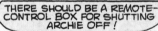

... I THINK IT'S ABOUT A SPACE ALIEN PRIVATE EYE WHO IS FIGHTING OFF A HOSTILE TAKEOVER OF HIS CORPORATION BY A FAMILY OF GOOF-UPS!

THERE SHOULD BE A REMOTE-CONTROL BOX FOR SHUTTING ARCHIE OFF!

THIS TELEVISION IS REALLY RAD!

I HAVE REMOTE CONTROLS FOR EVERYTHING! I'LL SHOW YOU!

2

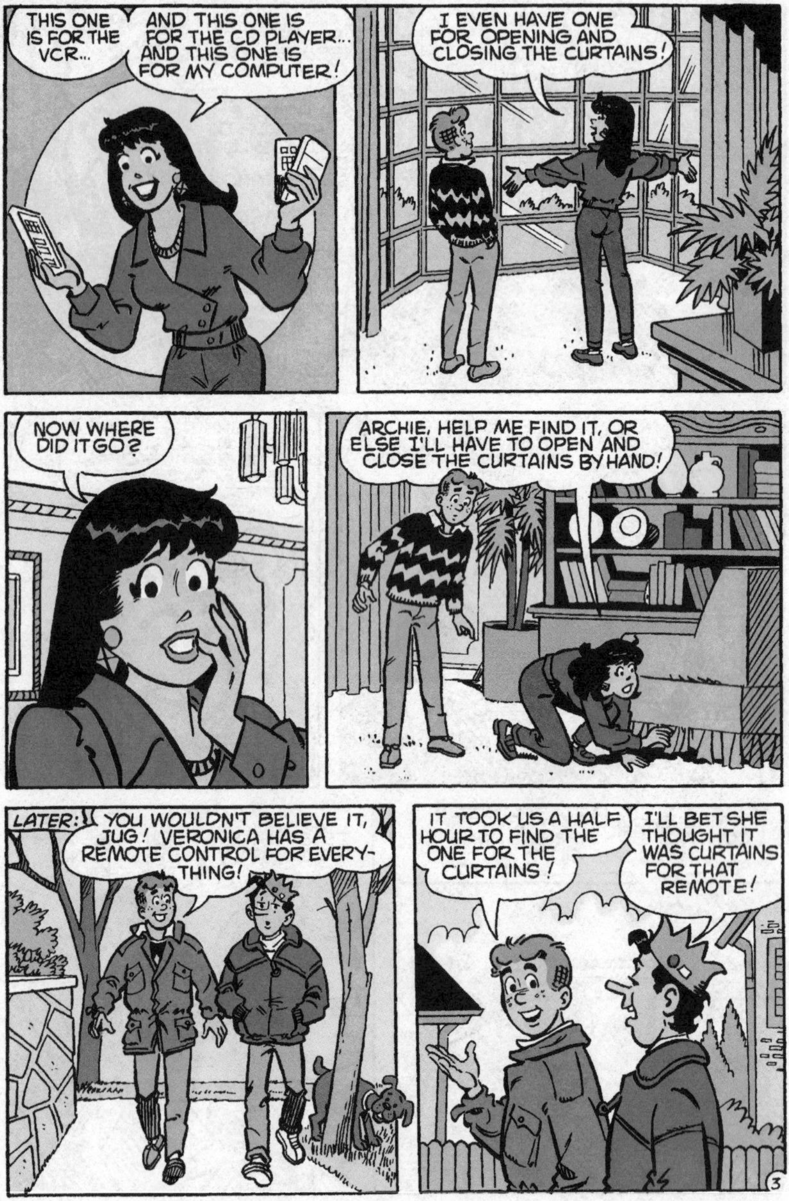
THIS ONE IS FOR THE VCR...
AND THIS ONE IS FOR THE CD PLAYER... AND THIS ONE IS FOR MY COMPUTER!
I EVEN HAVE ONE FOR OPENING AND CLOSING THE CURTAINS!
NOW WHERE DID IT GO?
ARCHIE, HELP ME FIND IT, OR ELSE I'LL HAVE TO OPEN AND CLOSE THE CURTAINS BY HAND!
LATER:
YOU WOULDN'T BELIEVE IT, JUG! VERONICA HAS A REMOTE CONTROL FOR EVERY-THING!
IT TOOK US A HALF HOUR TO FIND THE ONE FOR THE CURTAINS!
I'LL BET SHE THOUGHT IT WAS CURTAINS FOR THAT REMOTE!
3

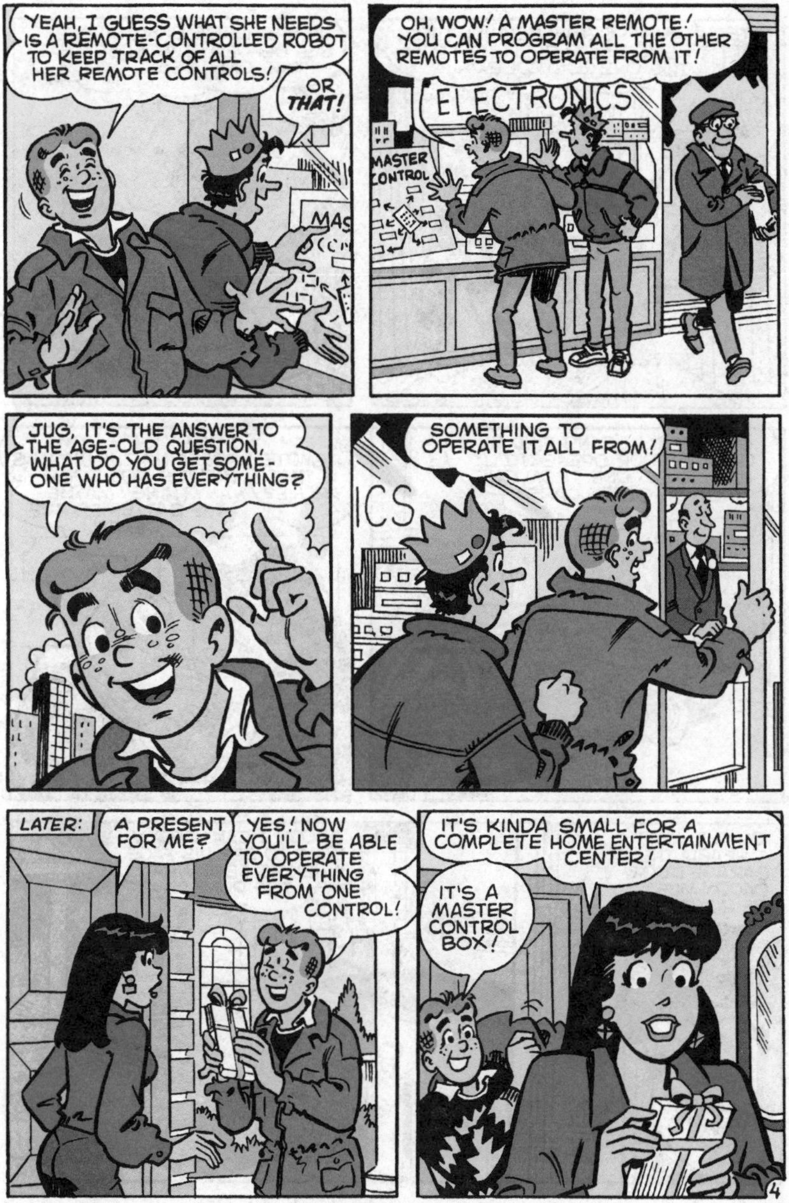
YEAH, I GUESS WHAT SHE NEEDS IS A REMOTE-CONTROLLED ROBOT TO KEEP TRACK OF ALL HER REMOTE CONTROLS!
OR *THAT!*
OH, WOW! A MASTER REMOTE! YOU CAN PROGRAM ALL THE OTHER REMOTES TO OPERATE FROM IT!
ELECTRONICS
MASTER CONTROL
JUG, IT'S THE ANSWER TO THE AGE-OLD QUESTION, WHAT DO YOU GET SOME-ONE WHO HAS EVERYTHING?
SOMETHING TO OPERATE IT ALL FROM!
ICS
LATER:
A PRESENT FOR ME?
YES! NOW YOU'LL BE ABLE TO OPERATE EVERYTHING FROM ONE CONTROL!
IT'S KINDA SMALL FOR A COMPLETE HOME ENTERTAINMENT CENTER!
IT'S A MASTER CONTROL BOX!
4

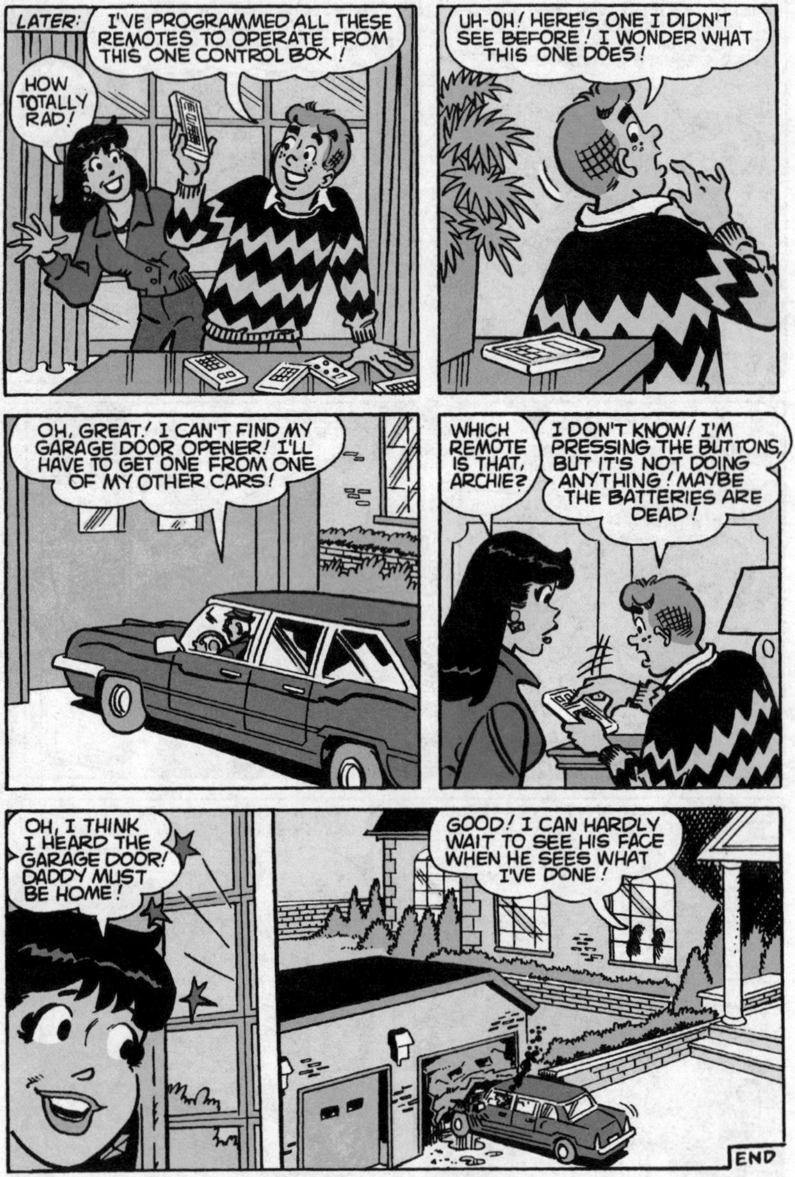
LATER:
I'VE PROGRAMMED ALL THESE REMOTES TO OPERATE FROM THIS ONE CONTROL BOX!
HOW TOTALLY RAD!
UH-OH! HERE'S ONE I DIDN'T SEE BEFORE! I WONDER WHAT THIS ONE DOES!
OH, GREAT! I CAN'T FIND MY GARAGE DOOR OPENER! I'LL HAVE TO GET ONE FROM ONE OF MY OTHER CARS!
WHICH REMOTE IS THAT, ARCHIE?
I DON'T KNOW! I'M PRESSING THE BUTTONS, BUT IT'S NOT DOING ANYTHING! MAYBE THE BATTERIES ARE DEAD!
OH, I THINK I HEARD THE GARAGE DOOR! DADDY MUST BE HOME!
GOOD! I CAN HARDLY WAIT TO SEE HIS FACE WHEN HE SEES WHAT I'VE DONE!
END

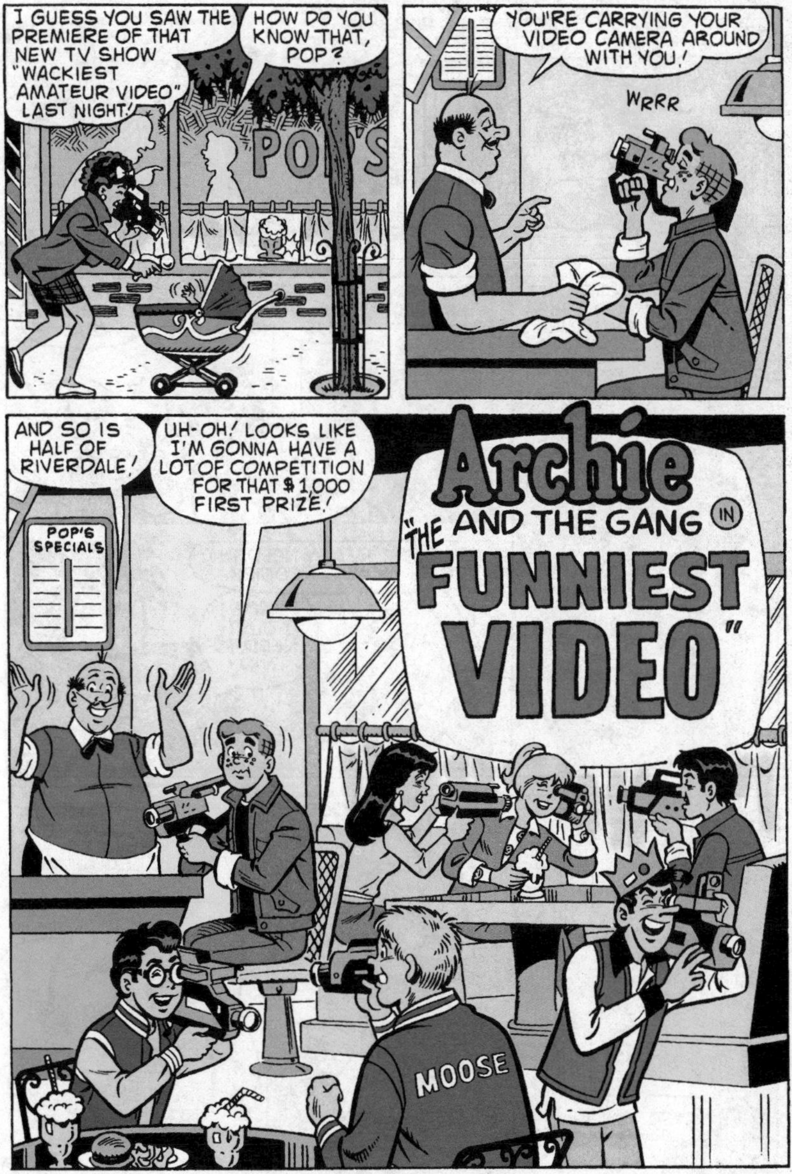
I GUESS YOU SAW THE PREMIERE OF THAT NEW TV SHOW "WACKIEST AMATEUR VIDEO" LAST NIGHT!
HOW DO YOU KNOW THAT, POP?
POP'S
YOU'RE CARRYING YOUR VIDEO CAMERA AROUND WITH YOU!
WRRR
AND SO IS HALF OF RIVERDALE!
UH-OH! LOOKS LIKE I'M GONNA HAVE A LOT OF COMPETITION FOR THAT $1,000 FIRST PRIZE!
POP'S SPECIALS
Archie AND THE GANG IN "THE FUNNIEST VIDEO"
MOOSE

Originally presented in EVERYTHING'S ARCHIE #154, March, 1991

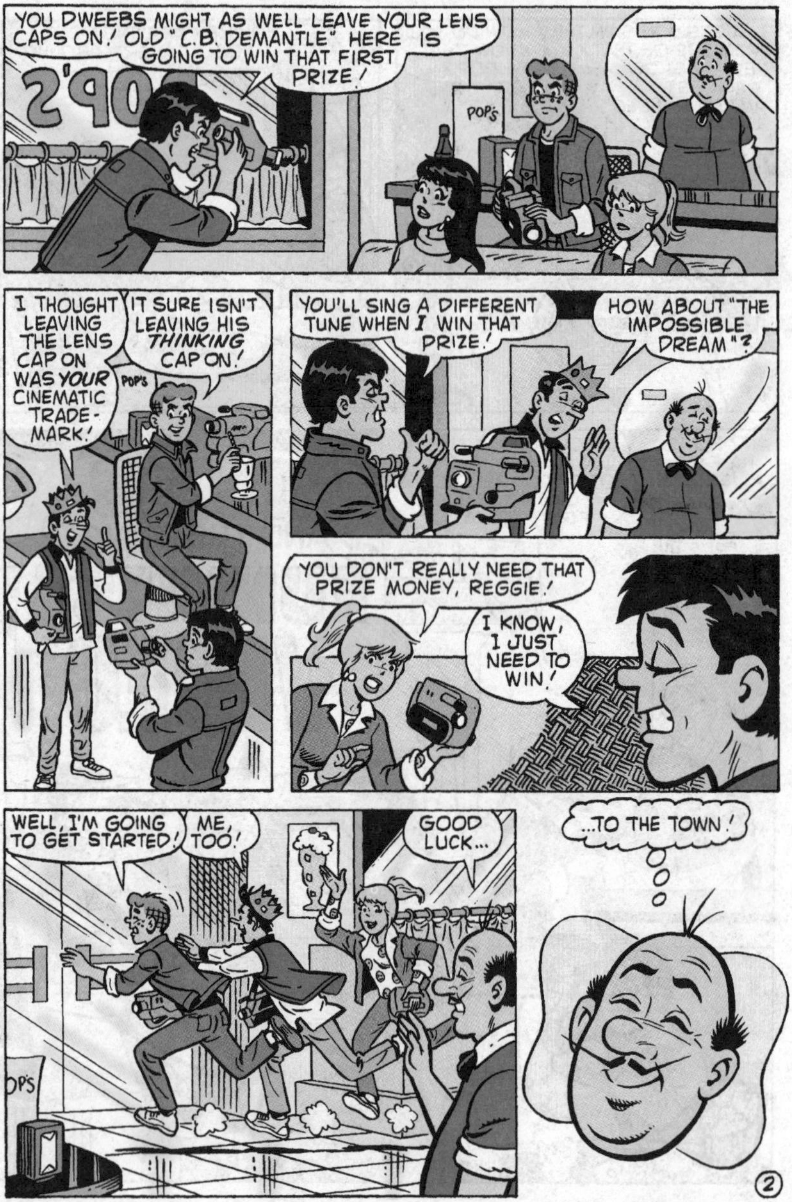
YOU DWEEBS MIGHT AS WELL LEAVE YOUR LENS CAPS ON! OLD "C.B. DEMANTLE" HERE IS GOING TO WIN THAT FIRST PRIZE!
POP'S
POP'S
I THOUGHT LEAVING THE LENS CAP ON WAS YOUR CINEMATIC TRADE-MARK!
IT SURE ISN'T LEAVING HIS THINKING CAP ON!
POP'S
YOU'LL SING A DIFFERENT TUNE WHEN I WIN THAT PRIZE!
HOW ABOUT "THE IMPOSSIBLE DREAM"?
YOU DON'T REALLY NEED THAT PRIZE MONEY, REGGIE!
I KNOW, I JUST NEED TO WIN!
WELL, I'M GOING TO GET STARTED!
ME, TOO!
GOOD LUCK...
...TO THE TOWN!
2

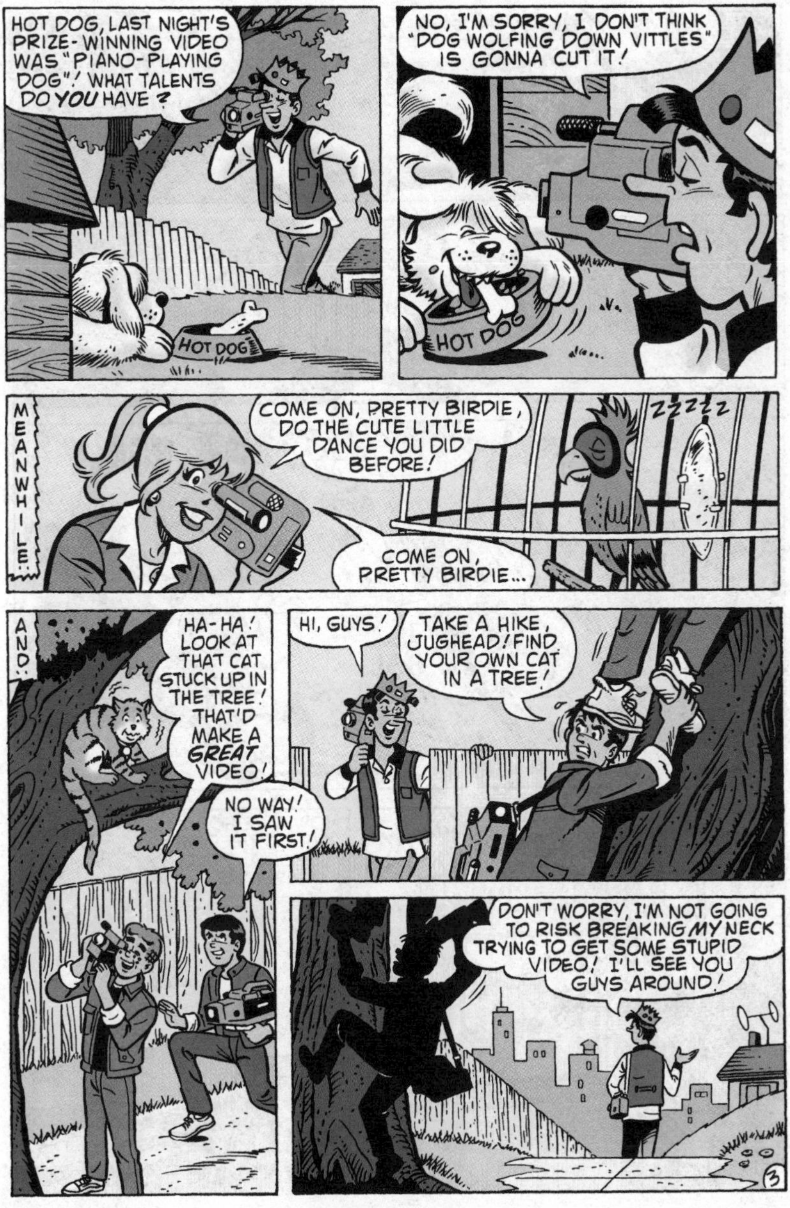
HOT DOG, LAST NIGHT'S PRIZE-WINNING VIDEO WAS "PIANO-PLAYING DOG"! WHAT TALENTS DO YOU HAVE?
HOT DOG
NO, I'M SORRY, I DON'T THINK "DOG WOLFING DOWN VITTLES" IS GONNA CUT IT!
HOT DOG
MEANWHILE:
COME ON, PRETTY BIRDIE, DO THE CUTE LITTLE DANCE YOU DID BEFORE!
ZZZZZ
COME ON, PRETTY BIRDIE...
AND:
HA-HA! LOOK AT THAT CAT STUCK UP IN THE TREE! THAT'D MAKE A GREAT VIDEO!
NO WAY! I SAW IT FIRST!
HI, GUYS!
TAKE A HIKE, JUGHEAD! FIND YOUR OWN CAT IN A TREE!
DON'T WORRY, I'M NOT GOING TO RISK BREAKING MY NECK TRYING TO GET SOME STUPID VIDEO! I'LL SEE YOU GUYS AROUND!
3

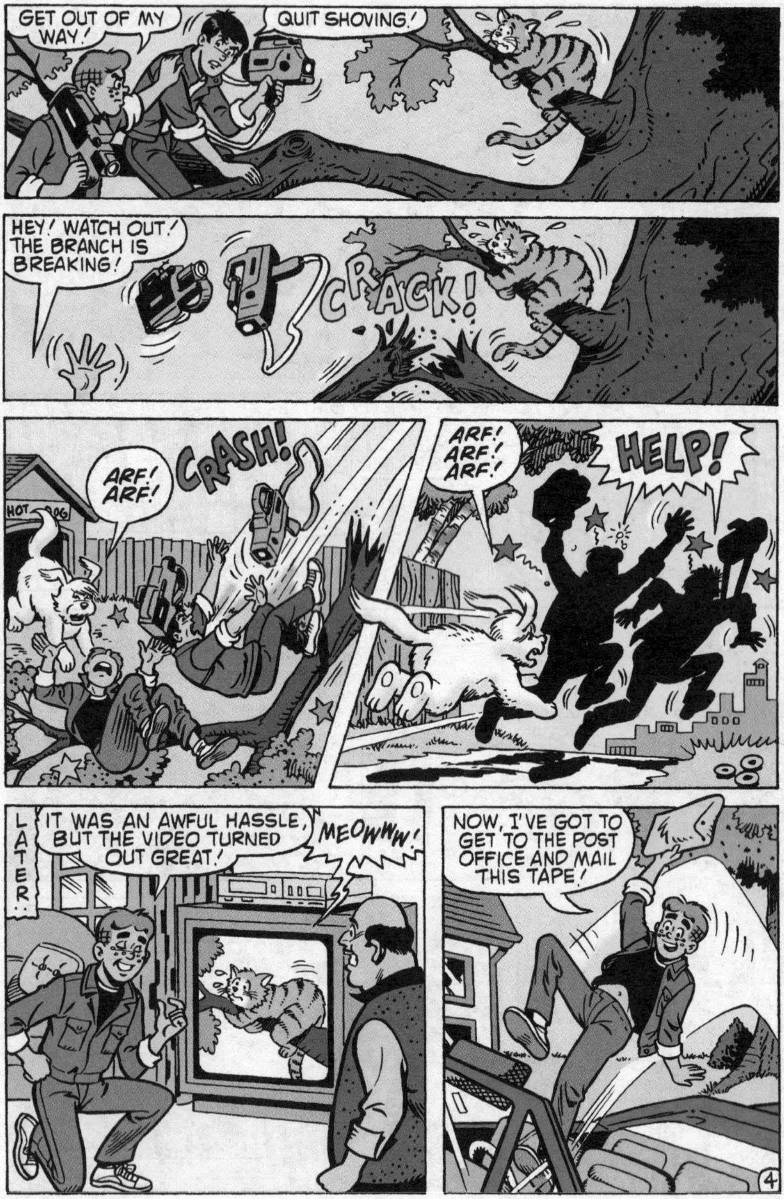
GET OUT OF MY WAY!
QUIT SHOVING!
HEY! WATCH OUT! THE BRANCH IS BREAKING!
CRACK!
ARF! ARF!
CRASH!
HOT DOG
ARF! ARF! ARF!
HELP!
LATER:
IT WAS AN AWFUL HASSLE, BUT THE VIDEO TURNED OUT GREAT!
MEOWWW!
NOW, I'VE GOT TO GET TO THE POST OFFICE AND MAIL THIS TAPE!
4

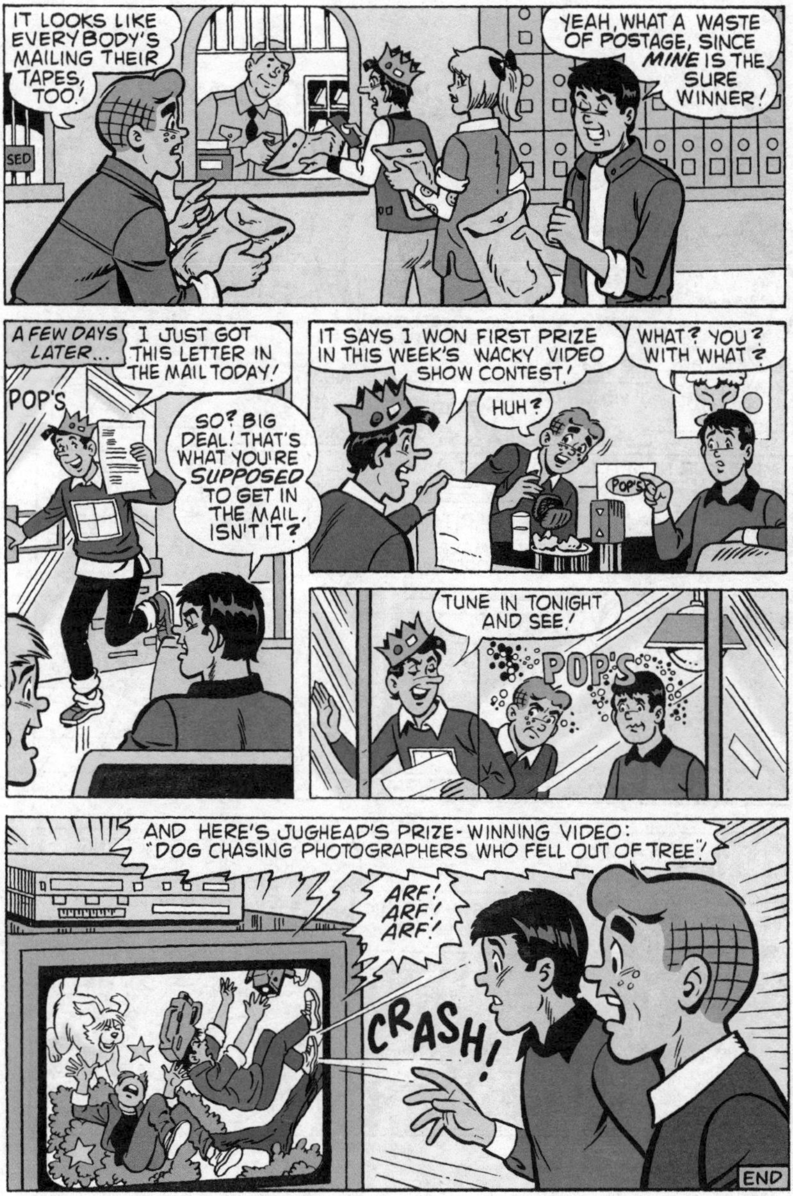
IT LOOKS LIKE EVERYBODY'S MAILING THEIR TAPES, TOO!
YEAH, WHAT A WASTE OF POSTAGE, SINCE MINE IS THE SURE WINNER!
A FEW DAYS LATER...
I JUST GOT THIS LETTER IN THE MAIL TODAY!
POP'S
SO? BIG DEAL! THAT'S WHAT YOU'RE SUPPOSED TO GET IN THE MAIL, ISN'T IT?
IT SAYS I WON FIRST PRIZE IN THIS WEEK'S WACKY VIDEO SHOW CONTEST!
HUH?
WHAT? YOU? WITH WHAT?
POP'S
TUNE IN TONIGHT AND SEE!
POP'S
AND HERE'S JUGHEAD'S PRIZE-WINNING VIDEO: "DOG CHASING PHOTOGRAPHERS WHO FELL OUT OF TREE"!
ARF! ARF! ARF!
CRASH!
END

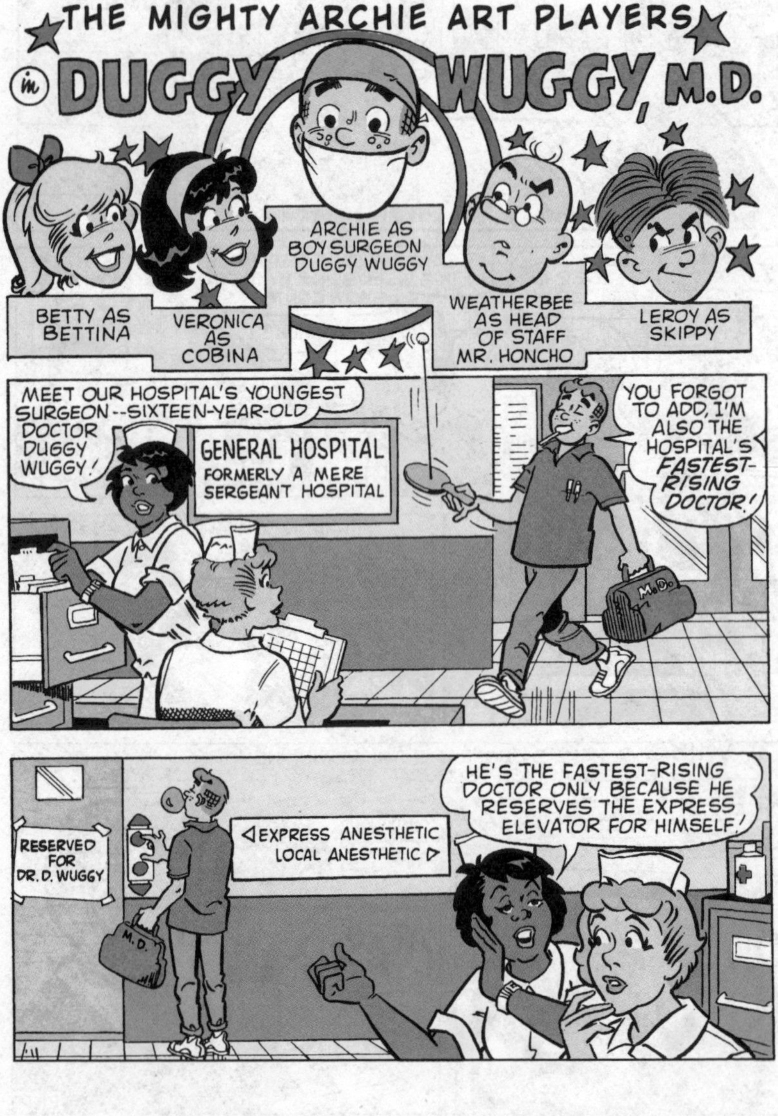
THE MIGHTY ARCHIE ART PLAYERS
in DUGGY WUGGY, M.D.
ARCHIE AS BOY SURGEON DUGGY WUGGY
BETTY AS BETTINA
VERONICA AS COBINA
WEATHERBEE AS HEAD OF STAFF MR. HONCHO
LEROY AS SKIPPY
MEET OUR HOSPITAL'S YOUNGEST SURGEON--SIXTEEN-YEAR-OLD DOCTOR DUGGY WUGGY!
GENERAL HOSPITAL
FORMERLY A MERE SERGEANT HOSPITAL
YOU FORGOT TO ADD, I'M ALSO THE HOSPITAL'S FASTEST-RISING DOCTOR!
M.D.
RESERVED FOR DR. D. WUGGY
EXPRESS ANESTHETIC
LOCAL ANESTHETIC
M.D.
HE'S THE FASTEST-RISING DOCTOR ONLY BECAUSE HE RESERVES THE EXPRESS ELEVATOR FOR HIMSELF!

Originally presented in LAUGH #27, April, 1991

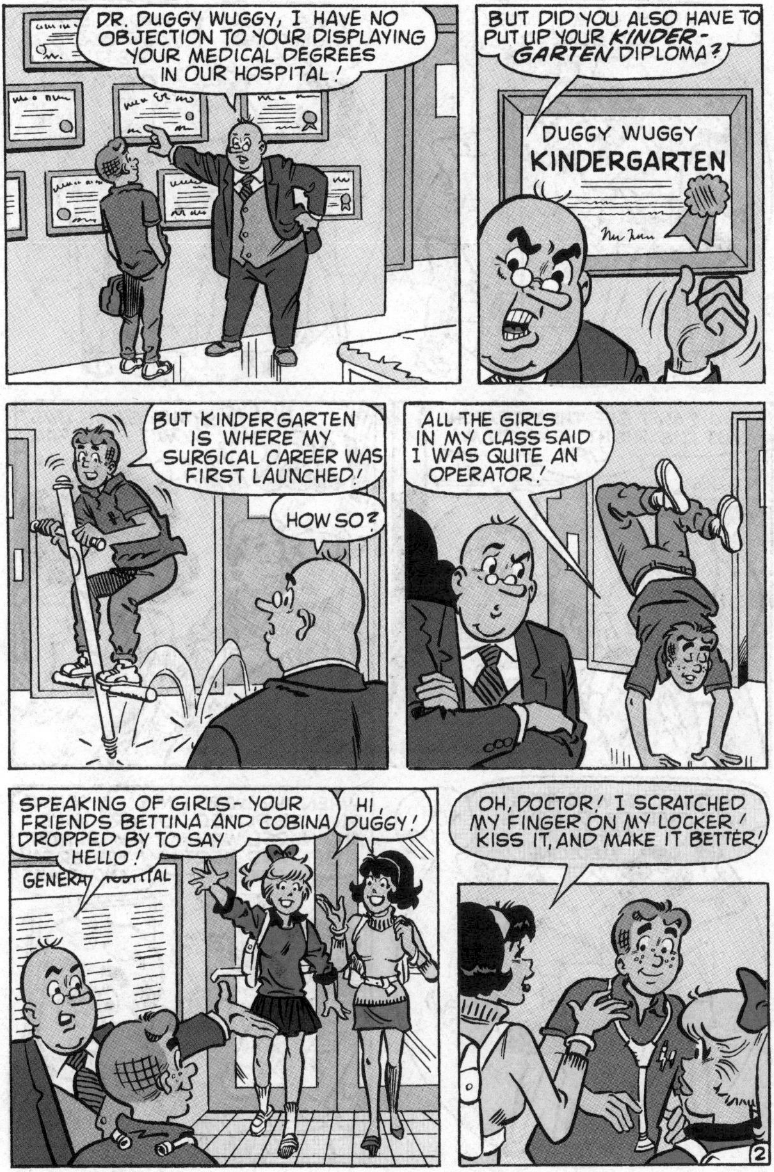
DR. DUGGY WUGGY, I HAVE NO OBJECTION TO YOUR DISPLAYING YOUR MEDICAL DEGREES IN OUR HOSPITAL!
BUT DID YOU ALSO HAVE TO PUT UP YOUR KINDER-GARTEN DIPLOMA?
DUGGY WUGGY
KINDERGARTEN
BUT KINDERGARTEN IS WHERE MY SURGICAL CAREER WAS FIRST LAUNCHED!
HOW SO?
ALL THE GIRLS IN MY CLASS SAID I WAS QUITE AN OPERATOR!
SPEAKING OF GIRLS- YOUR FRIENDS BETTINA AND COBINA DROPPED BY TO SAY HELLO!
HI, DUGGY!
OH, DOCTOR! I SCRATCHED MY FINGER ON MY LOCKER! KISS IT, AND MAKE IT BETTER!
2

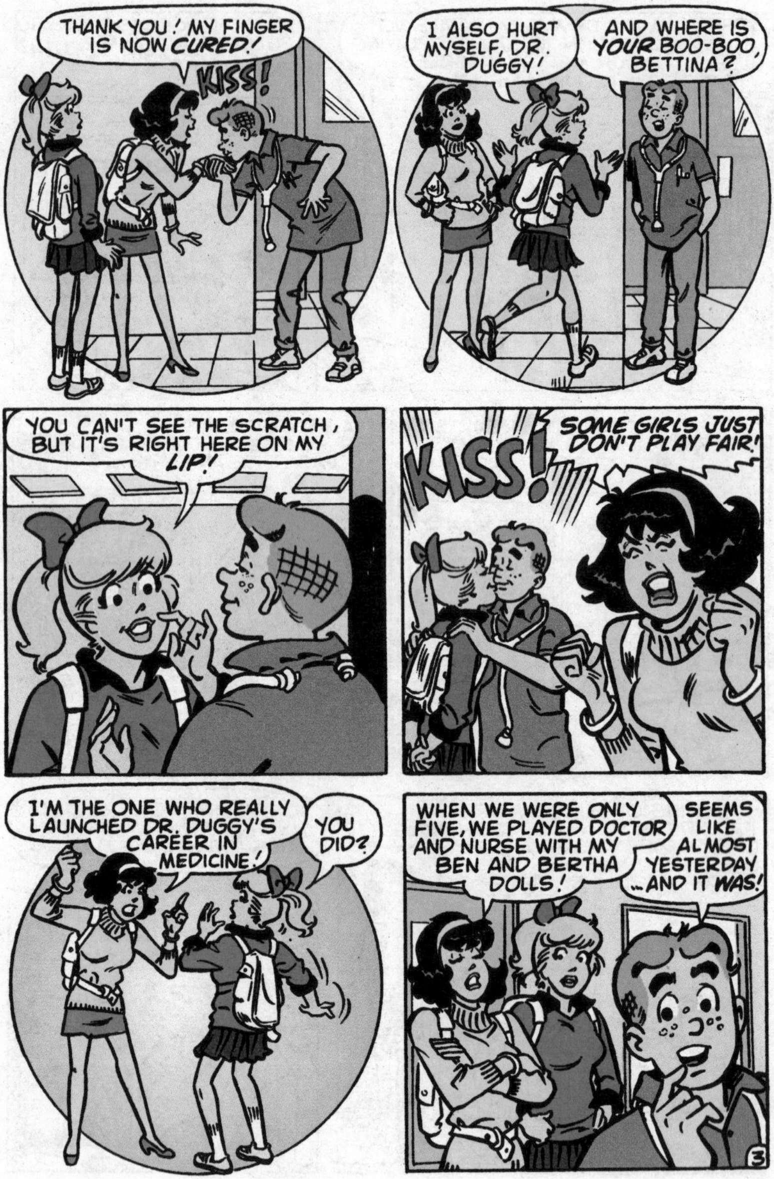
THANK YOU! MY FINGER IS NOW CURED!
KISS!
I ALSO HURT MYSELF, DR. DUGGY!
AND WHERE IS YOUR BOO-BOO, BETTINA?
YOU CAN'T SEE THE SCRATCH, BUT IT'S RIGHT HERE ON MY LIP!
KISS!
SOME GIRLS JUST DON'T PLAY FAIR!
I'M THE ONE WHO REALLY LAUNCHED DR. DUGGY'S CAREER IN MEDICINE!
YOU DID?
WHEN WE WERE ONLY FIVE, WE PLAYED DOCTOR AND NURSE WITH MY BEN AND BERTHA DOLLS!
SEEMS LIKE ALMOST YESTERDAY ...AND IT WAS!
3

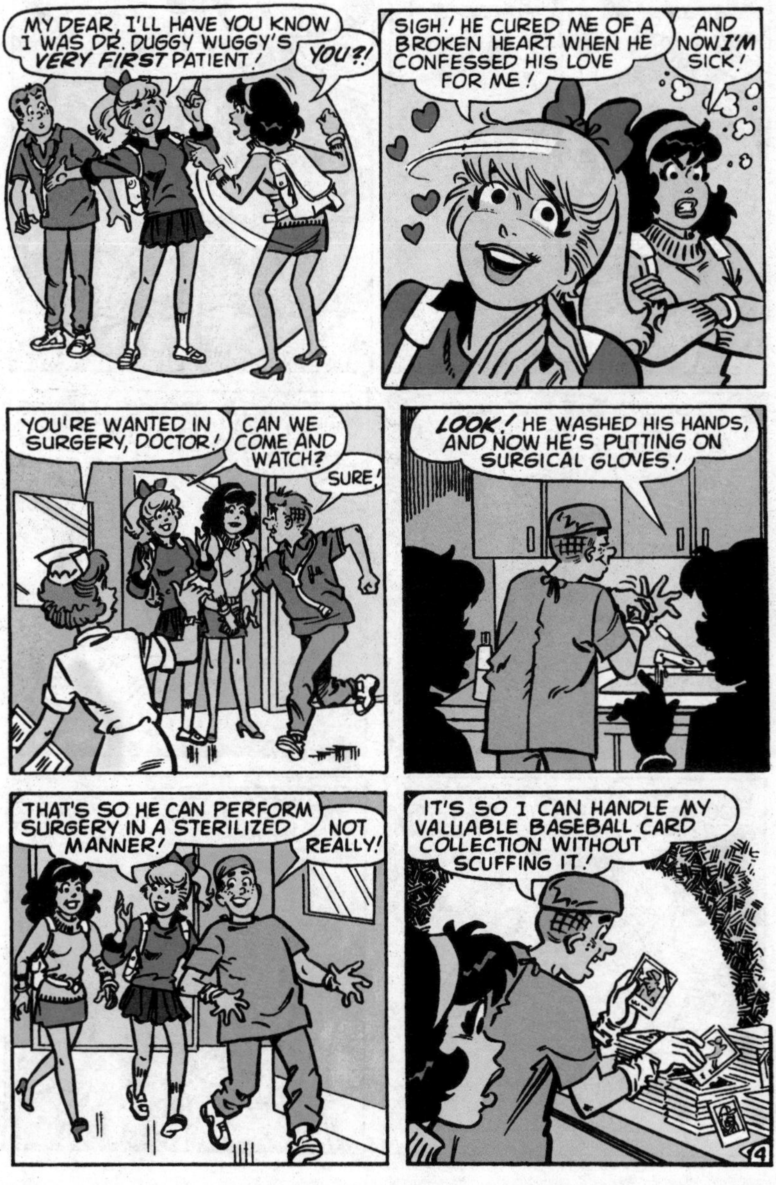

MY DEAR, I'LL HAVE YOU KNOW I WAS DR. DUGGY WUGGY'S VERY FIRST PATIENT!
YOU?!
SIGH! HE CURED ME OF A BROKEN HEART WHEN HE CONFESSED HIS LOVE FOR ME!
AND NOW I'M SICK!
YOU'RE WANTED IN SURGERY, DOCTOR!
CAN WE COME AND WATCH?
SURE!
LOOK! HE WASHED HIS HANDS, AND NOW HE'S PUTTING ON SURGICAL GLOVES!
THAT'S SO HE CAN PERFORM SURGERY IN A STERILIZED MANNER!
NOT REALLY!
IT'S SO I CAN HANDLE MY VALUABLE BASEBALL CARD COLLECTION WITHOUT SCUFFING IT!
4

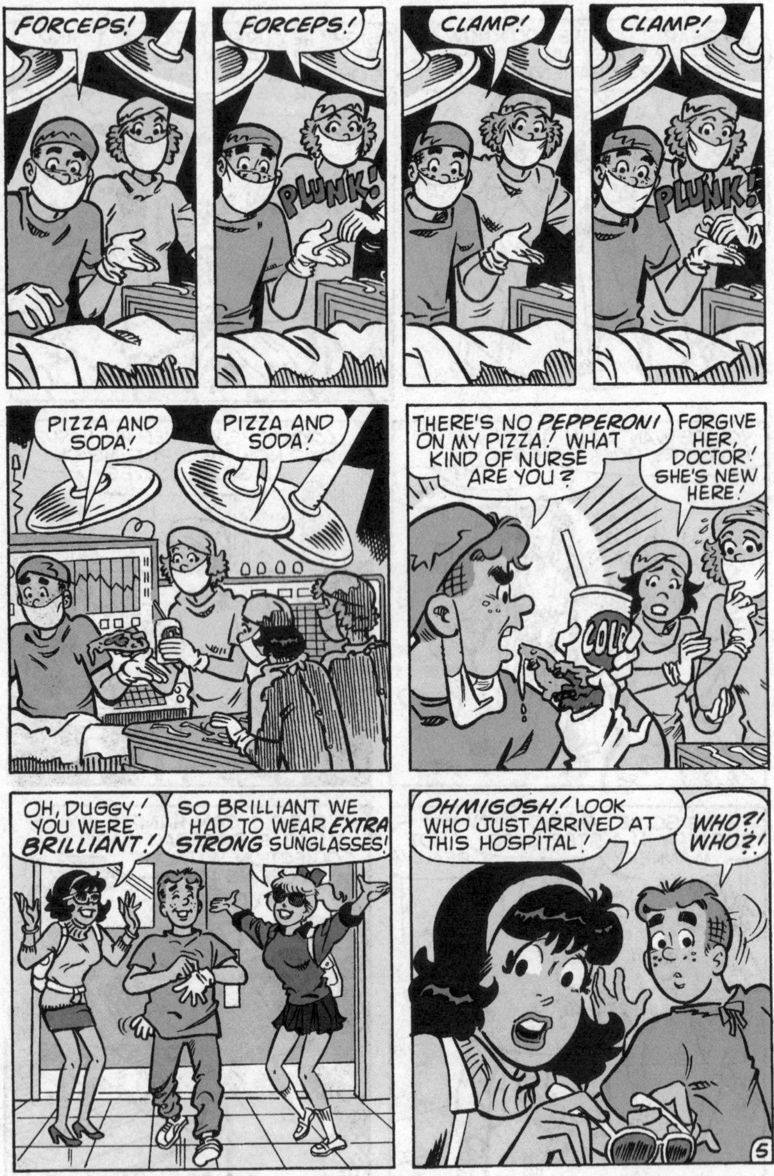
FORCEPS!
FORCEPS!
PLUNK!
CLAMP!
CLAMP!
PLUNK!
PIZZA AND SODA!
PIZZA AND SODA!
THERE'S NO PEPPERONI ON MY PIZZA! WHAT KIND OF NURSE ARE YOU?
FORGIVE HER, DOCTOR! SHE'S NEW HERE!
OH, DUGGY! YOU WERE BRILLIANT!
SO BRILLIANT WE HAD TO WEAR EXTRA STRONG SUNGLASSES!
OHMIGOSH! LOOK WHO JUST ARRIVED AT THIS HOSPITAL!
WHO?! WHO?!
5

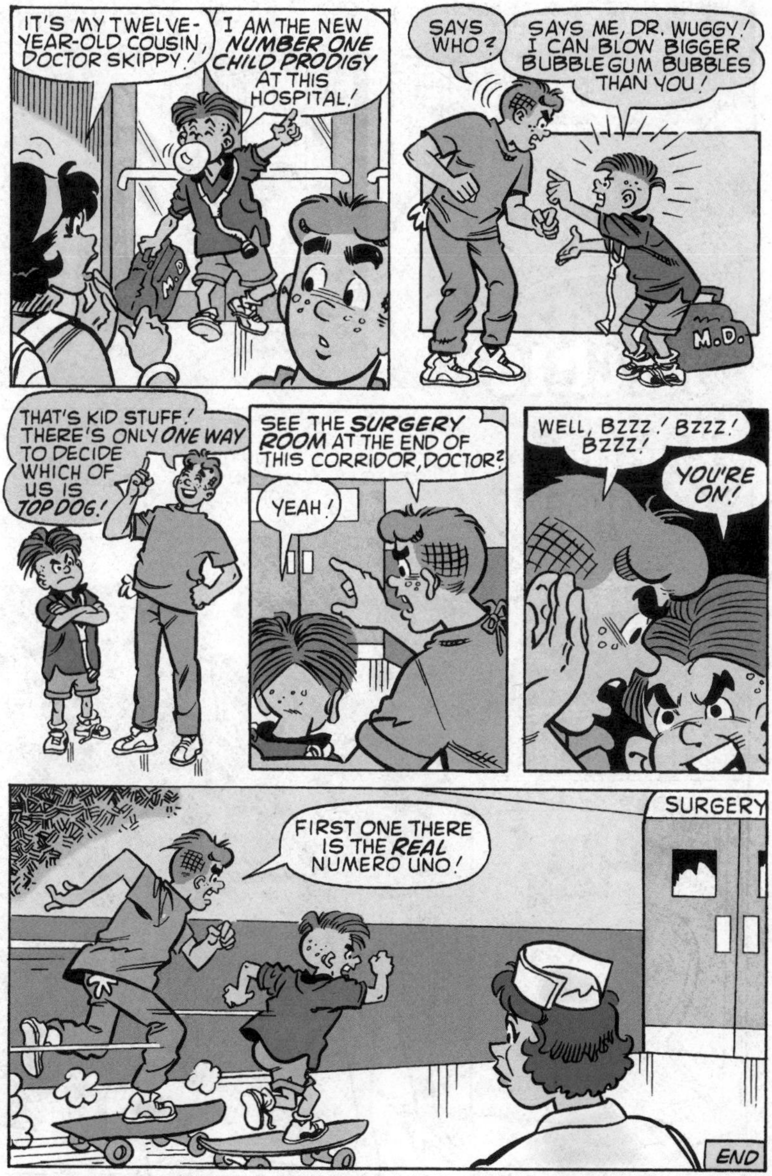
IT'S MY TWELVE-YEAR-OLD COUSIN, DOCTOR SKIPPY!
I AM THE NEW NUMBER ONE CHILD PRODIGY AT THIS HOSPITAL!
M.D
SAYS WHO?
SAYS ME, DR. WUGGY! I CAN BLOW BIGGER BUBBLEGUM BUBBLES THAN YOU!
M.D.
THAT'S KID STUFF! THERE'S ONLY ONE WAY TO DECIDE WHICH OF US IS TOP DOG!
SEE THE SURGERY ROOM AT THE END OF THIS CORRIDOR, DOCTOR?
YEAH!
WELL, BZZZ! BZZZ! BZZZ!
YOU'RE ON!
SURGERY
FIRST ONE THERE IS THE REAL NUMERO UNO!
END

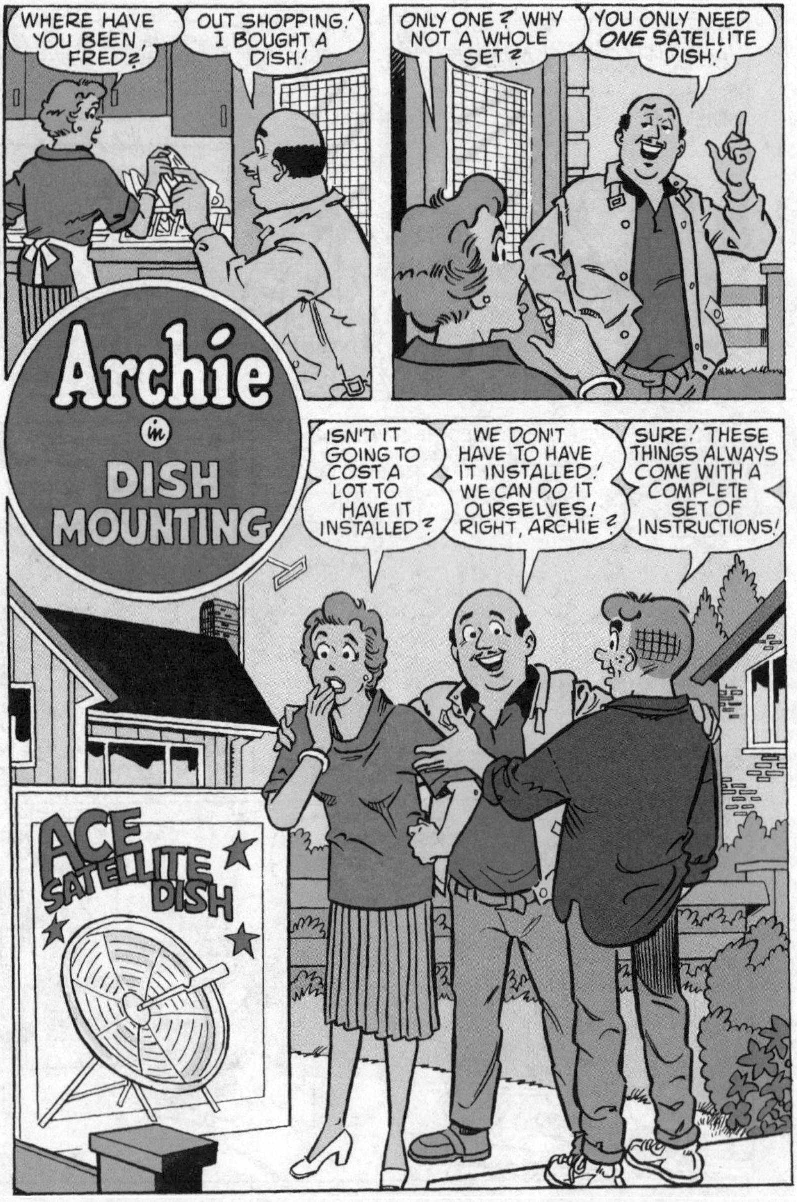
WHERE HAVE YOU BEEN, FRED?
OUT SHOPPING! I BOUGHT A DISH!
ONLY ONE? WHY NOT A WHOLE SET?
YOU ONLY NEED ONE SATELLITE DISH!
Archie in DISH MOUNTING
ISN'T IT GOING TO COST A LOT TO HAVE IT INSTALLED?
WE DON'T HAVE TO HAVE IT INSTALLED! WE CAN DO IT OURSELVES! RIGHT, ARCHIE?
SURE! THESE THINGS ALWAYS COME WITH A COMPLETE SET OF INSTRUCTIONS!
ACE SATELLITE DISH

Originally presented in ARCHIE #389, July, 1991

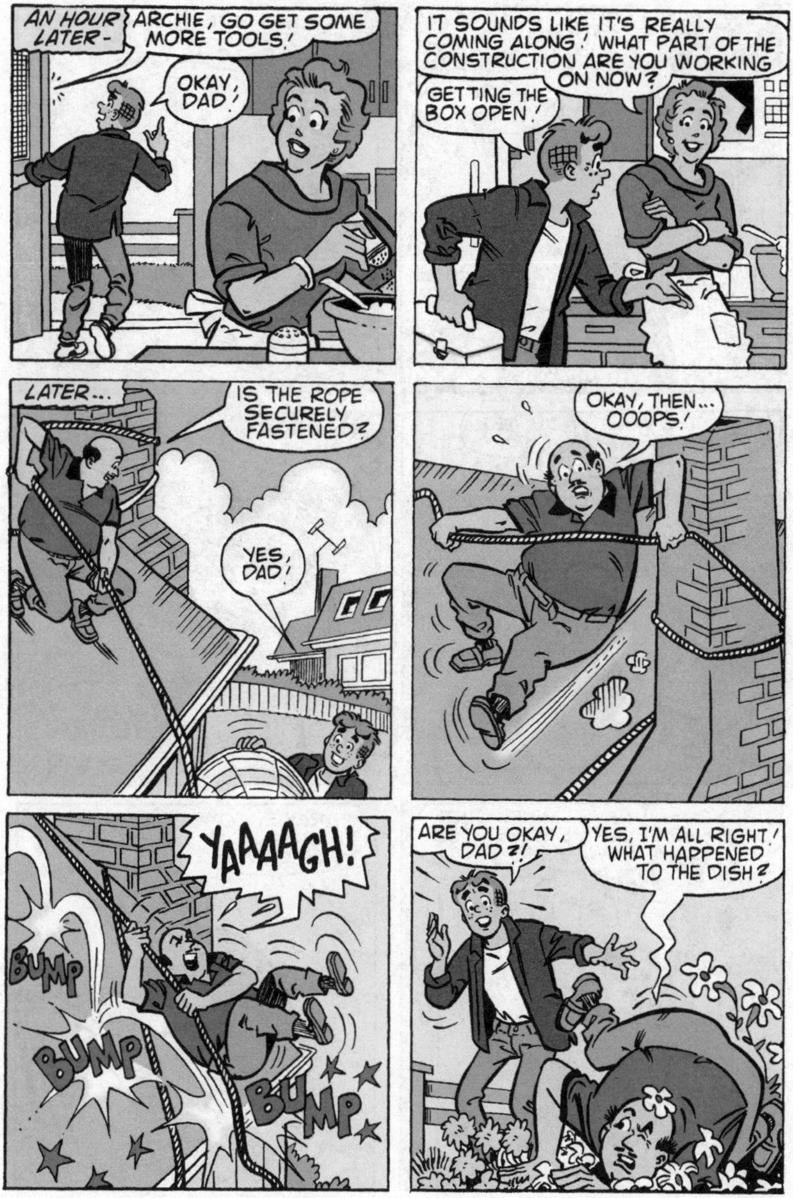
AN HOUR LATER-
ARCHIE, GO GET SOME MORE TOOLS!
OKAY, DAD!
IT SOUNDS LIKE IT'S REALLY COMING ALONG! WHAT PART OF THE CONSTRUCTION ARE YOU WORKING ON NOW?
GETTING THE BOX OPEN!
LATER...
IS THE ROPE SECURELY FASTENED?
YES, DAD!
OKAY, THEN... OOOPS!
YAAAAGH!
BUMP
BUMP
BUMP
ARE YOU OKAY, DAD?!
YES, I'M ALL RIGHT! WHAT HAPPENED TO THE DISH?

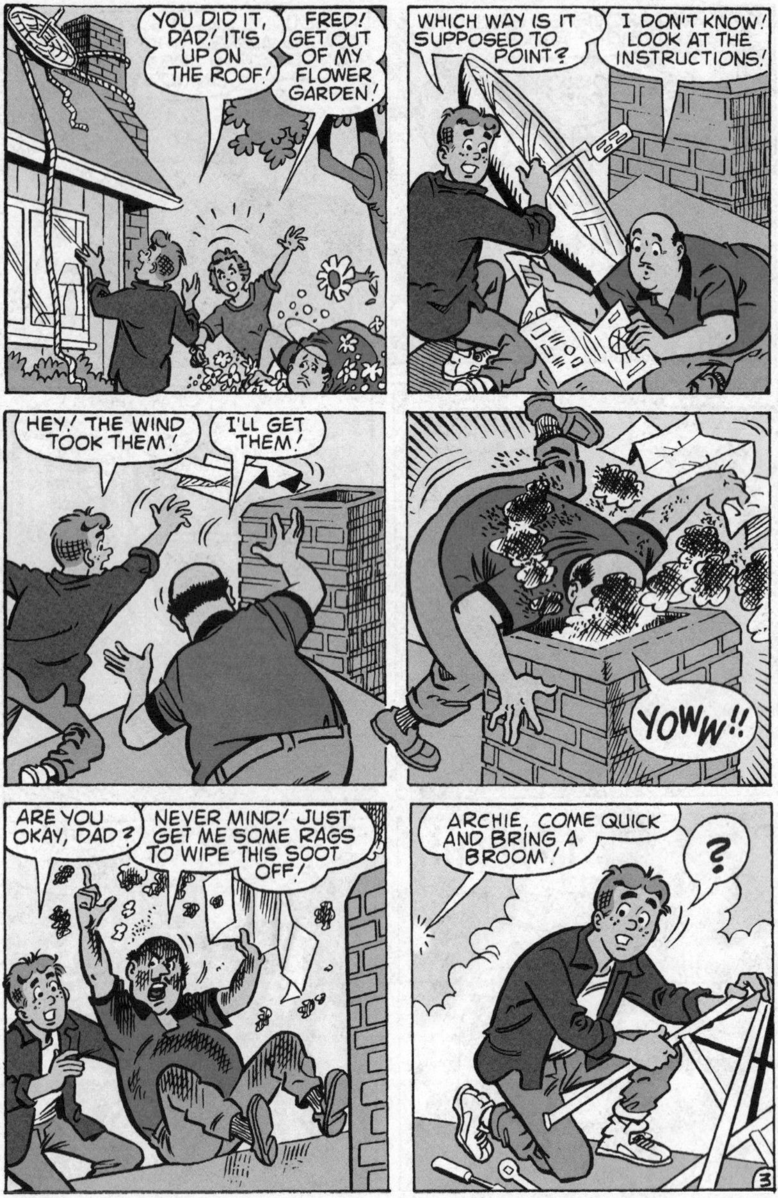
YOU DID IT, DAD! IT'S UP ON THE ROOF!
FRED! GET OUT OF MY FLOWER GARDEN!
WHICH WAY IS IT SUPPOSED TO POINT?
I DON'T KNOW! LOOK AT THE INSTRUCTIONS!
HEY! THE WIND TOOK THEM!
I'LL GET THEM!
YOWW!!
ARE YOU OKAY, DAD?
NEVER MIND! JUST GET ME SOME RAGS TO WIPE THIS SOOT OFF!
ARCHIE, COME QUICK AND BRING A BROOM!
?
3

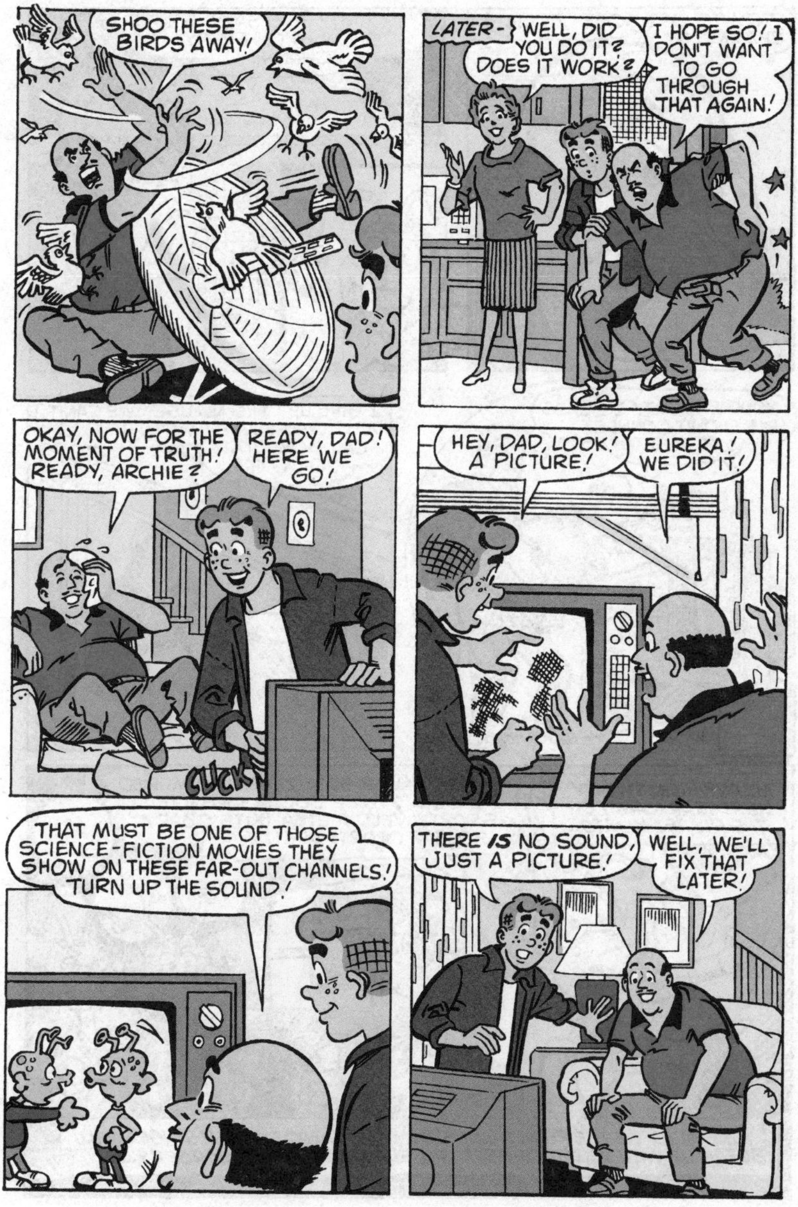
SHOO THESE BIRDS AWAY!
LATER-
WELL, DID YOU DO IT? DOES IT WORK?
I HOPE SO! I DON'T WANT TO GO THROUGH THAT AGAIN!
OKAY, NOW FOR THE MOMENT OF TRUTH! READY, ARCHIE?
READY, DAD! HERE WE GO!
CLICK
HEY, DAD, LOOK! A PICTURE!
EUREKA! WE DID IT!
THAT MUST BE ONE OF THOSE SCIENCE-FICTION MOVIES THEY SHOW ON THESE FAR-OUT CHANNELS! TURN UP THE SOUND!
THERE *IS* NO SOUND, JUST A PICTURE!
WELL, WE'LL FIX THAT LATER!

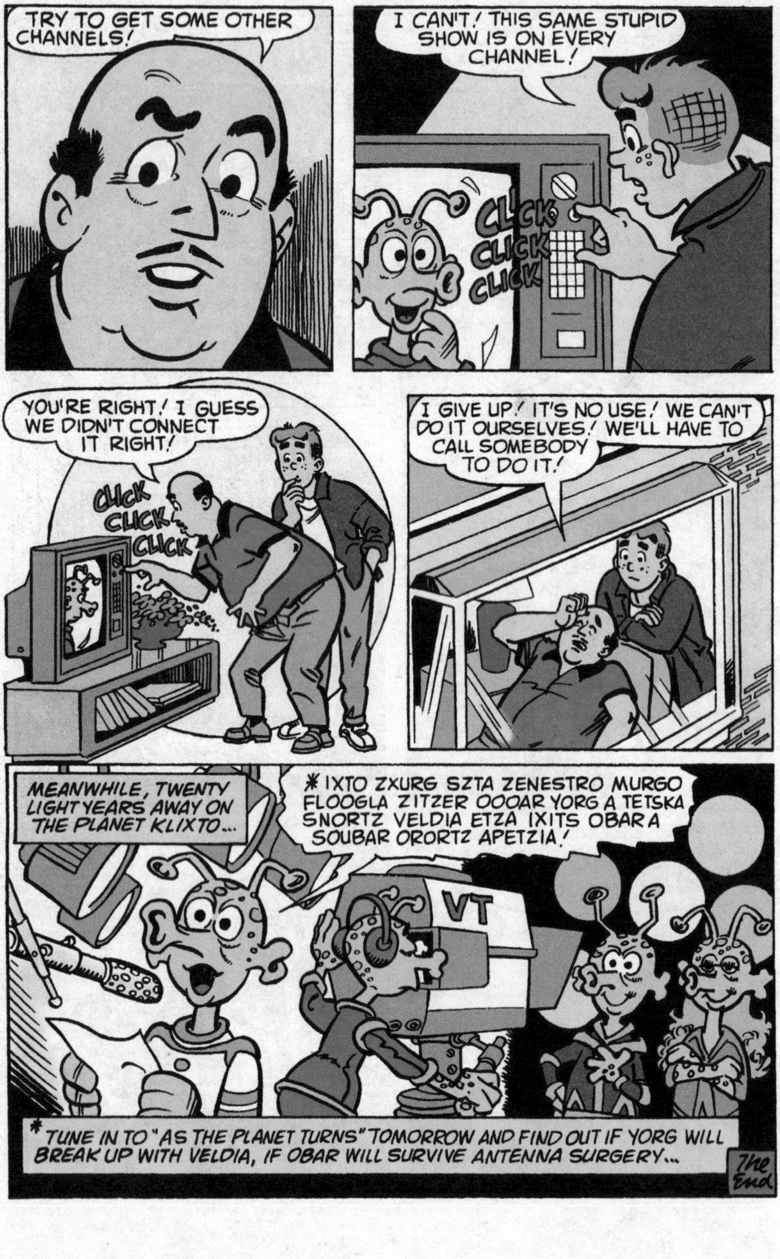
TRY TO GET SOME OTHER CHANNELS!
I CAN'T! THIS SAME STUPID SHOW IS ON EVERY CHANNEL!
CLICK CLICK CLICK
YOU'RE RIGHT! I GUESS WE DIDN'T CONNECT IT RIGHT!
CLICK CLICK CLICK
I GIVE UP! IT'S NO USE! WE CAN'T DO IT OURSELVES! WE'LL HAVE TO CALL SOMEBODY TO DO IT!
MEANWHILE, TWENTY LIGHT YEARS AWAY ON THE PLANET KLIXTO...
* IXTO ZXURG SZTA ZENESTRO MURGO FLOOGLA ZITZER OOOAR YORG A TETSKA SNORTZ VELDIA ETZA IXITS OBAR A SOUBAR ORORTZ APETZIA!
VT
* TUNE IN TO "AS THE PLANET TURNS" TOMORROW AND FIND OUT IF YORG WILL BREAK UP WITH VELDIA, IF OBAR WILL SURVIVE ANTENNA SURGERY...
The End

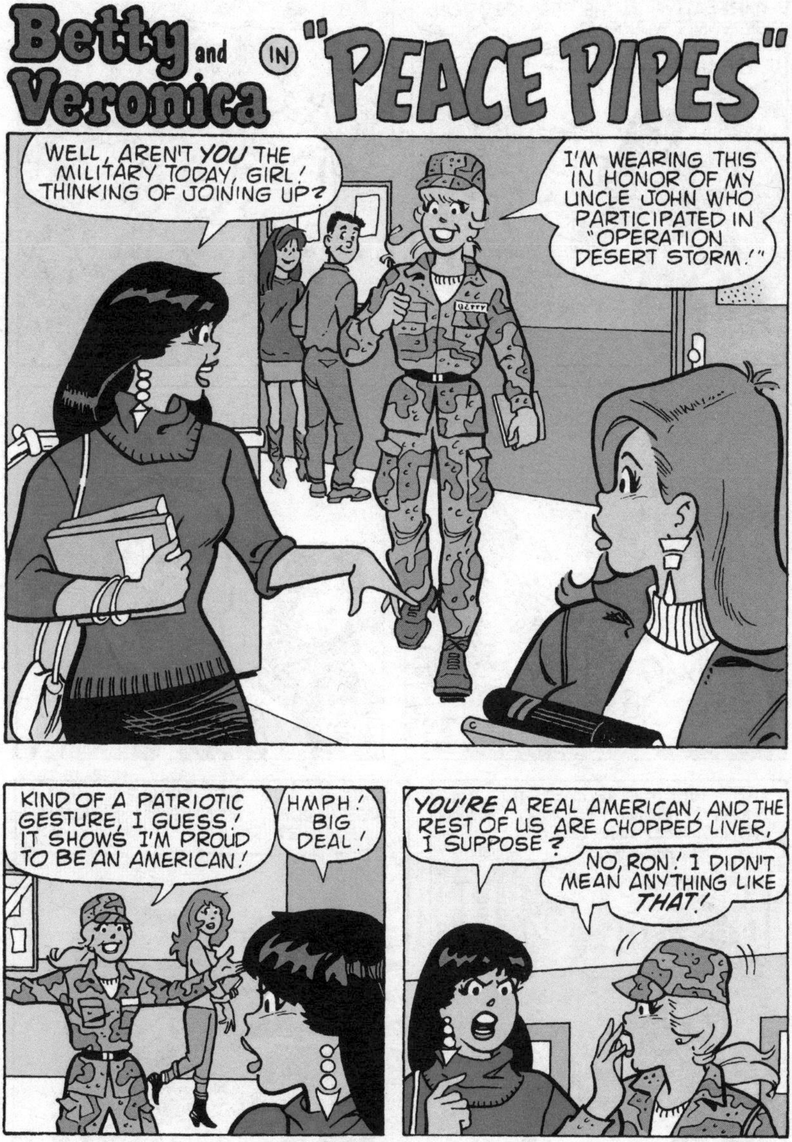
Betty and Veronica IN "PEACE PIPES"
WELL, AREN'T YOU THE MILITARY TODAY, GIRL! THINKING OF JOINING UP?
I'M WEARING THIS IN HONOR OF MY UNCLE JOHN WHO PARTICIPATED IN "OPERATION DESERT STORM!"
KIND OF A PATRIOTIC GESTURE, I GUESS! IT SHOWS I'M PROUD TO BE AN AMERICAN!
HMPH! BIG DEAL!
YOU'RE A REAL AMERICAN, AND THE REST OF US ARE CHOPPED LIVER, I SUPPOSE?
NO, RON! I DIDN'T MEAN ANYTHING LIKE THAT!

Originally presented in BETTY & VERONICA #47, January, 1992

JUST BECAUSE YOU HAVE A RELATIVE IN THE SERVICE, DOESN'T MAKE YOU ANY BETTER THAN THE REST OF US!

NO, RON...!

NICE TOUCH, BETTY! I LIKE IT!

Y-YOU DO, SIR?

A WALKING ADVERTISEMENT FOR OUR PROUD HERITAGE! MOST PRAISEWORTHY!

MY UNCLE IS IN THE SERVICE!

I WISH MORE PEOPLE WOULD DEMONSTRATE PRIDE IN THEIR FAMILY BACKGROUND!

HAH! WHEN IT COMES TO FAMILY BACKGROUND, WE LODGES ARE SECOND TO NONE!

LOOK AT THAT LOWER LIP, ARCH! QUEEN RONNIE IS PERTURBED!

WHAT'S WRONG, LUV?

2

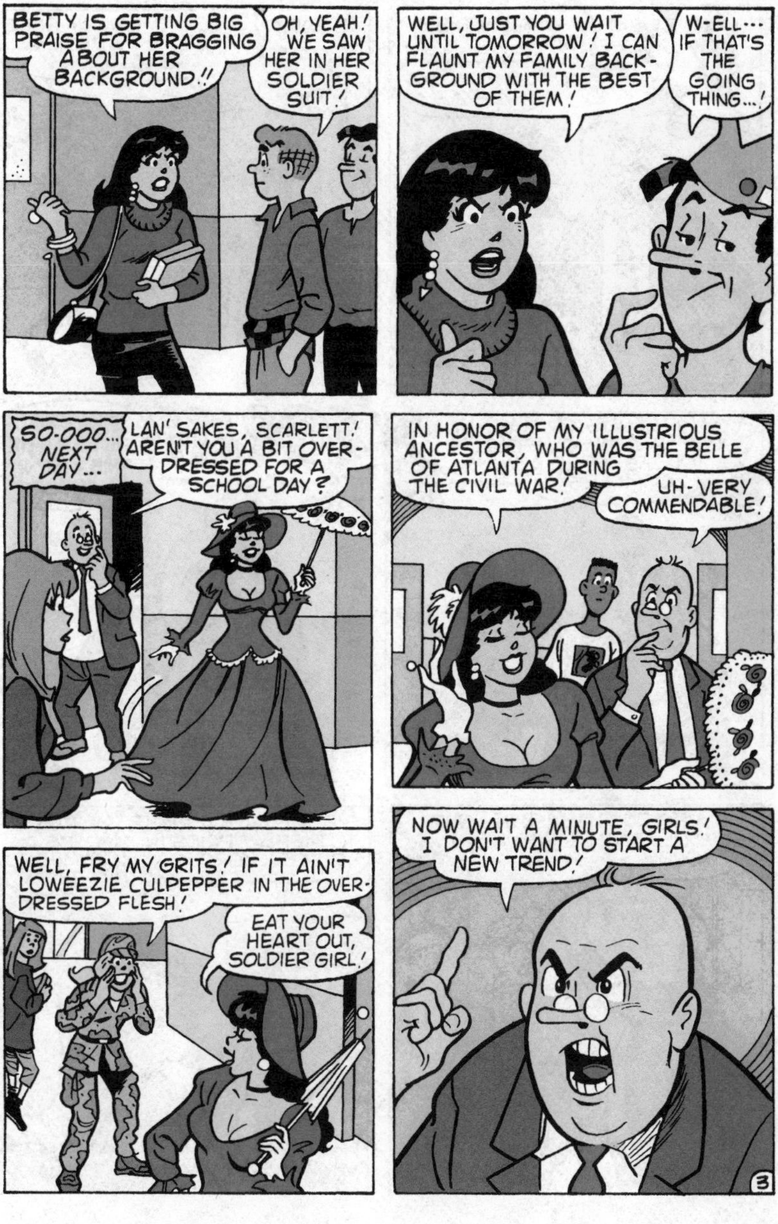
BETTY IS GETTING BIG PRAISE FOR BRAGGING ABOUT HER BACKGROUND!!
OH, YEAH! WE SAW HER IN HER SOLDIER SUIT!
WELL, JUST YOU WAIT UNTIL TOMORROW! I CAN FLAUNT MY FAMILY BACK-GROUND WITH THE BEST OF THEM!
W-ELL... IF THAT'S THE GOING THING...!
SO-OOO... NEXT DAY...
LAN' SAKES, SCARLETT! AREN'T YOU A BIT OVER-DRESSED FOR A SCHOOL DAY?
IN HONOR OF MY ILLUSTRIOUS ANCESTOR, WHO WAS THE BELLE OF ATLANTA DURING THE CIVIL WAR!
UH-VERY COMMENDABLE!
WELL, FRY MY GRITS! IF IT AIN'T LOWEEZIE CULPEPPER IN THE OVER-DRESSED FLESH!
EAT YOUR HEART OUT, SOLDIER GIRL!
NOW WAIT A MINUTE, GIRLS! I DON'T WANT TO START A NEW TREND!
3

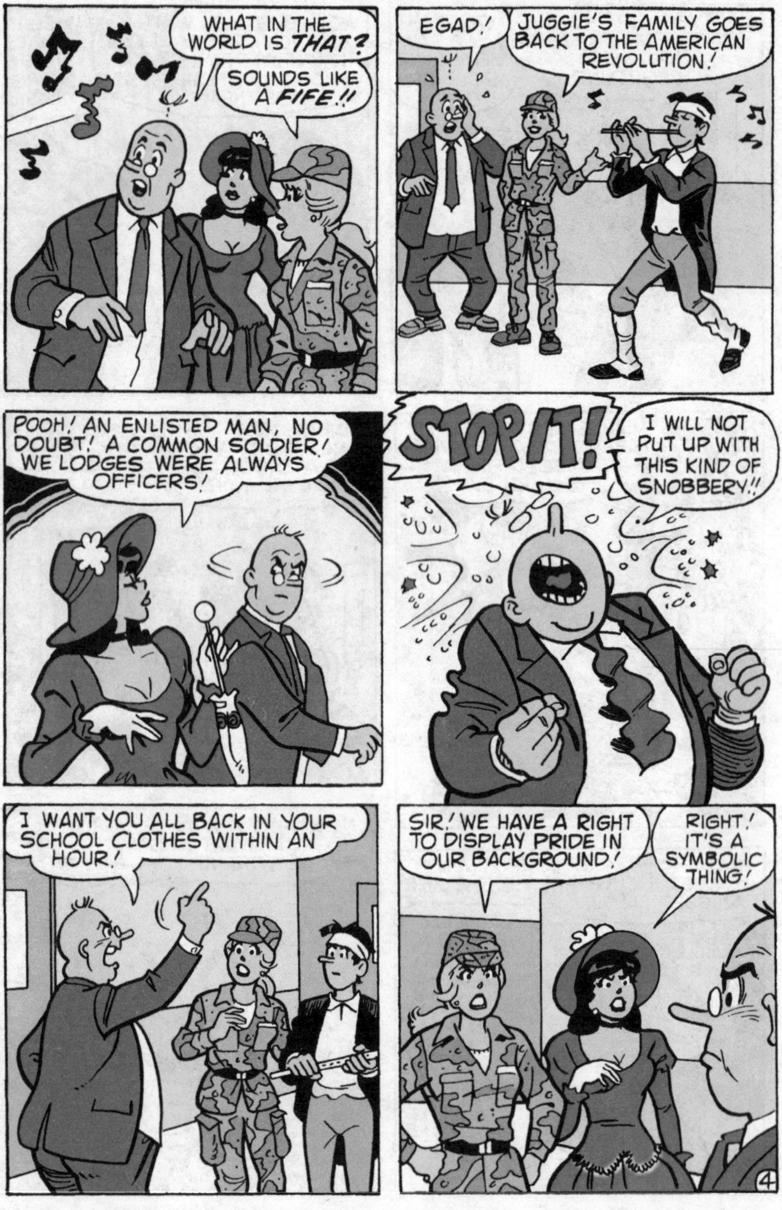
WHAT IN THE WORLD IS *THAT*?
SOUNDS LIKE A *FIFE*!!
EGAD!
JUGGIE'S FAMILY GOES BACK TO THE AMERICAN REVOLUTION!
POOH! AN ENLISTED MAN, NO DOUBT! A COMMON SOLDIER! WE LODGES WERE ALWAYS OFFICERS!
STOP IT!
I WILL NOT PUT UP WITH THIS KIND OF SNOBBERY!!
I WANT YOU ALL BACK IN YOUR SCHOOL CLOTHES WITHIN AN HOUR!
SIR! WE HAVE A RIGHT TO DISPLAY PRIDE IN OUR BACKGROUND!
RIGHT! IT'S A SYMBOLIC THING!
4

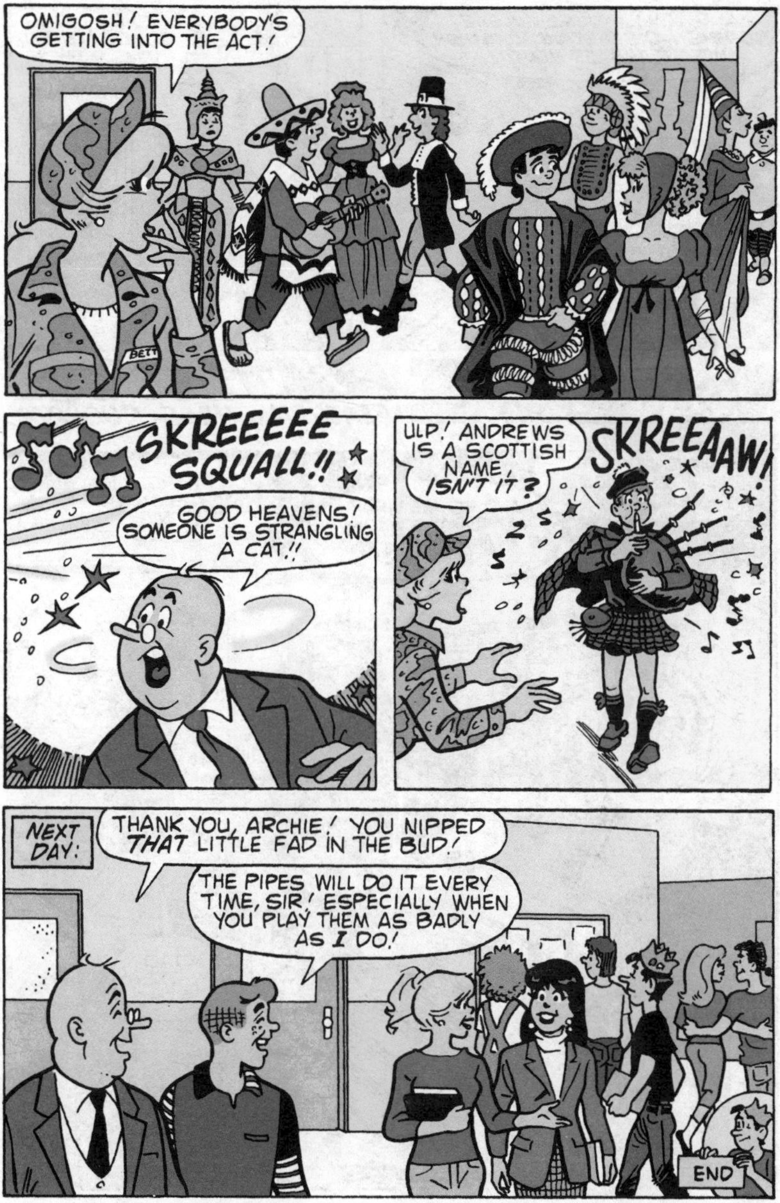
OMIGOSH! EVERYBODY'S GETTING INTO THE ACT!
SKREEEEEE SQUALL!!
GOOD HEAVENS! SOMEONE IS STRANGLING A CAT!!
ULP! ANDREWS IS A SCOTTISH NAME, ISN'T IT?
SKREEAAW!
NEXT DAY:
THANK YOU, ARCHIE! YOU NIPPED THAT LITTLE FAD IN THE BUD!
THE PIPES WILL DO IT EVERY TIME, SIR! ESPECIALLY WHEN YOU PLAY THEM AS BADLY AS I DO!
END

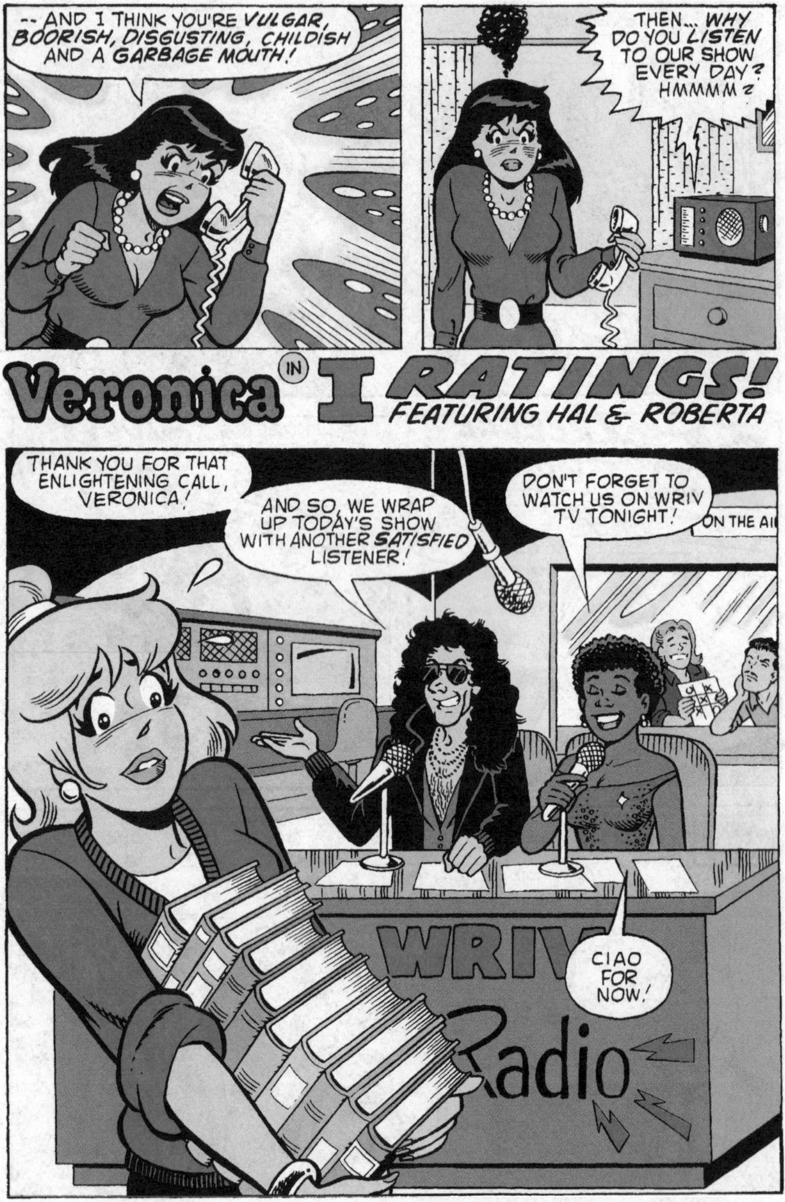
-- AND I THINK YOU'RE VULGAR, BOORISH, DISGUSTING, CHILDISH AND A GARBAGE MOUTH!
THEN... WHY DO YOU LISTEN TO OUR SHOW EVERY DAY? HMMMM?
Veronica IN I RATINGS! FEATURING HAL & ROBERTA
THANK YOU FOR THAT ENLIGHTENING CALL, VERONICA!
AND SO, WE WRAP UP TODAY'S SHOW WITH ANOTHER SATISFIED LISTENER!
DON'T FORGET TO WATCH US ON WRIV TV TONIGHT!
ON THE AI
WRIV
CIAO FOR NOW!
Radio

Originally presented in VERONICA #20, April, 1992

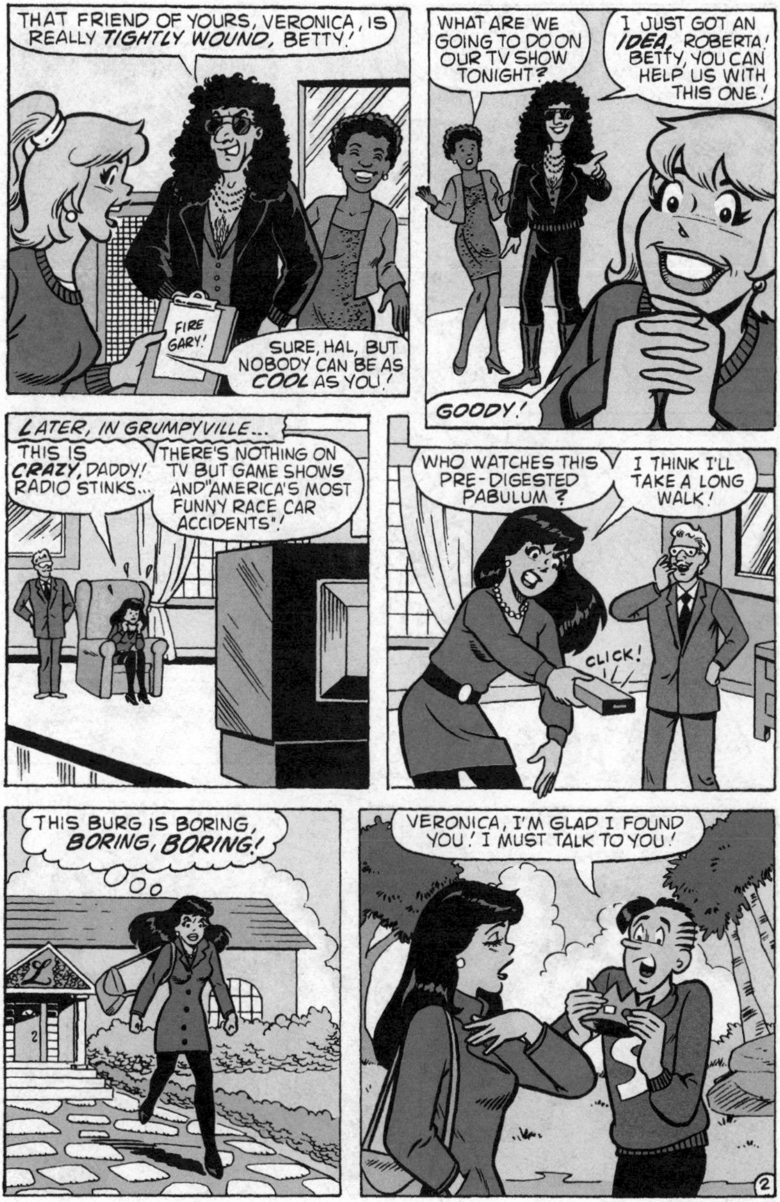
THAT FRIEND OF YOURS, VERONICA, IS REALLY TIGHTLY WOUND, BETTY!
FIRE GARY!
SURE, HAL, BUT NOBODY CAN BE AS COOL AS YOU!
WHAT ARE WE GOING TO DO ON OUR TV SHOW TONIGHT?
I JUST GOT AN IDEA, ROBERTA! BETTY, YOU CAN HELP US WITH THIS ONE!
GOODY!
LATER, IN GRUMPYVILLE...
THIS IS CRAZY, DADDY! RADIO STINKS...
THERE'S NOTHING ON TV BUT GAME SHOWS AND "AMERICA'S MOST FUNNY RACE CAR ACCIDENTS"!
WHO WATCHES THIS PRE-DIGESTED PABULUM?
I THINK I'LL TAKE A LONG WALK!
CLICK!
THIS BURG IS BORING, BORING, BORING!
VERONICA, I'M GLAD I FOUND YOU! I MUST TALK TO YOU!
2

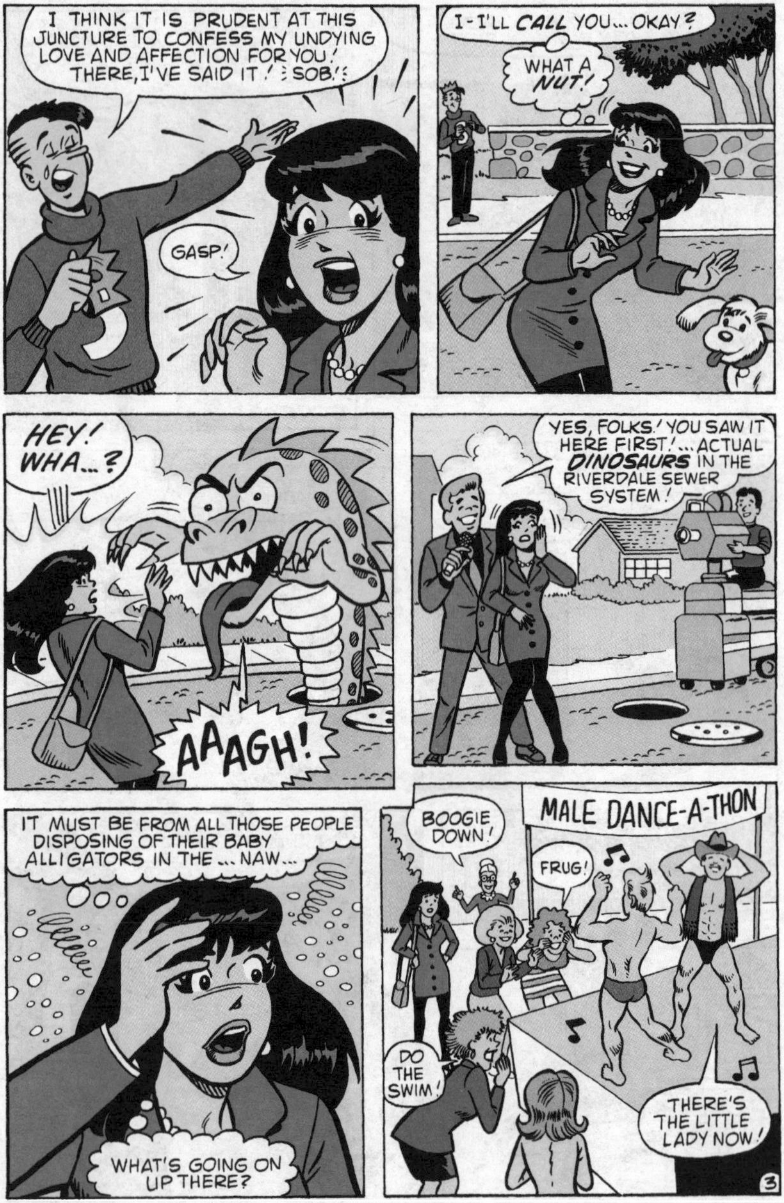
I THINK IT IS PRUDENT AT THIS JUNCTURE TO CONFESS MY UNDYING LOVE AND AFFECTION FOR YOU! THERE, I'VE SAID IT! SOB!
GASP!
I-I'LL CALL YOU... OKAY?
WHAT A NUT!
HEY! WHA...?
AAAGH!
YES, FOLKS! YOU SAW IT HERE FIRST! ... ACTUAL DINOSAURS IN THE RIVERDALE SEWER SYSTEM!
IT MUST BE FROM ALL THOSE PEOPLE DISPOSING OF THEIR BABY ALLIGATORS IN THE ... NAW...
WHAT'S GOING ON UP THERE?
MALE DANCE-A-THON
BOOGIE DOWN!
FRUG!
DO THE SWIM!
THERE'S THE LITTLE LADY NOW!
3

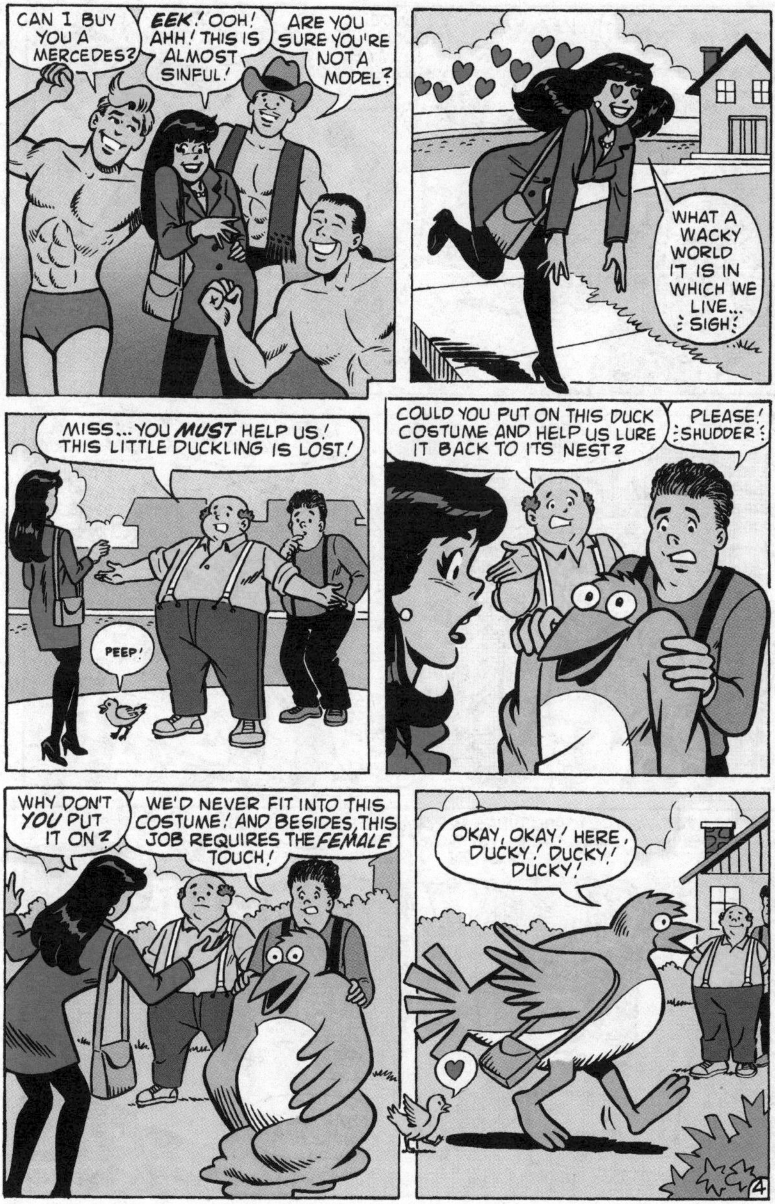
CAN I BUY YOU A MERCEDES?
EEK! OOH! AHH! THIS IS ALMOST SINFUL!
ARE YOU SURE YOU'RE NOT A MODEL?
WHAT A WACKY WORLD IT IS IN WHICH WE LIVE... SIGH!
MISS... YOU MUST HELP US! THIS LITTLE DUCKLING IS LOST!
PEEP!
COULD YOU PUT ON THIS DUCK COSTUME AND HELP US LURE IT BACK TO ITS NEST?
PLEASE! SHUDDER!
WHY DON'T YOU PUT IT ON?
WE'D NEVER FIT INTO THIS COSTUME! AND BESIDES, THIS JOB REQUIRES THE FEMALE TOUCH!
OKAY, OKAY! HERE, DUCKY! DUCKY! DUCKY!
4

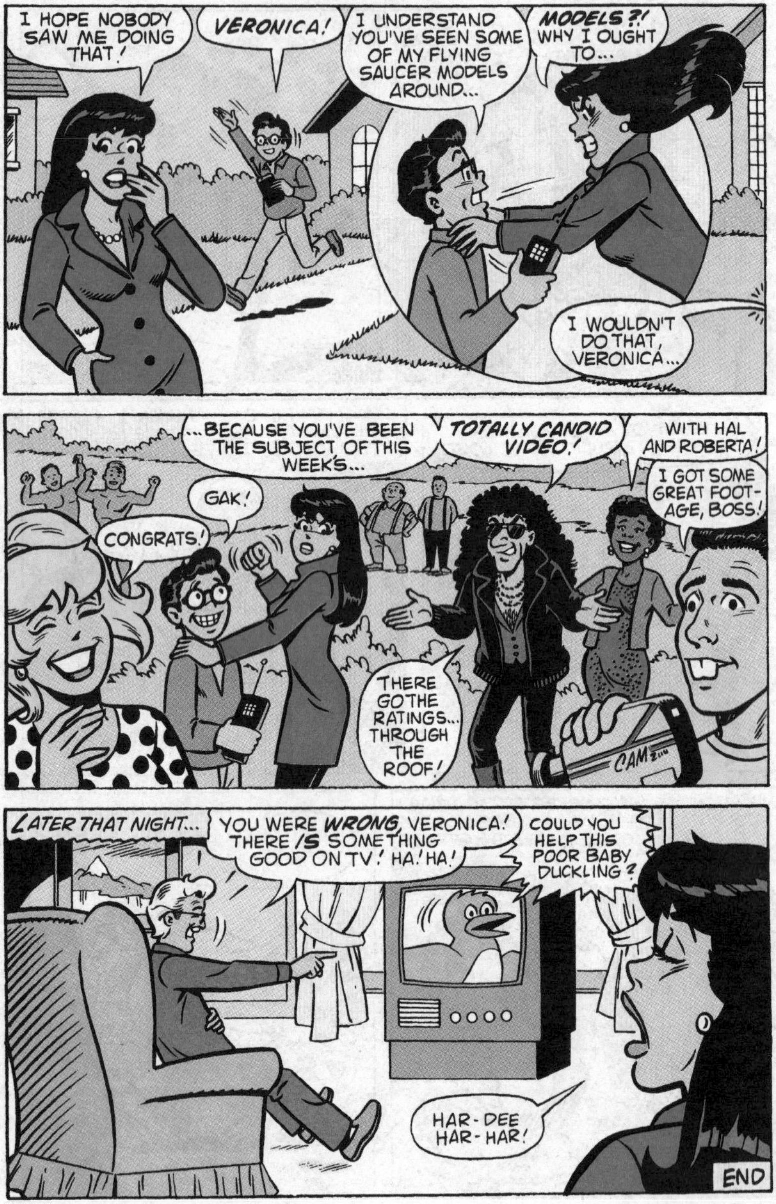
I HOPE NOBODY SAW ME DOING THAT!
VERONICA!
I UNDERSTAND YOU'VE SEEN SOME OF MY FLYING SAUCER MODELS AROUND...
MODELS?! WHY I OUGHT TO...
I WOULDN'T DO THAT, VERONICA...
...BECAUSE YOU'VE BEEN THE SUBJECT OF THIS WEEK'S...
TOTALLY CANDID VIDEO!
WITH HAL AND ROBERTA!
I GOT SOME GREAT FOOTAGE, BOSS!
GAK!
CONGRATS!
THERE GO THE RATINGS... THROUGH THE ROOF!
CAM
LATER THAT NIGHT...
YOU WERE WRONG, VERONICA! THERE IS SOMETHING GOOD ON TV! HA! HA!
COULD YOU HELP THIS POOR BABY DUCKLING?
HAR-DEE HAR-HAR!
END

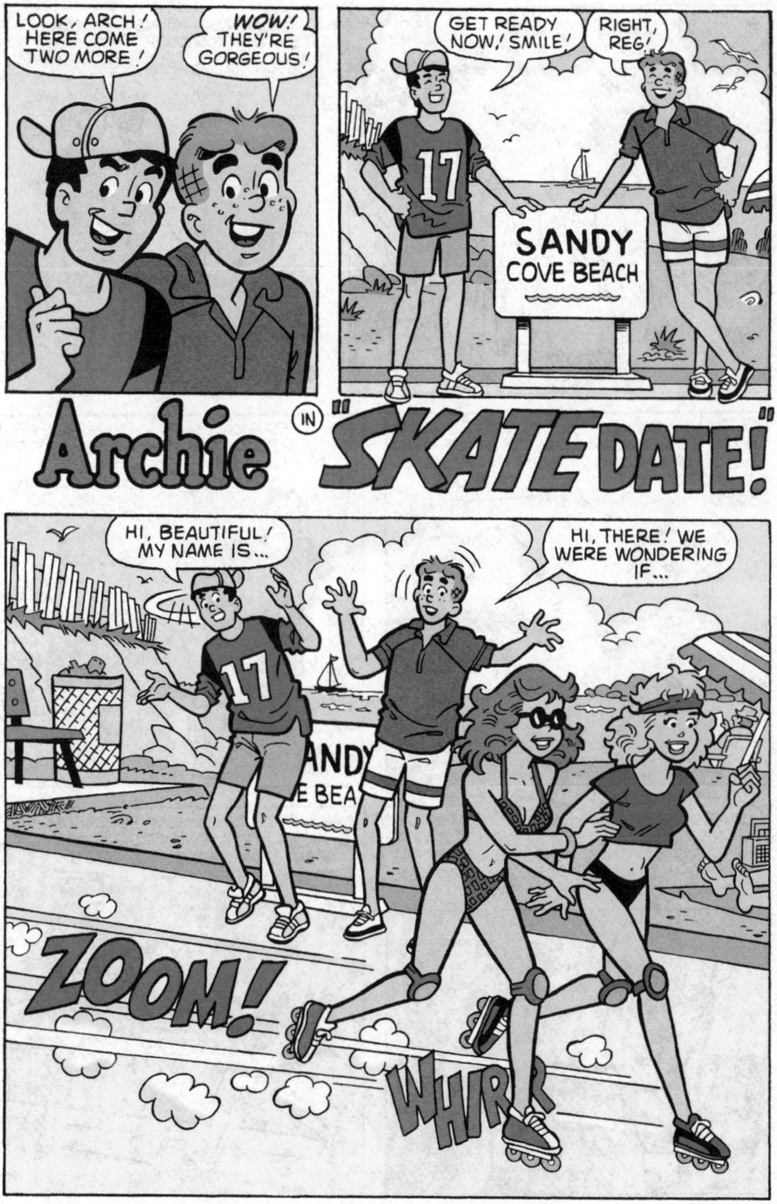
LOOK, ARCH! HERE COME TWO MORE!
WOW! THEY'RE GORGEOUS!
GET READY NOW! SMILE!
RIGHT, REG!
SANDY COVE BEACH
Archie IN "SKATE DATE!"
HI, BEAUTIFUL! MY NAME IS...
HI, THERE! WE WERE WONDERING IF...
ZOOM!
WHIRR

Originally presented in ARCHIE #404, October, 1992

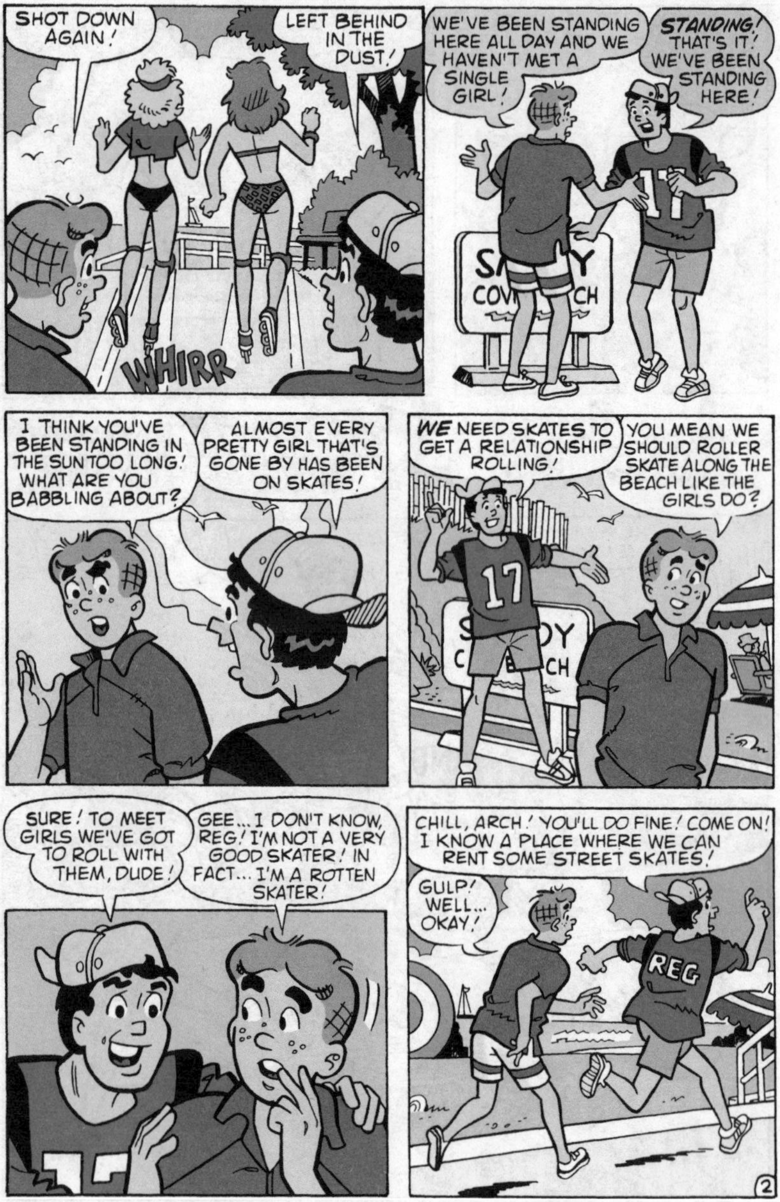
SHOT DOWN AGAIN!
LEFT BEHIND IN THE DUST!
WHIRR
WE'VE BEEN STANDING HERE ALL DAY AND WE HAVEN'T MET A SINGLE GIRL!
STANDING! THAT'S IT! WE'VE BEEN STANDING HERE!
I THINK YOU'VE BEEN STANDING IN THE SUN TOO LONG! WHAT ARE YOU BABBLING ABOUT?
ALMOST EVERY PRETTY GIRL THAT'S GONE BY HAS BEEN ON SKATES!
WE NEED SKATES TO GET A RELATIONSHIP ROLLING!
YOU MEAN WE SHOULD ROLLER SKATE ALONG THE BEACH LIKE THE GIRLS DO?
SURE! TO MEET GIRLS WE'VE GOT TO ROLL WITH THEM, DUDE!
GEE... I DON'T KNOW, REG! I'M NOT A VERY GOOD SKATER! IN FACT... I'M A ROTTEN SKATER!
CHILL, ARCH! YOU'LL DO FINE! COME ON! I KNOW A PLACE WHERE WE CAN RENT SOME STREET SKATES!
GULP! WELL... OKAY!
REG
2

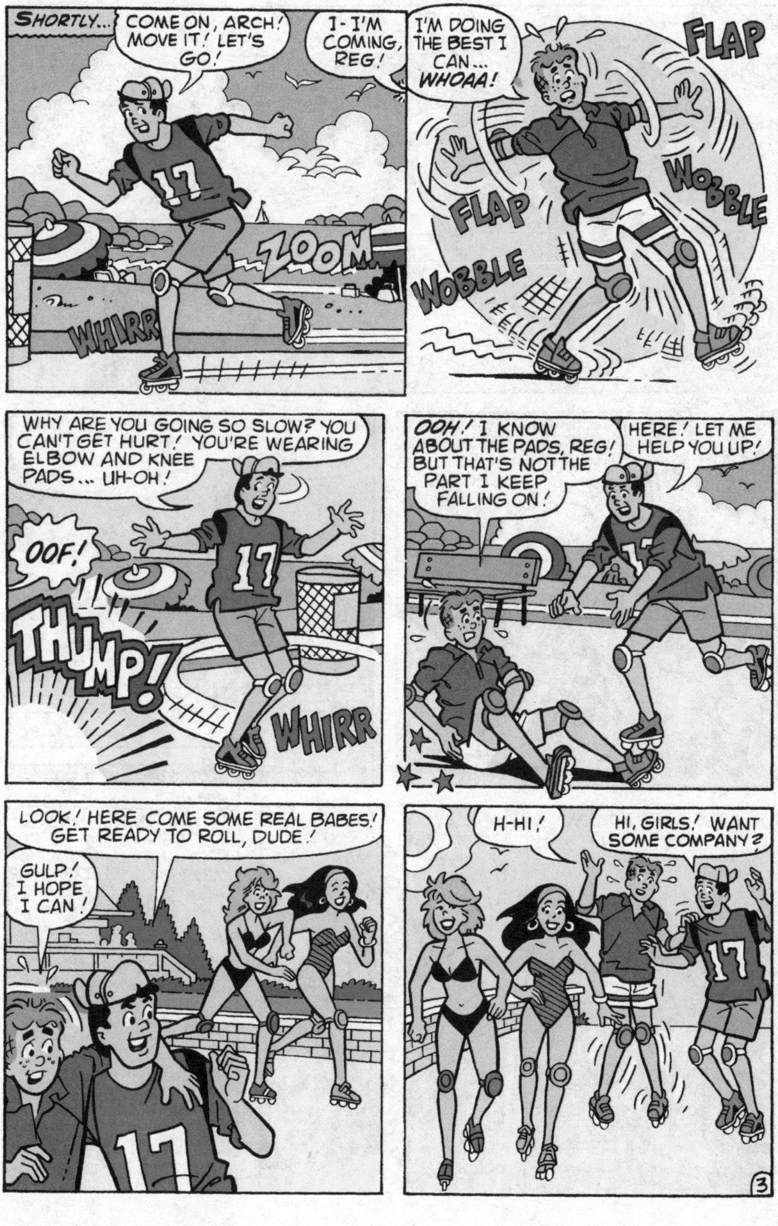
SHORTLY...
COME ON, ARCH! MOVE IT! LET'S GO!
I-I'M COMING, REG!
ZOOM
WHIRR
I'M DOING THE BEST I CAN... WHOAA!
FLAP
FLAP
WOBBLE
WOBBLE
WHY ARE YOU GOING SO SLOW? YOU CAN'T GET HURT! YOU'RE WEARING ELBOW AND KNEE PADS... UH-OH!
OOF!
THUMP!
WHIRR
OOH! I KNOW ABOUT THE PADS, REG! BUT THAT'S NOT THE PART I KEEP FALLING ON!
HERE! LET ME HELP YOU UP!
LOOK! HERE COME SOME REAL BABES! GET READY TO ROLL, DUDE!
GULP! I HOPE I CAN!
H-HI!
HI, GIRLS! WANT SOME COMPANY?
3

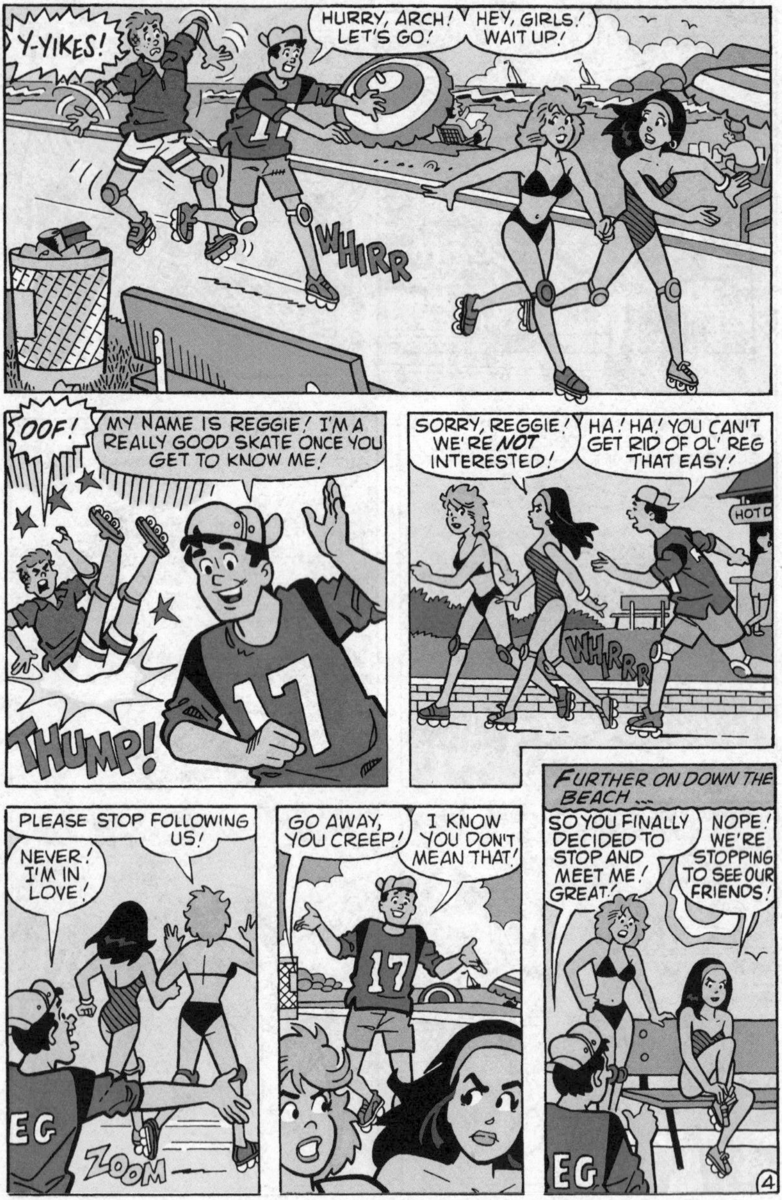
Y-YIKES!
HURRY, ARCH! LET'S GO!
HEY, GIRLS! WAIT UP!
WHIRR
OOF!
MY NAME IS REGGIE! I'M A REALLY GOOD SKATE ONCE YOU GET TO KNOW ME!
THUMP!
SORRY, REGGIE! WE'RE NOT INTERESTED!
HA! HA! YOU CAN'T GET RID OF OL' REG THAT EASY!
WHIRRR
PLEASE STOP FOLLOWING US!
NEVER! I'M IN LOVE!
ZOOM
GO AWAY, YOU CREEP!
I KNOW YOU DON'T MEAN THAT!
FURTHER ON DOWN THE BEACH ...
SO YOU FINALLY DECIDED TO STOP AND MEET ME! GREAT!
NOPE! WE'RE STOPPING TO SEE OUR FRIENDS!
4

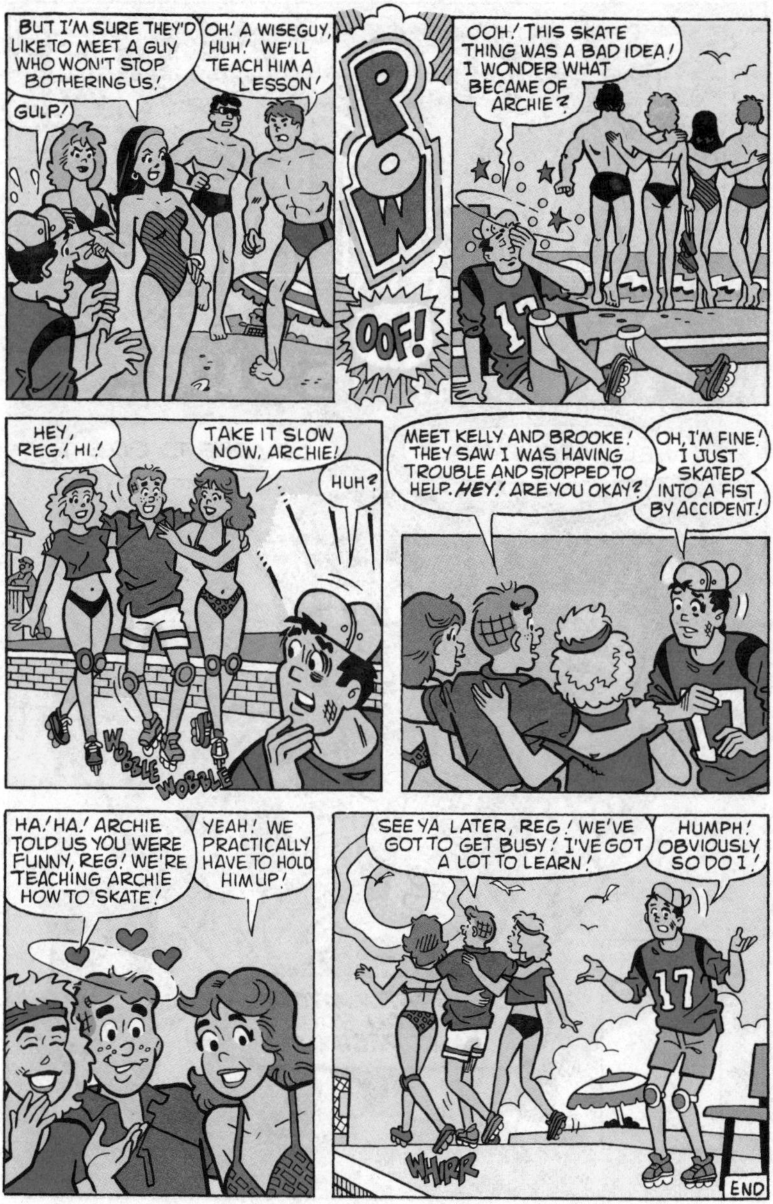
BUT I'M SURE THEY'D LIKE TO MEET A GUY WHO WON'T STOP BOTHERING US!
OH! A WISEGUY, HUH! WE'LL TEACH HIM A LESSON!
GULP!
POW
OOF!
OOH! THIS SKATE THING WAS A BAD IDEA! I WONDER WHAT BECAME OF ARCHIE?
HEY, REG! HI!
TAKE IT SLOW NOW, ARCHIE!
HUH?
WOBBLE WOBBLE
MEET KELLY AND BROOKE! THEY SAW I WAS HAVING TROUBLE AND STOPPED TO HELP. HEY! ARE YOU OKAY?
OH, I'M FINE! I JUST SKATED INTO A FIST BY ACCIDENT!
HA! HA! ARCHIE TOLD US YOU WERE FUNNY, REG! WE'RE TEACHING ARCHIE HOW TO SKATE!
YEAH! WE PRACTICALLY HAVE TO HOLD HIM UP!
SEE YA LATER, REG! WE'VE GOT TO GET BUSY! I'VE GOT A LOT TO LEARN!
HUMPH! OBVIOUSLY SO DO I!
WHIRR
END

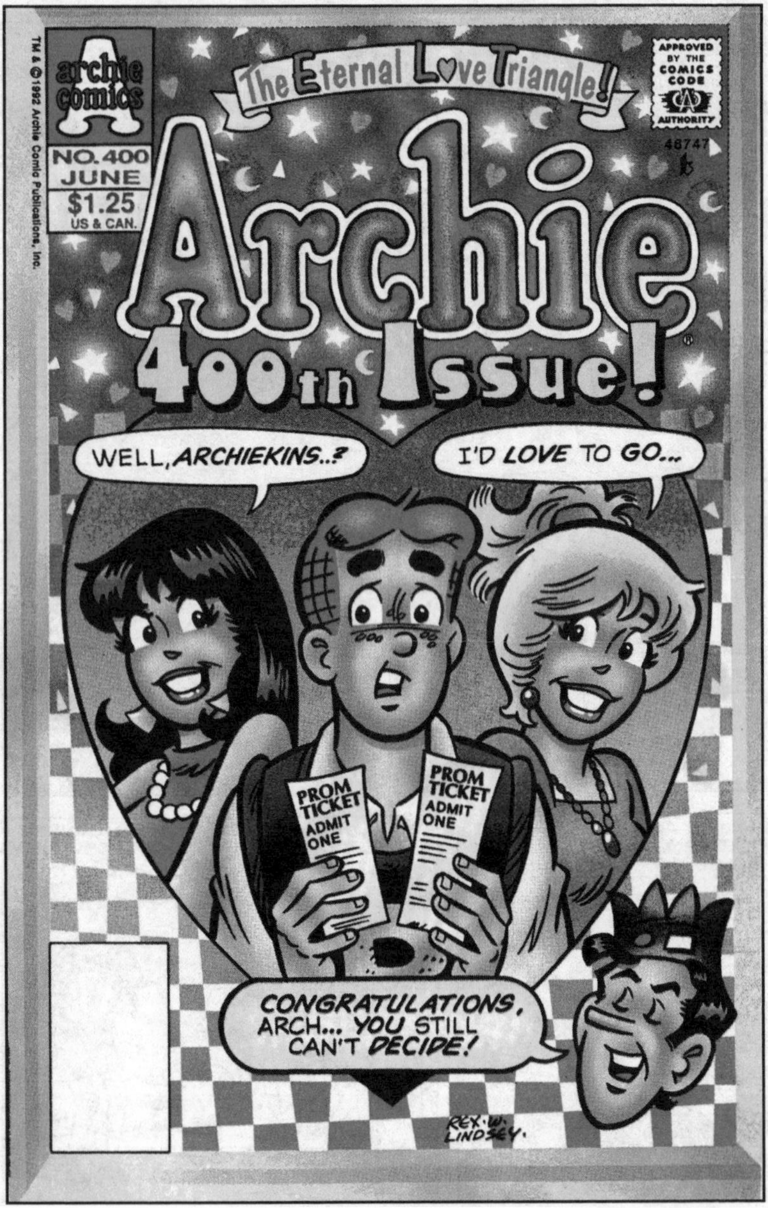
archie comics
NO. 400
JUNE
$1.25
US & CAN.
TM & © 1992 Archie Comic Publications, Inc.
The Eternal Love Triangle!
APPROVED BY THE COMICS CODE AUTHORITY
Archie
400th Issue!
WELL, ARCHIEKINS..?
I'D LOVE TO GO...
PROM TICKET ADMIT ONE
PROM TICKET ADMIT ONE
CONGRATULATIONS, ARCH... YOU STILL CAN'T DECIDE!
REX. W. LINDSEY.

Originally printed in 1992

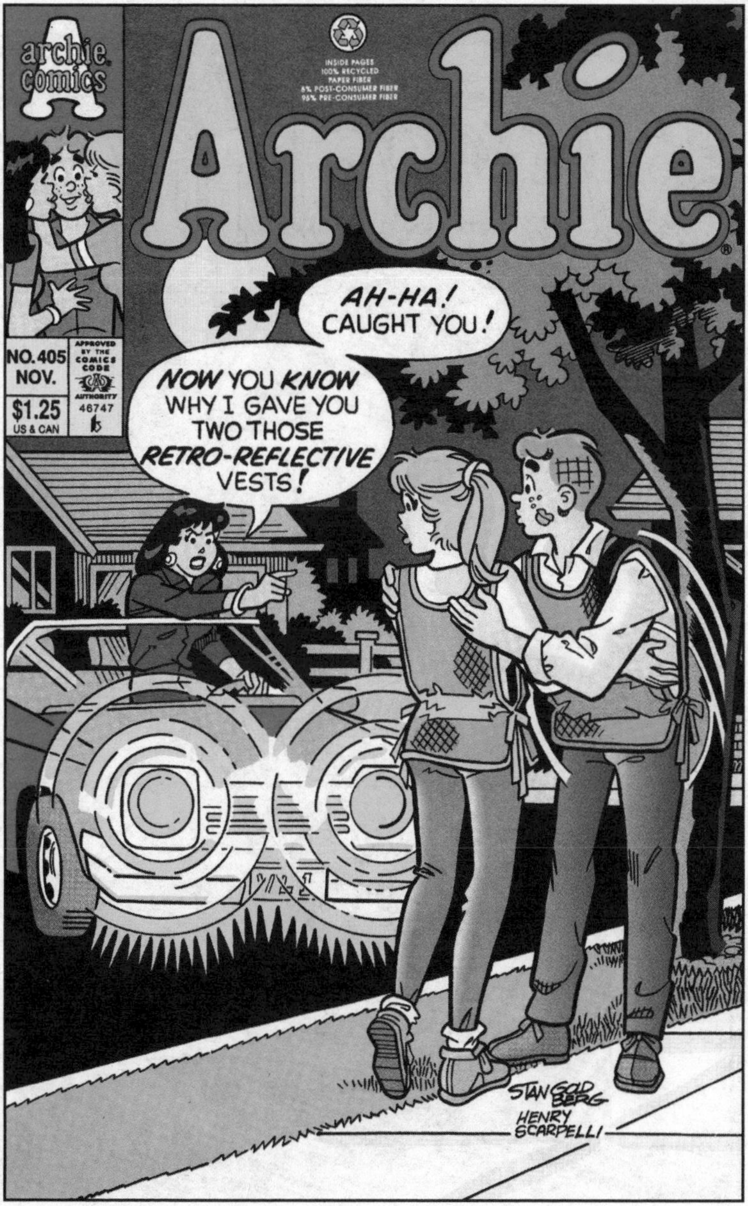
archie comics
Archie
INSIDE PAGES 100% RECYCLED PAPER FIBER 5% POST-CONSUMER FIBER 95% PRE-CONSUMER FIBER
NO. 405 NOV.
$1.25 US & CAN
APPROVED BY THE COMICS CODE AUTHORITY
AH-HA! CAUGHT YOU!
NOW YOU KNOW WHY I GAVE YOU TWO THOSE RETRO-REFLECTIVE VESTS!
STAN GOLDBERG
HENRY SCARPELLI

Originally printed in 1992

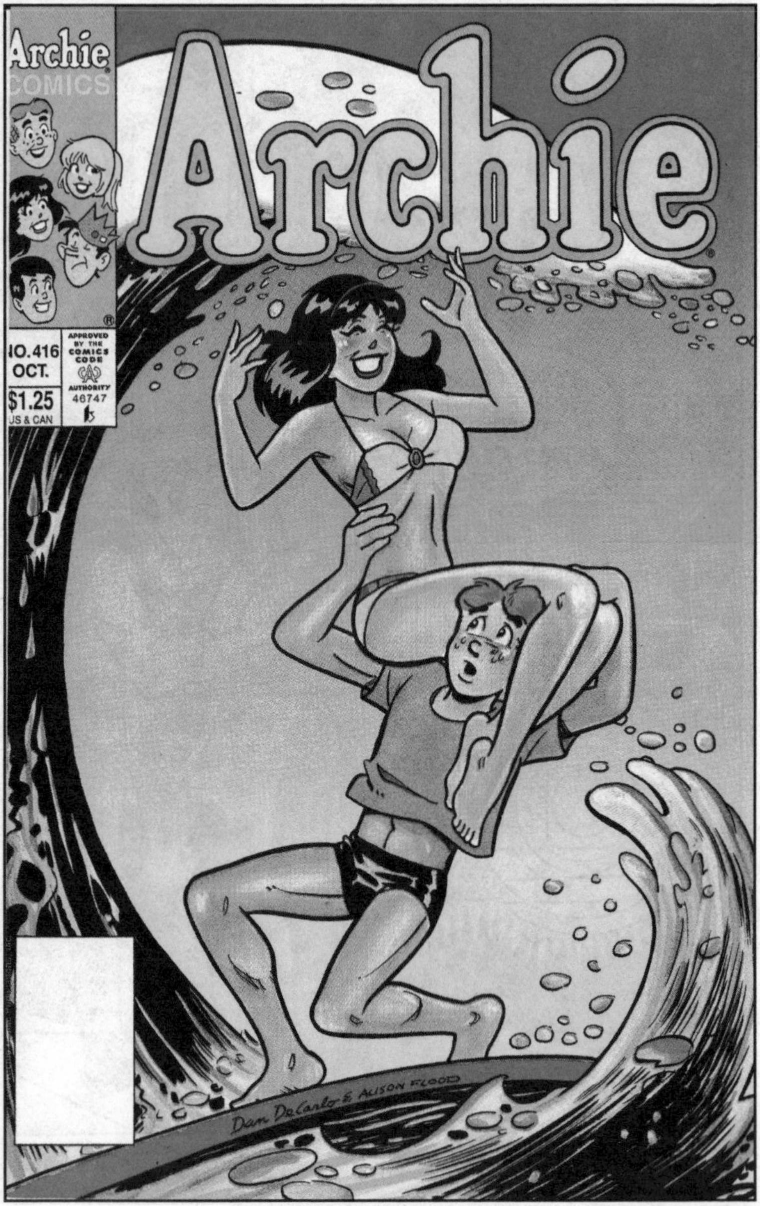
Archie
COMICS
Archie
NO.416
OCT.
$1.25
US & CAN
APPROVED BY THE COMICS CODE AUTHORITY
46747
Dan DeCarlo & Alison Flood

Originally printed in 1993

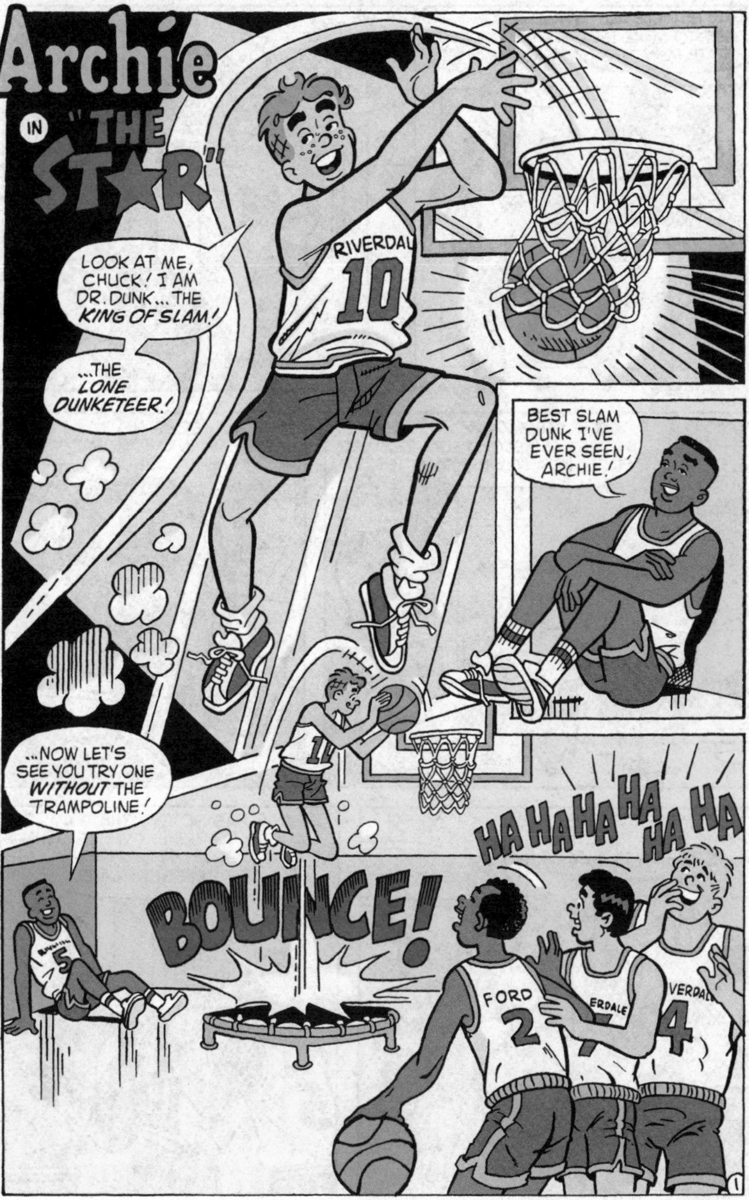

Archie
IN "THE STAR"
LOOK AT ME, CHUCK! I AM DR. DUNK... THE KING OF SLAM!
...THE LONE DUNKETEER!
RIVERDAL
10
BEST SLAM DUNK I'VE EVER SEEN, ARCHIE!
...NOW LET'S SEE YOU TRY ONE WITHOUT THE TRAMPOLINE!
HA HA HA HA HA HA HA
BOUNCE!
FORD
2
ERDALE
VERDAL
4


Originally presented in ARCHIE #411, May, 1993

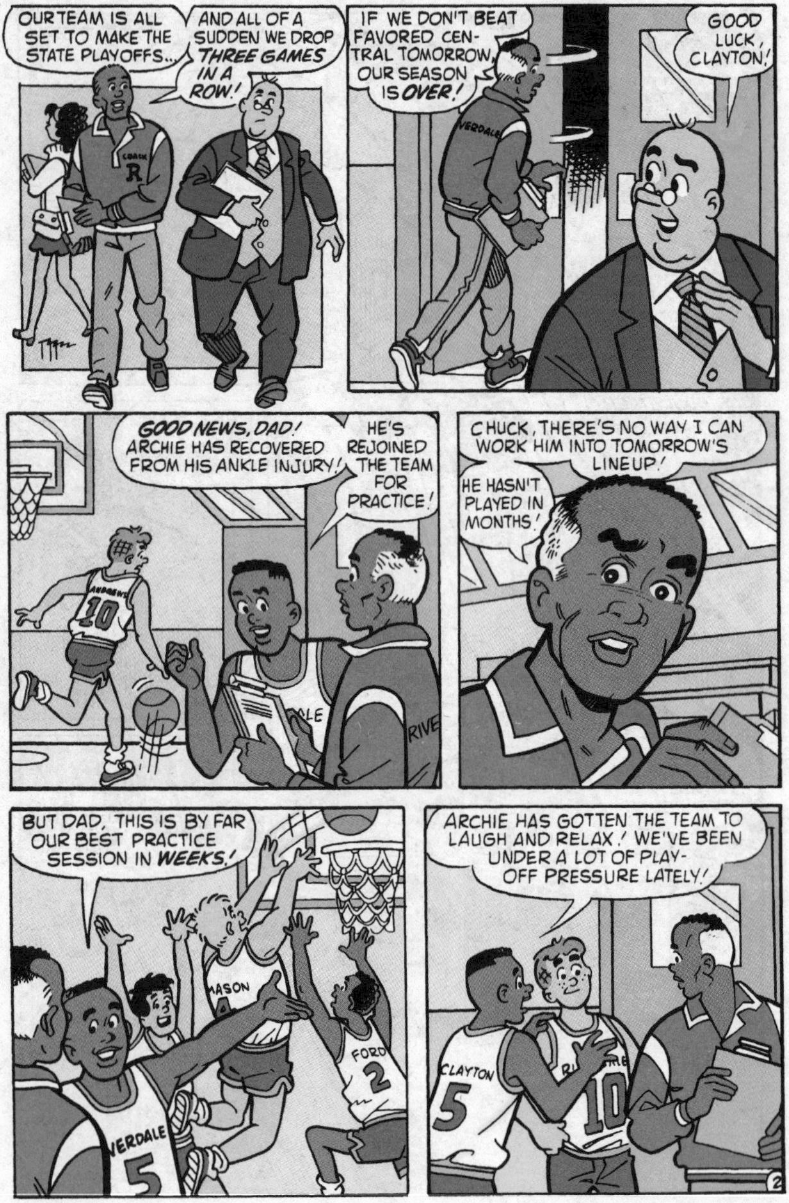
OUR TEAM IS ALL SET TO MAKE THE STATE PLAYOFFS...
AND ALL OF A SUDDEN WE DROP THREE GAMES IN A ROW!
IF WE DON'T BEAT FAVORED CEN-TRAL TOMORROW, OUR SEASON IS OVER!
GOOD LUCK, CLAYTON!
GOOD NEWS, DAD! ARCHIE HAS RECOVERED FROM HIS ANKLE INJURY!
HE'S REJOINED THE TEAM FOR PRACTICE!
CHUCK, THERE'S NO WAY I CAN WORK HIM INTO TOMORROW'S LINEUP!
HE HASN'T PLAYED IN MONTHS!
BUT DAD, THIS IS BY FAR OUR BEST PRACTICE SESSION IN WEEKS!
ARCHIE HAS GOTTEN THE TEAM TO LAUGH AND RELAX! WE'VE BEEN UNDER A LOT OF PLAY-OFF PRESSURE LATELY!
2

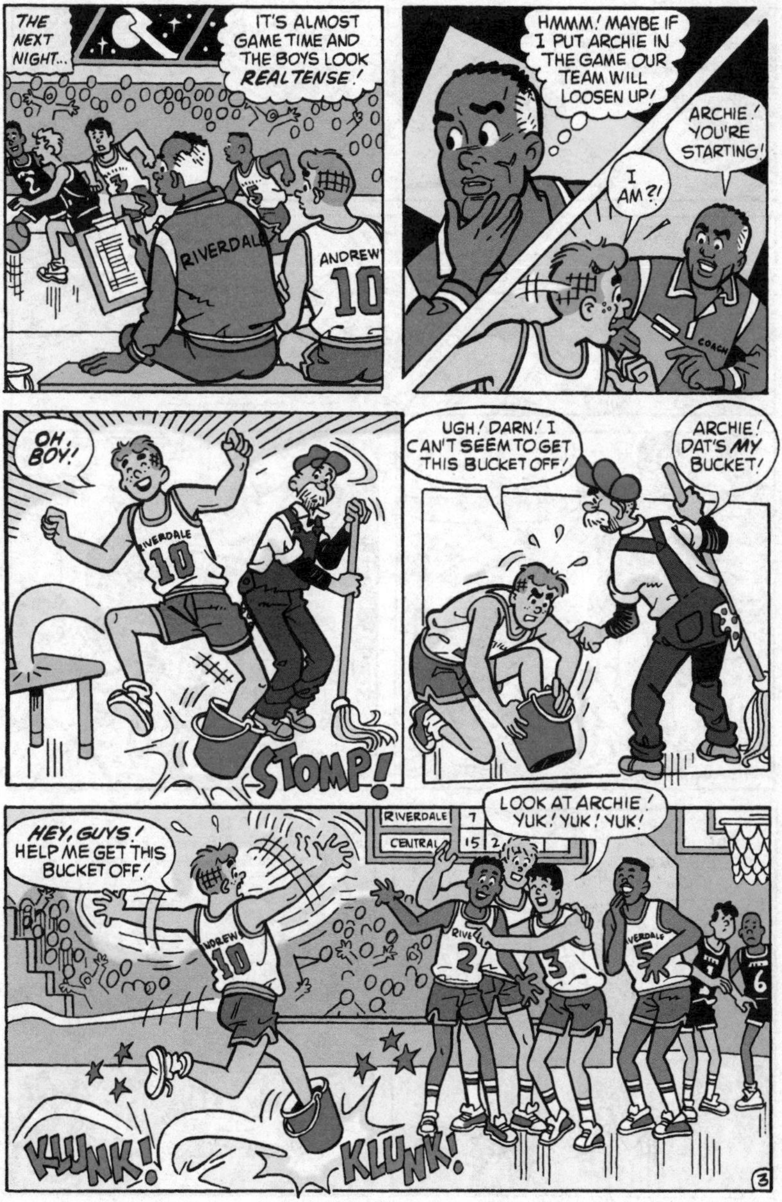
THE NEXT NIGHT...
IT'S ALMOST GAME TIME AND THE BOYS LOOK *REAL TENSE*!
RIVERDALE
ANDREWS
10
HMMM! MAYBE IF I PUT ARCHIE IN THE GAME OUR TEAM WILL LOOSEN UP!
ARCHIE! YOU'RE STARTING!
I AM?!
COACH
OH, BOY!
STOMP!
UGH! DARN! I CAN'T SEEM TO GET THIS BUCKET OFF!
ARCHIE! DAT'S *MY* BUCKET!
HEY, GUYS! HELP ME GET THIS BUCKET OFF!
RIVERDALE 7
CENTRAL 15
LOOK AT ARCHIE! YUK! YUK! YUK!
KLUNK!
KLUNK!
3

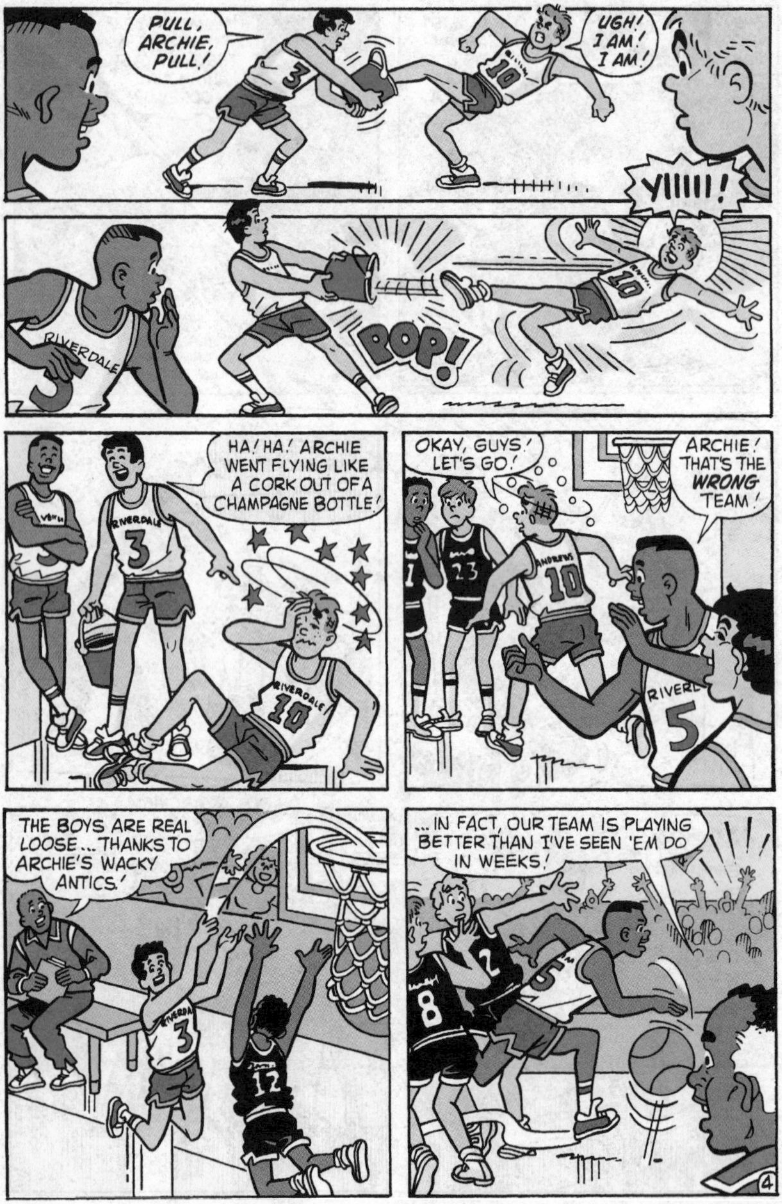
PULL, ARCHIE, PULL!
UGH! I AM! I AM!
YIIIII!
POP!
HA! HA! ARCHIE WENT FLYING LIKE A CORK OUT OF A CHAMPAGNE BOTTLE!
OKAY, GUYS! LET'S GO!
ARCHIE! THAT'S THE WRONG TEAM!
THE BOYS ARE REAL LOOSE... THANKS TO ARCHIE'S WACKY ANTICS!
... IN FACT, OUR TEAM IS PLAYING BETTER THAN I'VE SEEN 'EM DO IN WEEKS!
4

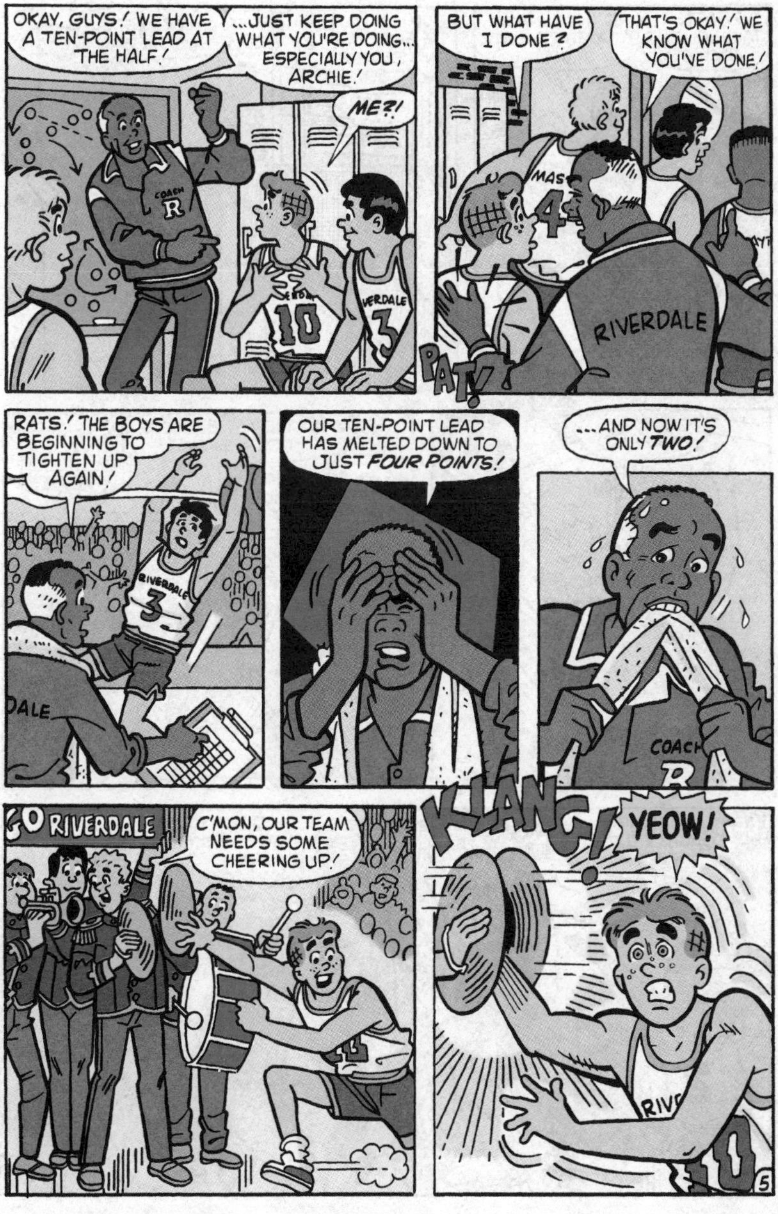
OKAY, GUYS! WE HAVE A TEN-POINT LEAD AT THE HALF!
...JUST KEEP DOING WHAT YOU'RE DOING... ESPECIALLY YOU, ARCHIE!
ME?!
BUT WHAT HAVE I DONE?
THAT'S OKAY! WE KNOW WHAT YOU'VE DONE!
PAT!
RIVERDALE
RATS! THE BOYS ARE BEGINNING TO TIGHTEN UP AGAIN!
OUR TEN-POINT LEAD HAS MELTED DOWN TO JUST FOUR POINTS!
...AND NOW IT'S ONLY TWO!
GO RIVERDALE
C'MON, OUR TEAM NEEDS SOME CHEERING UP!
KLANG!
YEOW!
5

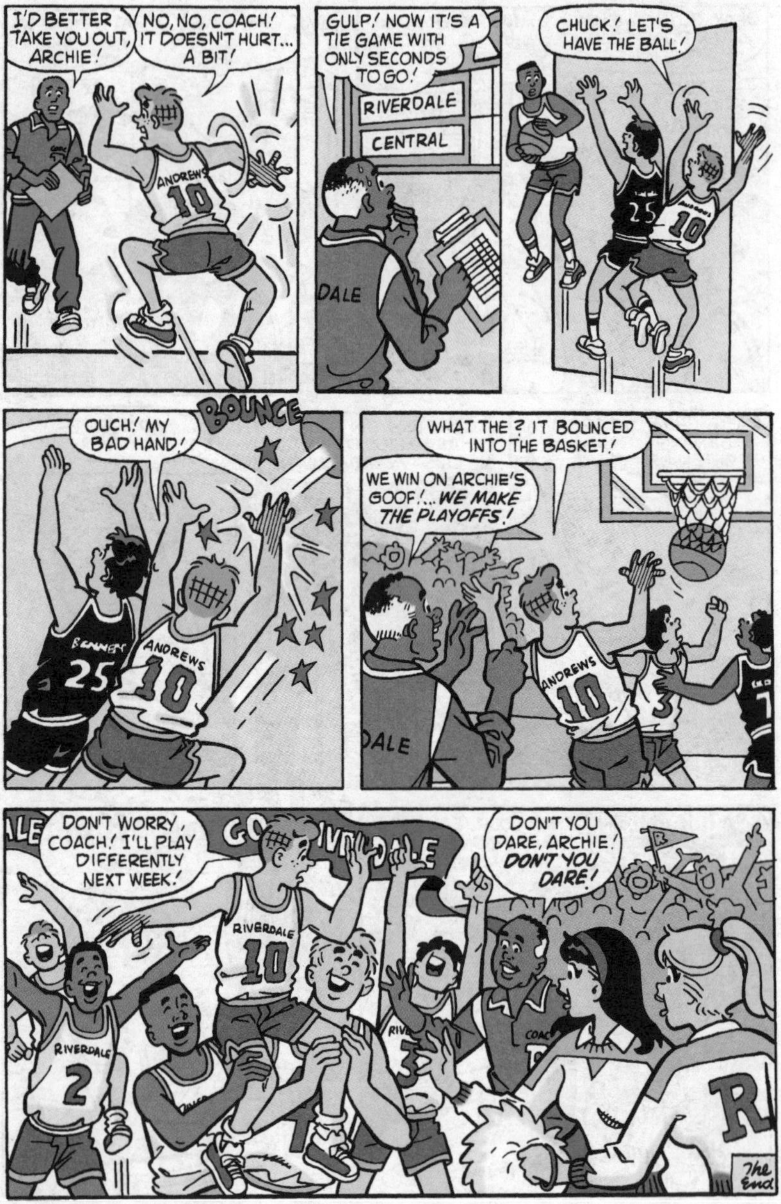
I'D BETTER TAKE YOU OUT, ARCHIE!
NO, NO, COACH! IT DOESN'T HURT... A BIT!
ANDREWS 10
GULP! NOW IT'S A TIE GAME WITH ONLY SECONDS TO GO!
RIVERDALE
CENTRAL
CHUCK! LET'S HAVE THE BALL!
OUCH! MY BAD HAND!
BOUNCE
WHAT THE ? IT BOUNCED INTO THE BASKET!
WE WIN ON ARCHIE'S GOOF!... WE MAKE THE PLAYOFFS!
DON'T WORRY, COACH! I'LL PLAY DIFFERENTLY NEXT WEEK!
DON'T YOU DARE, ARCHIE! DON'T YOU DARE!
The End

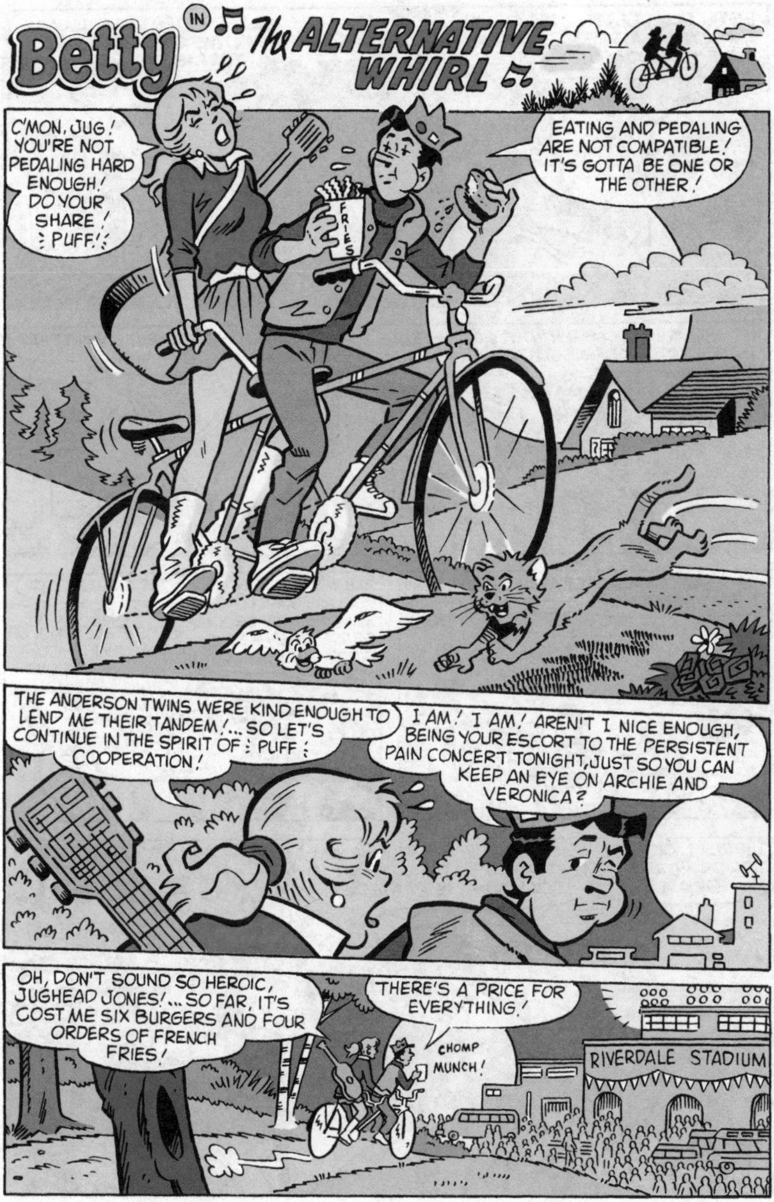
Betty
IN
The ALTERNATIVE WHIRL
C'MON, JUG! YOU'RE NOT PEDALING HARD ENOUGH! DO YOUR SHARE! PUFF!
FRIES
EATING AND PEDALING ARE NOT COMPATIBLE! IT'S GOTTA BE ONE OR THE OTHER!
THE ANDERSON TWINS WERE KIND ENOUGH TO LEND ME THEIR TANDEM!... SO LET'S CONTINUE IN THE SPIRIT OF PUFF COOPERATION!
I AM! I AM! AREN'T I NICE ENOUGH, BEING YOUR ESCORT TO THE PERSISTENT PAIN CONCERT TONIGHT, JUST SO YOU CAN KEEP AN EYE ON ARCHIE AND VERONICA?
OH, DON'T SOUND SO HEROIC, JUGHEAD JONES!... SO FAR, IT'S COST ME SIX BURGERS AND FOUR ORDERS OF FRENCH FRIES!
THERE'S A PRICE FOR EVERYTHING!
CHOMP MUNCH!
RIVERDALE STADIUM

Originally presented in BETTY #6, June, 1993

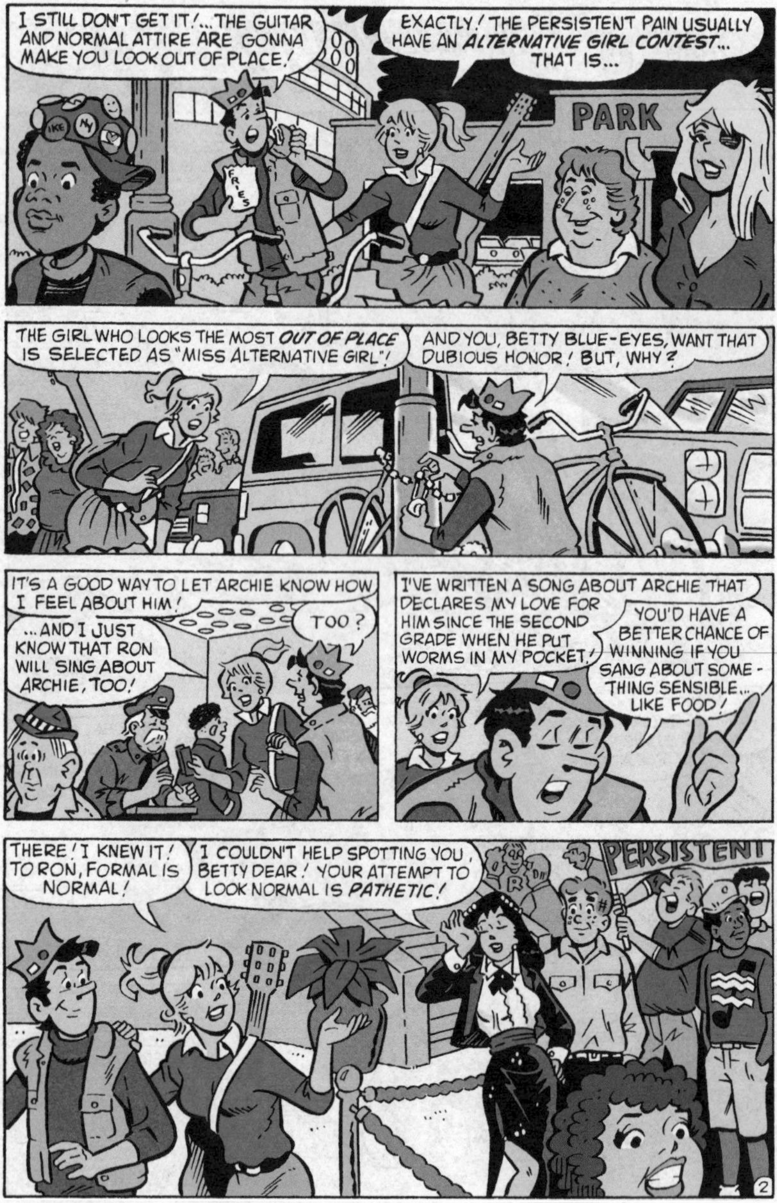
I STILL DON'T GET IT!... THE GUITAR AND NORMAL ATTIRE ARE GONNA MAKE YOU LOOK OUT OF PLACE!
EXACTLY! THE PERSISTENT PAIN USUALLY HAVE AN ALTERNATIVE GIRL CONTEST... THAT IS...
PARK
FRIES
THE GIRL WHO LOOKS THE MOST OUT OF PLACE IS SELECTED AS "MISS ALTERNATIVE GIRL"!
AND YOU, BETTY BLUE-EYES, WANT THAT DUBIOUS HONOR! BUT, WHY?
IT'S A GOOD WAY TO LET ARCHIE KNOW HOW I FEEL ABOUT HIM!
...AND I JUST KNOW THAT RON WILL SING ABOUT ARCHIE, TOO!
TOO?
I'VE WRITTEN A SONG ABOUT ARCHIE THAT DECLARES MY LOVE FOR HIM SINCE THE SECOND GRADE WHEN HE PUT WORMS IN MY POCKET!
YOU'D HAVE A BETTER CHANCE OF WINNING IF YOU SANG ABOUT SOME-THING SENSIBLE... LIKE FOOD!
THERE! I KNEW IT! TO RON, FORMAL IS NORMAL!
I COULDN'T HELP SPOTTING YOU, BETTY DEAR! YOUR ATTEMPT TO LOOK NORMAL IS PATHETIC!
PERSISTENT
2

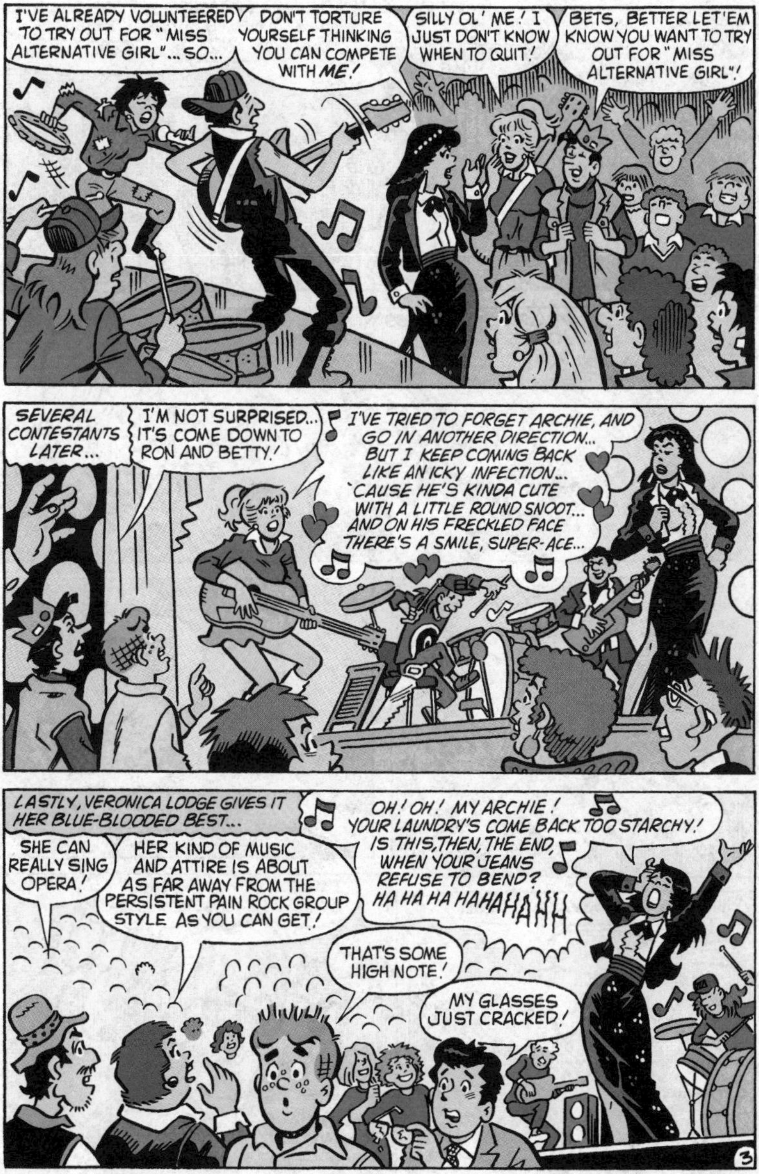
I'VE ALREADY VOLUNTEERED TO TRY OUT FOR "MISS ALTERNATIVE GIRL"... SO...
DON'T TORTURE YOURSELF THINKING YOU CAN COMPETE WITH *ME*!
SILLY OL' ME! I JUST DON'T KNOW WHEN TO QUIT!
BETS, BETTER LET'EM KNOW YOU WANT TO TRY OUT FOR "MISS ALTERNATIVE GIRL"!
SEVERAL CONTESTANTS LATER...
I'M NOT SURPRISED... IT'S COME DOWN TO RON AND BETTY!
I'VE TRIED TO FORGET ARCHIE, AND GO IN ANOTHER DIRECTION... BUT I KEEP COMING BACK LIKE AN ICKY INFECTION... 'CAUSE HE'S KINDA CUTE WITH A LITTLE ROUND SNOOT... AND ON HIS FRECKLED FACE THERE'S A SMILE, SUPER-ACE...
LASTLY, VERONICA LODGE GIVES IT HER BLUE-BLOODED BEST...
SHE CAN REALLY SING OPERA!
HER KIND OF MUSIC AND ATTIRE IS ABOUT AS FAR AWAY FROM THE PERSISTENT PAIN ROCK GROUP STYLE AS YOU CAN GET!
OH! OH! MY ARCHIE! YOUR LAUNDRY'S COME BACK TOO STARCHY! IS THIS, THEN, THE END, WHEN YOUR JEANS REFUSE TO BEND? HA HA HA HAHAHAHH
THAT'S SOME HIGH NOTE!
MY GLASSES JUST CRACKED!
3

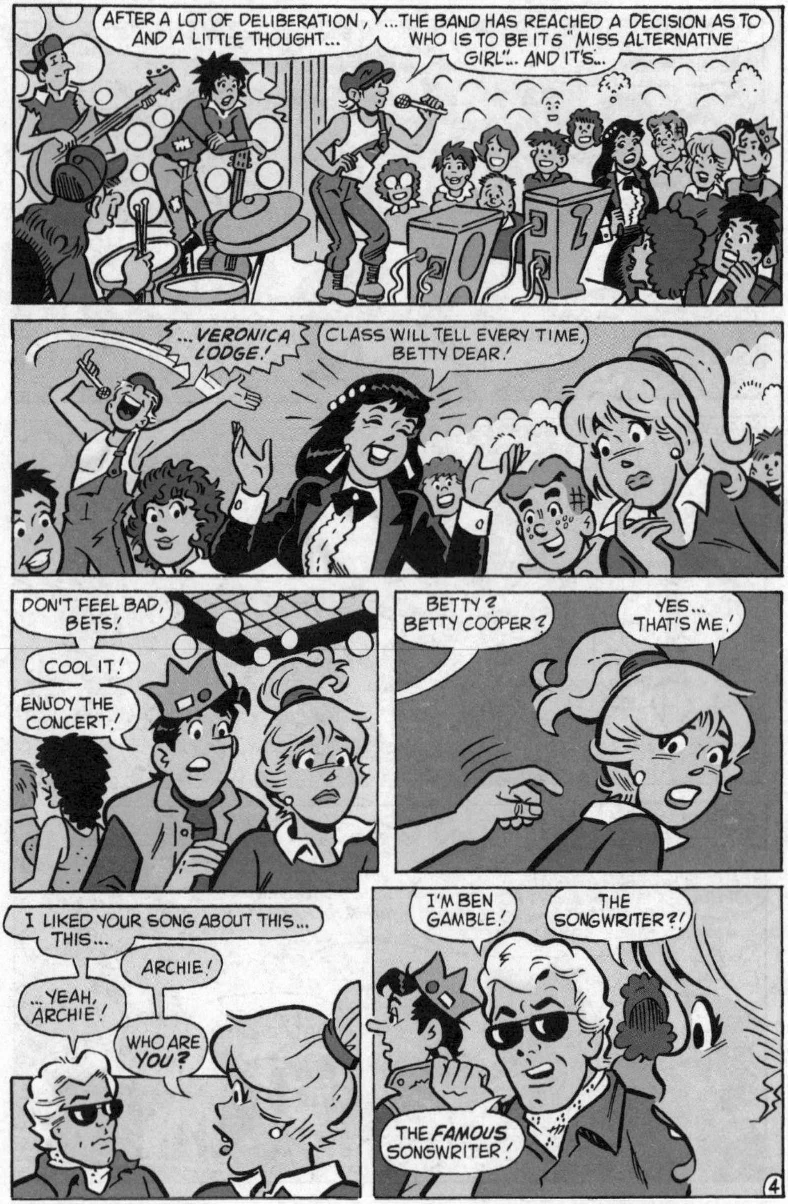
AFTER A LOT OF DELIBERATION, AND A LITTLE THOUGHT...
...THE BAND HAS REACHED A DECISION AS TO WHO IS TO BE ITS "MISS ALTERNATIVE GIRL"... AND IT'S...
...VERONICA LODGE!
CLASS WILL TELL EVERY TIME, BETTY DEAR!
DON'T FEEL BAD, BETS!
COOL IT!
ENJOY THE CONCERT!
BETTY? BETTY COOPER?
YES... THAT'S ME!
I LIKED YOUR SONG ABOUT THIS... THIS...
ARCHIE!
...YEAH, ARCHIE!
WHO ARE YOU?
I'M BEN GAMBLE!
THE SONGWRITER?!
THE FAMOUS SONGWRITER!
4

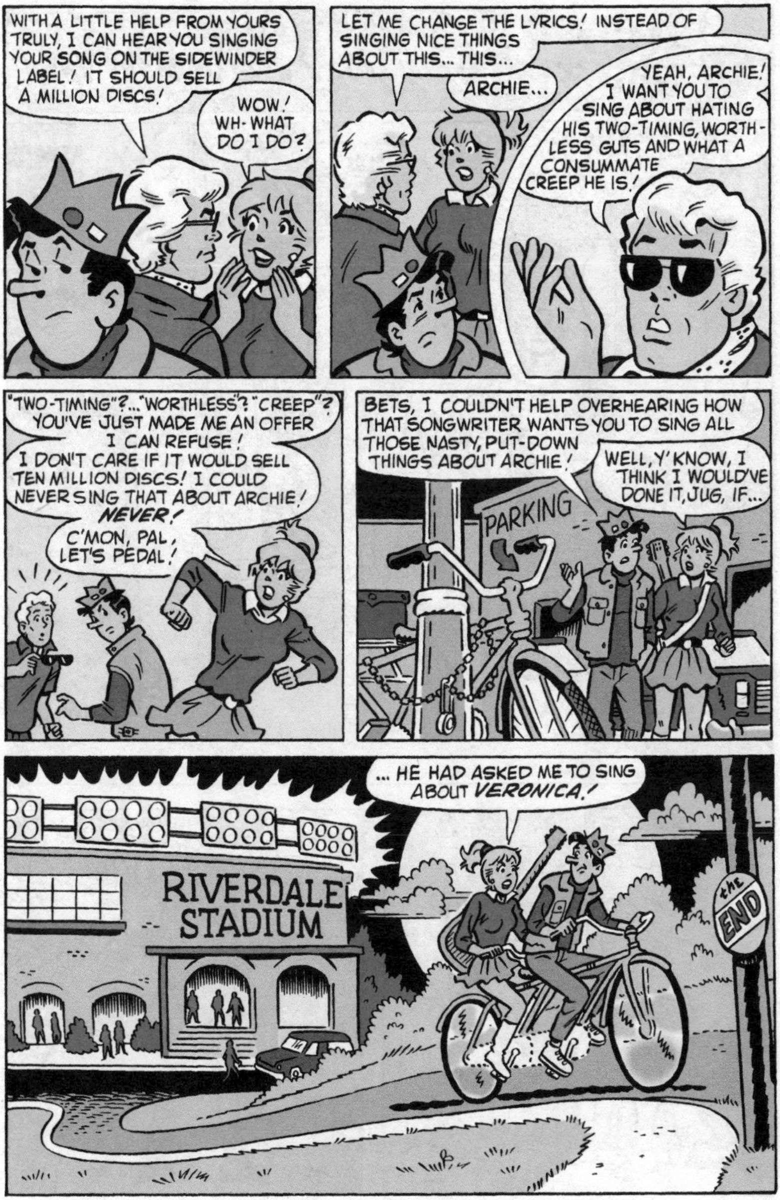
WITH A LITTLE HELP FROM YOURS TRULY, I CAN HEAR YOU SINGING YOUR SONG ON THE SIDEWINDER LABEL! IT SHOULD SELL A MILLION DISCS!
WOW! WH-WHAT DO I DO?
LET ME CHANGE THE LYRICS! INSTEAD OF SINGING NICE THINGS ABOUT THIS... THIS...
ARCHIE...
YEAH, ARCHIE! I WANT YOU TO SING ABOUT HATING HIS TWO-TIMING, WORTH-LESS GUTS AND WHAT A CONSUMMATE CREEP HE IS!
"TWO-TIMING"?..."WORTHLESS"? "CREEP"? YOU'VE JUST MADE ME AN OFFER I CAN REFUSE!
I DON'T CARE IF IT WOULD SELL TEN MILLION DISCS! I COULD NEVER SING THAT ABOUT ARCHIE! NEVER!
C'MON, PAL, LET'S PEDAL!
BETS, I COULDN'T HELP OVERHEARING HOW THAT SONGWRITER WANTS YOU TO SING ALL THOSE NASTY, PUT-DOWN THINGS ABOUT ARCHIE!
WELL, Y'KNOW, I THINK I WOULD'VE DONE IT, JUG, IF...
PARKING
... HE HAD ASKED ME TO SING ABOUT VERONICA!
RIVERDALE STADIUM
the END

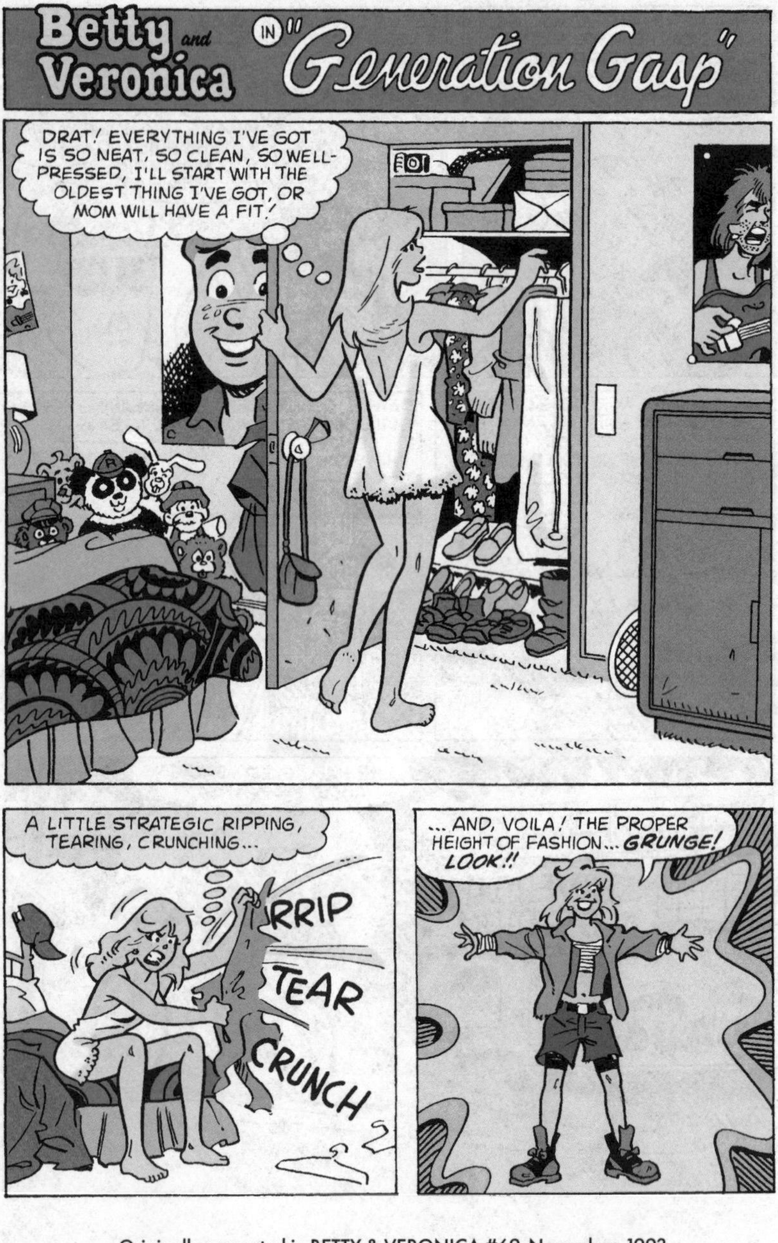
Betty and Veronica
IN "Generation Gasp"
DRAT! EVERYTHING I'VE GOT IS SO NEAT, SO CLEAN, SO WELL-PRESSED, I'LL START WITH THE OLDEST THING I'VE GOT, OR MOM WILL HAVE A FIT!
A LITTLE STRATEGIC RIPPING, TEARING, CRUNCHING...
RRIP
TEAR
CRUNCH
... AND, VOILA! THE PROPER HEIGHT OF FASHION... GRUNGE! LOOK!!

Originally presented in BETTY & VERONICA #69, November, 1993

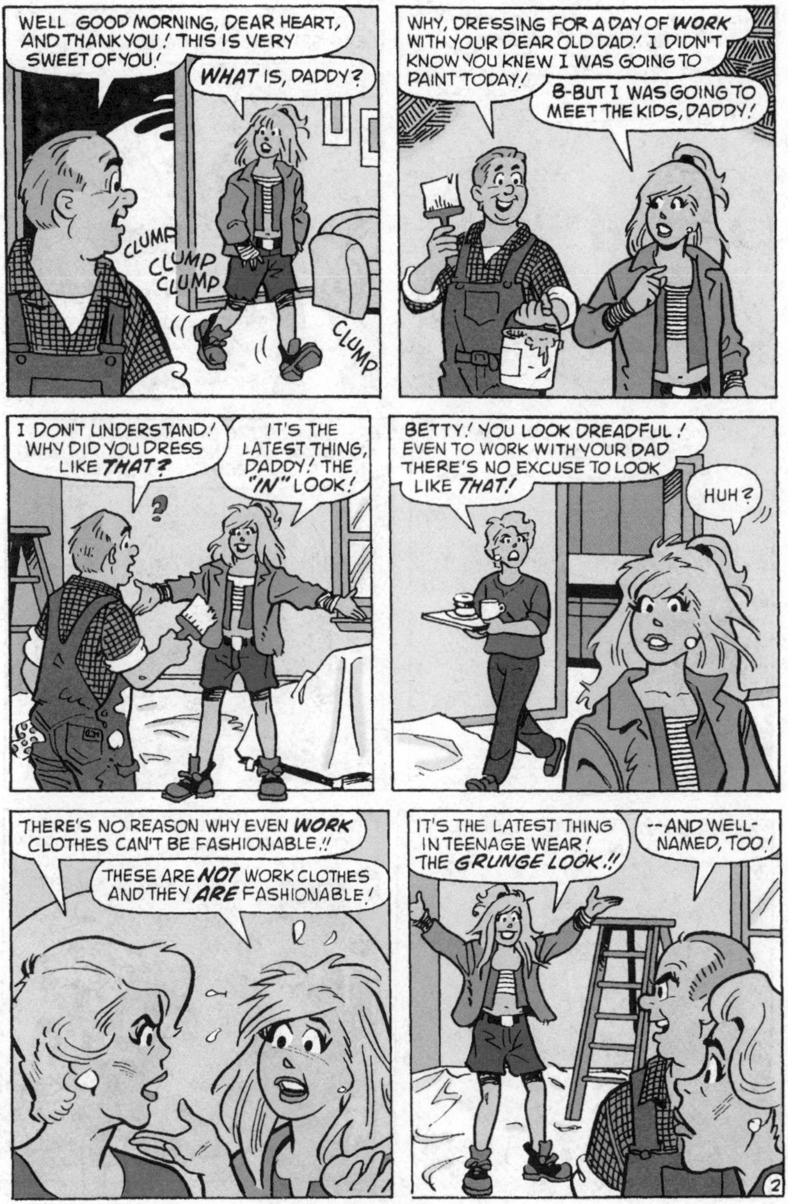
WELL GOOD MORNING, DEAR HEART, AND THANK YOU! THIS IS VERY SWEET OF YOU!
WHAT IS, DADDY?
CLUMP
CLUMP
CLUMP
CLUMP
WHY, DRESSING FOR A DAY OF WORK WITH YOUR DEAR OLD DAD! I DIDN'T KNOW YOU KNEW I WAS GOING TO PAINT TODAY!
B-BUT I WAS GOING TO MEET THE KIDS, DADDY!
I DON'T UNDERSTAND! WHY DID YOU DRESS LIKE THAT?
IT'S THE LATEST THING, DADDY! THE "IN" LOOK!
BETTY! YOU LOOK DREADFUL! EVEN TO WORK WITH YOUR DAD THERE'S NO EXCUSE TO LOOK LIKE THAT!
HUH?
THERE'S NO REASON WHY EVEN WORK CLOTHES CAN'T BE FASHIONABLE!!
THESE ARE NOT WORK CLOTHES AND THEY ARE FASHIONABLE!
IT'S THE LATEST THING IN TEENAGE WEAR! THE GRUNGE LOOK!!
--AND WELL-NAMED, TOO!
2

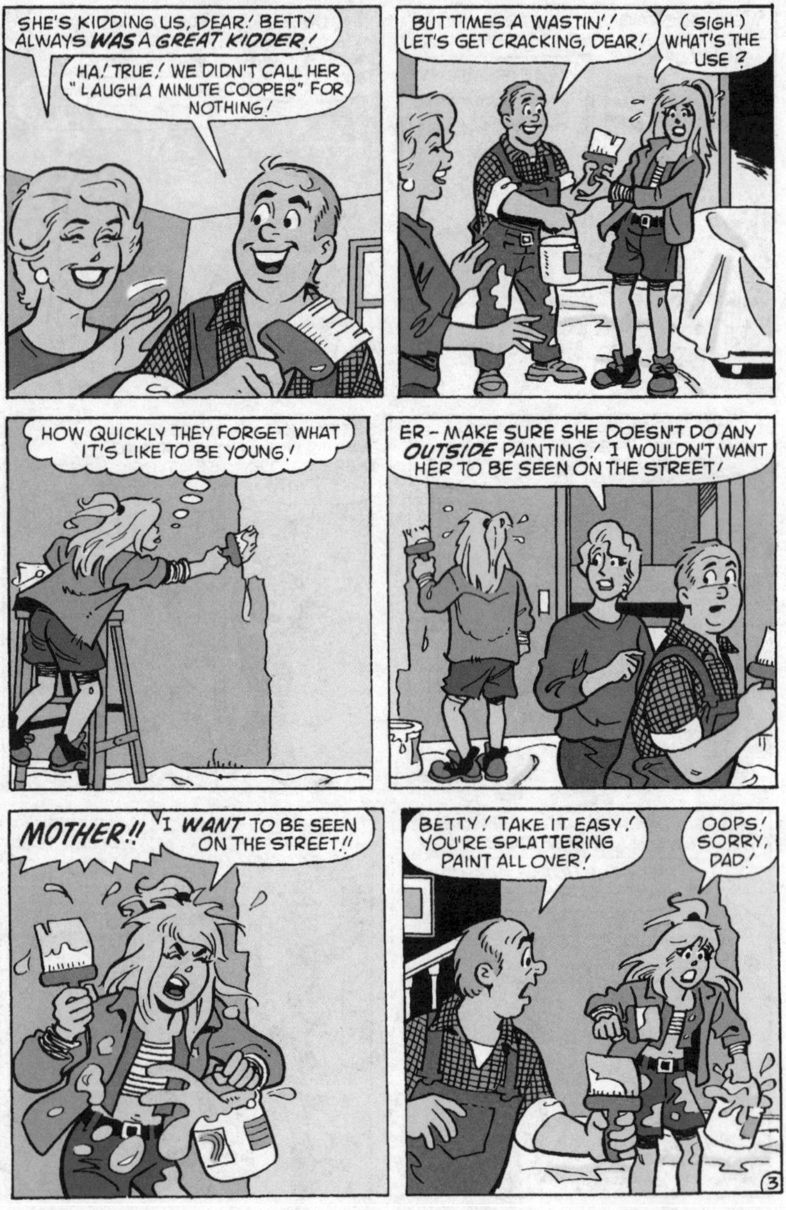
SHE'S KIDDING US, DEAR! BETTY ALWAYS WAS A GREAT KIDDER!
HA! TRUE! WE DIDN'T CALL HER "LAUGH A MINUTE COOPER" FOR NOTHING!
BUT TIMES A WASTIN'! LET'S GET CRACKING, DEAR!
(SIGH) WHAT'S THE USE?
HOW QUICKLY THEY FORGET WHAT IT'S LIKE TO BE YOUNG!
ER - MAKE SURE SHE DOESN'T DO ANY OUTSIDE PAINTING! I WOULDN'T WANT HER TO BE SEEN ON THE STREET!
MOTHER!!
I WANT TO BE SEEN ON THE STREET!!
BETTY! TAKE IT EASY! YOU'RE SPLATTERING PAINT ALL OVER!
OOPS! SORRY, DAD!
3

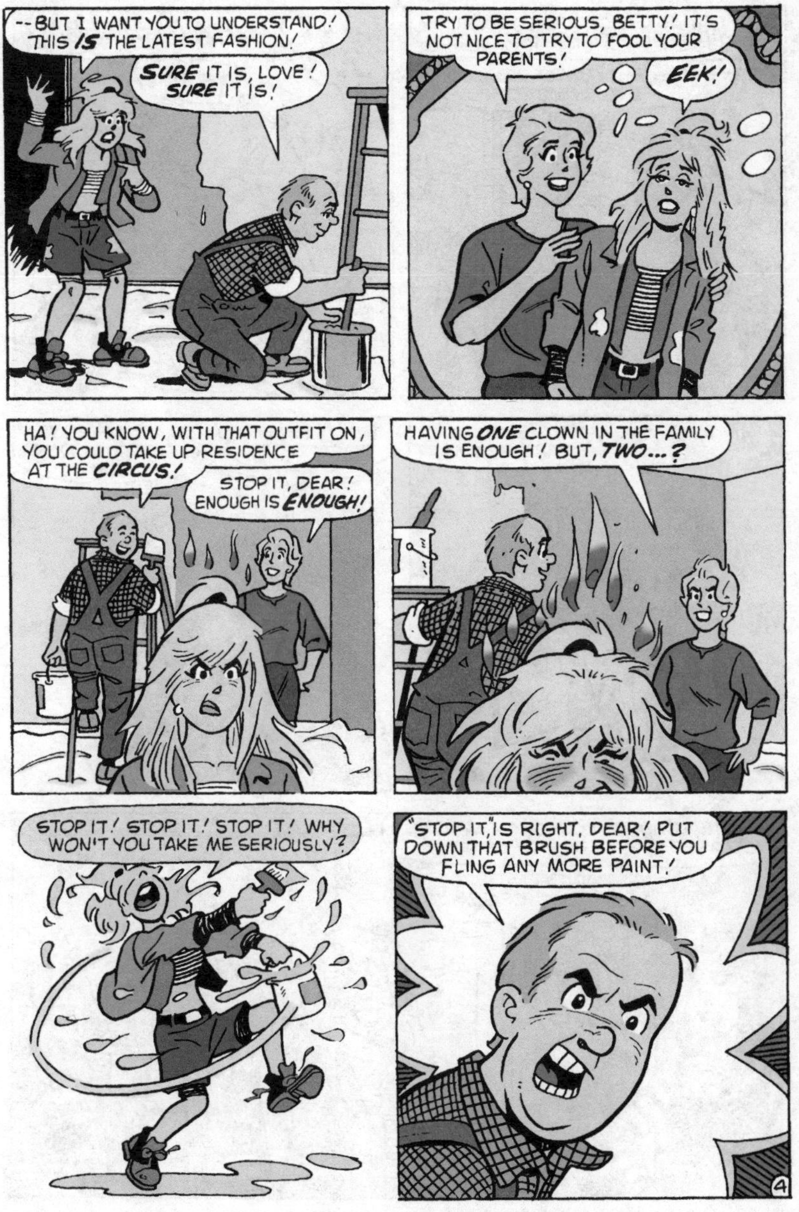
-- BUT I WANT YOU TO UNDERSTAND! THIS IS THE LATEST FASHION!
SURE IT IS, LOVE! SURE IT IS!
TRY TO BE SERIOUS, BETTY! IT'S NOT NICE TO TRY TO FOOL YOUR PARENTS!
EEK!
HA! YOU KNOW, WITH THAT OUTFIT ON, YOU COULD TAKE UP RESIDENCE AT THE CIRCUS!
STOP IT, DEAR! ENOUGH IS ENOUGH!
HAVING ONE CLOWN IN THE FAMILY IS ENOUGH! BUT, TWO...?
STOP IT! STOP IT! STOP IT! WHY WON'T YOU TAKE ME SERIOUSLY?
"STOP IT," IS RIGHT, DEAR! PUT DOWN THAT BRUSH BEFORE YOU FLING ANY MORE PAINT!
4

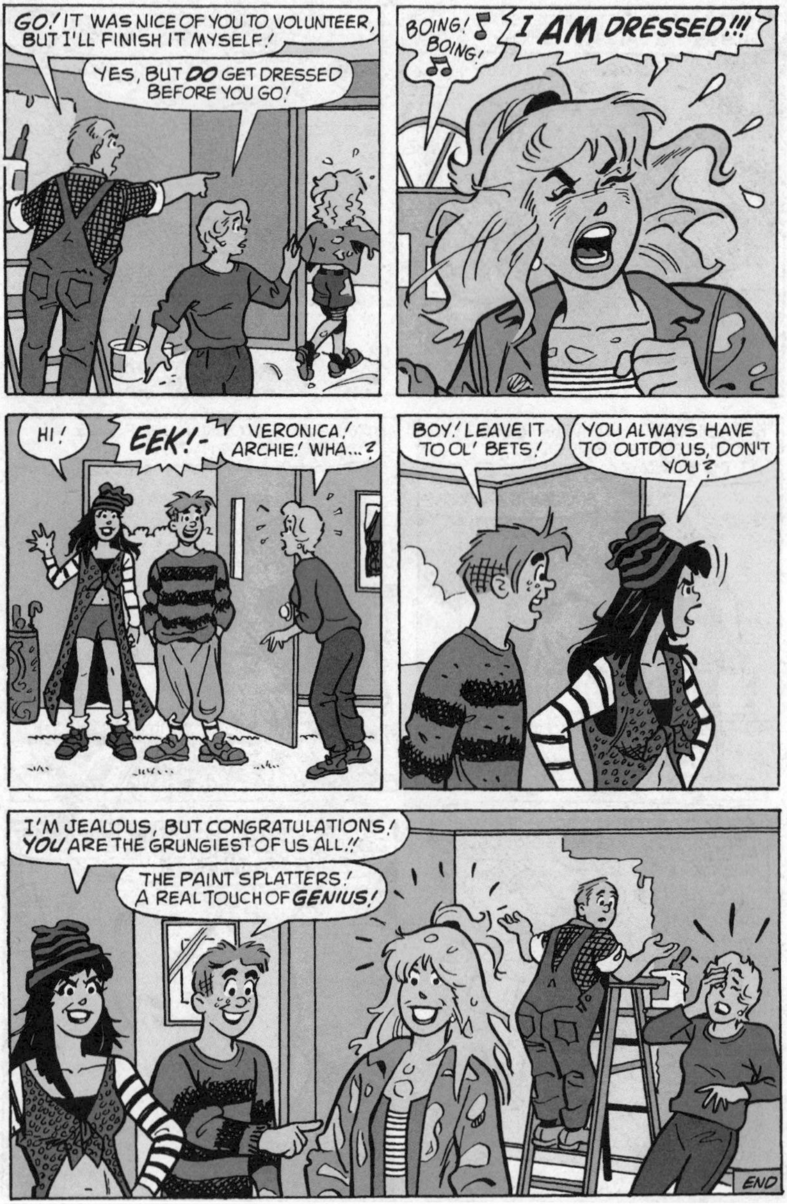
GO! IT WAS NICE OF YOU TO VOLUNTEER, BUT I'LL FINISH IT MYSELF!
YES, BUT DO GET DRESSED BEFORE YOU GO!
BOING! BOING!
I AM DRESSED!!!
HI!
EEK!-
VERONICA! ARCHIE! WHA...?
BOY! LEAVE IT TO OL' BETS!
YOU ALWAYS HAVE TO OUTDO US, DON'T YOU?
I'M JEALOUS, BUT CONGRATULATIONS! YOU ARE THE GRUNGIEST OF US ALL!!
THE PAINT SPLATTERS! A REAL TOUCH OF GENIUS!
END

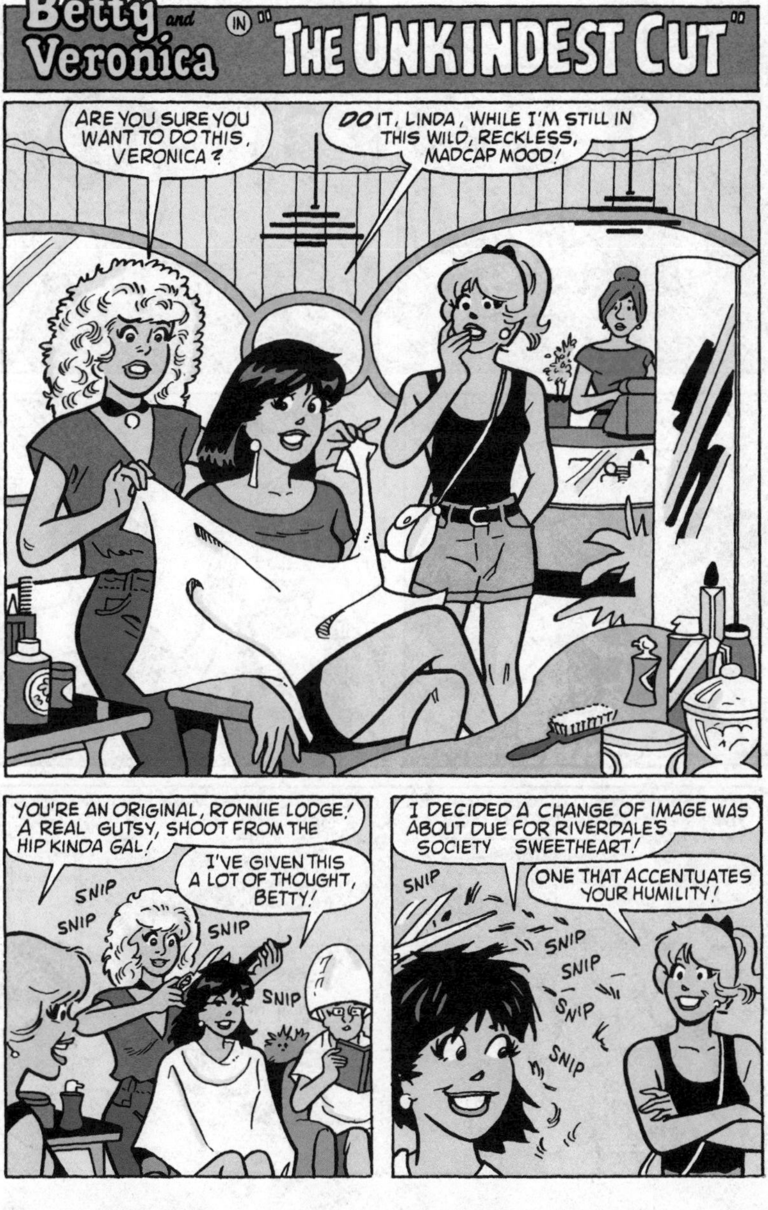
Betty and Veronica IN "THE UNKINDEST CUT"
ARE YOU SURE YOU WANT TO DO THIS, VERONICA?
DO IT, LINDA, WHILE I'M STILL IN THIS WILD, RECKLESS, MADCAP MOOD!
YOU'RE AN ORIGINAL, RONNIE LODGE! A REAL GUTSY, SHOOT FROM THE HIP KINDA GAL!
I'VE GIVEN THIS A LOT OF THOUGHT, BETTY!
SNIP
SNIP
SNIP
SNIP
I DECIDED A CHANGE OF IMAGE WAS ABOUT DUE FOR RIVERDALE'S SOCIETY SWEETHEART!
ONE THAT ACCENTUATES YOUR HUMILITY!
SNIP
SNIP
SNIP
SNIP
SNIP

Originally presented in BETTY & VERONICA #70, December, 1993

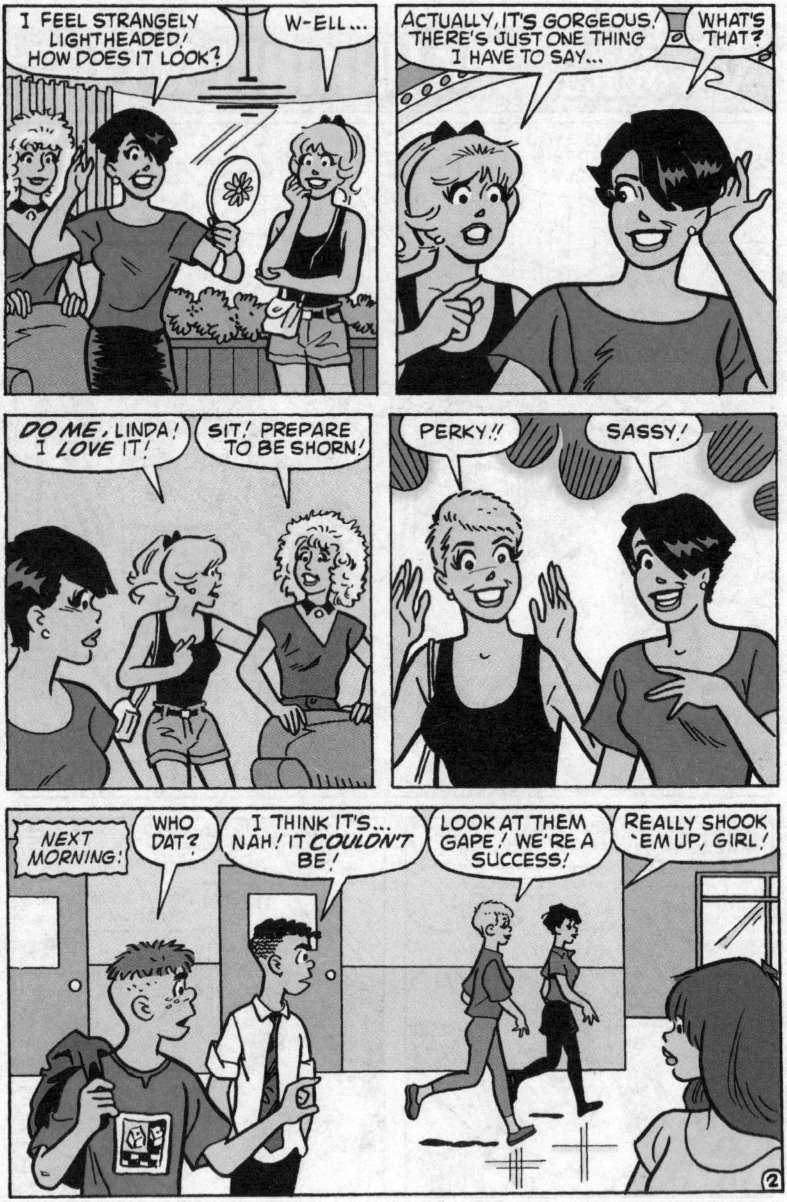
I FEEL STRANGELY LIGHTHEADED! HOW DOES IT LOOK?
W-ELL...
ACTUALLY, IT'S GORGEOUS! THERE'S JUST ONE THING I HAVE TO SAY...
WHAT'S THAT?
DO ME, LINDA! I LOVE IT!
SIT! PREPARE TO BE SHORN!
PERKY!!
SASSY!
NEXT MORNING!
WHO DAT?
I THINK IT'S... NAH! IT COULDN'T BE!
LOOK AT THEM GAPE! WE'RE A SUCCESS!
REALLY SHOOK 'EM UP, GIRL!
2

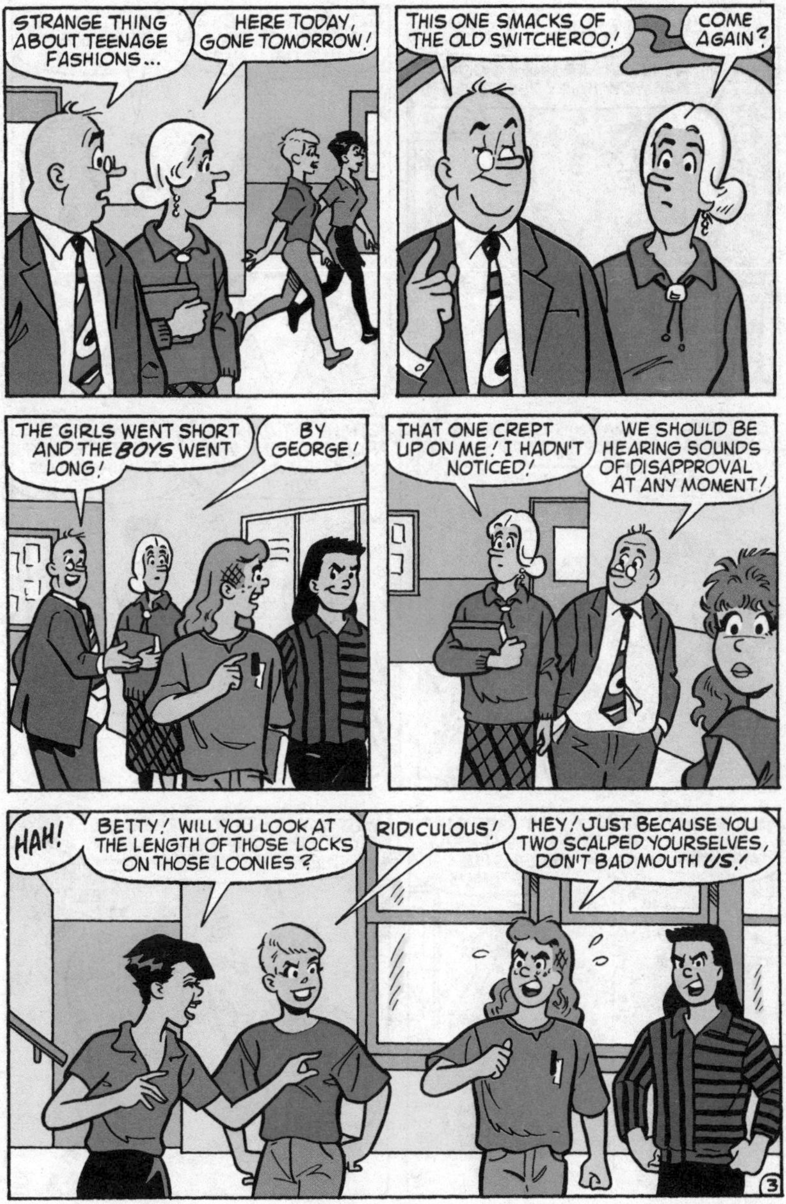
STRANGE THING ABOUT TEENAGE FASHIONS...
HERE TODAY, GONE TOMORROW!
THIS ONE SMACKS OF THE OLD SWITCHEROO!
COME AGAIN?
THE GIRLS WENT SHORT AND THE BOYS WENT LONG!
BY GEORGE!
THAT ONE CREPT UP ON ME! I HADN'T NOTICED!
WE SHOULD BE HEARING SOUNDS OF DISAPPROVAL AT ANY MOMENT!
HAH!
BETTY! WILL YOU LOOK AT THE LENGTH OF THOSE LOCKS ON THOSE LOONIES?
RIDICULOUS!
HEY! JUST BECAUSE YOU TWO SCALPED YOURSELVES, DON'T BAD MOUTH US!
3

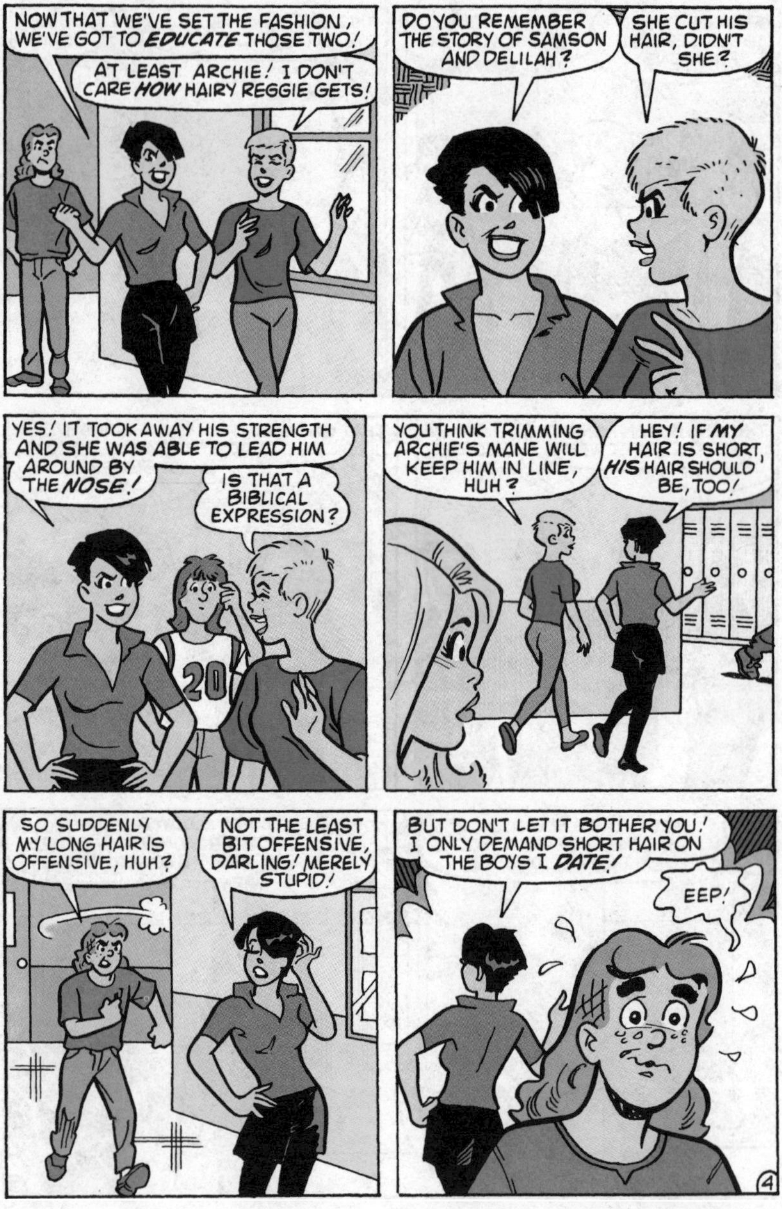
NOW THAT WE'VE SET THE FASHION, WE'VE GOT TO *EDUCATE* THOSE TWO!
AT LEAST ARCHIE! I DON'T CARE *HOW* HAIRY REGGIE GETS!
DO YOU REMEMBER THE STORY OF SAMSON AND DELILAH?
SHE CUT HIS HAIR, DIDN'T SHE?
YES! IT TOOK AWAY HIS STRENGTH AND SHE WAS ABLE TO LEAD HIM AROUND BY THE *NOSE*!
IS THAT A BIBLICAL EXPRESSION?
20
YOU THINK TRIMMING ARCHIE'S MANE WILL KEEP HIM IN LINE, HUH?
HEY! IF *MY* HAIR IS SHORT, *HIS* HAIR SHOULD BE, TOO!
SO SUDDENLY MY LONG HAIR IS OFFENSIVE, HUH?
NOT THE LEAST BIT OFFENSIVE, DARLING! MERELY STUPID!
BUT DON'T LET IT BOTHER YOU! I ONLY DEMAND SHORT HAIR ON THE BOYS I *DATE*!
EEP!
4

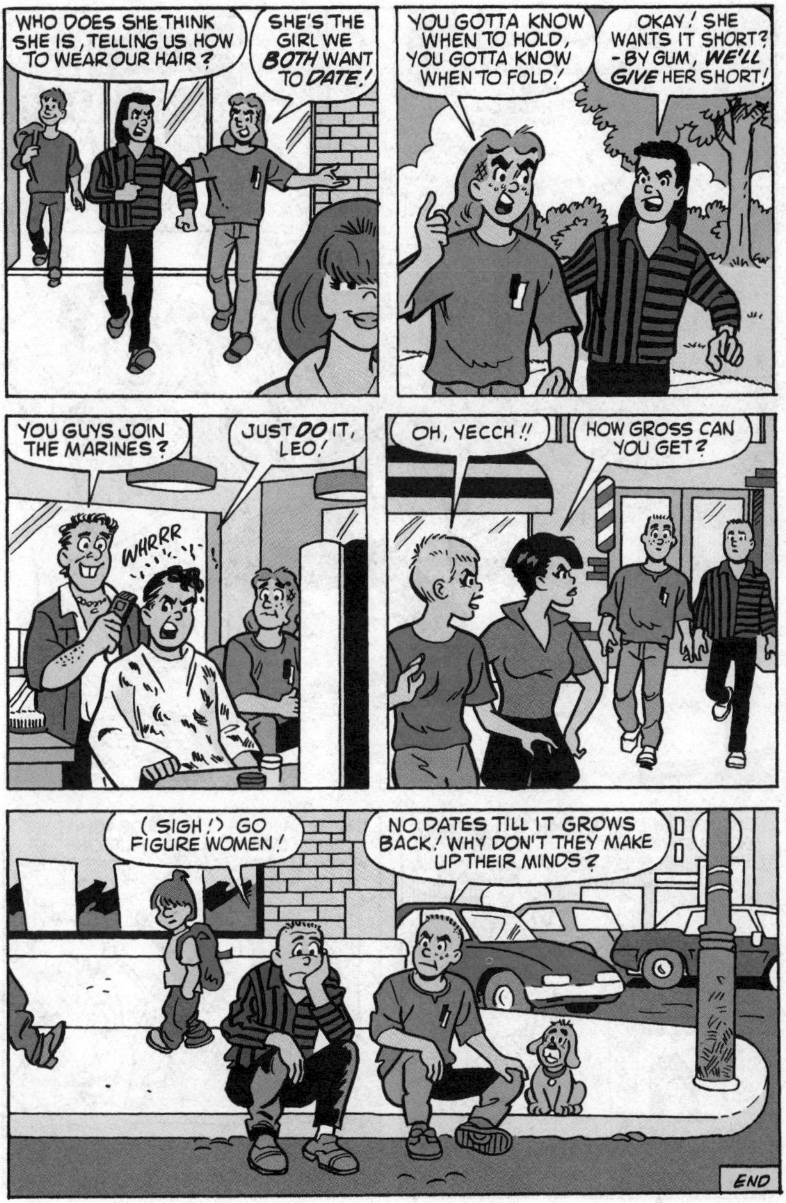
WHO DOES SHE THINK SHE IS, TELLING US HOW TO WEAR OUR HAIR?
SHE'S THE GIRL WE BOTH WANT TO DATE!
YOU GOTTA KNOW WHEN TO HOLD, YOU GOTTA KNOW WHEN TO FOLD!
OKAY! SHE WANTS IT SHORT? - BY GUM, WE'LL GIVE HER SHORT!
YOU GUYS JOIN THE MARINES?
JUST DO IT, LEO!
WHRRR
OH, YECCH!!
HOW GROSS CAN YOU GET?
(SIGH!) GO FIGURE WOMEN!
NO DATES TILL IT GROWS BACK! WHY DON'T THEY MAKE UP THEIR MINDS?
END

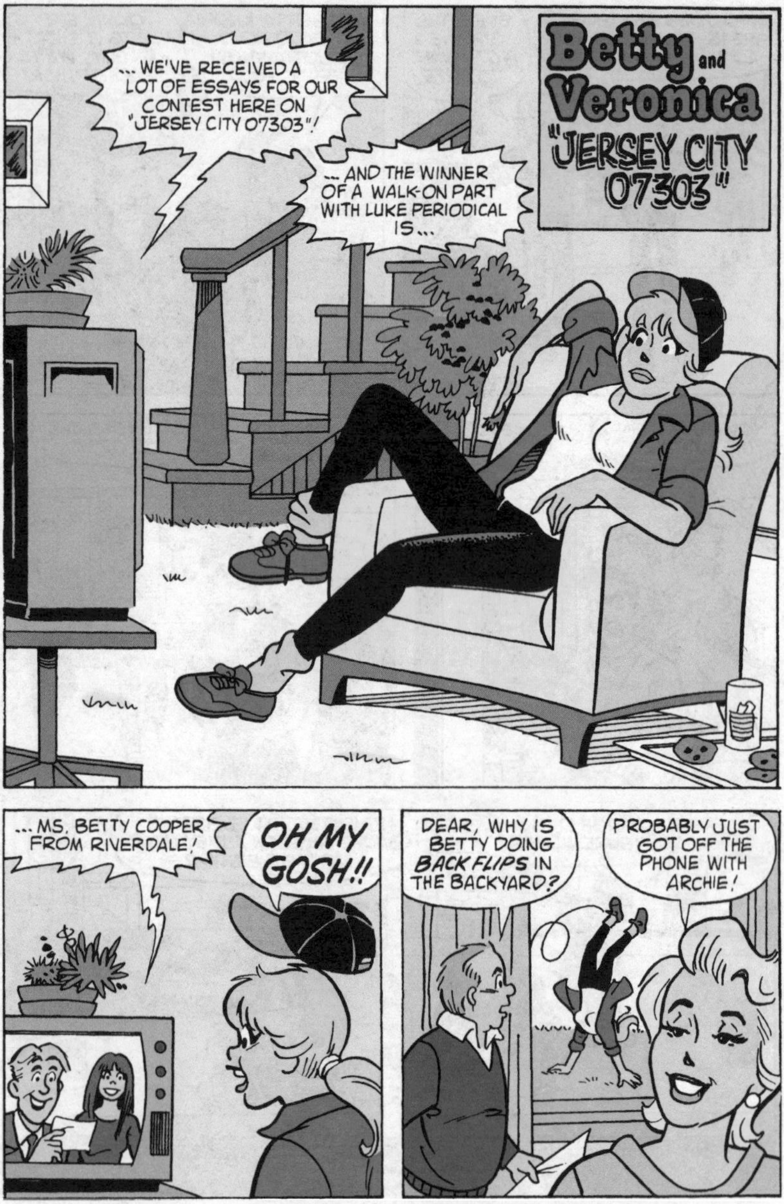
Betty and Veronica
"JERSEY CITY 07303"
... WE'VE RECEIVED A LOT OF ESSAYS FOR OUR CONTEST HERE ON "JERSEY CITY 07303"!
... AND THE WINNER OF A WALK-ON PART WITH LUKE PERIODICAL IS...
... MS. BETTY COOPER FROM RIVERDALE!
OH MY GOSH!!
DEAR, WHY IS BETTY DOING BACK FLIPS IN THE BACKYARD?
PROBABLY JUST GOT OFF THE PHONE WITH ARCHIE!

Originally presented in BETTY & VERONICA SPECTACULAR #7, April, 1994

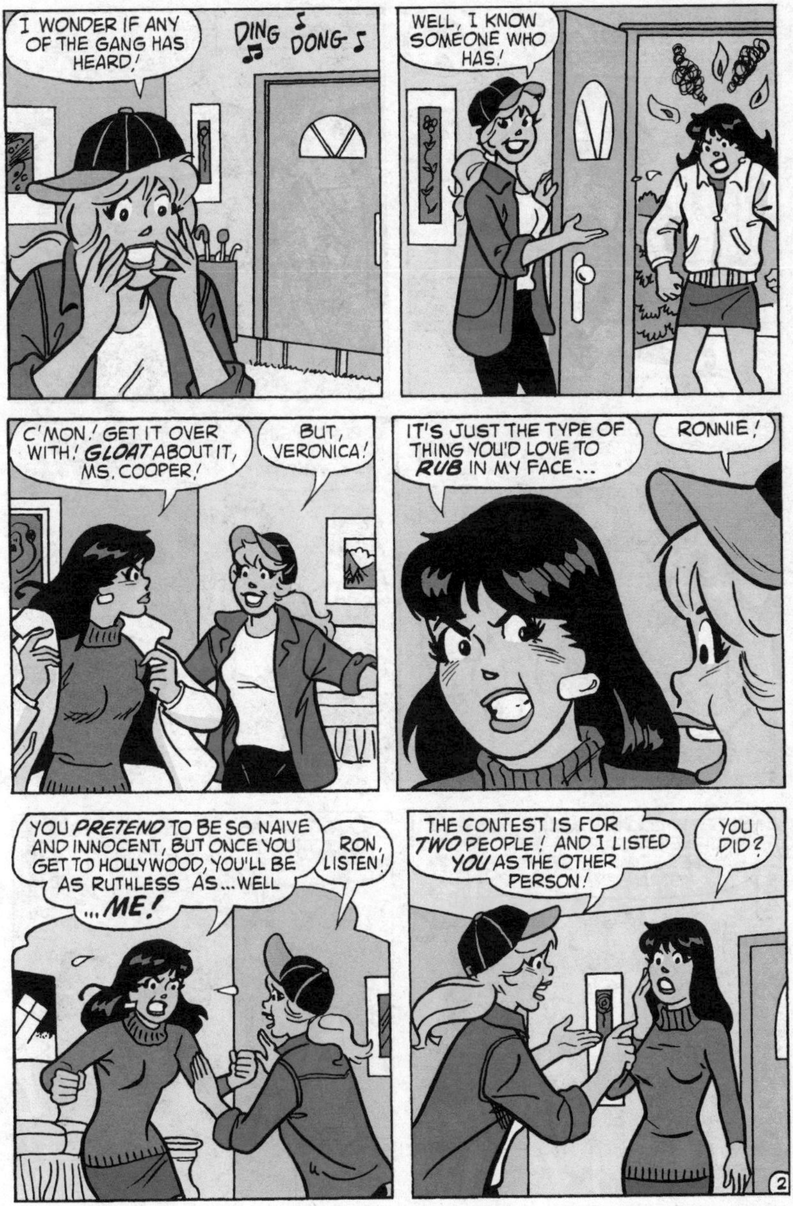
I WONDER IF ANY OF THE GANG HAS HEARD!
DING DONG
WELL, I KNOW SOMEONE WHO HAS!
C'MON! GET IT OVER WITH! GLOAT ABOUT IT, MS. COOPER!
BUT, VERONICA!
IT'S JUST THE TYPE OF THING YOU'D LOVE TO RUB IN MY FACE...
RONNIE!
YOU PRETEND TO BE SO NAIVE AND INNOCENT, BUT ONCE YOU GET TO HOLLYWOOD, YOU'LL BE AS RUTHLESS AS...WELL ...ME!
RON, LISTEN!
THE CONTEST IS FOR TWO PEOPLE! AND I LISTED YOU AS THE OTHER PERSON!
YOU DID?
2

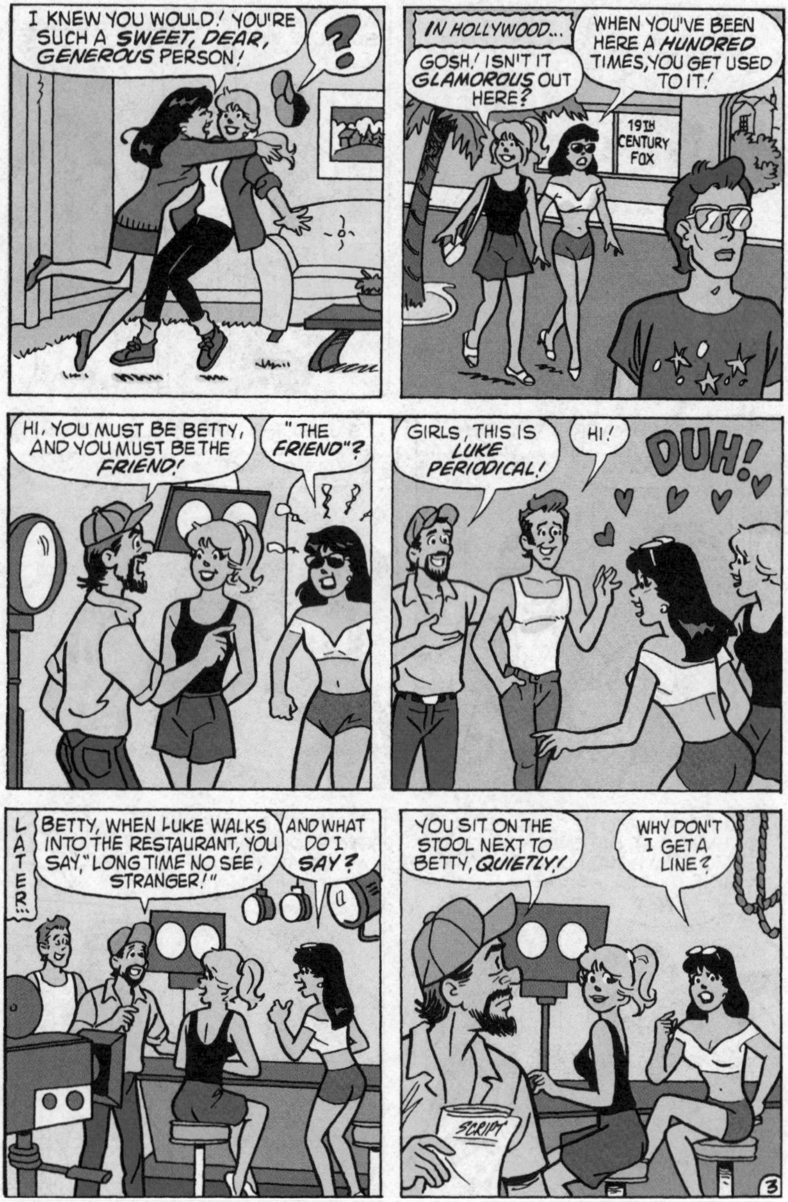
I KNEW YOU WOULD! YOU'RE SUCH A SWEET, DEAR, GENEROUS PERSON!
?
IN HOLLYWOOD...
GOSH! ISN'T IT GLAMOROUS OUT HERE?
WHEN YOU'VE BEEN HERE A HUNDRED TIMES, YOU GET USED TO IT!
19TH CENTURY FOX
HI, YOU MUST BE BETTY, AND YOU MUST BE THE FRIEND!
"THE FRIEND"?
GIRLS, THIS IS LUKE PERIODICAL!
HI!
DUH!
LATER...
BETTY, WHEN LUKE WALKS INTO THE RESTAURANT, YOU SAY, "LONG TIME NO SEE, STRANGER!"
AND WHAT DO I SAY?
YOU SIT ON THE STOOL NEXT TO BETTY, QUIETLY!
WHY DON'T I GET A LINE?
SCRIPT
3

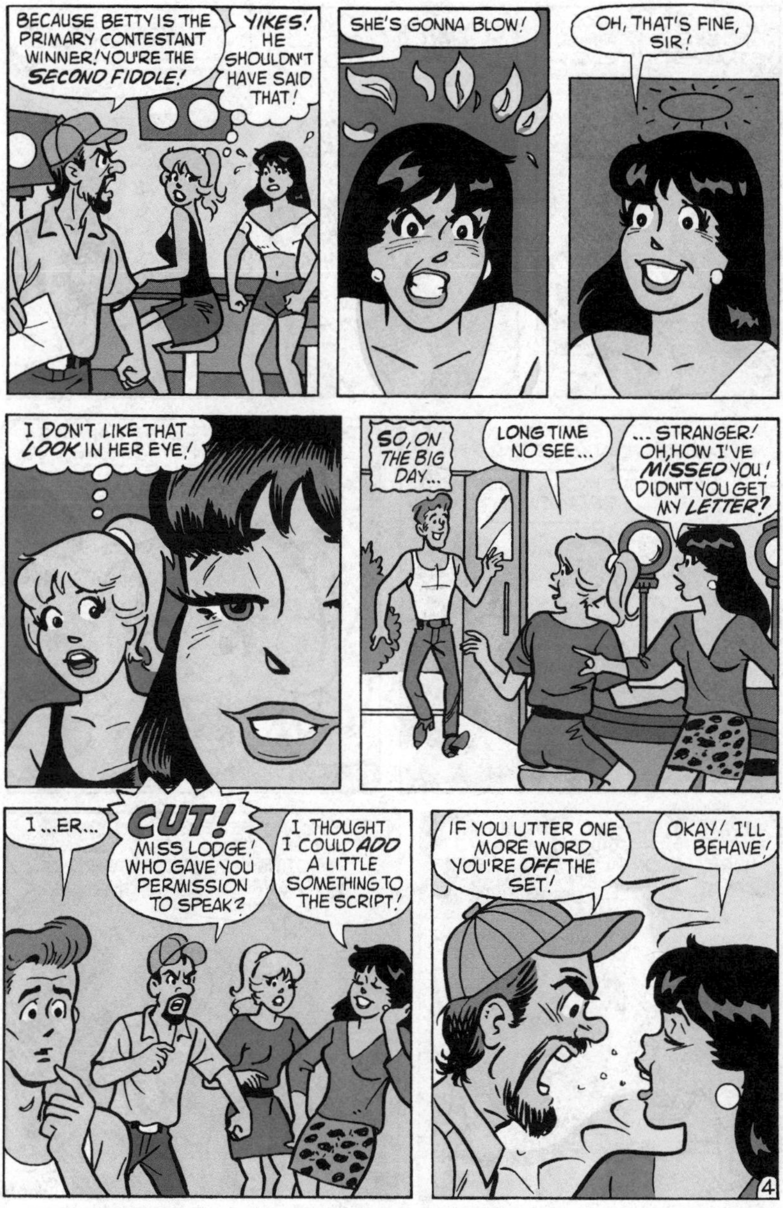
BECAUSE BETTY IS THE PRIMARY CONTESTANT WINNER! YOU'RE THE SECOND FIDDLE!
YIKES! HE SHOULDN'T HAVE SAID THAT!
SHE'S GONNA BLOW!
OH, THAT'S FINE, SIR!
I DON'T LIKE THAT LOOK IN HER EYE!
SO, ON THE BIG DAY...
LONG TIME NO SEE...
... STRANGER! OH, HOW I'VE MISSED YOU! DIDN'T YOU GET MY LETTER?
I ...ER...
CUT! MISS LODGE! WHO GAVE YOU PERMISSION TO SPEAK?
I THOUGHT I COULD ADD A LITTLE SOMETHING TO THE SCRIPT!
IF YOU UTTER ONE MORE WORD YOU'RE OFF THE SET!
OKAY! I'LL BEHAVE!
4

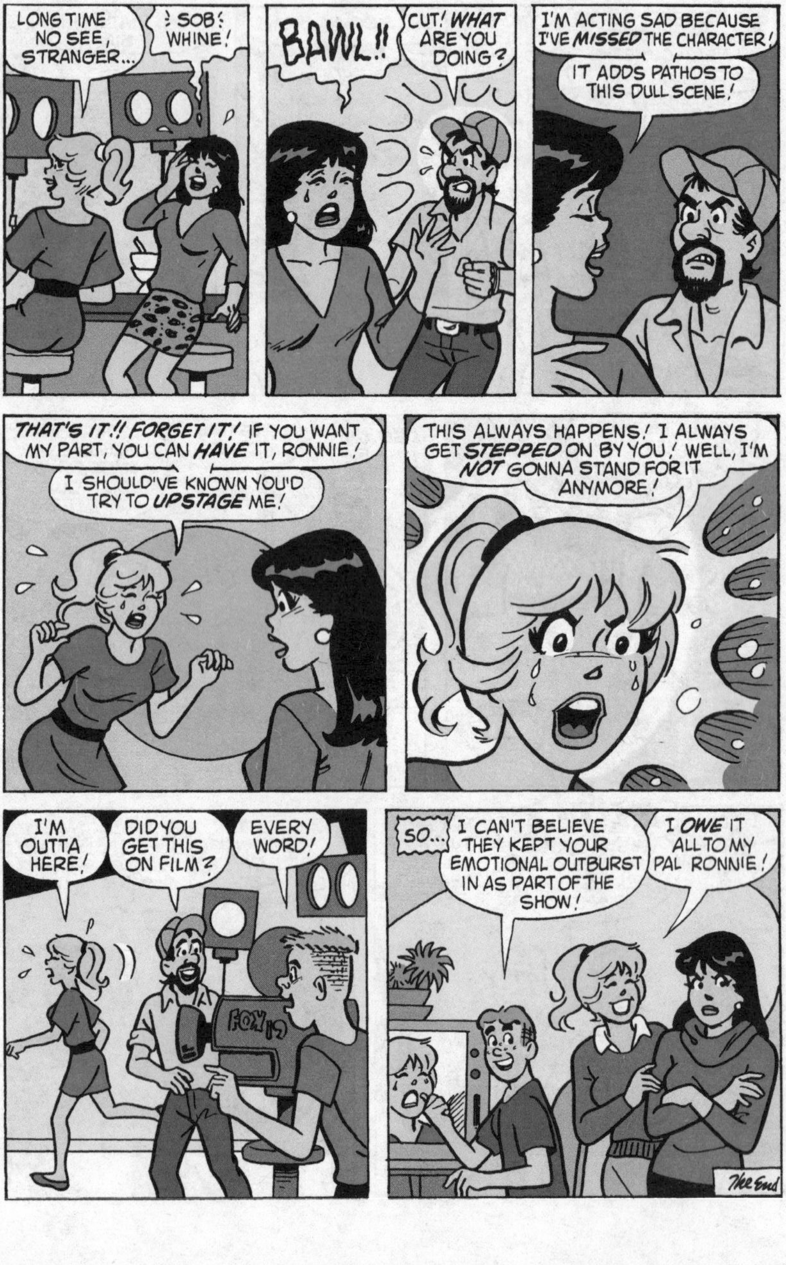
LONG TIME NO SEE, STRANGER...
SOB WHINE!
BAWL!!
CUT! WHAT ARE YOU DOING?
I'M ACTING SAD BECAUSE I'VE MISSED THE CHARACTER!
IT ADDS PATHOS TO THIS DULL SCENE!
THAT'S IT!! FORGET IT! IF YOU WANT MY PART, YOU CAN HAVE IT, RONNIE!
I SHOULD'VE KNOWN YOU'D TRY TO UPSTAGE ME!
THIS ALWAYS HAPPENS! I ALWAYS GET STEPPED ON BY YOU! WELL, I'M NOT GONNA STAND FOR IT ANYMORE!
I'M OUTTA HERE!
DID YOU GET THIS ON FILM?
EVERY WORD!
FOX 19
SO...
I CAN'T BELIEVE THEY KEPT YOUR EMOTIONAL OUTBURST IN AS PART OF THE SHOW!
I OWE IT ALL TO MY PAL RONNIE!
The End

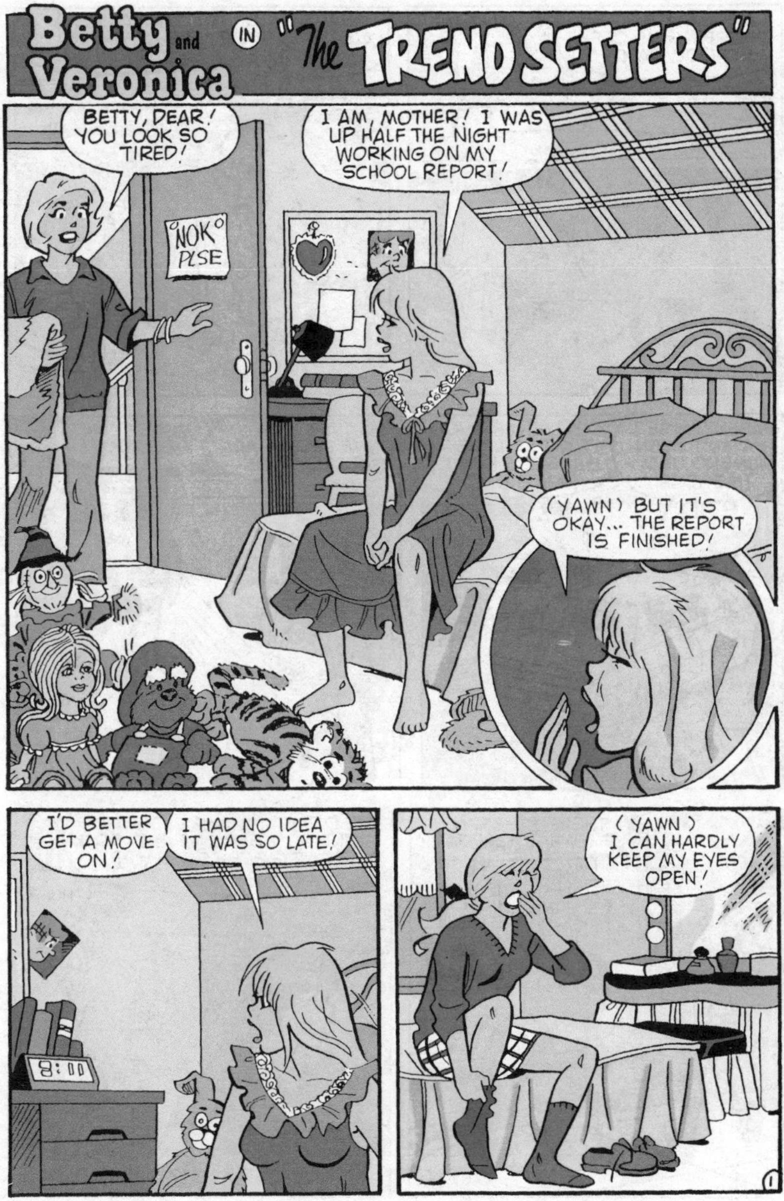
Betty and Veronica
IN "The TREND SETTERS"
BETTY, DEAR! YOU LOOK SO TIRED!
I AM, MOTHER! I WAS UP HALF THE NIGHT WORKING ON MY SCHOOL REPORT!
NOK PLSE
(YAWN) BUT IT'S OKAY... THE REPORT IS FINISHED!
I'D BETTER GET A MOVE ON!
I HAD NO IDEA IT WAS SO LATE!
8:00
(YAWN) I CAN HARDLY KEEP MY EYES OPEN!
1

Originally presented in BETTY & VERONICA #76, June, 1994

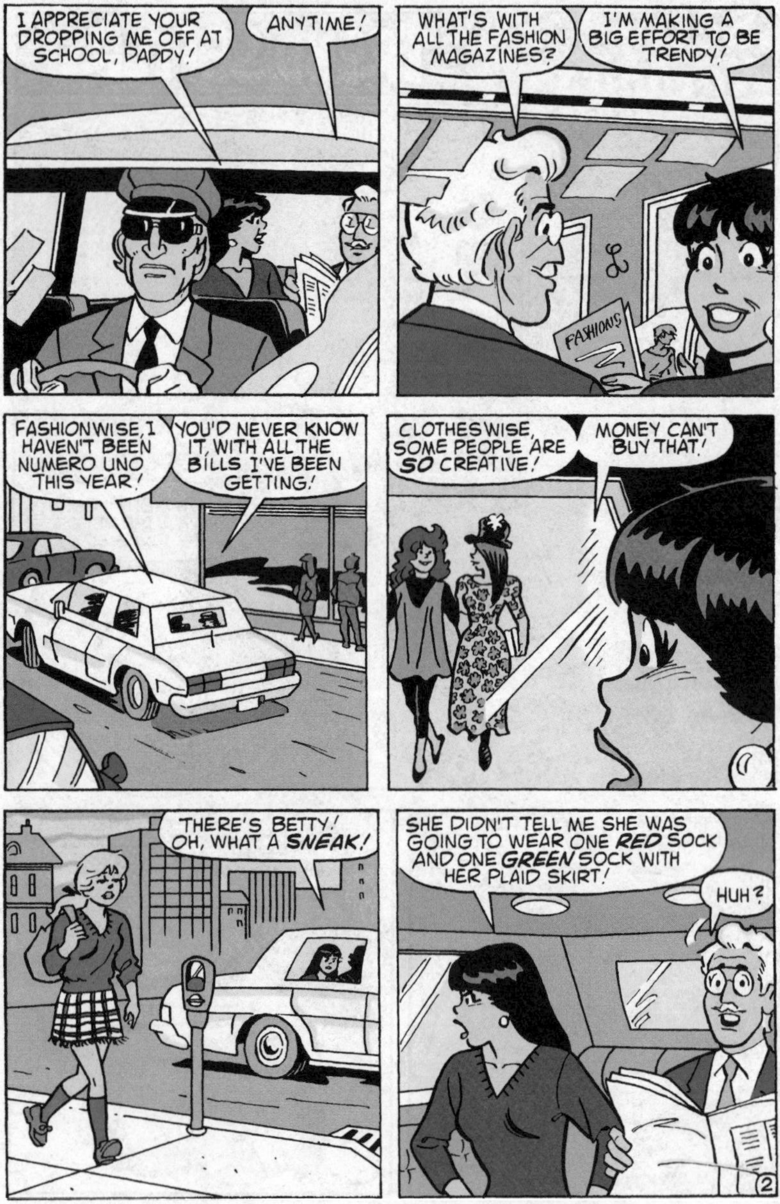
I APPRECIATE YOUR DROPPING ME OFF AT SCHOOL, DADDY!
ANYTIME!
WHAT'S WITH ALL THE FASHION MAGAZINES?
I'M MAKING A BIG EFFORT TO BE TRENDY!
FASHIONS
FASHIONWISE, I HAVEN'T BEEN NUMERO UNO THIS YEAR!
YOU'D NEVER KNOW IT, WITH ALL THE BILLS I'VE BEEN GETTING!
CLOTHESWISE, SOME PEOPLE ARE SO CREATIVE!
MONEY CAN'T BUY THAT!
THERE'S BETTY! OH, WHAT A SNEAK!
SHE DIDN'T TELL ME SHE WAS GOING TO WEAR ONE RED SOCK AND ONE GREEN SOCK WITH HER PLAID SKIRT!
HUH?
2

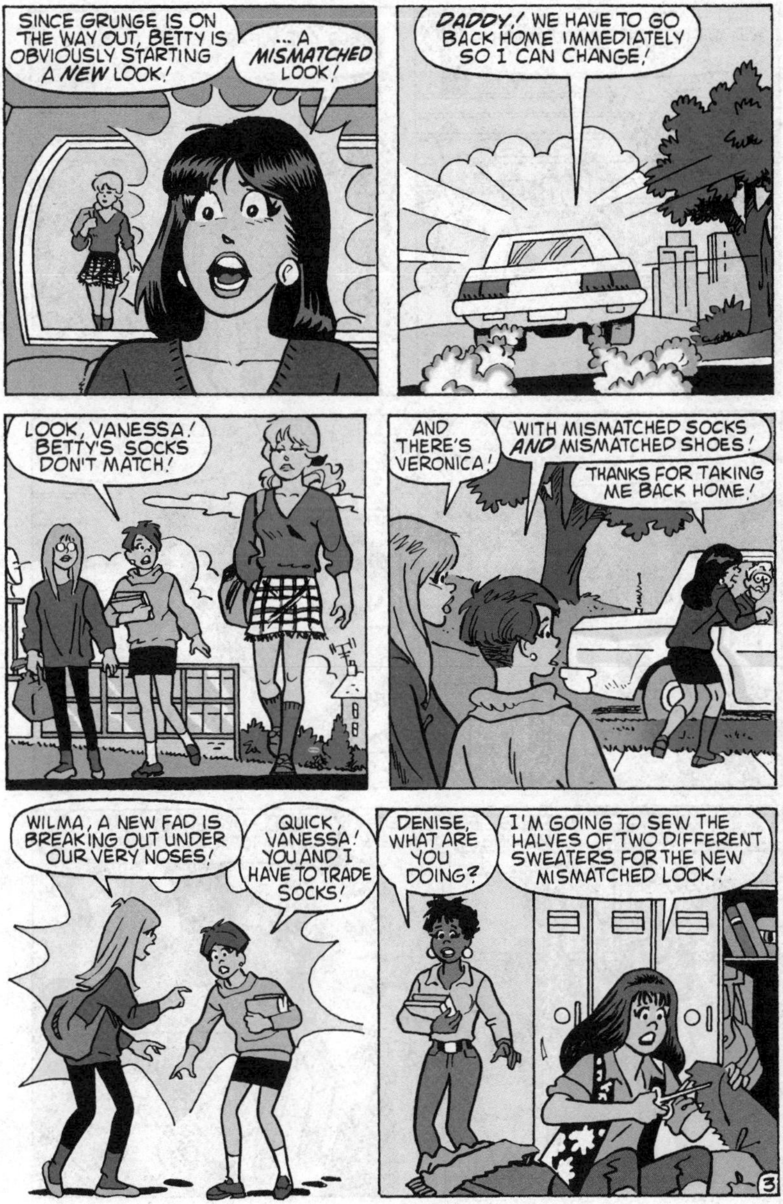
SINCE GRUNGE IS ON THE WAY OUT, BETTY IS OBVIOUSLY STARTING A NEW LOOK!
... A MISMATCHED LOOK!
DADDY! WE HAVE TO GO BACK HOME IMMEDIATELY SO I CAN CHANGE!
LOOK, VANESSA! BETTY'S SOCKS DON'T MATCH!
AND THERE'S VERONICA!
WITH MISMATCHED SOCKS AND MISMATCHED SHOES!
THANKS FOR TAKING ME BACK HOME!
WILMA, A NEW FAD IS BREAKING OUT UNDER OUR VERY NOSES!
QUICK, VANESSA! YOU AND I HAVE TO TRADE SOCKS!
DENISE, WHAT ARE YOU DOING?
I'M GOING TO SEW THE HALVES OF TWO DIFFERENT SWEATERS FOR THE NEW MISMATCHED LOOK!
3

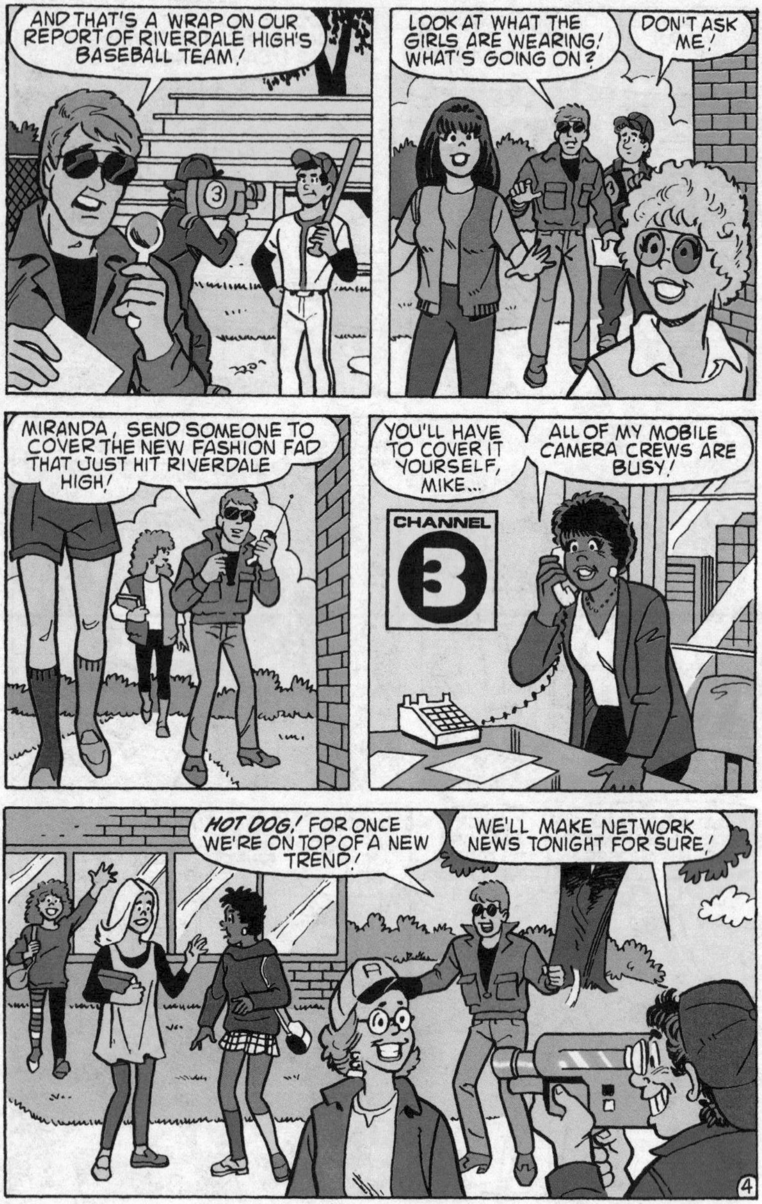
AND THAT'S A WRAP ON OUR REPORT OF RIVERDALE HIGH'S BASEBALL TEAM!
3
LOOK AT WHAT THE GIRLS ARE WEARING! WHAT'S GOING ON?
DON'T ASK ME!
MIRANDA, SEND SOMEONE TO COVER THE NEW FASHION FAD THAT JUST HIT RIVERDALE HIGH!
YOU'LL HAVE TO COVER IT YOURSELF, MIKE...
ALL OF MY MOBILE CAMERA CREWS ARE BUSY!
CHANNEL 3
HOT DOG! FOR ONCE WE'RE ON TOP OF A NEW TREND!
WE'LL MAKE NETWORK NEWS TONIGHT FOR SURE!
A
4

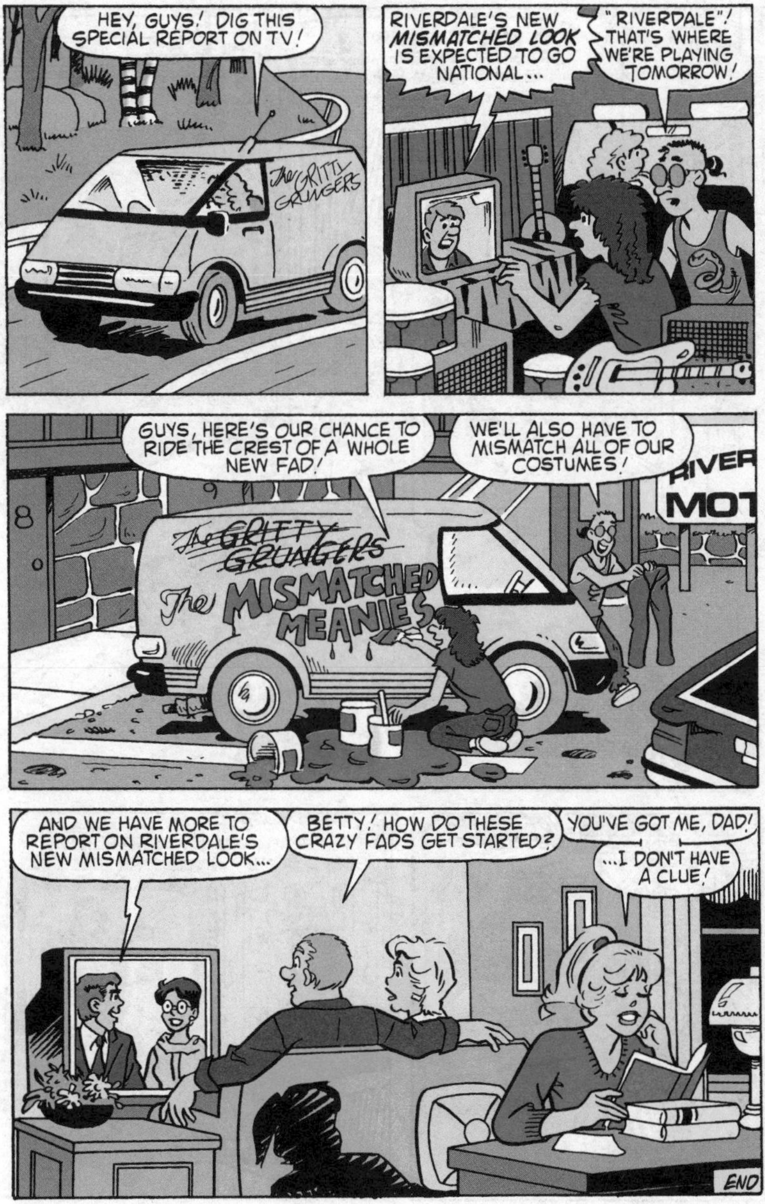
HEY, GUYS! DIG THIS SPECIAL REPORT ON TV!
The GRITTY GRUNGERS
RIVERDALE'S NEW MISMATCHED LOOK IS EXPECTED TO GO NATIONAL...
"RIVERDALE"! THAT'S WHERE WE'RE PLAYING TOMORROW!
GUYS, HERE'S OUR CHANCE TO RIDE THE CREST OF A WHOLE NEW FAD!
WE'LL ALSO HAVE TO MISMATCH ALL OF OUR COSTUMES!
The GRITTY GRUNGERS
The MISMATCHED MEANIES
RIVER
MOT
AND WE HAVE MORE TO REPORT ON RIVERDALE'S NEW MISMATCHED LOOK...
BETTY! HOW DO THESE CRAZY FADS GET STARTED?
YOU'VE GOT ME, DAD!
...I DON'T HAVE A CLUE!
END

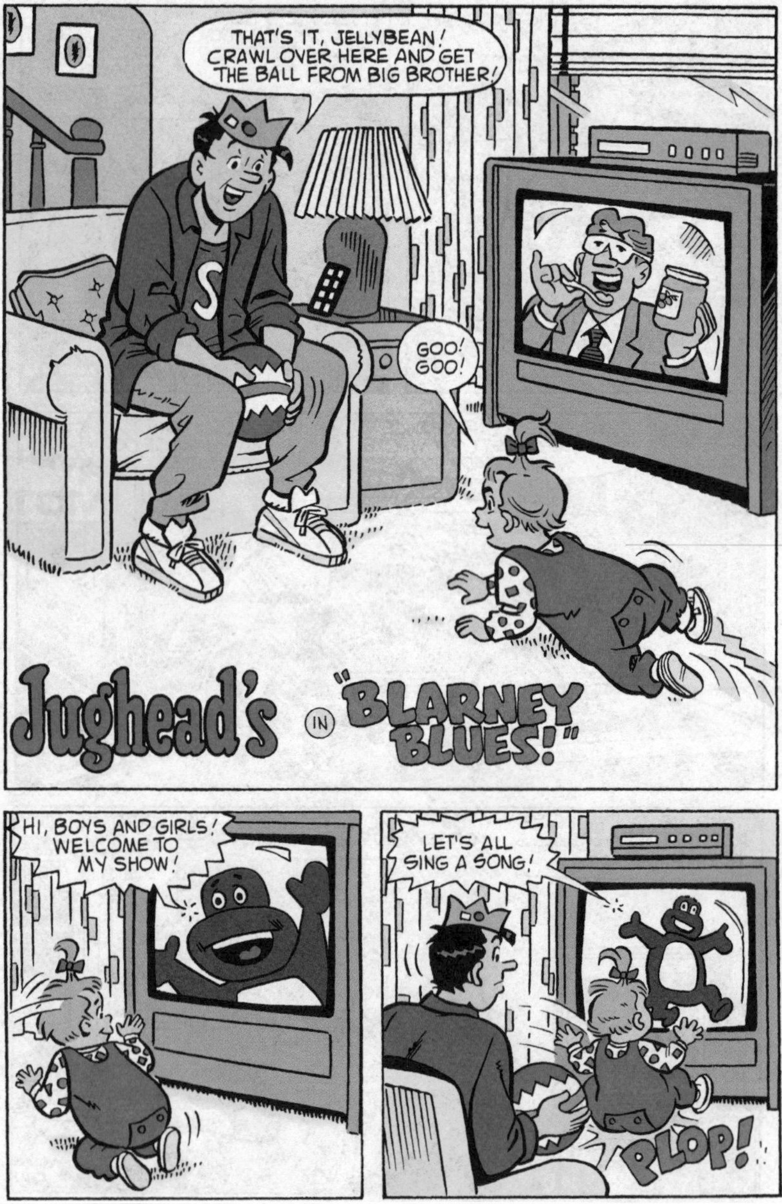
THAT'S IT, JELLYBEAN! CRAWL OVER HERE AND GET THE BALL FROM BIG BROTHER!
GOO! GOO!
Jughead's IN "BLARNEY BLUES!"
HI, BOYS AND GIRLS! WELCOME TO MY SHOW!
LET'S ALL SING A SONG!
PLOP!

Originally presented in JUGHEAD #57, June, 1994

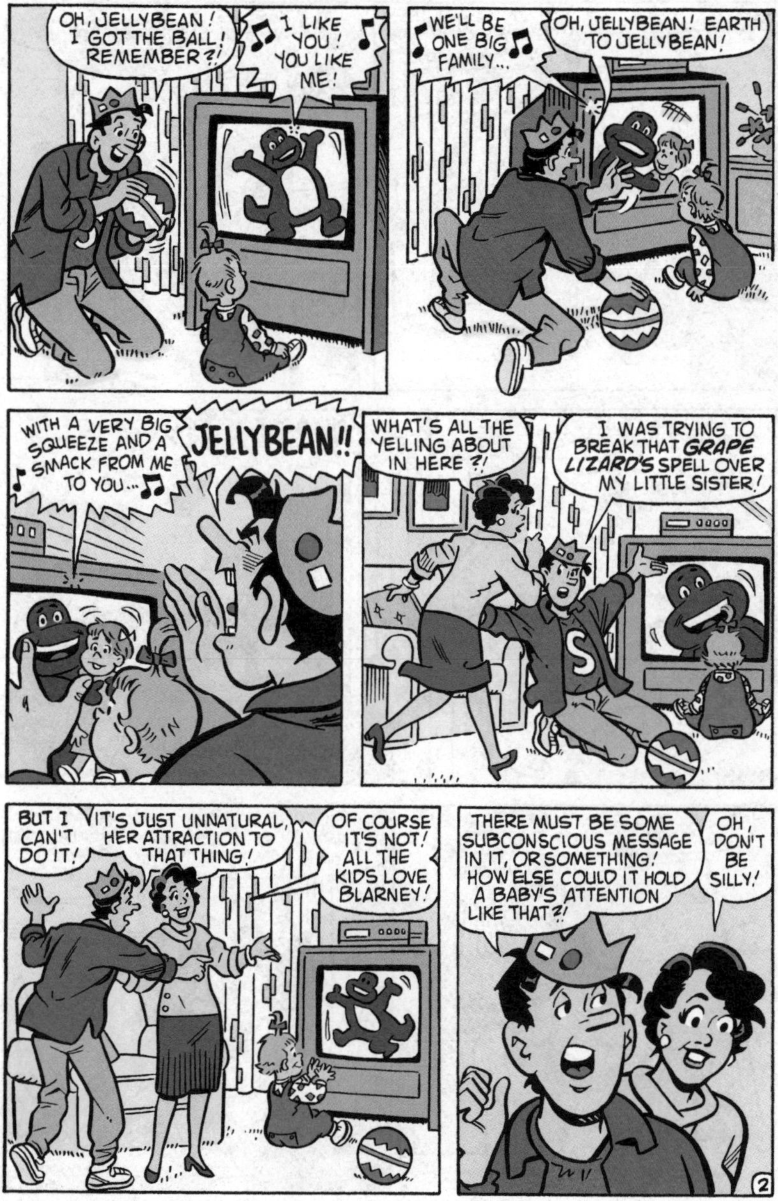
OH, JELLYBEAN! I GOT THE BALL! REMEMBER?!
I LIKE YOU! YOU LIKE ME!
WE'LL BE ONE BIG FAMILY...
OH, JELLYBEAN! EARTH TO JELLYBEAN!
WITH A VERY BIG SQUEEZE AND A SMACK FROM ME TO YOU...
JELLYBEAN!!
WHAT'S ALL THE YELLING ABOUT IN HERE?!
I WAS TRYING TO BREAK THAT GRAPE LIZARD'S SPELL OVER MY LITTLE SISTER!
BUT I CAN'T DO IT!
IT'S JUST UNNATURAL, HER ATTRACTION TO THAT THING!
OF COURSE IT'S NOT! ALL THE KIDS LOVE BLARNEY!
THERE MUST BE SOME SUBCONSCIOUS MESSAGE IN IT, OR SOMETHING! HOW ELSE COULD IT HOLD A BABY'S ATTENTION LIKE THAT?!
OH, DON'T BE SILLY!
2

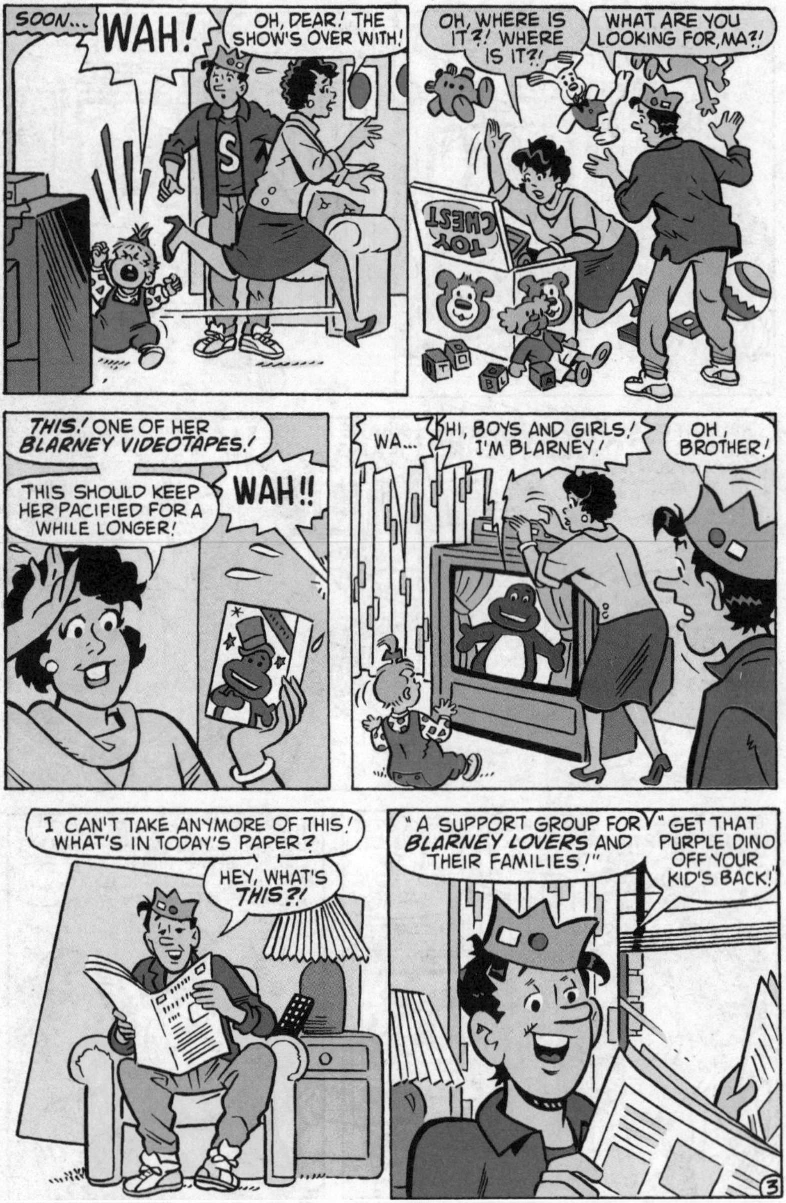
SOON...
WAH!
OH, DEAR! THE SHOW'S OVER WITH!
OH, WHERE IS IT?! WHERE IS IT?!
WHAT ARE YOU LOOKING FOR, MA?!
TOY CHEST
THIS! ONE OF HER BLARNEY VIDEOTAPES!
THIS SHOULD KEEP HER PACIFIED FOR A WHILE LONGER!
WAH!!
WA...
HI, BOYS AND GIRLS! I'M BLARNEY!
OH, BROTHER!
I CAN'T TAKE ANYMORE OF THIS! WHAT'S IN TODAY'S PAPER?
HEY, WHAT'S THIS?!
"A SUPPORT GROUP FOR BLARNEY LOVERS AND THEIR FAMILIES!"
"GET THAT PURPLE DINO OFF YOUR KID'S BACK!"
3

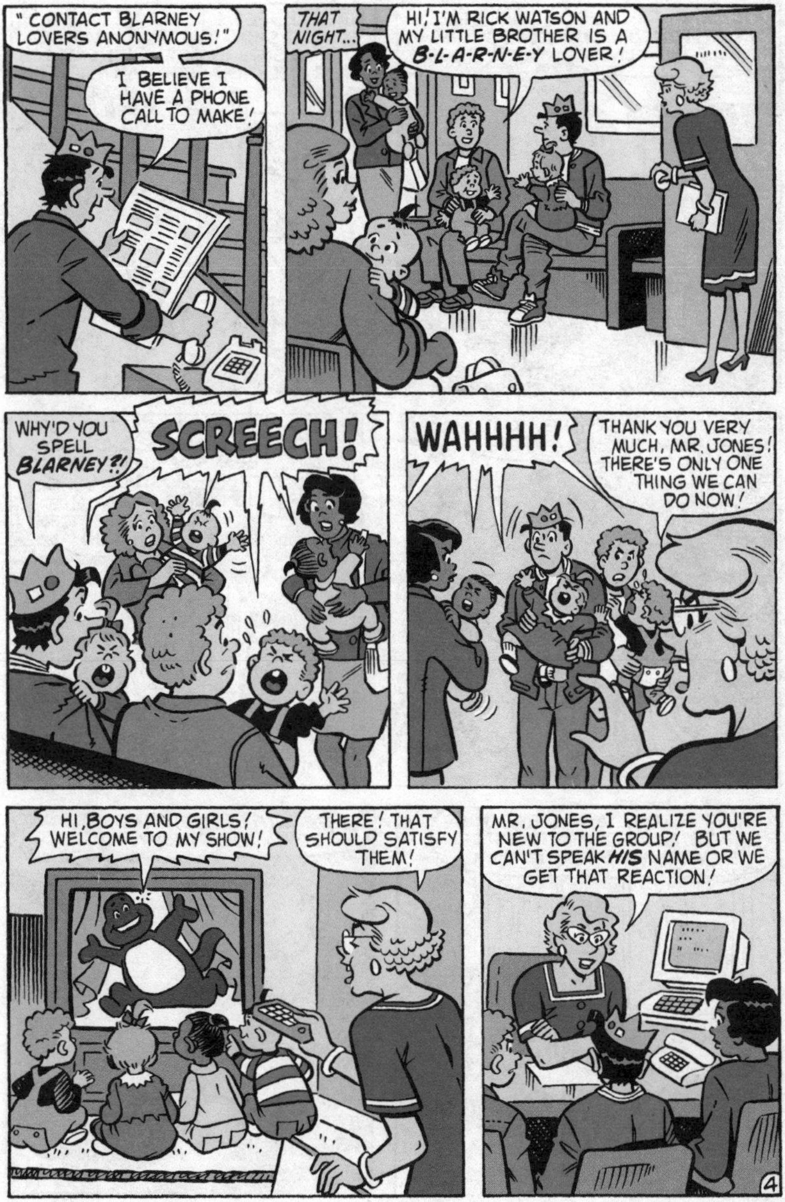
"CONTACT BLARNEY LOVERS ANONYMOUS!"
I BELIEVE I HAVE A PHONE CALL TO MAKE!
THAT NIGHT...
HI! I'M RICK WATSON AND MY LITTLE BROTHER IS A B-L-A-R-N-E-Y LOVER!
WHY'D YOU SPELL BLARNEY?!
SCREECH!
WAHHHH!
THANK YOU VERY MUCH, MR. JONES! THERE'S ONLY ONE THING WE CAN DO NOW!
HI, BOYS AND GIRLS! WELCOME TO MY SHOW!
THERE! THAT SHOULD SATISFY THEM!
MR. JONES, I REALIZE YOU'RE NEW TO THE GROUP! BUT WE CAN'T SPEAK HIS NAME OR WE GET THAT REACTION!
4

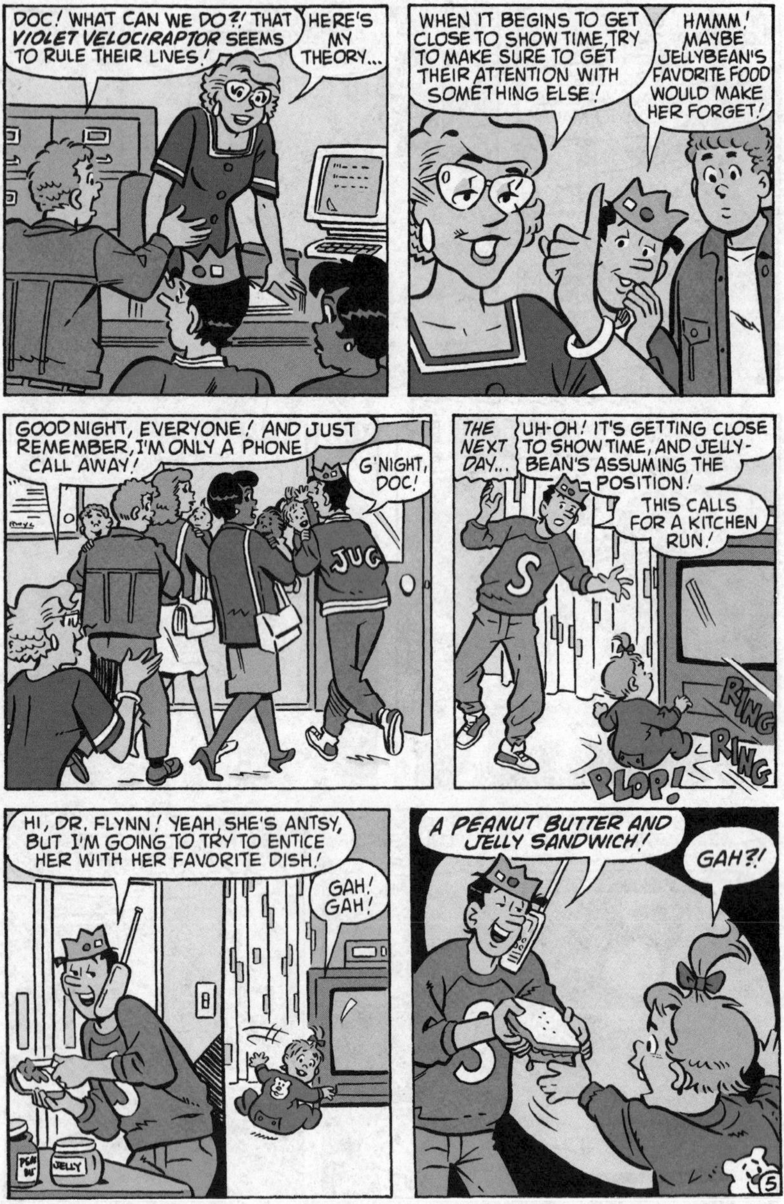
DOC! WHAT CAN WE DO?! THAT *VIOLET VELOCIRAPTOR* SEEMS TO RULE THEIR LIVES!
HERE'S MY THEORY...
WHEN IT BEGINS TO GET CLOSE TO SHOW TIME, TRY TO MAKE SURE TO GET THEIR ATTENTION WITH SOMETHING ELSE!
HMMM! MAYBE JELLYBEAN'S FAVORITE FOOD WOULD MAKE HER FORGET!
GOOD NIGHT, EVERYONE! AND JUST REMEMBER, I'M ONLY A PHONE CALL AWAY!
G'NIGHT, DOC!
JUG
*THE NEXT DAY...*
UH-OH! IT'S GETTING CLOSE TO SHOW TIME, AND JELLY-BEAN'S ASSUMING THE POSITION!
THIS CALLS FOR A KITCHEN RUN!
RING
RING
PLOP!
HI, DR. FLYNN! YEAH, SHE'S ANTSY, BUT I'M GOING TO TRY TO ENTICE HER WITH HER FAVORITE DISH!
GAH! GAH!
JELLY
*A PEANUT BUTTER AND JELLY SANDWICH!*
GAH?!
5

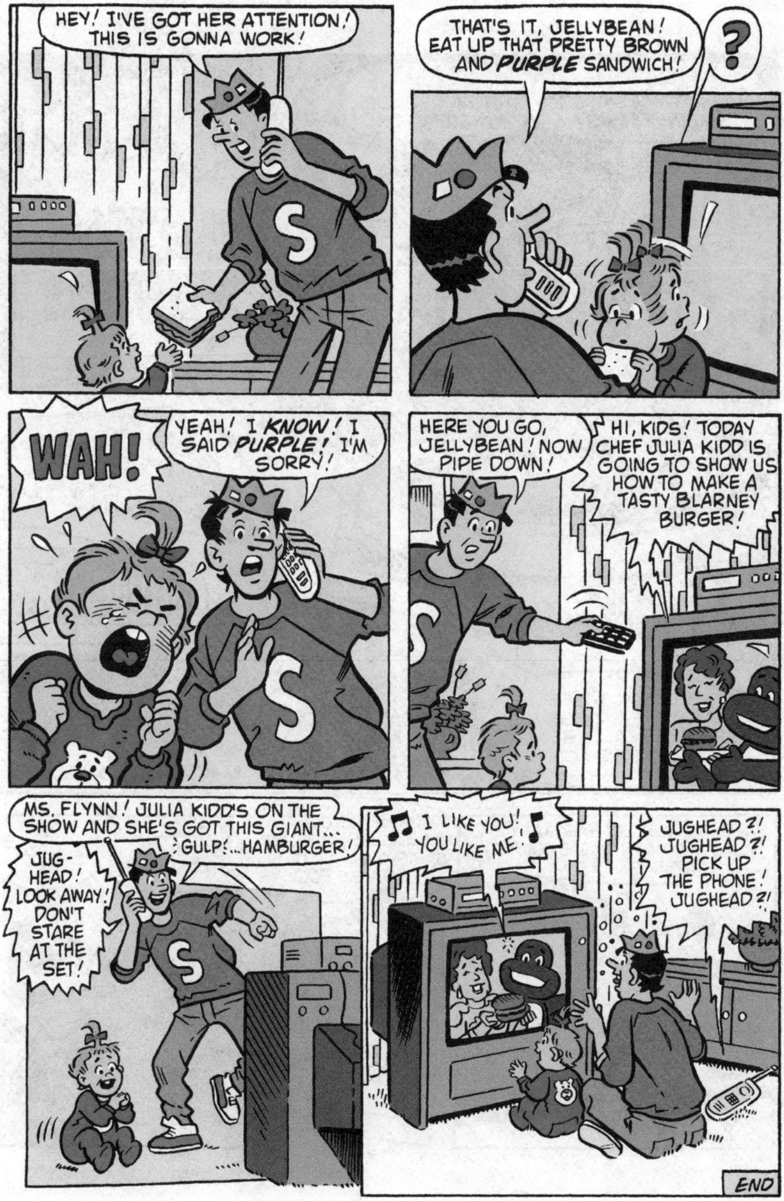
HEY! I'VE GOT HER ATTENTION! THIS IS GONNA WORK!
THAT'S IT, JELLYBEAN! EAT UP THAT PRETTY BROWN AND PURPLE SANDWICH!
?
WAH!
YEAH! I KNOW! I SAID PURPLE! I'M SORRY!
HERE YOU GO, JELLYBEAN! NOW PIPE DOWN!
HI, KIDS! TODAY CHEF JULIA KIDD IS GOING TO SHOW US HOW TO MAKE A TASTY BLARNEY BURGER!
MS. FLYNN! JULIA KIDD'S ON THE SHOW AND SHE'S GOT THIS GIANT... GULP!...HAMBURGER!
JUG-HEAD! LOOK AWAY! DON'T STARE AT THE SET!
I LIKE YOU! YOU LIKE ME!
JUGHEAD?! JUGHEAD?! PICK UP THE PHONE! JUGHEAD?!
END

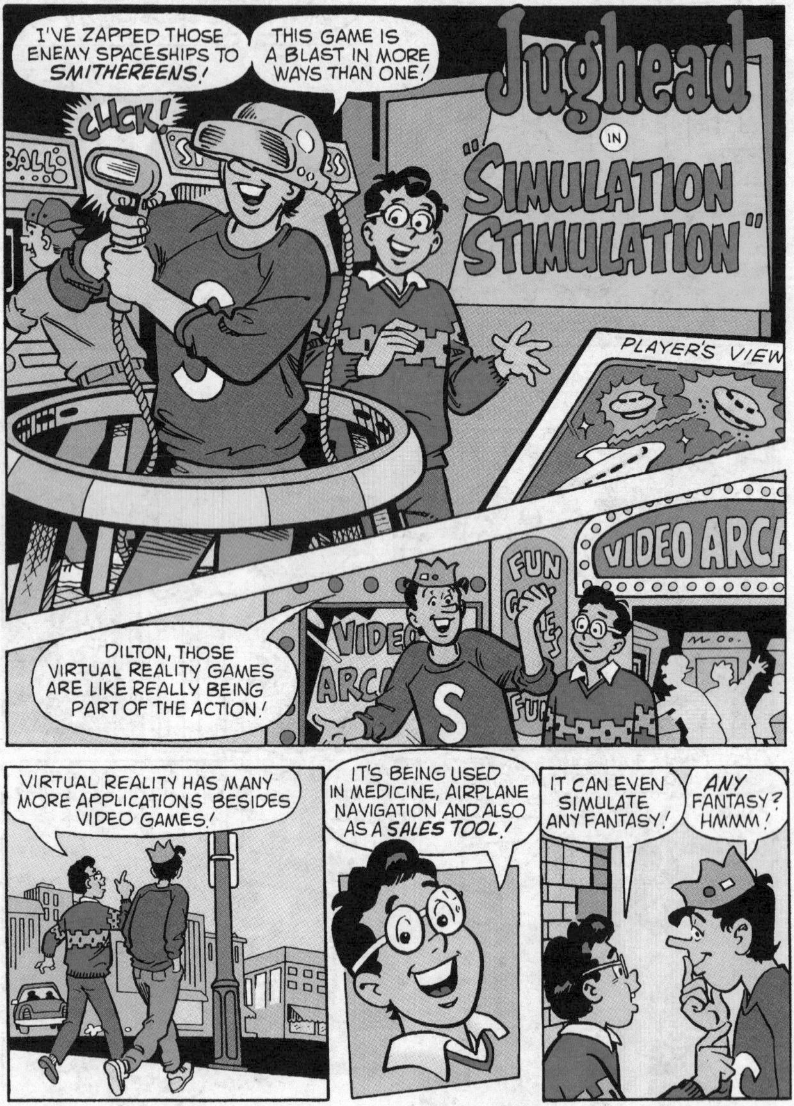
I'VE ZAPPED THOSE ENEMY SPACESHIPS TO SMITHEREENS!
THIS GAME IS A BLAST IN MORE WAYS THAN ONE!
Jughead
IN
"SIMULATION STIMULATION"
CLICK!
PLAYER'S VIEW
VIDEO ARCA
FUN
DILTON, THOSE VIRTUAL REALITY GAMES ARE LIKE REALLY BEING PART OF THE ACTION!
VIRTUAL REALITY HAS MANY MORE APPLICATIONS BESIDES VIDEO GAMES!
IT'S BEING USED IN MEDICINE, AIRPLANE NAVIGATION AND ALSO AS A SALES TOOL!
IT CAN EVEN SIMULATE ANY FANTASY!
ANY FANTASY? HMMM!

Originally presented in JUGHEAD #58, July, 1994

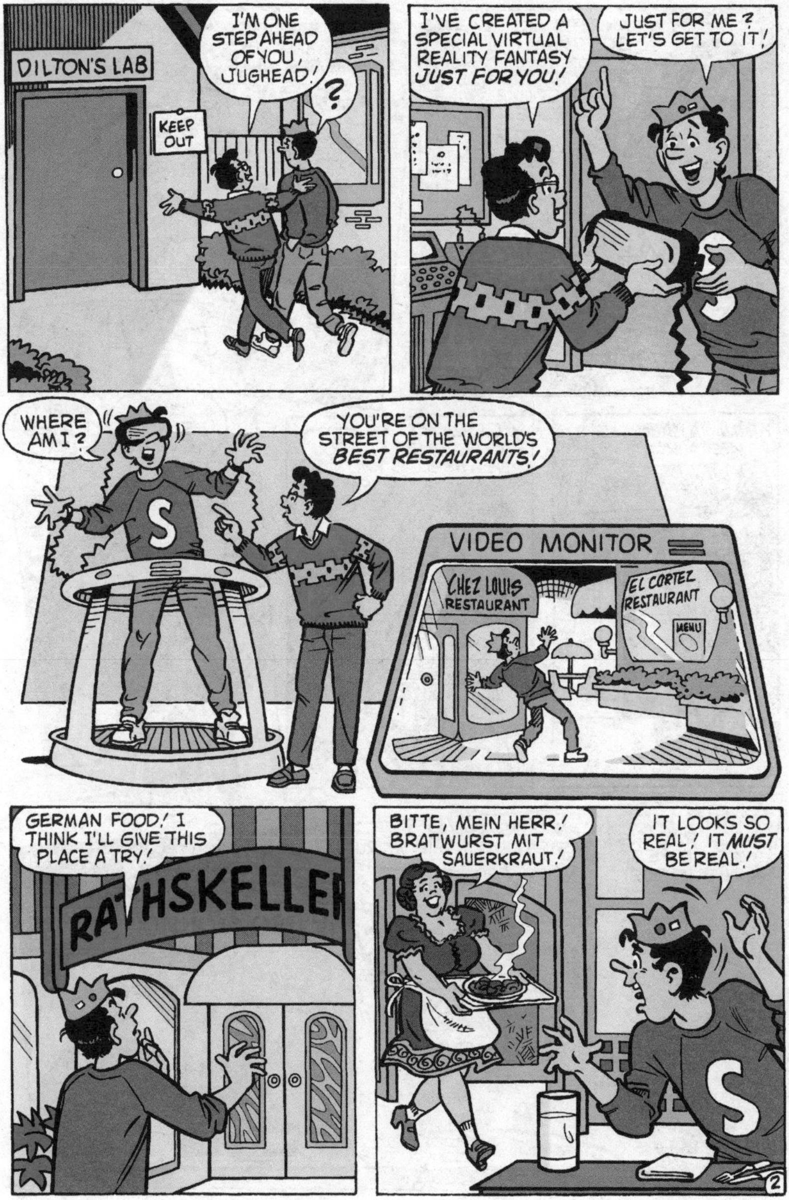
DILTON'S LAB
KEEP OUT
I'M ONE STEP AHEAD OF YOU, JUGHEAD!
?
I'VE CREATED A SPECIAL VIRTUAL REALITY FANTASY JUST FOR YOU!
JUST FOR ME? LET'S GET TO IT!
WHERE AM I?
YOU'RE ON THE STREET OF THE WORLD'S BEST RESTAURANTS!
VIDEO MONITOR
CHEZ LOUIS RESTAURANT
EL CORTEZ RESTAURANT
MENU
GERMAN FOOD! I THINK I'LL GIVE THIS PLACE A TRY!
RATHSKELLER
BITTE, MEIN HERR! BRATWURST MIT SAUERKRAUT!
IT LOOKS SO REAL! IT MUST BE REAL!
2

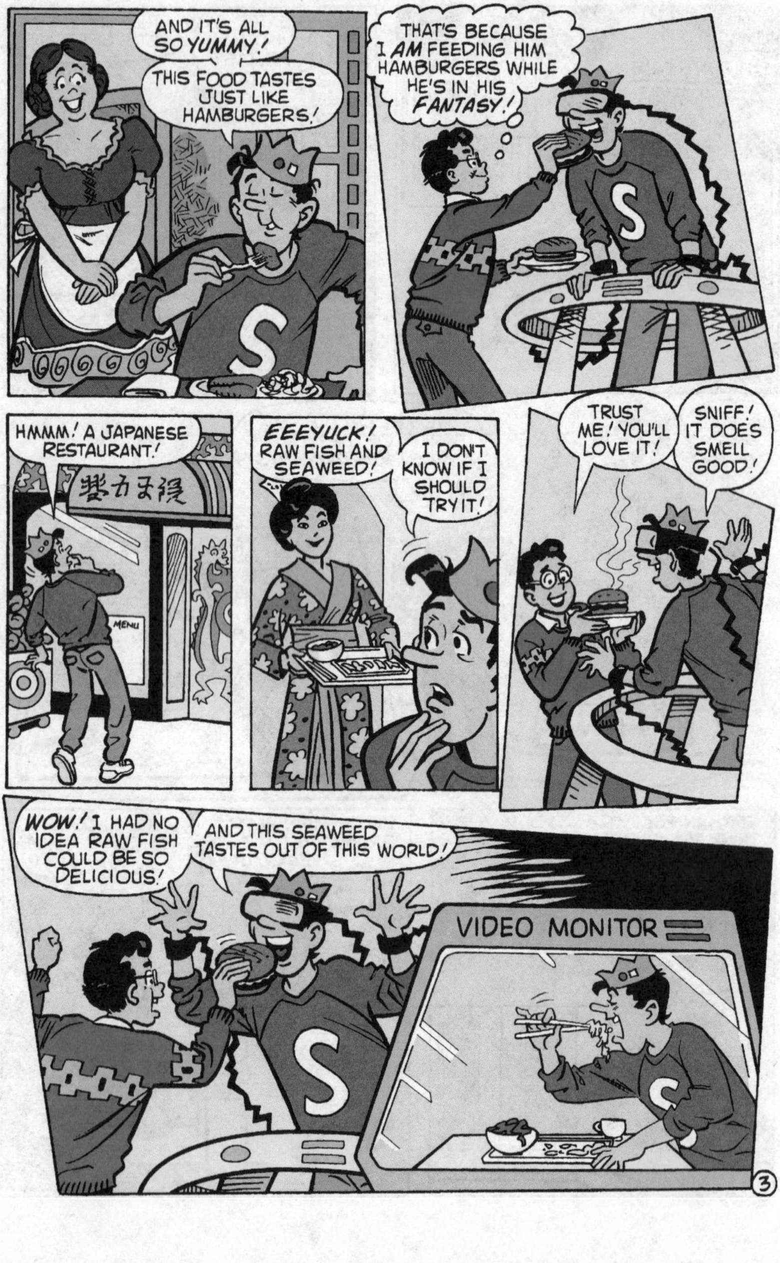
AND IT'S ALL SO YUMMY!
THIS FOOD TASTES JUST LIKE HAMBURGERS!
THAT'S BECAUSE I AM FEEDING HIM HAMBURGERS WHILE HE'S IN HIS FANTASY!
HMMM! A JAPANESE RESTAURANT!
MENU
EEEYUCK! RAW FISH AND SEAWEED!
I DON'T KNOW IF I SHOULD TRY IT!
TRUST ME! YOU'LL LOVE IT!
SNIFF! IT DOES SMELL GOOD!
WOW! I HAD NO IDEA RAW FISH COULD BE SO DELICIOUS!
AND THIS SEAWEED TASTES OUT OF THIS WORLD!
VIDEO MONITOR
3

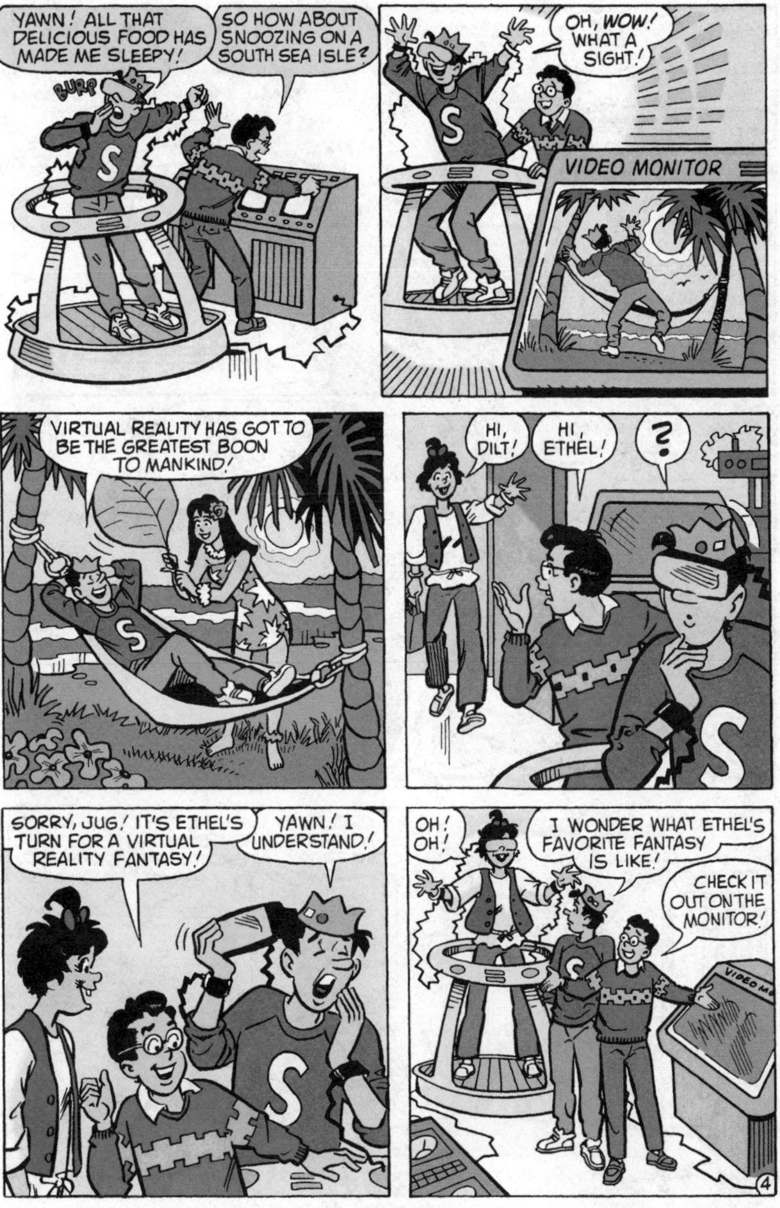
YAWN! ALL THAT DELICIOUS FOOD HAS MADE ME SLEEPY!
BURP
SO HOW ABOUT SNOOZING ON A SOUTH SEA ISLE?
OH, WOW! WHAT A SIGHT!
VIDEO MONITOR
VIRTUAL REALITY HAS GOT TO BE THE GREATEST BOON TO MANKIND!
HI, DILT!
HI, ETHEL!
?
SORRY, JUG! IT'S ETHEL'S TURN FOR A VIRTUAL REALITY FANTASY!
YAWN! I UNDERSTAND!
OH! OH!
I WONDER WHAT ETHEL'S FAVORITE FANTASY IS LIKE!
CHECK IT OUT ON THE MONITOR!
4

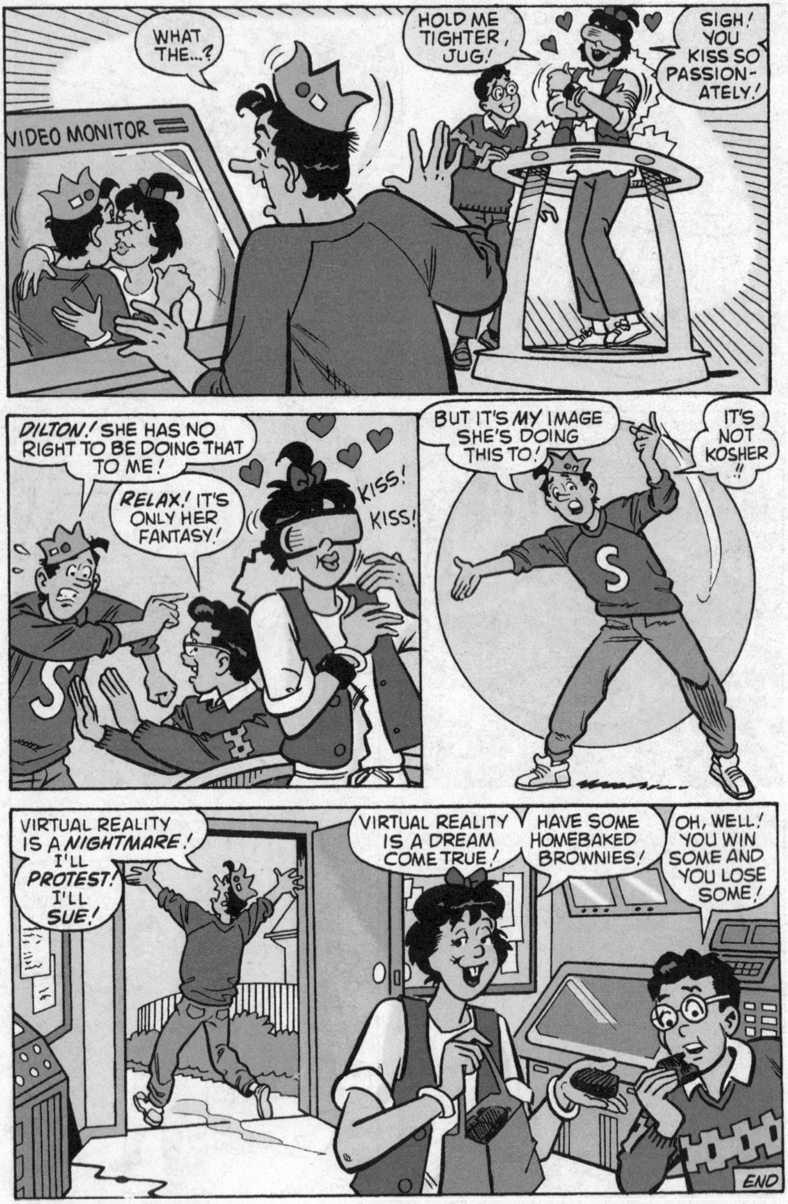
WHAT THE...?
VIDEO MONITOR
HOLD ME TIGHTER, JUG!
SIGH! YOU KISS SO PASSION-ATELY!
DILTON! SHE HAS NO RIGHT TO BE DOING THAT TO ME!
RELAX! IT'S ONLY HER FANTASY!
KISS! KISS!
BUT IT'S MY IMAGE SHE'S DOING THIS TO!
IT'S NOT KOSHER!!
VIRTUAL REALITY IS A NIGHTMARE! I'LL PROTEST! I'LL SUE!
VIRTUAL REALITY IS A DREAM COME TRUE!
HAVE SOME HOMEBAKED BROWNIES!
OH, WELL! YOU WIN SOME AND YOU LOSE SOME!
END

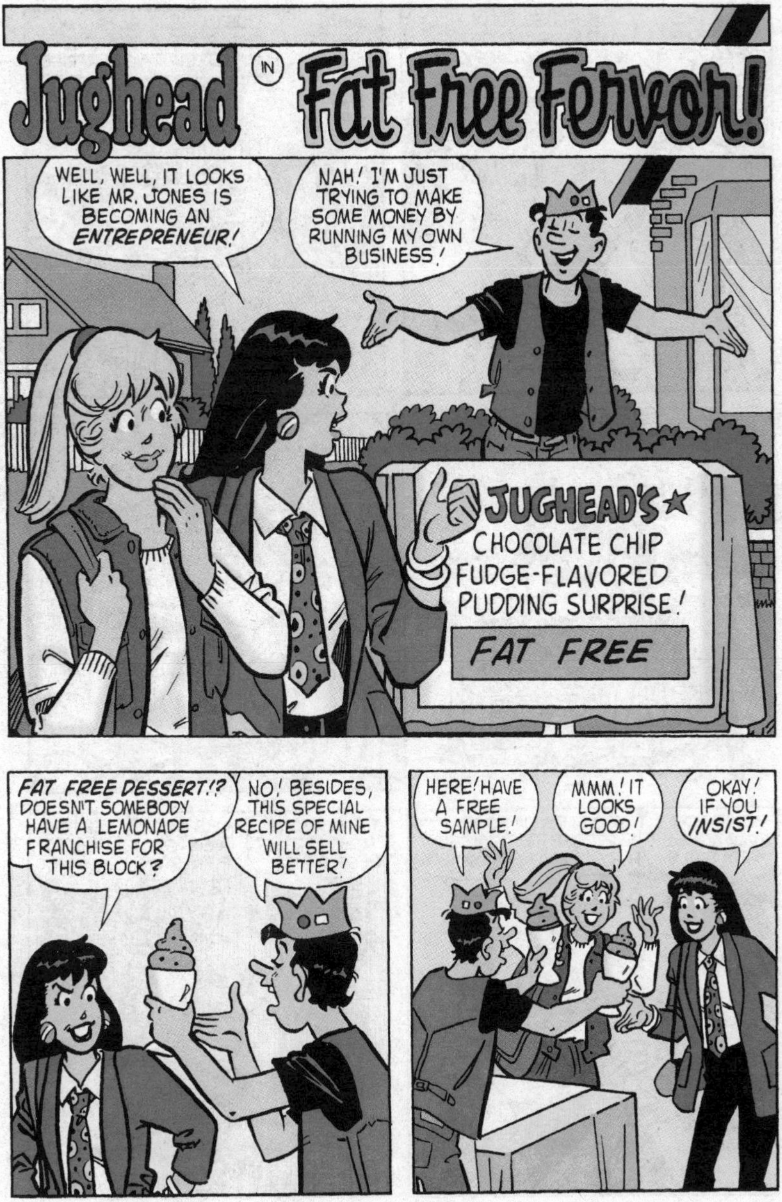
Jughead IN Fat Free Fervor!
WELL, WELL, IT LOOKS LIKE MR. JONES IS BECOMING AN ENTREPRENEUR!
NAH! I'M JUST TRYING TO MAKE SOME MONEY BY RUNNING MY OWN BUSINESS!
JUGHEAD'S
CHOCOLATE CHIP FUDGE-FLAVORED PUDDING SURPRISE!
FAT FREE
FAT FREE DESSERT!? DOESN'T SOMEBODY HAVE A LEMONADE FRANCHISE FOR THIS BLOCK?
NO! BESIDES, THIS SPECIAL RECIPE OF MINE WILL SELL BETTER!
HERE! HAVE A FREE SAMPLE!
MMM! IT LOOKS GOOD!
OKAY! IF YOU INSIST!

Originally presented in JUGHEAD #61, October, 1994

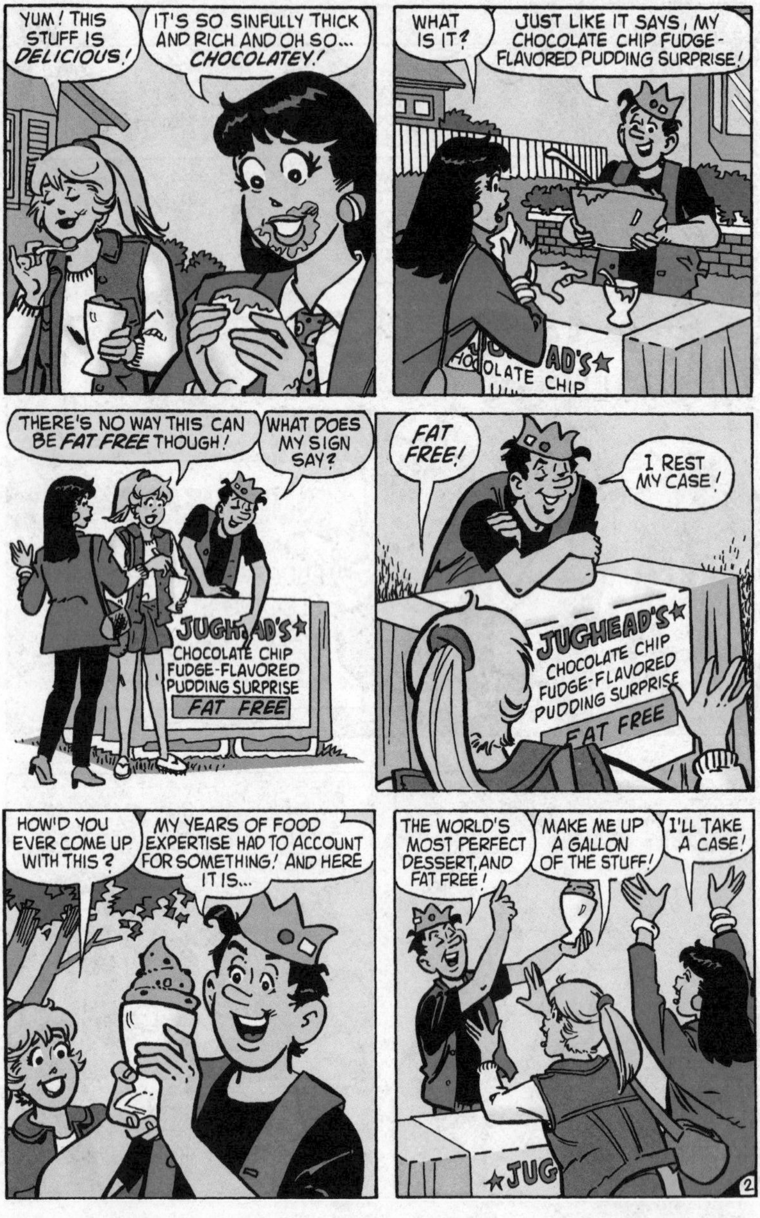
YUM! THIS STUFF IS DELICIOUS!
IT'S SO SINFULLY THICK AND RICH AND OH SO... CHOCOLATEY!
WHAT IS IT?
JUST LIKE IT SAYS, MY CHOCOLATE CHIP FUDGE-FLAVORED PUDDING SURPRISE!
THERE'S NO WAY THIS CAN BE FAT FREE THOUGH!
WHAT DOES MY SIGN SAY?
JUGHEAD'S CHOCOLATE CHIP FUDGE-FLAVORED PUDDING SURPRISE
FAT FREE
FAT FREE!
I REST MY CASE!
HOW'D YOU EVER COME UP WITH THIS?
MY YEARS OF FOOD EXPERTISE HAD TO ACCOUNT FOR SOMETHING! AND HERE IT IS...
THE WORLD'S MOST PERFECT DESSERT, AND FAT FREE!
MAKE ME UP A GALLON OF THE STUFF!
I'LL TAKE A CASE!
2

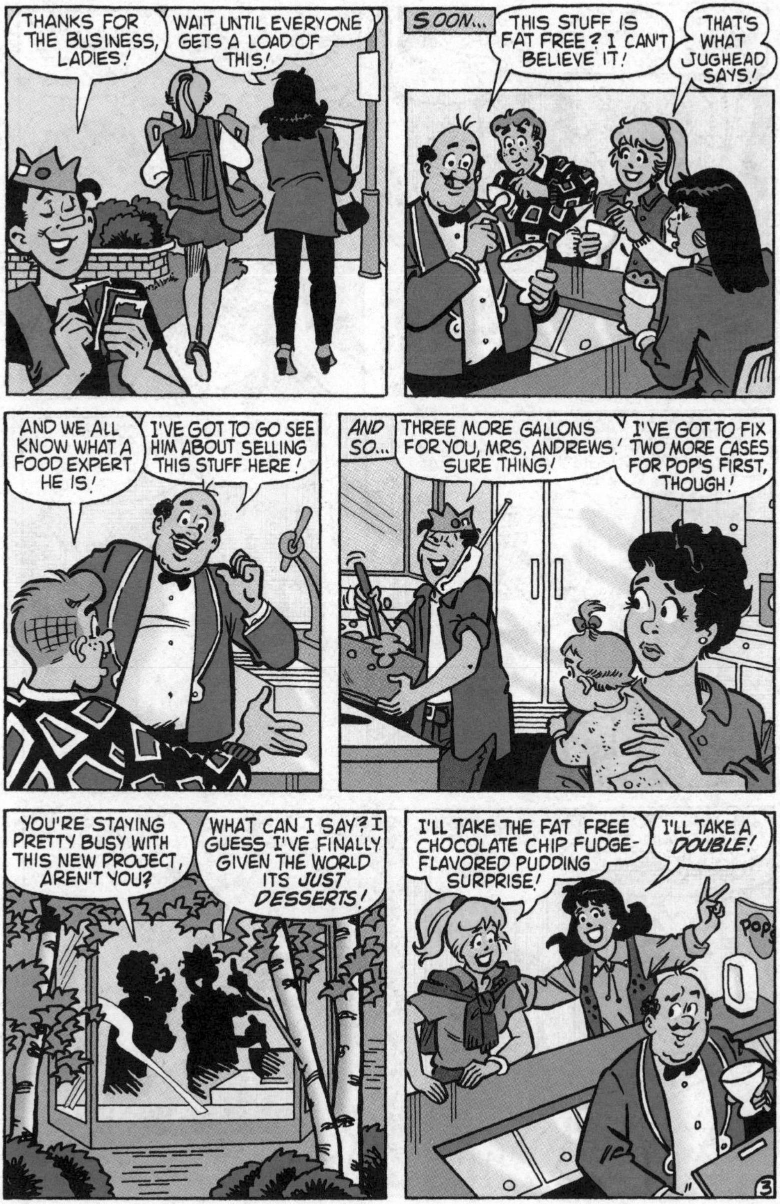
THANKS FOR THE BUSINESS, LADIES!
WAIT UNTIL EVERYONE GETS A LOAD OF THIS!
SOON...
THIS STUFF IS FAT FREE? I CAN'T BELIEVE IT!
THAT'S WHAT JUGHEAD SAYS!
AND WE ALL KNOW WHAT A FOOD EXPERT HE IS!
I'VE GOT TO GO SEE HIM ABOUT SELLING THIS STUFF HERE!
AND SO...
THREE MORE GALLONS FOR YOU, MRS. ANDREWS! SURE THING!
I'VE GOT TO FIX TWO MORE CASES FOR POP'S FIRST, THOUGH!
YOU'RE STAYING PRETTY BUSY WITH THIS NEW PROJECT, AREN'T YOU?
WHAT CAN I SAY? I GUESS I'VE FINALLY GIVEN THE WORLD ITS *JUST DESSERTS*!
I'LL TAKE THE FAT FREE CHOCOLATE CHIP FUDGE-FLAVORED PUDDING SURPRISE!
I'LL TAKE A *DOUBLE*!
POP'S
3

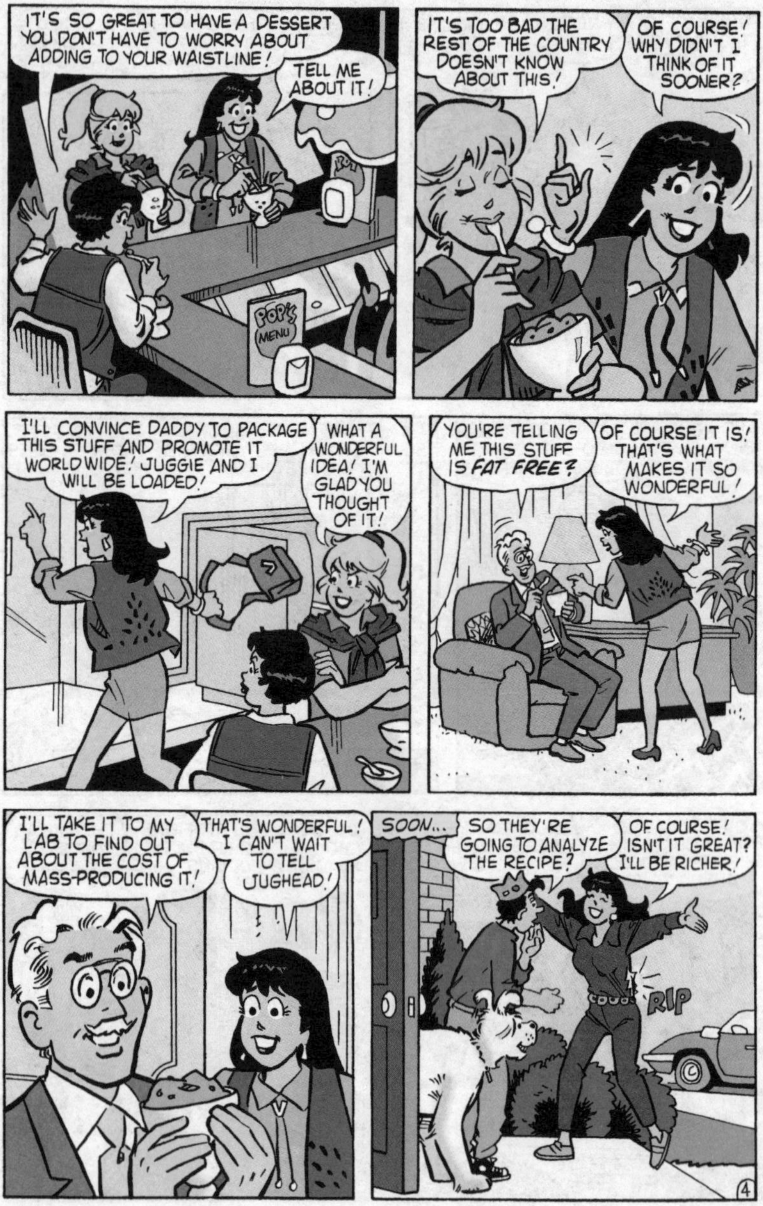
IT'S SO GREAT TO HAVE A DESSERT YOU DON'T HAVE TO WORRY ABOUT ADDING TO YOUR WAISTLINE!
TELL ME ABOUT IT!
POP'S MENU
IT'S TOO BAD THE REST OF THE COUNTRY DOESN'T KNOW ABOUT THIS!
OF COURSE! WHY DIDN'T I THINK OF IT SOONER?
I'LL CONVINCE DADDY TO PACKAGE THIS STUFF AND PROMOTE IT WORLDWIDE! JUGGIE AND I WILL BE LOADED!
WHAT A WONDERFUL IDEA! I'M GLAD YOU THOUGHT OF IT!
YOU'RE TELLING ME THIS STUFF IS FAT FREE?
OF COURSE IT IS! THAT'S WHAT MAKES IT SO WONDERFUL!
I'LL TAKE IT TO MY LAB TO FIND OUT ABOUT THE COST OF MASS-PRODUCING IT!
THAT'S WONDERFUL! I CAN'T WAIT TO TELL JUGHEAD!
SOON...
SO THEY'RE GOING TO ANALYZE THE RECIPE?
OF COURSE! ISN'T IT GREAT? I'LL BE RICHER!
RIP
4

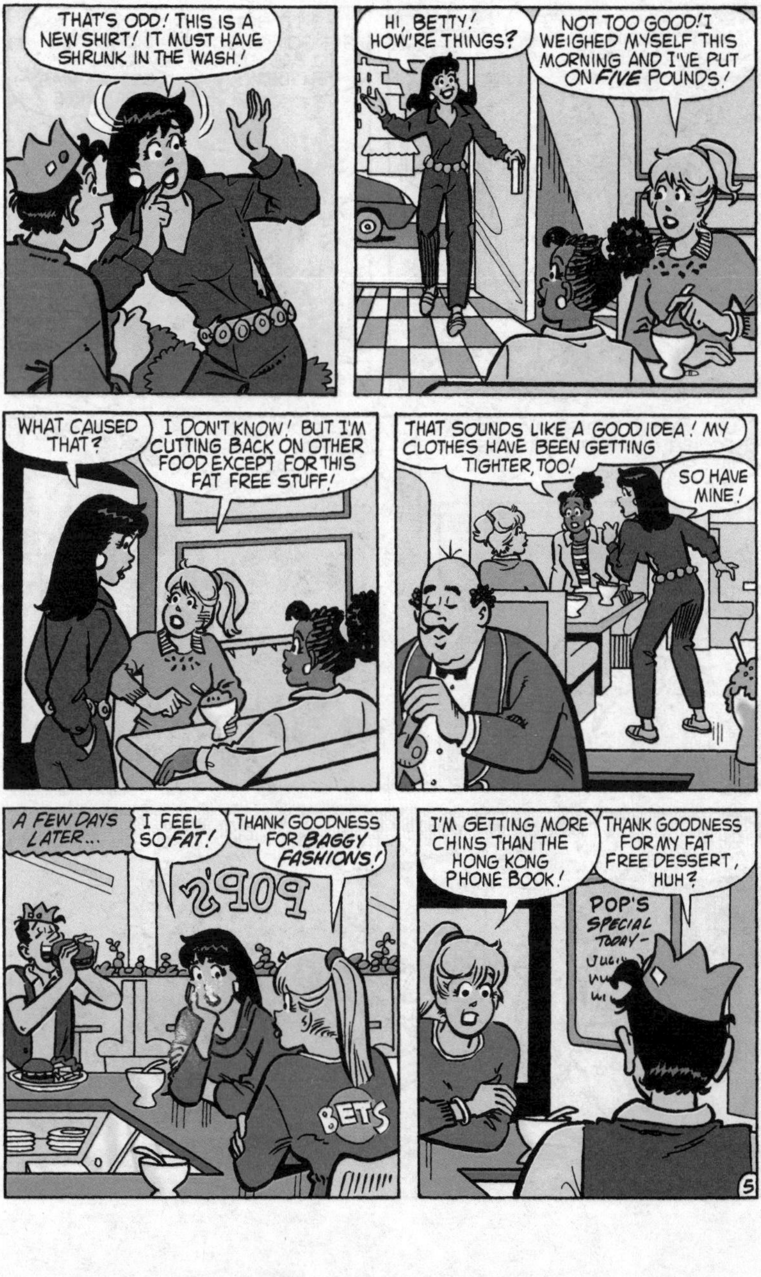
THAT'S ODD! THIS IS A NEW SHIRT! IT MUST HAVE SHRUNK IN THE WASH!
HI, BETTY! HOW'RE THINGS?
NOT TOO GOOD! I WEIGHED MYSELF THIS MORNING AND I'VE PUT ON FIVE POUNDS!
WHAT CAUSED THAT?
I DON'T KNOW! BUT I'M CUTTING BACK ON OTHER FOOD EXCEPT FOR THIS FAT FREE STUFF!
THAT SOUNDS LIKE A GOOD IDEA! MY CLOTHES HAVE BEEN GETTING TIGHTER, TOO!
SO HAVE MINE!
A FEW DAYS LATER...
I FEEL SO FAT!
THANK GOODNESS FOR BAGGY FASHIONS!
POP'S
BETS
I'M GETTING MORE CHINS THAN THE HONG KONG PHONE BOOK!
THANK GOODNESS FOR MY FAT FREE DESSERT, HUH?
POP'S SPECIAL TODAY-
5

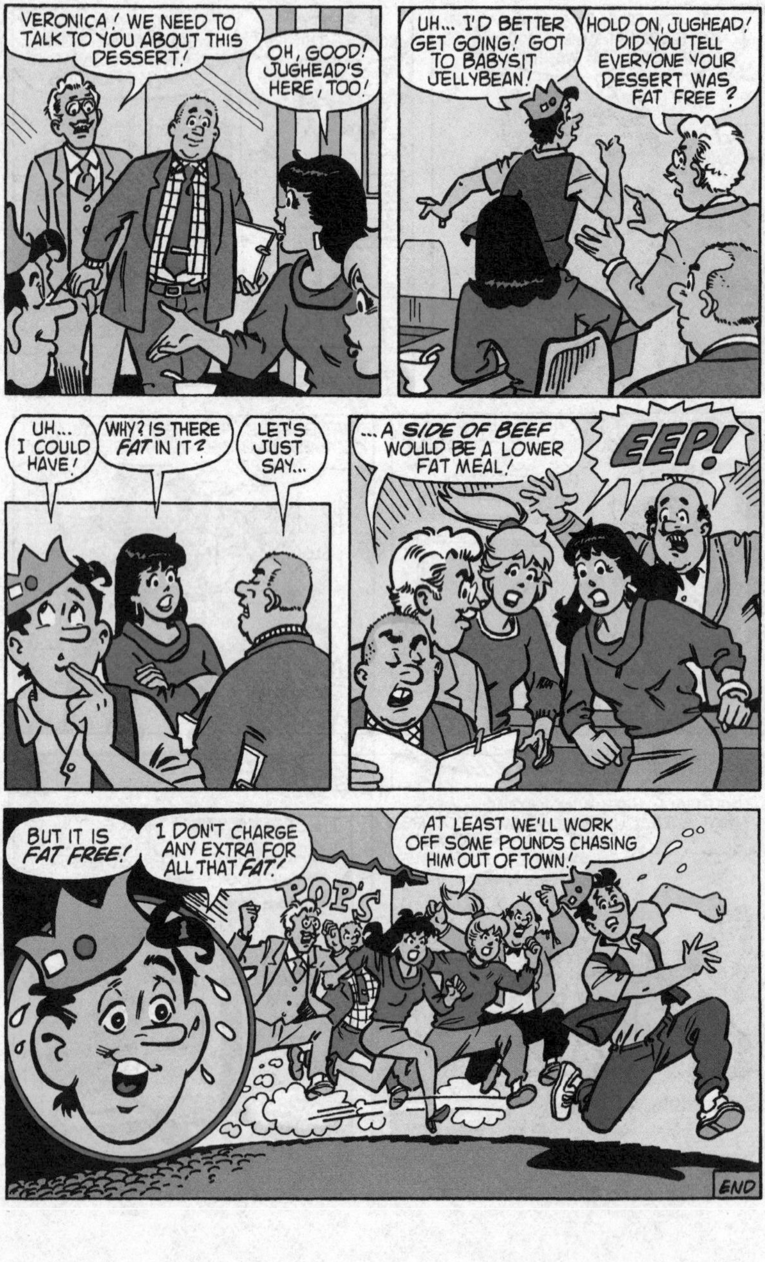
VERONICA! WE NEED TO TALK TO YOU ABOUT THIS DESSERT!
OH, GOOD! JUGHEAD'S HERE, TOO!
UH... I'D BETTER GET GOING! GOT TO BABYSIT JELLYBEAN!
HOLD ON, JUGHEAD! DID YOU TELL EVERYONE YOUR DESSERT WAS FAT FREE ?
UH... I COULD HAVE!
WHY? IS THERE FAT IN IT?
LET'S JUST SAY...
...A SIDE OF BEEF WOULD BE A LOWER FAT MEAL!
EEP!
BUT IT IS FAT FREE!
I DON'T CHARGE ANY EXTRA FOR ALL THAT FAT!
AT LEAST WE'LL WORK OFF SOME POUNDS CHASING HIM OUT OF TOWN!
POP'S
END

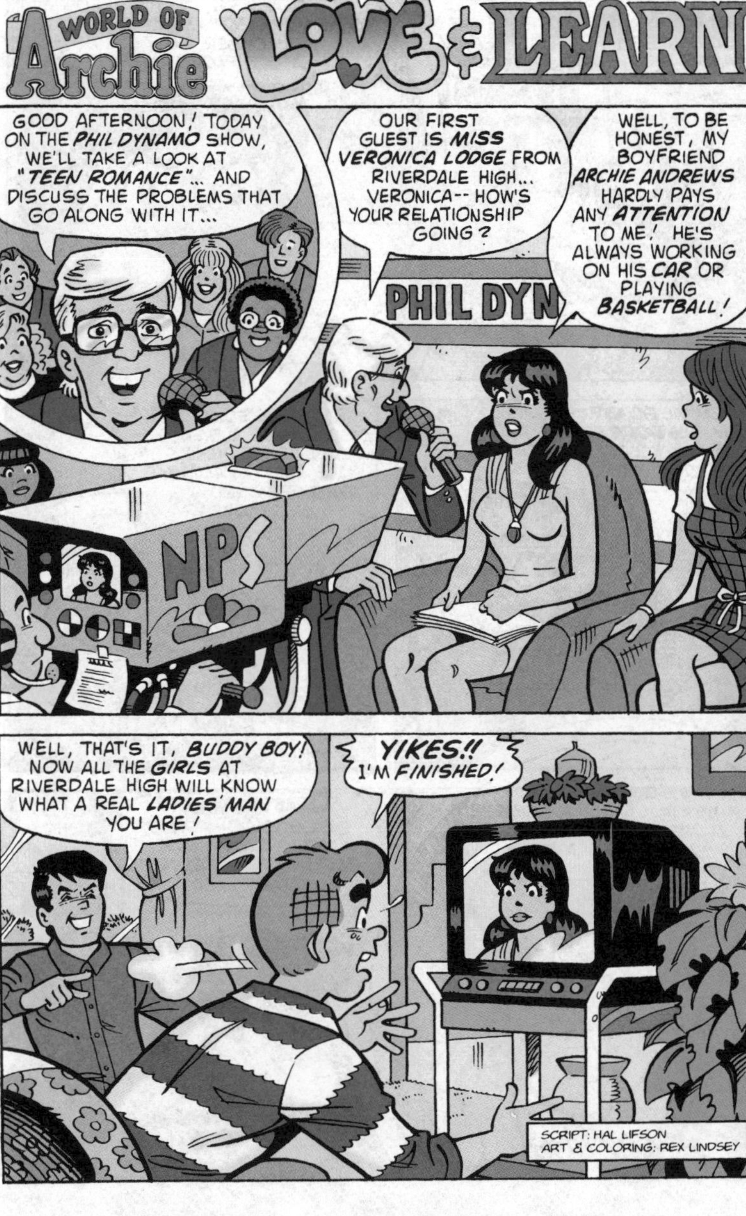
WORLD OF Archie
LOVE & LEARN
GOOD AFTERNOON! TODAY ON THE PHIL DYNAMO SHOW, WE'LL TAKE A LOOK AT "TEEN ROMANCE"... AND DISCUSS THE PROBLEMS THAT GO ALONG WITH IT...
OUR FIRST GUEST IS MISS VERONICA LODGE FROM RIVERDALE HIGH... VERONICA-- HOW'S YOUR RELATIONSHIP GOING?
WELL, TO BE HONEST, MY BOYFRIEND ARCHIE ANDREWS HARDLY PAYS ANY ATTENTION TO ME! HE'S ALWAYS WORKING ON HIS CAR OR PLAYING BASKETBALL!
PHIL DYN
NPS
WELL, THAT'S IT, BUDDY BOY! NOW ALL THE GIRLS AT RIVERDALE HIGH WILL KNOW WHAT A REAL LADIES' MAN YOU ARE!
YIKES!! I'M FINISHED!
SCRIPT: HAL LIFSON
ART & COLORING: REX LINDSEY

Originally presented in WORLD OF ARCHIE #22, March, 1996

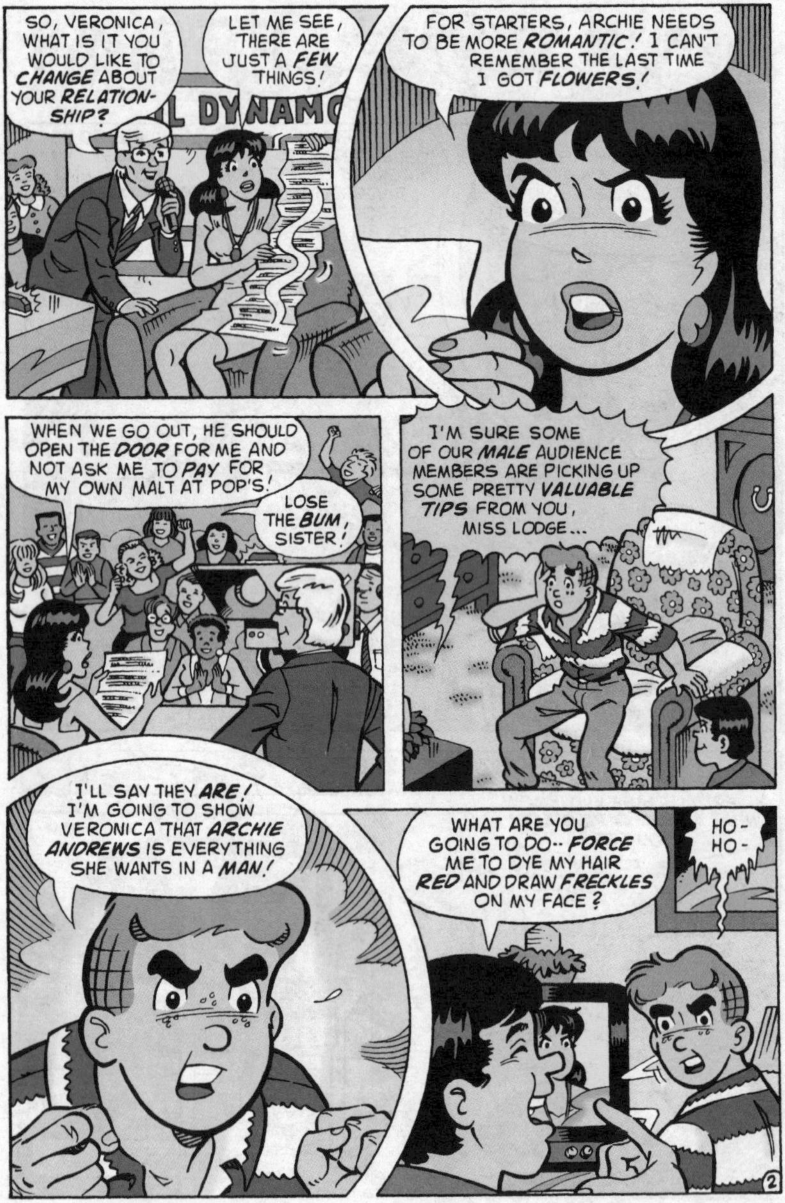
SO, VERONICA, WHAT IS IT YOU WOULD LIKE TO CHANGE ABOUT YOUR RELATION-SHIP?
LET ME SEE, THERE ARE JUST A FEW THINGS!
FOR STARTERS, ARCHIE NEEDS TO BE MORE ROMANTIC! I CAN'T REMEMBER THE LAST TIME I GOT FLOWERS!
WHEN WE GO OUT, HE SHOULD OPEN THE DOOR FOR ME AND NOT ASK ME TO PAY FOR MY OWN MALT AT POP'S!
LOSE THE BUM, SISTER!
I'M SURE SOME OF OUR MALE AUDIENCE MEMBERS ARE PICKING UP SOME PRETTY VALUABLE TIPS FROM YOU, MISS LODGE...
I'LL SAY THEY ARE! I'M GOING TO SHOW VERONICA THAT ARCHIE ANDREWS IS EVERYTHING SHE WANTS IN A MAN!
WHAT ARE YOU GOING TO DO-- FORCE ME TO DYE MY HAIR RED AND DRAW FRECKLES ON MY FACE?
HO-HO-
2

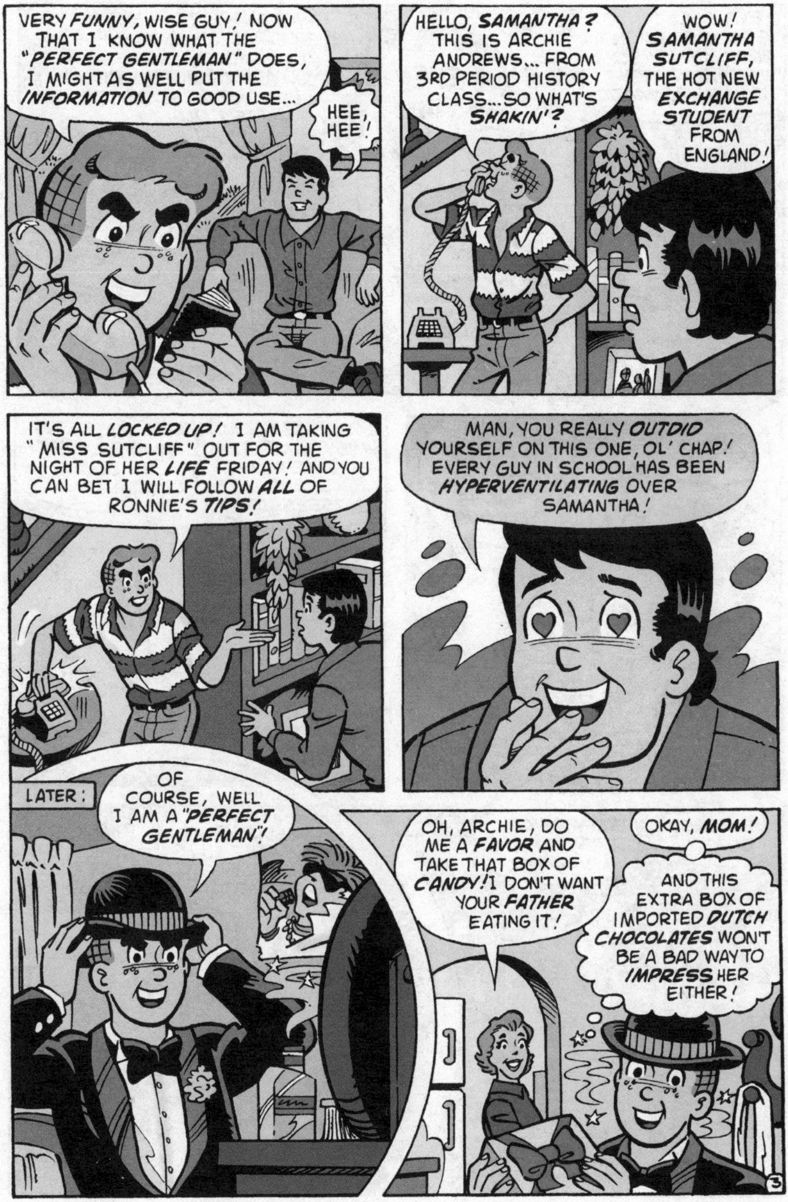
VERY FUNNY, WISE GUY! NOW THAT I KNOW WHAT THE "PERFECT GENTLEMAN" DOES, I MIGHT AS WELL PUT THE INFORMATION TO GOOD USE...
HEE, HEE!
HELLO, SAMANTHA? THIS IS ARCHIE ANDREWS... FROM 3RD PERIOD HISTORY CLASS... SO WHAT'S SHAKIN'?
WOW! SAMANTHA SUTCLIFF, THE HOT NEW EXCHANGE STUDENT FROM ENGLAND!
IT'S ALL LOCKED UP! I AM TAKING "MISS SUTCLIFF" OUT FOR THE NIGHT OF HER LIFE FRIDAY! AND YOU CAN BET I WILL FOLLOW ALL OF RONNIE'S TIPS!
MAN, YOU REALLY OUTDID YOURSELF ON THIS ONE, OL' CHAP! EVERY GUY IN SCHOOL HAS BEEN HYPERVENTILATING OVER SAMANTHA!
LATER:
OF COURSE, WELL I AM A "PERFECT GENTLEMAN"!
OH, ARCHIE, DO ME A FAVOR AND TAKE THAT BOX OF CANDY! I DON'T WANT YOUR FATHER EATING IT!
OKAY, MOM!
AND THIS EXTRA BOX OF IMPORTED DUTCH CHOCOLATES WON'T BE A BAD WAY TO IMPRESS HER EITHER!
3

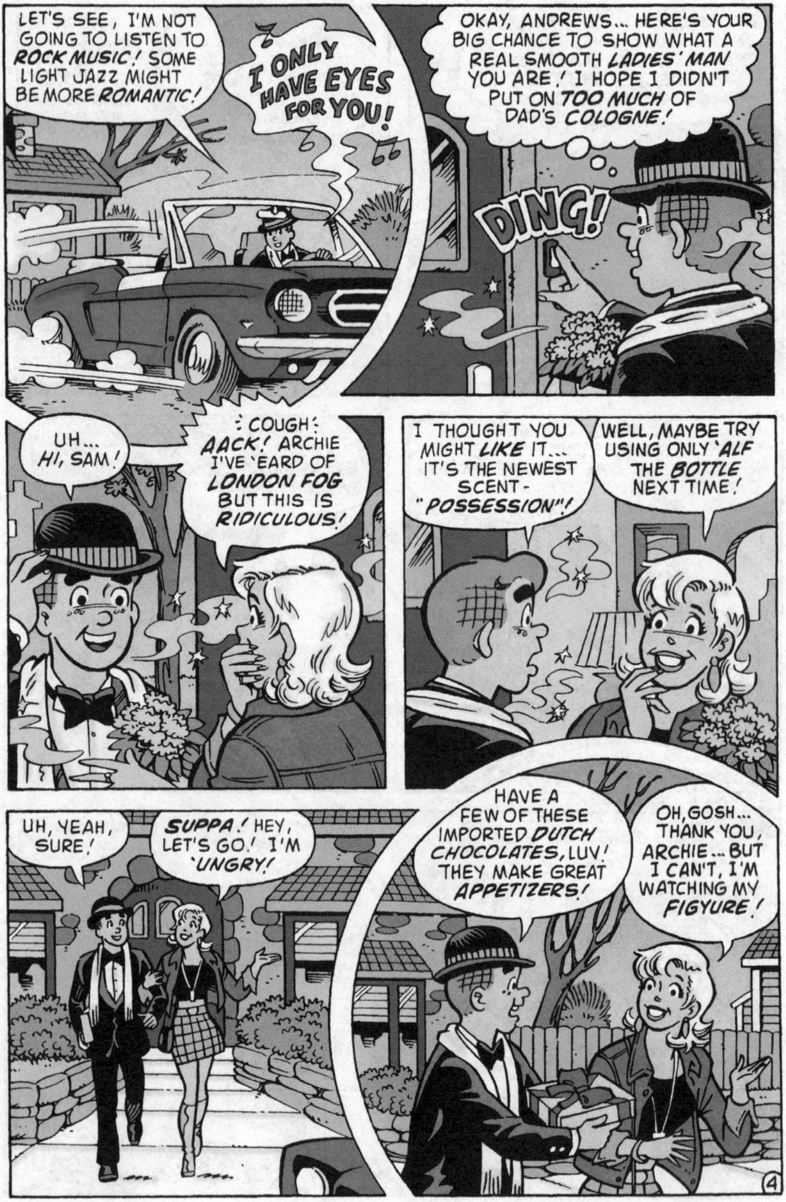

LET'S SEE, I'M NOT GOING TO LISTEN TO ROCK MUSIC! SOME LIGHT JAZZ MIGHT BE MORE ROMANTIC!
I ONLY HAVE EYES FOR YOU!
OKAY, ANDREWS... HERE'S YOUR BIG CHANCE TO SHOW WHAT A REAL SMOOTH LADIES' MAN YOU ARE! I HOPE I DIDN'T PUT ON TOO MUCH OF DAD'S COLOGNE!
DING!
UH... HI, SAM!
COUGH AACK! ARCHIE I'VE 'EARD OF LONDON FOG BUT THIS IS RIDICULOUS!
I THOUGHT YOU MIGHT LIKE IT... IT'S THE NEWEST SCENT - "POSSESSION"!
WELL, MAYBE TRY USING ONLY 'ALF THE BOTTLE NEXT TIME!
UH, YEAH, SURE!
SUPPA! HEY, LET'S GO! I'M 'UNGRY!
HAVE A FEW OF THESE IMPORTED DUTCH CHOCOLATES, LUV! THEY MAKE GREAT APPETIZERS!
OH, GOSH... THANK YOU, ARCHIE... BUT I CAN'T, I'M WATCHING MY FIGYURE!
4

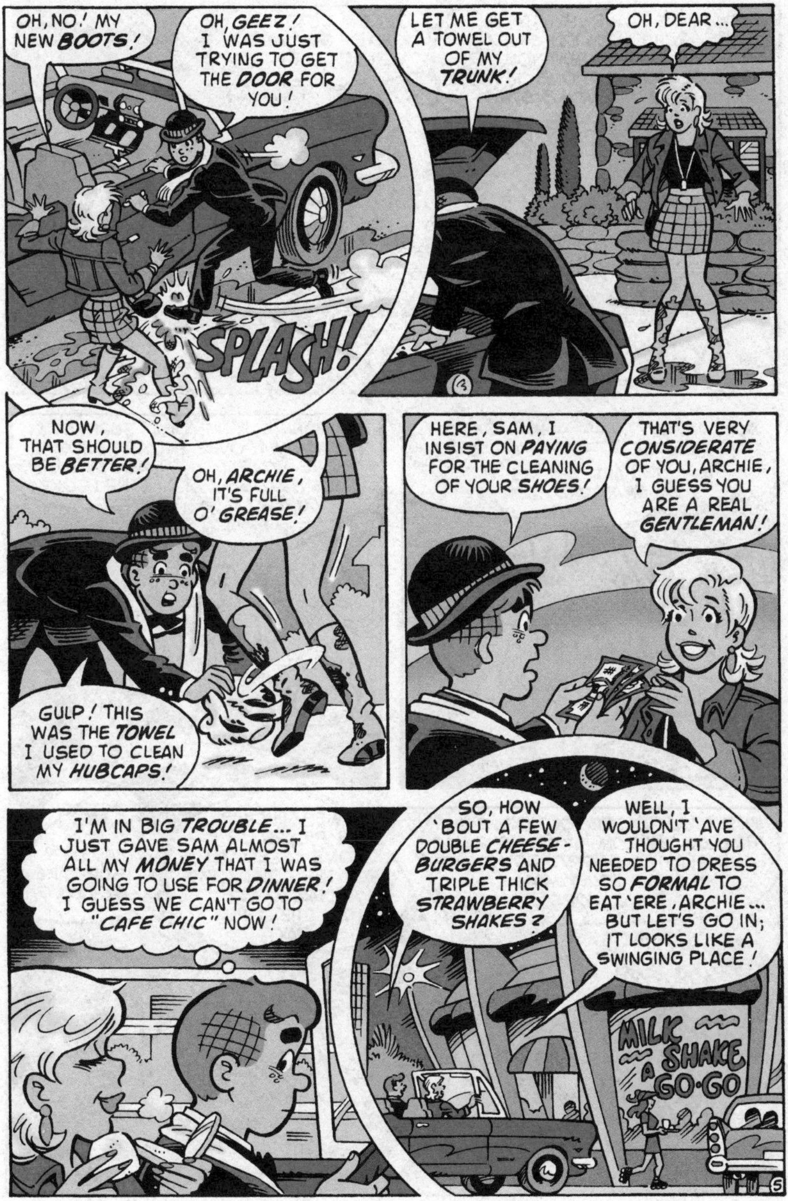
OH, NO! MY NEW BOOTS!
OH, GEEZ! I WAS JUST TRYING TO GET THE DOOR FOR YOU!
SPLASH!
LET ME GET A TOWEL OUT OF MY TRUNK!
OH, DEAR...
NOW, THAT SHOULD BE BETTER!
OH, ARCHIE, IT'S FULL O' GREASE!
GULP! THIS WAS THE TOWEL I USED TO CLEAN MY HUBCAPS!
HERE, SAM, I INSIST ON PAYING FOR THE CLEANING OF YOUR SHOES!
THAT'S VERY CONSIDERATE OF YOU, ARCHIE, I GUESS YOU ARE A REAL GENTLEMAN!
I'M IN BIG TROUBLE... I JUST GAVE SAM ALMOST ALL MY MONEY THAT I WAS GOING TO USE FOR DINNER! I GUESS WE CAN'T GO TO "CAFE CHIC" NOW!
SO, HOW 'BOUT A FEW DOUBLE CHEESE-BURGERS AND TRIPLE THICK STRAWBERRY SHAKES?
WELL, I WOULDN'T 'AVE THOUGHT YOU NEEDED TO DRESS SO FORMAL TO EAT 'ERE, ARCHIE... BUT LET'S GO IN; IT LOOKS LIKE A SWINGING PLACE!
MILK SHAKE A GO-GO
5

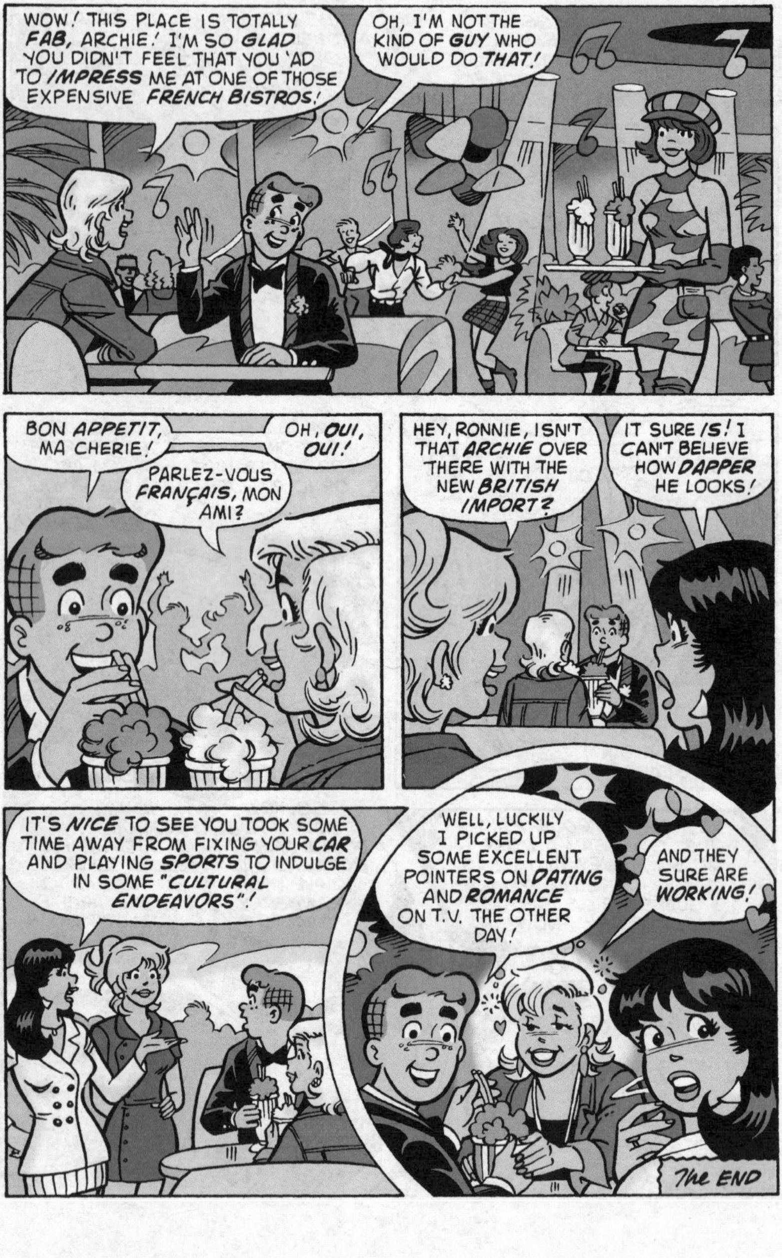
WOW! THIS PLACE IS TOTALLY FAB, ARCHIE! I'M SO GLAD YOU DIDN'T FEEL THAT YOU 'AD TO IMPRESS ME AT ONE OF THOSE EXPENSIVE FRENCH BISTROS!
OH, I'M NOT THE KIND OF GUY WHO WOULD DO THAT!
BON APPETIT, MA CHERIE!
OH, OUI, OUI!
PARLEZ-VOUS FRANÇAIS, MON AMI?
HEY, RONNIE, ISN'T THAT ARCHIE OVER THERE WITH THE NEW BRITISH IMPORT?
IT SURE IS! I CAN'T BELIEVE HOW DAPPER HE LOOKS!
IT'S NICE TO SEE YOU TOOK SOME TIME AWAY FROM FIXING YOUR CAR AND PLAYING SPORTS TO INDULGE IN SOME "CULTURAL ENDEAVORS"!
WELL, LUCKILY I PICKED UP SOME EXCELLENT POINTERS ON DATING AND ROMANCE ON T.V. THE OTHER DAY!
AND THEY SURE ARE WORKING!
The END

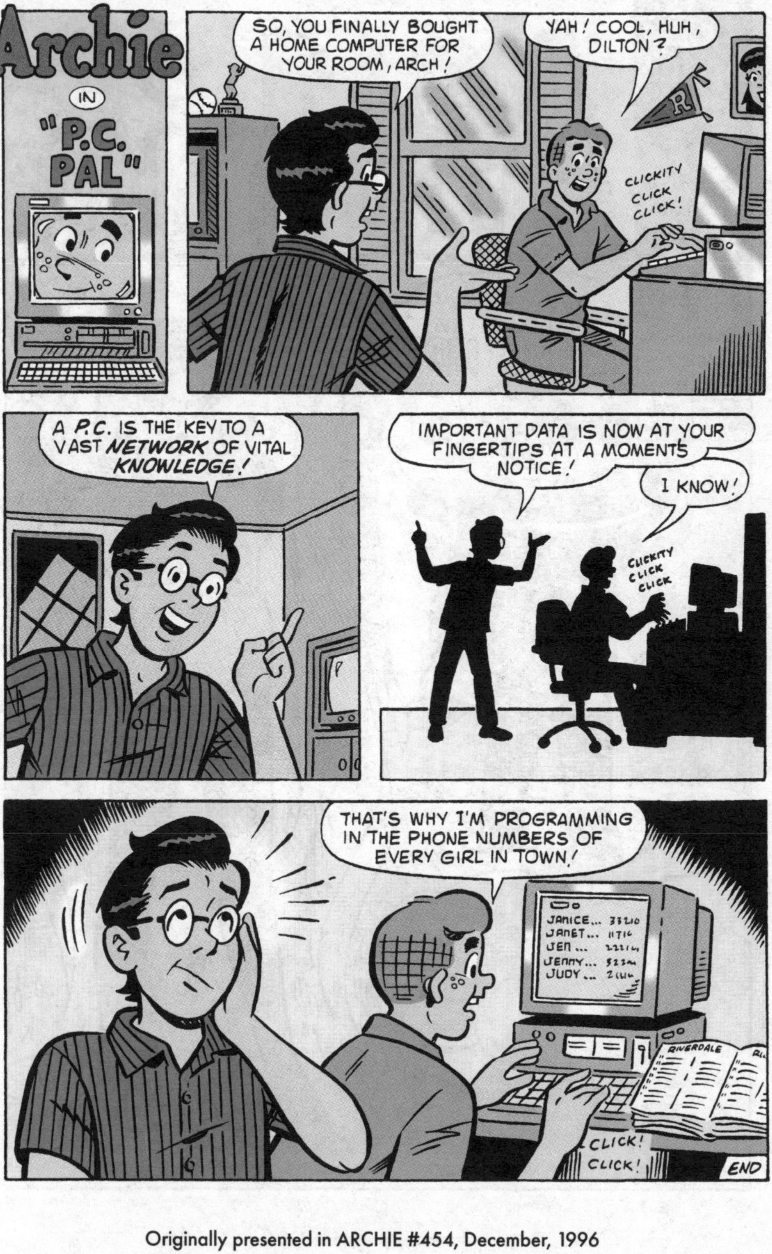
Archie
IN
"P.C. PAL"
SO, YOU FINALLY BOUGHT A HOME COMPUTER FOR YOUR ROOM, ARCH!
YAH! COOL, HUH, DILTON?
CLICKITY CLICK CLICK!
A P.C. IS THE KEY TO A VAST NETWORK OF VITAL KNOWLEDGE!
IMPORTANT DATA IS NOW AT YOUR FINGERTIPS AT A MOMENT'S NOTICE!
I KNOW!
CLICKITY CLICK CLICK
THAT'S WHY I'M PROGRAMMING IN THE PHONE NUMBERS OF EVERY GIRL IN TOWN!
JANICE...
JANET...
JEN...
JENNY...
JUDY...
RIVERDALE
CLICK!
CLICK!
END

Originally presented in ARCHIE #454, December, 1996

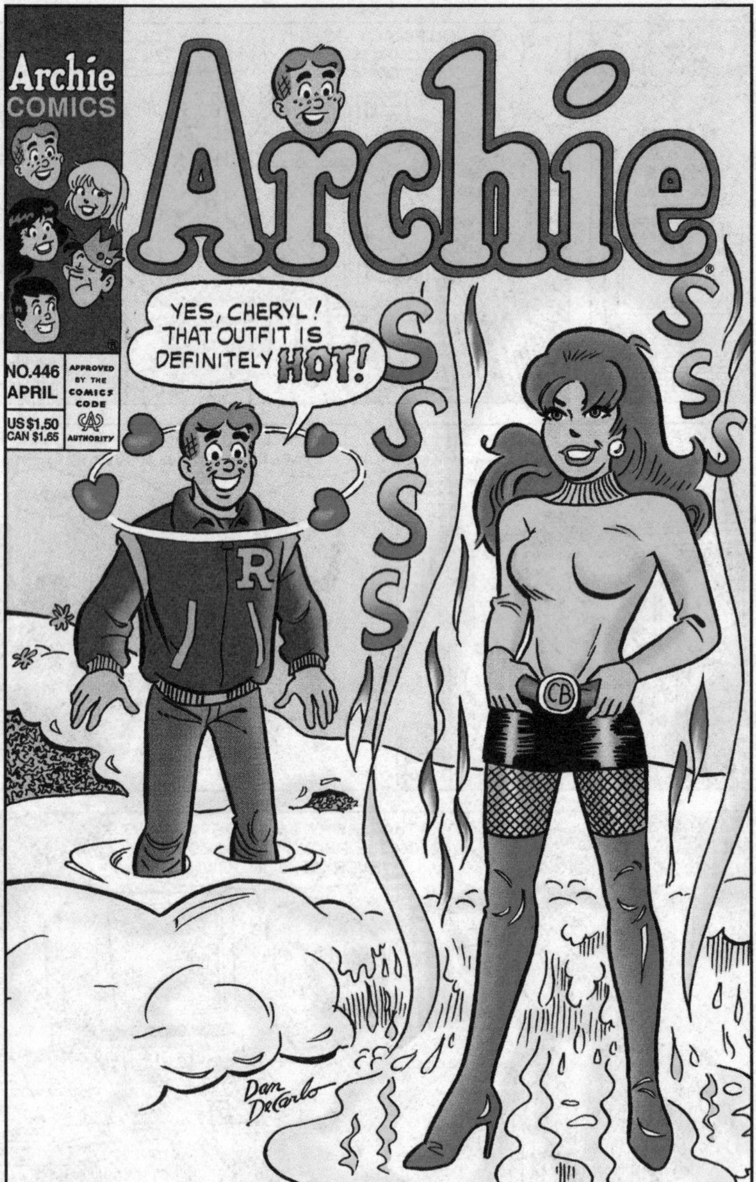
Archie COMICS
Archie
NO.446
APRIL
APPROVED BY THE COMICS CODE AUTHORITY
US $1.50
CAN $1.65
YES, CHERYL! THAT OUTFIT IS DEFINITELY HOT!
S S S S S
S S S S
CB
Dan DeCarlo

Originally printed in 1996

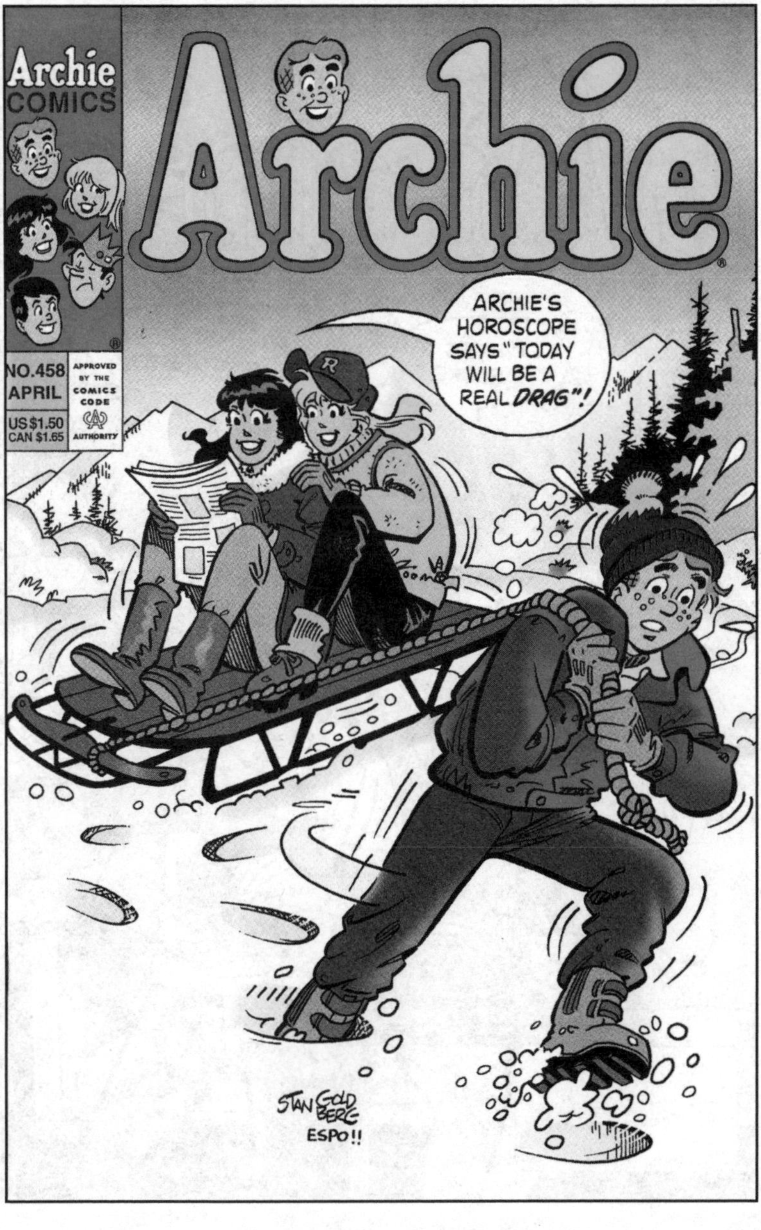
Archie COMICS
Archie
NO.458 APRIL
US $1.50 CAN $1.65
APPROVED BY THE COMICS CODE AUTHORITY
ARCHIE'S HOROSCOPE SAYS "TODAY WILL BE A REAL DRAG"!
STAN GOLDBERG
ESPO!!

Originally printed in 1997

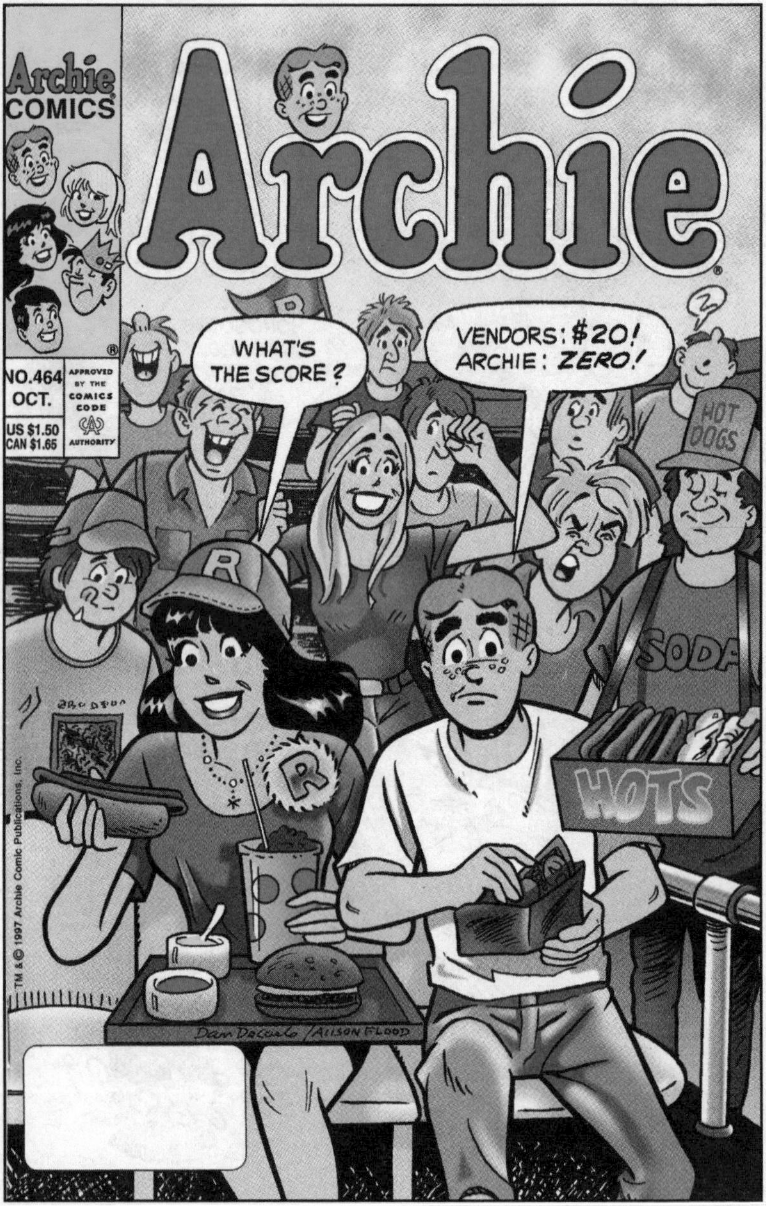
Archie COMICS
Archie
NO.464 OCT.
US $1.50 CAN $1.65
APPROVED BY THE COMICS CODE AUTHORITY
WHAT'S THE SCORE ?
VENDORS: $20! ARCHIE: ZERO!
HOT DOGS
SODA
HOTS
TM & © 1997 Archie Comic Publications, Inc.

Originally printed in 1997

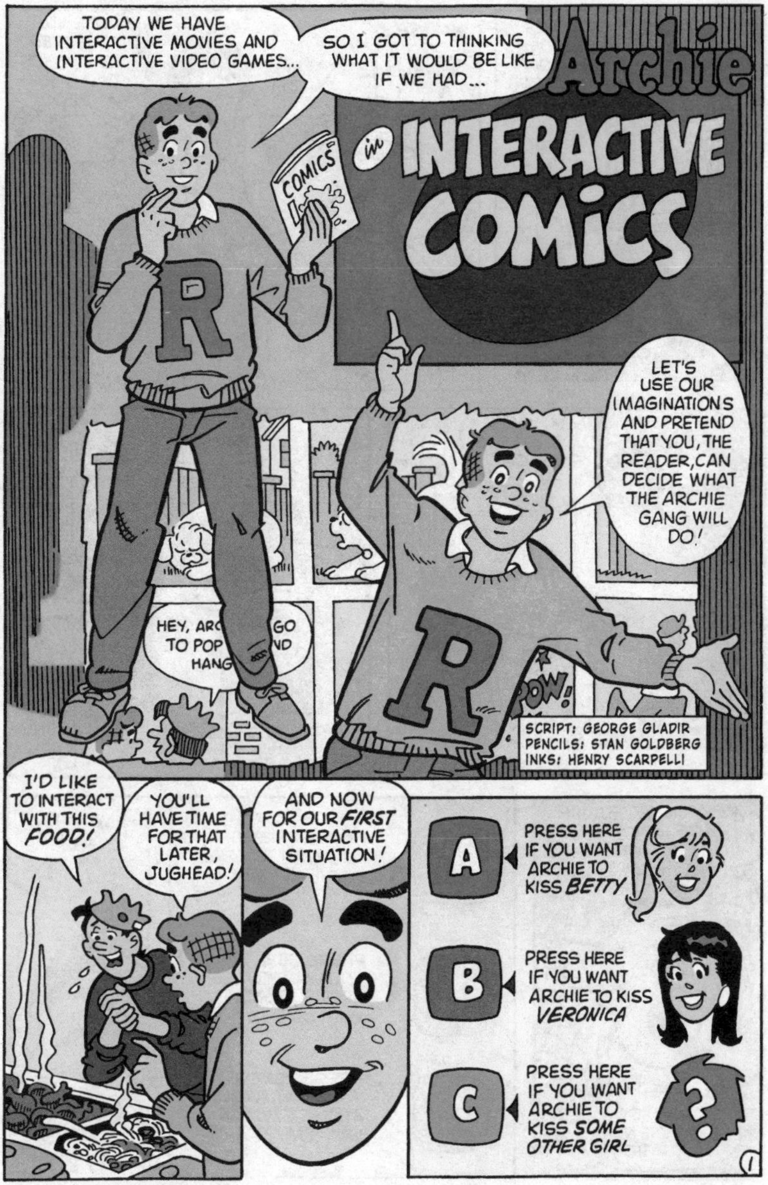
TODAY WE HAVE INTERACTIVE MOVIES AND INTERACTIVE VIDEO GAMES...
SO I GOT TO THINKING WHAT IT WOULD BE LIKE IF WE HAD...
Archie in INTERACTIVE COMICS
COMICS
LET'S USE OUR IMAGINATIONS AND PRETEND THAT YOU, THE READER, CAN DECIDE WHAT THE ARCHIE GANG WILL DO!
SCRIPT: GEORGE GLADIR
PENCILS: STAN GOLDBERG
INKS: HENRY SCARPELLI
I'D LIKE TO INTERACT WITH THIS FOOD!
YOU'LL HAVE TIME FOR THAT LATER, JUGHEAD!
AND NOW FOR OUR FIRST INTERACTIVE SITUATION!
A
PRESS HERE IF YOU WANT ARCHIE TO KISS BETTY
B
PRESS HERE IF YOU WANT ARCHIE TO KISS VERONICA
C
PRESS HERE IF YOU WANT ARCHIE TO KISS SOME OTHER GIRL
1

Originally presented in ARCHIE #457, March, 1997

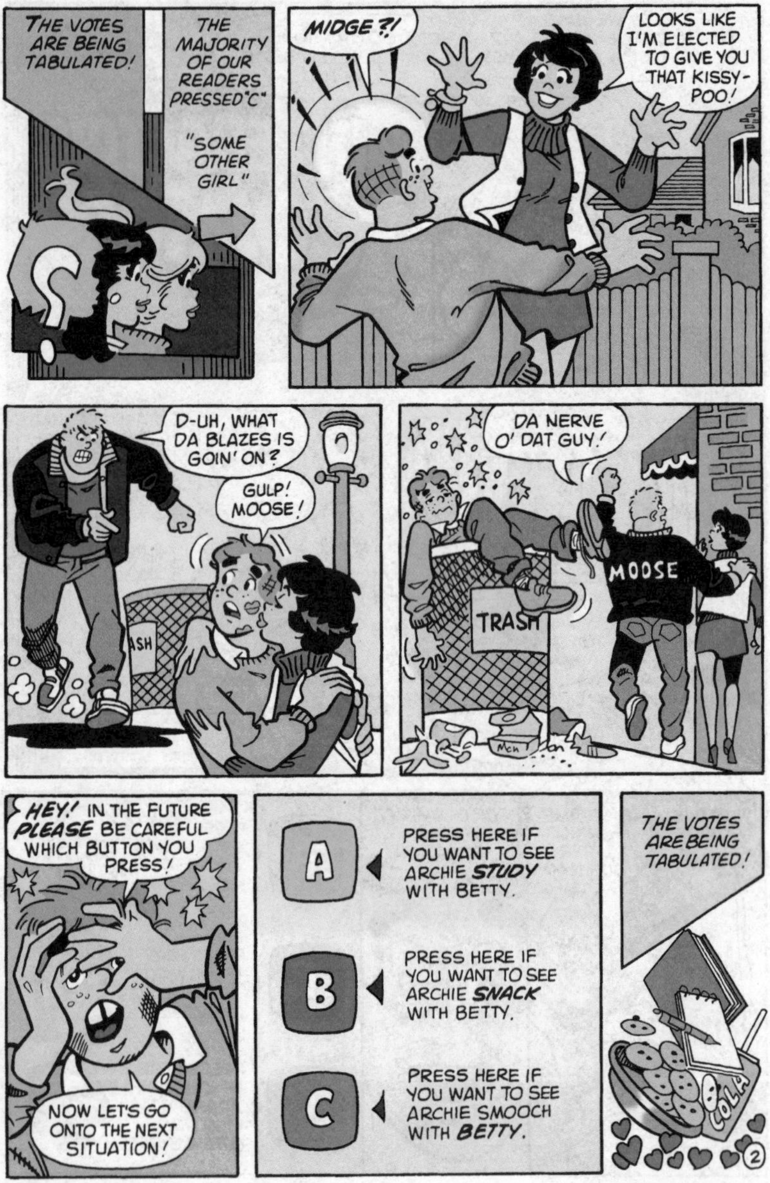
THE VOTES ARE BEING TABULATED!
THE MAJORITY OF OUR READERS PRESSED "C"
"SOME OTHER GIRL"
MIDGE ?!
LOOKS LIKE I'M ELECTED TO GIVE YOU THAT KISSY-POO!
D-UH, WHAT DA BLAZES IS GOIN' ON?
GULP! MOOSE!
TRASH
DA NERVE O' DAT GUY!
MOOSE
TRASH
HEY! IN THE FUTURE PLEASE BE CAREFUL WHICH BUTTON YOU PRESS!
NOW LET'S GO ONTO THE NEXT SITUATION!
A
PRESS HERE IF YOU WANT TO SEE ARCHIE STUDY WITH BETTY.
B
PRESS HERE IF YOU WANT TO SEE ARCHIE SNACK WITH BETTY.
C
PRESS HERE IF YOU WANT TO SEE ARCHIE SMOOCH WITH BETTY.
THE VOTES ARE BEING TABULATED!
COLA
2

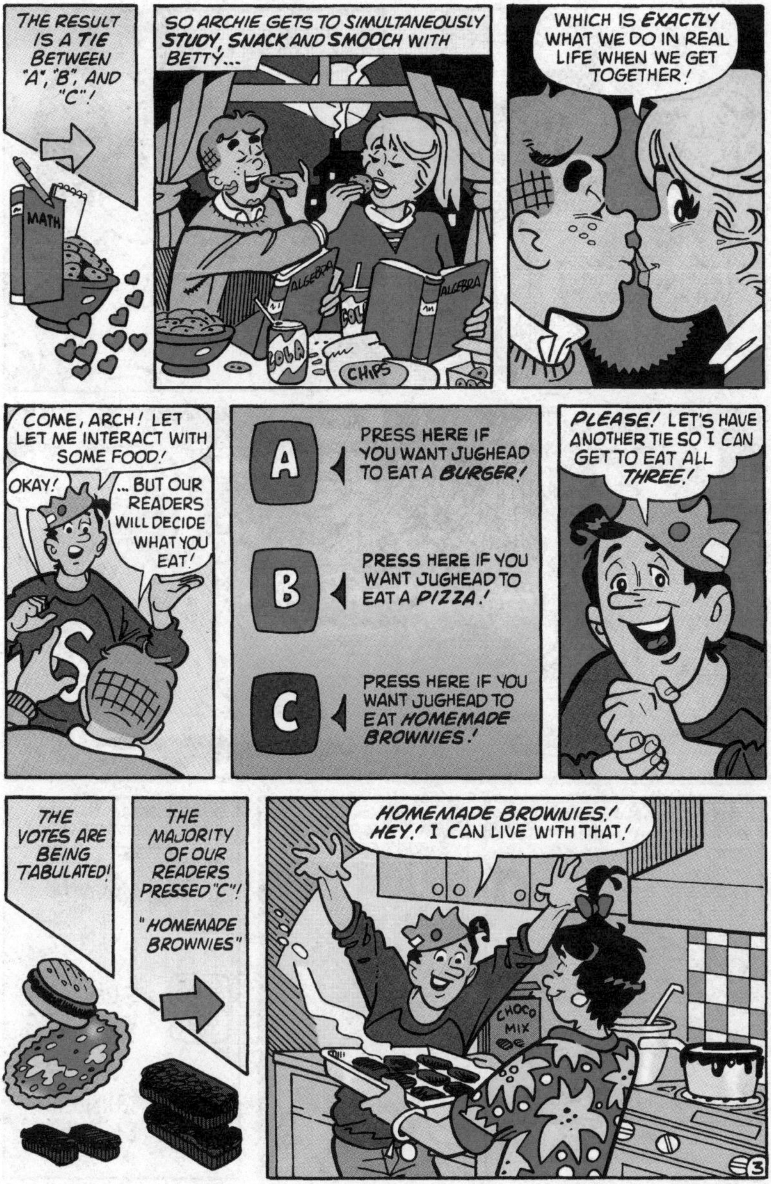
THE RESULT IS A TIE BETWEEN "A", "B", AND "C"!
MATH
SO ARCHIE GETS TO SIMULTANEOUSLY STUDY, SNACK AND SMOOCH WITH BETTY...
ALGEBRA
ALGEBRA
COLA
CHIPS
WHICH IS EXACTLY WHAT WE DO IN REAL LIFE WHEN WE GET TOGETHER!
COME, ARCH! LET LET ME INTERACT WITH SOME FOOD!
OKAY!
... BUT OUR READERS WILL DECIDE WHAT YOU EAT!
A
PRESS HERE IF YOU WANT JUGHEAD TO EAT A BURGER!
B
PRESS HERE IF YOU WANT JUGHEAD TO EAT A PIZZA!
C
PRESS HERE IF YOU WANT JUGHEAD TO EAT HOMEMADE BROWNIES!
PLEASE! LET'S HAVE ANOTHER TIE SO I CAN GET TO EAT ALL THREE!
THE VOTES ARE BEING TABULATED!
THE MAJORITY OF OUR READERS PRESSED "C"!
"HOMEMADE BROWNIES"
HOMEMADE BROWNIES! HEY! I CAN LIVE WITH THAT!
CHOCO MIX
3

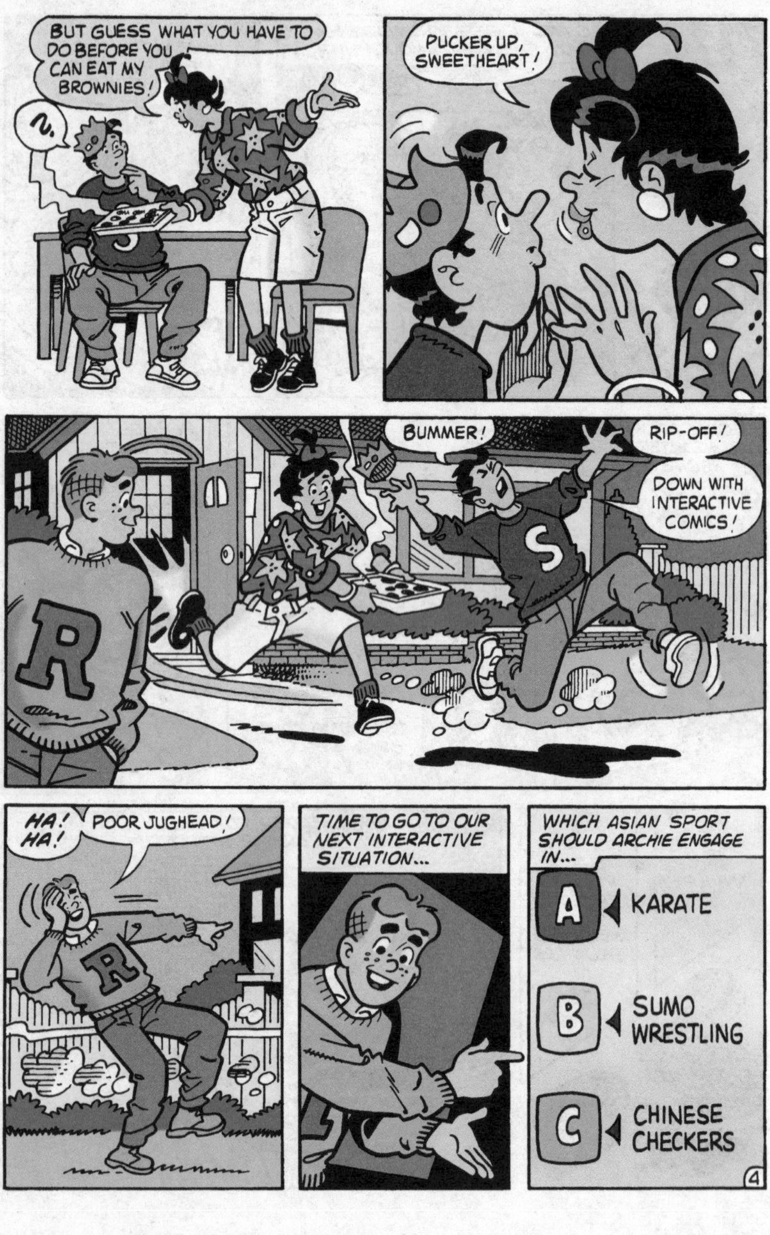
BUT GUESS WHAT YOU HAVE TO DO BEFORE YOU CAN EAT MY BROWNIES!
?
PUCKER UP, SWEETHEART!
BUMMER!
RIP-OFF!
DOWN WITH INTERACTIVE COMICS!
HA! HA!
POOR JUGHEAD!
TIME TO GO TO OUR NEXT INTERACTIVE SITUATION...
WHICH ASIAN SPORT SHOULD ARCHIE ENGAGE IN...
A KARATE
B SUMO WRESTLING
C CHINESE CHECKERS
4

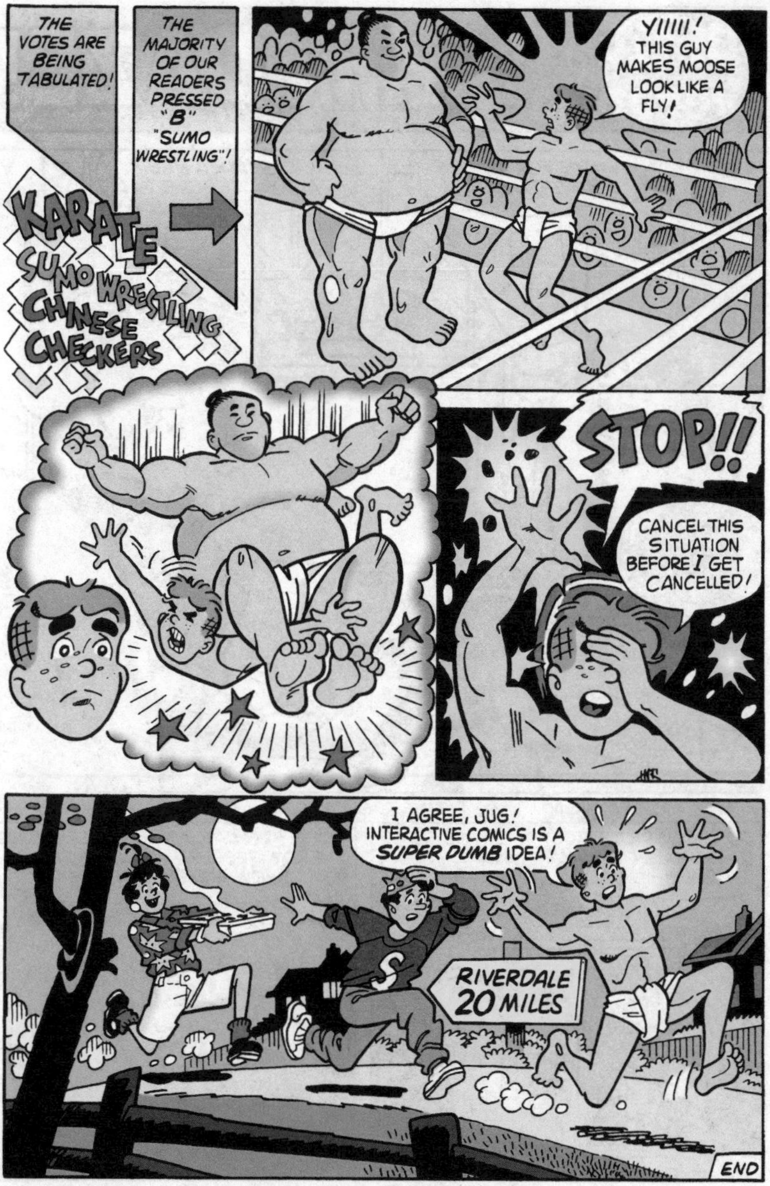
THE VOTES ARE BEING TABULATED!
THE MAJORITY OF OUR READERS PRESSED "B" "SUMO WRESTLING"!
KARATE
SUMO WRESTLING
CHINESE CHECKERS
YIIIII! THIS GUY MAKES MOOSE LOOK LIKE A FLY!
STOP!!
CANCEL THIS SITUATION BEFORE I GET CANCELLED!
I AGREE, JUG! INTERACTIVE COMICS IS A SUPER DUMB IDEA!
RIVERDALE 20 MILES
END

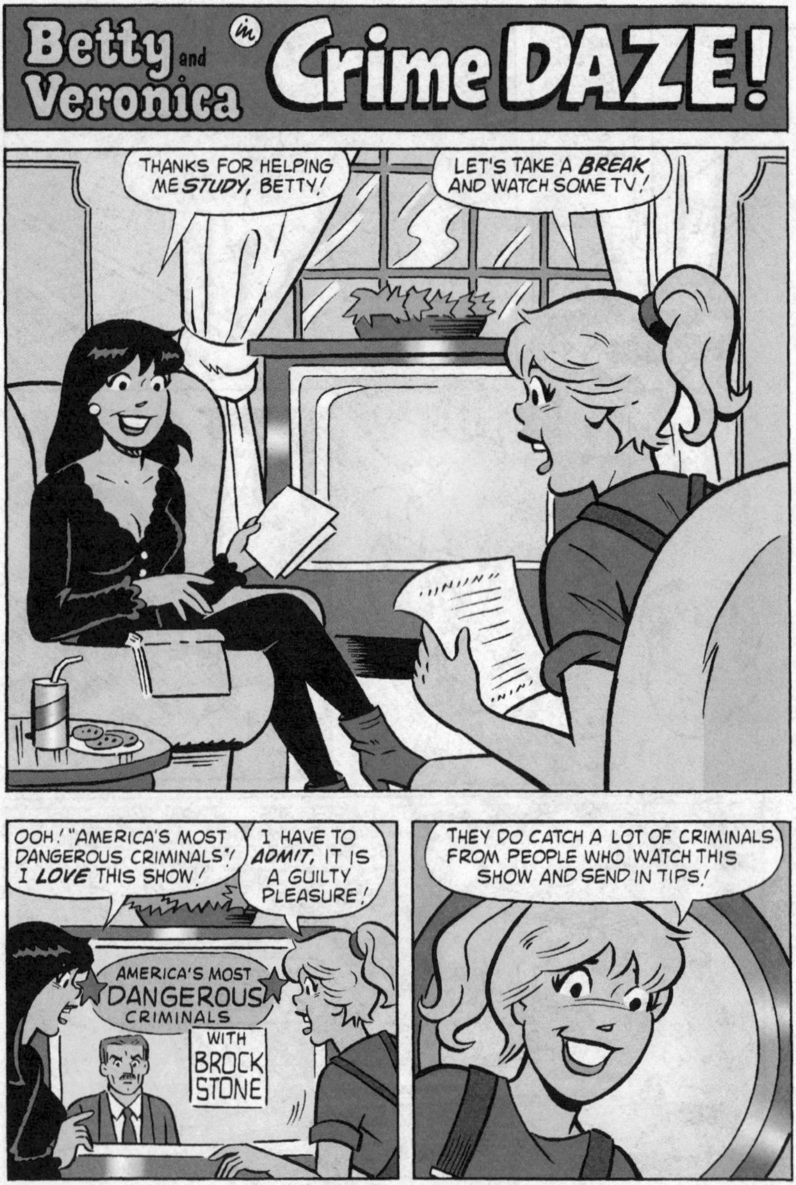
Betty and Veronica in Crime DAZE!
THANKS FOR HELPING ME STUDY, BETTY!
LET'S TAKE A BREAK AND WATCH SOME TV!
OOH! "AMERICA'S MOST DANGEROUS CRIMINALS"! I LOVE THIS SHOW!
I HAVE TO ADMIT, IT IS A GUILTY PLEASURE!
AMERICA'S MOST DANGEROUS CRIMINALS
WITH BROCK STONE
THEY DO CATCH A LOT OF CRIMINALS FROM PEOPLE WHO WATCH THIS SHOW AND SEND IN TIPS!

Originally presented in BETTY & VERONICA SPECTACULAR #24, July, 1997

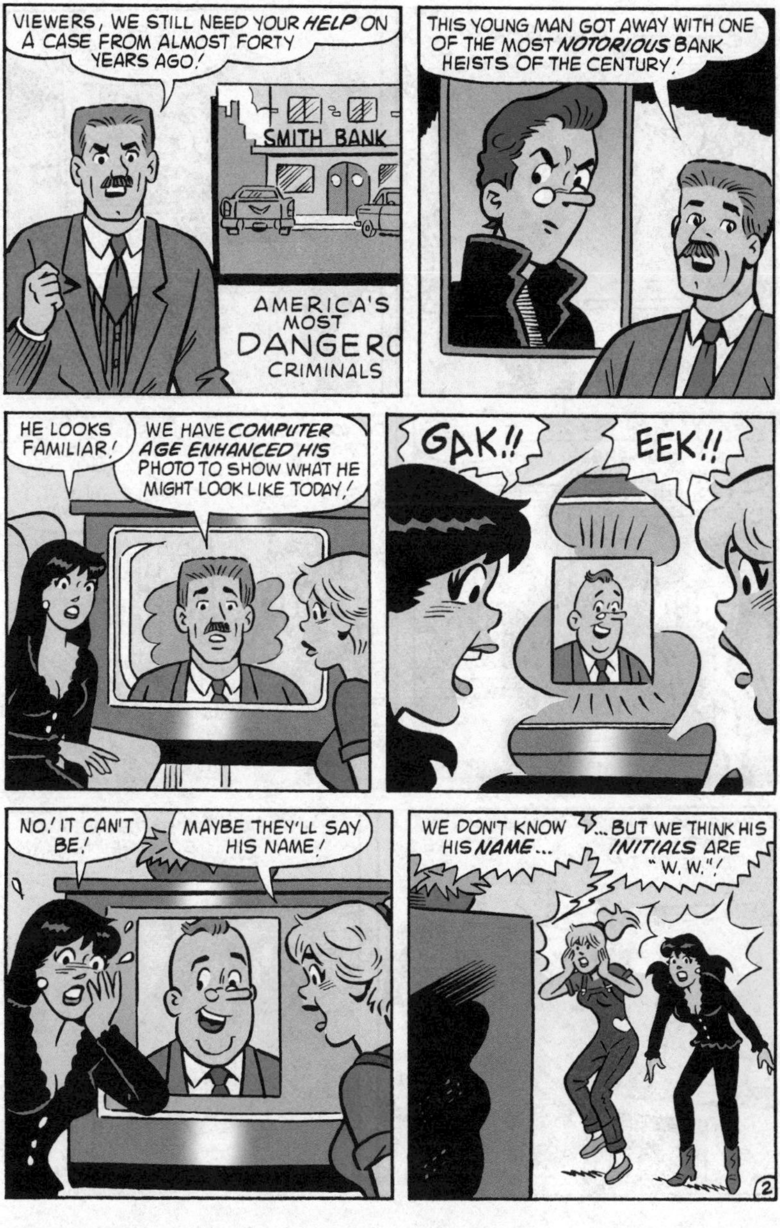
VIEWERS, WE STILL NEED YOUR HELP ON A CASE FROM ALMOST FORTY YEARS AGO!
SMITH BANK
AMERICA'S MOST DANGERO CRIMINALS
THIS YOUNG MAN GOT AWAY WITH ONE OF THE MOST NOTORIOUS BANK HEISTS OF THE CENTURY!
HE LOOKS FAMILIAR!
WE HAVE COMPUTER AGE ENHANCED HIS PHOTO TO SHOW WHAT HE MIGHT LOOK LIKE TODAY!
GAK!!
EEK!!
NO! IT CAN'T BE!
MAYBE THEY'LL SAY HIS NAME!
WE DON'T KNOW HIS NAME...
...BUT WE THINK HIS INITIALS ARE "W. W."!
2

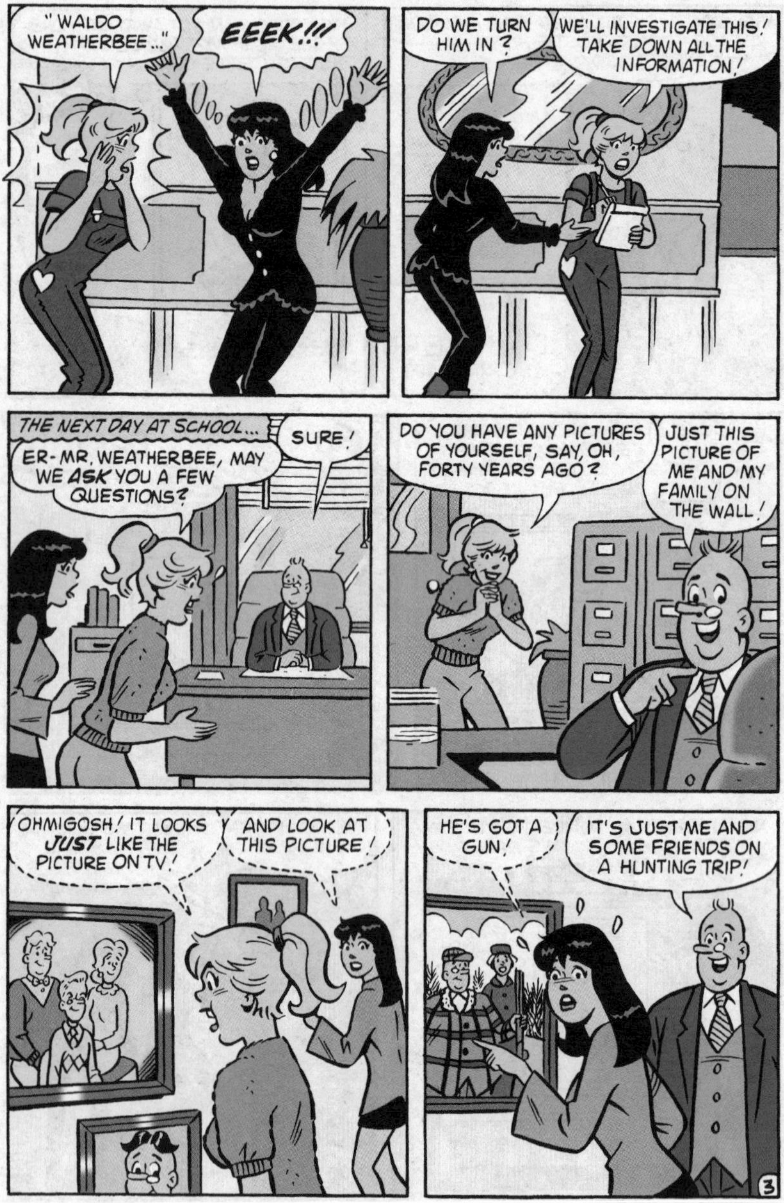
"WALDO WEATHERBEE..."
EEEK!!!
DO WE TURN HIM IN?
WE'LL INVESTIGATE THIS! TAKE DOWN ALL THE INFORMATION!
THE NEXT DAY AT SCHOOL...
ER- MR. WEATHERBEE, MAY WE ASK YOU A FEW QUESTIONS?
SURE!
DO YOU HAVE ANY PICTURES OF YOURSELF, SAY, OH, FORTY YEARS AGO?
JUST THIS PICTURE OF ME AND MY FAMILY ON THE WALL!
OHMIGOSH! IT LOOKS JUST LIKE THE PICTURE ON TV!
AND LOOK AT THIS PICTURE!
HE'S GOT A GUN!
IT'S JUST ME AND SOME FRIENDS ON A HUNTING TRIP!
3

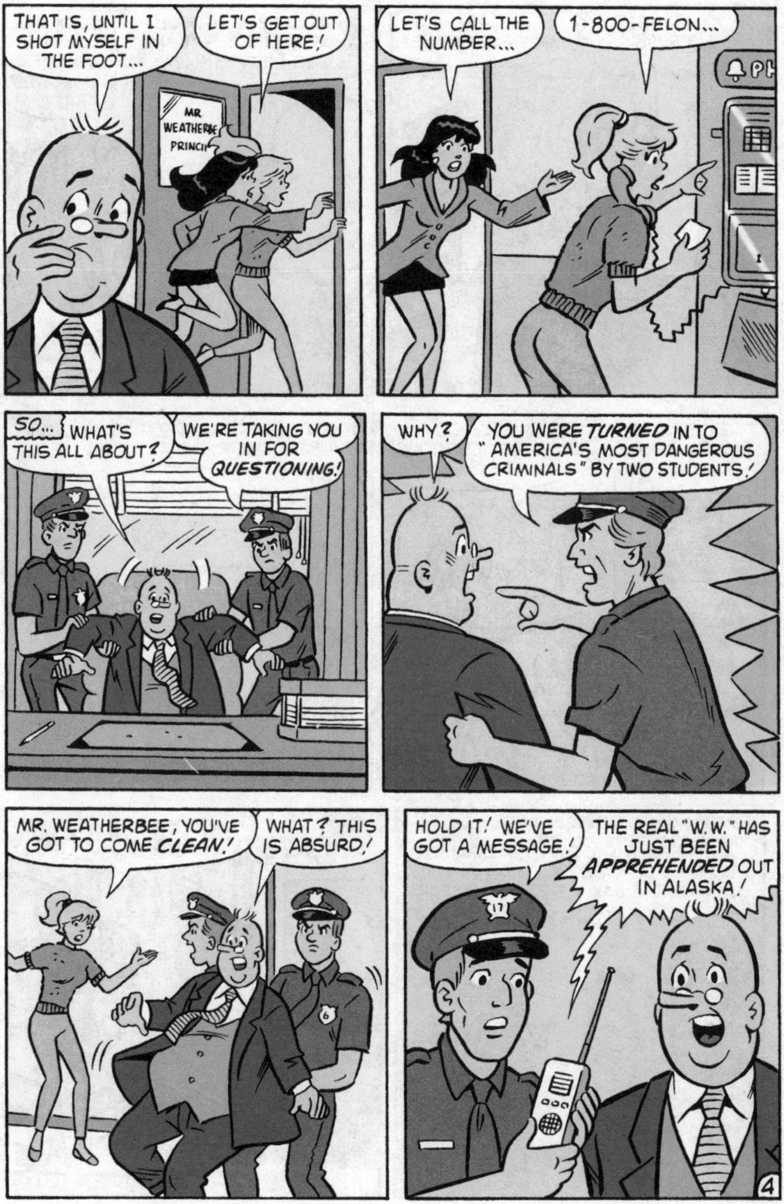
THAT IS, UNTIL I SHOT MYSELF IN THE FOOT...
LET'S GET OUT OF HERE!
MR. WEATHERBE PRINCI
LET'S CALL THE NUMBER...
1-800-FELON...
SO... WHAT'S THIS ALL ABOUT?
WE'RE TAKING YOU IN FOR QUESTIONING!
WHY?
YOU WERE TURNED IN TO "AMERICA'S MOST DANGEROUS CRIMINALS" BY TWO STUDENTS!
MR. WEATHERBEE, YOU'VE GOT TO COME CLEAN!
WHAT? THIS IS ABSURD!
HOLD IT! WE'VE GOT A MESSAGE!
THE REAL "W.W." HAS JUST BEEN APPREHENDED OUT IN ALASKA!
4

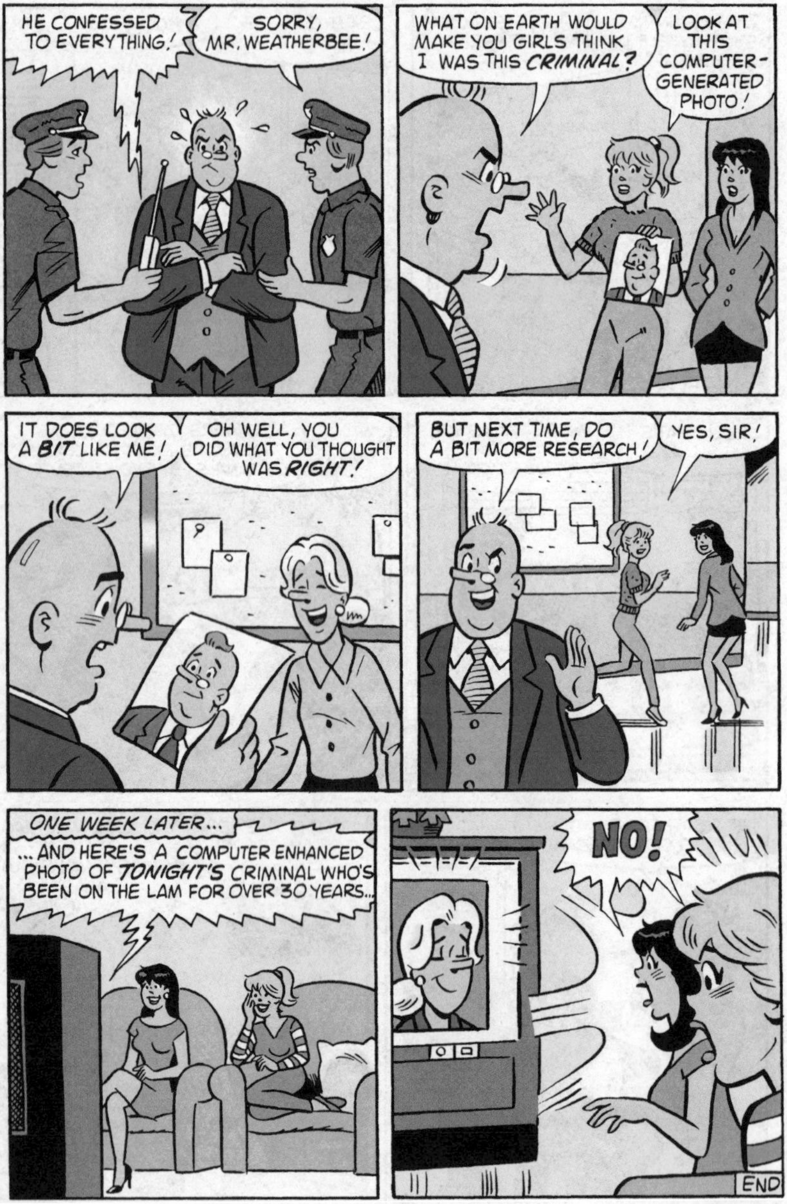
HE CONFESSED TO EVERYTHING!
SORRY, MR. WEATHERBEE!
WHAT ON EARTH WOULD MAKE YOU GIRLS THINK I WAS THIS CRIMINAL?
LOOK AT THIS COMPUTER-GENERATED PHOTO!
IT DOES LOOK A BIT LIKE ME!
OH WELL, YOU DID WHAT YOU THOUGHT WAS RIGHT!
BUT NEXT TIME, DO A BIT MORE RESEARCH!
YES, SIR!
ONE WEEK LATER...
...AND HERE'S A COMPUTER ENHANCED PHOTO OF TONIGHT'S CRIMINAL WHO'S BEEN ON THE LAM FOR OVER 30 YEARS...
NO!
END

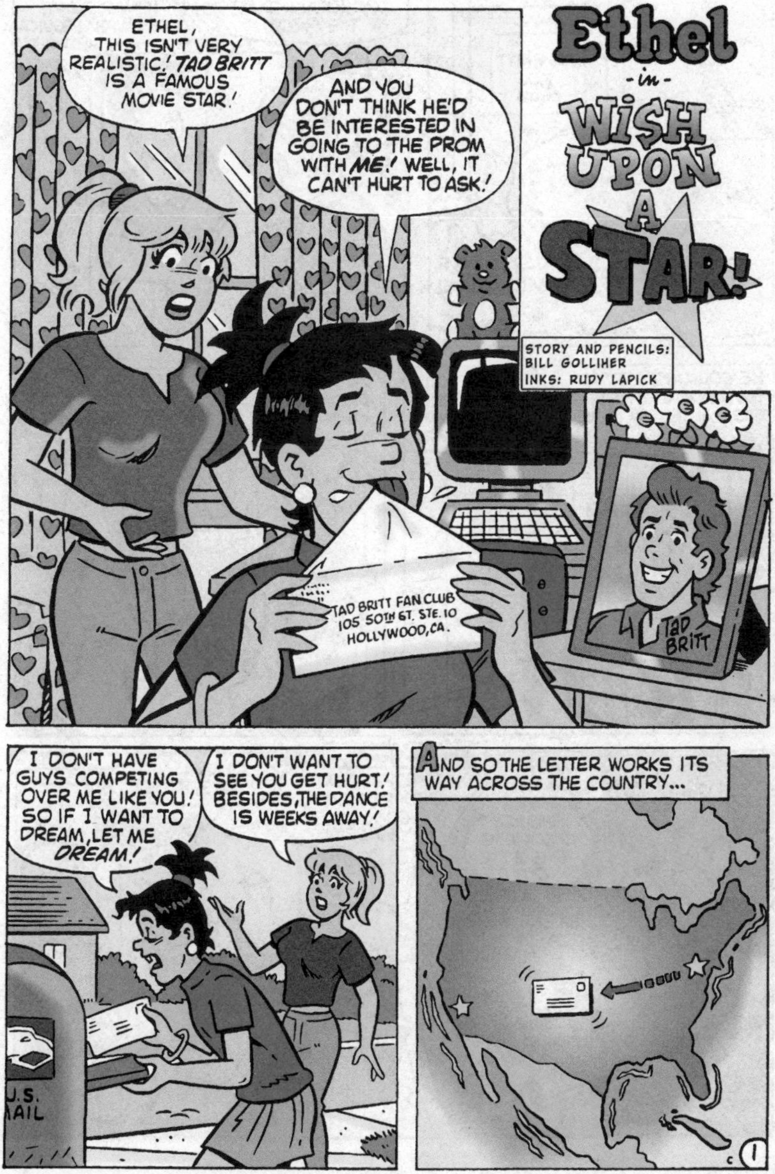

ETHEL, THIS ISN'T VERY REALISTIC! TAD BRITT IS A FAMOUS MOVIE STAR!
AND YOU DON'T THINK HE'D BE INTERESTED IN GOING TO THE PROM WITH ME! WELL, IT CAN'T HURT TO ASK!
Ethel -in- WISH UPON A STAR!
STORY AND PENCILS: BILL GOLLIHER
INKS: RUDY LAPICK
TAD BRITT FAN CLUB 105 50TH ST. STE.10 HOLLYWOOD, CA.
TAD BRITT
I DON'T HAVE GUYS COMPETING OVER ME LIKE YOU! SO IF I WANT TO DREAM, LET ME DREAM!
I DON'T WANT TO SEE YOU GET HURT! BESIDES, THE DANCE IS WEEKS AWAY!
U.S. MAIL
AND SO THE LETTER WORKS ITS WAY ACROSS THE COUNTRY...
1


Originally presented in ARCHIE & FRIENDS #24, August, 1997

UNTIL...
TAD BRITT FAN CLUB
U.S. MAIL
U.S. MAIL
U.S. MAIL
U.S. MAIL
U.S. MAIL
ETHEL, DID YOU HEAR? ARCHIE ASKED ME TO THE PROM!
THAT'S GREAT!! HOW DID THAT HAPPEN WITH VERONICA AROUND?!
HE COULDN'T AFFORD THE DESIGNER TUXEDO SHE WANTED HIM TO WEAR, SO SHE'S GOING WITH REGGIE!
MAYBE YOU SHOULD SEND HER A THANK YOU CARD!
ANY NEWS FROM YOU KNOW WHO?
NO! YOU WERE RIGHT! IT WAS A LONG SHOT!
?
TAD?! WHO'S THAT? MAYBE I SHOULD CHECK THIS DISKETTE OUT!
ETHEL + TAD
THE NEXT DAY...
ETHEL, YOU DROPPED THIS BY YOUR LOCKER YESTERDAY!
OH... UH... THANKS, REGGIE!
2

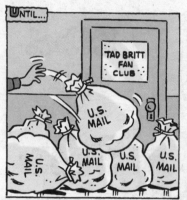

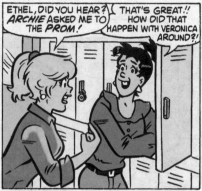

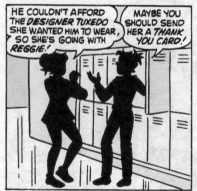

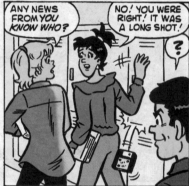

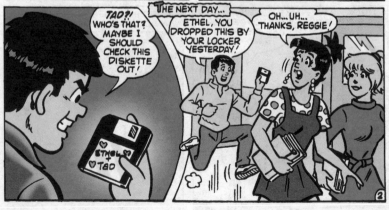

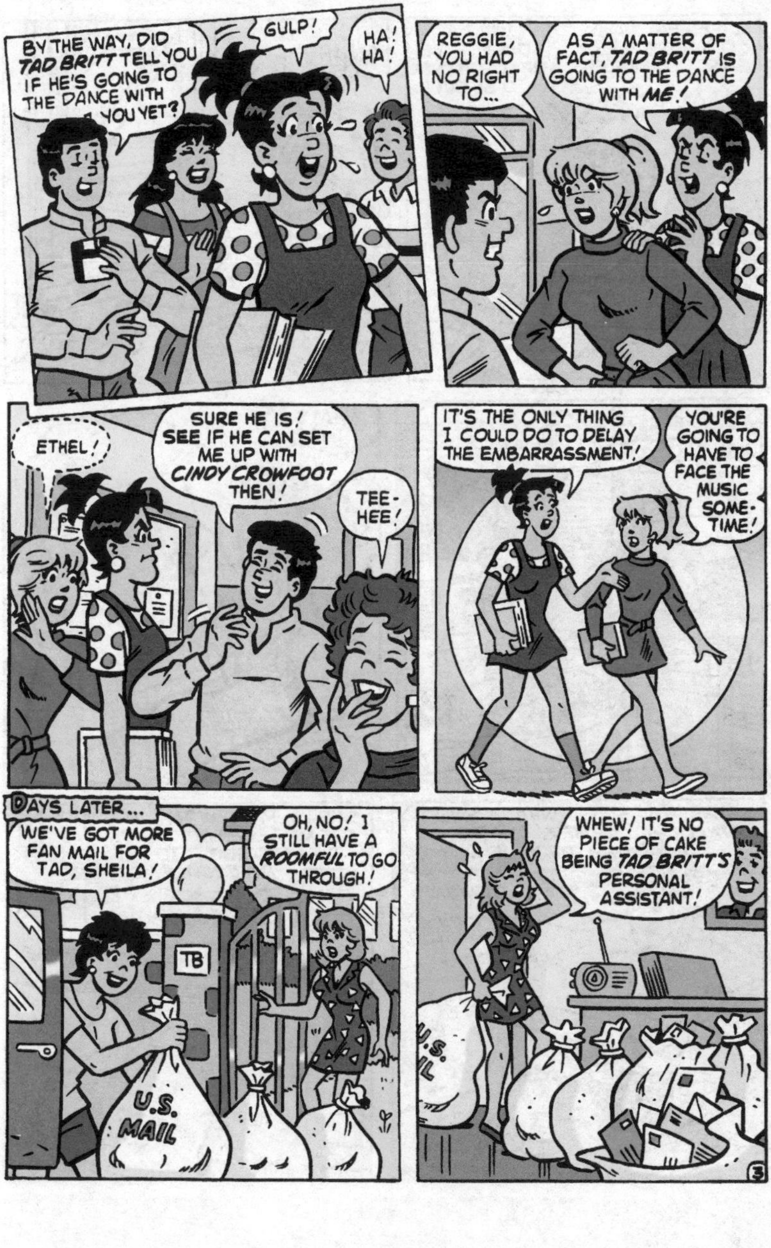
BY THE WAY, DID TAD BRITT TELL YOU IF HE'S GOING TO THE DANCE WITH YOU YET?
GULP!
HA! HA!
REGGIE, YOU HAD NO RIGHT TO...
AS A MATTER OF FACT, TAD BRITT IS GOING TO THE DANCE WITH ME!
ETHEL!
SURE HE IS! SEE IF HE CAN SET ME UP WITH CINDY CROWFOOT THEN!
TEE-HEE!
IT'S THE ONLY THING I COULD DO TO DELAY THE EMBARRASSMENT!
YOU'RE GOING TO HAVE TO FACE THE MUSIC SOME-TIME!
DAYS LATER...
WE'VE GOT MORE FAN MAIL FOR TAD, SHEILA!
OH, NO! I STILL HAVE A ROOMFUL TO GO THROUGH!
TB
U.S. MAIL
WHEW! IT'S NO PIECE OF CAKE BEING TAD BRITT'S PERSONAL ASSISTANT!
3

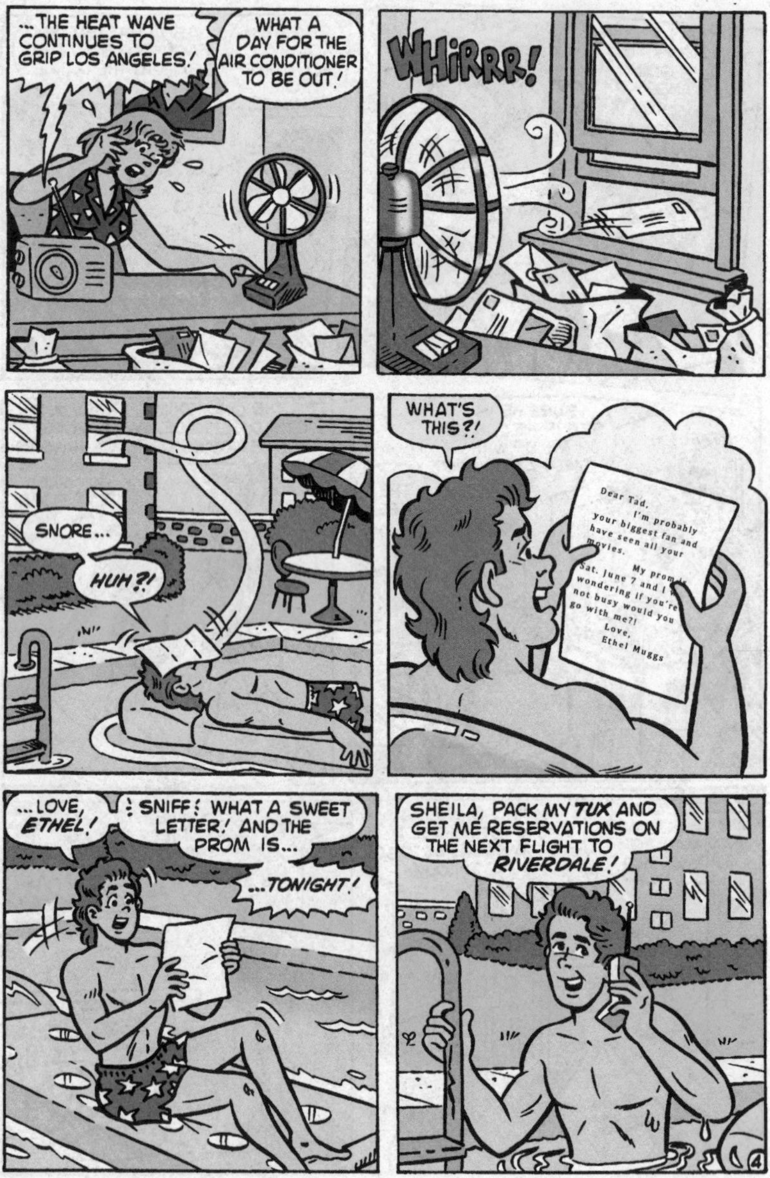
...THE HEAT WAVE CONTINUES TO GRIP LOS ANGELES!
WHAT A DAY FOR THE AIR CONDITIONER TO BE OUT!
WHIRRR!
SNORE...
HUH?!
WHAT'S THIS?!
Dear Tad,
I'm probably
your biggest fan and
have seen all your
movies.
My prom
Sat. June 7 and I
wondering if you're
not busy would you
go with me?!
Love,
Ethel Muggs
...LOVE, ETHEL!
SNIFF! WHAT A SWEET LETTER! AND THE PROM IS...
...TONIGHT!
SHEILA, PACK MY TUX AND GET ME RESERVATIONS ON THE NEXT FLIGHT TO RIVERDALE!
4

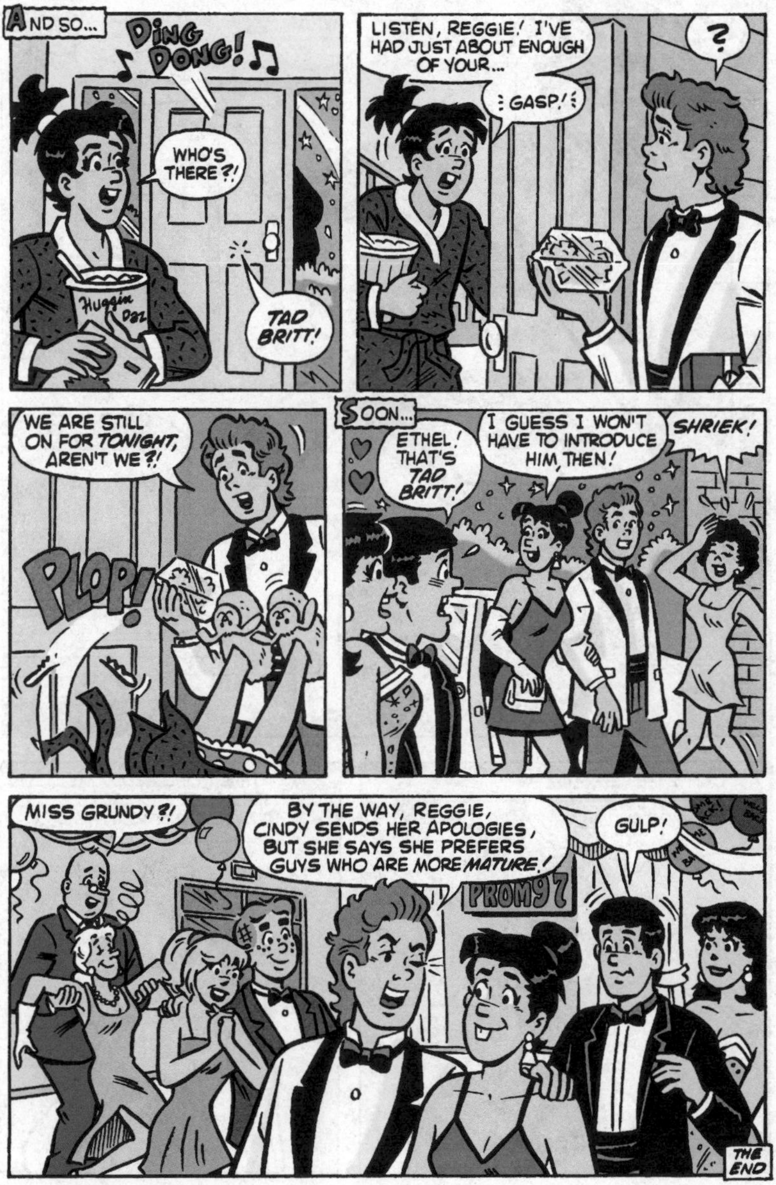
AND SO...
DING DONG!
WHO'S THERE?!
TAD BRITT!
LISTEN, REGGIE! I'VE HAD JUST ABOUT ENOUGH OF YOUR...
GASP!
?
WE ARE STILL ON FOR TONIGHT, AREN'T WE?!
PLOP!
SOON...
ETHEL! THAT'S TAD BRITT!
I GUESS I WON'T HAVE TO INTRODUCE HIM, THEN!
SHRIEK!
MISS GRUNDY?!
BY THE WAY, REGGIE, CINDY SENDS HER APOLOGIES, BUT SHE SAYS SHE PREFERS GUYS WHO ARE MORE MATURE!
GULP!
PROM 97
THE END

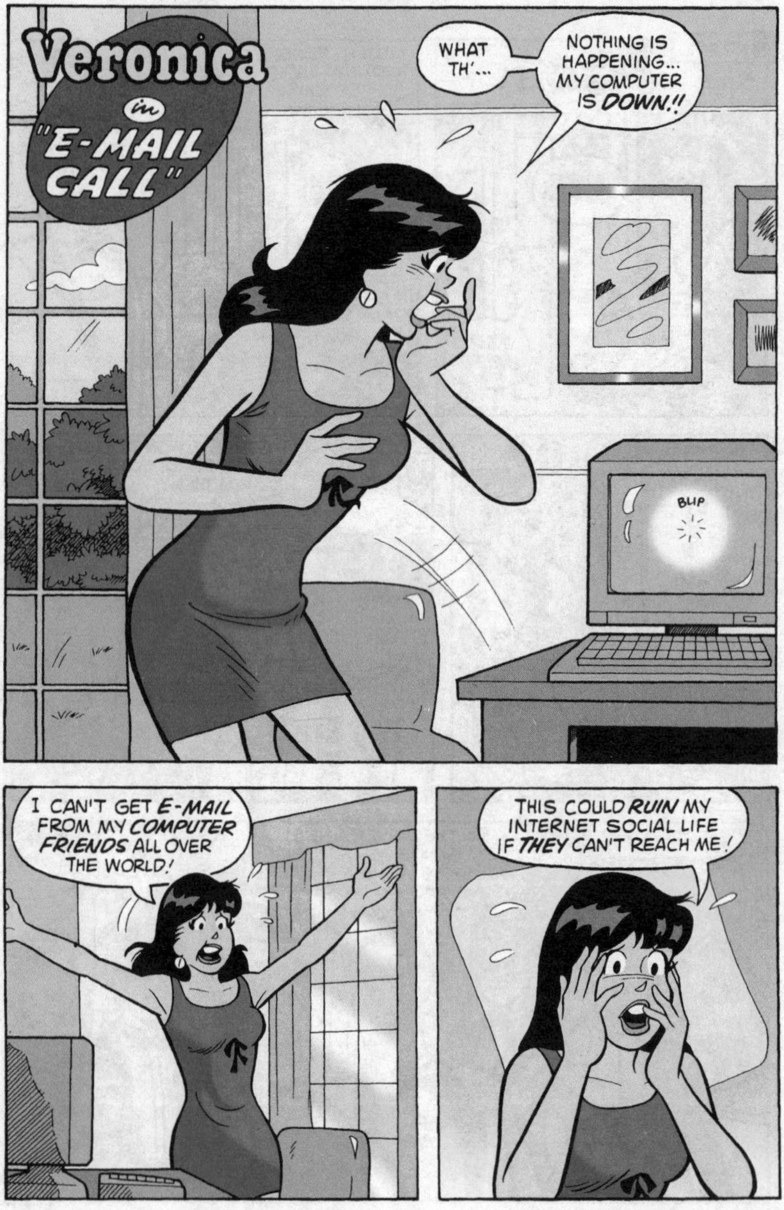
Veronica
in
"E-MAIL CALL"
WHAT TH'...
NOTHING IS HAPPENING... MY COMPUTER IS DOWN!!
BLIP
I CAN'T GET E-MAIL FROM MY COMPUTER FRIENDS ALL OVER THE WORLD!
THIS COULD RUIN MY INTERNET SOCIAL LIFE IF THEY CAN'T REACH ME!

Originally presented in VERONICA #68, October, 1997

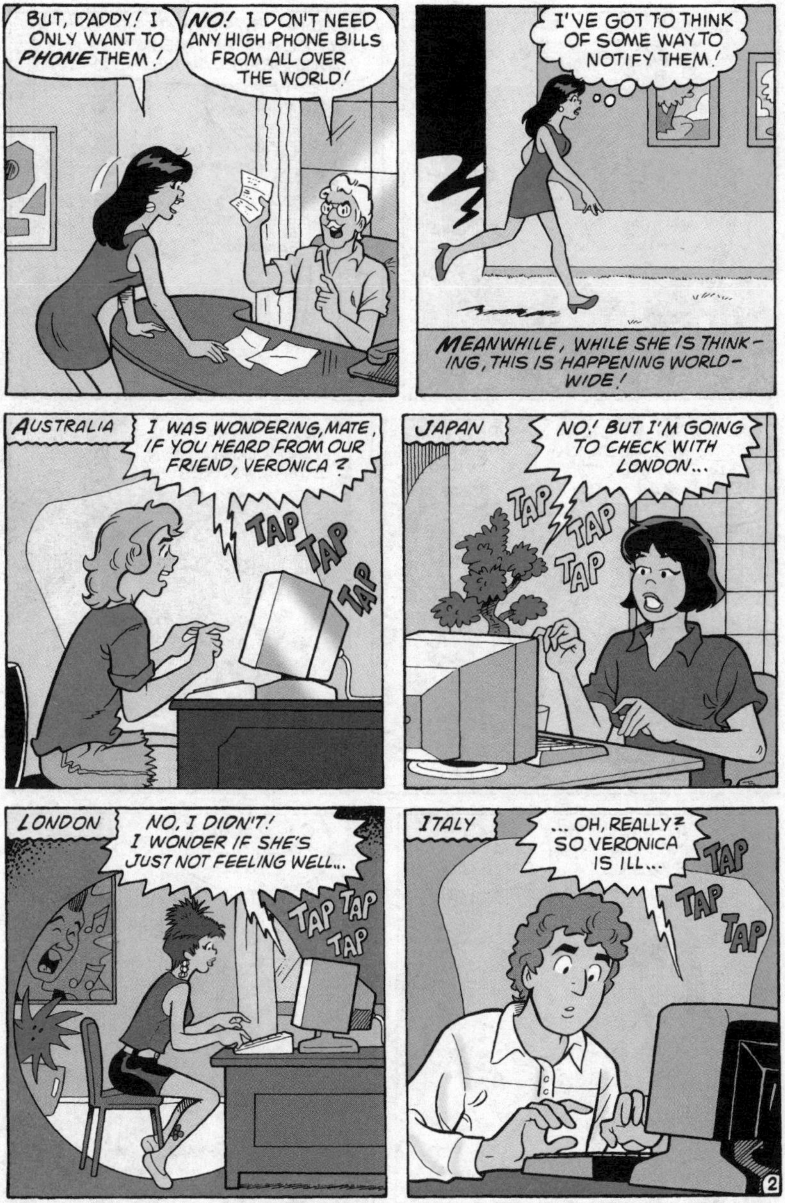
BUT, DADDY! I ONLY WANT TO PHONE THEM!
NO! I DON'T NEED ANY HIGH PHONE BILLS FROM ALL OVER THE WORLD!
I'VE GOT TO THINK OF SOME WAY TO NOTIFY THEM!
MEANWHILE, WHILE SHE IS THINKING, THIS IS HAPPENING WORLD-WIDE!
AUSTRALIA
I WAS WONDERING, MATE, IF YOU HEARD FROM OUR FRIEND, VERONICA?
TAP TAP TAP
JAPAN
NO! BUT I'M GOING TO CHECK WITH LONDON...
TAP TAP TAP
LONDON
NO, I DIDN'T! I WONDER IF SHE'S JUST NOT FEELING WELL...
TAP TAP TAP
ITALY
...OH, REALLY? SO VERONICA IS ILL...
TAP TAP TAP
2

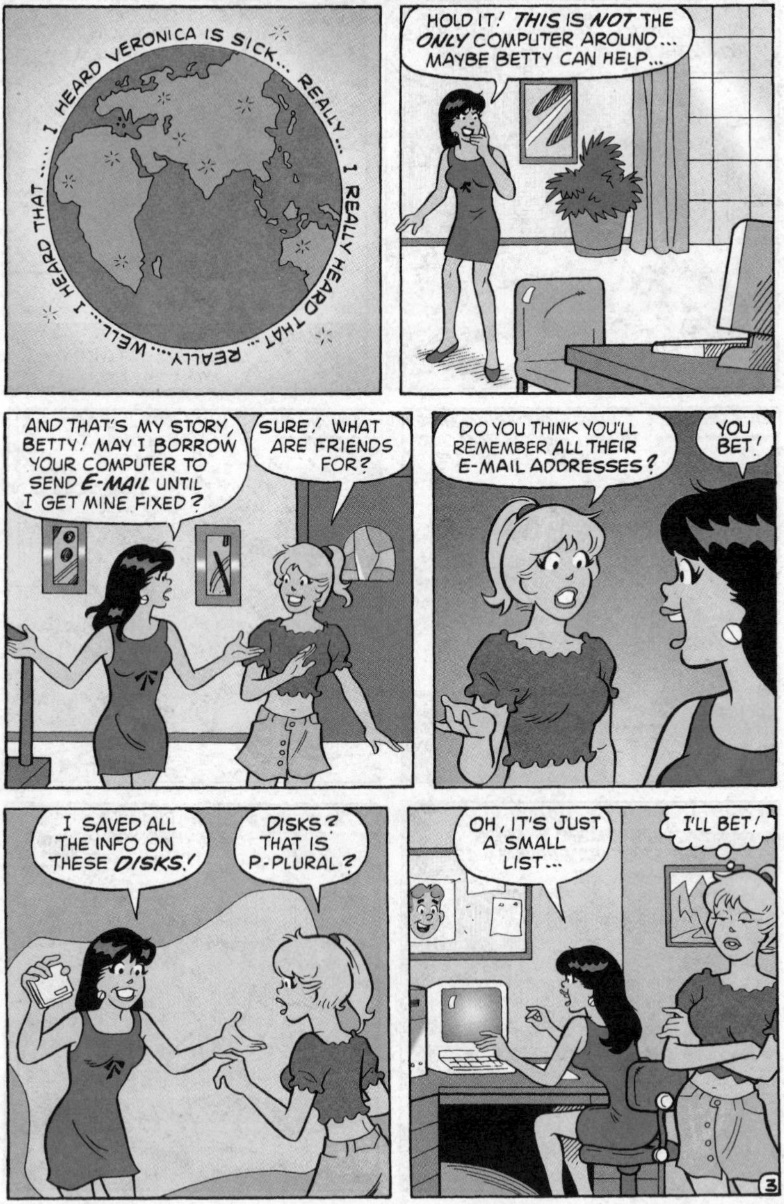
I HEARD VERONICA IS SICK... REALLY... I REALLY HEARD THAT... REALLY.... WELL.... I HEARD THAT..... I
HOLD IT! THIS IS NOT THE ONLY COMPUTER AROUND... MAYBE BETTY CAN HELP...
AND THAT'S MY STORY, BETTY! MAY I BORROW YOUR COMPUTER TO SEND E-MAIL UNTIL I GET MINE FIXED?
SURE! WHAT ARE FRIENDS FOR?
DO YOU THINK YOU'LL REMEMBER ALL THEIR E-MAIL ADDRESSES?
YOU BET!
I SAVED ALL THE INFO ON THESE DISKS!
DISKS? THAT IS P-PLURAL?
OH, IT'S JUST A SMALL LIST...
I'LL BET!
3

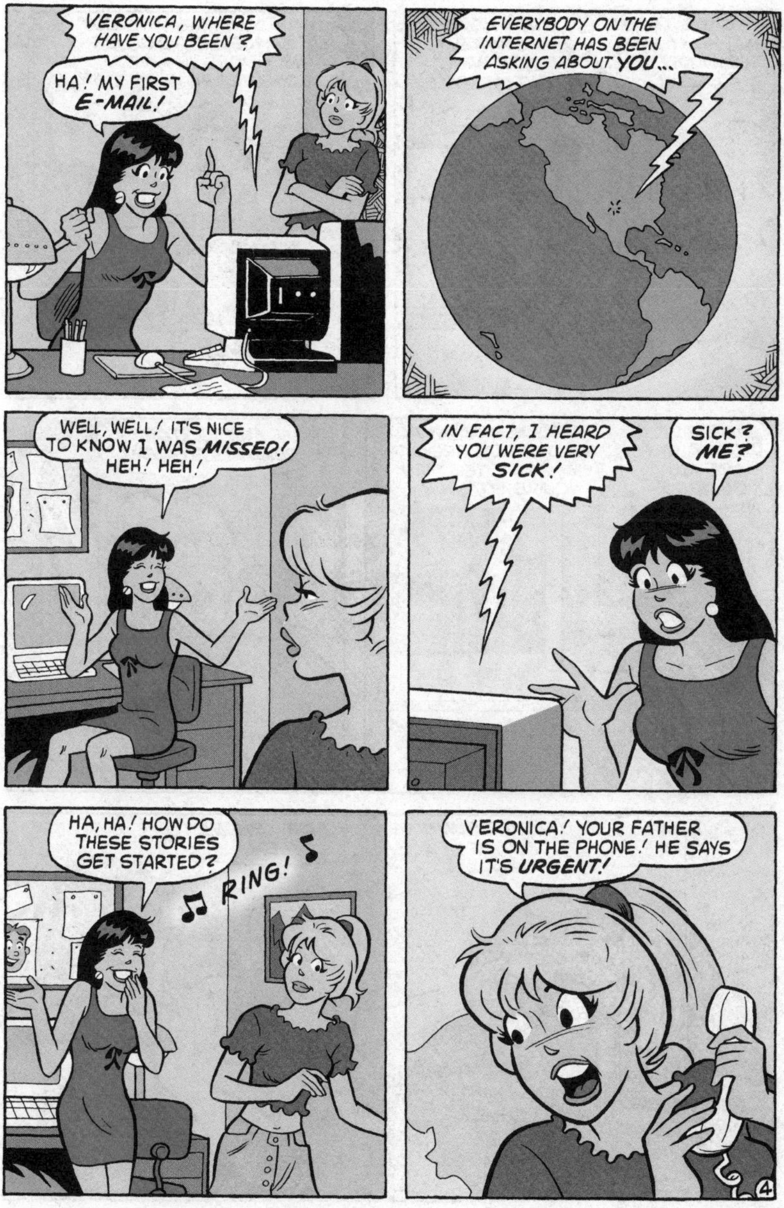
VERONICA, WHERE HAVE YOU BEEN?
HA! MY FIRST E-MAIL!
EVERYBODY ON THE INTERNET HAS BEEN ASKING ABOUT YOU...
WELL, WELL! IT'S NICE TO KNOW I WAS MISSED! HEH! HEH!
IN FACT, I HEARD YOU WERE VERY SICK!
SICK? ME?
HA, HA! HOW DO THESE STORIES GET STARTED?
RING!
VERONICA! YOUR FATHER IS ON THE PHONE! HE SAYS IT'S URGENT!
4

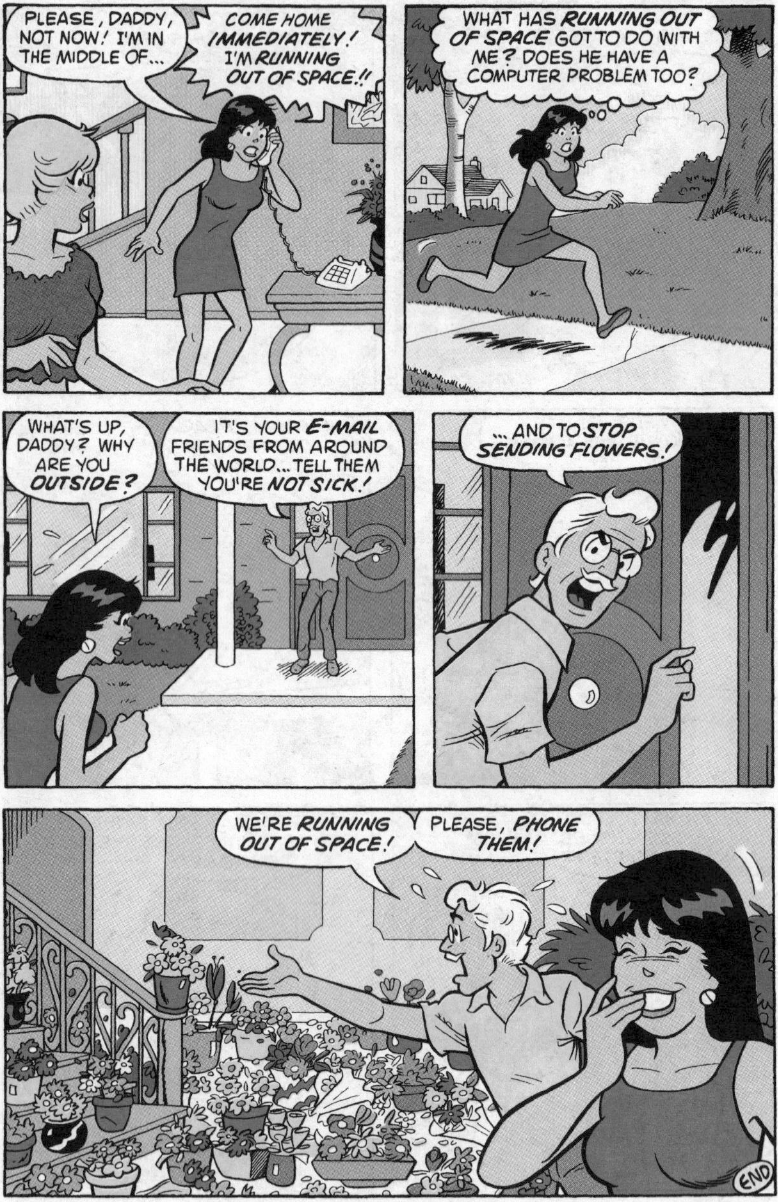
PLEASE, DADDY, NOT NOW! I'M IN THE MIDDLE OF...
COME HOME IMMEDIATELY! I'M RUNNING OUT OF SPACE!!
WHAT HAS RUNNING OUT OF SPACE GOT TO DO WITH ME? DOES HE HAVE A COMPUTER PROBLEM TOO?
WHAT'S UP, DADDY? WHY ARE YOU OUTSIDE?
IT'S YOUR E-MAIL FRIENDS FROM AROUND THE WORLD...TELL THEM YOU'RE NOT SICK!
...AND TO STOP SENDING FLOWERS!
WE'RE RUNNING OUT OF SPACE!
PLEASE, PHONE THEM!
END

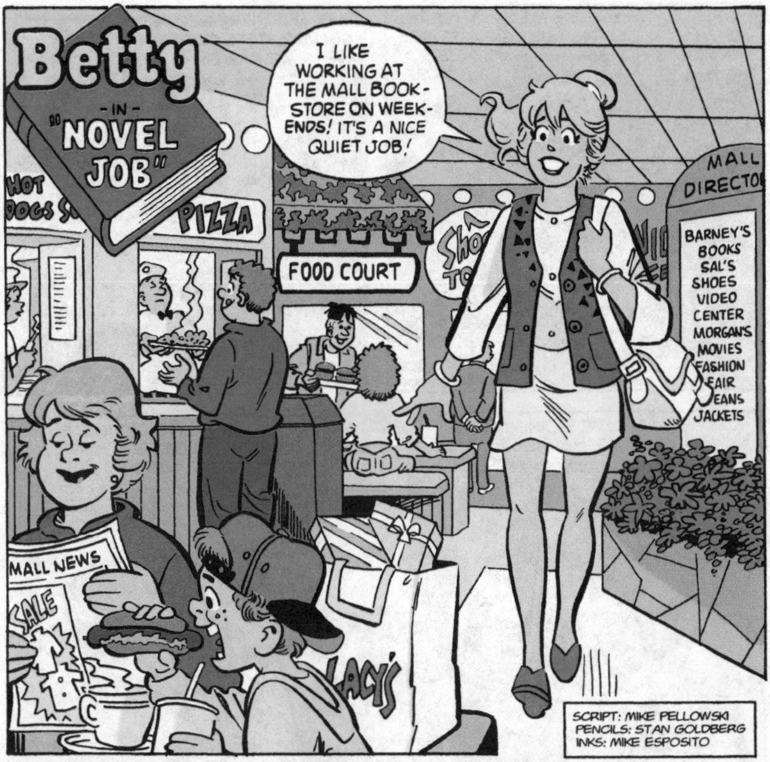
Betty
-IN-
"NOVEL JOB"
I LIKE WORKING AT THE MALL BOOK-STORE ON WEEK-ENDS! IT'S A NICE QUIET JOB!
HOT DOGS
PIZZA
FOOD COURT
MALL DIRECTO
BARNEY'S BOOKS
SAL'S SHOES
VIDEO CENTER
MORGAN'S MOVIES
FASHION FAIR
JEANS JACKETS
MALL NEWS
SALE
LACY'S
SCRIPT: MIKE PELLOWSKI
PENCILS: STAN GOLDBERG
INKS: MIKE ESPOSITO

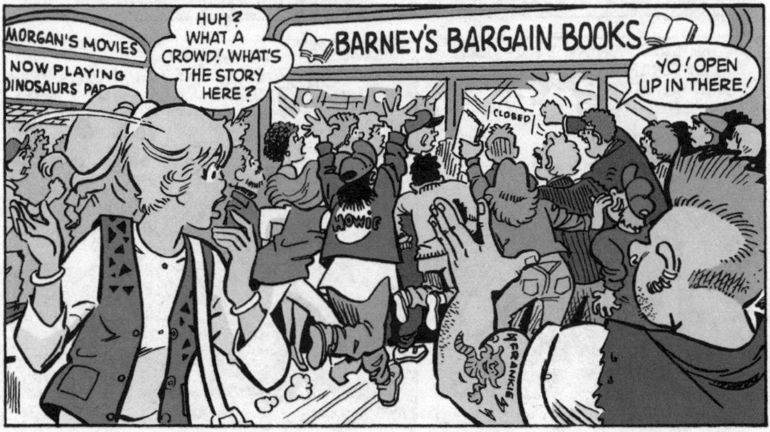
MORGAN'S MOVIES
NOW PLAYING
DINOSAURS PA
HUH? WHAT A CROWD! WHAT'S THE STORY HERE?
BARNEY'S BARGAIN BOOKS
YO! OPEN UP IN THERE!
CLOSED
HOWIE
FRANKIE

Originally presented in BETTY #56, December, 1997

LIKE... IS *HE* HERE YET?

EXCUSE ME! COMING THROUGH!

YEAH, DUDE! *HE'S* IN THE STORE!

WHY ARE THERE SECURITY GUARDS AT THE DOOR WITH MR. BARNEY?

CLOSED

WHAT'S GOING ON, MR. BARNEY?

LET HER THROUGH, GUYS! THAT'S BETTY COOPER! SHE WORKS HERE!

BEST SELLERS LIST

GUARD

AT THE LAST MINUTE I WAS ABLE TO SCHEDULE A CELEBRITY BOOK SIGNING APPEARANCE!

BY WHO?

SCI-FI

HOWIE SEVERE!

HOWIE SEVERE, THE FAMOUS SHOCK D.J.?

DUCK BUMPS BOOKS

READ "PETTY THEFT"

DANIELLE IRONS 'LOVE YA'

LOVE YA

HOWIE SEVERE   IN PERSON

NO. **1** BEST SELLER

"WOWIE HOWIE TELLS ALL"

2

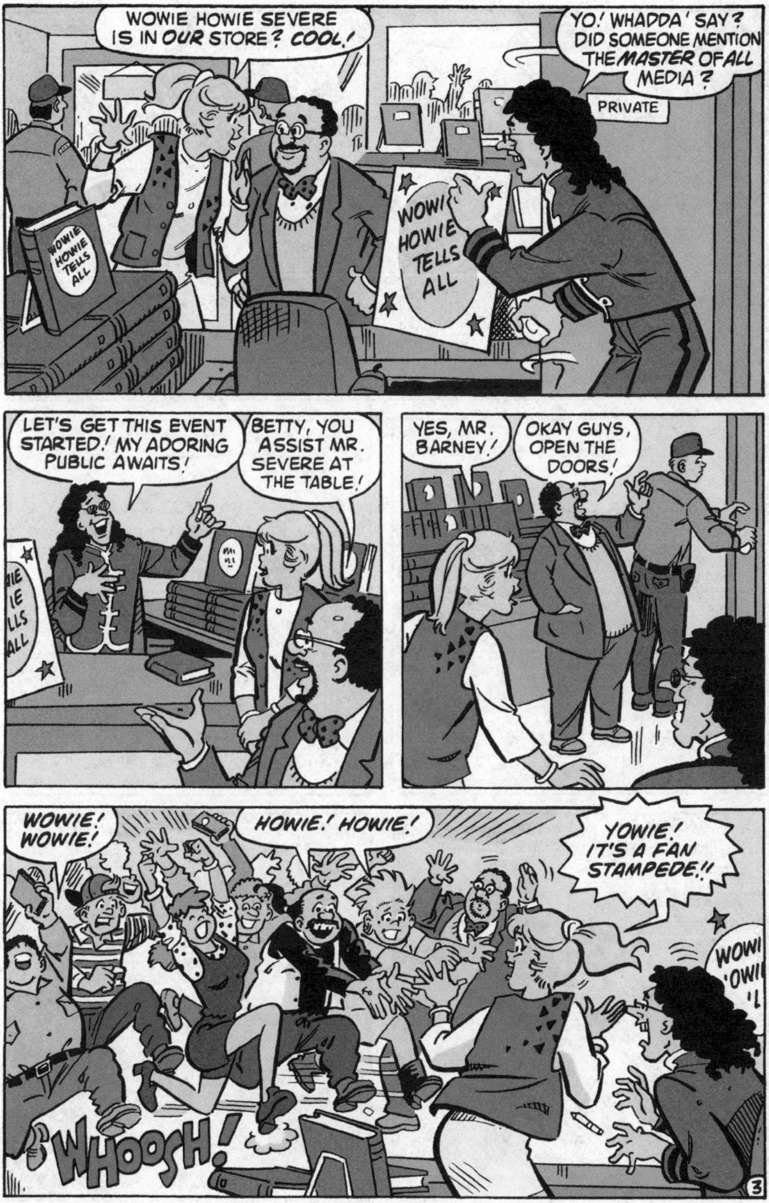
WOWIE HOWIE SEVERE IS IN OUR STORE? COOL!
YO! WHADDA' SAY? DID SOMEONE MENTION THE MASTER OF ALL MEDIA?
PRIVATE
WOWIE HOWIE TELLS ALL
WOWIE HOWIE TELLS ALL
LET'S GET THIS EVENT STARTED! MY ADORING PUBLIC AWAITS!
BETTY, YOU ASSIST MR. SEVERE AT THE TABLE!
YES, MR. BARNEY!
OKAY GUYS, OPEN THE DOORS!
WOWIE! WOWIE!
HOWIE! HOWIE!
YOWIE! IT'S A FAN STAMPEDE!!
WHOOSH!
3

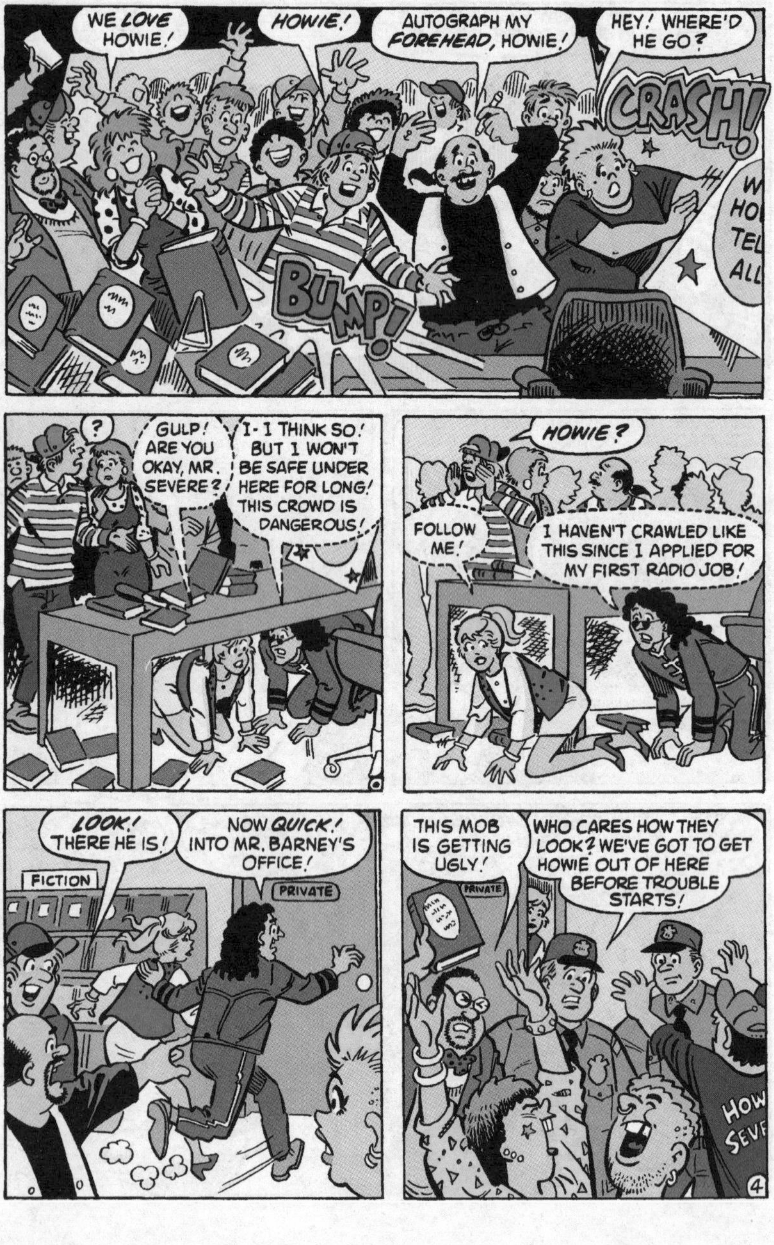
WE LOVE HOWIE!
HOWIE!
AUTOGRAPH MY FOREHEAD, HOWIE!
HEY! WHERE'D HE GO?
CRASH!
BUMP!
GULP! ARE YOU OKAY, MR. SEVERE?
I- I THINK SO! BUT I WON'T BE SAFE UNDER HERE FOR LONG! THIS CROWD IS DANGEROUS!
HOWIE?
FOLLOW ME!
I HAVEN'T CRAWLED LIKE THIS SINCE I APPLIED FOR MY FIRST RADIO JOB!
LOOK! THERE HE IS!
NOW QUICK! INTO MR. BARNEY'S OFFICE!
FICTION
PRIVATE
THIS MOB IS GETTING UGLY!
WHO CARES HOW THEY LOOK? WE'VE GOT TO GET HOWIE OUT OF HERE BEFORE TROUBLE STARTS!
PRIVATE
4

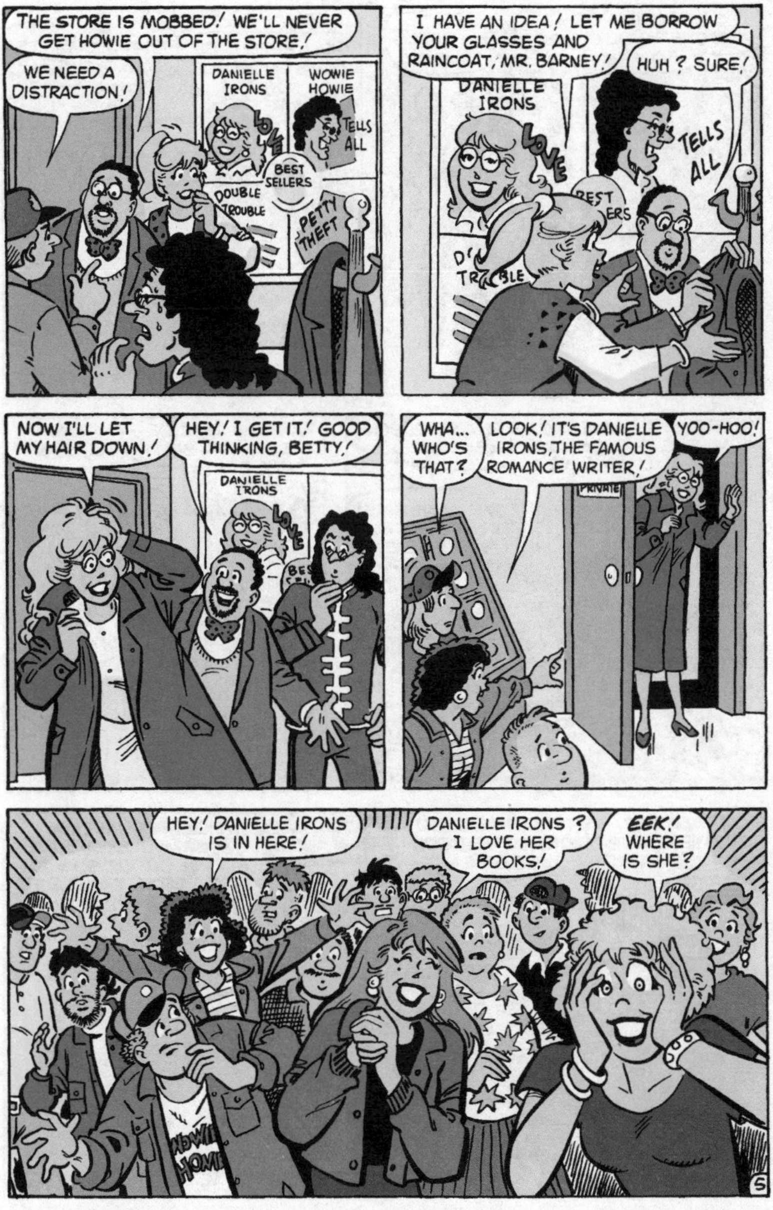
THE STORE IS MOBBED! WE'LL NEVER GET HOWIE OUT OF THE STORE!
WE NEED A DISTRACTION!
DANIELLE IRONS
WOWIE HOWIE
LOVE
TELLS ALL
BEST SELLERS
DOUBLE TROUBLE
PETTY THEFT
I HAVE AN IDEA! LET ME BORROW YOUR GLASSES AND RAINCOAT, MR. BARNEY!
HUH ? SURE!
NOW I'LL LET MY HAIR DOWN!
HEY! I GET IT! GOOD THINKING, BETTY!
WHA... WHO'S THAT?
LOOK! IT'S DANIELLE IRONS, THE FAMOUS ROMANCE WRITER!
YOO-HOO!
PRIVATE
HEY! DANIELLE IRONS IS IN HERE!
DANIELLE IRONS ? I LOVE HER BOOKS!
EEK! WHERE IS SHE?
5

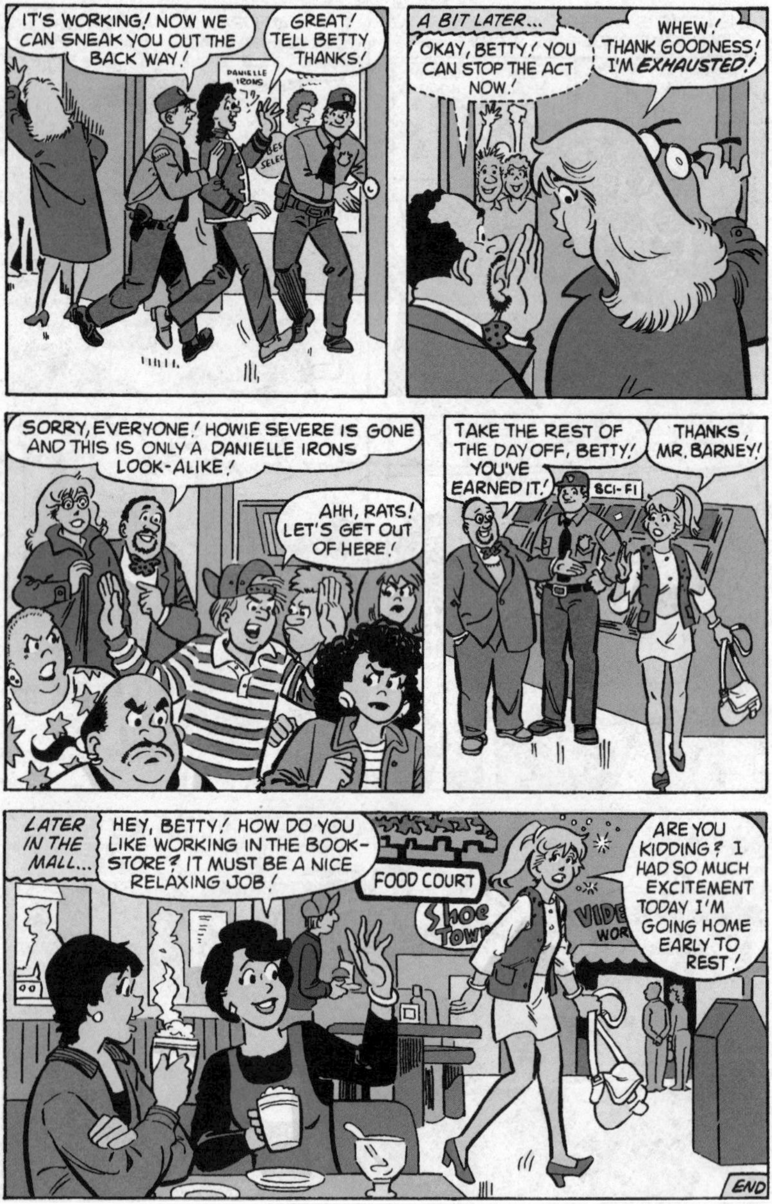
IT'S WORKING! NOW WE CAN SNEAK YOU OUT THE BACK WAY!
GREAT! TELL BETTY THANKS!
DANIELLE IRONS
A BIT LATER...
OKAY, BETTY! YOU CAN STOP THE ACT NOW!
WHEW! THANK GOODNESS! I'M *EXHAUSTED*!
SORRY, EVERYONE! HOWIE SEVERE IS GONE AND THIS IS ONLY A DANIELLE IRONS LOOK-ALIKE!
AHH, RATS! LET'S GET OUT OF HERE!
TAKE THE REST OF THE DAY OFF, BETTY! YOU'VE EARNED IT!
THANKS, MR. BARNEY!
SCI-FI
LATER IN THE MALL...
HEY, BETTY! HOW DO YOU LIKE WORKING IN THE BOOK-STORE? IT MUST BE A NICE RELAXING JOB!
FOOD COURT
ARE YOU KIDDING? I HAD SO MUCH EXCITEMENT TODAY I'M GOING HOME EARLY TO REST!
END

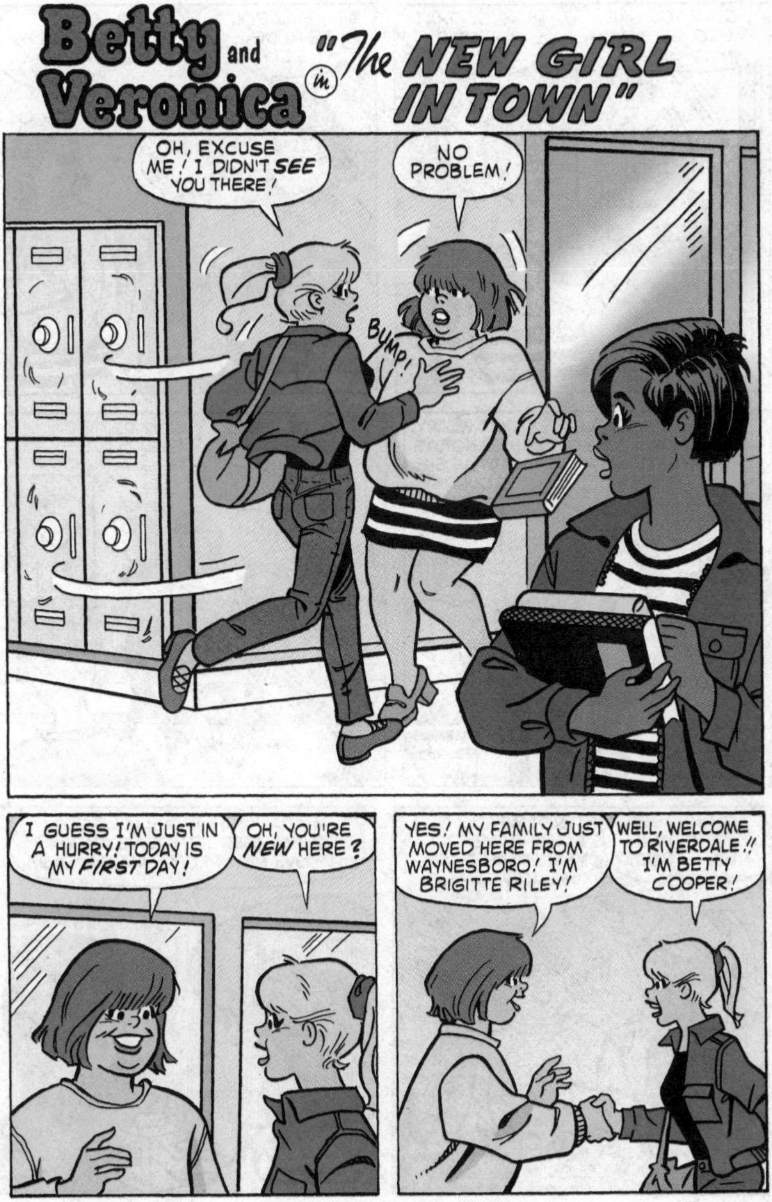
Betty and Veronica
in
"The NEW GIRL IN TOWN"
OH, EXCUSE ME! I DIDN'T SEE YOU THERE!
NO PROBLEM!
BUMP!
I GUESS I'M JUST IN A HURRY! TODAY IS MY FIRST DAY!
OH, YOU'RE NEW HERE?
YES! MY FAMILY JUST MOVED HERE FROM WAYNESBORO! I'M BRIGITTE RILEY!
WELL, WELCOME TO RIVERDALE!! I'M BETTY COOPER!

Originally presented in BETTY & VERONICA #119, January, 1998

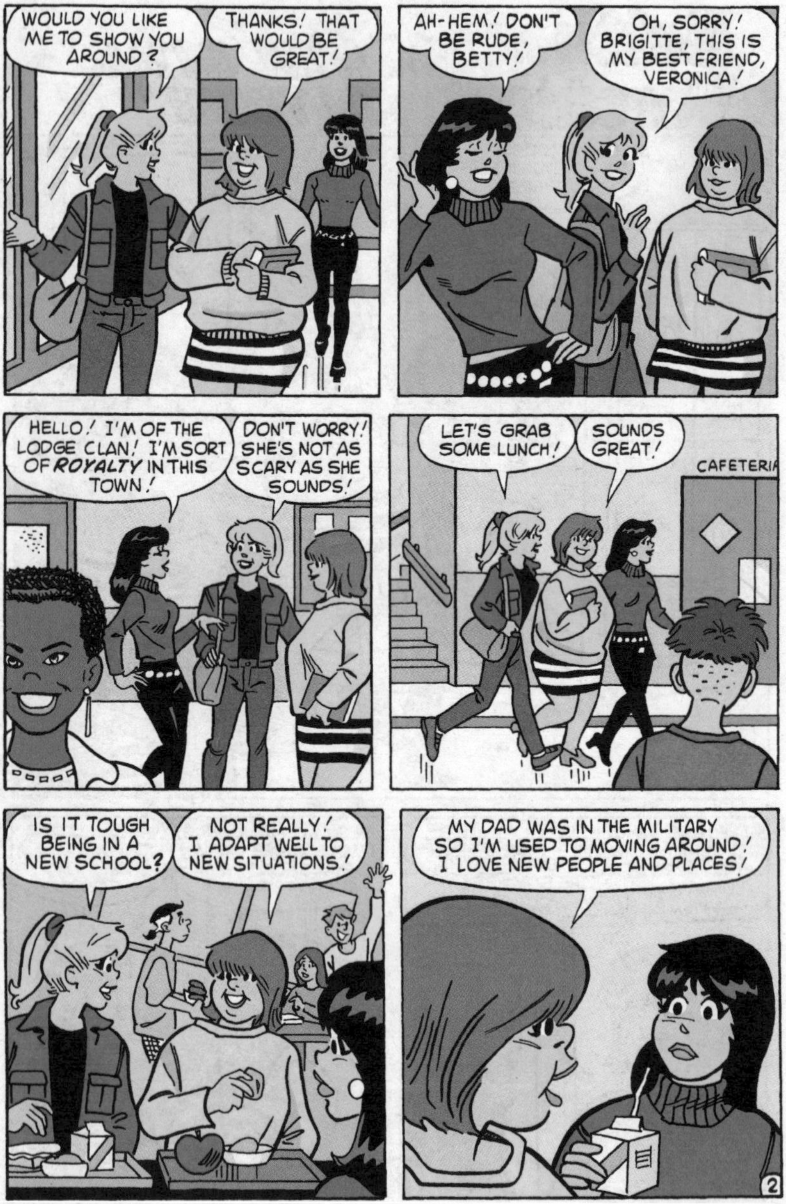
WOULD YOU LIKE ME TO SHOW YOU AROUND?
THANKS! THAT WOULD BE GREAT!
AH-HEM! DON'T BE RUDE, BETTY!
OH, SORRY! BRIGITTE, THIS IS MY BEST FRIEND, VERONICA!
HELLO! I'M OF THE LODGE CLAN! I'M SORT OF *ROYALTY* IN THIS TOWN!
DON'T WORRY! SHE'S NOT AS SCARY AS SHE SOUNDS!
LET'S GRAB SOME LUNCH!
SOUNDS GREAT!
CAFETERIA
IS IT TOUGH BEING IN A NEW SCHOOL?
NOT REALLY! I ADAPT WELL TO NEW SITUATIONS!
MY DAD WAS IN THE MILITARY SO I'M USED TO MOVING AROUND! I LOVE NEW PEOPLE AND PLACES!
2

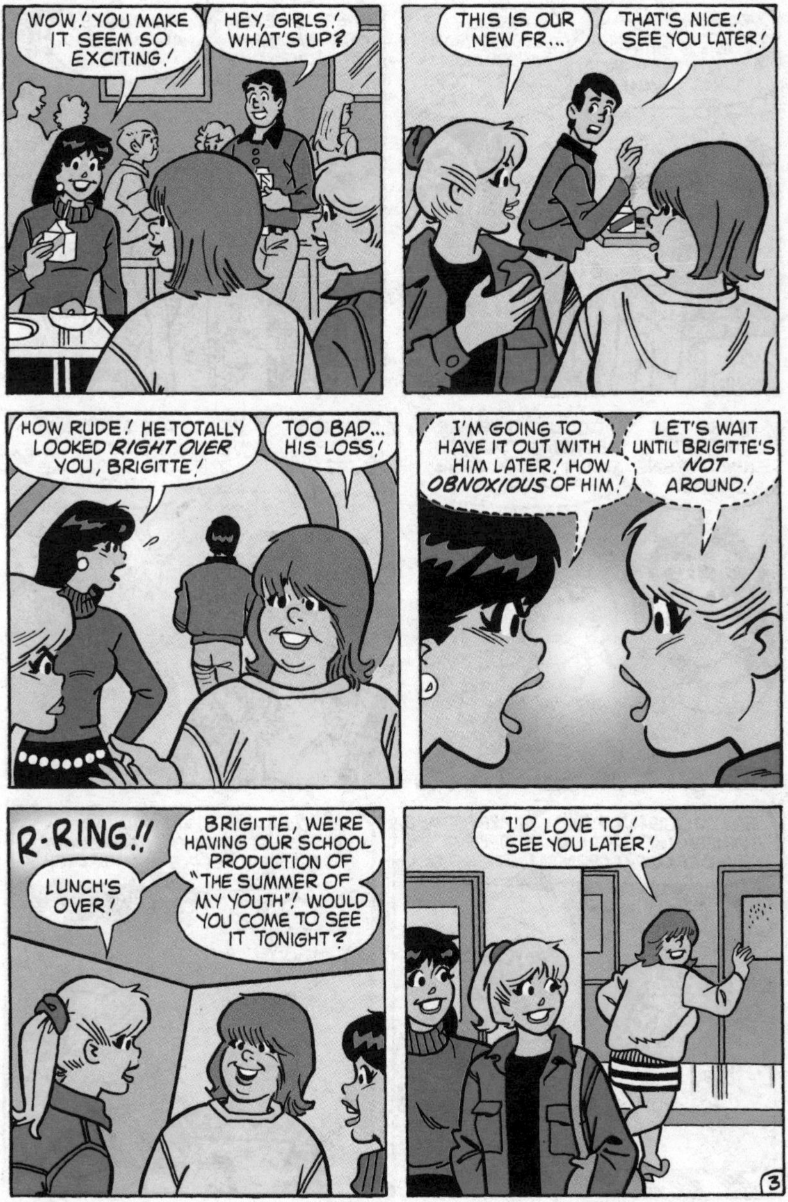
WOW! YOU MAKE IT SEEM SO EXCITING!
HEY, GIRLS! WHAT'S UP?
THIS IS OUR NEW FR...
THAT'S NICE! SEE YOU LATER!
HOW RUDE! HE TOTALLY LOOKED RIGHT OVER YOU, BRIGITTE!
TOO BAD... HIS LOSS!
I'M GOING TO HAVE IT OUT WITH HIM LATER! HOW OBNOXIOUS OF HIM!
LET'S WAIT UNTIL BRIGITTE'S NOT AROUND!
R-RING!!
LUNCH'S OVER!
BRIGITTE, WE'RE HAVING OUR SCHOOL PRODUCTION OF "THE SUMMER OF MY YOUTH"! WOULD YOU COME TO SEE IT TONIGHT?
I'D LOVE TO! SEE YOU LATER!
3

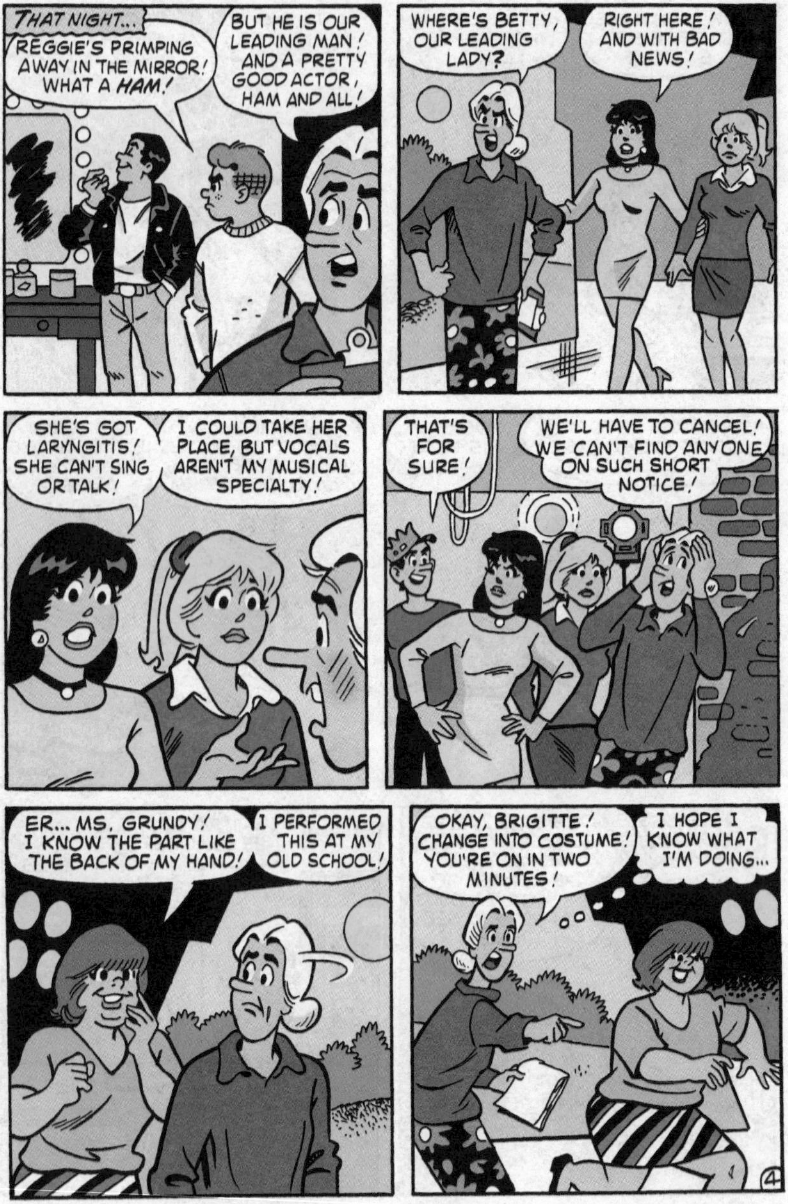
THAT NIGHT...
REGGIE'S PRIMPING AWAY IN THE MIRROR! WHAT A HAM!
BUT HE IS OUR LEADING MAN! AND A PRETTY GOOD ACTOR, HAM AND ALL!
WHERE'S BETTY, OUR LEADING LADY?
RIGHT HERE! AND WITH BAD NEWS!
SHE'S GOT LARYNGITIS! SHE CAN'T SING OR TALK!
I COULD TAKE HER PLACE, BUT VOCALS AREN'T MY MUSICAL SPECIALTY!
THAT'S FOR SURE!
WE'LL HAVE TO CANCEL! WE CAN'T FIND ANYONE ON SUCH SHORT NOTICE!
ER... MS. GRUNDY! I KNOW THE PART LIKE THE BACK OF MY HAND!
I PERFORMED THIS AT MY OLD SCHOOL!
OKAY, BRIGITTE! CHANGE INTO COSTUME! YOU'RE ON IN TWO MINUTES!
I HOPE I KNOW WHAT I'M DOING...
4

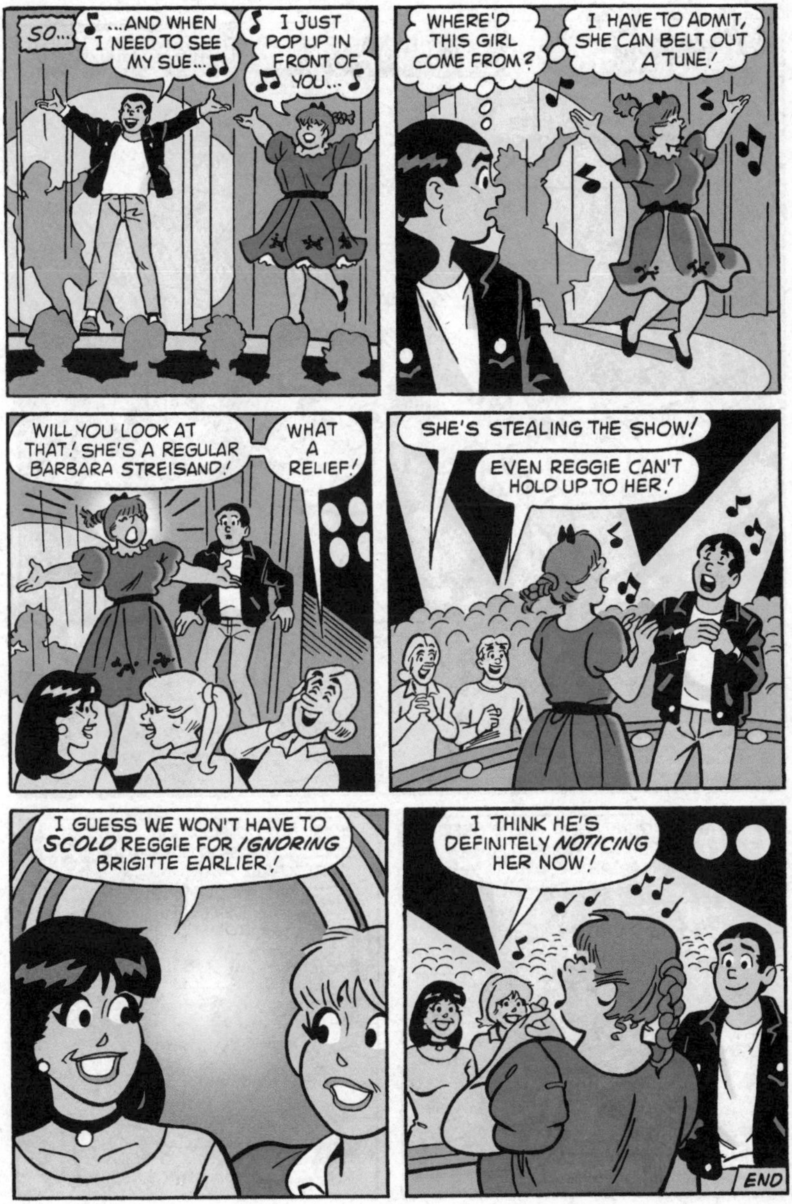
SO...
...AND WHEN I NEED TO SEE MY SUE...
I JUST POP UP IN FRONT OF YOU...
WHERE'D THIS GIRL COME FROM?
I HAVE TO ADMIT, SHE CAN BELT OUT A TUNE!
WILL YOU LOOK AT THAT! SHE'S A REGULAR BARBARA STREISAND!
WHAT A RELIEF!
SHE'S STEALING THE SHOW!
EVEN REGGIE CAN'T HOLD UP TO HER!
I GUESS WE WON'T HAVE TO SCOLD REGGIE FOR IGNORING BRIGITTE EARLIER!
I THINK HE'S DEFINITELY NOTICING HER NOW!
END

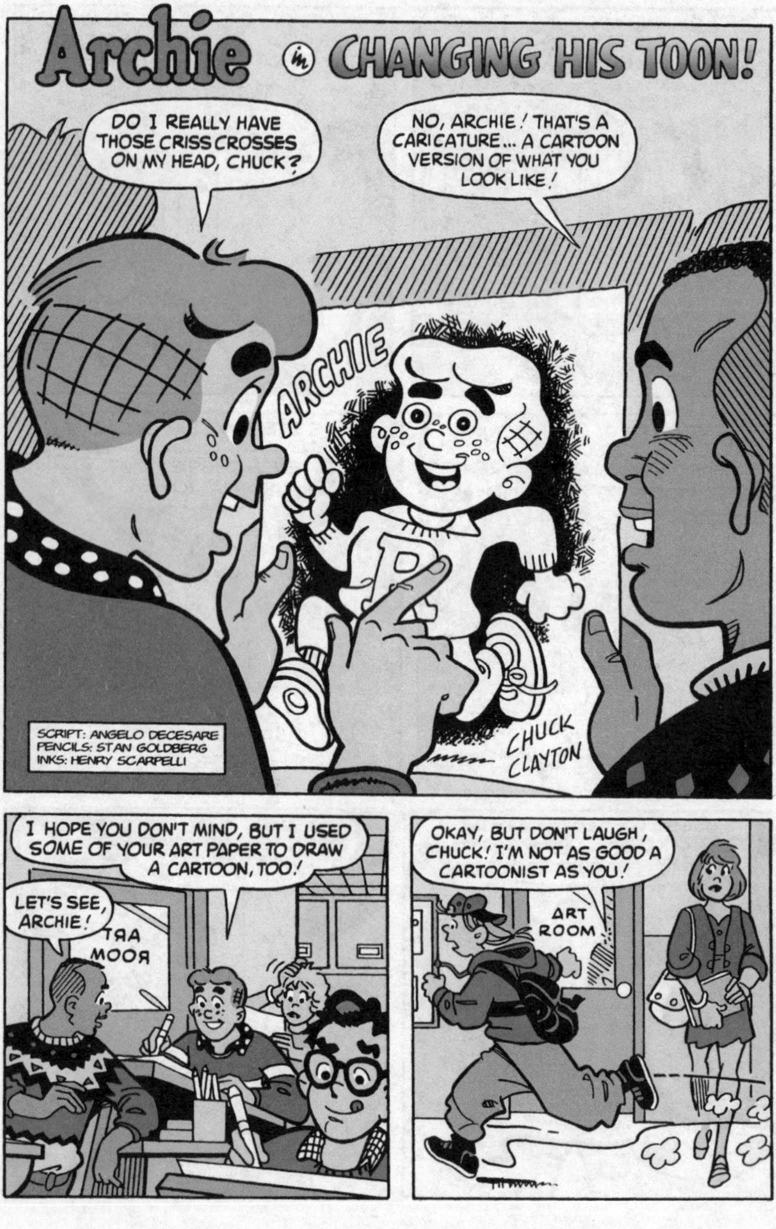
Archie in CHANGING HIS TOON!
DO I REALLY HAVE THOSE CRISS CROSSES ON MY HEAD, CHUCK?
NO, ARCHIE! THAT'S A CARICATURE... A CARTOON VERSION OF WHAT YOU LOOK LIKE!
ARCHIE
CHUCK CLAYTON
SCRIPT: ANGELO DECESARE
PENCILS: STAN GOLDBERG
INKS: HENRY SCARPELLI
I HOPE YOU DON'T MIND, BUT I USED SOME OF YOUR ART PAPER TO DRAW A CARTOON, TOO!
LET'S SEE, ARCHIE!
OKAY, BUT DON'T LAUGH, CHUCK! I'M NOT AS GOOD A CARTOONIST AS YOU!
ART ROOM

Originally presented in ARCHIE #470, April, 1998

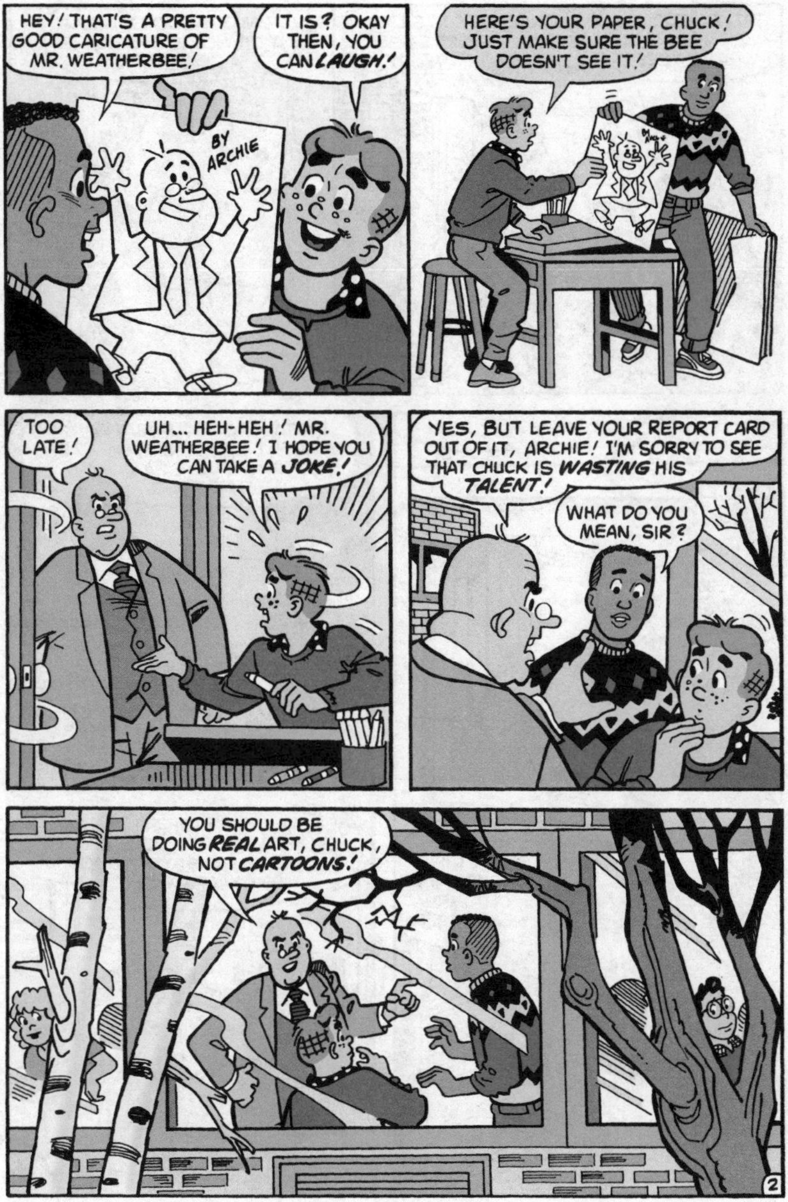
HEY! THAT'S A PRETTY GOOD CARICATURE OF MR. WEATHERBEE!
IT IS? OKAY THEN, YOU CAN LAUGH!
BY ARCHIE
HERE'S YOUR PAPER, CHUCK! JUST MAKE SURE THE BEE DOESN'T SEE IT!
TOO LATE!
UH... HEH-HEH! MR. WEATHERBEE! I HOPE YOU CAN TAKE A JOKE!
YES, BUT LEAVE YOUR REPORT CARD OUT OF IT, ARCHIE! I'M SORRY TO SEE THAT CHUCK IS WASTING HIS TALENT!
WHAT DO YOU MEAN, SIR?
YOU SHOULD BE DOING REAL ART, CHUCK, NOT CARTOONS!
2

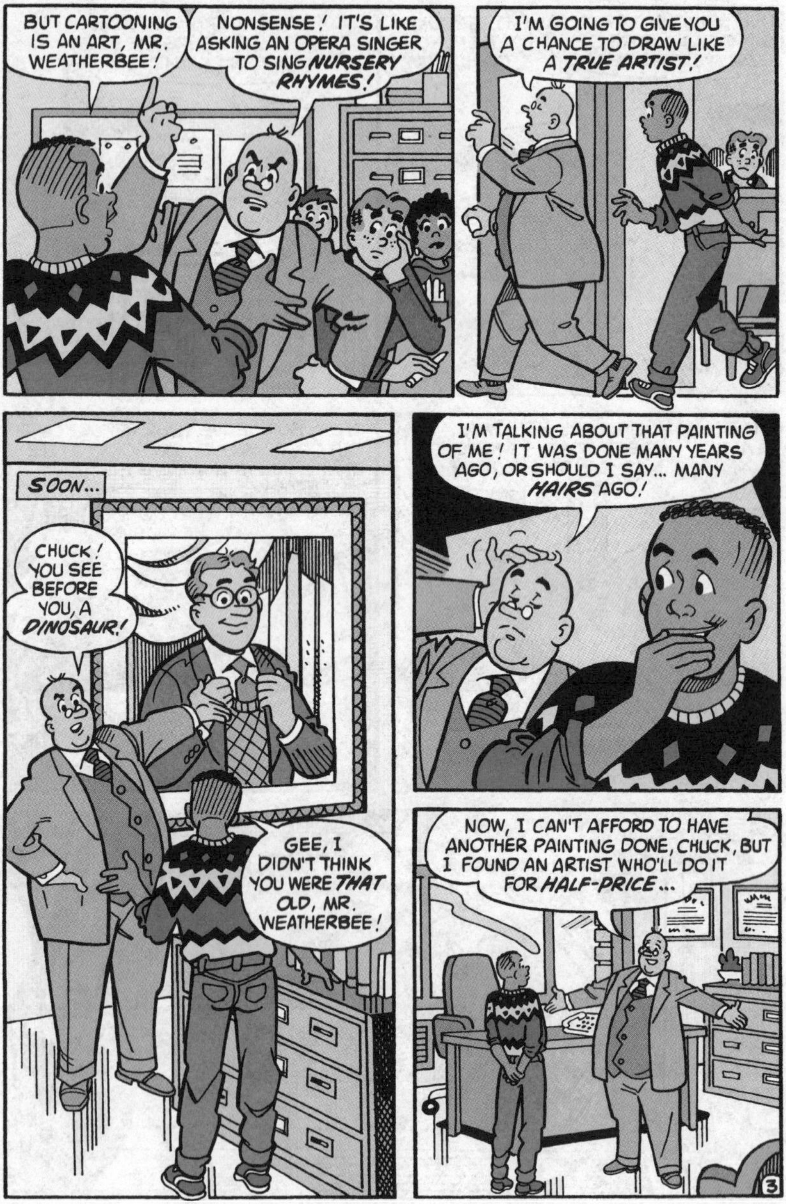
BUT CARTOONING IS AN ART, MR. WEATHERBEE!
NONSENSE! IT'S LIKE ASKING AN OPERA SINGER TO SING NURSERY RHYMES!
I'M GOING TO GIVE YOU A CHANCE TO DRAW LIKE A TRUE ARTIST!
SOON...
CHUCK! YOU SEE BEFORE YOU, A DINOSAUR!
GEE, I DIDN'T THINK YOU WERE THAT OLD, MR. WEATHERBEE!
I'M TALKING ABOUT THAT PAINTING OF ME! IT WAS DONE MANY YEARS AGO, OR SHOULD I SAY... MANY HAIRS AGO!
NOW, I CAN'T AFFORD TO HAVE ANOTHER PAINTING DONE, CHUCK, BUT I FOUND AN ARTIST WHO'LL DO IT FOR HALF-PRICE...
3

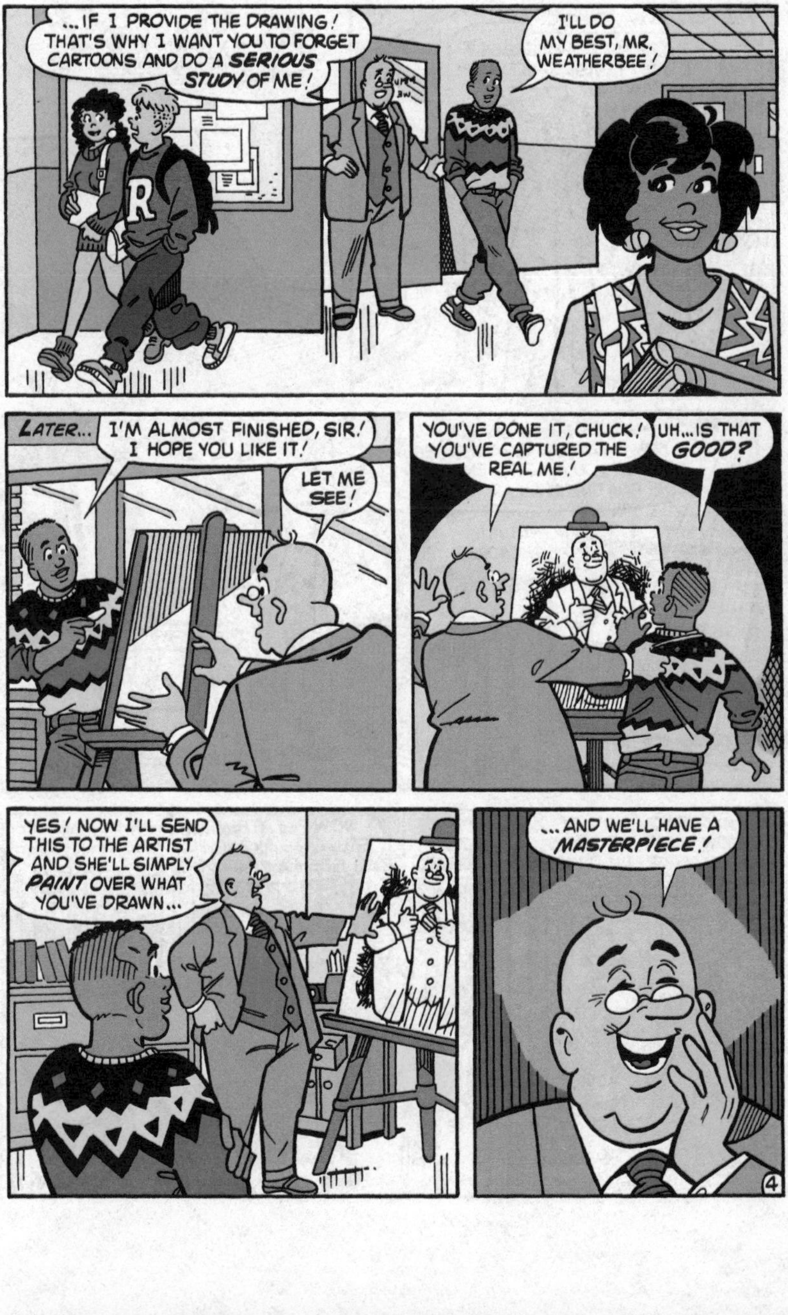
...IF I PROVIDE THE DRAWING! THAT'S WHY I WANT YOU TO FORGET CARTOONS AND DO A SERIOUS STUDY OF ME!
I'LL DO MY BEST, MR. WEATHERBEE!
LATER...
I'M ALMOST FINISHED, SIR! I HOPE YOU LIKE IT!
LET ME SEE!
YOU'VE DONE IT, CHUCK! YOU'VE CAPTURED THE REAL ME!
UH...IS THAT GOOD?
YES! NOW I'LL SEND THIS TO THE ARTIST AND SHE'LL SIMPLY PAINT OVER WHAT YOU'VE DRAWN...
...AND WE'LL HAVE A MASTERPIECE!
4

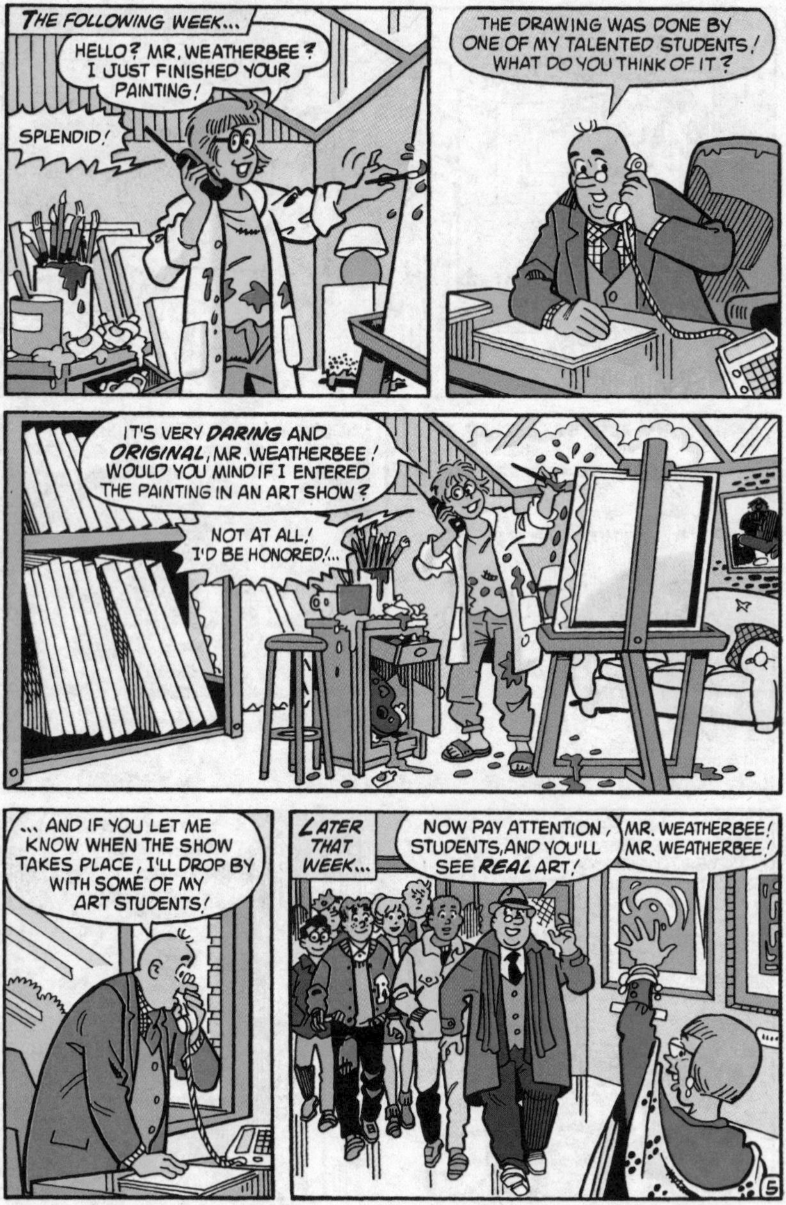
THE FOLLOWING WEEK...
HELLO? MR. WEATHERBEE? I JUST FINISHED YOUR PAINTING!
SPLENDID!
THE DRAWING WAS DONE BY ONE OF MY TALENTED STUDENTS! WHAT DO YOU THINK OF IT?
IT'S VERY DARING AND ORIGINAL, MR. WEATHERBEE! WOULD YOU MIND IF I ENTERED THE PAINTING IN AN ART SHOW?
NOT AT ALL! I'D BE HONORED!...
... AND IF YOU LET ME KNOW WHEN THE SHOW TAKES PLACE, I'LL DROP BY WITH SOME OF MY ART STUDENTS!
LATER THAT WEEK...
NOW PAY ATTENTION, STUDENTS, AND YOU'LL SEE REAL ART!
MR. WEATHERBEE! MR. WEATHERBEE!
5

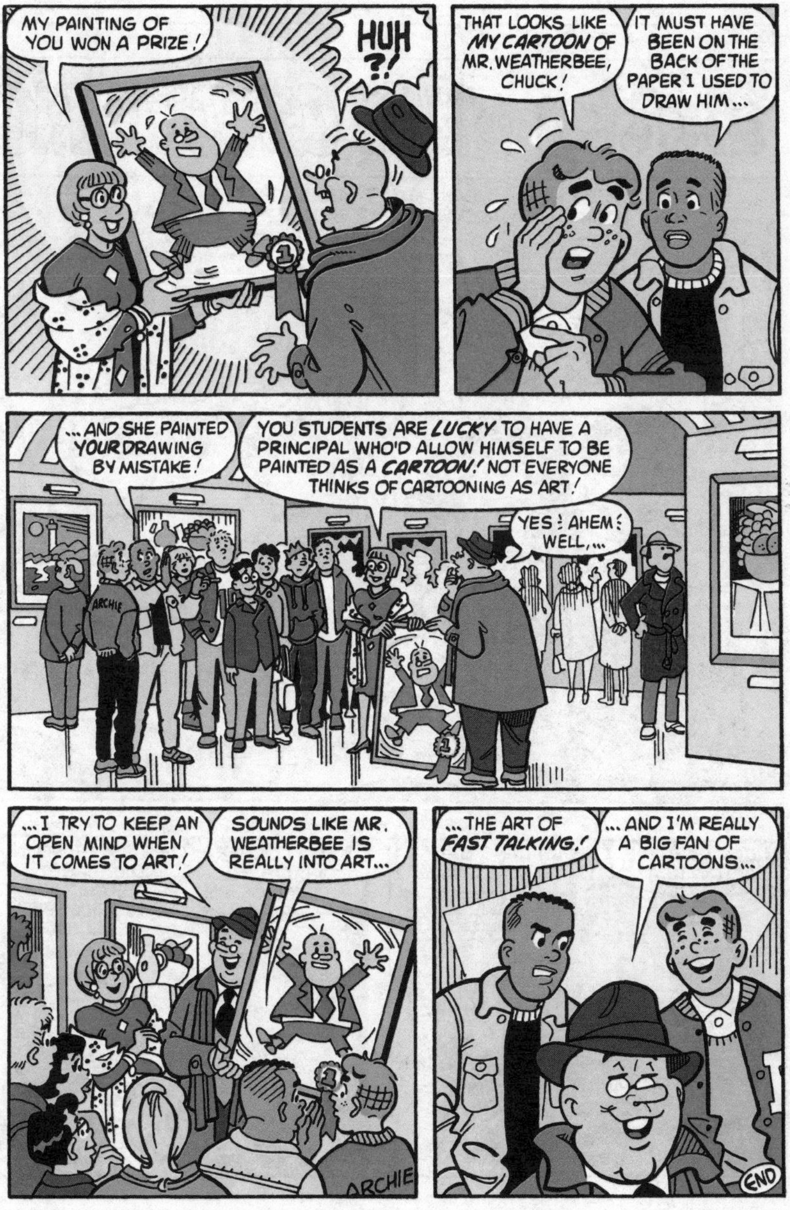
MY PAINTING OF YOU WON A PRIZE!
HUH ?!
THAT LOOKS LIKE MY CARTOON OF MR. WEATHERBEE, CHUCK!
IT MUST HAVE BEEN ON THE BACK OF THE PAPER I USED TO DRAW HIM...
...AND SHE PAINTED YOUR DRAWING BY MISTAKE!
YOU STUDENTS ARE LUCKY TO HAVE A PRINCIPAL WHO'D ALLOW HIMSELF TO BE PAINTED AS A CARTOON! NOT EVERYONE THINKS OF CARTOONING AS ART!
YES! AHEM! WELL,...
ARCHIE
...I TRY TO KEEP AN OPEN MIND WHEN IT COMES TO ART!
SOUNDS LIKE MR. WEATHERBEE IS REALLY INTO ART...
ARCHIE
...THE ART OF FAST TALKING!
...AND I'M REALLY A BIG FAN OF CARTOONS...
END

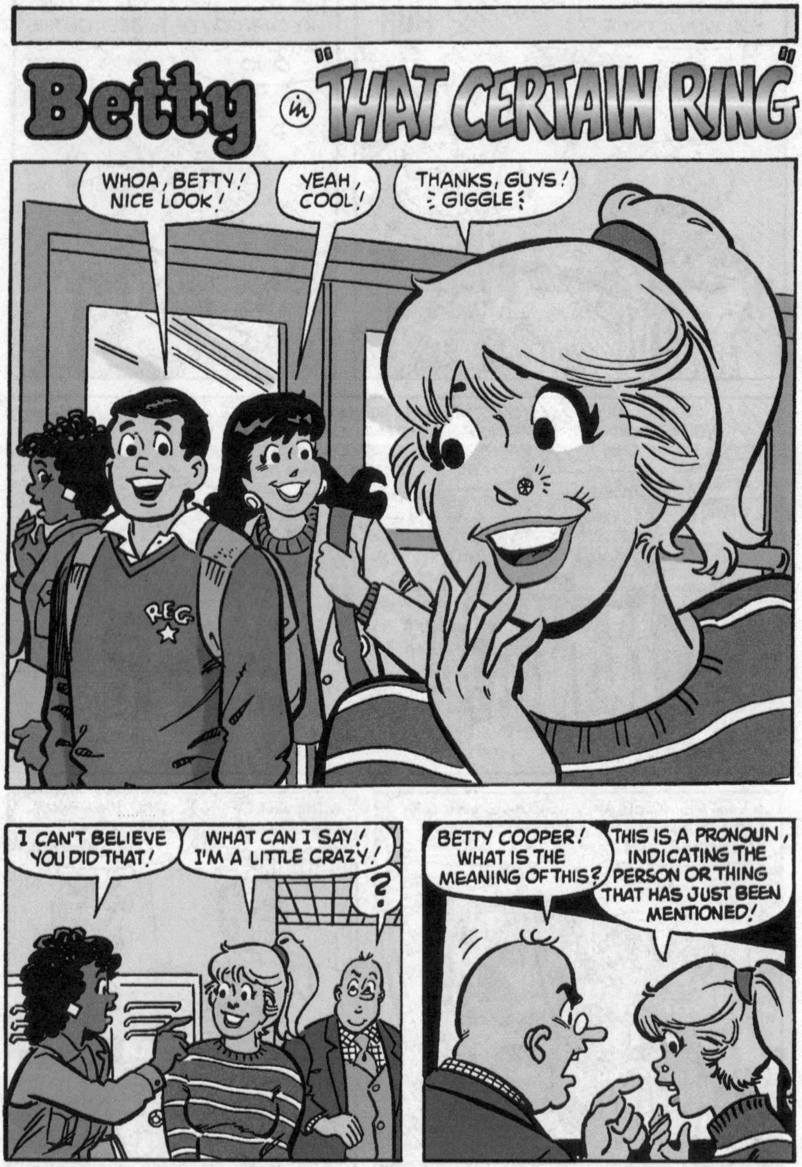
Betty in "THAT CERTAIN RING"
WHOA, BETTY! NICE LOOK!
YEAH, COOL!
THANKS, GUYS! ⁝GIGGLE⁝
I CAN'T BELIEVE YOU DID THAT!
WHAT CAN I SAY! I'M A LITTLE CRAZY!
?
BETTY COOPER! WHAT IS THE MEANING OF THIS?
THIS IS A PRONOUN, INDICATING THE PERSON OR THING THAT HAS JUST BEEN MENTIONED!

Originally presented in BETTY #62, June, 1998

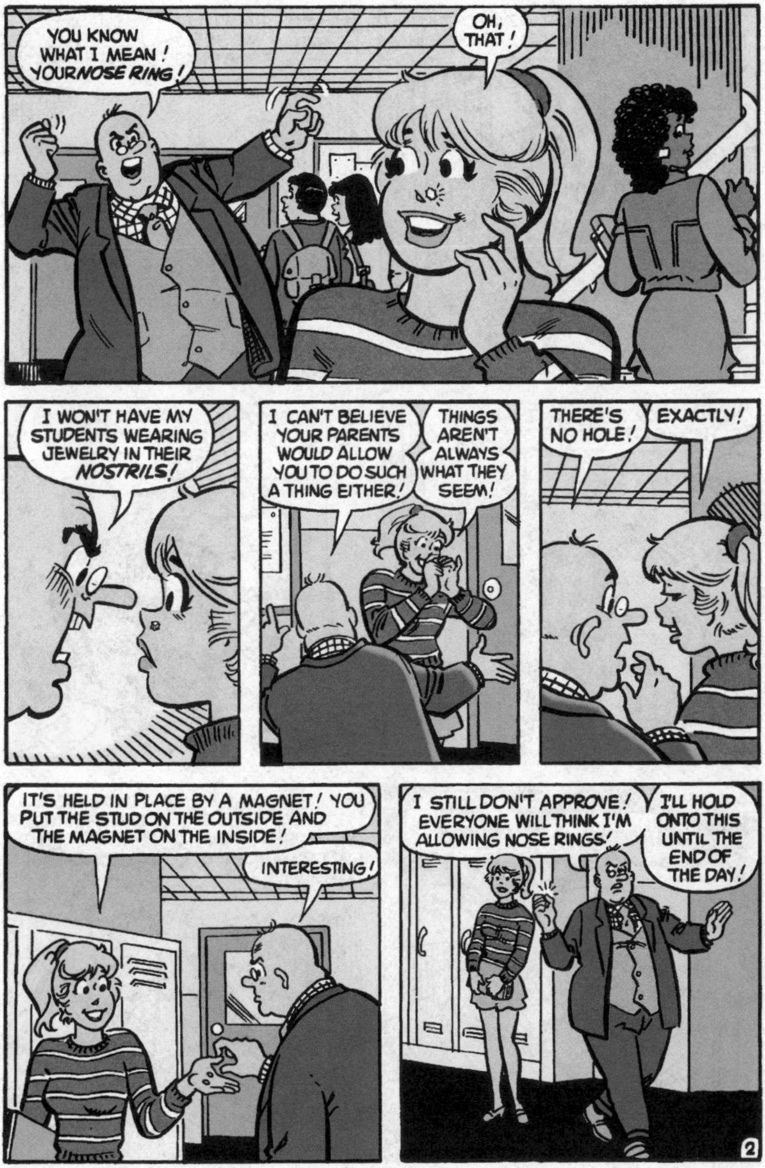
YOU KNOW WHAT I MEAN! YOUR NOSE RING!
OH, THAT!
I WON'T HAVE MY STUDENTS WEARING JEWELRY IN THEIR NOSTRILS!
I CAN'T BELIEVE YOUR PARENTS WOULD ALLOW YOU TO DO SUCH A THING EITHER!
THINGS AREN'T ALWAYS WHAT THEY SEEM!
THERE'S NO HOLE!
EXACTLY!
IT'S HELD IN PLACE BY A MAGNET! YOU PUT THE STUD ON THE OUTSIDE AND THE MAGNET ON THE INSIDE!
INTERESTING!
I STILL DON'T APPROVE! EVERYONE WILL THINK I'M ALLOWING NOSE RINGS!
I'LL HOLD ONTO THIS UNTIL THE END OF THE DAY!
2

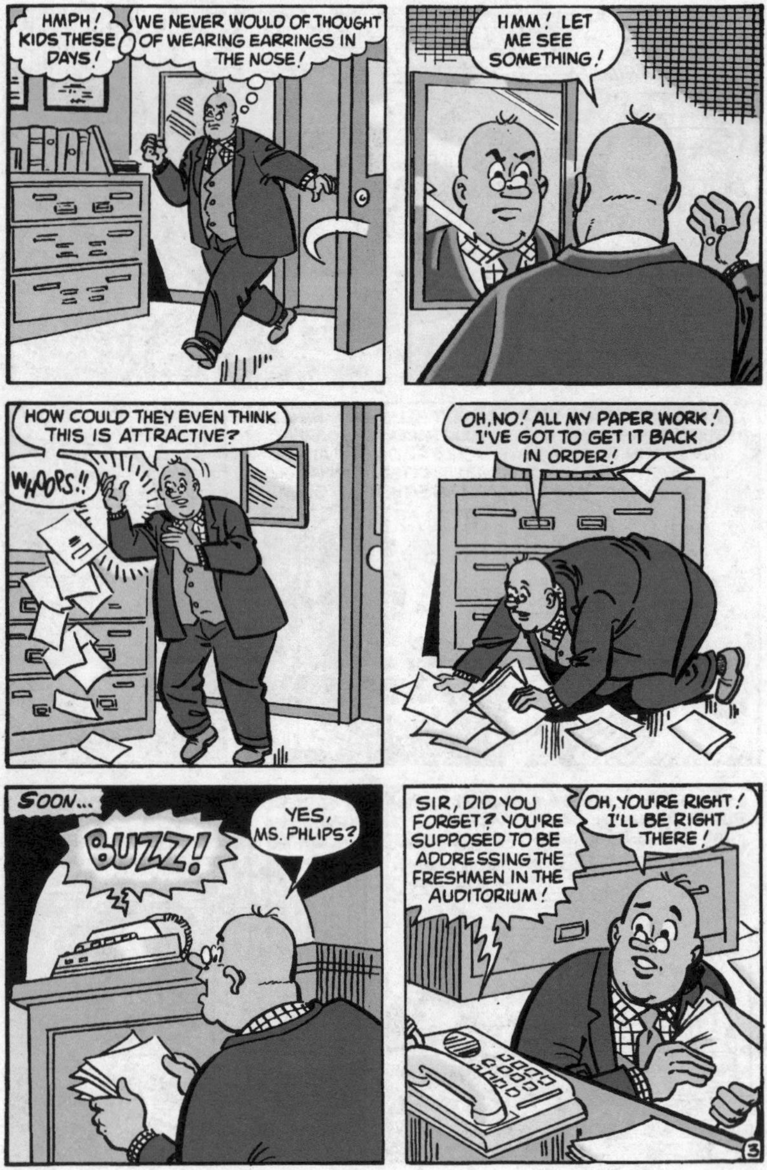
HMPH! KIDS THESE DAYS!
WE NEVER WOULD OF THOUGHT OF WEARING EARRINGS IN THE NOSE!
HMM! LET ME SEE SOMETHING!
HOW COULD THEY EVEN THINK THIS IS ATTRACTIVE?
WHOOPS!!
OH, NO! ALL MY PAPER WORK! I'VE GOT TO GET IT BACK IN ORDER!
SOON...
BUZZ!
YES, MS. PHLIPS?
SIR, DID YOU FORGET? YOU'RE SUPPOSED TO BE ADDRESSING THE FRESHMEN IN THE AUDITORIUM!
OH, YOU'RE RIGHT! I'LL BE RIGHT THERE!
3

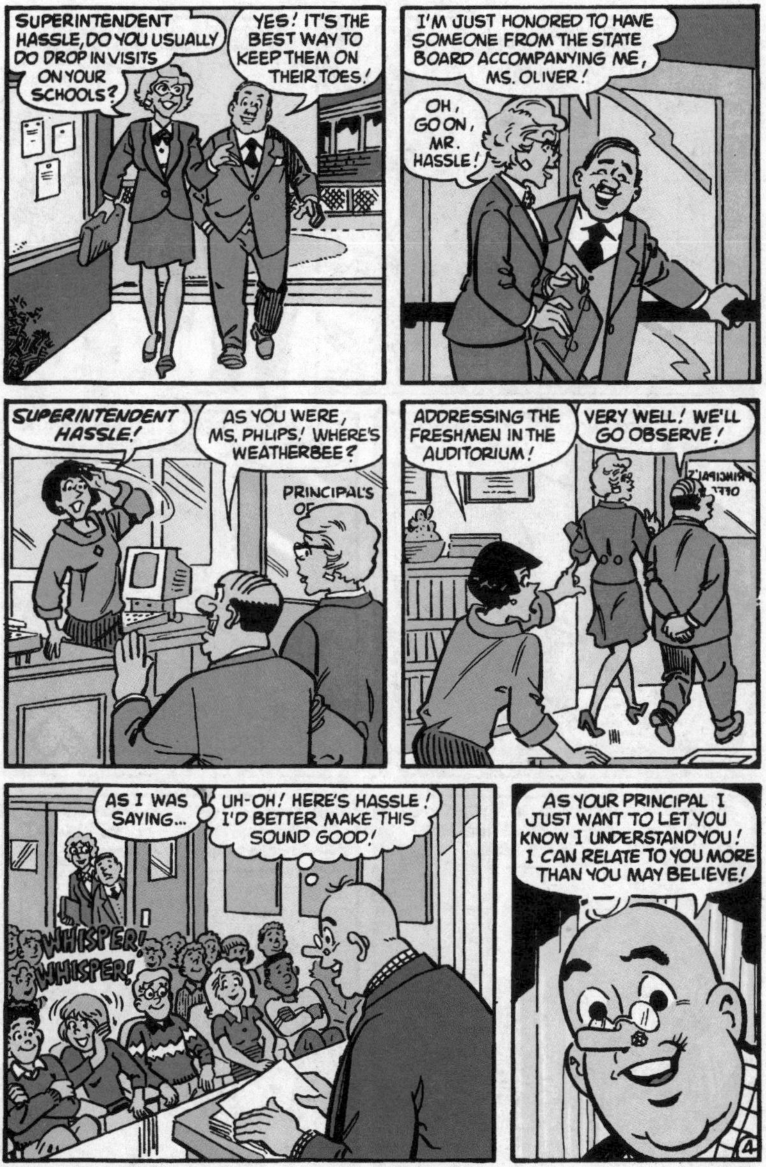
SUPERINTENDENT HASSLE, DO YOU USUALLY DO DROP IN VISITS ON YOUR SCHOOLS?
YES! IT'S THE BEST WAY TO KEEP THEM ON THEIR TOES!
I'M JUST HONORED TO HAVE SOMEONE FROM THE STATE BOARD ACCOMPANYING ME, MS. OLIVER!
OH, GO ON, MR. HASSLE!
SUPERINTENDENT HASSLE!
AS YOU WERE, MS. PHLIPS! WHERE'S WEATHERBEE?
PRINCIPAL'S OF
ADDRESSING THE FRESHMEN IN THE AUDITORIUM!
VERY WELL! WE'LL GO OBSERVE!
AS I WAS SAYING...
UH-OH! HERE'S HASSLE! I'D BETTER MAKE THIS SOUND GOOD!
WHISPER! WHISPER!
AS YOUR PRINCIPAL I JUST WANT TO LET YOU KNOW I UNDERSTAND YOU! I CAN RELATE TO YOU MORE THAN YOU MAY BELIEVE!
4

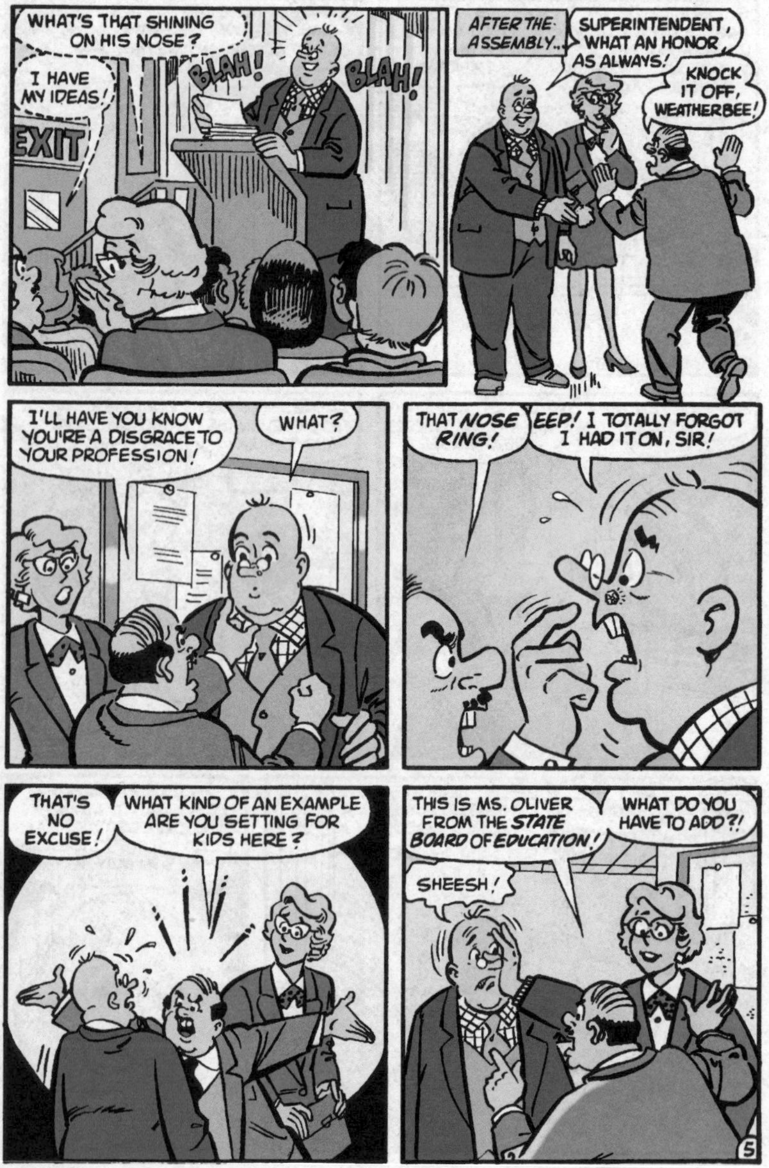
WHAT'S THAT SHINING ON HIS NOSE?
I HAVE MY IDEAS!
BLAH!
BLAH!
EXIT
AFTER THE ASSEMBLY...
SUPERINTENDENT, WHAT AN HONOR AS ALWAYS!
KNOCK IT OFF, WEATHERBEE!
I'LL HAVE YOU KNOW YOU'RE A DISGRACE TO YOUR PROFESSION!
WHAT?
THAT NOSE RING!
EEP! I TOTALLY FORGOT I HAD IT ON, SIR!
THAT'S NO EXCUSE!
WHAT KIND OF AN EXAMPLE ARE YOU SETTING FOR KIDS HERE?
THIS IS MS. OLIVER FROM THE STATE BOARD OF EDUCATION!
WHAT DO YOU HAVE TO ADD?!
SHEESH!
5

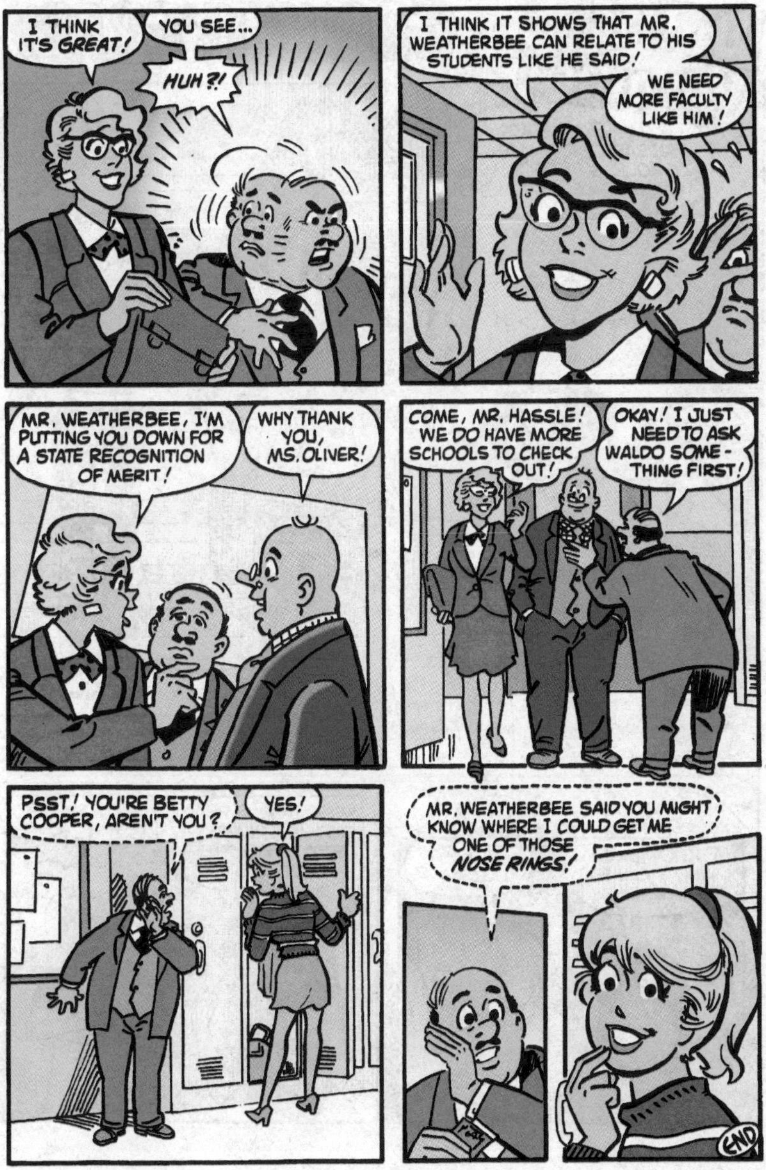
I THINK IT'S GREAT!
YOU SEE...
HUH?!
I THINK IT SHOWS THAT MR. WEATHERBEE CAN RELATE TO HIS STUDENTS LIKE HE SAID!
WE NEED MORE FACULTY LIKE HIM!
MR. WEATHERBEE, I'M PUTTING YOU DOWN FOR A STATE RECOGNITION OF MERIT!
WHY THANK YOU, MS. OLIVER!
COME, MR. HASSLE! WE DO HAVE MORE SCHOOLS TO CHECK OUT!
OKAY! I JUST NEED TO ASK WALDO SOME-THING FIRST!
PSST! YOU'RE BETTY COOPER, AREN'T YOU?
YES!
MR. WEATHERBEE SAID YOU MIGHT KNOW WHERE I COULD GET ME ONE OF THOSE NOSE RINGS!
END

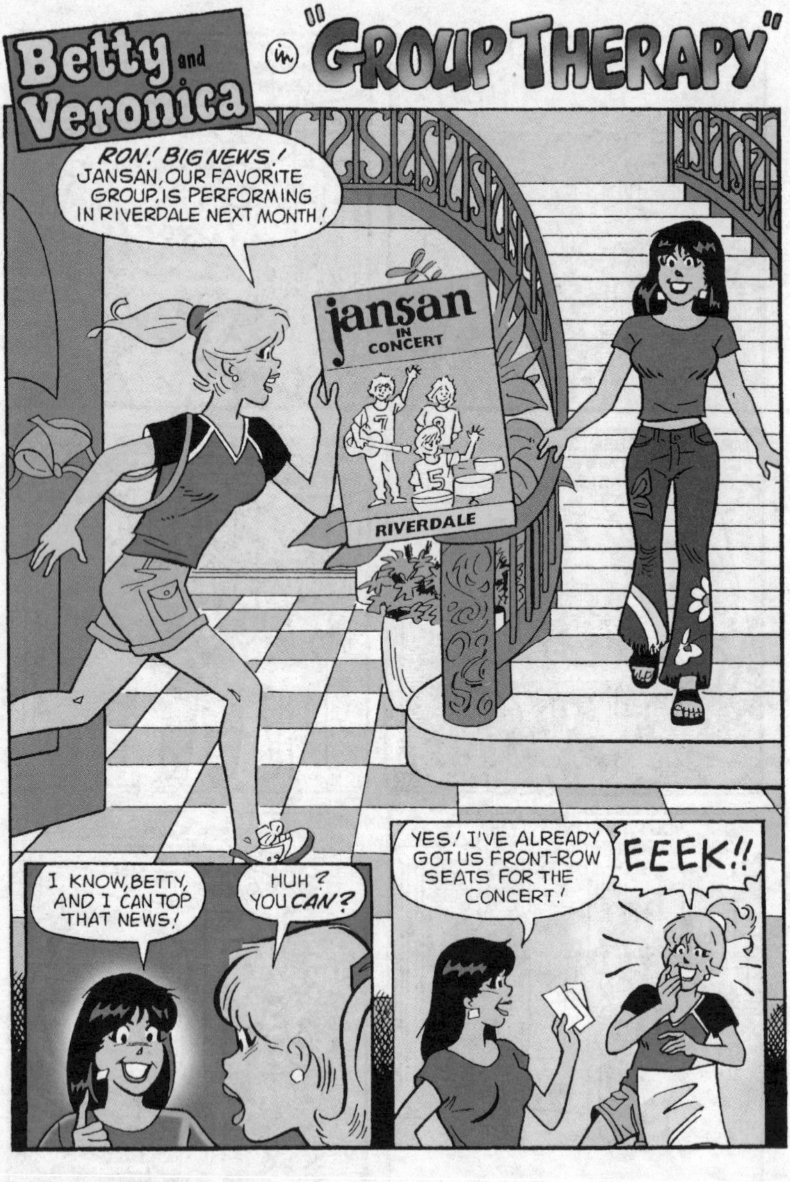
Betty and Veronica
in "GROUP THERAPY"
RON! BIG NEWS! JANSAN, OUR FAVORITE GROUP, IS PERFORMING IN RIVERDALE NEXT MONTH!
jansan IN CONCERT
RIVERDALE
I KNOW, BETTY, AND I CAN TOP THAT NEWS!
HUH? YOU CAN?
YES! I'VE ALREADY GOT US FRONT-ROW SEATS FOR THE CONCERT!
EEEK!!

Originally presented in BETTY & VERONICA #126, July, 1998

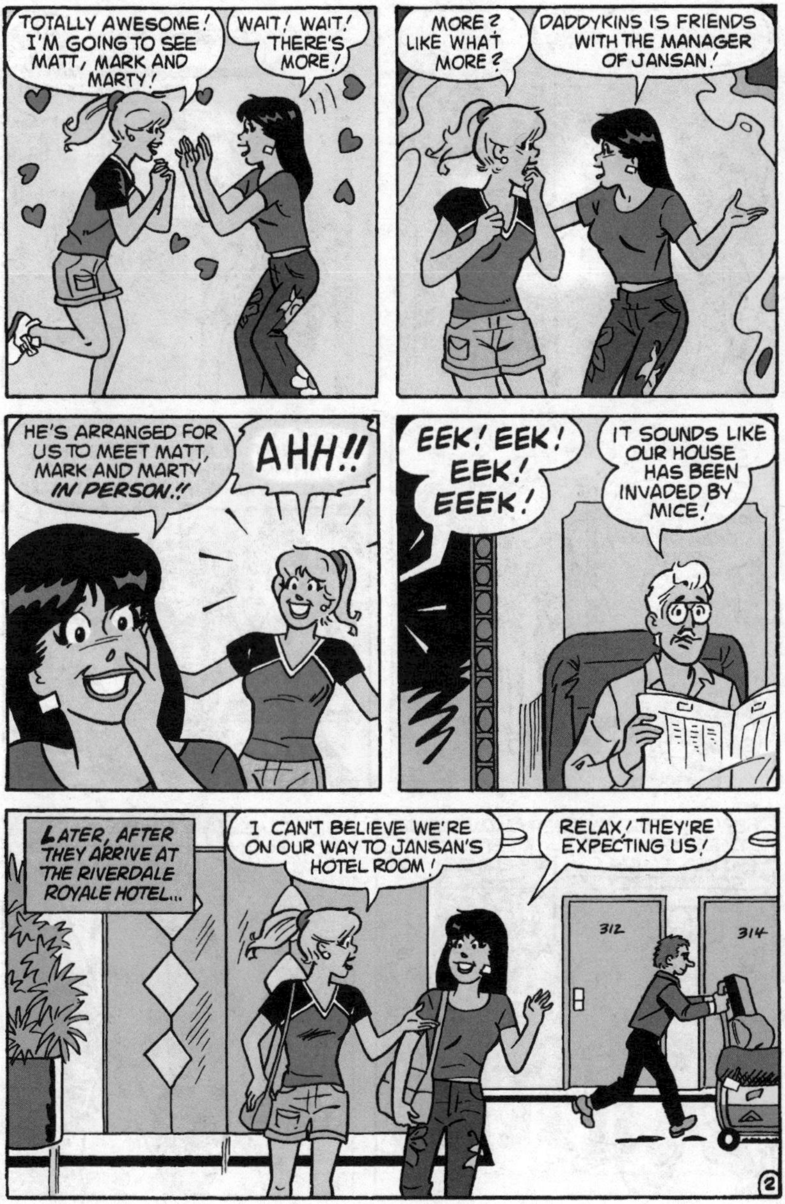
TOTALLY AWESOME! I'M GOING TO SEE MATT, MARK AND MARTY!
WAIT! WAIT! THERE'S MORE!
MORE? LIKE WHAT MORE?
DADDYKINS IS FRIENDS WITH THE MANAGER OF JANSAN!
HE'S ARRANGED FOR US TO MEET MATT, MARK AND MARTY IN PERSON.!!
AHH!!
EEK! EEK! EEK! EEEK!
IT SOUNDS LIKE OUR HOUSE HAS BEEN INVADED BY MICE!
LATER, AFTER THEY ARRIVE AT THE RIVERDALE ROYALE HOTEL...
I CAN'T BELIEVE WE'RE ON OUR WAY TO JANSAN'S HOTEL ROOM!
RELAX! THEY'RE EXPECTING US!
312
314
2

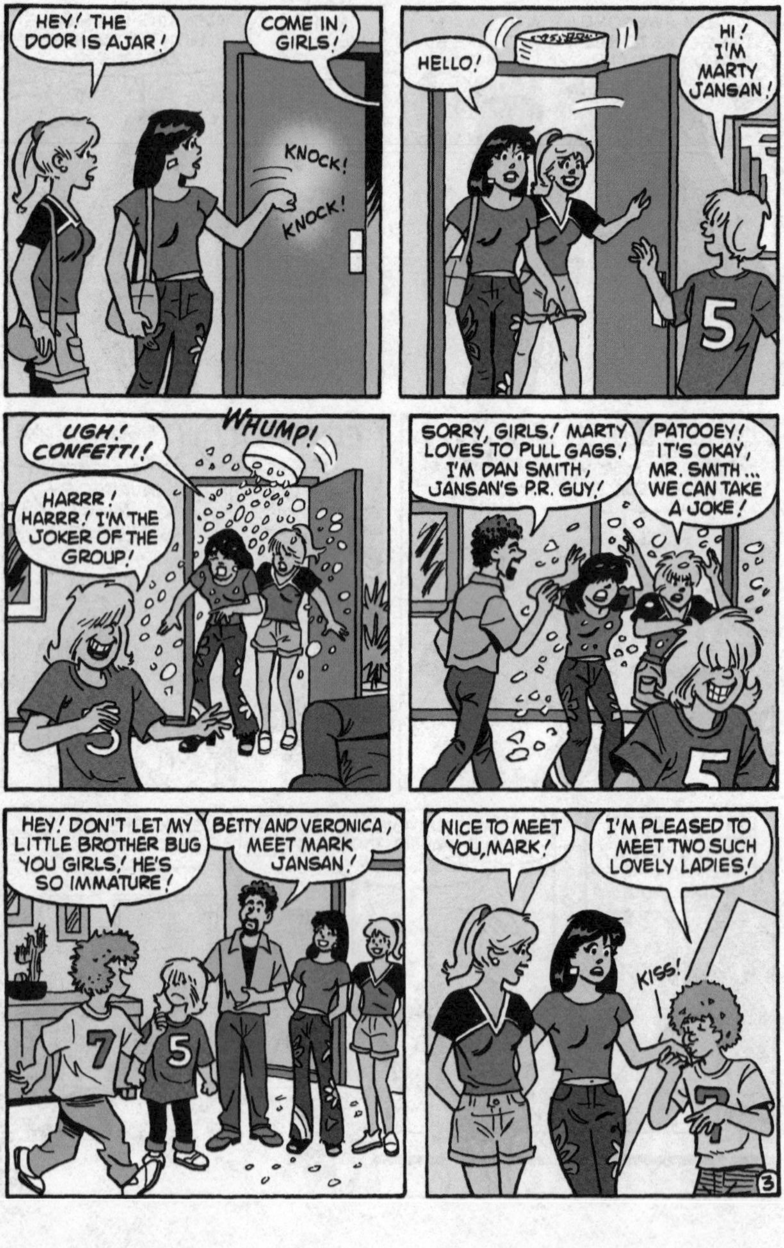
HEY! THE DOOR IS AJAR!
COME IN, GIRLS!
KNOCK! KNOCK!
HELLO!
HI! I'M MARTY JANSAN!
UGH! CONFETTI!
WHUMP!
HARRR! HARRR! I'M THE JOKER OF THE GROUP!
SORRY, GIRLS! MARTY LOVES TO PULL GAGS! I'M DAN SMITH, JANSAN'S P.R. GUY!
PATOOEY! IT'S OKAY, MR. SMITH... WE CAN TAKE A JOKE!
HEY! DON'T LET MY LITTLE BROTHER BUG YOU GIRLS! HE'S SO IMMATURE!
BETTY AND VERONICA, MEET MARK JANSAN!
NICE TO MEET YOU, MARK!
I'M PLEASED TO MEET TWO SUCH LOVELY LADIES!
KISS!
3

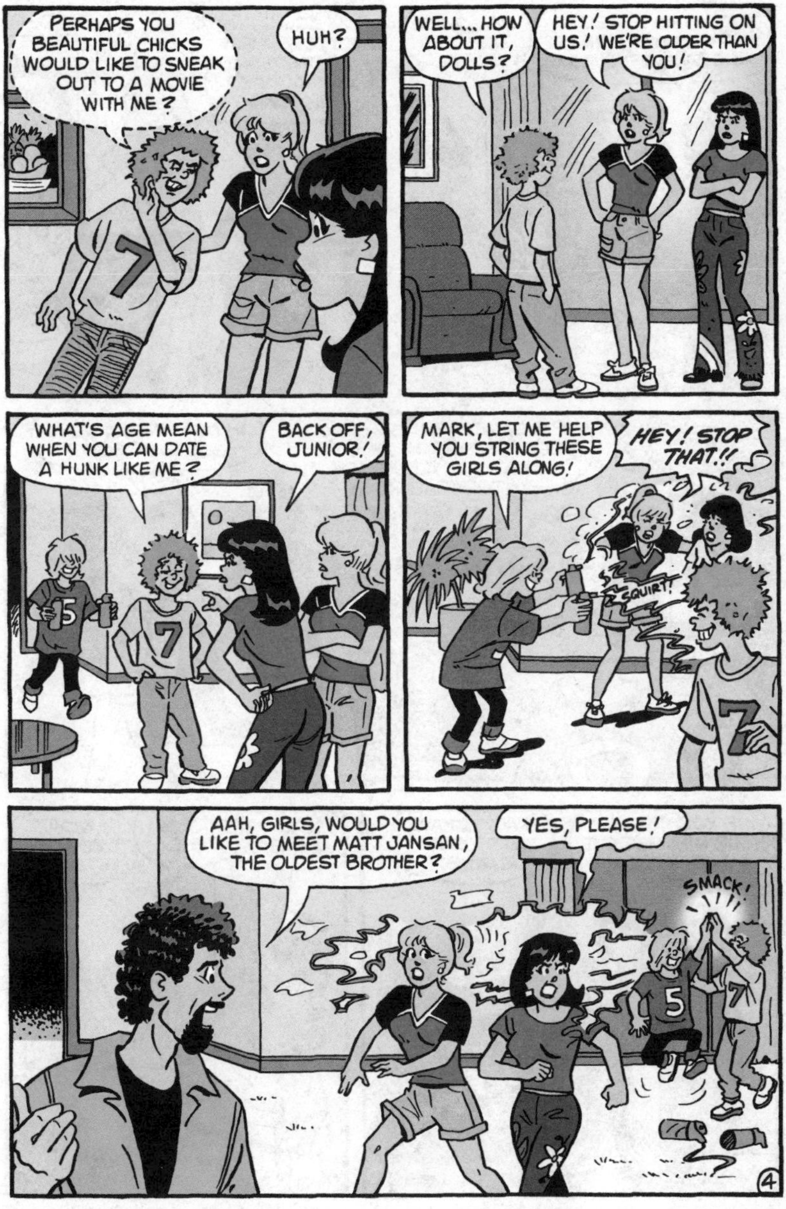
PERHAPS YOU BEAUTIFUL CHICKS WOULD LIKE TO SNEAK OUT TO A MOVIE WITH ME?
HUH?
WELL... HOW ABOUT IT, DOLLS?
HEY! STOP HITTING ON US! WE'RE OLDER THAN YOU!
WHAT'S AGE MEAN WHEN YOU CAN DATE A HUNK LIKE ME?
BACK OFF, JUNIOR!
MARK, LET ME HELP YOU STRING THESE GIRLS ALONG!
HEY! STOP THAT!!
SQUIRT!
AAH, GIRLS, WOULD YOU LIKE TO MEET MATT JANSAN, THE OLDEST BROTHER?
YES, PLEASE!
SMACK!
4

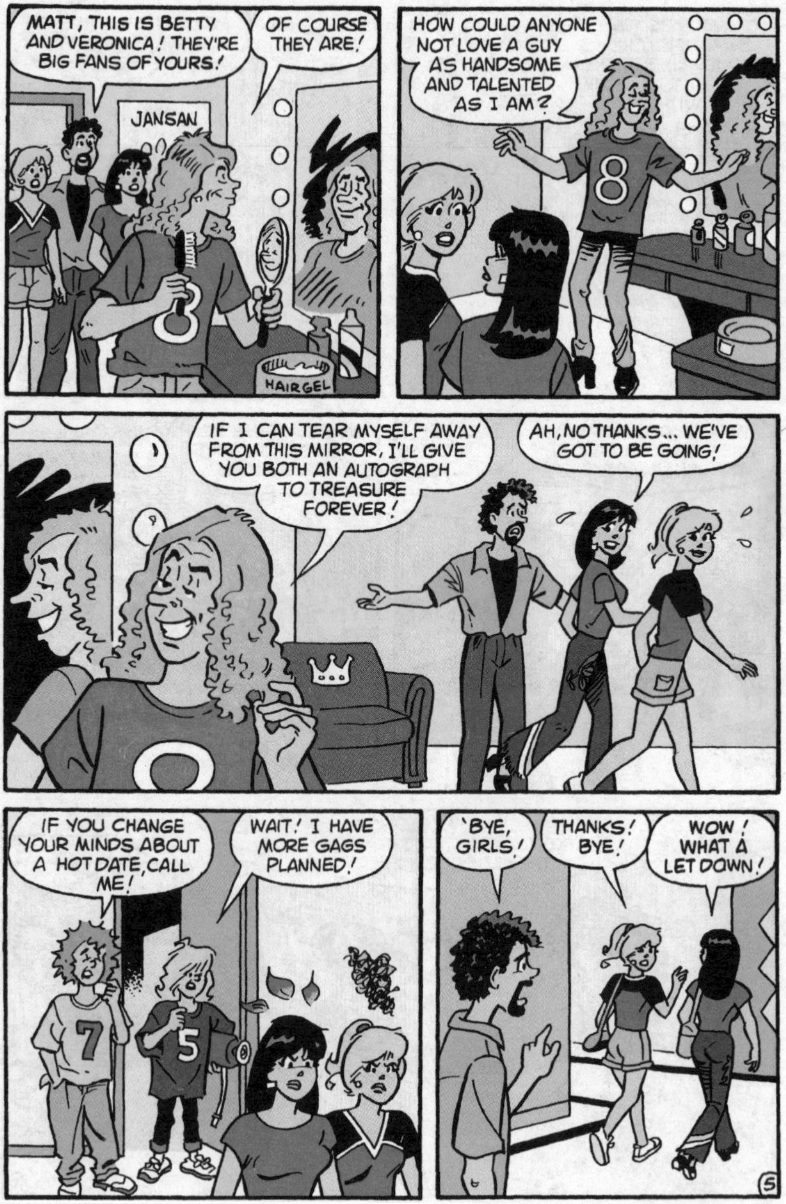
MATT, THIS IS BETTY AND VERONICA! THEY'RE BIG FANS OF YOURS!
OF COURSE THEY ARE!
JANSAN
HAIRGEL
HOW COULD ANYONE NOT LOVE A GUY AS HANDSOME AND TALENTED AS I AM?
IF I CAN TEAR MYSELF AWAY FROM THIS MIRROR, I'LL GIVE YOU BOTH AN AUTOGRAPH TO TREASURE FOREVER!
AH, NO THANKS... WE'VE GOT TO BE GOING!
IF YOU CHANGE YOUR MINDS ABOUT A HOT DATE, CALL ME!
WAIT! I HAVE MORE GAGS PLANNED!
'BYE, GIRLS!
THANKS! BYE!
WOW! WHAT A LET DOWN!
5

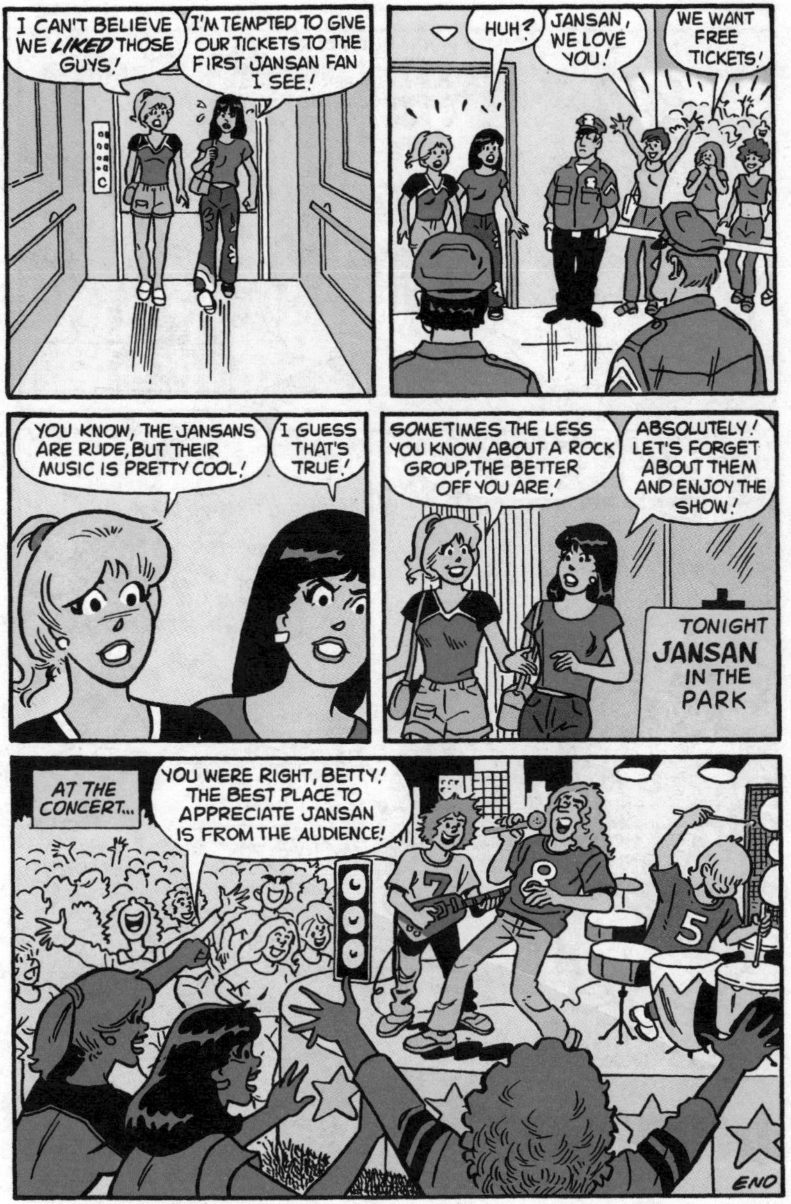
I CAN'T BELIEVE WE *LIKED* THOSE GUYS!
I'M TEMPTED TO GIVE OUR TICKETS TO THE FIRST JANSAN FAN I SEE!
HUH?
JANSAN, WE LOVE YOU!
WE WANT FREE TICKETS!
YOU KNOW, THE JANSANS ARE RUDE, BUT THEIR MUSIC IS PRETTY COOL!
I GUESS THAT'S TRUE!
SOMETIMES THE LESS YOU KNOW ABOUT A ROCK GROUP, THE BETTER OFF YOU ARE!
ABSOLUTELY! LET'S FORGET ABOUT THEM AND ENJOY THE SHOW!
TONIGHT JANSAN IN THE PARK
AT THE CONCERT...
YOU WERE RIGHT, BETTY! THE BEST PLACE TO APPRECIATE JANSAN IS FROM THE AUDIENCE!
ENO

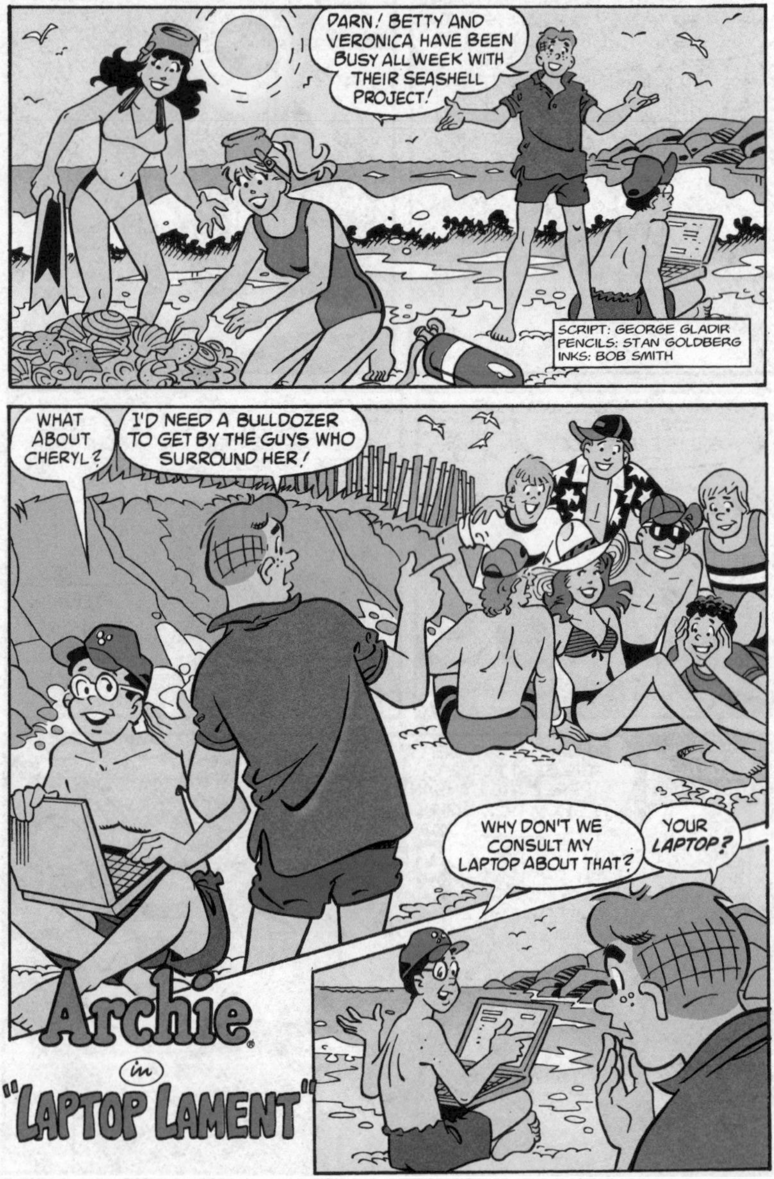
DARN! BETTY AND VERONICA HAVE BEEN BUSY ALL WEEK WITH THEIR SEASHELL PROJECT!
SCRIPT: GEORGE GLADIR
PENCILS: STAN GOLDBERG
INKS: BOB SMITH
WHAT ABOUT CHERYL?
I'D NEED A BULLDOZER TO GET BY THE GUYS WHO SURROUND HER!
WHY DON'T WE CONSULT MY LAPTOP ABOUT THAT?
YOUR LAPTOP?
Archie
in
"LAPTOP LAMENT"

Originally presented in ARCHIE #475, September, 1998

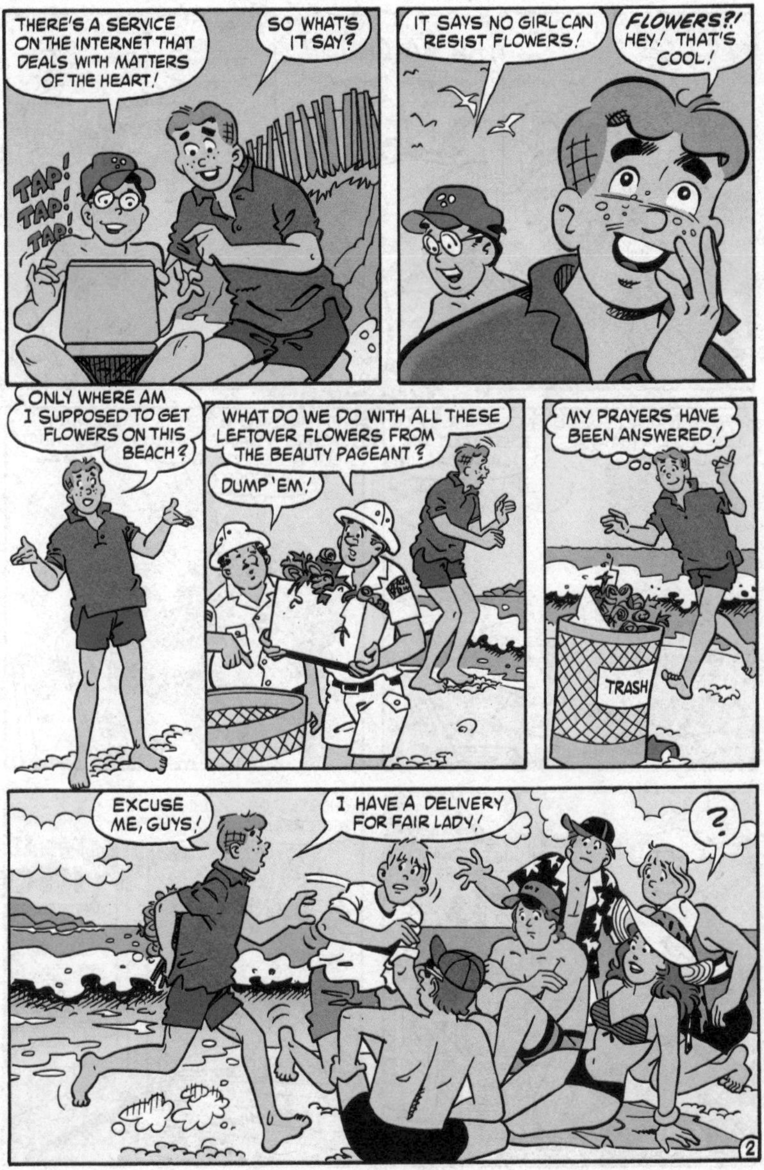
THERE'S A SERVICE ON THE INTERNET THAT DEALS WITH MATTERS OF THE HEART!
SO WHAT'S IT SAY?
TAP! TAP! TAP!
IT SAYS NO GIRL CAN RESIST FLOWERS!
FLOWERS?! HEY! THAT'S COOL!
ONLY WHERE AM I SUPPOSED TO GET FLOWERS ON THIS BEACH?
WHAT DO WE DO WITH ALL THESE LEFTOVER FLOWERS FROM THE BEAUTY PAGEANT?
DUMP 'EM!
MY PRAYERS HAVE BEEN ANSWERED!
TRASH
EXCUSE ME, GUYS!
I HAVE A DELIVERY FOR FAIR LADY!
?
2

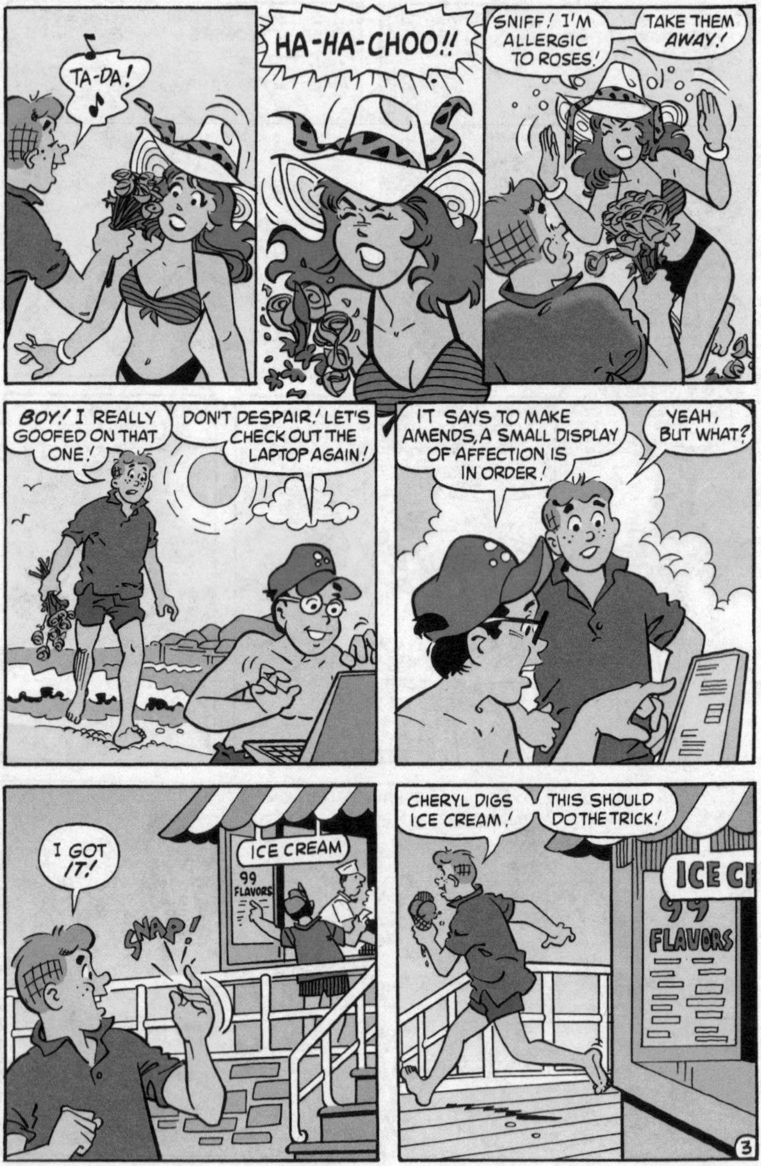
TA-DA!
HA-HA-CHOO!!
SNIFF! I'M ALLERGIC TO ROSES!
TAKE THEM AWAY!
BOY! I REALLY GOOFED ON THAT ONE!
DON'T DESPAIR! LET'S CHECK OUT THE LAPTOP AGAIN!
IT SAYS TO MAKE AMENDS, A SMALL DISPLAY OF AFFECTION IS IN ORDER!
YEAH, BUT WHAT?
I GOT IT!
SNAP!
ICE CREAM
99 FLAVORS
CHERYL DIGS ICE CREAM!
THIS SHOULD DO THE TRICK!
ICE C
99
FLAVORS
3

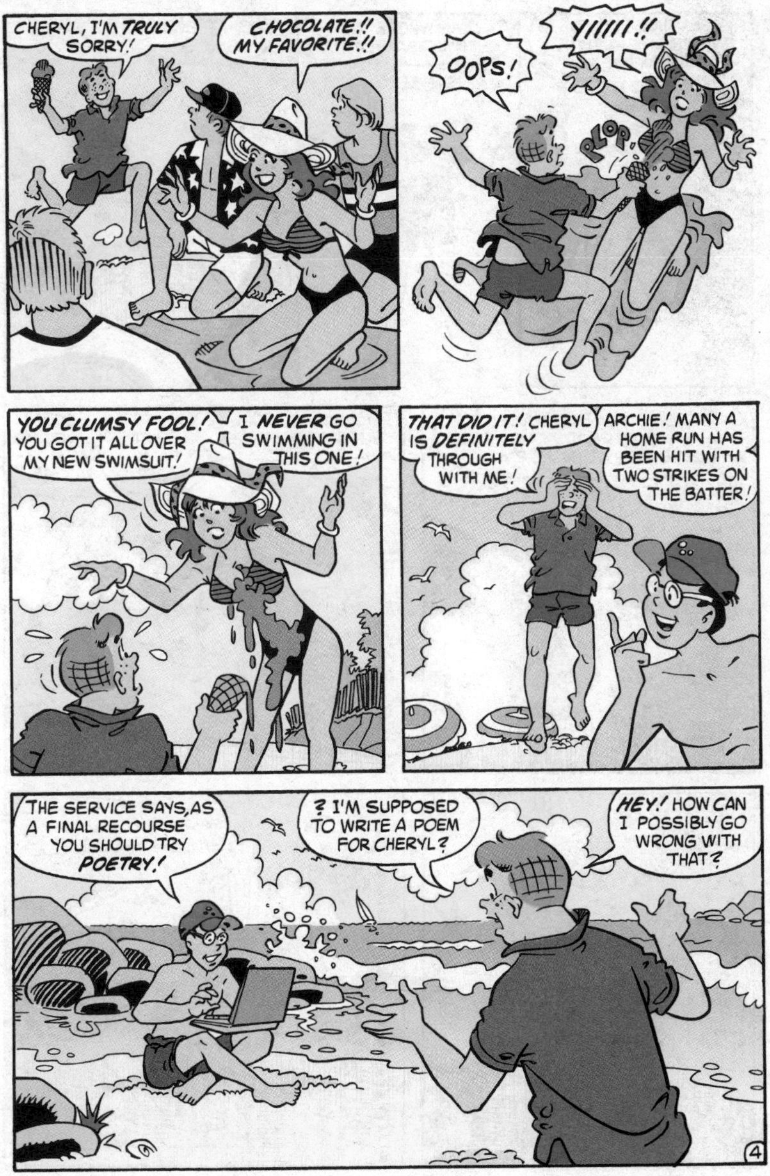
CHERYL, I'M TRULY SORRY!
CHOCOLATE!! MY FAVORITE!!
OOPS!
YIIIII!!
PLOP!
YOU CLUMSY FOOL! YOU GOT IT ALL OVER MY NEW SWIMSUIT!
I NEVER GO SWIMMING IN THIS ONE!
THAT DID IT! CHERYL IS DEFINITELY THROUGH WITH ME!
ARCHIE! MANY A HOME RUN HAS BEEN HIT WITH TWO STRIKES ON THE BATTER!
THE SERVICE SAYS, AS A FINAL RECOURSE YOU SHOULD TRY POETRY!
? I'M SUPPOSED TO WRITE A POEM FOR CHERYL?
HEY! HOW CAN I POSSIBLY GO WRONG WITH THAT?
4

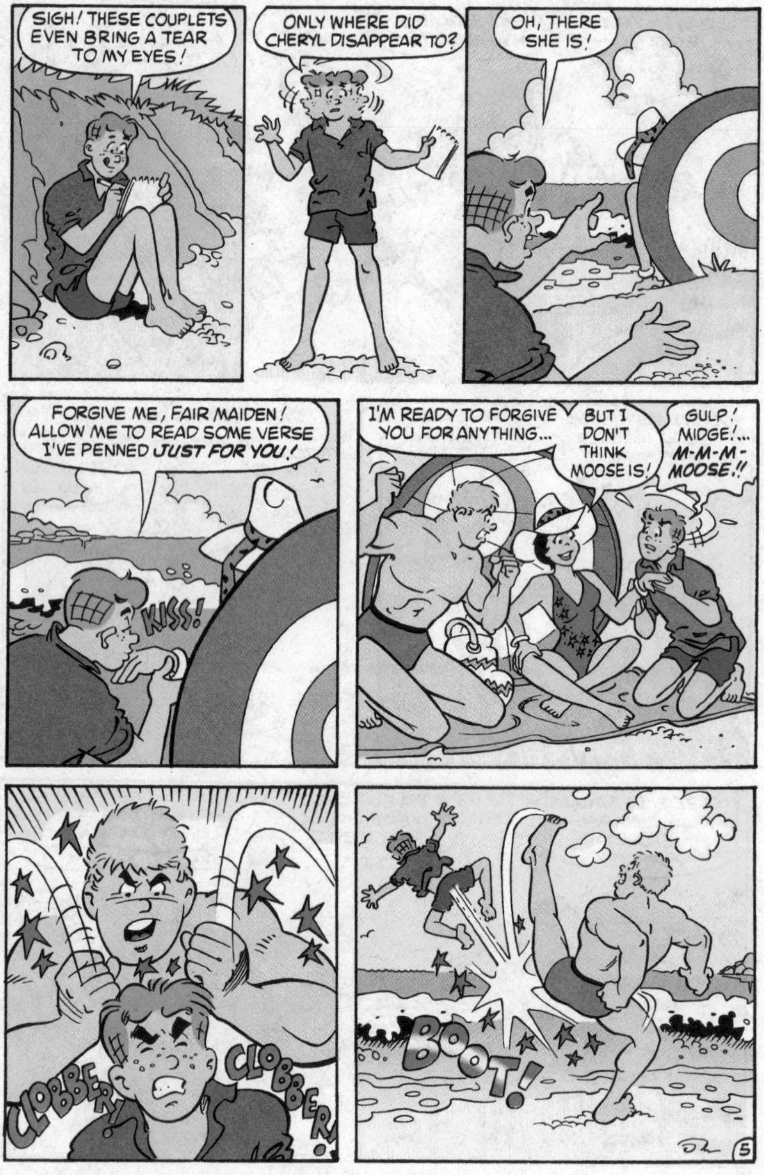
SIGH! THESE COUPLETS EVEN BRING A TEAR TO MY EYES!
ONLY WHERE DID CHERYL DISAPPEAR TO?
OH, THERE SHE IS!
FORGIVE ME, FAIR MAIDEN! ALLOW ME TO READ SOME VERSE I'VE PENNED JUST FOR YOU!
KISS!
I'M READY TO FORGIVE YOU FOR ANYTHING...
BUT I DON'T THINK MOOSE IS!
GULP! MIDGE!... M-M-M-MOOSE!!
CLOBBER!
CLOBBER!
BOOT!
5

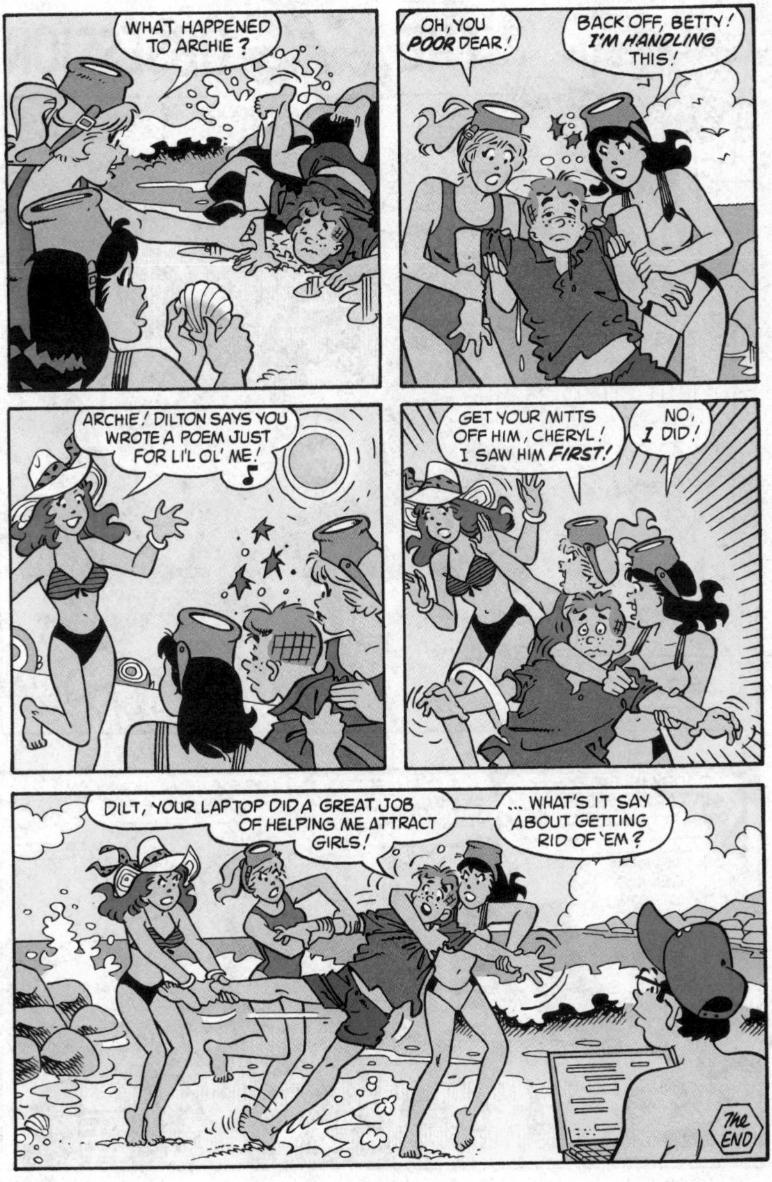
WHAT HAPPENED TO ARCHIE?
OH, YOU POOR DEAR!
BACK OFF, BETTY! I'M HANDLING THIS!
ARCHIE! DILTON SAYS YOU WROTE A POEM JUST FOR LI'L OL' ME!
GET YOUR MITTS OFF HIM, CHERYL! I SAW HIM FIRST!
NO, I DID!
DILT, YOUR LAPTOP DID A GREAT JOB OF HELPING ME ATTRACT GIRLS!
... WHAT'S IT SAY ABOUT GETTING RID OF 'EM?
THE END

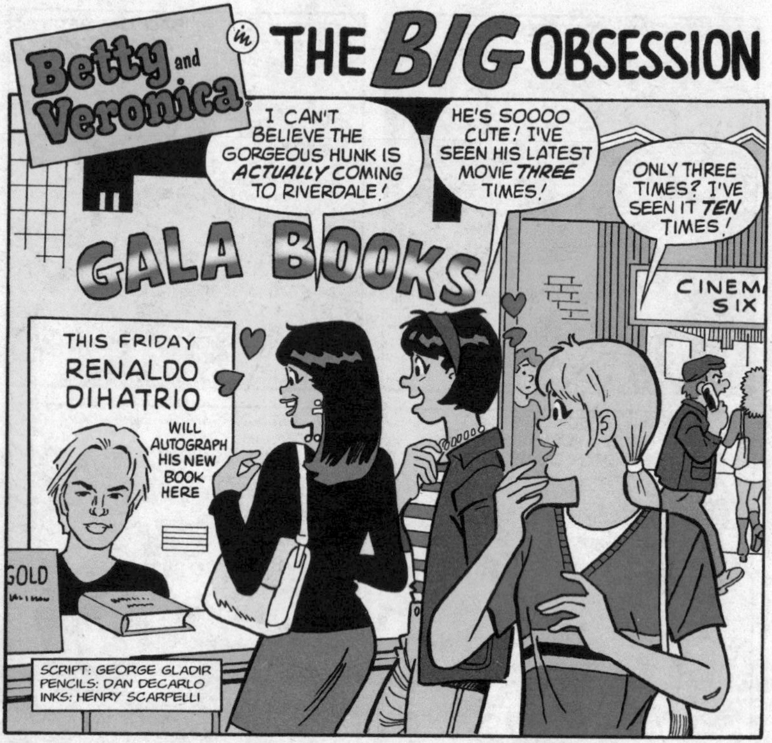
Betty and Veronica in
THE BIG OBSESSION
I CAN'T BELIEVE THE GORGEOUS HUNK IS ACTUALLY COMING TO RIVERDALE!
HE'S SOOOO CUTE! I'VE SEEN HIS LATEST MOVIE THREE TIMES!
ONLY THREE TIMES? I'VE SEEN IT TEN TIMES!
GALA BOOKS
CINEMA SIX
THIS FRIDAY RENALDO DIHATRIO
WILL AUTOGRAPH HIS NEW BOOK HERE
GOLD
SCRIPT: GEORGE GLADIR
PENCILS: DAN DECARLO
INKS: HENRY SCARPELLI

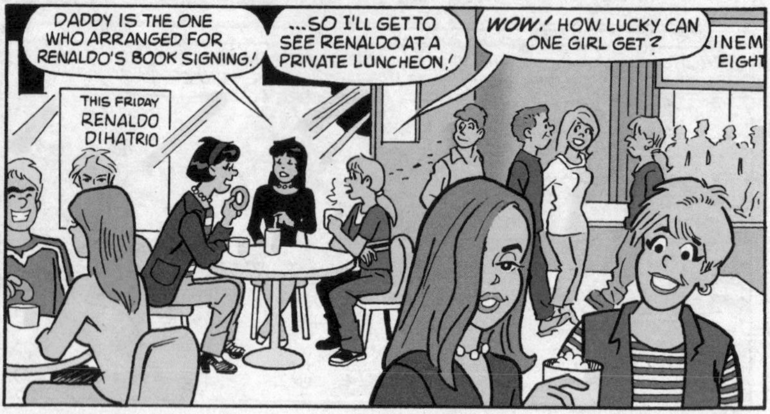
DADDY IS THE ONE WHO ARRANGED FOR RENALDO'S BOOK SIGNING!
...SO I'LL GET TO SEE RENALDO AT A PRIVATE LUNCHEON!
WOW! HOW LUCKY CAN ONE GIRL GET?
THIS FRIDAY RENALDO DIHATRIO
CINEMA EIGHT

Originally presented in BETTY & VERONICA #129, November, 1998

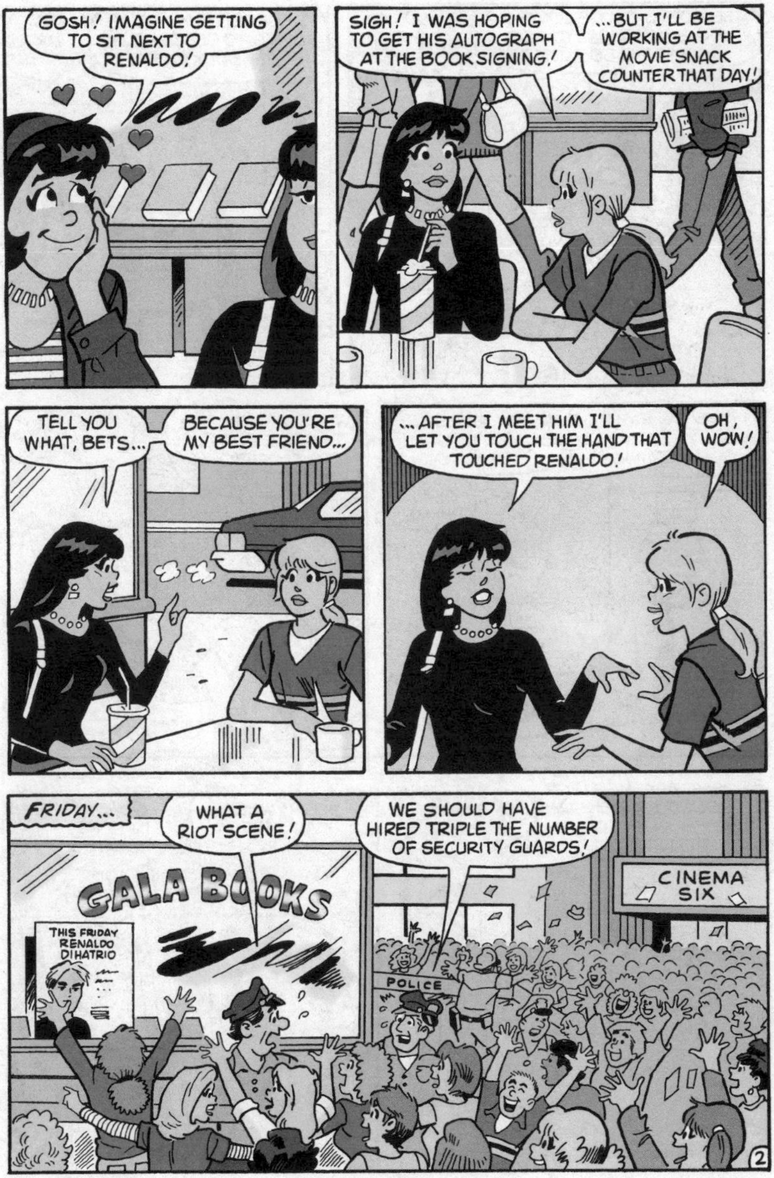
GOSH! IMAGINE GETTING TO SIT NEXT TO RENALDO!
SIGH! I WAS HOPING TO GET HIS AUTOGRAPH AT THE BOOK SIGNING!
...BUT I'LL BE WORKING AT THE MOVIE SNACK COUNTER THAT DAY!
TELL YOU WHAT, BETS...
BECAUSE YOU'RE MY BEST FRIEND...
...AFTER I MEET HIM I'LL LET YOU TOUCH THE HAND THAT TOUCHED RENALDO!
OH, WOW!
FRIDAY...
WHAT A RIOT SCENE!
WE SHOULD HAVE HIRED TRIPLE THE NUMBER OF SECURITY GUARDS!
GALA BOOKS
THIS FRIDAY RENALDO DIHATRIO
CINEMA SIX
POLICE
2

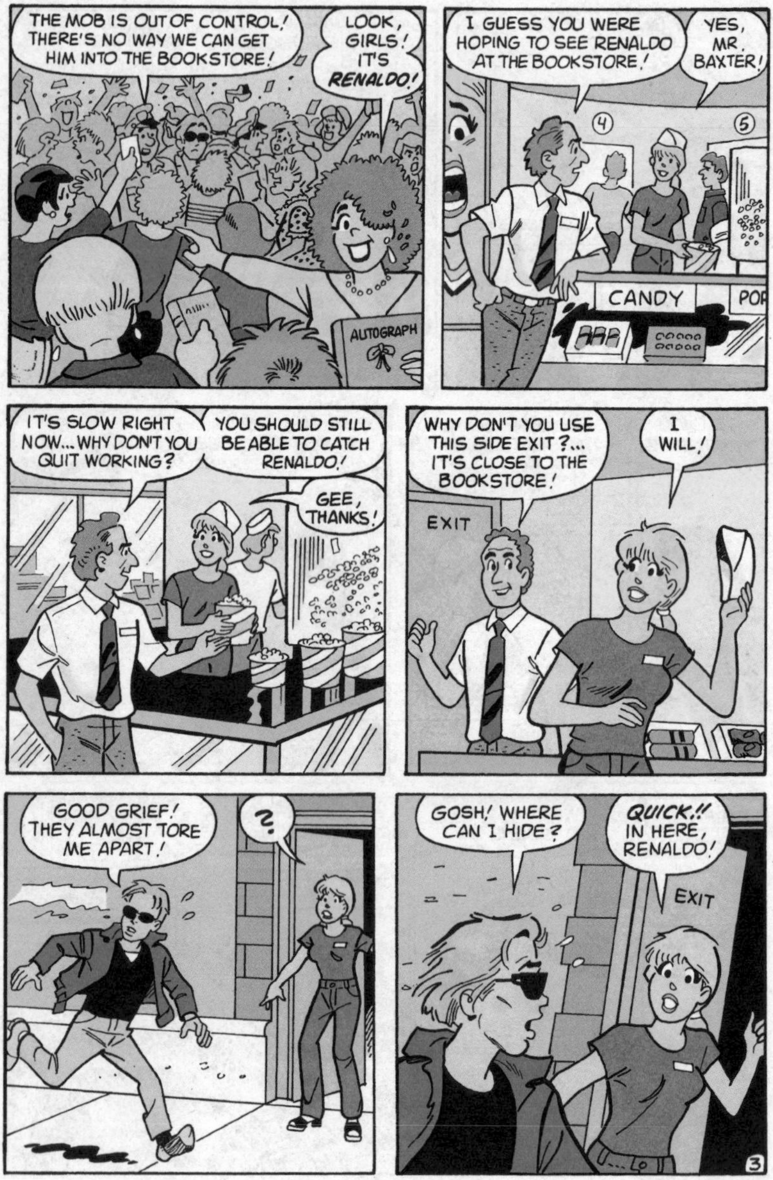
THE MOB IS OUT OF CONTROL! THERE'S NO WAY WE CAN GET HIM INTO THE BOOKSTORE!
LOOK, GIRLS! IT'S RENALDO!
AUTOGRAPH
I GUESS YOU WERE HOPING TO SEE RENALDO AT THE BOOKSTORE!
YES, MR. BAXTER!
4
5
CANDY
IT'S SLOW RIGHT NOW... WHY DON'T YOU QUIT WORKING?
YOU SHOULD STILL BE ABLE TO CATCH RENALDO!
GEE, THANKS!
WHY DON'T YOU USE THIS SIDE EXIT?... IT'S CLOSE TO THE BOOKSTORE!
I WILL!
EXIT
GOOD GRIEF! THEY ALMOST TORE ME APART!
?
GOSH! WHERE CAN I HIDE?
QUICK!! IN HERE, RENALDO!
EXIT
3

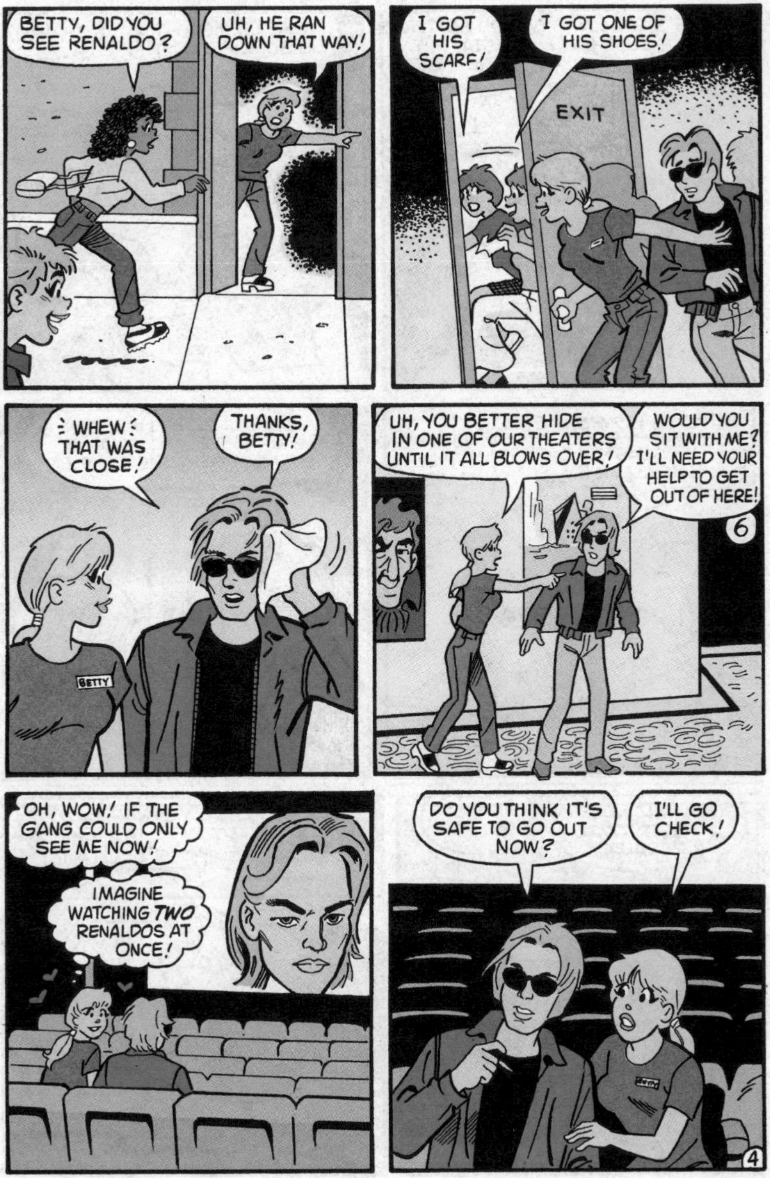
BETTY, DID YOU SEE RENALDO?
UH, HE RAN DOWN THAT WAY!
I GOT HIS SCARF!
I GOT ONE OF HIS SHOES!
EXIT
WHEW! THAT WAS CLOSE!
THANKS, BETTY!
BETTY
UH, YOU BETTER HIDE IN ONE OF OUR THEATERS UNTIL IT ALL BLOWS OVER!
WOULD YOU SIT WITH ME? I'LL NEED YOUR HELP TO GET OUT OF HERE!
6
OH, WOW! IF THE GANG COULD ONLY SEE ME NOW!
IMAGINE WATCHING TWO RENALDOS AT ONCE!
DO YOU THINK IT'S SAFE TO GO OUT NOW?
I'LL GO CHECK!
4

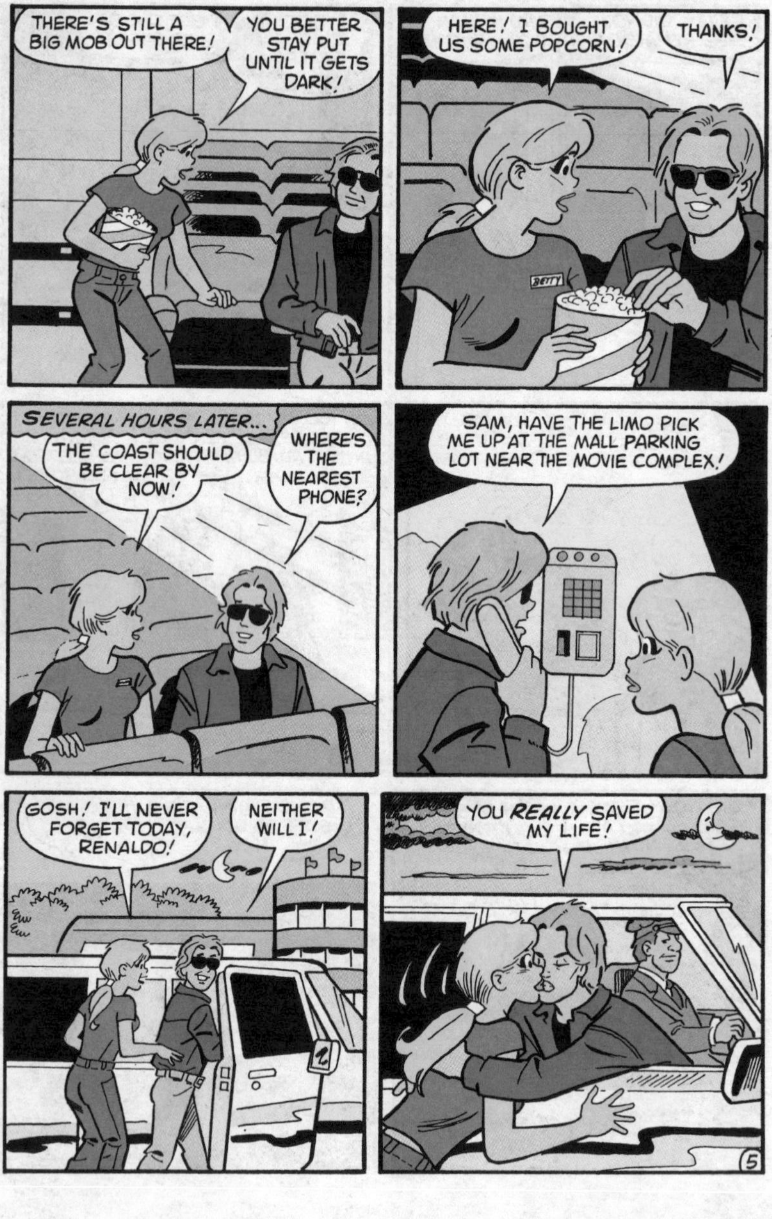
THERE'S STILL A BIG MOB OUT THERE!
YOU BETTER STAY PUT UNTIL IT GETS DARK!
HERE! I BOUGHT US SOME POPCORN!
THANKS!
BETTY
SEVERAL HOURS LATER...
THE COAST SHOULD BE CLEAR BY NOW!
WHERE'S THE NEAREST PHONE?
SAM, HAVE THE LIMO PICK ME UP AT THE MALL PARKING LOT NEAR THE MOVIE COMPLEX!
GOSH! I'LL NEVER FORGET TODAY, RENALDO!
NEITHER WILL I!
YOU REALLY SAVED MY LIFE!
5

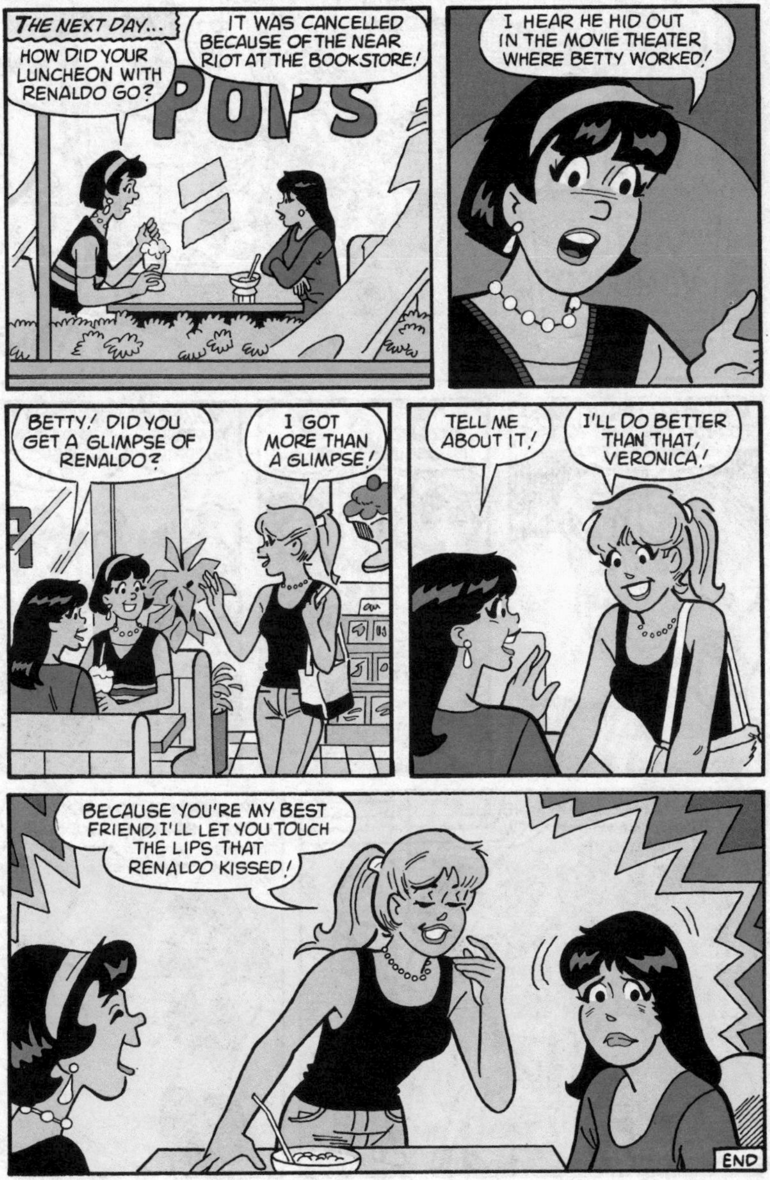
THE NEXT DAY...
HOW DID YOUR LUNCHEON WITH RENALDO GO?
IT WAS CANCELLED BECAUSE OF THE NEAR RIOT AT THE BOOKSTORE!
POP'S
I HEAR HE HID OUT IN THE MOVIE THEATER WHERE BETTY WORKED!
BETTY! DID YOU GET A GLIMPSE OF RENALDO?
I GOT MORE THAN A GLIMPSE!
TELL ME ABOUT IT!
I'LL DO BETTER THAN THAT, VERONICA!
BECAUSE YOU'RE MY BEST FRIEND, I'LL LET YOU TOUCH THE LIPS THAT RENALDO KISSED!
END

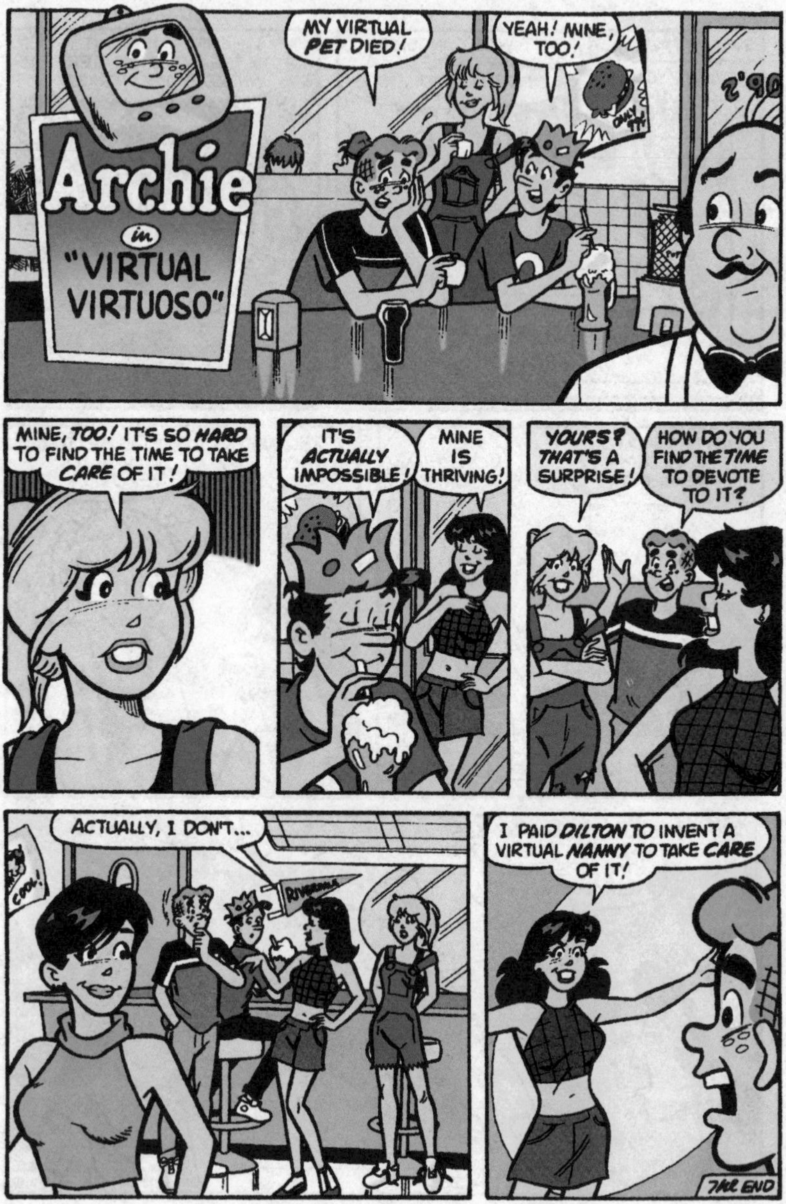
Archie
in
"VIRTUAL VIRTUOSO"
MY VIRTUAL PET DIED!
YEAH! MINE, TOO!
ONLY 99¢
MINE, TOO! IT'S SO HARD TO FIND THE TIME TO TAKE CARE OF IT!
IT'S ACTUALLY IMPOSSIBLE!
MINE IS THRIVING!
YOURS? THAT'S A SURPRISE!
HOW DO YOU FIND THE TIME TO DEVOTE TO IT?
ACTUALLY, I DON'T...
COOL!
I PAID DILTON TO INVENT A VIRTUAL NANNY TO TAKE CARE OF IT!
THE END

Originally presented in JUGHEAD #110, November, 1998

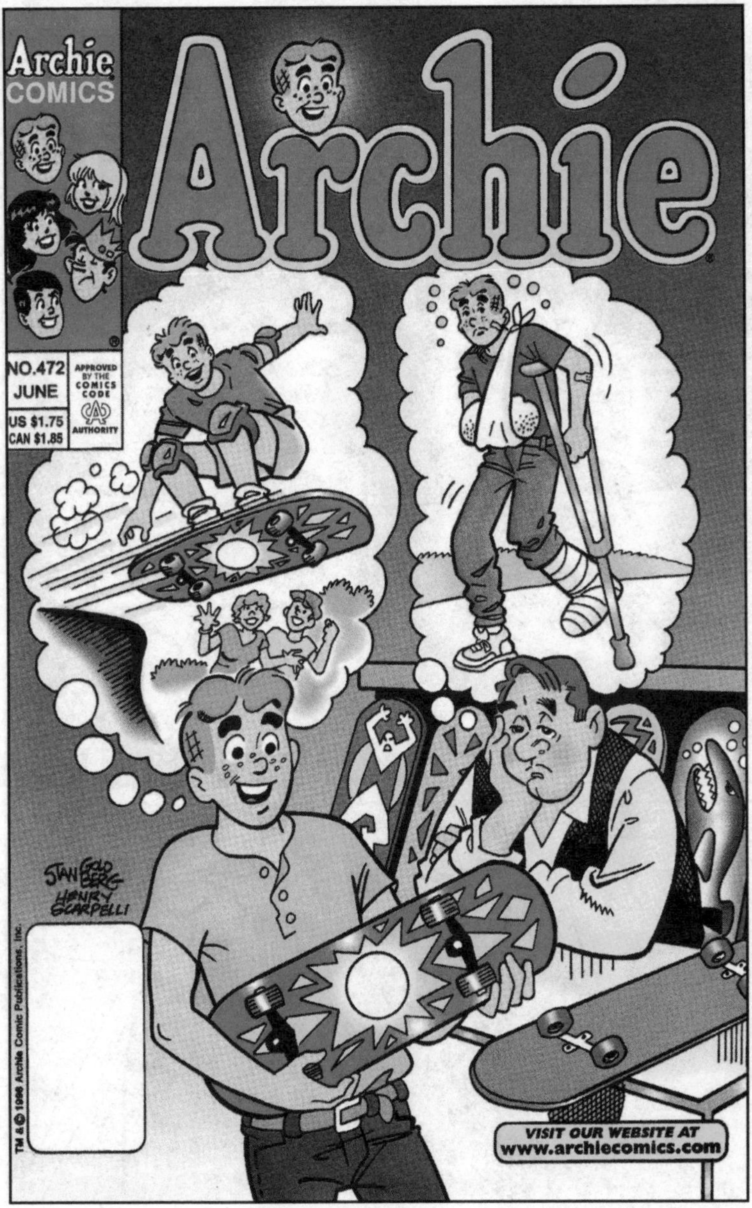
Archie COMICS
Archie
NO.472
JUNE
US $1.75
CAN $1.85
APPROVED BY THE COMICS CODE AUTHORITY
STAN GOLDBERG
HENRY SCARPELLI
TM & © 1998 Archie Comic Publications, Inc.
VISIT OUR WEBSITE AT
www.archiecomics.com

Originally printed in 1998

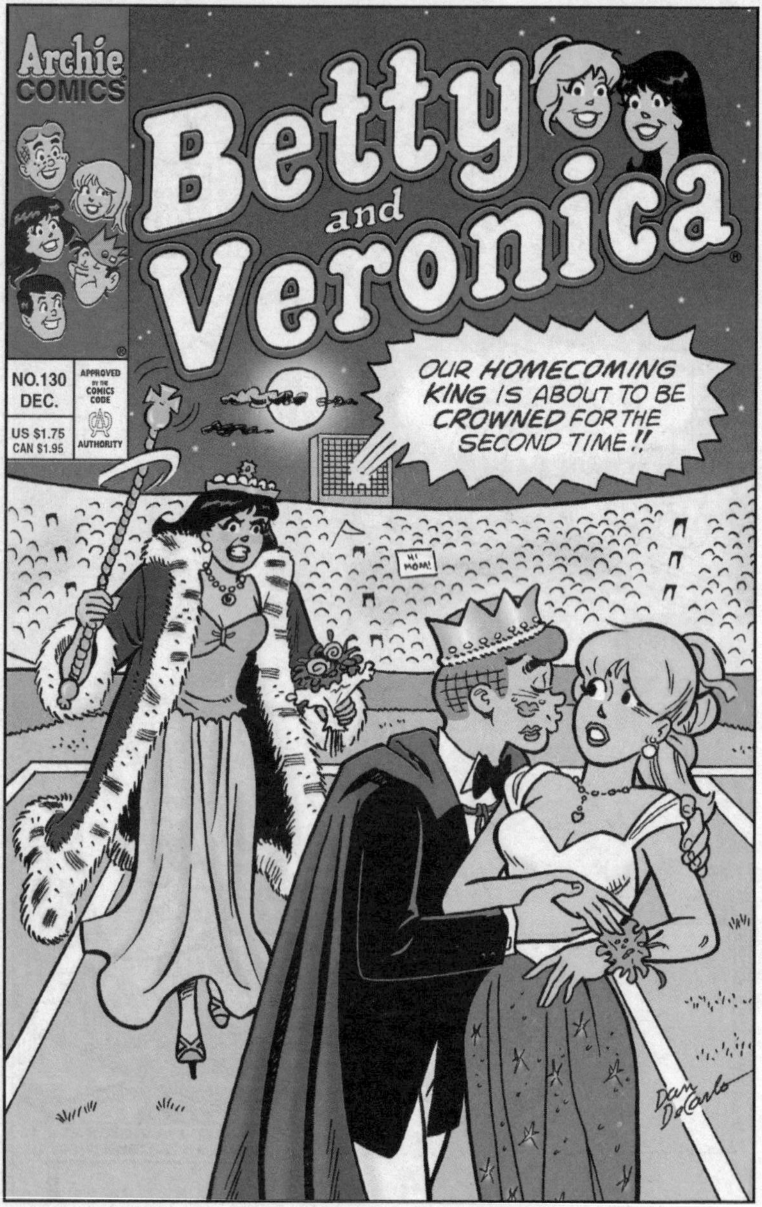
Archie COMICS
Betty and Veronica
NO.130 DEC.
US $1.75 CAN $1.95
APPROVED BY THE COMICS CODE AUTHORITY
OUR HOMECOMING KING IS ABOUT TO BE CROWNED FOR THE SECOND TIME!!
HI MOM!
Dan DeCarlo

Originally printed in 1998

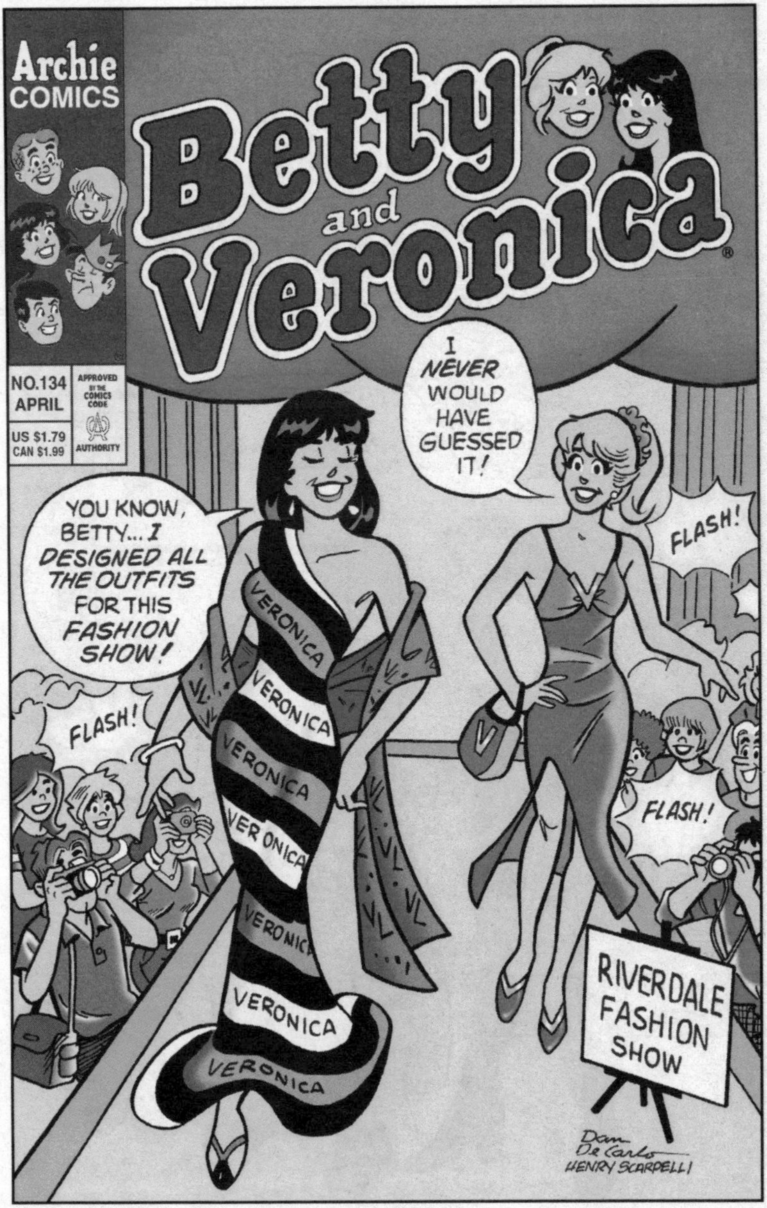
Archie COMICS
Betty and Veronica
NO.134 APRIL
US $1.79 CAN $1.99
APPROVED BY THE COMICS CODE AUTHORITY
YOU KNOW, BETTY... I DESIGNED ALL THE OUTFITS FOR THIS FASHION SHOW!
I NEVER WOULD HAVE GUESSED IT!
FLASH!
FLASH!
FLASH!
VERONICA
RIVERDALE FASHION SHOW
Dan DeCarlo
HENRY SCARPELLI

Originally printed in 1999

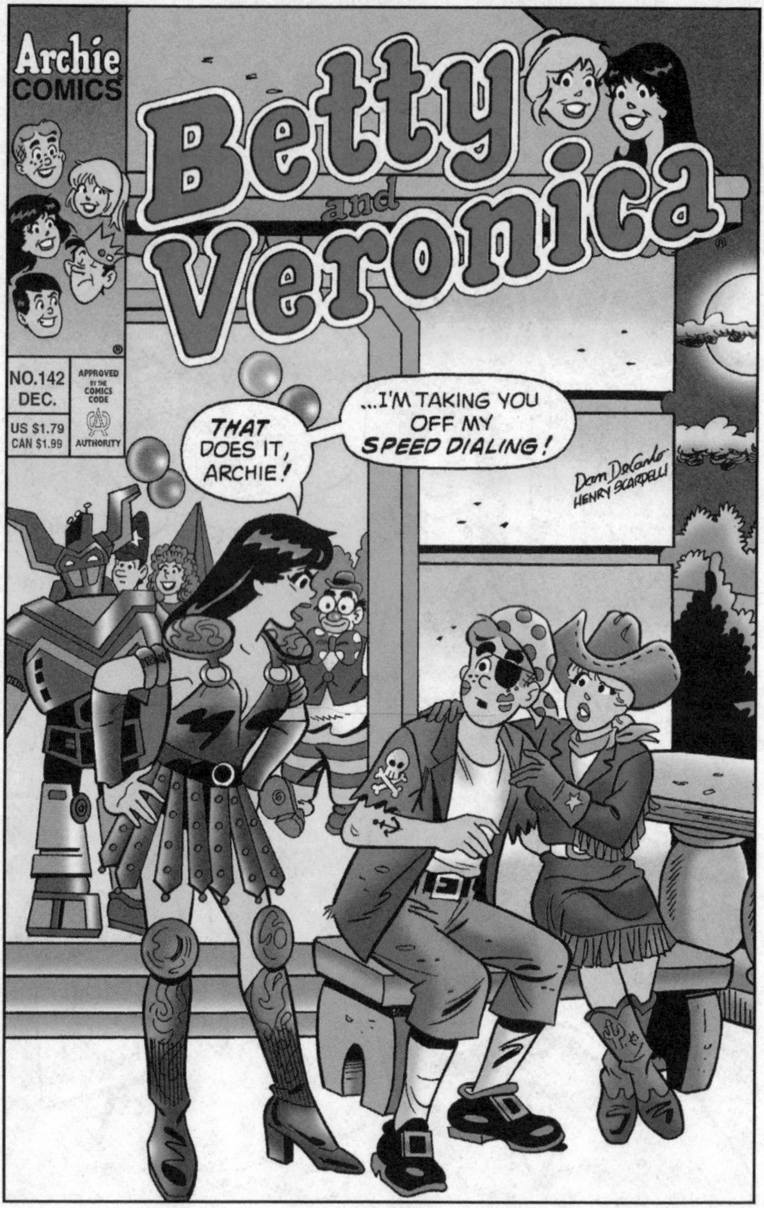
Archie
COMICS
Betty and Veronica
NO.142
DEC.
US $1.79
CAN $1.99
APPROVED BY THE COMICS CODE AUTHORITY
THAT DOES IT, ARCHIE!
...I'M TAKING YOU OFF MY SPEED DIALING!
Dan DeCarlo
HENRY SCARPELLI

Originally printed in 1999

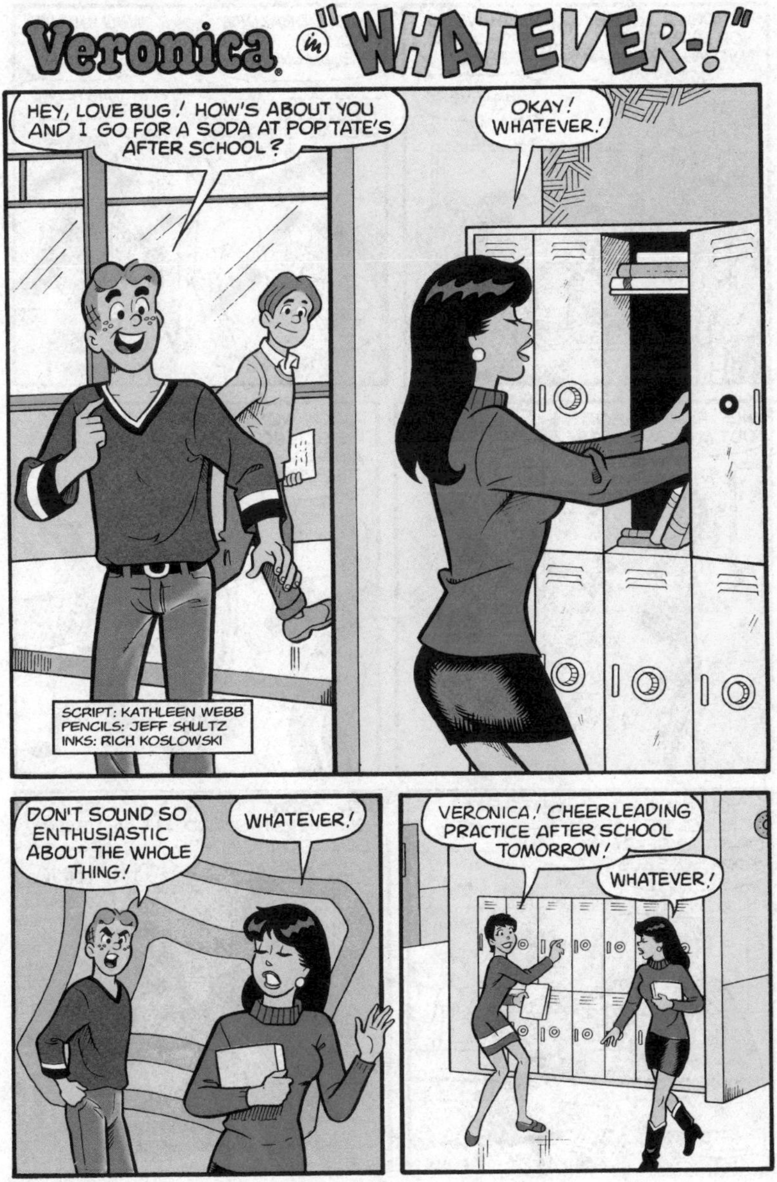
Veronica in "WHATEVER-!"
HEY, LOVE BUG! HOW'S ABOUT YOU AND I GO FOR A SODA AT POP TATE'S AFTER SCHOOL?
OKAY! WHATEVER!
SCRIPT: KATHLEEN WEBB
PENCILS: JEFF SHULTZ
INKS: RICH KOSLOWSKI
DON'T SOUND SO ENTHUSIASTIC ABOUT THE WHOLE THING!
WHATEVER!
VERONICA! CHEERLEADING PRACTICE AFTER SCHOOL TOMORROW!
WHATEVER!

Originally presented in VERONICA #85, March, 1999

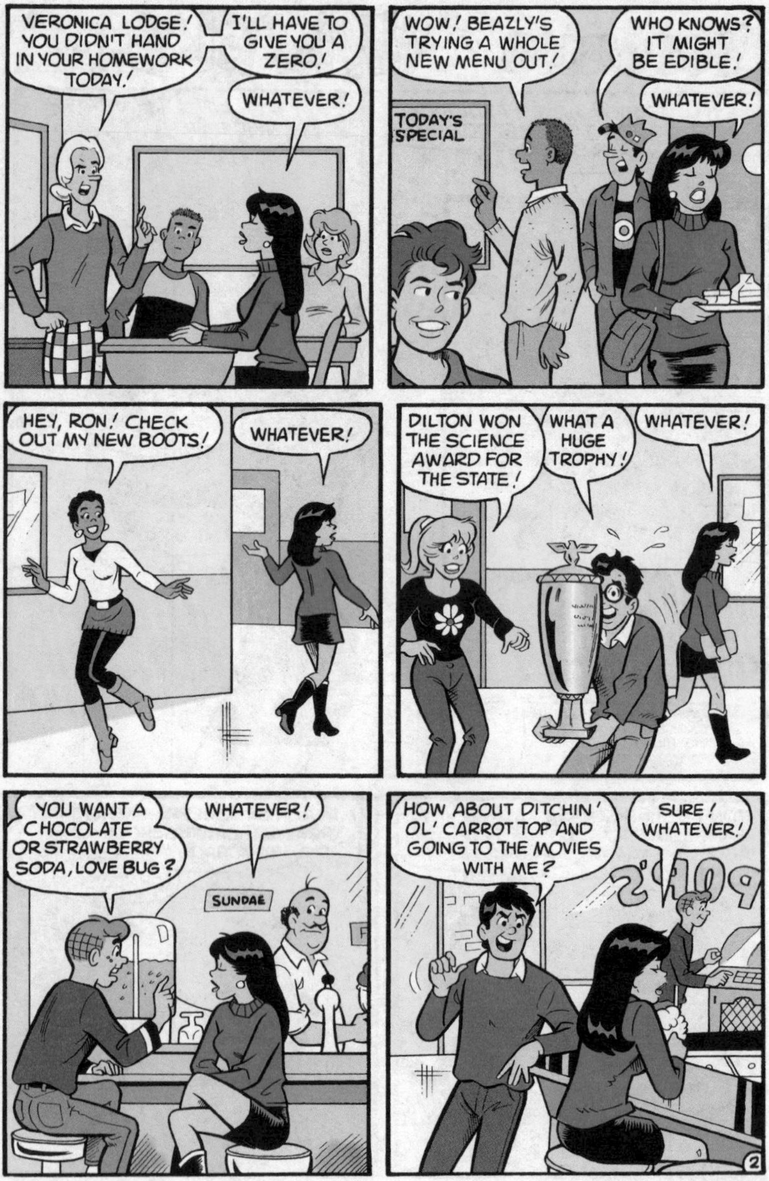
VERONICA LODGE! YOU DIDN'T HAND IN YOUR HOMEWORK TODAY!
I'LL HAVE TO GIVE YOU A ZERO!
WHATEVER!
WOW! BEAZLY'S TRYING A WHOLE NEW MENU OUT!
TODAY'S SPECIAL
WHO KNOWS? IT MIGHT BE EDIBLE!
WHATEVER!
HEY, RON! CHECK OUT MY NEW BOOTS!
WHATEVER!
DILTON WON THE SCIENCE AWARD FOR THE STATE!
WHAT A HUGE TROPHY!
WHATEVER!
YOU WANT A CHOCOLATE OR STRAWBERRY SODA, LOVE BUG?
WHATEVER!
SUNDAE
HOW ABOUT DITCHIN' OL' CARROT TOP AND GOING TO THE MOVIES WITH ME?
SURE! WHATEVER!
2

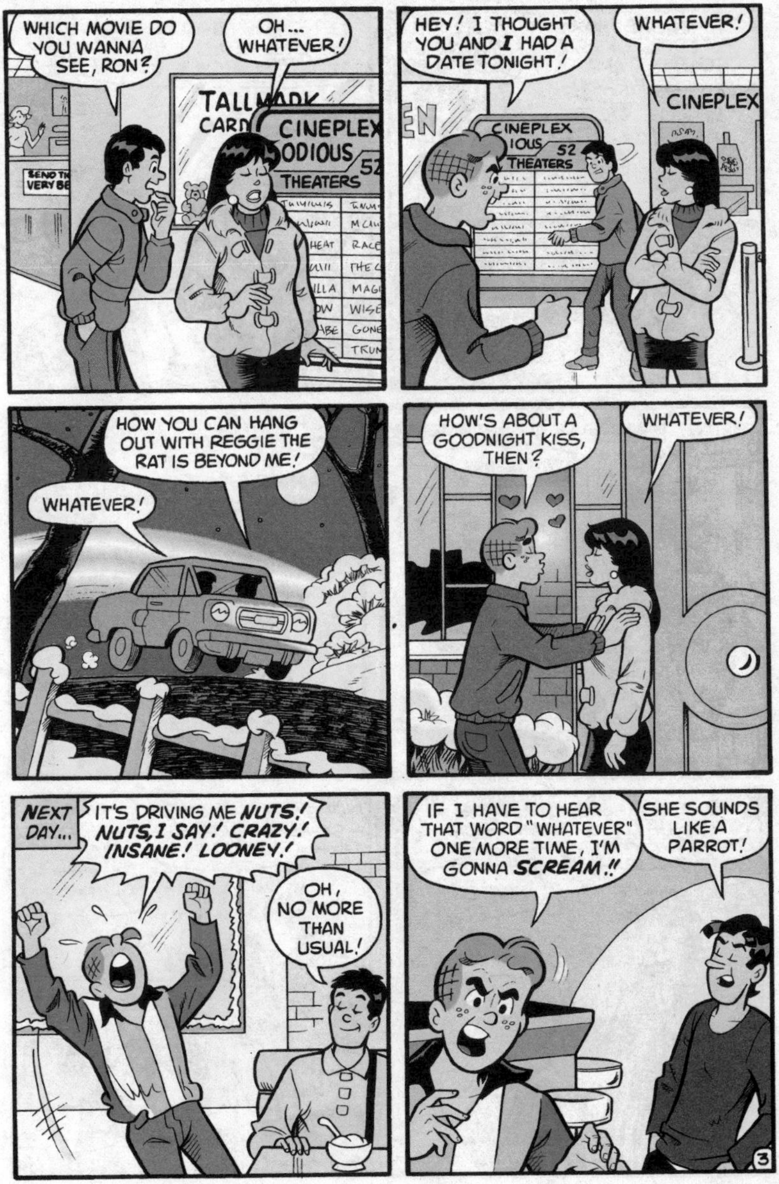
WHICH MOVIE DO YOU WANNA SEE, RON?
OH... WHATEVER!
TALLMADK
CARD
CINEPLEX ODIOUS 52 THEATERS
HEY! I THOUGHT YOU AND I HAD A DATE TONIGHT!
WHATEVER!
CINEPLEX
HOW YOU CAN HANG OUT WITH REGGIE THE RAT IS BEYOND ME!
WHATEVER!
HOW'S ABOUT A GOODNIGHT KISS, THEN?
WHATEVER!
NEXT DAY...
IT'S DRIVING ME NUTS! NUTS, I SAY! CRAZY! INSANE! LOONEY!
OH, NO MORE THAN USUAL!
IF I HAVE TO HEAR THAT WORD "WHATEVER" ONE MORE TIME, I'M GONNA SCREAM!!
SHE SOUNDS LIKE A PARROT!
3

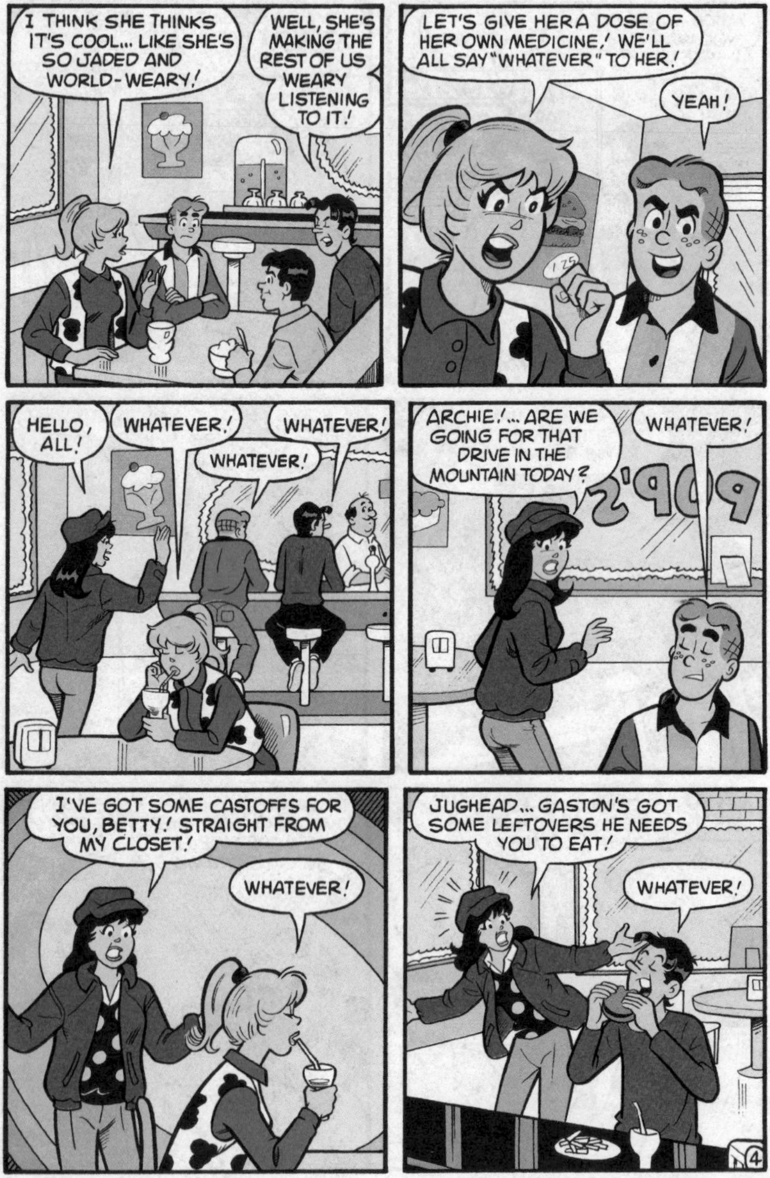
I THINK SHE THINKS IT'S COOL... LIKE SHE'S SO JADED AND WORLD-WEARY!
WELL, SHE'S MAKING THE REST OF US WEARY LISTENING TO IT!
LET'S GIVE HER A DOSE OF HER OWN MEDICINE! WE'LL ALL SAY "WHATEVER" TO HER!
YEAH!
HELLO, ALL!
WHATEVER!
WHATEVER!
WHATEVER!
ARCHIE!... ARE WE GOING FOR THAT DRIVE IN THE MOUNTAIN TODAY?
WHATEVER!
POP'S
I'VE GOT SOME CASTOFFS FOR YOU, BETTY! STRAIGHT FROM MY CLOSET!
WHATEVER!
JUGHEAD... GASTON'S GOT SOME LEFTOVERS HE NEEDS YOU TO EAT!
WHATEVER!
4

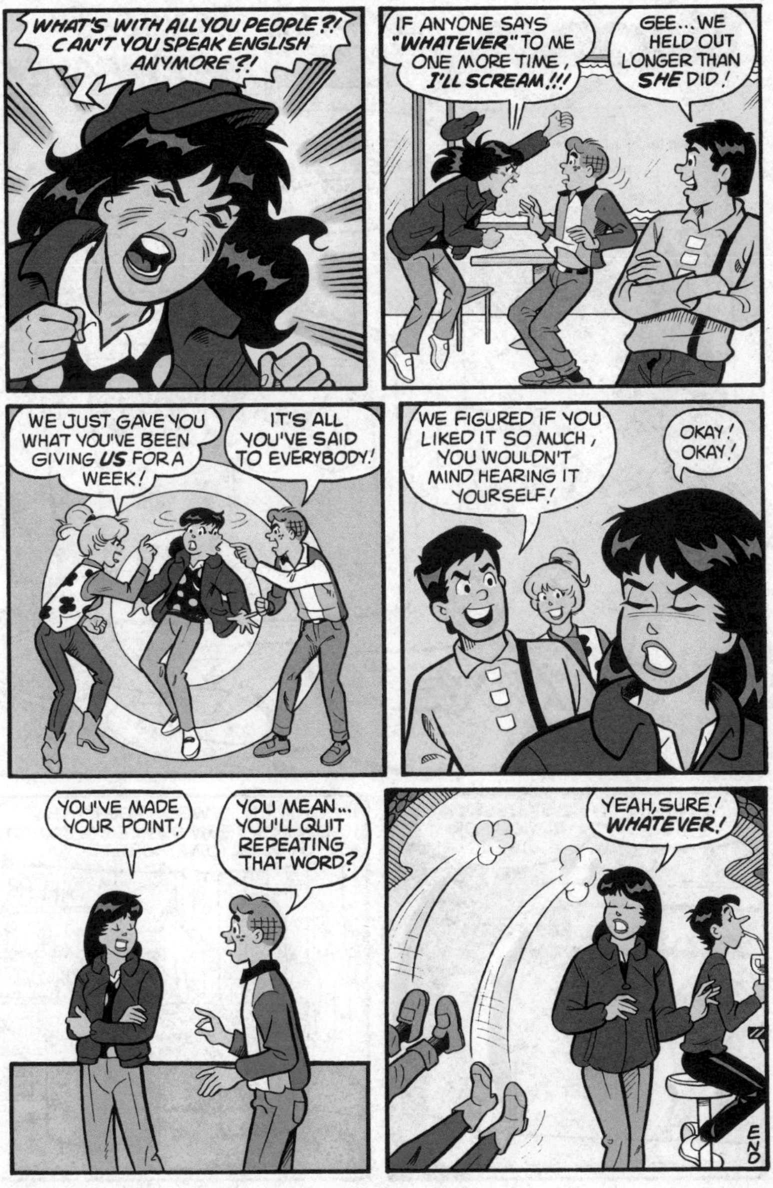
WHAT'S WITH ALL YOU PEOPLE?! CAN'T YOU SPEAK ENGLISH ANYMORE?!
IF ANYONE SAYS "WHATEVER" TO ME ONE MORE TIME, I'LL SCREAM!!!
GEE... WE HELD OUT LONGER THAN SHE DID!
WE JUST GAVE YOU WHAT YOU'VE BEEN GIVING US FOR A WEEK!
IT'S ALL YOU'VE SAID TO EVERYBODY!
WE FIGURED IF YOU LIKED IT SO MUCH, YOU WOULDN'T MIND HEARING IT YOURSELF!
OKAY! OKAY!
YOU'VE MADE YOUR POINT!
YOU MEAN... YOU'LL QUIT REPEATING THAT WORD?
YEAH, SURE! WHATEVER!
END

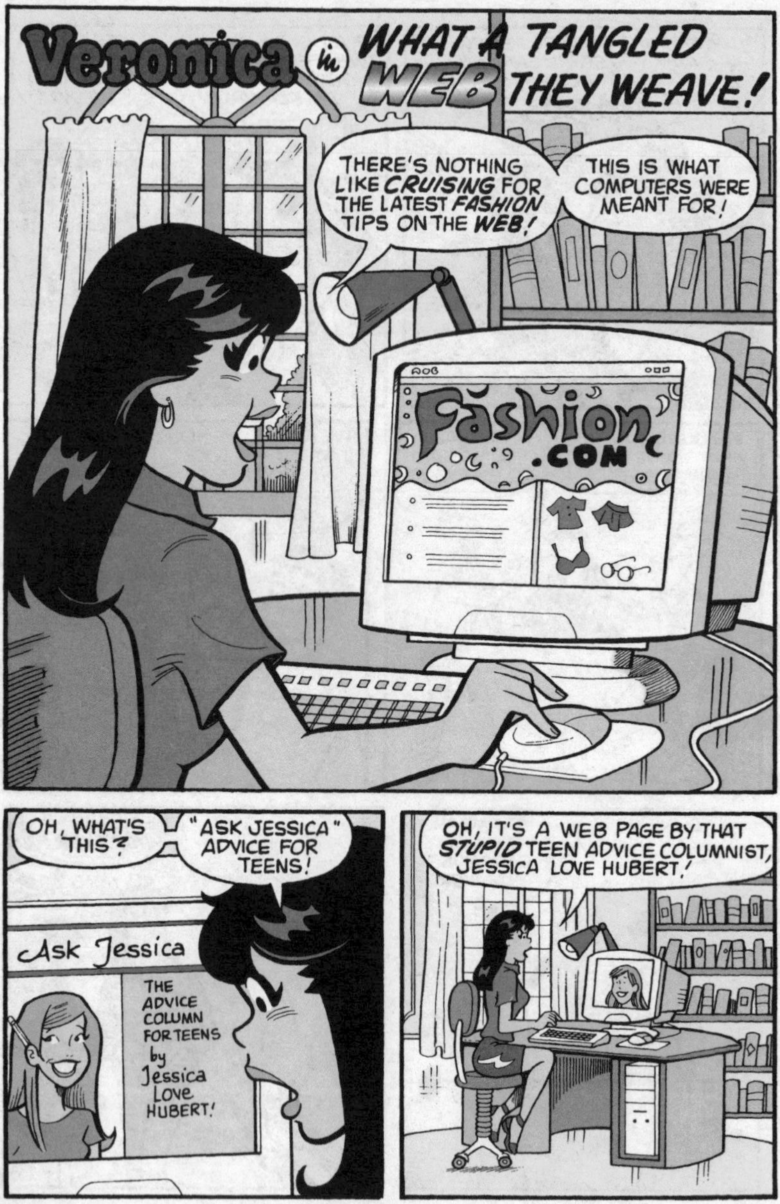
Veronica in WHAT A TANGLED WEB THEY WEAVE!
THERE'S NOTHING LIKE CRUISING FOR THE LATEST FASHION TIPS ON THE WEB!
THIS IS WHAT COMPUTERS WERE MEANT FOR!
Fashion .COM
OH, WHAT'S THIS?
"ASK JESSICA" ADVICE FOR TEENS!
Ask Jessica
THE ADVICE COLUMN FOR TEENS by Jessica Love HUBERT!
OH, IT'S A WEB PAGE BY THAT STUPID TEEN ADVICE COLUMNIST, JESSICA LOVE HUBERT!

Originally presented in VERONICA #89, July, 1999

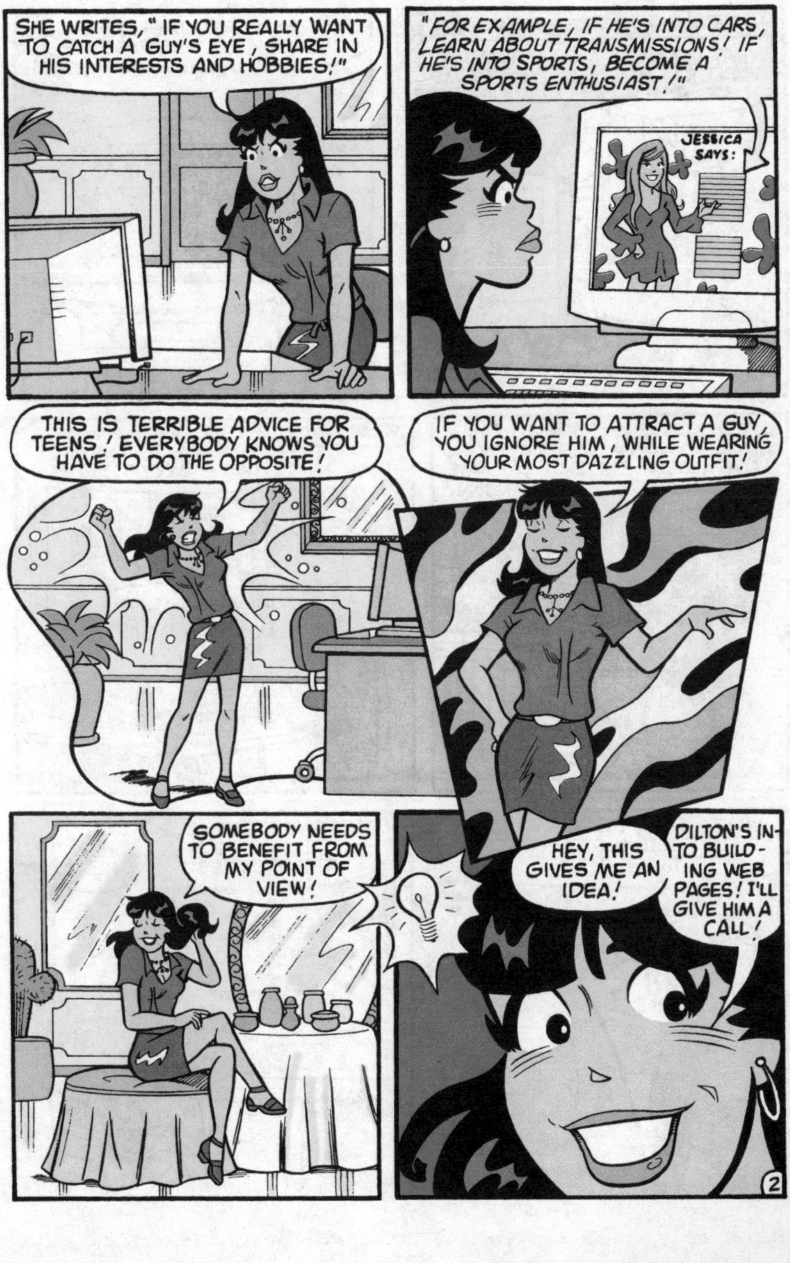
SHE WRITES, " IF YOU REALLY WANT TO CATCH A GUY'S EYE, SHARE IN HIS INTERESTS AND HOBBIES!"
"FOR EXAMPLE, IF HE'S INTO CARS, LEARN ABOUT TRANSMISSIONS! IF HE'S INTO SPORTS, BECOME A SPORTS ENTHUSIAST!"
JESSICA SAYS:
THIS IS TERRIBLE ADVICE FOR TEENS! EVERYBODY KNOWS YOU HAVE TO DO THE OPPOSITE!
IF YOU WANT TO ATTRACT A GUY, YOU IGNORE HIM, WHILE WEARING YOUR MOST DAZZLING OUTFIT!
SOMEBODY NEEDS TO BENEFIT FROM MY POINT OF VIEW!
HEY, THIS GIVES ME AN IDEA!
DILTON'S INTO BUILDING WEB PAGES! I'LL GIVE HIM A CALL!
2

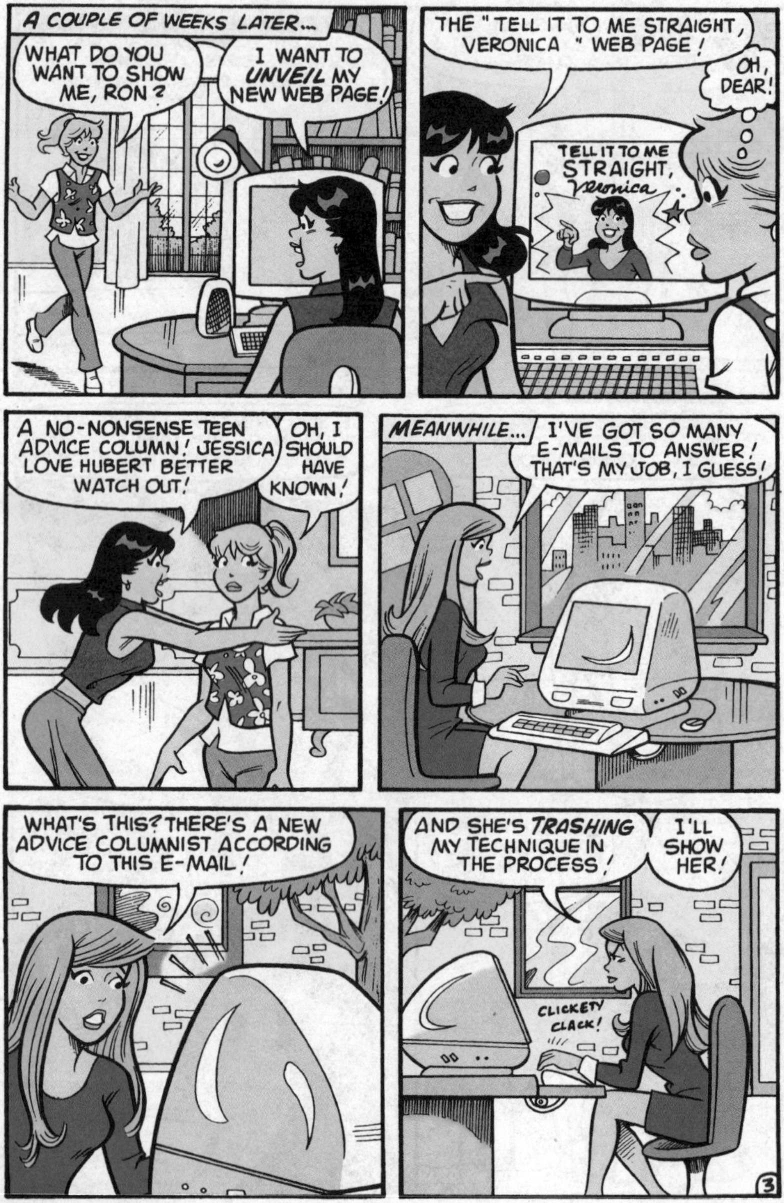
A COUPLE OF WEEKS LATER...
WHAT DO YOU WANT TO SHOW ME, RON?
I WANT TO UNVEIL MY NEW WEB PAGE!
THE "TELL IT TO ME STRAIGHT, VERONICA" WEB PAGE!
OH, DEAR!
TELL IT TO ME STRAIGHT, Veronica
A NO-NONSENSE TEEN ADVICE COLUMN! JESSICA LOVE HUBERT BETTER WATCH OUT!
OH, I SHOULD HAVE KNOWN!
MEANWHILE...
I'VE GOT SO MANY E-MAILS TO ANSWER! THAT'S MY JOB, I GUESS!
WHAT'S THIS? THERE'S A NEW ADVICE COLUMNIST ACCORDING TO THIS E-MAIL!
AND SHE'S TRASHING MY TECHNIQUE IN THE PROCESS!
I'LL SHOW HER!
CLICKETY CLACK!
3

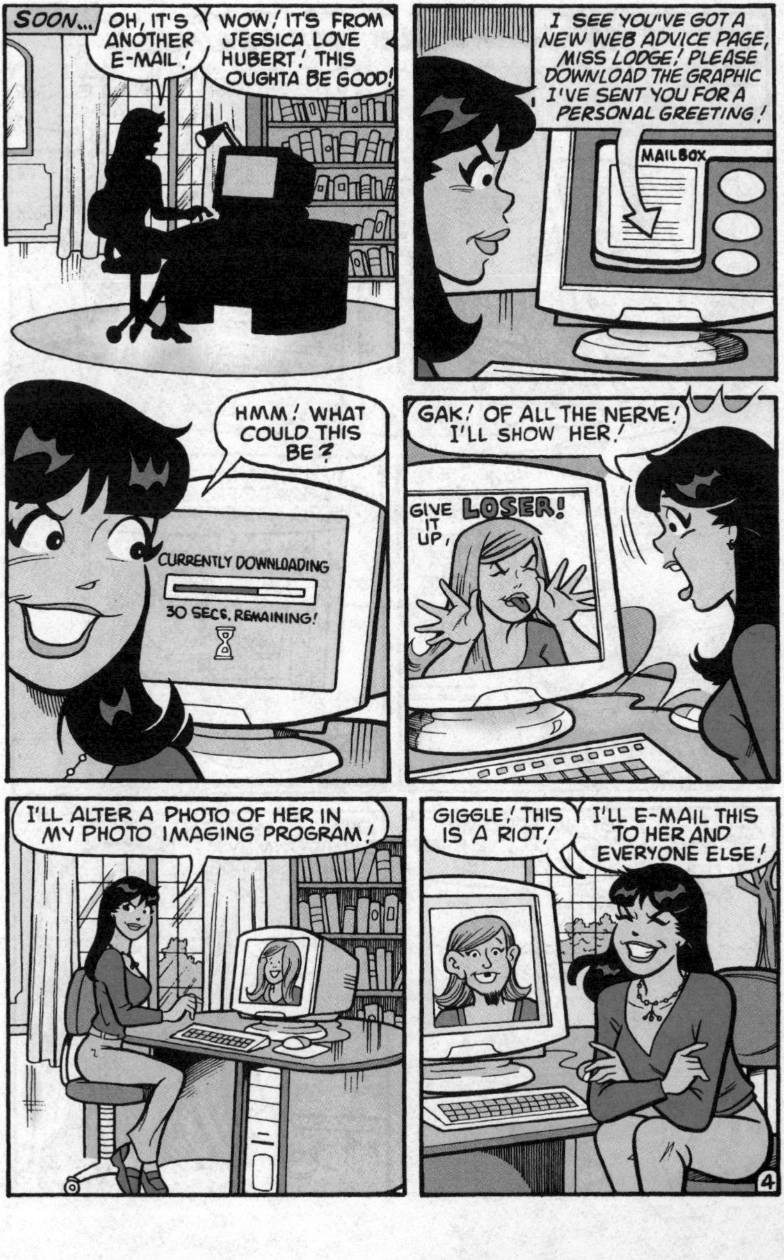
SOON...
OH, IT'S ANOTHER E-MAIL!
WOW! IT'S FROM JESSICA LOVE HUBERT! THIS OUGHTA BE GOOD!
I SEE YOU'VE GOT A NEW WEB ADVICE PAGE, MISS LODGE! PLEASE DOWNLOAD THE GRAPHIC I'VE SENT YOU FOR A PERSONAL GREETING!
MAILBOX
HMM! WHAT COULD THIS BE?
CURRENTLY DOWNLOADING
30 SECS. REMAINING!
GAK! OF ALL THE NERVE! I'LL SHOW HER!
GIVE IT UP, LOSER!
I'LL ALTER A PHOTO OF HER IN MY PHOTO IMAGING PROGRAM!
GIGGLE! THIS IS A RIOT!
I'LL E-MAIL THIS TO HER AND EVERYONE ELSE!
4

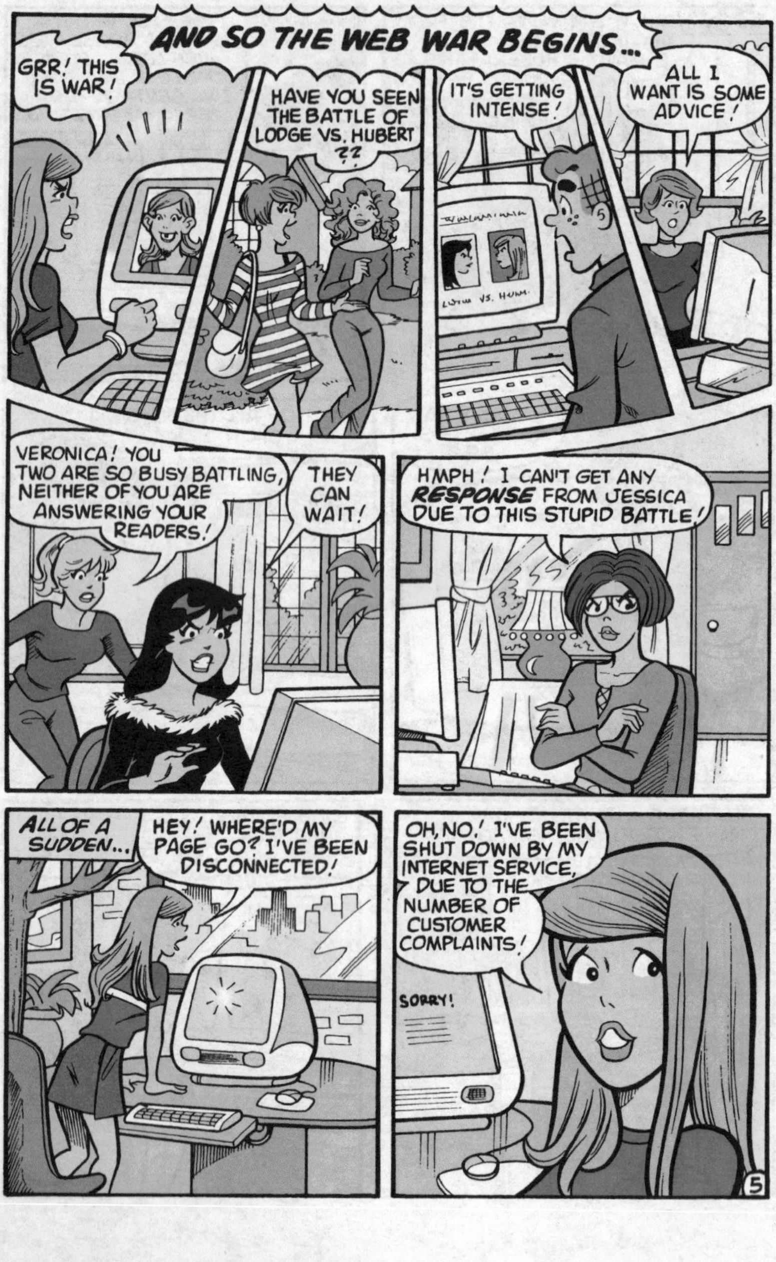
AND SO THE WEB WAR BEGINS...
GRR! THIS IS WAR!
HAVE YOU SEEN THE BATTLE OF LODGE VS. HUBERT ??
IT'S GETTING INTENSE!
ALL I WANT IS SOME ADVICE!
VERONICA! YOU TWO ARE SO BUSY BATTLING, NEITHER OF YOU ARE ANSWERING YOUR READERS!
THEY CAN WAIT!
HMPH! I CAN'T GET ANY RESPONSE FROM JESSICA DUE TO THIS STUPID BATTLE!
ALL OF A SUDDEN...
HEY! WHERE'D MY PAGE GO? I'VE BEEN DISCONNECTED!
OH, NO! I'VE BEEN SHUT DOWN BY MY INTERNET SERVICE, DUE TO THE NUMBER OF CUSTOMER COMPLAINTS!
SORRY!
5

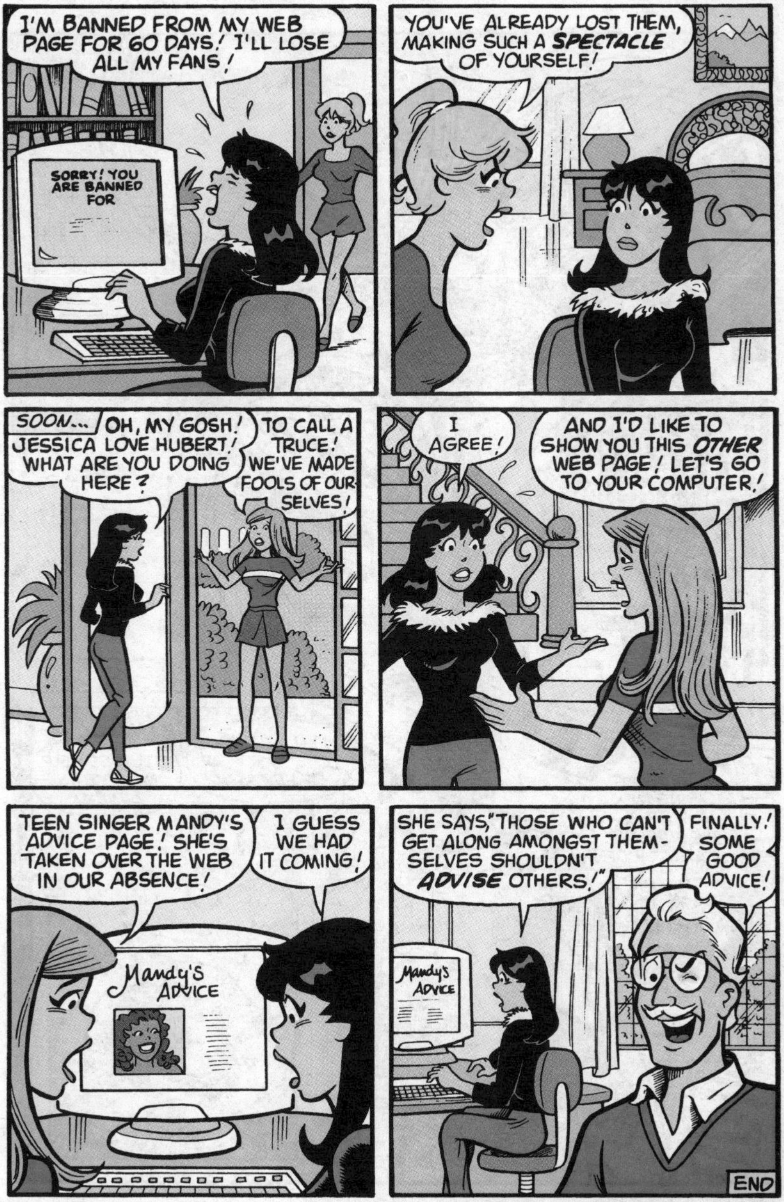
I'M BANNED FROM MY WEB PAGE FOR 60 DAYS! I'LL LOSE ALL MY FANS!
SORRY! YOU ARE BANNED FOR
YOU'VE ALREADY LOST THEM, MAKING SUCH A SPECTACLE OF YOURSELF!
SOON...
OH, MY GOSH! JESSICA LOVE HUBERT! WHAT ARE YOU DOING HERE?
TO CALL A TRUCE! WE'VE MADE FOOLS OF OUR-SELVES!
I AGREE!
AND I'D LIKE TO SHOW YOU THIS OTHER WEB PAGE! LET'S GO TO YOUR COMPUTER!
TEEN SINGER MANDY'S ADVICE PAGE! SHE'S TAKEN OVER THE WEB IN OUR ABSENCE!
I GUESS WE HAD IT COMING!
Mandy's ADVICE
SHE SAYS, "THOSE WHO CAN'T GET ALONG AMONGST THEM-SELVES SHOULDN'T ADVISE OTHERS!"
FINALLY! SOME GOOD ADVICE!
Mandy's ADVICE
END

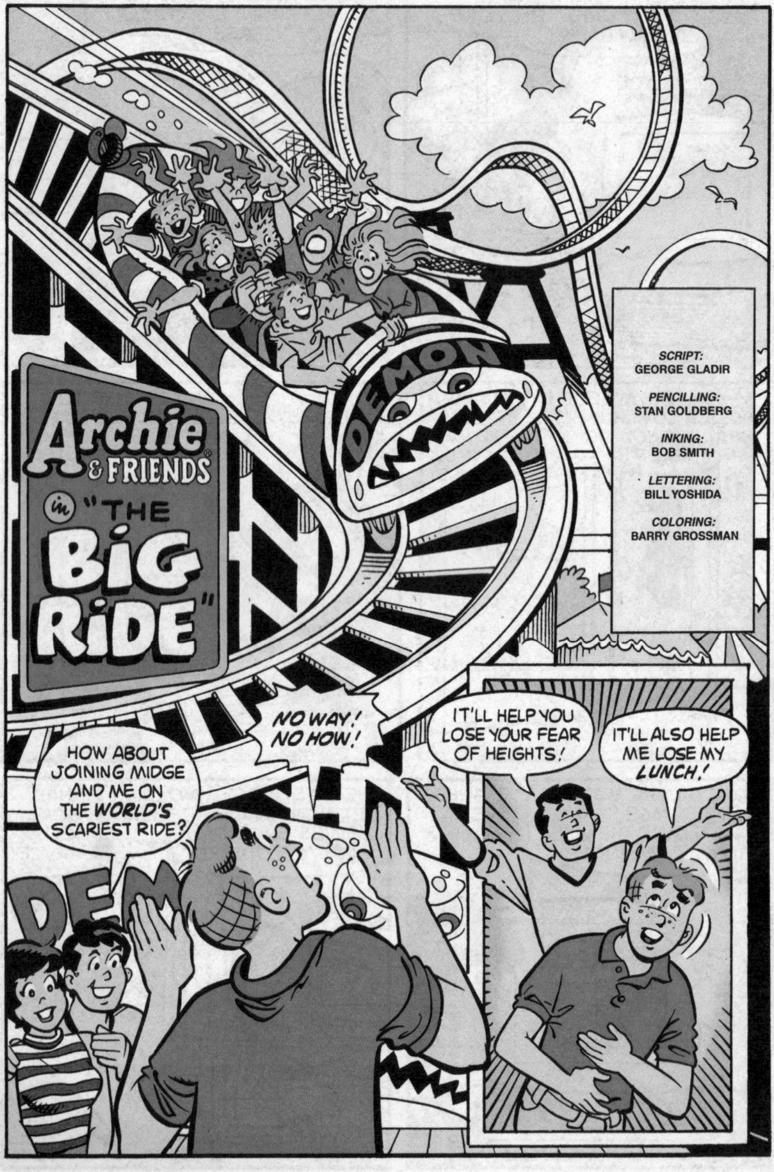
DEMON
Archie & FRIENDS in "THE BIG RIDE"
SCRIPT: GEORGE GLADIR
PENCILLING: STAN GOLDBERG
INKING: BOB SMITH
LETTERING: BILL YOSHIDA
COLORING: BARRY GROSSMAN
HOW ABOUT JOINING MIDGE AND ME ON THE WORLD'S SCARIEST RIDE?
NO WAY! NO HOW!
IT'LL HELP YOU LOSE YOUR FEAR OF HEIGHTS!
IT'LL ALSO HELP ME LOSE MY LUNCH!

Originally presented in ARCHIE & FRIENDS #38, December, 1999

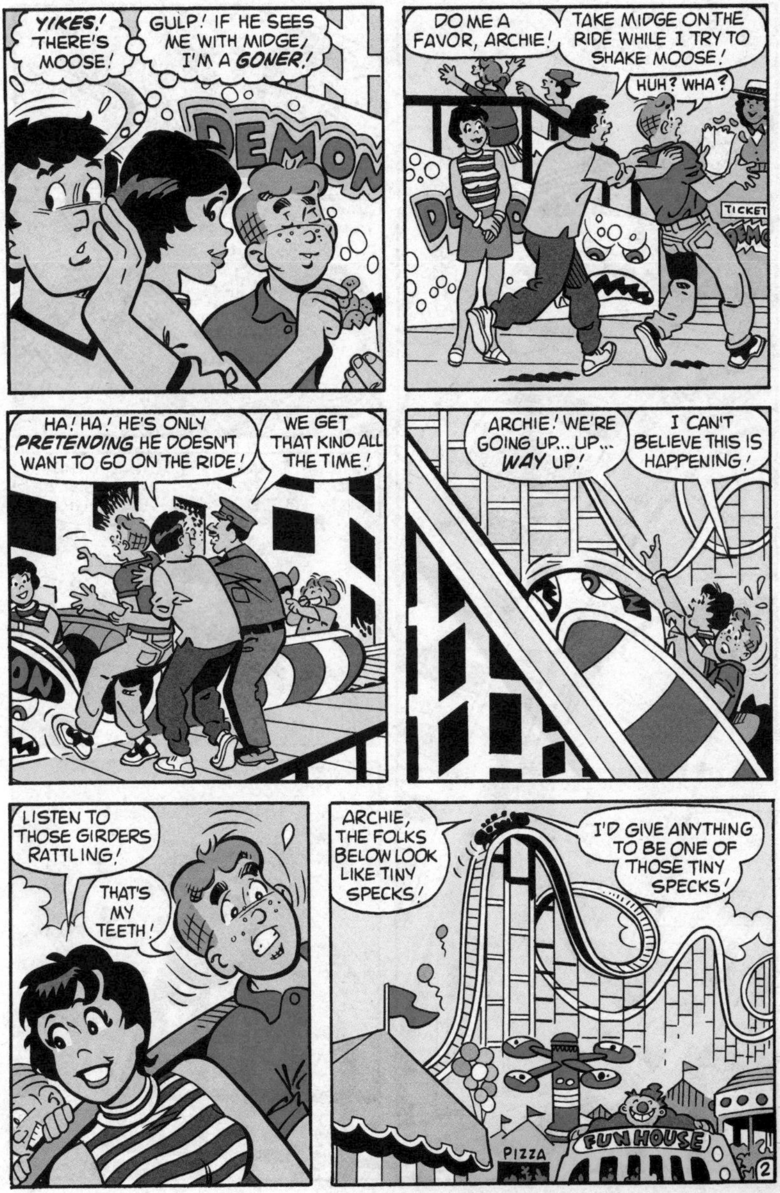
YIKES! THERE'S MOOSE!
GULP! IF HE SEES ME WITH MIDGE, I'M A GONER!
DEMON
DO ME A FAVOR, ARCHIE!
TAKE MIDGE ON THE RIDE WHILE I TRY TO SHAKE MOOSE!
HUH? WHA?
TICKET
HA! HA! HE'S ONLY PRETENDING HE DOESN'T WANT TO GO ON THE RIDE!
WE GET THAT KIND ALL THE TIME!
ARCHIE! WE'RE GOING UP... UP... WAY UP!
I CAN'T BELIEVE THIS IS HAPPENING!
LISTEN TO THOSE GIRDERS RATTLING!
THAT'S MY TEETH!
ARCHIE, THE FOLKS BELOW LOOK LIKE TINY SPECKS!
I'D GIVE ANYTHING TO BE ONE OF THOSE TINY SPECKS!
PIZZA
FUN HOUSE
2

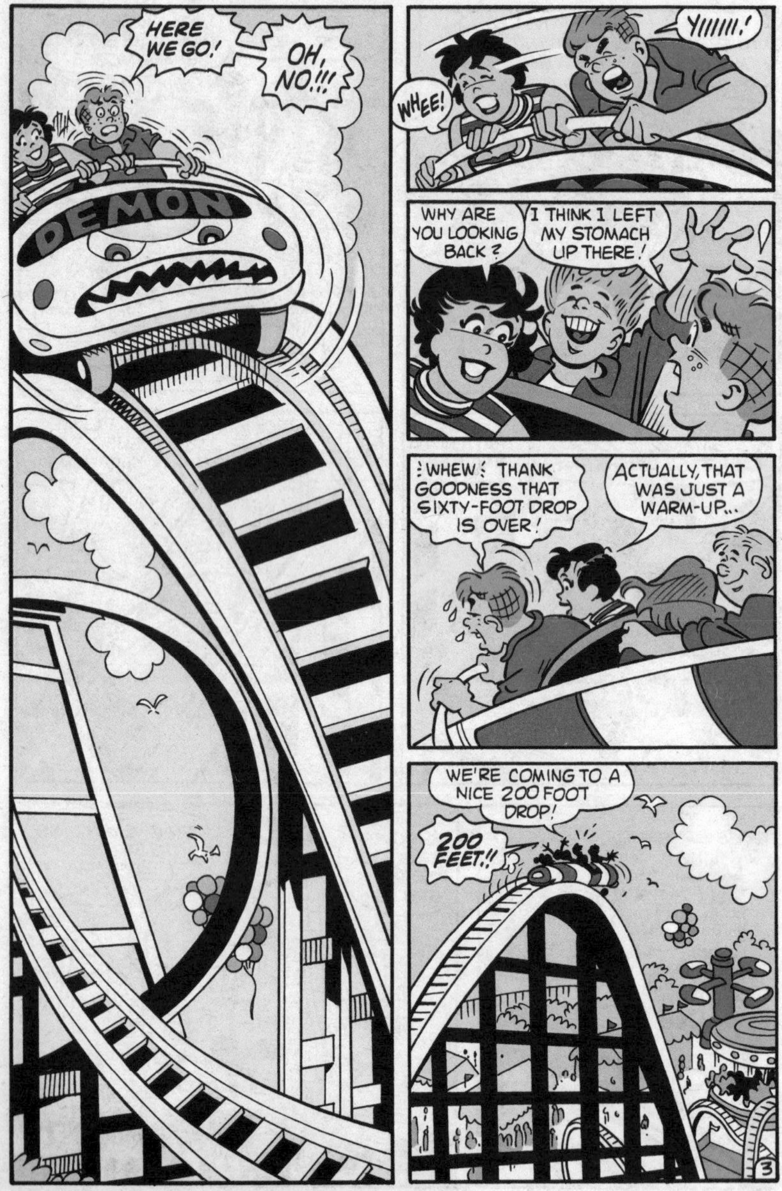
HERE WE GO!
OH, NO!!!
DEMON
YIIIIII!
WHEE!
WHY ARE YOU LOOKING BACK?
I THINK I LEFT MY STOMACH UP THERE!
WHEW! THANK GOODNESS THAT SIXTY-FOOT DROP IS OVER!
ACTUALLY, THAT WAS JUST A WARM-UP...
WE'RE COMING TO A NICE 200 FOOT DROP!
200 FEET!!
3

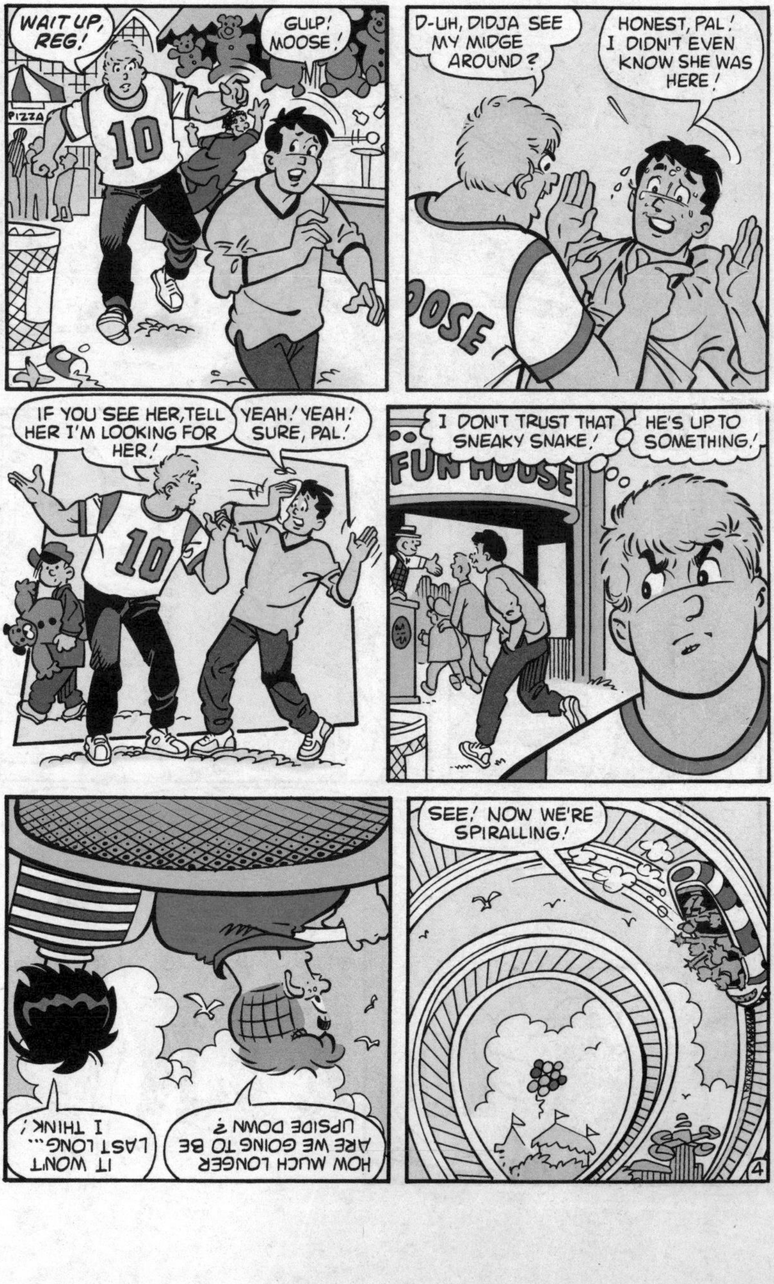
WAIT UP, REG!
GULP! MOOSE!
D-UH, DIDJA SEE MY MIDGE AROUND?
HONEST, PAL! I DIDN'T EVEN KNOW SHE WAS HERE!
MOOSE
IF YOU SEE HER, TELL HER I'M LOOKING FOR HER!
YEAH! YEAH! SURE, PAL!
I DON'T TRUST THAT SNEAKY SNAKE!
HE'S UP TO SOMETHING!
FUN HOUSE
HOW MUCH LONGER ARE WE GOING TO BE UPSIDE DOWN?
IT WON'T LAST LONG... I THINK!
SEE! NOW WE'RE SPIRALLING!
4

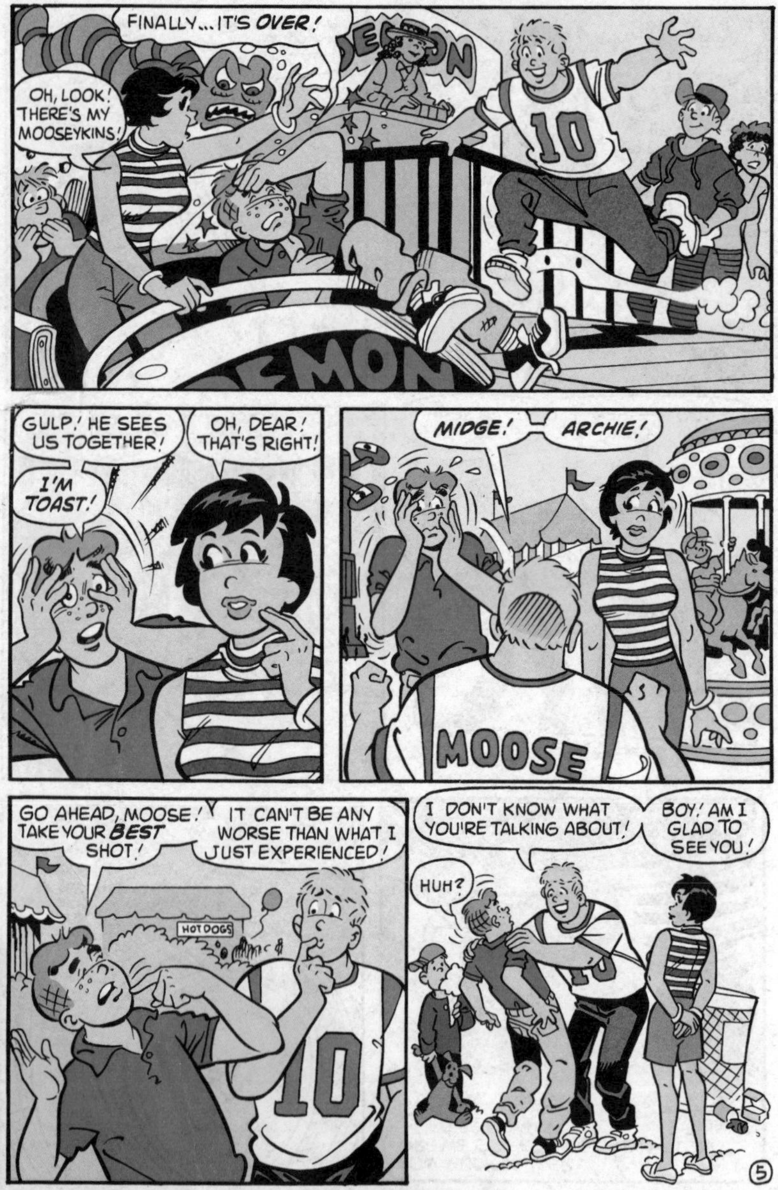
FINALLY... IT'S *OVER*!
OH, LOOK! THERE'S MY MOOSEYKINS!
10
GULP! HE SEES US TOGETHER!
*I'M TOAST!*
OH, DEAR! THAT'S RIGHT!
*MIDGE!*
*ARCHIE!*
MOOSE
GO AHEAD, MOOSE! TAKE YOUR *BEST* SHOT!
IT CAN'T BE ANY WORSE THAN WHAT I JUST EXPERIENCED!
HOT DOGS
10
I DON'T KNOW WHAT YOU'RE TALKING ABOUT!
HUH?
BOY! AM I GLAD TO SEE YOU!
5

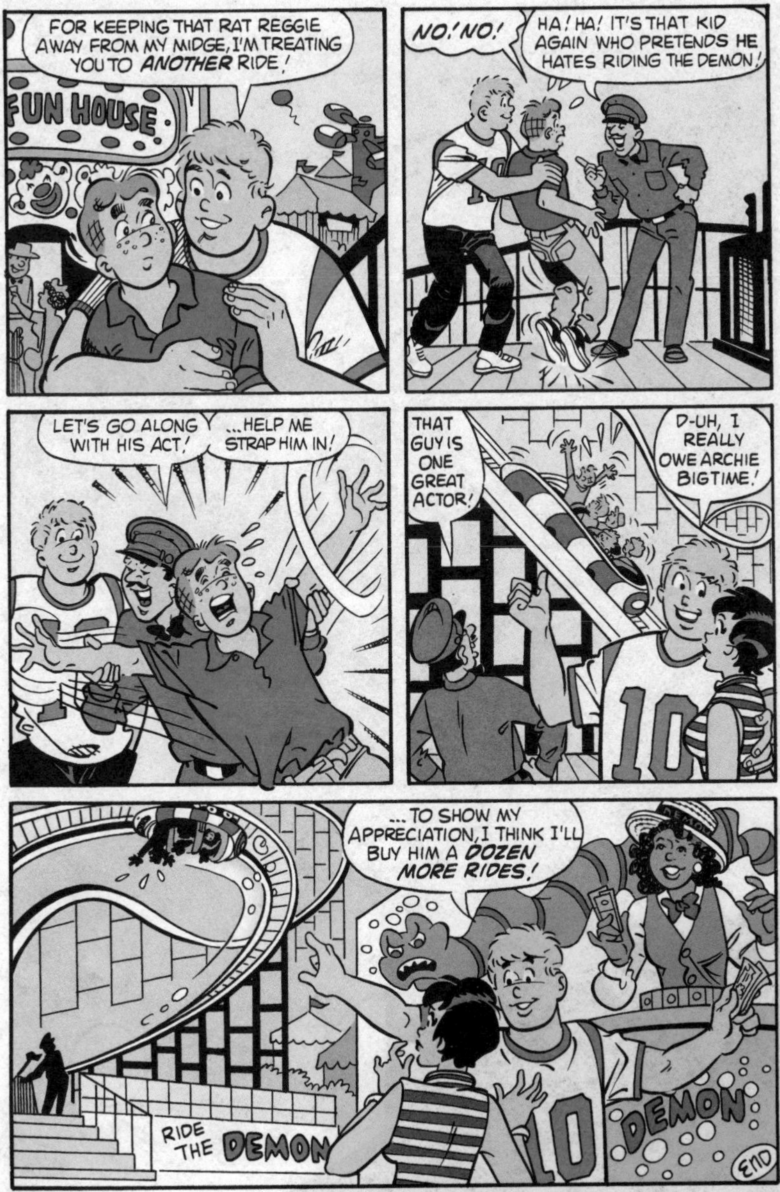
FOR KEEPING THAT RAT REGGIE AWAY FROM MY MIDGE, I'M TREATING YOU TO ANOTHER RIDE!
FUN HOUSE
NO! NO!
HA! HA! IT'S THAT KID AGAIN WHO PRETENDS HE HATES RIDING THE DEMON!
LET'S GO ALONG WITH HIS ACT!
...HELP ME STRAP HIM IN!
THAT GUY IS ONE GREAT ACTOR!
D-UH, I REALLY OWE ARCHIE BIGTIME!
...TO SHOW MY APPRECIATION, I THINK I'LL BUY HIM A DOZEN MORE RIDES!
RIDE THE DEMON
DEMON
END